Lamia

Lamia

tristan travis, jr.

E. P. DUTTON, INC.   NEW YORK

Published in the United States by
E. P. Dutton, Inc.,
2 Park Avenue, New York, N.Y. 10016

Library of Congress Cataloging in Publication Data

Travis, Tristan.
  Lamia.

  I. Title.
  PS3570.R353L3   813'.54   82-2415
                                  AACR2

ISBN: 0-525-24113-2

Designed by Nicola Mazzella

10 9 8 7 6 5 4 3 2 1

First Edition

*To Lamia, who let me love,
who let me live.*

Acknowledgments

Some very special people who certainly share the blame: Mary Dennis, Murray and Judy Moulding, Rick DeMarinis and Nona Beryl.

And through the island nightly do I range,
Or in the green sea mate with
Monsters strange . . .

—William Morris
The Lady of the Land

The horrors waited outside patiently. Even policemen,
the horrors thought. We get even policemen, in the end.

—Donald Barthelme
The Policemen's Ball (1970)

Es vet zich oys-hailen far der chasseneh.

—Rose Frank (1967)

Lamia

part one

1

Harold Bledsoe knew he didn't have the balls, but he followed her anyway.

He opened a can of beer from a six-pack on the seat beside him, waited for the gray '64 Plymouth to pull out of the big A&P parking lot—it was her parents' car—then eased in behind it a couple of blocks later when she caught a light at Pulaski. He stayed close behind her for the next mile or so till they reached the Kennedy. There, after they'd both merged onto the expressway, he fell back again, the sparse, late-night, westbound traffic allowing him to keep track of her from a distance.

He drained the can of beer, hurled it out the window. He left his hand outside for a moment, spread his fingers in the rush of humid night air; it felt as though he'd plunged them into a warm swift river.

Switching to the outer lane to pass a slow-moving semi—didn't want to let her get too far ahead—he tore loose another can from the six-pack, pressed it to his face before opening it. The cool metal felt good against his thick cheeks. He rolled it slowly up and down from his damp brows to his high, thinning hairline. First real night of summer, he thought.

Half a mile from Higgins Road, he stepped on it, pushed his fire-red Mustang all the way up to eighty-five. The gap closed rapidly between them. By the time her turn signal began blinking, the distance separating them had shrunk to a few car lengths. He stabbed the brakes, maintained that distance as they both veered north down the exit ramp.

Mary Jo Rudkus. Stuck-up blond bitch! She had it coming. They both worked at the A&P. She was a checkout, one of three girls running the night registers. Four months she'd worked there now, and still she barely said hi to him. He'd come up and bag for her every chance he got, and she could care less, acted like he was some kind of low-life creep, like she was doing him a big-ass favor just letting him stuff grocery she'd rung up. College twat—they were all the same. She went to Triton Junior over in River Grove. Troy Franklin, he went there too. Whenever he bagged for her she practically pulled down her pants for him.

At the intersection of Cumberland Avenue, they both stopped for a light. He reached over and opened his glove compartment, took out a handgun wrapped in a chamois. He removed the chamois, laid the gun in his lap.

He had to admit she turned him on. Not just tits and ass, either. She had a real pretty face and her teeth, they were so white it looked like they were a photograph or something. She wasn't a real blonde. He'd overheard Franklin talking about her to some of the other flyers back in the receiving room: He'd gone out with her a few times, claimed she had a nigger's beard between her legs. It didn't matter, though, because what Harold liked most about her was her hands. They were so small, so thin and frail-looking. And she chewed her nails, chewed them real good, made her fingers look like little rubber erasers. It was kind of crazy, but he liked to watch them work, the way they picked and poked through the items, counted out the change.

The light turned green. She pulled away, reopened the gap between them. He knew he wasn't much to look at: not much hair, a beer gut—a lot older than she was, too. Still, she definitely had it coming. . . .

Dee Road was next. She speeded up, made the turn through a yellow light. He swatted the steering wheel angrily as the yellow light changed red. He'd been daydreaming, slipped too far behind. Slowing, he saw there was no cross traffic, ran through the light, taking the corner with a loud whine from his tires. As he sped after her, he checked the rearview mirror for cops. Breathed with relief when none appeared. A gun on his lap, an open beer in his hand—no time to be stopped for a lousy traffic violation!

They were already winding through Chippewa Woods when he overtook her. A pair of oncoming headlights appeared around a bend. He waited for the lights to pass, then closed in. Two car lengths . . . a car length . . . less than a car length . . .

Now or never. There was only another mile or so of the preserve. She lived in a housing complex just beyond the north end. This was the last chance—the perfect spot, a secluded stretch of road bordered on both sides by unlit forest. Twice before he'd followed her here. Twice before he'd backed off, lost his nerve.

He took a final swig of beer, threw out the can. Then he leaned forward, grasped the wheel tensely in both hands, flashed his brights. He closed the gap to a few feet. Not too hard, he cautioned himself. No real damage—just enough to jolt her, piss her off. He braced himself. He shot ahead.

The bumpers struck with a resounding clunk. The two cars hung together for a moment, then came apart. The Plymouth lurched to the center of the road, the girl apparently wrenching the wheel with a startled jerk. He debated knocking into her again, applied his brakes instead. Moments later he saw her own brake lights flare. She was slowing, pulling over. . . .

4

It worked! Just like he'd read about in the papers: out West, the Mojave Marauder, a California rapist who used to tool up behind women driving alone at night in the desert. He'd bump into 'em and the stupid cunts'd stop every time and then he'd take 'em off behind some sand dune and do 'em up. Harold had read about it a couple of years ago. And now here he was actually doing it himself!

The two vehicles rolled to a halt, half a dozen yards separating them on the road's broad gravel shoulder. Mary Jo Rudkus sat waiting behind the wheel, confused, uncertain. She turned in her seat, stared back at him, was blinded by his brights. When he didn't get out, she finally climbed out herself, walked to the rear of her car and inspected the damage.

Her license plate had been knocked loose, hung down sideways almost touching the ground. Might be a ding in her bumper too, but he couldn't be sure from where he sat. Nothing serious. Even so he could tell she was starting to heat up, anger rapidly replacing her confusion. She leaned over, felt the bumper. She straightened, turned his way with both hands on her hips.

He had the gun in his hand now. All he had to do was go out there and shove it in her face. He'd make her get in his car and then drive her way out Touhy Avenue to the country. He'd park in a cornfield. He'd make her take her clothes off and just sit there all naked and embarrassed for a while. Then he'd make her go to town on him. Get her to touch him with those little hands—those little eraser-tip fingers of hers. When he was screwing her, he'd ask her if he was better than Troy Franklin. He'd make her say yes and then when they were finished he'd tell her that he was going to shoot her anyway. She'd beg and cry and promise she wouldn't tell nobody—maybe even promise to be his girl friend—but it wouldn't make any difference, because he'd know all the time she was just a lying, stuck-up college twat. He'd shoot her outside so he didn't mess up his car. He'd march her out into the middle of the cornfield and shoot her where some stupid farmer wouldn't find her till the fall harvest.

He reached for the door, swung it open. She was still standing by her rear bumper, was squinting, looking right at him, shielding her eyes from the lights with a raised hand. He made no move to get out.

His stomach knotted. Cold beads of sweat broke out on his forehead. A numbness crept into his arms, settled in his wrists. Suddenly he was very close to throwing up, could feel the beer churning inside him.

She lowered her hand, still squinting, started walking toward him.

Shit! He knew in an instant that he couldn't face her—couldn't possibly go through with it! He slammed the door shut again, slammed the Mustang into reverse and fishtailed backward in a shower of dust and gravel. Moments later he was speeding back to the city, the distant, glimmering Chicago skyline of 1967.

"What are you looking at?"

"Huh?"

"I said, 'Whatcha think you're looking at?' "

"Looking at?"

"You heard me, Lieutenant."

Detective Lieutenant John Valjohn adjusted his wire-rimmed glasses, gazed in bewildered silence across the narrow breadth of a urinal separating him from his immediate superior, Captain Maxwell Howland of Homicide. It was true Valjohn had heard him; it also was true he had no idea what the captain was talking about. They both stood in the third-floor men's room of the Chicago Police Department, relieving themselves.

"You some kind of pervert or something you gotta gawk at somebody taking a leak?"

"Gawk?" Now he was thoroughly confused. He may have glanced in Howland's direction when he'd first walked up and unzipped his fly—he'd picked an end urinal, the farthest away from his superior, who already was firmly planted in front of the middle fixture—but he certainly hadn't gawked. At least he didn't think he had. Actually his mind had been miles away, wearily resifting through bits of tired old evidence on the case he was working.

"Don't play dumb with me. You looked over at me. And then your eyes, they went down *you know where!*"

"Now hold on a second, Captain—"

"You hold on a second, Lieutenant! I just wanna know why you gotta gawk at someone else's privates. I mean, watching your own ain't enough?"

"Jesus!"

"Maybe you think I don't measure up—is that it? Is that the big deal? I mean, hell, why don'tcha get down there with a ruler an' do the job right? Be my guest."

The lieutenant looked at the ceiling, closed his eyes.

"You people—you really think you got it made in that department, don't you?"

"I don't believe this," Valjohn whispered to the ceiling, his eyes still closed.

"You don't believe this? Well, let me tell you what you better believe, Lieutenant! You better believe you ain't got it made in *this* department—and I'm talking about Homicide now! Maybe you can pull this kind of crap around your faggoty universities, but it sure don't go around here. Not on the Force. Not while Max Howland's still alive and kicking!"

"Look, if you think—"

"Never mind what I think. I'm just telling you what don't go around here. No way, nohow, no, sir! So just forget it!"

Valjohn sensed the futility of further conversation. He shrugged, continued his business at hand.

Howland finished, fumbled himself back into his trousers, carefully shielding himself from view, and zipped up. He proceeded to fart. One long, loud blast followed by a riffle of several short, overlapping ones. Smiling complacently, he made to leave, took a couple of steps, stopped and swung around.

"Let me see your piece," he said.

Valjohn stared at the wall in front of him. Ceramic tile. The grout was old, chipping out. He slowly turned his head, contemplated the man standing there. Howland was a short, stocky man, a fireplug with cauliflower ears. He had a wide, square-set jaw, wore a flattop crew cut that made his head look like it was all right angles, like it hadn't been taken out of its box yet. Late forties, early fifties, chewed a stubby black cigar.

"I beg your pardon?"

"I said, 'Lemme see your piece.' "

Done urinating, he shook a few times, zipped up, and strolled over to the row of sinks across the room.

"Sorry, Captain, too late." He grinned, patted his fly. "All tucked in for the night."

"Very funny, Lieutenant. Now suppose you whip it out so I can see it."

Valjohn hesitated, still feigning a mock grin. Howland glowered.

"Wow, you had me worried there for a minute, Captain. I thought—"

"I know what you thought. Now hurry up and lemme see it."

Valjohn lightly frisked himself with both hands. He shook his head.

"Sorry—it doesn't seem to be on my person today."

"It doesn't seem to be on your person today," Howland snorted triumphantly. He removed the cigar from his mouth, walked over to a sink and spat.

"You know, for a textbook-wonder cop you're pretty fucking stupid." He ran water flushing out the sink. "You know that?"

Valjohn began rinsing his hands. He knew what was coming, made a determined effort to keep calm.

"Ever hear of regulations, Lieutenant? Ever bother reading them?"

"I've read them, Captain."

"Good. Then you should know you're required to carry your gun at all times. On and off duty." Howland opened his jacket and flashed his own shoulder-holstered .38.

"Maybe you think them rules don't apply to you? I mean, you being such a hot-shit celebrity and everything—a cube cop or whatever the fuck it is they call you. Maybe you think them rules is just for the rest of us poor slobs out here directing traffic?"

Valjohn remained silent. He knew Howland wanted to get a rise out of him, would only provoke him further if he succeeded.

"Well, I'll tell you what I'm gonna do. I'm just gonna write you up a little old reprimand. You know, just a little old reminder you ain't quite the big Mr. Hot-shit dick you think you are." The captain glanced at his watch. "Too late today—you'll have a copy on your desk Monday morning."

Valjohn reached up to the towel dispenser and pulled the lever to advance a fresh portion of linen. It was jammed. He banged it a few times with a fist, pulled the lever again. Nothing happened. "Great," he muttered.

"My pleasure," Howland growled, stuck his cigar back in his mouth and strode out of the lavatory.

Detective Lieutenant John Valjohn dried his hands on the soiled linen that hung beneath the unit in a damp, twisted loop.

Clint Eastwood squinted. Extreme close-up. His eyes measured thirty feet across from pupil to pupil—filled the entire screen of the State Theater with his best wrinkle-puckered, bad-ass stare—

At that moment Lieutenant Mona Cobb put her hand on Lieutenant John Valjohn's knee, squeezed it. He glanced at her. She didn't return his glance, was too absorbed in the movie to look away. When Eastwood drew his gun and began shooting people, she squeezed his knee again—dug in her fingernails every time Clint's big six-gun spat lead.

Blam! Blam! Blam!

Valjohn twisted in his seat, was forced to reach down and grab her wrist.

"Sorry," she whispered, actually smiled at him for an instant. Then she was back gaping at the action on the screen.

Valjohn tried for the dozenth time to get involved in the movie. Failed. All he could see was Captain Maxwell Howland's ugly face snarling and sneering at him in the lavatory. Chewing him out like some half-baked rookie. The whole incident left him seething—furious with Howland for being such a jerk, furious with himself for playing into his hands. Why didn't he carry a gun? Maybe he did think he was Mr. Hot-shit—that he could pick and choose his own rules as he went along. Maybe Howland was right.

The picture ended. Everyone had been buried; there was no one left to shoot. Valjohn stood up. Mona remained seated staring at the credits. When the credits were over and the houselights came on, she still made no move to leave. He stood by awkwardly waiting. He cleared his throat. Finally he reached over and tapped her shoulder.

"Er, uh, Mona, you ready?"

She looked up at him, her eyes distant, shining, as though she were just emerging from some deep and rewarding religious experience. She nodded. She collected her purse and sweater, rose to her feet.

"Wow! That Eastwood—he really does a number on me. You know what I mean?"

Valjohn smiled obligingly. He followed her up the empty aisle.

Lieutenant Mona Cobb. One of thirty-four sworn woman officers on the CCPD (not counting meter maids). "Dickless Tracys," as they were affectionately labeled by their more traditional counterparts. Valjohn asked himself what he was doing out with her. She had to be at least a decade older than he—hell, maybe two—a divorcee, a three-time loser. She was tall, thick-bodied, breastless and waistless. While her face was not unattractive—he could ascribe a certain Modigliani charm to her long, thin nose and pointed chin—she did her best to conceal it, caking on the cosmetics

8

until she looked like a pastel portrait of herself. As for personality, well
. . . he didn't doubt for a single moment she was probably a "damn good"
cop and a "good old boy" to boot.

In the lobby they overtook the tail end of the crowd. A man jostled into
him as they moved toward the main exit. He heard the man mutter what
sounded like a racial slur. Valjohn turned.

"Excuse me?"

The man glared back but chose not to repeat it. He had a fat face with
small lobeless ears, thinning sandy hair, mad-dog eyes.

Valjohn shrugged and let it drop. This man's problems he could do
without. He walked away. Outside Mona hailed a cab. They headed north
to Rush Street.

So why wasn't he out tonight with some bright, young, lithesome lovely?
The answer was easy: Whoever she might be hadn't asked him, and Mona
had. Numerous times. Always in the past, however, he'd turned her down.
Not this time. Today, she'd managed to catch him shortly after his encoun-
ter with Howland in the john. She'd sauntered up to him in the hall—they
both worked on the same floor in the Bureau of Investigative Services—
and he'd finally run out of excuses. There was no doubt the captain's
baiting had gotten under his skin. His sex life was at a low ebb, he'd admit
it—though it hadn't quite sunk to the desperate levels Howland had so
politely intimated. It seemed ages since he'd been out on a date: not since
he'd taken over the case, and that was almost five months ago. He was
always too busy, too absorbed in his work. Twelve, sixteen hours a day. Six
and seven days a week. There just never seemed to be any time left over.

This weekend was going to be different, though. He was going to make
time—starting tonight with Mona. Things were pretty much at a standstill
in the case. There hadn't been an 1834 for a couple of months now. All
existing leads either dead-ended or disappeared into the realm of infinite
possibilities. His efforts, his long hours had accomplished very little in the
way of discernible results. He was discouraged; he was feeling flat. He
needed a break.

Tomorrow he was taking the day off, had agreed earlier in the week to
play golf with Bert Carlson from the lab . . . and besides, if Mona was
nothing else, she was a guaranteed 14-karat pushover—or so he'd been
told on more than one occasion. Over the years she'd been ritually tried
on and discarded by practically every available officer in the bureau. Some
not so available. So what the hell—who was he to be so damn choosy,
anyway?

They had dinner at Renalgo's, bar-hopped until midnight.

"My place or yours?" asked Mona after he'd paid the tab at Mike McDonald's.

"Lady's choice."

"What makes you think I'll be a lady?" She reached under the table and
squeezed his knee.

9

Valjohn flushed. "Just a wild guess, I guess." This time he didn't grab her hand away.

"Let's make it your place. Then you can show me your famous etchings."

"They're not exactly etchings."

"Well, whatever the hell they are."

Twenty minutes later Valjohn was opening the door of his bachelor flat and letting her in.

"Can I fix you a drink?" he asked, then remembered the liquor cabinet was empty—he was not much of an entertainer—or a drinker either, for that matter. The best he could offer her was a can of beer—one of two that had been taking up space in his refrigerator since last summer.

"Sure, I'll go another vodka gimlet."

She settled for a Bud.

"Tastes tinny," she complained, kicking off her heels and lounging back comfortably on the couch. "Now, why don't you trot out those etchings."

He explained again they weren't etchings, that they were called collages, that most of them were sizable and that if she really wanted to see them she'd have to go back to his studio in the rear of the apartment.

"I want to see 'em," she announced belligerently after draining her beer. She stood up abruptly. "Lead the way, Rembrandt."

Valjohn led the way, opened the door to his studio, a converted back bedroom, switched on the light. Mona took two steps forward and then one back.

"Jesus H. Christ, this place looks like the city dump!" She stood with wrinkled nose surveying the mess before her. There was barely room to walk. The floor was cluttered with boxes and jars, paper sacks, cans of paints and resins, piles of everything from newspaper clippings and photographs, police data and computer printouts to broken glass, shards of plastic, bits and pieces of wood and metal, sand, dirt and excelsior. Tools, brushes and palette knives lay scattered about. A small metal folding chair, the room's only furniture, lay on its side in a corner buried amid a stack of Masonite panels and lumber.

"You gotta be kidding me." Mona now was inspecting several of his finished works that just had come back from an exhibit in Philadelphia. They stood lined up against the near wall where he'd uncrated them earlier in the week.

"This is what all the fuss is about?" she asked incredulously. "What you're so famous for?"

Valjohn shrugged.

"I thought you were supposed to be some kind of artist or something —you know, like Rembrandt. I mean, it looks to me like a kindergarten kid could throw this junk together."

"Probably could." Valjohn smiled.

"I mean, I don't claim to be an art critic or nothing like that, but I sure as hell wouldn't want any of this junk hanging over my fireplace—my commode either, for that matter. No offense intended, you understand."

"I understand."

"I guess there must be plenty of people out there who feel differently, though, huh? Plenty of weirdos who really go for this stuff?"

Valjohn grunted.

"Well, so much for your etchings," she announced, stepping back and almost tripping over a can of turpentine. "We got better things to do than spend all night gawking at this junk—right?"

Valjohn winced. It was the second time that day someone had accused him of gawking.

"Right, Rembrandt?"

"Right," he mumbled.

She winked, reached out and pinched his backside.

"Not much of a workbench," declared Mona, wriggling out of her girdle and bounding with amazing swiftness onto his unmade bed. "Thought sure you'd have a king-size."

Valjohn, still untying his shoes, glanced up at her naked, unrestrained body stretched out across the rumpled covers of his economy twin, immediately wished he hadn't and looked away. He reminded himself to turn off the light before he climbed in after her.

"I have a confession to make, Rembrandt," she said, hoisting one of her heavily veined legs straight up over her head.

Valjohn kicked off his shoes, dropped his trousers, doing his best to avoid her with his eyes.

"This is my very first time ever."

He looked at her, remained politely silent.

"I mean, I've never done it with a Negro person before. My poor old man, he'd turn over in his grave if he ever found out." She still was holding a leg over her head, was examining painted toenails that looked as though she'd dipped them in Tabasco sauce.

"I won't tell him if you don't."

"'Course, you're not hardly colored at all. You don't talk colored, an' I'll bet my tan's darker than you are! 'Course, I guess you're not hardly white either. . . ."

"Maybe he'll only roll over on his side," consoled Valjohn, laying his trousers neatly across a chair.

"His side?"

"Your old man in his grave."

"Jesus! Can't you fold your clothes later?" She let her leg fall to the mattress with an impatient thud.

Valjohn nodded, tossed his shirt on the chair. He removed his glasses, set them on the nightstand. He started to turn off the light.

"Leave it!" she ordered, reached out and into his shorts, grasped him in a callused hand.

A moment later they were both wrestling among the sheets. Early in the

11

going Mona sent the nightstand crashing over with a wild kick. Valjohn scrambled out of bed to inspect the damage. Mercifully his glasses had bounced sideways up against the wall and were unharmed. Not so mercifully, the lamp also was all right—its shade knocked awry, but the bulb inside, a big hundred-watter, blazing brightly as ever. He picked up the stand, replaced the lamp and his glasses. He started to climb into bed again, thought for a moment and slid the stand farther toward the wall—beyond the range of Mona's flailing limbs. At this point she rolled over and begged him to bugger her.

"Come on, baby, plug me! Blast me in the old caboose!" She lay writhing on her stomach, arched her back and began slapping and kneading her own bared behind.

"Come on, baby-baby, bang me in the old coal bin! Roto-Rooter me!"

Valjohn felt himself going down like a circus tent on Sunday. When he sat on the edge of the bed, scratching his chin, she threw a tantrum, cried and cursed him, implored him to reconsider. It only served to deflate him further. She tried to goad him into beating her up. She pounded on his back with her fists, demanded that he "sap her in the chops!"

He calmly replied that he wasn't going to give her so much as a swift kick in the ass. She collapsed into a stupor of self-pity and despair.

He got up. He got dressed. She remained sprawled on the bed. He offered to give her a ride home. She told him to eat a big one.

"Suit yourself." He picked up the phone and called a cab.

"Some dick you are," she sulked later, gathering her undergarments and stuffing them into her purse.

On her way out the front door, the cab honking in the street below, she yelled back at him, "And as for an artist, I wouldn't let you paint my toenails! You . . . you couldn't paint your way out of a paper bag with a ten-foot pole! A ten-foot brush! A ten-foot limp goddamn black dick of a cocksuckin' bastard, which is what you are, buster! You know that?"

The door slammed behind her.

"If you say so, Mona," he said and sighed. He slowly undressed again, debated taking a shower. Took a shower.

Clint Eastwood squinted. Extreme close-up. His eyes measured thirty feet across from pupil to pupil—filled the entire screen of the State Theater with his best wrinkle-puckered, bad-ass stare.

This was the part Harold Bledsoe liked. That stare. He leaned forward on his seat in the center of the fifth row, felt the skin prickling at his scalp, prickling down his spine all the way to his rump. Three times today he'd sat through this scene. He knew those eyes.

Now the other eyes. The eyes of Eastwood's quarry. The anonymous gunfighters. They were tense, threatening, blinking-scared. The eyes of jackals.

"Blam! Blam! Blam!" A thirty-foot six-gun erupted smoke and fire across the screen like a cannon. Men flung up their hands, tumbled backward, spewed blood. Eastwood

calmly holstered his gun to a background din of exotic whistles and percussion beats, strolled down a dusty street littered with bodies. Harold Bledsoe wiped a fleshy palm across his damp forehead, tugged at a lobeless ear. Now, that was how to get things done! No hesitation. No cold feet. Just go ahead and do it!

When the houselights came on again, he looked around at the audience, the people leaving, their gutless, stupid faces. They didn't understand. Not the slightest notion. He rose, strode up the aisle. Who was he trying to kid? What made him think he was any different?

On his way out through the lobby, he bumped into a man, a mulatto with a white woman. The woman looked like a whore.

"Watch where you're going, you fucking four-eyed Brillo-head!" he growled, three quarters under his breath.

"Excuse me?" The man turned.

Harold glowered at him but said nothing. The man turned away.

Damn right! Coffee-skinned son-of-a-bitch, you better back off! He thought it, but he kept it to himself. For a brief moment he swelled his chest, almost believed it. Almost.

He walked four blocks to where he'd parked his car on Clark Street. On his way he cut across the Civic Center Plaza, stopped for a moment to look up at the Picasso statue. It towered above him several stories high, a structure of welded steel plates and rods, enigmatic and untitled. Children played on its broad, sloping base. "Crazy pile of junk," he muttered to himself. Just what the fuck was it supposed to be? It had maybe eyes and a nose, he could see that, all right, but not much else. For a brief moment he thought the eyes were staring at him.

There were two parking tickets waiting for him on the windshield of his Mustang. He hadn't fed the meter for four hours. He grabbed the tickets, wadded them into a ball, tossed them at a passing van. Who was he kidding? He walked out in the street, retrieved the tickets. Pulling them apart, smoothing them against his thigh, he unlocked his car door and climbed in.

Before driving off, he reached over and opened his glove compartment. He took out his handgun again. He removed the chamois, stuck the gun under his belt. He liked it there while he drove sometimes. He could feel the cool barrel between his legs. Against his penis. If a truck bullied him, or a cab honked, or some shithead pedestrian shook a fist, he'd reach down and grip the handle, squeeze it hard. That was all. That was enough.

It was almost seven-thirty. He decided to drive out to the lakefront. This late the beach would probably be deserted. He could fire off a few rounds while there still was light.

Driving east on Randolph to the outer drive, he reflected on last night and Mary Jo Rudkus. He couldn't bring himself to go to work today. He had no idea if she'd recognized him—whether she knew his car or not. Who knows? Maybe she had the cops there right now waiting for him. Naw, he doubted that. For what? A lousy bump on the fender? For knocking her license plate loose? No way. The other? Like what was he doing following her? So? A free country, a public road and all that bullshit. They couldn't prove a thing. No sweat. There was never any sweat. He was so fuckin' lightweight it made him sick.

13

His boss, Riley—that was something else. He was going to be plenty pissed off. Friday was produce day. He said he'd rather have his stockflyers miss two other days than leave him short Friday. This was the second week in a row Harold had missed it. He could just see that big, scrawny mick stomping up the aisle after him when he clocked in Monday. He'd start screaming and bitching about his absenteeism, then work right into everything: sloppy pricing, misshelving, smoke breaks, reading magazines in the crapper, attitude—what sort of example was he setting for the kids? Riley always laid that one on him (at thirty-six Harold was the oldest stockflyer on the floor by a good fifteen years). Maybe this time Riley'd pull his card. So screw it. He'd worked there since high school. Maybe it was time for a change.

Harold parked the car at the north end of Davis Beach and walked out to the shoreline. The beach was deserted. He walked farther north, climbed up on a breakwater that ran half a mile into Lake Michigan. He drew his gun.

The heft of the weapon, the lethal balance of hard metal in his hand made him feel strangely whole, somehow complete. He cocked the hammer with his thumb, aimed at a trough of smooth water between two swells, squeezed the trigger. The gun—an exact replica of an old frontier Colt .45—bucked in his hand; a circle of water exploded very close to where he'd sighted. Not bad, he thought. Not bad at all.

He cocked the hammer again, was about to fire another round when he became aware of a figure approaching from out on the breakwater. Harold released the hammer with his thumb and hurriedly stuffed the revolver out of sight beneath his shirt.

As the figure neared, Harold saw that it was a fisherman. He was old, shabbily dressed in a torn slicker, striped bibs and a soot-stained railroad cap. He carried a bait pail, a thermos bottle and two sets of rod and reel. A stringer of perch swung from his waist. Harold looked at his eyes. Even from a distance, he could see they were red, swollen from staring too long in the wind. They looked like open sores.

While the fisherman still was in front of him, Harold reached down and gripped the handle of his gun.

The fisherman walked with a shuffle, one leg slightly splayed, suggesting an arthritic hip. He appeared not to notice Harold.

Harold lifted the gun from under his shirt, pointed it at the swollen eyes. The old man stopped walking. He now looked directly at Harold, but his expression remained the same. One of great weariness, of resignation.

When he began walking again, Harold pulled the trigger.

The old man's head was knocked back from under his cap. He dropped abruptly to the ground. The bait pail, fishing gear and thermos bounced and clattered on the concrete walkway, but the man lay still—like a puppet with its strings cut.

Harold stared down at the lump of clothes at his feet. His gun stuck out of his hand, awkwardly tilted toward the sky. A gust of wind off the lake caught in his open mouth.

He tried to realize what had happened, what he'd just done. An accident! His finger —it must have slipped on the trigger! He jerked his head around to see if he'd been observed. The beach still was deserted. He scanned the marina on the other side of the breakwater with the same result. The shot had been deafening, still rang in his ears. Everyone in the city must have heard! He stood taut, trembling, waiting for the outraged citizens to appear, waiting for the police sirens, waiting for the revenge of angry old fishermen everywhere.

The wind continued to gust. Waves scattered against the stones below. The city was silent, far away.

He looked down again at the fisherman. The body lay on its back, its right leg bent up, pinned underneath. The head tilted back with the face turned to one side. At the top of the left cheek near the bridge of the nose, blood ran out of an ugly U-shaped wound—a trickle, nothing more. The eyes, open, bulged hysterically from the pressure of the slug churning inside the skull. For a moment, Harold still could see the face alive, the eyes alive. . . .

"Goddamn," he muttered. He waxed philosophic. "Goddamn."

Then he grinned. He knew his finger hadn't slipped; he knew it had been no accident. He'd felt a sudden urge to do it—and he'd done it! No fuss, no cold feet, no getting sick. He'd just gone ahead and done it! Simple as that. He blew smoke from the barrel of the gun, spun the cylinder. One shot, goddamnit! He was nobody to mess with. Riley better think twice about giving him shit at work. Lots of people better think twice.

"Think I'm kidding?" he spoke to the fisherman, nudged the body with the toe of his Wellington. "Hey, old man, you think I'm kidding?"

He grinned again, then laid the gun on the walk. He dragged the body by an ankle to the edge of the breakwater. He looked at the face one more time. Blood had run down a cheek and now dripped from the chin into the deep, wrinkled folds of the neck.

"Too bad, old man, you messed with the wrong guy this time," Harold pronounced solemnly. Then he dumped the body into the lake. He threw the bait pail, thermos and fishing poles as far out as he could heave them. Holding up the stringer of perch, he admired them, dropped them over the old man's body sloshing in the waves against the pilings.

He picked up his gun and started back for the car. It was after eight.

He'd already reached the car, taken the keys from his pocket and unlocked the door when he saw her. Mary Jo Rudkus. She was standing not thirty yards away in the center of the beach. Alone.

No, it wasn't Mary Jo Rudkus—he must have that cunt on the brain. It was a young chick with blond hair, though. He wondered if she'd heard the gunshot, seen him shoot the old man. He doubted it, was positive she hadn't been there earlier. Besides, she wasn't even aware of him. She stood detached, staring out across the lake, the wind blowing her long, golden hair like some model in a TV commercial. She was that beautiful. It was dusk, rapidly becoming night, but he was certain she was that beautiful.

He hesitated, then thrust the car keys back into his pocket. He saw the old man lying at his feet, the hysterical gaze of those protruding eyes and he knew she was his.

Squeezing the smooth handle of the weapon tucked between his legs, he walked slowly toward her.

2

Lieutenant John Valjohn awoke at seven-fifteen, reached out to shut off the alarm, realized it wasn't buzzing. Saturday. He was taking the day off. He rolled over and tried to go back to sleep. Ten minutes later he got up.

He felt hung over—though he didn't remember drinking all that much. He was hit with a sudden recollection of Lieutenant Cobb's great weltering bum and launched immediately into his morning exercises: thirty push-ups; thirty sit-ups; thirty lateral toe-touches. Then moving off the russet throw rug beside his bed, three vertical push-ups, heels against the wall, sliding up between a brightly colored Kandinsky print and an original sepia nude done by a girl friend in college.

After a long, hot shower followed by a short, cold one, he began to come around, brusquely dried himself in front of the full-length mirror paneling the bathroom door, was mildly satisfied with what he saw. Granted he was no overpowering physical specimen: at six feet and 165 pounds he'd never be mistaken in a locker room for a pro football player . . . well, maybe he could pass for a kicker or a small flankerback (providing they never got him out on the field with a ball or a stopwatch). For having just turned thirty a few weeks ago, though, he'd managed to keep in pretty fair shape. Was actually 5 pounds lighter than he'd weighed in college (didn't put away all those bottomless pitchers of beer anymore). He paused for a moment, lowered his gaze. Nothing like a cold shower to bring out the latent eunuch in a man. Too bad Howland couldn't see him now; might give him a new lease on life.

Not exactly a matinee idol's face, he observed while he shaved. Still, some women seemed to find it interesting. They weren't all Mona Cobbs, either. He studied his mouth closely. Not really cruel enough. Neither were his eyes. He looked into them without his glasses. Too warm, too sensitive. Better get a haircut pretty soon, he told himself as he edged his razor down a cheek, delicately outlining his regulation sideburns. His earlobes were barely evident in the lower fringes of what was rapidly becoming a mini-Afro, his hair a light, kinky puffball of cinnamon and ginger. Definitely taboo. Surprised Howland hadn't jumped all over him about it.

He rinsed his face and dried on a fresh towel. He hesitated a moment longer, staring again into those too-warm, too-sensitive eyes.

"Oink, oink," he said.

While he ate breakfast, three spoonfuls of leftover cottage cheese and tea from a crusty, twice-used bag (he really had to do some marketing), he read the morning paper. Most of the news was concerned with the war. Bombing raids had been stepped up along the VC supply trails. Two U.S. planes had been shot down near the Cambodian border. Antiwar demonstrations were scheduled today on a number of major campuses across the country.

Valjohn tossed the front section onto a pile of other newspapers that had gathered on the kitchen floor and turned to the sports news. He scanned several pages until he found what he was looking for: the PGA scores. This week it was the Cleveland Open. Billy Casper had a two-stroke lead at the end of thirty-six. Palmer and Zarley were tied for second.

Golf once had been a major passion in his life. Glancing farther down the scores, he recognized several names of players he'd competed against in college. A couple of them he'd beaten. He often wondered how he might have fared if he'd tried to make it on the tour. He was no Nicklaus—lacked the brutal power to humble those long par-fives. Still, he was a sound shot strategist, had a good repeating swing and a solid putting stroke. The way things had been going on the Force lately, maybe he should've given it a whirl. Besides, Charlie Sifford probably could use the company.

Before leaving the apartment, he went into his bedroom and opened the bottom drawer of his bureau. He brought out his revolver, a .357 Colt Python. A real cannon. He also brought out a holster, a basket-stamp hip-hugger, started to snap the holster on his belt, then remembered it didn't fit the gun. He'd won them both in a department raffle his first week on the Force. The firm that had donated them during National Law Enforcement Day offered to replace the holster, but he'd never gotten around to bringing it in. Returning the holster to the drawer, he tucked the revolver under his belt, whipped it out a couple of times, fast-drawing at himself in the mirror. Ridiculous. He felt ridiculous and the gun looked ridiculous. At least in *his* hand it did. He had absolutely no rapport with firearms, loathed the few required hours he'd endured firing the damn thing on the range during his rookie year.

He shoved the gun back in the bureau and closed the drawer. Howland and regulations would have to wait till Monday. No way was he going to pack it today; it would definitely interfere with his backswing.

Valjohn swung his battered '61 Volkswagen into Cog Hill's sprawling fifty-four-hole golfing complex and searched the pro shop area of the No. 3 course, Dub's Dread, where he was to meet Bert Carlson. Valjohn spotted the affable lab technician over by the ball washer near the first tee. Two men stood with him. One of them was Hans Glad, the department's PR director. The other man he didn't recognize. Valjohn swore lightly under his breath as he parked. So much for the friendly little game. Glad liked to play for serious stakes. The last time they'd golfed together Valjohn had been pressured into some heavy betting, had wound up taking him for a bundle. Glad would be champing at the bit to get even. Now Valjohn wished he'd gone to the range and hit some shags.

He put on his shoes, hauled out his bag of clubs from the back seat and started for the pro shop.

"Come on, John, shake it!" hollered Glad, waving to him. "We're on deck! We already paid your green fee."

Valjohn waved back. Great. No time for even a few practice putts.

"Hope you don't mind a foursome—Bert mentioned yesterday you were playing so I asked him if we could tag along. Maybe get up a chummy little Nassau." There was a distinct gleam in the director's eyes as they nodded greetings. "Oh, I'd like you to meet a friend of mine, Sergeant Vito Satucci. He's with the State Police down in Springfield. Crowd control. Up here for a few days visiting operations. Vito, this is Lieutenant John Valjohn from Homicide. He's the one I've been telling you about. Swings a pretty fair stick. Won the NCAA championship a few years back."

"Finished ninth," Valjohn corrected. He shook hands with Satucci, then took out his driver and hurriedly began limbering up.

"Might as well make things interesting," said Glad, already on his way to the tee blocks. "Vito and I'll take on you and Bert. Say . . . uh . . . five a point. Low ball, low total and proxies. How does that sound?"

"Sounds pretty steep. This is my first time out this year."

"Only played a couple of times myself," flimflammed Glad. "Old Plastic Face" they called him on the Force. He had soft, doughy features and could mold them into more expressions than a mime troupe.

"How do you like this guy, Vito? Last time we played together he plucks me like a wet chicken for a hundred bucks—"

"Sixty," corrected Valjohn.

"—And now he's gonna bury his money in an old shoe. Okay, so we'll make it two bucks a point."

There was no escape. Valjohn looked at his partner. Carlson shrugged.

Glad smiled, took a perfunctory practice swing and lined up his shot. Though he was tall he had a short, flat swing—mainly to accommodate the bulge of a sizable paunch, one that appeared both conspicuous and unnatural on his otherwise slender build. He hit one of his typical drives: low and short, not much over two hundred yards, but straight down the middle of the fairway and in good position for his next shot on a dogleg left. Still smiling, the director hitched up his bright red par-buster pants and strode from the tee. The man knew his game; he was no hacker.

Satucci was next. Valjohn watched the sergeant tee his ball up and take his stance. He had legs as big as Nicklaus's and shoulders that belonged on a linebacker. Definitely riot-squad material. He also had a deep tan and heavy golfing calluses on his right forefinger and thumb; Valjohn had noticed them when he shook hands. Glad obviously had picked himself a player.

Without benefit of a practice swing, Satucci sent a screamer off to the left. The ball flew low for the first hundred yards, then suddenly shot upward, as if it had been hit again. When it finally came down, it had carried a bunker 260 yards on the fly and landed in the fairway perfectly cutting the dogleg.

"Good poke," acknowledged Valjohn.

"That's my pahtnah!" chortled Glad.

Carlson, swinging hard trying to match Satucci's home run, sliced his drive into a cornfield on the right.

"Hey, Bert, spring planting's over with—hit again."

He topped his next drive off the heel.

"That's okay, Bert. You'll settle down," Valjohn spoke encouragement as he replaced his partner on the tee. He felt far from encouraged himself, however.

He stared down the fairway. There was no way he was going to match Satucci's drive—not with the first shot of the season. He took a practice swing. It felt wrong. He took another one and then another. It still felt wrong. What the hell, he thought, addressing the ball, maybe he'd get lucky. . . .

He didn't. He caught the ball thin and pulled it off line. He watched a puff of sand rise as the ball dove into the bunker. Satucci's drive had flown.

Glad grinned. "Cat box!" he said, and he and his partner zoomed off in their electric cart. Valjohn and Carlson followed on foot, Carlson pulling a cart, Valjohn with his bag slung over his shoulder.

"Sorry you got stuck with me," apologized Carlson as they walked down the fairway.

"Sorry I got stuck with myself is more like it."

"I didn't know Glad was going to turn this into the U.S. Open, or I'd have thought twice about letting him join us."

Valjohn nodded, then chose to change the subject. "Couldn't talk your old boss into coming along?"

"The ancient one? Are you kidding? He wouldn't be caught dead out here."

Valjohn laughed. More than once he'd had his ears burned listening to one of Moe Frank's tirades on golf. Inane, decadent—a game for *shleppers* and *shlemiels,* certainly not for a real *mensh.* Now, baseball—watching his precious White Sox perform—that was another matter. "He still laid up with that summer cold?"

"Yes and no. Yes, he's still coughing like a consumptive; no, he was back to work yesterday afternoon."

Valjohn shook his head. Moe Frank was his closest friend, both on and off the Force. What the old ex-lab chief needed most was a little of this game for *shleppers* and *shlemiels*—a chance to get outside and start soaking up some fresh air and sunshine.

Both Carlson and Valjohn mishit their next shots into the rough; Glad made it to the apron; Satucci lobbed an eight-iron three feet from the pin.

"That's my pahtnah!"

Valjohn watched Bert dribble his next shot into a trap. It was going to be a long afternoon.

Three holes later and eighteen dollars down, Valjohn was just climbing out of a small ravine where he'd dumped another errant drive, when a caddy drove up in a cart and asked if he was Lieutenant John Valjohn.

He nodded.

"You've got a phone call in the clubhouse. They said to tell you it's from headquarters and it's urgent."

"Deus ex machina," Valjohn said and grinned at Carlson, picked up his clubs and dumped them into the back of the boy's cart. "We've just been reprieved."

"1834?"

"Could be."

"Hey, what's going on?" called Glad, speeding up to them in his cart. He'd left Satucci farther down the fairway by his ball.

Valjohn told him.

"Do you have to take it right now? I mean, for chrissakes, we're right in the middle of a game."

"Said it was urgent." Valjohn climbed into the waiting cart.

"The Reaper?"

He shrugged.

Glad scowled in silence.

"Look, I'll try to make it back if I can. Otherwise go on without me."

"Ya, sure . . ." The director knew he wasn't coming back. His fish had thrown the hook.

"Tell Vito I enjoyed playing with him. Maybe we can do it again sometime."

He tapped the caddy on the shoulder and they drove off. "See you later, Bert."

Bert grinned and waved.

At the clubhouse, he tipped the surprised caddy a buck and took the call in the men's locker room.

"Could be sympathetic vibrations," he mused aloud, scratching his head with the phone. Sergeant Milton Stephansky, special dispatcher for Homicide, had just informed him of the latest developments in the case he was working, C-65-1834, otherwise known as the "Reaper killings." It was a sensational, high-priority investigation and the first one—high or low— he'd ever headed.

"What?"

"Echo killings. Copycats."

"If you say so, Lieutenant."

A distinct possibility, thought Valjohn, considering the nature of the murders and all the publicity of the gory details. And considering all the psychos roaming around loose in the city. The sadists could thrill with the killer; the masochists with the victims. The sado-masos could have it both ways. Something for everybody.

"Any makes?"

"Right," came the hoarse, gravel-voiced reply. He was hard enough to understand in person; over the phone it sounded like a breakdown in the connection. "Well"—Valjohn heard the snap of a clipboard, paper rustling —"the one in the alley over on the South Side, his name's Jimmy Lee Cook. Nigro. Twenty-three. Got a rap sheet a mile long. Juvenile court at thirteen. Auto theft. Put on pro. B. and E. Sent to St. Charles when he was fifteen. Later served two separate sentences: a year in Vandalia for aggravated battery; three more in Joliet for armed robbery. Paroled in '63. A couple of years back he was indicted on a rape-murder charge. Case never came to trial, was backlogged and finally thrown out by a judge on an arrest technicality. Since then a few minor parole violations; otherwise he's stayed out of trouble."

Typecast for the part, thought Valjohn, reflecting on the Reaper's victims. Every one of them was a convicted or suspected felon. The majority were rapists and murderers. There also were a few arsonists, a wanted kidnaper-extortionist, plus a couple of pimps—both with felonious assault records. Almost all were executors of violence in the inner city. Sixteen of them. And they all were dead.

"What about the other two?"

"Male Caucs. Skip Varner and Jeffrey Dix, Jr. Late twenties–early thirties. Both outa-staters. Tennessee. We're still checking 'em out."

"You sure about the MO?"

"Look," Stephansky growled, "I'm just sitting here on my fat ass taking calls. I don't have to be sure about nothing. Harris and Sweeney are sure. So is Gillian. Sexually abused. Standard 1834 mutilations."

Valjohn found himself scraping the floor with a shoe, his spikes shredding the composition tile. Three in one night! His investigation already was under fire. Now the flak was really going to fly. He wished he was back out on the course losing his life savings to Glad and his storm trooper. Some reprieve.

"So what else is new?" He managed a sigh.

"Housewife bludgeoned to death in Skokie. Body was stuffed in an incinerator, but she only burned from the waist up. Two teenage gang members shot, execution style, on the West Side. Mother in Bridgeport smothered her kid in her husband's VFW flag. Owner of a Loop liquor store was robbed and knifed in a Grant Park lavatory. Oh, ya, a fisherman was shot. They fished his body out of the lake by the Davis Breakwater not half an hour ago."

Summer definitely had arrived, thought Valjohn, reflecting on homicide's seasonal graph. The long, cold nights of winter nurtured arson and robbery, but murder thrived in the dog days.

"If I was you, though," came Stephansky's rasping voice, "I wouldn't be worrying about other people's murders. You're up to your ass in corpses all your own."

Twenty-five minutes later, Valjohn arrived at the first address, an alley just off Cottage Grove. Several blue-and-whites lined the street. An ambulance sat with its red light flashing. He recognized a midnight-blue XKE parked at the corner. The alley was cordoned off.

Valjohn parked his Volks alongside the ambulance. A patrolman at the alley entrance blew his whistle and waved him away. Valjohn climbed out of his car. The patrolman strode angrily toward him.

"Hey, whaddaya think you're doing? You can't park there!"

"Lieutenant Valjohn, Homicide," Valjohn said without bothering to show his gold.

"Uh . . . sorry, sir. Didn't recognize you."

"No sweat." He hadn't had time to change clothes, was still wearing his golf hat.

He shouldered through the inevitable crowd gathered on the sidewalk, was struck with the odd impression that he knew everyone there, that he'd seen them all before. They were homicide's ever-faithful fans: undaunted, loyal as old alums, never missed a game.

"What's the word, Lieutenant?"

"Who's the stiff?"

Reporters. The boys from the cop shop. They stood in a small group with a patrolman on the other side of the alley, in shirt sleeves sweating out the midday heat with the rest of the spectators. His first impulse was to keep walking, but he stopped to speak to them, the words of a recent directive from the superintendent resounding in his head: *A police force is no more and no less than the image it casts before the public eye.*

"All I know is what I read in the newspapers." He forced a smile—just like Old Plastic Face himself. He always felt intimidated by the press. He remembered what a hatchet job they'd done on his predecessor (not that he hadn't deserved it). Though they'd certainly done nothing as yet to harm his own career, he knew there were a few among them—particularly the older raggers—who definitely were after his scalp.

"How was the game today, Arnie?"

Valjohn glanced at Chick Screed of the *Trib*. Speaking of older raggers —hardboiled, crusty and snide, a Walter Winchell look-alike. The man was smiling at him, but his eyes were two pieces of flint. Closely allied with the police union, the FPOP, he regarded Valjohn as little better than scab labor.

"Brief," replied Valjohn, ignoring the sarcasm. "Only got to play a couple of holes." He searched the surrounding crowd for the roving eye of a hand-held and was relieved not to find one. Considering his attire, he could do very nicely without TV coverage.

"Most inconsiderate of the murderer." There were chuckles. "Do the city a favor and stick to your paintings, Rembrandt. Or maybe you're planning to crack this case with your putter?"

Valjohn was about to answer in his defense when a deep voice rumbled out, "Hey, look, Screed, hassle him over what he does his day off on your own time! What I want to know is what went down in that alley there. How about it, V.J., is our friend playing games again?"

The voice belonged to Grady McTague, a reporter for the *Times*. Crag-gy-faced, fortyish, he stood at least six-six—when he straightened from his bearish slouch, which was rarely. He'd just now pushed his way through the crowd to join the group. In contrast to the other reporters in white shirts and ties, he was dressed in faded, war-surplus fatigues and sported a battered, beige tam. It was his XKE parked on the corner. A friend in need.

"Maybe, maybe not. I'll give you a statement as soon as I've checked it out."

"You do that, Lieutenant," growled Screed, "and don't forget we've got afternoon deadlines to meet." Several of the other reporters chimed in, grumbling over deadlines and the paucity of information.

"Give the man a break," said McTague, coming to his aid again. "He just got here."

"How about shots?" Dick Tate of the *News* asked.

"Just as soon as we're finished processing."

"The victim?"

"I'll check it out. If it's the Reaper, though, you can forget pictures." There was more grumbling. Valjohn started to walk away.

"V.J.," McTague called after him, "I'll trade you even. Right now. My hat for yours."

"Throw in our cars and you've got yourself a deal."

The big Irishman grinned, held onto his hat with both hands.

The alley ran between two sooty-gray brick buildings. One housed a sheet-metal fabricating shop; the other, an upholstering firm. Valjohn proceeded between them slowly, trying to fix in his mind first impressions. The alley seemed quite ordinary. Its pavement was old, broken and uneven, crumbling in spots from the weight of heavy trucks. Thistly weeds grew up through tar-seamed cracks. Waste paper and scrap metal lay scattered about. A green-shaded security light hung crookedly from a utility pole; all that remained of the bulb was a dangling piece of wire filament.

Would this at last be the place where he'd find it—the key, the tiniest of clues, to unlock the secrets behind all these bewildering 1834 murders?

The body was located beyond a wooden loading dock that extended from the rear of the sheet-metal shop. It lay partially hidden among several empty steel drums and a stack of discarded heating ducts. Lieutenant Greg Harris and Mike Cochran, a police photographer, were measuring with a field tape the distance it lay from the center of the alley. Harris's partner, George Sweeney, was squatting nearby, probing a clotted pool of blood with his pencil.

Sweeney looked up and acknowledged Valjohn's presence with a grunt. "How goes it, George? We still solid?"

Sweeney straightened to his feet, nodding. Valjohn discerned the ever-present flicker of resentment in the older detective's eyes. Last February the officer in charge of the investigation, Joseph Blear, had been relieved of duty following charges of gross misconduct. Sweeney was next in line to head the case, but Valjohn had been chosen over him. A dull plodder, Sweeney had been with the Force almost twenty years, Valjohn less than four; he was an outsider, a special appointee who'd received his initial rating with virtually no practical police experience. Being black didn't exactly help matters.

Harris spotted him, added a notation to the diagram he was making on his clipboard and walked over, reeling in his tape. He was a year or two older than Valjohn, competent but inexperienced. He also was the most fastidious dresser on the force. Even now in the sultry heat he wore a three-piece charcoal-gray suit, Capper and Capper, the coat buttoned and his Countess Mara tie snugly knotted and straight. He looked every inch the junior partner in a brokerage firm. He closed his eyes and shook his head. A bear market.

Valjohn knew the greeting. It wasn't going to be a pretty sight. The other men stood back. They were bursting to speak but remained silent. . . .

That was the way he wanted it, the way he'd instructed them to be. During this initial stage of his investigation, he wanted no comments, no ideas or interpretations. Now while the scene still was solid, still closest to the way things had happened, he wanted his mind free of all perceptions other than his own.

The corpse of Jimmy Lee Cook lay sprawled on the pavement before him. He remembered the first time he'd viewed a Reaper victim. He'd gagged, doubled over as if someone had knocked the wind out of him, then stumbled away coughing—partly to fight off the nausea, partly to hide his embarrassment. That had been less than a year ago. Now after investigating five of these slayings, he was able to stare without looking away, to breathe evenly and keep the contents of his stomach from churning up into his throat. Now a seasoned veteran, he even felt an inane urge to nudge the body with his foot, as if kicking the tire of a used car.

Cook's face was turned upward, his head cradled in his right arm, which appeared to be broken. His eyes, glazed in death, protruded wide open, horrorstruck—"like the eyes of a toad that's just been stepped on." Or so Valjohn's predecessor, Joseph Blear, had described the appearance in an earlier case report. Valjohn thought about the old science-fiction myth, the one about a murder victim's eyes photographing the last thing they saw, permanently fixing on the retinas the image of the murderer in the act. Looking at Cook, he almost could believe it. All he would have to do now was remove the eyeballs, take them to the lab, develop them like a roll of microfilm and *voilà!* APB time.

The mouth. The mutilation of the mouth was the killer's signature. Cook's lips were gone, completely chewed away. What remained was a shredded hole that bared his teeth and gums, gave his face a ludicrous grin —a death's-head grin—as though he were leering insanely at his own demise.

Valjohn knelt down and closely inspected the throat. There were no bruises or cuts. The victim's shirt looked like a rag. It was ripped and tattered, smeared with blood. Several buttons were missing. Through the openings he could see familiar ridges of abraded flesh running parallel along the rib cage. The victim's left teat looked as if it had been chewed off.

He knew what the postmortem would reveal under that shirt: There would be broken ribs, maybe a fractured sternum, maybe even a collapsed lung. There would also be something that resembled an old, blown-out piece of inner tube that once had been the victim's heart. Massive myocardial rupture would be the diagnosis. The outer walls of both ventricles burst; the interventricular septum split. There would be torn papillary muscle and the sinus of Valsalva ruptured as well. The pericardial sac encasing the heart would be distended, bloated with aneurysmic blood— a situation, it would be ruled by the CC, that had brought on "immediate and indefeasible death." The heart, pressured in this sac, was unable to recover from systole, unable to fill—like a collapsed balloon held in a fist. As a simple pump, it failed; as a vital organ, it ceased to exist. And so had Jimmy Lee Cook.

Valjohn had been informed by a consultant cardiologist that, taken separately, any one of the ruptures was a relatively common occurrence in cardiopathology, happening most frequently among the elderly, those already suffering from ischemic and other forms of chronic heart disease. But so much damage happening in one organ at one time was phenomenal, perhaps unprecedented. It really was a statistical impossibility—particularly taking into account that all victims in the case were either young or middle-aged men. It was as though someone had pushed a button and the organ had simply self-destructed.

So how was it to be explained? Fear? Exertion? The Pheidippides syndrome? The magnitudes seemed implausible.

Valjohn took a deep breath and lowered his gaze. The victim's trousers had been pulled down to his knees. The narrow black belt still was buckled. It was broken, however, on the right side between the second and third loops. It suggested the trousers had been yanked down with a great deal of force, the worn leather of the belt parting over the right hip bone.

Cook wore no underclothing: traditional rapist attire. His genitals—or what was left of them—hung exposed over the upper portion of his left thigh, spilled down into a thickened brown pool of blood. His organs were unrecognizable as such. Rather they resembled some surrealistic blob, an amorphic grotesquerie in the background of a Dali landscape. There were patches of crusted semen spattered all over.

He stood up and stepped back. He looked down once more and tried to imagine what might have happened, tried to picture in his mind the outrageous act that could have reduced a strong-bodied male adult into the wreckage that lay at his feet. He had little success.

"I get the creeps every time I look at one of these poor bastards," said Harris after Valjohn had walked over to the other detectives.

Valjohn nodded.

"Not me," growled Sweeney. "Just another fuckin' asshole that got wiped."

Valjohn turned to the photographer. "Give me a series of overlapping shots starting here by this blood. Move in on the body—be sure to catch those buttons there." He pointed to a couple of white pearl disks lying in the middle of the alley. They appeared to match the ones on Cook's shirt. The path of Cook's struggle probably originated near where they were standing and proceeded across the alley to the steel drums.

While the photographer fiddled with his lens setting, Valjohn looked at him thoughtfully. "And Cochran, I don't want to see that face over there turning up in the *National Enquirer,* okay?"

The photographer looked up from his camera, his face reddening. He started to say something.

"Not an accusation." Valjohn waved him quiet. "Just some friendly advice." He turned back to Harris and Sweeney, who were smiling.

"What about witnesses?"

"Some people upstairs." Sweeney pointed to a row of tenement windows over the upholstery shop. "They said they heard a commotion down here last night, but they claimed it was too dark to see anything. Light on

26

the utility pole's been busted over a year. Nobody came down to investigate."

Valjohn nodded. Couldn't blame them. Not in this neighborhood.

"Matter of fact, the body wasn't discovered till late this morning. Around ten-thirty. Guy dumping trash from the shop here spotted a leg sticking out."

"How's the fix?"

"Pretty good. People upstairs pretty much agree it was around twelve-thirty they heard all the ruckus. That puts it between twelve and thirteen hours ago. I'd say that holds up with the blood color."

Valjohn glanced at the dried splash at their feet. It was faintly brown, turning black. Burnt umber, he thought, the somber shade of a Rembrandt palette.

"He ain't clammy, but I figure he's lost most of his body heat. As much as he's gonna lose on a scorcher like today. We'll give him a rigor test as soon as you want to break the scene."

Valjohn borrowed Harris's note pad. Pressed for time, he made a hurried sketch of the scene, concentrated on positioning the body in relationship to the buildings, the alley and a few surrounding objects. It was rough, haphazard; still it would make later viewings of photographs more meaningful.

"Okay, let's roll him for lividity."

They eased the body over on its stomach, face down. The side on which the body had been resting was noticeably discolored, even with the victim's dark-pigmented skin. A large purple blotch covered the left buttock. It looked like an immense birthmark.

"Always nice to be sure," observed Valjohn. The discoloration was caused by blood. When the heart stopped pumping, the blood settled into stagnant pools in the lowest levels of the body. If you found a corpse lying on his back with the telltale blotches on his stomach, you could be fairly certain the body had been moved after death.

"How about rigor?"

Harris took hold of the body at the hips while Sweeney began manipulating the limbs, starting with the arms and moving to the legs. When he got to the feet, he quit and stood up.

"He's still loose in the calves and ankles."

Thirteen hours looked good—though rigor mortis was tricky and by itself far from dependable as a gauge. Temperature affected the process, as did the size of the subject. Rigor moved swiftly through those who were physically weak or exhausted, slowly through those who were large and heavily muscled. People dying under extreme stress could develop the symptoms instantly. Valjohn recalled reading in a textbook on forensic medicine about a cavalryman who was shot in the head during a battle charge. The dead soldier froze in the saddle, had to be pried from his mount some time later, his sword still clutched in his hand.

The stage of rigor in Cook's body, coupled with the heat of the day, seemed to verify the theory that the victim had been murdered where he lay and that the murder had taken place sometime last night between midnight and one o'clock.

"Hey, look who's here," announced Harris, standing up.

Valjohn turned and glanced down the alley, saw the familiar bent figure of Moe Frank limping toward them. His presence came as a total surprise and Valjohn greeted him with a big grin. The ancient one. For fifteen years he'd headed the crime lab in Central Division, had stepped down from that position the same year Valjohn had joined the Force. Now Frank only worked part-time. Six weeks ago Valjohn had helped him celebrate his seventieth birthday with a fifth of *cordon bleu*.

Bright-eyed and wearing a grizzled goatee, Moe still was considered one of the keenest minds in the business—ancient or otherwise. Only last week Valjohn had talked him into assisting on the case. Frank had been hesitant. He'd planned to move to California in the fall with his mother—she was eighty-seven—and was wary of committing himself to any new and potentially long-term project, no matter how intriguing.

"What brings you to the battle zone?" asked Valjohn as Moe set down the black leather satchel he was carrying and began rubbing his knee. Even in his younger years Moe rarely ventured forth from the confines of his sanctum sanctorum, the security of his Bunsen burner, his test tubes and slides.

He broke into a hacking cough, then replied, "I'm not sure. It's been ten years since I dusted a scene." He gazed solemnly at the deceased, and his voice trailed off. "I'd forgotten what it was like . . . out here." He broke into a cough again.

"Count your blessings. How's your cold?"

"What cold?"

"How's the knee?"

"What knee?" he said. He grinned and gave it a quick rub. "Who's complaining? When the weather changes, I'll let you know. Right now, I'm fondling it out of gratitude." He still was recovering from a recent knee operation. The joint originally had been traumatized by a Capone gunman's bullet back in the thirties. Various doctors had tried to rebuild it; for nearly forty years he'd suffered through their failures. Finally in the early spring of this year he'd given up on it, had it fused solid as a ball bat. He seemed pleased with the results. He was free of pain and claimed to feel twenty years younger, though he did admit his walk was something less than an artistic success. "So I move like a drunken old goat trying to fornicate with itself," he'd contended his first day out of the hospital. "The important thing is I move."

"Moe, we're really pressed for time. Grab a few samples here if you like; then come on with me across town. It's a triple feature today."

While Moe began rummaging through his field kit, Valjohn stepped aside with Sweeney and Harris and listened to their assessments. Valjohn listened without comment. When they were finished he told them to take some men and cover the neighborhood, check out the local hangouts and try to establish where Cook had last been seen alive and if he was with anyone. Then he remembered the press. He couldn't spare the time to get hung up with them now. He put Sweeney in charge of issuing statements. "Level with them, but no speculation. Let them in the alley for pictures after the final cross-combing. Be sure to bag the body first, though."

He turned back to Moe, who was bent over the victim with scissors snipping away several snarls of pubic hair. The spindly old technician carefully tweezered them into a collecting vial. He capped the vial, put it in his bag. He then leaned forward, supporting himself on his hands and his good knee, his right leg extended stiffly to one side, lowered his head until only a few inches separated his face from the victim's private parts. He tottered there awkwardly for several moments.

"My, my," he finally muttered to himself. He straightened up. "Go ahead, Valjohnny, take a whiff.

"Go ahead." Moe grinned. "I thought I was too old even to remember." Valjohn knelt down.

The Pullman Hill Cemetery lawn was freshly cut; the grass around the markers and the scattered trees—mostly poplars and evergreens—appeared closely trimmed, neatly manicured. Valjohn gazed down a row of gravestones that dipped and then rose again over a gentle, tree-lined swell of land. A bluejay screeched discontent, flitted among the leafless upper branches of a huge dying elm. In the background the steady rush of traffic on Irving Park Road could be heard, hidden from view by a high stone fence. A jet in final descent for O'Hare passed low overhead. Valjohn watched it disappear in the trees, then returned his attention to the narrow gravel drive he stood upon . . .

. . . and to the two-tone '56 Chevy sedan—all four doors hanging wide open—parked in the middle of it.

Jeffrey Dix, Jr., and Skip Varner couldn't stop laughing. Just the other side of Decatur, Dix ran the car off the road—he was laughing that hard.

"Will you knock it off, Skip," he gasped, wrestling the car back onto the pavement. Varner was recounting the incident they'd had at a filling station on the outskirts of Shelby, Kentucky, the night before.

"I think y'all down a quart, sir," Varner mocked.

Dix guffawed. That's what the attendant seemed to be trying to say when he straightened up from under the hood. He stood there, staring, holding the dipstick in an outstretched hand, his mouth open, trying to form words with no voice. Dix had just brought a tire iron down on his head. The blow had glanced off, had torn loose a clot of hair and scalp but had failed to knock him down. He just stood there staring.

When Dix hit him again, he slammed the iron across the boy's temple with a baseball swing. The head had creased like a ripe melon.

29

"You shoulda waited till after he poured in the oil. That's what he was fixin' to do. Standin' there all googly-eyed. Hell, he warn't goin' nowheres. You shoulda waited."

"I tole you to knock it off," Dix said, his eyes brimming with tears. They'd been laughing on and off now for nearly nine hours. They'd go along for twenty or thirty miles in silence, and then Varner would make some smart-ass remark and they'd start in all over again. Dix's insides ached. That Varner really could do a job on him.

Moe was busy dusting for prints on the passenger side of the Chevy. Frank Gillian, one of the detectives on the scene, had just returned from interrogating a caretaker at his residence. Gillian, young, bright, an honors graduate from the police academy, stood now filling in Valjohn with some of the details: As of yet there were no witnesses. Discovery was made by a gravedigger named C. J. Claypool sometime around eleven. Evidently this was one of the cemetery's older and more remote sections; it didn't get many visitors. Claypool had driven behind the Chevy in his pickup on the way to a new gravesite. He was towing his backhoe on a flatbed. The driver's door on the Chevy was open so there wasn't enough room to get by. He honked his horn and waited for a few minutes. He figured somebody'd gotten out to place some flowers. When nobody showed he got suspicious, climbed from his truck for a closer look. After a peek through the Chevy's rear window, he ran back and jumped into his pickup, threw it into reverse and floored it. He forgot he was pulling a trailer.

"That's when he jackknifed the flatbed into that headstone over there," Gillian said, pointing across the lane to a gray marble obelisk that lay toppled over in the grass. There were deep tire tracks cut into the nearby sod. "He had to unhitch the trailer to turn around. Then he highballed it back to his house and called the police."

Valjohn smiled grimly.

They were headed for Chicago, had been driving nonstop ever since Shelby. The filling station had been good for a hundred and ten bucks. After they'd removed the keys and the dipstick from the attendant—he was still clutching the dipstick tightly in his hand—they'd dragged his body inside and dumped it under the lube racks. While they were emptying the till, another customer had driven up. Varner had gone out to the pumps and serviced him as if he'd been working there all his life. Even did his windshield.

It was after ten in the evening when they arrived in the city. They tried to locate a cousin of Dix's who lived on the West Side, but his address turned out to be phony. They drove around aimlessly for a number of blocks until they came to a row of taverns. They parked in front of the first one, waited to make sure they weren't in niggertown, then got out and went inside.

They drank whiskey and beer, played shuffleboard and listened to the jukebox.

When I was just a baby
My mama told me son,

30

Always be a good boy;
Don't ever play with guns.

Dix liked Johnny Cash. There was something about his voice that really got to him deep down. Made him feel sad and glad—all pissed off and mean-eyed proud at the same time.

But I shot a man in Reno
Just to watch him die. . . .

Dix kept dropping quarters in the jukebox, playing the same song over and over. Other patrons started complaining. In a game of partners on the shuffleboard, he took a swing at another player with one of the steel pucks. A mistake. The man was small, went down easy, but also he was a regular customer and had a lot of friends. One of them, a massive foundry worker, flattened Dix with a swipe of his forearm. He stomped him with a pair of steel-toed work boots till Dix quit rolling on the floor and lay still. A couple of other men picked him up and pitched him out the back door onto a trash heap.

Varner lay low for a few minutes—he didn't want to earn some of the same treatment—then he strolled out the back door. Dix was on all fours in the middle of the alley, spitting blood. When Varner tried to help him, he jerked his arm away. "Let's get the hell out of here," he said, getting up on his own.

Soon they were in their car again, driving aimlessly through the city. It was three thirty-five, Saturday morning.

"You talked to Officer Molinero already?"

Valjohn nodded.

"He was the one who found the other body out there on the grounds. Claypool never saw it."

"What about the front gate?"

"I checked with the caretaker," said Lieutenant Gillian. "His kid's supposed to lock it in the evening. Said he must've forgot last night. The kid's gone right now."

"Better check with him when he gets back. Find out if there was any particular reason he picked last night to forget."

For the second time that day Valjohn borrowed another detective's clipboard and sketch pad. He positioned the car in relationship to the drive and the surrounding markers. He also diagramed the blood path. It started in the car. The front seat and dash were spattered with burnt umber. A trail of it ran from the driver's side out across the grass. Valjohn knew where it led, paced it off: fifty-seven yards—a little half-wedge shot—over a winding row of graves.

They angled east on Ogden Avenue until they reached Damen. There they turned north, and Varner, who was driving, began to nod. He suggested they find a motel. Dix grumbled, said they could sleep in the car. Stemming a nosebleed with his

31

shirttail, he told Varner to pull over. While Varner was searching for a place to park, Dix spotted a blonde standing at a bus stop at the corner of Damen and Washington Boulevard.

"Ooee!" he squealed as they drove by her. "Go around the block quick!" He laughed, forgetting his nosebleed and aching sides. "That's what we need—a little hair pie!" He slapped Varner on the shoulder. Varner protested, claimed she'd never get into the car. He turned left; Dix climbed into the back seat.

They had to go around a double block. When they returned onto Damen, Varner was certain she'd be gone. He had no way of knowing the buses had stopped running hours ago.

"Hot fucking damn!" yelled Dix when he saw her still standing there. He ducked down behind the seat as Varner pulled up alongside her and rolled down his window. He offered her a lift. . . .

The trail of blood ended in a small, dark puddle beside the body of one of the victims. It was a scene right out of a late-night horror movie, thought Valjohn. All it lacked was Lugosi or Karloff lurking in the shadows. Skip Varner lay in a fetal position, back hunched up against the rough granite setting of a marble headstone, whose inscription read: F. Brawne. His face was drained, alabaster white. His throat slashed. Both hands, caked with dried blood, clutched at the wound—as if trying to hold back the torrential outpouring of his life. The wound was more of a gouge than a slash. The skin was shredded and torn—not the neat cut of a razor or sharp knife but more the work of a dull-bladed instrument wielded with considerable force.

Varner's wound had been inflicted while he was in the car, presumably in the driver's seat. One of his shoes, a size-ten loafer, was found wedged between the brake and clutch pedal. Since he chose to flee on foot, his assailant probably was a passenger. (The key still was in the ignition and the engine started promptly on examination.) The haste of his escape was clearly marked by his blood spoor.

Falling blood told a story all its own. When shed from a stationary person, the droplets which fell on the ground tended to be round and smooth. If a person was moving, the droplets became elliptical, with jagged edges. The faster the person moved, the more elliptical and jagged they became. Though blood in the grass was impossible to read, Varner had also shed it on several flat marker stones lying in his path. The drops, drying black in the sun, were very jagged and distorted.

There was nothing to indicate that his attacker had given chase. There was no sign of struggle outside the car. No other wounds. Considering the blood loss, Valjohn was amazed the man had been able to run as far as he had. Pure adrenaline, he mused. "Scared shitless," Gillian had commented earlier, noting Varner had soiled his pants.

Valjohn finished his sketches and walked back to the Chevy. Moe was standing by a rear door, staring into the car. Valjohn slipped into the front seat, being careful not to touch any prime metal surfaces, and joined Moe's gaze into the back seat. It was not hard to see why the gravedigger, Claypool, had freaked out when he'd peered through the window.

The body of Jeffrey Dix was in the most grotesque, most sordid attitude of any Valjohn had yet encountered. *Au naturel*—except for a single white sock—he was stuffed upside down between the seats. His head bore the brunt of his weight, pressed sideways against the floorboard; his neck, cocked sharply at right angles, looked broken. His torso rose straight up, with his buttocks arching slightly over the rear-seat ashtray. One leg extended to the ripped upholstery of the ceiling, the other was twisted unnaturally to one side—the foot with a sock, tangled in a passenger's hand strap. Dried blood striped the body like primitive ceremonial paint. It had gushed from his inverted loins and coursed in two separate streams down his abdomen and chest, congealed in a dark, shallow pool encircling his face.

Between his legs . . . another Dali landscape. This time there was an added touch, however. Dix's member had been removed, torn away and jammed into the ragged, lipless hole that was his mouth.

Valjohn glanced at Moe. Moe leaned inside gingerly on his stiff leg. Because of the victim's posture he did not have far to bend. He took a few short sniffs of the thickly matted pubic hair and straightened.

Valjohn looked at him.

"Gefilte fish," he announced simply.

"Gefilte fish?"

Valjohn pressed over the seat and took a few whiffs of his own. He pulled back, puzzled.

"Gefilte fish?"

"Gefilte fish."

—part two—

3

"Libby, honey, would you tend to Mrs. Fulsop for me? I'm swamped right now. Room 312—she's on the pan."

And of course Libby would, even though she was behind in her duties —it was almost eleven, and she still had three baths to give before she could start charting.

"Tell her to fizz off," said Debbie Turner from behind the drawn curtain of a patient she was catheterizing. "You're just as swamped as she is."

Libby smiled, clucked her tongue, but after carefully folding the last miter corner to the bed she was making and fluffing the pillow, she went to the aid of the abandoned Mrs. Fulsop.

"I'm afraid I've been a naughty girl," said the tiny, wizened old lady in 312. She lay with covers clutched up to her chin.

Libby smiled, walked to the bed, reached under the sheets and quickly removed her hand. Accidents will happen, she wanted to reassure her, but she could only cluck her tongue and continue smiling.

After flushing out the bedpan, she went to CSR and brought back a bath tray, a new nightie and clean linen.

By the time she'd given the rest of her morning baths, the lunch trays were rattling up the dumbwaiter. She would have to finish charting during her own lunch period. She did not bother to glance at herself in the wall

37

mirror as she entered the nursing station. She knew what she looked like; she also knew missing lunch would do her no great harm.

"Libby, I don't see why you put up with it," said Debbie three hours later in the elevator after they'd signed off. "I mean, girls like Barbara or Karen —they're only using you."

At street level they took the north service exit and walked across Hopkins Avenue to the residence hall.

"It's nice to help out friends, but those girls . . . just ask a favor of them once and watch how fast they disappear."

Libby smiled to herself as they rode the small residence elevator to their floor. She appreciated Debbie's concern, loved her for it, but Debbie never would understand how she felt. She, Libby, could no more ask a favor of her friends than she could refuse one asked of her. Of course, the other girls took advantage of her, but she didn't mind. It was what she did best: giving herself to others.

Stella Bernstick, the school's director, had just finished tacking a revision of her counseling hours to the bulletin board and was leaving commons when Libby and Debbie emerged from the elevator.

"Good afternoon, Miss Bernstick," greeted Debbie. Libby murmured an echo.

"Girls." Miss Bernstick nodded. She moved toward the elevator, then turned to watch them walk down the hallway to their rooms. How expressive their walks were, she mused. And how contrasting. Libby, dull, heavyset, plain as porridge, a poor student—she plodded along as if weighted down like a beast of burden. More than once Miss Bernstick had considered speaking to her about her posture. The way she slouched—it so accentuated her dumpiness. And Debbie, slim, vivacious, cute as a button, an excellent student—though at times a trifle impertinent—she seemed to bounce from the balls of her feet with an exuberant yet unmistakable feminine grace.

Suddenly she was reminded of Sandra Kane, Libby's ex-roommate, and a painful sadness swept through her. Poor Sandra . . . she too had had that high-spirited bounce. Miss Bernstick caught herself. None of that! She wasn't going to ruin the day; she would shove the whole episode out of her mind—right now!—before it dragged her down.

In the elevator Miss Bernstick reflected on Libby—or rather Crescent Elizabeth O'Leary, as her full name read on her enrollment card. She had scored the lowest grade on her entrance exam of anyone in her class—so low, in fact, that at first she was considered inadmissible. It was only after several last-minute vacancies opened up that she'd been reassessed and finally accepted—mainly on the weight of a letter from one of her former teachers and a recommendation from a doctor on the staff of a small hospital downstate where she'd served as a candy striper.

In her office, Miss Bernstick removed Libby's folder from the files, opened it on her desk. She sorted through its contents, came to the letter

38

from Libby's ex-teacher, a Miss Nancy Haas, thoughtfully scanned back over it. Along with strongly urging the school to consider Libby for enrollment, Miss Haas gave a brief but telling account of her former student's background. An abandoned child, taken in by relatives—then orphaned again by a family tragedy—the poor girl had obviously had a rough time of it. She'd finally been raised in a state institution near Macomb, had not left there until coming here to Windhaven last fall.

She was twenty-two—four years older than the usual freshman coming out of high school. Apparently there'd been early learning problems. She'd been presumed retarded as a child, had received no formal education until the time she entered the home. She was almost a teenager by then. It was at this point, according to Miss Haas, that largely through her own efforts and understanding, Libby had been reevaluated and given the necessary tutelage to eventually earn her high school diploma.

Miss Bernstick paused, then read once again Libby's application, the short vocational essay concluding it:

> There are so many of all of us who are strong and healthy and yet lots of people who are hurting and sick too. If God went to the trouble of making us, some of us ought to go to the trouble of helping and healing the sick people who often don't have nobody to care for them. I feel good when I am doing this. I know I'm not the smart kind of person with many answers, but I am not the kind of person who is afraid to work either.
>
> Also I have always wanted to be a nurse. Even when I was a little girl I wanted to be a nurse. It is nothing I just dreamed up on the spot. Windhaven School of Nursing is a good school of nursing and if I'm let in I will always try my hardest to be a good nurse. Also I don't care about making lots of money.

Miss Bernstick had been touched when she'd first read those words. Nowadays so many of the girls fell into two distinct categories: Either they were all business, somehow seeing the profession only in terms of salary, security, job status and promotion; or they were starry-eyed romanticists in love with the idea of being a nurse, but only, as many would quickly learn, from a safe distance.

Libby's essay was one of the few that conveyed an understanding of toil. Miss Bernstick still could remember at orientation shaking her hand, that strong, thick-callused grip—she'd never felt such a hand on a young girl. Libby's chores at that foster home—she understood it was in the country —must have included, along with feeding the chickens, shoeing horses and bulldogging!

At Windhaven Libby left no doubts about her capacity for work. Making beds, cleaning and scrubbing bedside areas, lifting patients into wheelchairs, bathing them (they clamored for her back rubs, for her strong hands to knead their bed-sore muscles), emptying refuse, carrying trays and running errands endlessly for everyone—doctors, patients, nurses, fellow students, visitors—everyone. Her performance was tireless. No menial task was beneath her. This slope-shouldered, thick-limbed girl was a throwback to the nurses of a bygone era, a martyr to the needs of both the suffering and the overdemanding alike.

Stella Bernstick reached up and stroked the lines in her brow that had been deeply etched from a lifetime of worrying over her girls. Looking at Libby's photograph, the plump, round face, the dull blue eyes, the sparse, weed-blond hair—she cut it shorter now to keep it less scraggly-looking; unfortunately it also made her head appear smaller, accentuating her hulking figure. Miss Bernstick could not help feeling a strong affection for this noble anachronism. But an anachronism she was.

It was 1965 and nursing had changed considerably since the days of a Bridget Divers or an Anna Etheridge. Modern methods and technology demanded a different kind of girl—one with a trained, questioning mind to cope with a more complex role of responsibilities. Today's nurse had to be able to think for herself and be academically sound. She had to have a knowledge of chemistry, anatomy, physiology, microbiology, pharmacology, psychology, sociology, ethics. . . .

Miss Bernstick thumbed through Libby's grades. She was definitely borderline. Though she'd managed to get through the first semester with C's —a D in physiology was balanced with a B in Nursing I—her midterm grades for this semester indicated imminent disaster. She was failing in every course except Nursing II, and there she'd fallen to a C.

Miss Bernstick closed the folder and drummed her fingers on the cover. In the past her policy toward borderline students had been one of hands off. To assist them or lighten their load in any way was to do both them and the school an injustice. A diploma was of little value to a girl if she couldn't pass the state board exam. No license meant three wasted years. For the school it meant reprimand from the Department of Education. Too many unqualified graduates and the school could lose its accreditation.

Realistically, Libby was a born practical nurse. She could study for a year and gain her certificate with ease—no license was required, no academic hurdles. But, of course, she had her heart set on becoming an R.N. . . .

Miss Bernstick returned the folder to the files. She walked over to the window and looked down on the street below, the steady stream of people pouring in and out of Windhaven General.

She knew it was coming. Only this time she didn't stop herself. She allowed her mind to fill with ghosts.

Sandra Kane. Sue Ann Simmons. Patsy Marussa. Three of them. Her girls. She remembered their faces, their bright eyes and laughter, their innocence, their eagerness to learn. She remembered each of them and all of them, and the tears came.

Last November. The weekend before Thanksgiving. It had been warm, unseasonably warm, and some of the students had decided to spend one last day at the beach before winter set in. Twenty-two of them, mostly upperclassmen, singing and in high spirits, clambered into a chartered bus on that fateful Saturday morning and drove off to the Indiana Sand Dunes Park. When the bus returned in the evening, there were only nineteen.

No one seemed to know what had happened to the other three. They had failed to show up at a prearranged departure time, and the bus driver, after waiting over two hours, finally left when it was dark. Miss Bernstick notified the State Police immediately.

According to those who returned, the bus had reached the park around eleven, and the girls had remained together through a picnic lunch and most of the early afternoon. Later, however, they'd separated into smaller groups to wander off and explore the beach and surrounding dunes.

The missing girls were last seen together by one of their classmates, Laura Hunt, who'd left them to go boating with strangers. Ironically, Laura had been warned by the other three not to go off with the men in their boat, but to remain with the group, where, as Miss Bernstick had so often instructed them, there was safety in numbers. Laura had gone off anyway and reported last seeing her three classmates walking north along the beach toward the upper dunes—a remote area that was virtually deserted that time of year.

Miss Bernstick spent a sleepless night waiting to hear of any new developments from the authorities. There were none. The next day she went to the park. Laura went with her and helped direct a search party that had been enlisted during the night. It was not until Sunday evening, after she and Laura had returned to Windhaven, that the fate of the missing girls finally was learned. And for once in her life, her worst fears fell short of the truth.

A deputy searching in the upper dunes had found one of the girls' shoes. Not far from the shoe was an area of sand that appeared freshly dug. It proved to be the shallow grave of Patsy Marussa. She'd been shot three times—twice in the chest and once in the leg. The other two girls, Sandra and Sue Ann, were found nearby. Sandra also had been shot; Sue Ann had been strangled. Though Patsy was still fully clothed, her two classmates had been stripped and buried together, their bodies arranged across one another in an obscene pose. There was evidence of sexual assault. The lab tests revealed one of the girls had been abused after death.

The grisly details sped unchecked through Miss Bernstick's mind until she was dizzy. She turned away from the window, her view of humanity rushing about on the street below, and walked unsteadily back to her desk and sat down. Struggling, she managed to focus her thoughts once again on Crescent Elizabeth O'Leary.

Sandra Kane had been Libby's "big sister," assigned as a volunteer upperclassman to look after her when she'd first entered school, to help acquaint her with things and make her feel at home. Sandra was a city girl. She was attractive, sparkling, outgoing and popular with her classmates. Libby was just the opposite. Surprisingly, the two girls had hit it off together. In late September, when Sandra's regular roommate had suddenly dropped out of school, Libby had moved in with her.

It now appeared that Sandra's friendship had been a big factor in Libby's early period of adjustment. She'd given her a sense of belonging, succeeded in drawing her out of herself, helping her to relax and overcome her crippling shyness. This confidence was reflected in the classroom, where her performance, though certainly nothing special, was at least mediocre.

Miss Bernstick's secretary knocked on the door and entered from the outer office. She asked if there was any correspondence to be typed before quitting time. Stella dismissed her with a wave.

The tragedy had seemed to hit Libby the hardest of anyone at school. Though they'd all suffered through an intense period of shock and mourning, Libby had sunk into a deep depression from which, Miss Bernstick felt, she'd never recovered.

With Sandra gone, Libby kept completely to herself. She roomed alone, rarely ventured out other than to attend her classes, work at the hospital and eat. She almost never visited the commons to chat or watch television. When she did speak to someone, it was seldom more than a few mumbled syllables. Whatever she did in her spare time, it certainly wasn't related to her schoolwork. Her plunging grades left little doubt in Miss Bernstick's mind that unless Libby snapped out of it soon, she would be dropped from school at the end of the term.

Stella snatched a faded two-week-old cineraria from her desk and threw it into the wastebasket. Then she stood up, straightened her hair and patted the thin row of cottony ringlets that fringed her forehead.

The time had come for her to do something—hands-off policy be damned! She'd never met a more deserving girl; she'd see her through this crisis if she had to tutor her herself!

The next day Miss Bernstick summoned Debbie Turner to her office. Debbie seemed as close to Libby as any of the other girls. Debbie also was in many ways similar to Sandra—popular, outgoing, a good student. Miss Bernstick discussed Libby's problems at length with her and was pleased to learn that Debbie shared her concern. When she solicited her help in the matter, Debbie offered it eagerly.

"You could start by moving in with her. I don't think rooming alone is doing her one bit of good."

Debbie was silent.

Stella knew she was asking a lot. Debbie and her present roommate, Frances Taylor, were close friends.

"Of course, that's just a suggestion. Why don't you think it over for a few days. Make your decision then."

Debbie'd already thought it over. "I guess if you think it'll really help . . ." She sighed.

"I'm certain it will, and the sooner it's done, the better. If you'd like, I'll speak to Frances for you. I'm sure she'll understand."

Debbie told her it was no problem. She offered to move in that day.

"Wonderful," said Stella, standing up. She shook the hand of her fellow conspirator and expressed how pleased she was with the outcome of their little chat.

"Oh, if you happen to see Libby in the dorm," she added, "please send her to me. There are some things I have to discuss with her."

Libby sat listening with head bowed, her thick hands folded together in her lap—looking very much, thought Miss Bernstick, as though she were deep in prayer. Miss Bernstick had just told her she was being placed on academic probation.

The director picked up a mimeographed copy of the imposed restrictions and read them off. They were designed to settle down the work habits of the wayward student. No weekend leaves were allowed. No late-night passes. No television after 8:00 P.M. Special study hall sign-ins were required in the afternoon and evening. Libby listened unmoved, head still bowed.

After Miss Bernstick had finished reading, she was silent for several moments. Then instead of handing the copy to Libby, she made a big show of tearing it up and throwing the pieces into the wastebasket. Libby raised her head, a look of puzzlement on her face.

"Libby, I'm afraid these restrictions really don't apply in your case. I think we both know assigning you to spend more time alone in your room would accomplish nothing. It would be like throwing Brer Rabbit into the briar patch, if you catch my meaning."

Libby stared at her with wide, unblinking eyes. Miss Bernstick wished she could read the thoughts behind them and then scolded herself for thinking of grazing cattle.

"So what I've done in your case is made up a special set of regulations. Nothing written down, but I think the gist of what I'm about to tell you should be easy enough to remember.

"First of all, as you already know, I've assigned Debbie Turner as your new roommate. She's a wonderful girl, and I think you'll both get along splendidly. In fact, I want you to make a special effort to be good friends. Confide in her. If things are troubling you, let her in on it. If you're having problems with your homework, don't be afraid to ask for help. Okay?"

Libby tried to smile.

"Okay?"

She mumbled, "Yes."

"Next, I think you've sadly neglected your social life. I want to see you spending more time in the lounge. Watch some television, gossip with the rest of the girls—or at least listen in. Go out with them to the movies. Go to some parties. I think it's nice to enjoy one's own company now and then, but I don't think you're enjoying it. There also are times when the company of others is needed. You've been moping around long enough, Libby. Do I make myself clear?"

43

Libby's eyes watered.

"Sandra and the other girls are gone, and we all loved them and miss them very much, but we're still here, and we have to go on living. Our duties are still before us, and if we don't perform them, who will? Do you still want to be a nurse, Libby?"

Libby wiped her eyes. She nodded her head vigorously.

4

As a child Crescent Elizabeth O'Leary made marvelous noises. She could whistle, click her tongue—pip, coo, chirk in an endless variety of sounds, a variety that far exceeded the normal range of infant utterances.

She was born on the prairie, in the house of her aunt and uncle on a small downstate farm wedged between two hillsides along the gumbo-brown banks of the La Moine River. One spring day, out of the blue, her mother had come to visit her only sister, Eudora O'Leary. She had stayed for two months, given birth to Crescent, and disappeared the following week, never to be seen or heard from again. Eudora's husband, Lloyd, was a poor tenant farmer who worked less than three hundred acres of another man's land to provide for a family that already included two offspring. Nevertheless, he and his wife would not think of turning Crescent over to the county home and strangers. Her mother might be worthless and a tramp, but still she was kin. And so was her daughter.

Eudora O'Leary found her niece's colorful intonations a vast improvement over the whooping and wailing that had so stridently expressed her own children's infancy. Crescent filled her tiny nursery, a converted stairwell closet, with lilting warbles, chirps, twits—strange, successive mordents by the hour. She seemingly had at her command an entire exotic language all her own. And she never cried.

When the O'Learys had company, they would invariably bring her out to perform. Sitting in someone's lap or crawling about on the rose print linoleum floor of the living room, she never failed to delight their guests with her melodious patter. She even charmed their landlord, Isaac Hoge, a niggardly old celibate who was not known for his fondness for children. Paying a visit to his tenant's stark clapboard dwelling one afternoon, he happened upon Crescent amusing herself on the porch. Though he'd come to lecture Lloyd for cracking a new coulter on his plow, he listened to Crescent's enchanting repertoire and soon forgot the purpose of his visit. He'd never heard anything like her before. "She's better'n a pet canary. Ought to be in the movies," he opined, shaking a bony finger at Crescent's aunt. "Or on TV—'The Mr. Ed Sullivan Show'!" He stayed for coffee and then for supper, never once mentioned his plow. From that time on he took a special interest in Crescent, referred to her as his "little songbird" and knocked ten dollars off the O'Learys' monthly rent. Eudora and Lloyd could not have been more proud of her if she'd been their own.

As Crescent grew older, however, her aunt and uncle began to worry. It occurred to them on her third birthday that she had yet to utter one word. No "Mama," no "Dada," no "wahwah"—not one sound that was even faintly reminiscent of human speech. In the months that followed Eudora O'Leary tried hard to get her to talk. She played games with her by the hour; she coaxed; she pleaded. But to no avail. Crescent could not —or would not. It was as though she were afraid to abandon her own special sounds, as though they formed a sanctuary, a part of her own little world that she would stubbornly cling to for the rest of her life.

By the time she was four, the O'Learys were convinced she was addle-headed.

They took her to the family doctor in the nearby town of Carthage. Dr. Abraham Whittle, a complacent septuagenarian and incurable sophist, could discover no physical defects. Her vocal cords were in perfect condition. So was her hearing. The O'Learys were not encouraged. The doctor did, however, offer them some words of hope: Her perversity might not be permanent. Like thumb sucking or bed wetting, there was a chance she still might outgrow it.

As they prepared to leave his office, the doctor handed Crescent a lollipop, patted her on the head and told the O'Learys to count their blessings. Crescent was, after all, a beautiful child, fit as a fiddle, and besides, he added with a wink, the world was too full of talk these days; perhaps her affliction was a blessing in disguise.

The resemblance was uncanny, thought Eudora one afternoon watching Crescent play in the yard. She was picking dandelions growing up through the center of a huge discarded tractor tire, carefully placing them in an old fruit jar. The hair was the same: rich, blond—a mixture of barley and rye. The same delicate clear skin, white as separated milk. And the features of the face—the impossibly green eyes—Eudora could almost see Crescent's

46

mother, Geraldine, her own little sister twenty years ago—now holding up that jar in both hands over her head, offering its bright yellow bouquet to the sun; watched her turn circles barefoot in the crabgrass until she was dizzy, until she'd changed back to Crescent, to Geraldine and finally, tumbling to the ground, giggling and rolling about, back again to Crescent.

Eudora, plain and dowdy, even felt a tinge of her old sibling jealousy. But though she'd often longed to be as pretty as her sister, she'd never wanted to be Geraldine. There was something strange about her, something lonely and sad. When they were kids growing up together on the farm near Griggsville—you could see it in her eyes even then, a kind of distance, as if part of her were always somewhere else, lost and searching. And how many times had she run off as a little girl? How many times had she been found wandering along some country road or playing by the river or sleeping in some distant field or woods? Mr. Barker, who had a neighboring farm on the ridge, joked that he put a bowl of milk on his porch every evening for stray dogs, cats and little Geraldine Cockroft. Jason Cockroft, their father, had finally built a picket fence around the yard. He said it was to keep his hounds from roaming, but everyone knew it was to keep little Geraldine penned up, to rest her mother's tired, fretful eyes.

Her parents doted upon her as though she were some miraculous gift they hadn't deserved—yet she remained wistful, never seeming to belong; and Eudora was sure one morning the family would wake up and find Geraldine gone for good, and it would seem almost as if she'd never really been there.

When she was fifteen Geraldine finally did run away for good. Or what amounted to the same thing, for it was eleven years before she returned, and by then there was nothing to return to. Their parents had been killed in a car wreck, the family farm sold to pay off debts. Eudora had left Griggsville, had married Lloyd, her high school sweetheart just home from the war, and they'd settled here near Carthage.

Eudora often had speculated on what had happened to her sister during those eleven years. She sometimes imagined her becoming rich and famous. One day she, Eudora, would be thumbing through a magazine and there would be a picture of Geraldine staring out at her with those big, wistful green eyes. She'd be a movie star or a fashion model, and she'd be dressed in diamonds and furs. Or maybe Lloyd and she would be driving along in the old Plymouth and suddenly they'd hear a familiar voice over the radio. She'd turn up the sound and, sure enough, it would be Geraldine singing a song on "Your Hit Parade"!

Eudora would brood over these fantasies, particularly when she was feeling trapped by the drabness of her own world. She would imagine herself rich and glamorous, and she would end up feeling bitter toward her husband and the tedious life he'd provided her. Then ashamed, she would swallow the bitterness and bristle with contempt for her sister, the one responsible for troubling her mind.

Eudora had questioned Geraldine after she showed up again, but her sister was as close-mouthed and aloof as always.

"I live up around Chicago," Geraldine confided. Nothing more. There was a hardness in her eyes now and the smell of alcohol on her breath. She was seven months pregnant, and she had a badly disfigured right ear. Her hair covered it most of the time, but Eudora had seen it "real good once" when they both were standing out by the garden in the wind. The upper shell was gone. All that remained was a thin, bony rim and an ugly twist of lobe.

Geraldine also refused to talk about Crescent's father. Again Eudora fantasized, saw him as the classic villain: handsome, dashing, rich and famous—an utter cad. Geraldine was madly in love with him, but he was already married. Because of his high position he wouldn't get a divorce. Geraldine had no alternative but to bear his child alone and in shame.

After her sister had run off again—this time leaving behind a newborn infant—Eudora visualized a different sort of man. He became a kind, generous individual, honorbound and loving. He adored Geraldine, was completely helpless under her spell. He offered her the world, but she ran away from him, just as she'd run away from everything else in her life that meant something. Miserable, desperate, he had no idea where she'd gone, where to begin looking. Perhaps he didn't even know she was with child. Would never know . . .

Eudora's fantasies bore little resemblance to the truth.

For eleven years Geraldine had lived "up around Chicago," just as she'd said. That included a string of dissolute, honky-tonk bars that stretched all the way from Cicero to Calumet City. By the time she was eighteen, she was already a seasoned barmaid, B-girl, stripper and hooker—had even performed in an eight-minute porno reel, costarring with a six-foot boa named Big Z.

As a stripper she became a headliner in a small West Side nightclub called the Club DeLaroo. There with her hair braided into pigtails and wielding an obscene pitchfork—its four tines resembling erect and circumcised penises—she danced under the name of Rebecca of Nookybrook Farm, three times nightly shed a red flannel jersey and bib overalls to the bump-and-grind refrain of a two-piece band:

Old MacDonald had a hard-on
Ee-ai, ee-ai, oh!
With a hump-hump here
And a hump-hump there.
Here a hump, there a hump,
Everywhere a hump-hump.
Old MacDonald had a hard-on
Ee-ai, ee-ai, ooo . . . ah . . . ooo!

She worked off and on for a number of years at the Club DeLaroo, had a long, tempestuous affair with the manager, a short, dark Sicilian with rings on every finger. Partly out of boredom and partly out of a need to assert her independence, she went back to turning tricks on the side. On one such occasion she contracted gonorrhea, proceeded to give it to the Sicilian. Enraged, he broke her nose with the back of his hand, threatened to kill her if he ever saw her again. She fled without packing a suitcase.

Sick of Chicago, she got a job as a hostess in a dance club, The Wallflower, on the Near North Side. Her plan was to work a few months, save some money, then move to Miami or Los Angeles.

One night driving to work, she pulled into a parking lot a block east of The Wallflower, was met by an attendant who directed her to a space in the unlit rear of the lot beside the blackened brick wall of a fire-gutted warehouse. She thought it strange at the time. Though she parked her '37 De Soto regularly in the lot, no one had ever assisted her in the past. A white-haired old man usually was the only one on duty after eight, and he never ventured from the rent shed where he sat all night, listening to his radio.

She'd already had a few drinks. When the attendant held open the door for her, she carelessly dismissed her suspicions and slid from behind the wheel. He was a large man, wore a green work shirt and a red-visored baseball cap. His sleeves were rolled up revealing one forearm dark and hirsute, the other withered and slick with burn scars. As she stood up she noticed that his face, which had appeared strangely lopsided through the window, also was covered with burn scars. The right side, the skin of his cheek and forehead, was badly discolored, mottled gray and yellow and drawn bone-tight. A pale cicatrix pulled his lower eyelid down and joined it to the corner of his mouth, giving him an unnatural sneer. He did not step aside to let her by.

For a moment they stood staring at one another without a word. She started to speak, at the same time reached for his arm to push him aside. He grabbed her by the shoulders and threw her back down across the seat. She tried to cry out, but his fists hammered about her head until she was silent. He hauled her semiconscious from the car, her head striking the running board as she pitched to the ground. There in a bedding of cinders and gravel, he raped her. Brutally. Drooling, growling, cursing, he licked, sucked and chewed her flesh. When his fury was spent, he began strangling her with her orange silk scarf.

Headlights flashed on the warehouse wall behind them. He looked up to see another car pulling into the lot, flung her head back in the cinders and fled.

Geraldine couldn't move. Her arms and legs belonged to someone else. She lay on the ground on her back, her chest heaving and shuddering. She coughed and spit up. She rolled her head. Thirty minutes after the attack, when she was discovered by two youths—they'd heard her labored breathing from a neighboring row of cars—she still lay there.

The two boys, both in their middle teens, stood over her in dumbfounded silence. One of them carried a flashlight and a screwdriver wrapped in a sweatshirt; the other, a barracks bag. They were systematically looting the cars in the lot—taking any valuables left on the seats, breaking open and emptying the glove compartments. The youth with the flashlight switched it on. He could see her face was battered, swollen and bleeding; her hair tangled and smeared with blood and cinders. One of her ears looked nearly chewed off. He swung the beam of light down her body. The front of her blouse was torn open, her dress hiked up above her waist. She lay with her arms at her sides, her legs outstretched, slightly spread.

The youth carrying the bag told his friend to douse the light. He set down his bag and knelt over her, stared at the shadow of her sex. In the moonlight her white legs seemed to glow. He unzipped his pants.

"You crazy bastard!" his friend hissed gleefully.

Two hours later several patrons returning from The Wallflower found Geraldine wandering in a daze among the parked cars. They were part of a construction crew working on a nearby bridge project. They'd just been hustled for a big bar tab, thrown out of the club, and they were in a drunken, ugly mood. One of the men recognized Geraldine as a Wallflower hostess. She had, in fact, played him for a number of drinks a week earlier.

He winked at his buddies—the evening wasn't over yet. He put his arm around her and gently but firmly led her to his car. While he was opening the door, he suddenly grabbed her by the hair. Then he threw her into the back seat, lunged on top of her. The other men, four in all, stood around nervously joking and laughing, each waiting his turn.

The old man found her early the next morning when he left the shed to go home. She was raving incoherently, had crawled under a '39 La Salle and refused to come out. He tried to coax her, but she only crawled farther under and peered out at him like some wild, cornered animal. He called the police.

Geraldine recovered from her ordeal with surprising speed. She spent five days in Cook County Hospital, two of those under observation in the psycho ward. Most of her injuries were superficial, though she did lose three quarters of her right ear. They also cleared up her gonorrhea. She didn't learn until a month later that she was pregnant.

Her first thoughts were for getting an abortion. Several girls at the club had had them. They were expensive, but she wrote down names and addresses, made appointments.

The weeks went by; the months went by. She did nothing. As the fetus grew in her body, a notion grew in her head: She would have the child. Not that she wanted to be a mother—the idea was abhorrent to her. Nor had she grown fond of the fetus itself. She still regarded it as a tumor—the whelp of an incubus. Rather she desired to give birth for sentiments that defied her understanding, sentiments that were as strong as they were remote and unclear to her. She desired to give birth to herself, to purge herself of herself. In her mind, the child she carried became everything she despised about her life, everything she longed to escape from. To bring it into the world and then to run from it, to abandon her own likeness— that somehow filled her with promise. It would be her final resolution to flight, the ultimate assertion of her independence.

She pondered the alternatives that would face her after delivery. She would not abandon the infant in the streets. Nor would she leave it on the traditional doorstep of a stranger. She would seek out her own roots, return downstate to her home.

One morning in early May, she loaded the De Soto with her few belongings and herself—she was seven months along—and drove out of the city.

Sometime before her fifth birthday, Crescent fell into a state of abject silence. Her aunt and uncle had become increasingly distressed with her inability to speak, increasingly disenchanted with her marvelous noises. She no longer flourished as their little songbird. She'd become instead an idiot child, an object of pity, a source of embarrassment and shame. Whenever someone came to visit now, she was carefully kept hidden away, playing outside or shut up in her tiny room.

Even when there was no company, her aunt could barely stand having her around. The moment Crescent opened her mouth her aunt would snap at her, demand her to be still or to take her freakish chatter elsewhere.

Eudora had solemnly prayed that the doctor would discover something organically wrong with the child, something that could be seen and dealt with or at least understood. When he hadn't, she found herself giving way to new feelings. She began to perceive Crescent as somehow tainted spiritually—just like her mother. It was almost as if God were punishing Crescent for her mother's sins, her selfishness and irresponsibility.

"Hey, Goonybird, Ma says to knock it off!"

When Crescent's noises had become too loud for the thin plasterboard walls of her room, Kevin, the oldest of the O'Leary children, would pound on the door and yell at her.

"Goonybird! Goonybird!" Kevin's sister, Sarah Ann, would mimic from wherever she was playing nearby. It was Crescent's nickname, one Kevin had given her a long time ago but had been forbidden to use. Lately he'd learned he could get away with it, and soon he, Sarah Ann and all their friends were shouting it out with glee.

Crescent retreated farther and farther into herself, avoided the other children, avoided her aunt, whom she'd once followed around the house like a weaning kitten. Outside playing in the barnyard with the pigs and chickens or wandering in a nearby grove of towering oaks—these were her favorite places now, secluded, the only places left where she could raise her voice, sing her secret songs into the wind without fear of ridicule or rebuke. But even here she eventually fell mute, the silence growing from within, swelling up in her throat, self-imposed, choking her with loneliness.

As the months went by, her steadfast smile faded. Her laughter was forgotten. She moved through the day with dull, listless submission. At night her sleep was fitful, burdened with terrible dreams that left her whimpering, twisting in the covers. She began eating her hair, sucking on the long, golden strands, chewing off the tips; ate her fingernails, paint chips, string, rubber bands, crumbs and peelings of all kinds lying on the kitchen floor, grass, weeds and dried chicken droppings in the yard, caulking tar and cinders from the barn. She developed a tic: Her right eyelid would wink and flutter like the wings of a freshly pinned butterfly.

Her appearance changed. She grew pale. Her eyes dulled. Her hair turned drab as summer dust. The O'Learys took little notice.

In the early spring of Crescent's sixth year, about the time the last snows had melted and the fields were still filled with muddy pools, Sarah Ann became ill. A plump, boisterous girl, she grew listless and tired. Her robust appetite dwindled away until her mealtimes included little more than a few indifferent mouthfuls, a recital of lame excuses. Her mother's initial relief —Sarah Ann always had eaten too much—changed to growing concern when she saw how rapidly her daughter was losing weight, how pale and drawn she looked. It seemed as though she'd contracted Crescent's malady, only in a much more accelerated form.

Before the fields had dried out, Sarah Ann started running a fever. The O'Learys decided it was time to take her into town to visit Dr. Whittle. Though Eudora could see no reason for her sister's daughter being reexamined—she was convinced there was nothing medicine could do for her —Sarah Ann wanted the company, and Crescent wound up tagging along.

Pica was not unusual among children, the old physician informed Eudora, referring to Crescent's deviant eating habits. She would outgrow it in time. All she needed was plenty of fresh air and sunshine. Then noting her uneven, straggly hair, he decided she might have hair balls in her stomach and prescribed an appropriate emetic.

Dr. Whittle conceded that Sarah Ann was legitimately ill, diagnosed her ailment as glandular fever. She had the customary symptoms: a mild, persistent temperature, pain and swelling in her lymph nodes, a swollen spleen. He recommended a dietary supplement and plenty of rest. There was no cause for worry; it was nothing serious.

Two weeks passed. Then two more. Sarah Ann's condition failed to improve. Her fever hung on. She continued losing weight. The pain and swelling in her glands spread to her bronchial nodes, causing a cough. The cough developed slowly, increased until by the end of the fourth week she was having paroxysmal fits, vomiting.

Dr. Whittle finally made one of his rare house calls (a practice he'd scrupulously avoided since Roosevelt's election to a second term). This time when he examined her, he took a sample of her blood and sent it to the county laboratory. An overabundance of white lymphocytes was discovered. Dr. Whittle rediagnosed her case as mononucleosis complicated

52

with whooping cough. He failed, however, to take a sample of her sputum for positive identification.

Sarah Ann was given anti-spasmodics and sedatives for her convulsions. She also received penicillin shots to combat the disease and prevent further complications of pneumonia. Dr. Whittle again reassured the O'Learys not to worry; things were well in hand. He reestimated her convalescence to run eight weeks.

Sarah Ann showed signs of improvement for several days. Her fever subsided, as did her cough and much of the pain and swelling in her glands. About the time her parents believed she would soon be up and around again, her condition took an abrupt and ugly turn for the worse.

She complained one day of a new ache, a tenderness deep in her bones. Two unaccountable bruises—large, yellowish-purple splotches—appeared on her body. The next night she awoke hemorrhaging profusely from her nose and mouth, choking on her own blood. Lloyd wrapped her in his overcoat and rushed her twenty miles to the municipal hospital in Macomb.

Two days later the O'Learys learned she was dying of leukemia. Instead of eight weeks to recover, she now was given eight weeks to live.

Crescent had never been very close to her stricken cousin. Both Sarah Ann and Kevin always had treated her as an outsider, an intruder. Where Kevin's hostility toward her was general, directed toward anyone he considered his inferior, including his sister, Sarah Ann's was personal, and derived from a very real sense of rivalry. Crescent had usurped her role as the baby of the family. Through Crescent she had learned that she was not pretty, but pudgy and plain. She brimmed with resentment, and when Crescent finally fell out of favor, Sarah Ann had rejoiced.

In the hospital Sarah Ann's attitude toward her little cousin changed. She would joke and reminisce warmly about the "silly Goonybird," ask her parents what new mischief she was getting into. Had she made any new noises lately? Had she quit eating her hair? Sarah Ann even tattled on her brother, told them how Kevin always picked on Crescent when he came home from school and no grown-ups were around. Then she would invariably ask if Crescent were coming to visit her. "We'll see," her mother would allow. On her next visit, when she'd show up with Lloyd or Kevin but without Crescent, Sarah Ann would pout and carry on the whole time they were there.

Eudora finally gave in. She did not like to take Crescent out in public, was sure other people could discern her idiocy, her sullied soul. She felt them staring—winced as though she herself were somehow responsible. Nevertheless, she could not long deny her dying daughter's wishes and began bringing Crescent nearly every visit, which was daily.

Sarah Ann was pleased with all the new attention suddenly shown her, but she also knew she was very sick. She could feel something wrong—not just the pain—but something else, like a strange emptiness deep inside. It was a feeling she had never had before, and yet now that it was there, she could not imagine ever again being without it. At night, when she was alone, she was afraid.

As the weeks went by she grew more and more attached to her little cousin. Everyone else made her feel funny, self-conscious and queer, like an animal in the zoo. Healthy, smiling, they would come and stand over her bed. They would stare down at her and look glad it was she lying there instead of them. She didn't know why, but Crescent made her feel differently. Poor Goonybird. Poor, poor, dumb Goonybird. Sarah Ann could relax with her. She could be herself.

When Crescent came to visit, well scrubbed and neatly dressed, she would run up to the bed and kiss her cousin on the cheek. Then she would sit back in a chair and listen attentively as Sarah Ann would talk and talk and talk to her—something Sarah Ann never had done at home. She introduced her to everyone in the ward as her baby sister, never once referring to her nickname.

One day she explained to a nurse that although Crescent was dumb, she had once been able to speak as well as anybody but that she'd stuck her tongue out at a preacher, and a big crow had swooped down from the sky and pecked it out. A six-year-old boy with a heart murmur in the bed next to Sarah Ann's wanted to know what had happened to her tongue. Had the crow eaten it? No! she was quick to inform him, the crow had not eaten it. The preacher had found it wiggling on the ground, had put it in a jar and someday, when Crescent was "growed up" and had learned better manners, he would give it back to her.

"Wonderful," the nurse said.

"Aw, that tongue won't never work again." The boy remained skeptical. "Not after being kept in an old jar for a whole bunch of years."

"You don't know nothing about tongues!" Sarah Ann yelled defiantly. "It'll work again—good as new!"

"No it won't."

"Will too, will too! Liars don't know false from true!"

The nurse was forced to intervene. She broke up their bickering by pulling closed the privacy curtain that hung between them.

Sarah Ann lay back on her pillows and fell fast asleep. The short outburst had drained her meager store of energy. Crescent sat watching over her. She felt her tongue wiggling in a secret corner of her mouth and thought about crows, the jars of preachers. She thought about better manners and being "growed up."

From the vantage of her cousin's bedside, Crescent received her earliest impressions of the calling. Almost every day for not quite two months, she watched the women in uniform moving about the ward, tending to the needs of the patients. She recognized their expertise, their authority: Her aunt and uncle yielded the charge of their daughter to them without question.

Crescent felt awe, but also a peculiar ambivalence. For though nurses fussed over Sarah Ann at every opportunity, still her condition failed to improve. The disease continued to flourish. It seemed to thrive on the very attention given her. She lost weight steadily. Her face was sunken, ashen. A network of delicate blue veins stood out on her forehead and temples. Her neck was so scrawny it barely could support her head, and her frail wrists looked almost transparent.

The nurses—death hung about them. Crescent could sense it in their manner, in their gentle, assured control, the clinical order that surrounded them. It both frightened and fascinated her. Sarah Ann was going to die —the grown-ups said different, but Crescent didn't believe them—she was going to die and somehow it was all right. There was nothing to worry about. Not in the ward of death's sweet attendants. She was in good hands. The nurses were in charge.

Crescent already had encountered death on the farm. She had seen chickens with their heads wrung off, thrashing about on the ground. She had heard pigs being slaughtered: Lloyd, his overalls and boots spattered in blood, had chased her away from the barn where she'd come to investigate the squealing.

One of the dogs, Duke, had been run over by a car on the main road. He'd managed to crawl back to the yard, dragging a trail in the dust with his crushed hindquarters. When Kevin tried to touch him, he'd growled and snapped. Kevin had run off to find help. Crescent had remained, keeping a safe distance a few feet away, staring at the dog.

Duke had sat halfway up, supporting himself with his forepaws. Panting heavily, his eyes slowly closed, his head drooping lower and lower until his tongue touched the grass. Then, like her uncle fighting sleep on the sofa after supper, he jerked his head up only to have his eyes slowly close again and his head begin to droop. He repeated the process several times before his head finally touched the ground and stayed there. With a great heave of his splintered chest, his panting ceased. His eyes opened wide, fastened on Crescent in one instant of desperate intimacy; in the next instant, still wide open, they became empty reflections, unblinking mirrors of grass, trees and sky.

Kevin returned with Lloyd, who stood over Duke, nudged him with the toe of his boot. "Deader'n a doornail," he solemnly pronounced. He took the body and wrapped it in an old grain sack and buried it behind the corn crib.

Sarah Ann had cried when Kevin told her worms were going to eat Duke. He told her they'd eat her too, just as soon as she died. Sobbing, she ran into the house and into her mother's arms, begged her to make Kevin take back what he'd said. It was all a horrible lie. Her mother scolded Kevin and told Sarah Ann of course it was a lie. Good dogs, just like good little girls, went to heaven after they died. And God didn't allow any worms in heaven.

Several weeks later, Kevin dug up Duke and showed him to both Sarah

Ann and Crescent. He was all rotten and stinking and covered with wriggling worms. When Kevin's mother found out what he'd done, she made Lloyd take him to the tool shed and give him a good licking with his belt.

Crescent wondered if that was how it would happen to Sarah Ann: One day her head would get heavier and heavier until she couldn't hold it up any longer, and it would droop down—just like Duke's—until her tongue touched the pillow. Her thin chest would heave and her breathing would stop. Her eyes would open wide for that one instant, would fasten on Crescent sitting there, would blaze their secrets to her and then turn to glass. Lloyd would come forward and nudge her with his boot, tell everybody she was "deader'n a doornail"—even though she hadn't had her neck wrung, or her throat slit, or been hit by a car on the highway; even though she lay, instead of on the dusty ground, in a nice clean hospital bed with her pillows fluffed regularly and freshly peeled oranges on her bedstand —and he'd carry her away, wrap her in a grain sack and bury her behind the corn crib because that's where the worms were waiting and maybe Kevin would dig her up later and his mother would make Lloyd give him another licking because Sarah Ann would look just like Duke and smell just like him too.

It didn't happen that way. When the end drew near, Crescent and Kevin had not been allowed to visit the hospital. One weekend Eudora had gone to stay with her daughter and hadn't returned until it was all over Wednesday morning. That had been the first week in July. Lloyd was busy cultivating, Kevin was out of school for the summer and Crescent had just turned six.

Sarah Ann's death filled her mother with great bitterness. What had she done to deserve such grief? What sin had she committed? She was a God-fearing woman. She went to church on Sunday. In the past ten years she'd been saved no less than seven times—twice in four months in '45 when the High Water Evangelists had come through town and set up their big tent on the fairgrounds in late spring and then again in early fall. Hadn't she worked hard all her life? Hadn't she sacrificed and toiled to make her husband a decent home and raise a family? Was it a sin to be dirt poor? And why her child and not Geraldine's? Her sister, who'd never done anything for anybody but herself? Who'd never been saved even once, who'd sinned and then abandoned her own child, dumped her here for Eudora to raise so she could go off gallivanting God-knows-where, footloose and fancy free? It didn't make sense. It wasn't right. She felt duped, betrayed. The resentment grew in her and festered.

One evening Crescent sat at the kitchen table with the rest of the family eating supper. She had just dipped a slab of buttered bread in the gravy on her plate and was about to take a bite when Eudora hit her. For no apparent reason, Eudora had slapped her full in the face. Crescent's head recoiled; she was almost dislodged from her chair. The bread went flying, spattered gravy down the front of her dress.

Stunned, totally bewildered, she stared wide-eyed at her aunt, lifted a hand to her stinging cheek. It was the first time a grown-up had ever struck her.

Eudora, wide-eyed, stared back. She too was stunned, could not believe what she'd just done.

"How's come you did that?" asked Lloyd, looking over a spoonful of yellow-wax bush beans.

Eudora's eyes brimmed with tears. She ignored her husband, reached out and pulled Crescent to her bosom, hugged and kissed her.

"Aunt Dora's sorry, sorry, sorry! She didn't mean to hit you, honey. She didn't mean it."

A few days later Eudora was scrubbing her pots and skillets in the kitchen sink when she happened to look out the rear window and see Kevin and Crescent playing together near the garden. He was being much too rough, was pulling and jerking her about by the arm like a rag doll. Eudora threw down her wad of steel wool and strode to the back door. The boy had a mean streak in him a mile wide. Lord knows how many times he'd made Sarah Ann's short life miserable. She started to swing open the door and holler—then inexplicably stopped, just stood there holding it ajar, peering through the screen.

Kevin had knocked Crescent to the ground and was sitting on her. Pinning her shoulders with his knees, he freed his hands to torment her, pulled her hair, pinched her nose and cheeks, slapped her. Eudora watched mesmerized, unable to move or speak. She watched her son stuff clumps of dirt and grass into the child's mouth. Crescent struggled to free herself, writhed and kicked, but he was four years older than she and weighed nearly twice as much.

Tiring of his sport, he started to climb off her, hesitated, glancing furtively about to make sure they still were alone, then gave her a hard punch in the face with a fist. He bounded up and dashed across the yard— almost as if expecting her to cry out. A few moments passed. Silence prevailed. He slowed to a walk, smiled at himself, then disappeared around a shed.

Crescent sat up, coughing and gagging, spitting out dirt and grass. Her nose was bleeding where Kevin had struck her. She wiped it with her small hands, looked at the smear of dirt and blood. There were no tears. Not one muffled sob.

Eudora eased the screen door shut and returned to the sink. She resumed her scrubbing, vigorously scoured the depths of her blackest pot and tried not to think of what she'd just seen: the spectacle of herself standing in the doorway, watching it all happen . . . failing to intervene.

"Dora's sorry, sorry, sorry! She didn't mean to hurt you, honey, you know that."

Crescent felt her aunt's arms wrapping around her, drawing her to her, felt her hands gently stroking her face, her hair. She also felt a sharp, throbbing pain in her right eye where her aunt had just hit her.

Moments earlier Eudora had been sitting in the living room, thumbing through a Sears catalogue. She'd heard tiny footsteps behind her, and she'd looked up absently, half expecting to see Sarah Ann skip into the room. When she saw that it was Crescent, realized that Sarah Ann never would come skipping up behind her again, she struck out, swung her hand partially closed, smacking Crescent just under her right eye and knocking her to the floor.

Immediately penitent, Eudora had sprung forward to help Crescent to her feet again. Now tenderly consoling her, she led her to the bathroom, where she ran cold water in the sink and carefully dabbed at her eye—reddened and already puffing up—with a dampened washcloth.

After dinner that evening while the family sat around in the living room, Lloyd asked his wife how Crescent had come by her black eye. It was swollen almost shut by then.

"How should I know?" she snapped back at him. "Probably stuck her nose somewhere it don't belong."

Kevin, sprawled on the floor oiling his BB gun, looked up with a grin. "Dumb Goonybird," he jeered.

Crescent was not sent to school in the fall. How could a poor, ignorant halfwit learn to read and write when she couldn't even talk? As her aunt's animosity continued to grow, she found herself on the receiving end of more and more capricious blows. Kevin too sensed that she had somehow become "fair game." While he did not openly assault her in the presence of his parents, he rarely hesitated in their absence. Slaps, punches, shoves and kicks became a part of her everyday existence. She was forced to skulk and slink about the house as though she were some small foraging creature. She would scamper off at the sound of footsteps, shut herself in closets, cower behind furniture. The bruises and abrasions began to accumulate on her body, her spindly arms and legs, like pockmarks of some strange, virulent disease.

One evening in the middle of October, she came to the supper table to find no place set for her. When she attempted to pull out her chair and sit down, her aunt gave her a sharp-knuckled rap on the arm. Crescent stood there, motionless, confused—unsure of what was expected of her. Without looking at her, Eudora continued eating as though nothing had happened. Nearly a minute passed. Finally Crescent again tried to sit in her chair. Again Eudora rapped her, this time harder, on the side of the head, causing her to wince and stumble backward.

"How's come you done that?" asked Lloyd.

" 'Cause I don't want her here eating at the table with us."

"How's come?"

" 'Cause I don't . . . and I don't, that's all! Now, stay out of what don't concern you."

Lloyd started to mumble something, went back to shoveling down his potatoes. Kevin sniggered.

Crescent still stood there, looked from her aunt to her uncle and back to her aunt.

"So go on—shoo! Get out of here!" yawped Eudora, taking another swipe at her. Crescent scurried out of the kitchen.

"I don't see as what's wrong her being here."

"I told you to stay out of this, Lloyd, and I mean it. I can't stand the sight of her—she drives me crazy! The dogs and cats, they don't eat at the table. Well, she don't talk no better'n they do. I'll tell you if the good Lord wanted her here eating with decent folk, he'd give her a tongue to talk with. It's plain enough she don't belong."

From that point on Crescent no longer ate with the family. Eudora fixed her a plate after the family was finished eating. She continued to fix her a plate for the next week. After that she decided she couldn't be bothered. Crescent was left to sneak about the kitchen, mousing table scraps and leftovers, for herself.

In the last week of November, she suffered a broken arm and two cracked ribs. It had been necessary for Eudora to take her into town to the doctor. Eudora decided to clean her up first. She was caked with dirt and grime, hadn't been bathed since June, the day of her last visit with Sarah Ann in the hospital.

Eudora laid out one of Sarah Ann's old dresses; most of Crescent's clothes had deteriorated into unsightly rags. Eudora filled the tub with hot water—so hot she could barely stand to immerse her hands. Then she stripped Crescent and dumped her in, furiously began scrubbing her with a stiff-bristled brush and a cake of lixum. The dirt came and so did the skin. Crescent struggled. Eventually she grew limp—the scalding water, her broken arm, her aunt's brutal scrubbing—she was overcome with pain and mercifully receded into a numbing stupor.

"She fell down the stairs," Eudora told Dr. Whittle without batting an eye. It was, after all, the truth. She did not elaborate. She did not explain how earlier she'd discovered Crescent playing upstairs in Sarah Ann's bedroom (Crescent still occupied the stairwell closet; Lloyd had suggested she move into the vacated bedroom months ago, but Eudora had been bitterly opposed), how she'd caught her with a box of her daughter's favorite ribbons, all of them dumped out and scattered on the floor. She did not tell how she'd descended on the child in a fury, pummeled and kicked her, yanked her to her feet by her hair, carried her—still by her hair —out of the room to the top of the stairs; how there, hesitating only long enough to swing her forward, she'd heaved her down—watched, as if in a savage dream, the child bouncing and banging all the way to the bottom, until she came to rest on her back, her right arm twisted and pinned beneath her.

Dr. Whittle had nodded, reflecting on the steep stairways of rural American architecture and the countless broken limbs they'd delivered him over the years. While he made a cast for her arm, he did notice a number of other marks on her, suspicious cuts and bruises. The scabs and discolorations indicated they were not part of her recent accident. He did ask how she'd come by them.

"Oh, she's always falling down, always bumping into things," Eudora clucked nervously. "She ain't got the sense God give a goat."

Dr. Whittle did look long and hard over the tops of his bifocals at the worn, crimp-faced woman standing in his office. But he said nothing more.

A summer drought stretching into late fall spelled difficult times for the O'Learys. The harvest had been reduced to a fraction of its normal yield and coupled with this, Isaac Hoge's brother, the O'Learys' new landlord, doubled the rent. (Old Isaac finally had succumbed to a series of strokes he'd suffered over the past two years.) Through the winter months money ran low. When spring came Eudora got a job in town, on an assembly line, canning meatballs.

Crescent was locked in the basement while her aunt worked during the day. The basement's cold stone walls were wet with seepage, its crumbling cement floor cluttered with junk. The air, thick as whey, choked her with a stench of mildew, rotten eggs and coal dust. A small, solitary window behind the furnace let in the only light.

At first she was locked up only in the morning when her aunt left for work and then released again as soon as she returned in the middle of the afternoon. Gradually, however, her periods of confinement lengthened. Eudora would take longer and longer each day to let her out. By mid-May Crescent was only allowed upstairs in the evening to eat and sleep.

Then one evening her aunt unbolted the cellar door, slid a pan of food on the top step where Crescent stood waiting . . . and slammed the door in her face.

She was not let out the next day either. Or the next. Weeks went by; months.

Not long after she was eight, Lloyd, in a moment of rare courage, brought her outside during an early-afternoon break in his field chores. She stood just off the front porch in the tall grass, her eyes dazzled by the sun, the bright summer landscape. She coughed, stumbled to hold herself upright. A fresh, cleansing breeze cut into her lungs like sharp scissors.

Her uncle stared at her in disbelief. She looked so pathetic squinting at the daylight, trembling and clutching herself in both hands, half naked in rags, her skin chalk white and covered with sores, her hair a tangled rat's nest. He wiped his windburned and grimy face on a sweat-soaked sleeve. He looked away in shame.

Her reprieve was short-lived. A car appeared on the trunk road, a thick tail of dust billowing up behind it. Frightened that someone might see her —or worse yet, that it might be his wife returning home early from work —he scooped up Crescent in one arm and hurriedly carried her back into

60

the house, set her gently down on the basement's top step and just as gently shut the door.

This time she remained locked up for almost three years. When she emerged again, it was in the arms of strangers and she was eleven years old. She was carried out into a strange night of flashing lights and leaping shadows. She was never to return to her prison under the house again.

5

Barbara Peltson, a load of books under her arms, ducked her head into the third-floor lounge of the Windhaven School of Nursing and called, "Hey, I'm going over to Marshall Field's. Anybody feel like shopping?"

"Have I got time to change?" asked Sally Krannert, who still was in uniform.

"Sure, they're open till eight tonight."

Sally stood up, tossed a copy of *Cosmopolitan* on an end table and had walked halfway across the room when a feeble voice called after her.

She stopped. Barbara peered back into the room.

Tucked away in a corner divan, gazing up from her physiology text, sat Libby O'Leary.

"Uh . . . I said, 'May I come along too?' "

Sally looked at Barbara. Barbara looked at Sally. Libby sitting in the lounge was puzzling in itself. That she'd just spoken to them was nothing short of mind-boggling.

"If . . . if it's all right with you," she added, looking down again at the book in her lap.

Sally giggled.

Barbara jabbed her in the arm and managed to speak.

"Er . . . why, sure, Libby, come on. There's always room for one more."

That began the first day of the special probation prescribed by Miss

Bernstick. Libby continued to frequent the lounge, went on numerous shopping jaunts about the city with girls from her floor. In the evenings she joined her new roommate, Debbie Turner, and Frances Taylor for a ritual cup of coffee and rolls at a corner Howard Johnson's. During the months of April and May, Libby saw nineteen movies, three concerts, one ballet; visited the Adler Planetarium, the Lincoln Park Zoo and the Museum of Science and Industry.

One Sunday night she and Debbie and Frances went into the Loop to see *The Boston Strangler*. Halfway through the movie Libby felt sick. She excused herself and waited in the powder room until the feature ended. Afterward Debbie apologized for her choice in movies. She admitted the only reason she and Frances had sat through it was because they had "a thing" for Tony Curtis. Libby made light of it, blamed her absence on the veal cutlets she'd had for supper at the "Windy Cafe," the hospital's infamous commissary. Sandra Kane's name was not mentioned.

On the evening of May 15, Stella Bernstick watched Libby come forward to receive her cap and candle. Head lowered, she plodded down the aisle as if in full harness, as if pulling some massive, invisible plow. Her eyes glanced up only once to thank Miss Bernstick as she accepted the symbolic accouterments of her calling. Then head lowered again, she plowed a new furrow back up the aisle to her seat.

A few minutes later Stella Bernstick was looking out across the upturned faces reciting the Florence Nightingale Pledge. Each girl held a lit candle in front of her. It was always at this moment, the drone of their voices in unison, that Miss Bernstick was touched most deeply by the spirit of her girls.

I will abstain from whatever is deleterious and mischievous. . . . I will do all in my power to maintain and elevate the standard of my profession . . . and will not take or knowingly administer any harmful drug. . . .

She found Libby's face, large, moonlike—perhaps she imagined it, but it seemed to outshine the others, as though she were not merely reflecting the flickering light she held before her but giving off a radiance all her own. Miss Bernstick smiled at the illusion. She was proud of the progress Libby was making. Though it still was too early to tell about her grades, at least she was making an effort to come out of her shell and socialize. Certainly much of the credit belonged to Debbie.

The ceremony ended with a hymn, "A Mighty Fortress Is Our God." Miss Bernstick felt moisture cloud her eyes as she watched another class of freshmen snuff their candles and file out of the chapel into the waiting night.

"Why not?" asked Debbie. Libby stood by the sink. She had just soaked her cap in perma-starch and handed it to Debbie. Debbie wadded up the wet linen into a ball and hurled it across the bathroom.

"Splop!" The missile struck the shower wall with resounding impact, stuck fast. Debbie walked over to the wall and plastered the glob out on the smooth, green tiles.

"You flatten it out like so . . . being sure to smooth out all the wrinkles. . . . There . . . then let it harden overnight. Tomorrow morning it'll be stiff as a board. Peel it off, fold it, pin the three corners and *voilà!* O'Leary is crowned nurse for a day! Now tell me why you won't go to the party."

Libby didn't answer.

"Come on, not the silent treatment. Why not?"

"Oh, Debbie," she said, opening the sink's drain.

"Don't 'Oh, Debbie' me. I want to know why not."

"I don't know. I've never been on a date before."

"So there's a first time for everything. You want to get married and have kids someday, don't you?"

Libby was sure that she didn't, but she managed to nod her head.

"Then how do you expect to meet the future Mr. Right if you won't go out in the first place?"

Libby could think of nothing to say. The drain gurgled as the sink emptied.

"Now, Stan's a nice guy—I've met him myself—and he's a good friend of David's. I mean, he's no crudo or creep or anything like that. He's just looking for someone to go to the party with. . . . So what do you say? Come on—you'll have a great time."

"Debbie, please?"

"Miss Bernstick would want you to go."

"No, please? Maybe some other time."

"Why later? Why not now?"

"I just don't feel like it, that's all. I'm sorry but I just don't want to go."

Debbie shrugged her shoulders. She recognized the tone that had entered Libby's voice. It was hopeless to continue.

"Suit yourself. But you'll be missing a really fun time." Debbie walked out of the bathroom. Libby slowly dried her hands. She avoided looking in the mirror.

Two days later Libby read the morning assignment sheet in the NS, noting that a Mr. Arnold T. Weintraub had been scheduled to her care. Mr. Weintraub, a middle-aged cardiac, had suffered his second severe attack in six months. He was listed maximum quiescent. She felt a faint twinge of apprehension. Making his bed would be difficult. He would have to be spoon-fed. Then came the matter of his bath. . . .

As the morning progressed, Libby found herself lingering with other patients. She had fed Mr. Weintraub his breakfast, had told him she would be back shortly to make his bed and bathe him. That had been over an hour ago. She could put it off no longer. Preparing a bath tray, she entered his room.

"I thought you'd abandoned me, young lady," Mr. Weintraub reproached her good-naturedly. He was a medium-sized man, heavyset with a florid face that smiled easily. His hair was black, close-cropped at the sides and balding on top.

Libby smiled weakly, setting the tray on the rollo-stand. She cranked his bed to a forty-five-degree angle so that he lay upright and then started to pull the privacy curtain around them.

"No need for that." Weintraub laughed jovially. "He hasn't woken up since they dumped him there. That was two days ago."

Libby glanced at the occupant in the other bed. Amid a battery of IV tubes and drains lay a man with the yellowest skin she'd ever seen. His labored breathing filled the room. She continued pulling the curtain closed.

"Looks like he's been dipped in butterscotch, don't it? Let that be a lesson to you, young lady: That's what comes from too many happy hours at the old martini mixer."

The liver, thought Libby, remembering an illustration from a pathology textbook. Until now she'd always thought the color of that picture an exaggeration.

"I know why you want the curtain pulled." Weintraub winked. "You want me alone in here all to yourself."

She flinched. Then she tried to smile, failed so miserably she had to turn away.

She washed his face first, his neck and shoulders. She washed each arm, holding it extended above him by the wrist. Weintraub lay still, inert, an overstuffed mannequin with sparkling gray eyes and dentured grin.

When she began scrubbing his chest and stomach, a rich lather of soap worked up in his thick, curly mat of body hair.

"Think hair on a man's chest is sexy?" asked the mannequin.

Libby was silent.

"Aw, come on—you must have some preference."

She rinsed the washcloth in the basin and began wiping the suds from his chest. Inside, in the pit of her stomach, she could feel the tension building.

"Come on. You can speak frankly. I won't hold it against you."

She continued rinsing.

"I know, the truth is you'd rather see less hair down there and more on top, right?" He arched his eyebrows, indicating the bald expanse of his forehead.

The truth was Libby had no preference, nor at that moment could have expressed one even if she had. As she rinsed and dried off his upper body, she felt her apprehension rapidly burgeoning into panic.

She did his feet next. He giggled, accused her of being a sadist. She managed to smile grimly as she worked the cloth between his toes. She did his calves, his knees and partway up his thighs. Then again she rinsed and dried him off.

The moment she dreaded was at hand. She returned to the washcloth in the basin, slowly soaped it with the small rectangular cake of hospital Ivory.

If Mr. Weintraub had been a regular patient, she would now hand him the washcloth and tell him to "finish up." But Mr. Weintraub was not a regular patient. He was a max. q., and that meant he was allowed no exertion of any avoidable kind. Maintaining the delicate etiquette of a hospital bath was clearly avoidable. Libby alone would have to finish the bath, would have to ply the cloth between his legs. . . .

She glanced at him. The smile seemed to have left his eyes, resettled at the corners of his mouth. His lips, thick and moist as link sausage, parted into what resembled a horrid leer. She looked quickly away. The contact of his eyes burned holes in her courage. She stood trembling, hesitant, clutching the washcloth before her in both hands.

"You all right?" asked Weintraub.

She clenched her jaw, told herself from some fleeting vantage point in her mind that she was being silly and unprofessional. In a burst of will, she flung back the covers and beheld his private parts.

Her will wavered. Frantically she plunged the cloth between his loins, closed her eyes and scrubbed.

"Jesus Christ!" shrieked Weintraub, lurching halfway out of bed. "Easy! Easy does it!"

Libby stuttered contrition, reduced the fury of her purge to the meekest of daubs and pats. She was a museum curator now dusting prehistoric relics. Glassy-eyed, she took his member between her thumb and forefinger, lifted it carefully to one side and gently laved his groin.

After rinsing the cloth in the basin, she returned to discover a shocking change taking place. His member was no longer lying limp and passive, but was growing—swelling huge and crooked.

Undaunted, intent on ending the ordeal as quickly as possible, she forged ahead, lifted the member again to one side and began rinsing his groin. The shunned organ gave a sudden twitch and flopped autonomously forward, striking her across the wrist. Startled, she lurched backward, knocking over the bath tray. The tray, basin and soap dish fell to the floor with a resounding clatter.

She wrenched open the curtain and bolted from the room. Her patient was left exposed to the hallway, open-mouthed, clutching his chest.

Coming down the hallway at that moment was Gaylord Radzim, an orderly from surgery. He watched as Libby burst from room 302, nearly colliding with his litter, and ran down the corridor to the far end, where she stopped and leaned against the wall, holding herself.

Radzim, a short, swarthy young man with curly black hair and guilt-quick eyes, was one of an indeterminate number of inveterate sadists who gravitated toward hospital work. Radzim himself found his job at Windhaven General so rewarding, so filled with the pain and anguish of his fellow man, that he supplemented his regular hours by working as a night attendant in the morgue. Rude and abusive to both nurses and patients alike, he derived a special glee from tormenting students. An acute shortage of skilled male help on the floors, however, forced the hospital to keep him on, and though his conduct had been reported numerous times, seldom was he disciplined.

The hospital's death litter, which Radzim was now pushing, was an ingenious apparatus of discretion. It closely resembled an ordinary ward litter, its bedding clean and neatly folded back on top as if ready to transport some new patient to X ray or surgery. The bedding, however, never was used. It was a sham, a false bottom. Beneath it and behind heavy sheets which draped the sides hung a lower berth. Here the hospital's irredeemable failures could be transported hidden from view down the hallways and elevators to the morgue. The design was wasted on Radzim, however, for he always managed to leave an arm or a leg dangling out from under the sheets. He then would slowly roll the cart along the corridor of a terminal cancer ward, lingering with his grim cargo before each open door.

And now approaching Libby at the end of the corridor, he glanced quickly around to make sure he was unobserved, then grabbed the hand of an occupant he carried hidden underneath and veered the litter toward her. He barely missed her backside as he rolled the cart by. Holding the deceased's hand by its stubby middle finger, he thrust it upward and vigorously goosed her.

The hallway echoed her shrieking inhalation. She straightened from the wall and spun around, dashed into the nearby lavatory without even glancing at the offender. Radzim, himself startled, dropped the hand and sped out of the ward, banging the litter through the swinging doors at a run.

Libby forfeited her breakfast in the toilet. She leaned over the bowl for some time afterward, coughing, sobbing. Slowly her hysteria—along with her nausea—subsided. She stood up. She walked over to the sink and washed her face. She looked at herself in the mirror. Her face was blotched and puffy. She looked quickly away, avoided meeting her eyes. There were times she could not bear looking into them, times when she discovered something lurking there, something from her past and yet of nothing she could remember, a strangeness—a familiarity—that both confused and frightened her. She knew it would be there now.

She wanted desperately to return to the dorm, to be alone and clear her thoughts. She was being silly—she knew it—but she couldn't help herself. How did she ever expect to become a nurse if she couldn't manage such a simple task? She fought the impulse to run.

"Well, hello there!" exclaimed Weintraub, a broad, sheepish grin on his face as she reentered room 302. The curtain hung wide open where she'd fled through it, several hooks pulled off the overhead rail. The floor was a mess where she'd knocked over the bath tray. The man in the other bed, still breathing heavily, lay unmoved, facing the wall. For some reason he did not appear quite so yellow. Everything else was exactly as she'd left it.

"I finished myself." Weintraub held up the washcloth. He also had covered himself.

"I'm very sorry, Mr. . . . Mr. . . ." She'd forgotten his name.

"Mr. Weintraub."

"I'm very sorry. I don't know what happened. I guess I got sick."

"Don't let it bother you, kid. Could have happened to anybody." She looked at him, saw the genuine concern in his eyes. How could she ever have imagined that face leering?

"Did . . . did you ring for assistance?" she asked as she stooped over to pick up the basin and soap dish.

"Nope. Figured you'd be back. No sense anybody else sticking their noses in here, right?" She gave him an appreciative smile.

"I'd better get a mop," she said, making up her mind at that exact moment to speak to Debbie. She would ask her if it was not too late to change her mind about the party.

Debbie called Carla Boswell. It was her fiancé who was giving the party. Debbie asked her if she could round up a date for Libby. Stan, the date Debbie had originally intended for her roommate, was already going with someone else. Carla said she'd see what she could do. Late Saturday afternoon, a few hours before the party, she called back that she'd finally found somebody.

That evening, when Debbie and Libby stepped out of the elevator, Alan Farber looked up from the front desk where he'd been flirting with a cute junior receptionist. Instinctively he knew which girl was his date. He resisted a strong impulse to turn and run on the spot, hated himself for not obeying it. She was a dog. A real dog. No, he thought after a moment, lowering his scrutiny from her moony face to her body, the loose gray flannel shift she was wearing that failed to conceal the breadth of her hips —make that a cow. A real heifer.

Debbie's boyfriend, David, who'd been standing in the foyer, came forward and met the girls along with Farber. After an awkward introduction, David offered to go out and hail a cab. Farber, who had a car parked nearby on a side street, chose not to mention it. No reason saddling himself for the whole evening. Under his breath he cursed his friend, Jim Brookston, who had fixed him up.

He looked at Libby as they walked outside and promised himself this would be his last blind date ever. Then he took her arm and helped stuff her into the back seat of a green Checker David had just waved over to the curb.

Libby had read the disappointment in her date's face the moment she'd seen him. She would have had to be blind to miss it. Nevertheless, it failed to upset her. She had no illusions. The moment Alan Farber drew in a corner of his mouth and glanced at the ceiling, he became irrelevant.

Farber was no more disappointed with Libby than Debbie was with him. She recognized his type instantly: twenty-eight or twenty-nine, a seasoned veteran of the Rush Street singles bars. He was way out of Libby's league —what was he doing on a blind date anyway? Debbie felt anger and frustration, wished she could have called a halt to the evening right then and there. Carla was such a nit! No, no sense blaming Carla. It was she herself who'd pushed Libby into this.

Before Farber climbed into the cab, Debbie tugged his arm. He hesitated, turned to her.

"Give her a break. It's her first date," she entreated with a whisper.

"Beautiful," muttered Farber. He slid into the back seat alongside Libby. Debbie and David followed.

On the way to the party, while the four of them scrunched together in the back seat, Debbie tried to start a conversation. Farber eased his arm around her shoulder. Now she was more on the order of what he'd expected. Her date didn't look all that cool either.

Debbie lifted his arm off her, gave him an icy glance. Poor Libby! There was no way she was going to be spared tonight. They rode the rest of the way in silence.

"What're you drinking?" Farber asked Libby after he'd removed her coat. Debbie watched him politely hang it in a closet, was momentarily encouraged.

"Rum? Bourbon? Gin?"

Libby looked at Debbie. Libby hated alcohol. She had tasted beer once when she was out with the girls, and it had made her tongue swell.

"Beer? Coke? Water?"

Finally she shook her head. She was not the least bit thirsty. "I guess I don't want anything, thank you."

"Beautiful." Farber shrugged. Well, he'd made an effort. "Excuse me," he said and wandered off.

"Hey, fella, don't you know there's a leash law in this town?"

Farber turned to see Jim Brookston, the party's host, and several of his pals grinning at him. "I can't wait to do *you* a favor sometime, Brookston."

"Don't blame me, Al. I never said I knew her. 'She's a friend of a friend of Carla's'—that's all I ever told you."

"A hot-pants nurse—right?"

Brookston snorted, nearly spilled the drink he was holding, slapped Farber on the back. Several minutes of joke-telling followed, involving such items as crutches, bedpans and iron lungs as well as gunnysacks, wheelbarrows and spurs. Farber gave them all the finger and proceeded into the kitchen to mix himself a drink.

"Libby, you should have let Alan bring you a drink. Guys like to wait on their dates," said Debbie, trying to make it sound as though Libby had chased him away. She knew, of course, that it wouldn't have mattered what her roommate did or didn't do. Poor Libby! If only Stan still had been free.

He was a friend, he knew about her problems and would have been thoughtful and understanding. Damn!

Libby smiled at Debbie. She knew her roommate was fretting over her. She wished there were some way she could tell her to relax and enjoy herself. She couldn't care less about Alan Farber.

David held up Debbie's drink in the living room and motioned for her to join him. Debbie reached out, took Libby's hand and led her in to mingle with the other guests.

They were in an apartment on the fortieth floor of one of the twin Marina Towers. The living room, large, distinctively semicircular to conform with the building's outer geometry, was jammed with people. Other rooms opened tangentially from it. These too were jammed with people. The decor was Spanish rustic, with blocky wooden furniture, fiesta-red carpet and drapes. A number of matching paintings—highly stylized impressions of bullfights—hung about on the curved walls. A Beatles album, turned up high in the background, could barely be heard above the drone of voices and laughter.

Libby followed Debbie and David from the living room to the kitchen, to the bedroom, to another bedroom, to the living room, to the balcony, back to the living room, back to the kitchen, back to the bedroom, to the other bedroom, to the living room, to the balcony. . . .

They were part of a steady flow of people, a central artery of tinkling glasses and waving cigarettes, smiles, winks and handshakes, of shifting glances, laughter, shouts, screeches and endless chitchat.

"Great party, Jim!"

"That was the host," buzzed Debbie in Libby's ear. "Carla's fiancé. He just passed his prelims. That's why he's throwing this bash. He's going to be a lawyer."

Libby nodded, smiled. She had no idea to whom Debbie was referring. She was overwhelmed by so many people; their faces swarmed in her mind. The only lawyer she'd ever known was a patient, an elderly man who'd died of a brain tumor. She wondered as she recalled his dull, sightless eyes and shriveled form whether he too had once had such a party.

There were fewer people on the balcony. Though mid-May, the night still had the chill of early spring. A young man in a faded denim jacket was playing a twelve-string guitar. Several people sat around him on aluminum lawn chairs. He was singing a song about the hardship of being black in America. He was white but gave the impression he wished he were black, at least while strumming his twelve-string guitar.

David, Debbie and Libby listened to him for a while, then moved over to the wrought-iron railing and looked out at the night skyline of the city.

"What a view!" exclaimed Debbie. "Wow, I can't believe I'm here, partying it up in Marina Towers."

Libby had difficulty sharing her roommate's enthusiasm—either for the party or for the building itself. Famous landmark or not, she found something unsettling about its thrusting, scalloped columns. She much preferred the city's more traditional structures, the staid rectangles and cubes like the big Hilton Hotel on Michigan Avenue or the Merchandise Mart.

When David and Debbie were ready to go inside again, Libby asked them to go without her. She knew they must be tired of her tagging along; she told them she wanted to stand in the fresh air a while longer. Debbie objected but finally patted her hand and said, "Well, don't stay out here too long or you'll catch pneumonia."

Left to herself, Libby gazed down at the Chicago River directly below the balcony. Fulsome green in the light of day, it now cleft the city to the lake in Stygian blackness. She followed its course eastward, counted five bridges dimly lit with traffic. Across the river she looked down into the Loop, could see part of the "loop" itself marching up Lake Street on steel trestles, turning south down Wabash Avenue to encircle the downtown with its dingy green sheds and elevated, glistening rails. She could see the bright diffusion of light above the buildings that lined State Street and glimpse through a gap in the rooftops the flashing neon of several movie marquees.

She peered into the windows of a nearby skyscraper, watched people moving about in their rooms directly across from her. Juxtaposed against the night, they seemed like prisoners walled up in concrete and glass.

As she continued staring she began to feel a curious sense of detachment. A sudden rush of exhilaration swept through her. She was suspended in space, aloft, floating free from all structures—free almost from the burden of her own body.

As quickly as it had come, the exhilaration passed. In its place she felt the cold night air and a colder sense of foreboding.

Nervously she searched among the lights and shadows of the downtown buildings, raised her eyes to include the surrounding ghettos, the ribbons of streetlights fading into the distant industrial glow of the outer city. She looked to the dark rim of the lake beyond.

Abruptly she glanced over her shoulder, saw that she now was alone on the balcony; the guitar player and his small audience had stepped inside. Yet she was not alone. A presence had joined her. She couldn't see it, touch it, couldn't identify it, but it was there, all around her . . . vague . . . threatening . . . malevolent. . . .

She shuddered, gripped the iron railing tightly in her hands. Then she let it go and spun around, walked away. She was anxious to be inside again, to be with others and hear laughter and music.

"Have you been out there all this time? Krikeez! You must be an ice cube!" Debbie greeted her as she stepped through the sliding-glass doorway.

Libby smiled, shivering, and nodded.

"You ready to leave?"

"Whenever you want to is fine with me." The truth of the matter was she'd been ready to leave earlier: Now she felt more like staying, actually wanted to be with people.

"Let me go find David. We'll meet you in the front hall."

As Libby made her way across the living room, she saw Alan Farber sitting with a girl over by the stereo. The girl was pretty with spidery eyes and wore a Loyola T-shirt. They were sharing the same foam-rubber cushion on the floor. Farber looked up, saw Libby and looked quickly away.

She found a vacant stool in the vestibule, a red-leathered taboret. She sat down. It felt good to get off her feet. She watched the party flow by. There was less movement now; more people had arrived and the flow had clogged to a weak trickle.

Debbie was gone for some time. While Libby sat waiting, she discovered a copy of *Playboy* under the stool. She picked it up and thumbed through it. The glittering people cavorting about its pages amazed her: They seemed unreal, so far removed from the drab segment of humanity that made up her world at the hospital.

She read a few of the jokes, but they didn't make much sense to her. She pulled out the centerfold and glanced at the Playmate of the Month: An auburn-haired beauty smiled out at her. Completely nude except for a pair of bedroom slippers, the girl was kneeling on a golden chaise longue. Her ample backside curved toward the camera, while her upper torso turned away so that one breast hung in profile. Her face, faintly plump, pubescent, looked back three-quarters full.

Libby stared at the girl's eyes and then gave a start. Plum blue, captured in a stranger's face, they were the eyes of her poor murdered roommate, Sandra Kane! And even though the auburn-haired girl still was smiling, the eyes—Sandra's eyes—were filled with such sorrow, such loneliness. They peered out at her like those of a sad clown with a painted face.

Fighting back a sob, Libby quickly closed the centerfold and put the magazine down.

"How'd you like to go to another party?" called Debbie, emerging from the living room with David in tow.

Libby stood up.

"Not like this brawl—just a small, quiet get-together. Some friends of David's asked us over. It's right down the hall. You're invited." Debbie didn't mention Libby's date.

"If it's what you want to do, that's okay."

"Not us, silly—what do you want to do? David can take you back to the dorm in a cab right now. Can't you, David?"

But the last thing Libby wanted to be was a problem.

Apart from the crushing throng of people, David's friends' apartment was almost identical to the one they'd just left; it even had the same Spanish decor. Posters (instead of paintings) of bullfights decorated the walls. The Rolling Stones played on a small portable stereo.

"Who's for getting stoned?" announced the host as Libby, Debbie and David walked into the living room.

72

"Got some outa-sight grass." Gary Chambers, one of three Northwest-ern grad students who lived here, looked around the room at the small group of familiar faces. He spotted Libby.

"Whoa! Hold on—is everybody cool here?"

"It's all right, Gary, she's my roommate," said Debbie, coming to her defense.

"Can't be too careful these days. The mayor's fuzz is everywhere."

There were burbles of shared laughter from the group.

Soon they were all forming a small circle in the center of the room, plopping down on brightly colored pillows already scattered about the floor. The fiesta-red drapes were pulled. Someone went to check to make sure the front door was chained.

"Welcome to theater in the round, fans," said Chambers, returning from a bedroom with his stash. "Starring the one and only dynamite rag." He sat down in the middle of the circle and began rolling. Everyone giggled and tittered. "I kid you not—this is rally raunchy shee-yee-yit!"

"You don't have to smoke if you don't want to," whispered Debbie to her roommate. Libby glanced at the host busily at work, at the crumbly makings in his plastic bag. It looked like alfalfa silage, she thought.

"Is . . . is that marijuana?" she whispered back to Debbie. She'd heard Debbie and the other girls talk about it before—how they smoked it at parties and got high, an experience she vaguely understood to be pleasura-ble. She also knew it was illegal.

Debbie grinned and winked.

Breaking the law didn't bother Libby. What did concern her were the words she had just recited not even a week ago at capping ceremony:

I will abstain from whatever is deleterious and mischievous . . . and will not take or knowingly administer any harmful drug. . . .

"What about the Pledge?"

"The what?"

"Florence Nightingale's pledge."

Debbie snorted. "Oh, my God, Libby, you're such a pumpkin! That means hard stuff—morphine, cocaine—pot's nothing like that. It's like booze."

"Better'n booze," piped in David over Debbie's shoulder. "There's no hangover."

When the host finished rolling the first joint, he lit it, took a deep drag and passed it around. He immediately began rolling another. The first joint came to David, who took a drag and handed it to Debbie. She also took a drag, then offered it to Libby.

Libby hesitated. She'd never even smoked tobacco.

"Hey, move it or lose it, will ya," a voice sounded from across the circle. "Good times are going up in smoke."

"You don't have to if you don't want to," Debbie said.

Libby reached out and took it. She remembered the chill that had swept through her when she was alone on the balcony at the other party. She wanted very much to join in.

"Hey, take a hit and pass it on!"

Besides, she couldn't believe Debbie would be offering it to her or smoking it herself if it really were harmful.

"Keep it moving, keep it moving!"

She lifted the joint to her lips, took a quick puff and passed it to the person on her left, a young man with long blond hair and a black, droopy moustache. The young man, who'd been watching her, said, "Not like that, like this." He proceeded to take a long drag, his mouth parted at the corners noisily sucking in air. "Then hold it in as long as you can," he gasped, straining to hold it in as long as he could. He passed the joint on to his left.

When it came around again, a mere stub of its original length, he told Libby to smoke it as though she were sipping hot soup.

Libby smiled, placed the stub between her lips and sipped hot soup. This time the smoke filled her lungs. The sensation was harsh and hot but not intolerable. When she started to exhale, her mentor nudged her, told her to keep it in. Which she did. Her capacity for holding her breath was exceptional. She'd once terrified a counselor at the home by staying under-water in a swimming quarry for two and a half minutes. Now she sat perfectly still, didn't exhale until it was her turn again.

"Far out," her friend laughed. "You'll be a pothead before you know it!"

"How do you feel?" asked Debbie handing her a newly rolled joint.

"Fine. I feel fine."

"Man, Gary, where'd you score this rag?"

"South of the border. Pure Canal Zone!"

There was a clamor of appreciative voices.

Libby watched the joint pass around the circle. Everyone seemed to be having a good time—joking and laughing. Their eyes shining. She decided she too was having a good time. It was not like the other party. She felt included here. She was glad she hadn't gone home.

"Wow!" moaned Debbie. "What a rush!" She was rocking back and forth on her haunches. When David handed her another joint, she ex-claimed, "Time out!" and passed it on to Libby without taking a hit. Libby smiled at her to let her know how much she was enjoying herself. She filled her lungs with smoke and dutifully held her breath, heroically held her breath, until again it was her turn. Actually she didn't care all that much about the smoking itself, couldn't understand why everyone carried on so about it. Not that she was complaining—it just didn't seem all that great. All that anything . . .

On the next time around, when she turned to pass the joint, the young man on her left handed her another one coming from the other direction. No sooner had she removed its moist, twisted end from her lips than

Debbie was nudging her to take a third one. The host was busily rolling a fourth.

Libby's throat began to burn. She coughed, choked on the next breath of smoke and decided she'd had enough.

The burning in her throat grew worse. With every breath she felt a tightening soreness. The lining of her throat was scorched—shriveling and cracking like the skin of a roasted goose.

"No, thank you," she heard herself rasp. Debbie had just offered her another joint. Her roommate had begun smoking again, was holding her breath, shook her head, gesticulated with the glowing brand. Libby took it, passed it quickly on.

She was on fire now. The flames in her throat had spread to her lungs, seared them. She coughed again, couldn't stop. The hot smoke clung to her insides. Her eyes watered, her whole body shook in a fit of deep, painful hacks. She had to stand up. If she remained on the floor any longer, she would suffocate.

Getting to her feet was not easy. Her own body had become an obstacle —a great unwieldy load. It took all the effort she could muster to maneuver from her pillow, to straighten her knees and lift her head. Once upright she felt dizzy, faint, was sure she was going to collapse. She trembled, swayed. A period of time elapsed which she had no memory of, no recollection of other than that it had existed and she had not.

"Are you all right?" said Mr. Weintraub from his hospital bed, waiting for her to finish his bath. Libby continued to tremble and sway. Gradually she became aware of her surroundings again . . . the poster of a bullfight on the far wall . . . the fiesta-red drapes. . . .

"Are you all right?"

Libby looked down and saw Debbie clutching her dress at the hem, her eyes puffy but wide with concern. The room was stifling. She felt captured in Debbie's grasp.

"I . . . I have to go to the bathroom." She pulled free, managed to step back over her pillow without stumbling and traipsed out of the room.

She was standing in front of the bathroom mirror. For how long? She didn't know. She had lost all sense of time. Or rather it had lost all sense of her, for it raged about like some wild beast, dragged her back and forth through the years while she stood there, helpless, gripping the sink in both hands.

She was a little girl again. She was walking in a pasture. The sun was high in the sky and very hot. In the distance she could hear the thunka-thunka-thunka of her uncle's tractor working the bottomlands.

A snake silently slithered away at her feet. She almost stepped on it, jumped back, watched it quickly disappear in the tall grass.

Then her aunt was calling her name from the house. She turned, saw Eudora standing on the back porch, shielding her eyes in the sunlight. She walked toward her, feeling the sun burning down on the tips of her shoulders. A cloud of gnats swirled up from a clump of thickets along the fence line. High above, a crow beat its way through the bright sky with black, jagged wings, cried out:

Caw haw! Caw haw!

. . . And suddenly there was no sky, no sun. She was lying in semidarkness on a pile of rags, an old, shredded mattress. Her eyes searched through the dim light, slowly recognized the dark stone walls, the damp, crumbling floor—even the cluttered outline of junk surrounding her: pieces of broken furniture, empty crates and egg cartons stacked to the rafters, an old butter churn, the broken blades of a windmill propped against a pile of mildewed seed bags. Her nostrils clogged with dank, familiar smells.

Once again she was in the O'Learys' basement. Once again a prisoner.

Voices upstairs. The cellar door opened. She heard footsteps descending. It was her cousin, Kevin, and Jimmy Tanner, a boy from a neighboring farm. She tensed and swallowed hard, recalling visits from Kevin and his friends in the past. They were bored, had come to amuse themselves.

"Gooo-neee . . . Oh, Gooo-neee . . . Where are you?"

It did no good to hide. Only added to their sport.

"There you are, you dumb Goonybird! Is that all you do—lie around and sleep all day?"

Kevin and his friend eased their way past the furnace, their eyes not yet accustomed to the gloom. They shuffled closer until they were standing over her, lying on her mattress at their feet.

"Jeez, it stinks down here," said the Tanner boy. He jabbed at an empty egg carton with a long, pointed stick he'd brought with him, succeeded in piercing it. He tossed it over his head.

"She ain't got no bathroom. She goes right on the floor. Over in that corner there." Kevin wrinkled his nose and nodded toward the furnace. He was carrying a large paper sack.

"We brung you a present, didn't we, Jimmy?" Kevin held up the sack. Jimmy snickered.

"It's right here in this sack. But first you gotta do something for us." He looked at Jimmy; Jimmy grinned.

"First you gotta pull down your pants. . . . So go on, pull 'em down. Then you get your present. Honest." He shook the sack. "It's real nice—what you've always wanted."

Jimmy guffawed.

She turned away from them, tried to burrow deep into her bedding of rags.

"Now, that ain't very nice—going back to sleep while you got company. I just guess we'll have to take them old pants down ourselves."

Kevin carefully placed the sack by the wall, then grabbed her by her ankles. She kicked out.

"Grab her other leg!" he yelled at his friend. The two of them managed to subdue her. They pulled her toward them and rolled her over on her back. Kevin reached down with a free hand and seized her tattered undergarment, yanked it hard, tearing it off. It was the only thing she wore, the only clothing given her. ("Can't have you running around naked as a jaybird—even in the basement. This is a decent, God-fearing house," her aunt had remonstrated one evening, handing her a new pair of panties along with her meal at the top of the stairs. After that she'd received a clean pair every other month.)

"See, she's got hair, just like I told you."

"Not much," said the Tanner boy, peering at the sparse tuft between her legs. "Nothing like Marlene Hausserman's. I seen her naked once swimming over at Clement's Pond. She had a whole bunch—all black and curly. I seen Otho Baker screw her."

"Oh, sure, I bet. They just sold you tickets an' let you watch, huh?"

"Naw, I was hiding in the cattails. They was out on the raft."

"I'd of been there, I'd've swum out and asked him to move over."

The Tanner boy laughed, then asked, "Think we ought to screw her?"

"Goonybird? You crazy?"

"Sure, why not? My older brother, Donny, he screwed a carp once."

"A carp?"

"Yep, slit its belly open with a knife. Use to fuck chickens the same way."

"He's crazy. Anyway, my folks'd kill me if they found out."

"Aw, bet they wouldn't care. They keep her down here with all the rats, don't they?"

"They'd care plenty. My ma's funny about stuff like that. She's got an awful lotta religion."

"Who's gonna find out? She can't talk, she can't snitch."

Kevin was silent. "I don't know . . ." he finally mumbled. He let go of her leg and reached for the sack. He opened it, peered inside. Then he stuck in his hand and withdrew its content, a three-foot-long garter snake.

"You gonna do what you said?" the Tanner boy snorted with glee.

"Gooo-neee . . . look what we brrrung you." He held the snake by the tail, dangled it over her head. She looked up at the frightened creature, its black eyes darting, its yellow-striped body twisting from one side to the other, trying to free itself from her cousin's grip.

Kevin slowly lowered it. She closed her eyes, felt it drape across her face, the touch of its cool, smooth underbelly sliding over the bridge of her nose, across her forehead, into her hair.

"You gonna do it? You gonna put it where you said?"

Kevin grinned. He lifted it from her face and flopped it down on her chest. She felt it slither across her flat, budding breasts, her stomach. It slipped off her hip. He flopped it on her stomach a second time. Once more it slipped off.

When she felt it again, her eyes jerked open. He was dangling it between her legs.

Immediately she began to kick and thrash. The Tanner boy, caught off guard, lost his grip and fell back. She half rose up, then tried to roll over and once again burrow into her bedding.

"Come on, Jimmy! Can't you hold her still no better'n that?"

Jimmy recovered, grabbed her ankles and flung her over. This time he knelt on her stomach, held one leg down with both hands. Kevin knelt on her other leg.

"That's more like it. . . . What's the matter, Goonybird? Don't you like your little present? He just wants to be friends. Don't you, snaky?"

He lowered the snake again until it touched the shadows of her sex.

"Go on, snaky. See the nice, warm hole to hide in? Go on now, you just crawl inside there."

The snake flicked out its tongue warily, arched its body J-shaped. Every time Kevin swung its head forward, it twisted away, tried to slither across her thigh.

"Aw, he ain't going to do it."

"Maybe it ain't open wide enough. Here, hold the snake for a second."

Kevin reached down and thrust three fingers of his right hand into her, dug her apart. Her eyes watered in pain. She bit her lip until she tasted the salt of her blood, but she uttered no sound.

When Kevin took back the snake, he seized it this time just behind the head. The body wrapped around his arm. He leaned forward and shoved the head into her separated flesh.

"Haw! Do it—stuff him up her old crack till he comes out her mouth!"

He continued shoving, used both hands to work his grip farther down the snake's neck, forcing more and more of the creature's length inside her. She endured the pain, jammed her hands into the rips of her mattress, clutched and tore at the stuffing.

She felt the snake turn—inside her—like the twitching of her own inner muscles. As Kevin pressed forward again, it doubled back on itself, emerged suddenly and bit his hand. Cursing, he yanked it up and flung it against the basement wall. It dropped to the floor, stunned.

Kevin got up and retrieved it. He hurled it against the wall a second time.

"Hey, look! Its insides are coming out."

He stared down at the injured creature lying by the base of the wall— at the wriggling mass of protoplasm that had just been discharged from a rent near its tail.

"Them ain't its insides. Them are babies. It's having babies."

The other boy climbed off Crescent for a closer look.

"No wonder he don't want to crawl up her crack—it's a girl snake."

Kevin stepped on its middle. More baby snakes spurted out. The Tanner boy giggled. He stomped on them, mashing them to a pulp of blood and scales on the concrete floor. The mother snake came alive, twisted up and bit at Kevin's shoe.

"Stupid old snake," he muttered. Keeping it pinned beneath his heel, he took out a pocket knife and began stabbing the creature. The Tanner boy picked up his pointed stick, joined in the fun.

Kevin removed his foot. The snake drew itself up into a feeble coil of defense. Blood and entrails oozed from a number of deep punctures in its sides.

"Hey, I know what," said the Tanner boy, and he dug a book of matches from his pocket. He lit the whole book at once, used the blaze to set fire to the sharp end of his stick. Then he proceeded to burn the snake, jabbed the flaming point into its wounds. The snake, near death, sluggishly rolled from side to side. Finally the Tanner boy pinned the animal with his foot, jammed the burning stick down its mouth.

Crescent, left alone, had turned over and reburied herself in the folds of her mattress, tried to hide away like a tiny insect. Now something compelled her to dig herself out, to sit upright and lean forward and bear witness to the death of the creature that only moments earlier had been twisting inside her.

The snake writhed in a final burst of agony. It wrapped its tail around the stick, futilely struggled to disgorge it from its seared gullet. Kevin and his friend howled with laughter. It appeared as though the snake were fighting with the stick, trying to swallow it whole.

Crescent had risen to her feet now, was staring transfixed. Even in the basement's dim light, she could see the creature's eyes . . . looked into them . . .

And almost instantly felt her thoughts disintegrate. Explode. She moaned, struggled to keep her balance. Choked on burning wood. In agony she let out a cry—found her voice, so long locked deep within—a wailing shriek that shook the basement walls. She lunged forward.

The Tanner boy had just lifted the stick with the dead snake still entwined, was about to flog it against the furnace—when she fell upon him. Caught off balance, he went down under a flurry of pummeling arms and scratching nails. He tried to get her off. Failed. Tried to fight back, contain her blows. Failed again. Though he was Kevin's age and nearly twice her size, he could not begin to match the fury of her attack. Overwhelmed, he shrank on the floor, huddled to protect himself with his arms and legs.

Kevin watched the scuffle with surprise, then amusement: The spectacle of his little halfwit cousin soundly thrashing his friend and peer. He taunted and jeered him, threw egg cartons at both of them. At last he decided he'd seen enough. He grabbed her by her foot and started to pull her off. She kicked free; then from a crouch sprang at him, clawing and screaming crazy noises.

Kevin found himself backing away—not so much from the force of her attack as from the look in her eyes. It was something beyond anger, something beyond hatred. He suddenly felt hollow and confused.

As he continued to give ground, she abruptly halted her attack and burst into tears. She bent over, vomited. Her cousin stood dumbstruck staring at her. He struggled to break his gaze, laughed nervously to hide the uneasiness he still felt. He circled around her, stumbled over a coal scuttle, managed to keep his balance. When he reached the stairs he called to his friend.

The Tanner boy got up slowly. He was cut and bleeding about the face. His shirt was torn, and he bled from an elbow. He sidled warily by her; she was hunched over on all fours now, coughing and heaving. He stumbled over the coal scuttle and went down, sprang to his feet again, dashed the remaining distance to the stairs, expecting to feel her leap on his back at any instant.

"Yagh! Dumb Goonybird!" Kevin shouted out defiantly. He picked up an old, empty paint can and threw it in her direction. Then he followed his friend who already had run past him up the stairs, now stood in the doorway waiting to slam the door behind them.

She crawled back onto her mattress. The tears and nausea had left her dizzy, exhausted. She collapsed face down. She tried to comprehend what had just happened, fell fast asleep instead. When she awoke it was several hours later. She had a throbbing headache. A feeble gray light filtered through the window. It soon would be night. Overhead she could hear the O'Learys moving about. They'd finished dinner. Her aunt was still banging around in the kitchen. Lloyd and Kevin had retired to the living room.

She could smell her own dinner: pork scraps, boiled potato skins and gravy; the plate already was sitting on the top of the stairs. Usually she was ravenous, pouncing on her food the moment her aunt set it down. Now she lay still and made no attempt to get up.

A sharp pain struck her in the lower abdomen. She rolled over on her side, doubled up as more cramps stabbed through her. Presently she felt a strange seeping between her legs.

She reached down, held up her fingers—warm, sticky, scarlet in the fading light. Blood. The snake must have bitten her. Deep inside.

When she shifted her position, the flow of blood increased. It gushed. A dark stain spread beneath her. She held her breath, lay rigid, terrified that the bleeding wouldn't stop—not until every last drop of her blood was drained, until she lay there cold and lifeless like a slaughtered calf.

Even after the bleeding did stop, she was afraid to move, continued to lie there until once again she fell asleep.

She awoke breathing and coughing smoke. Eyes watering, her head still aching, she sat up. It was night. The window was aglow with pale moonlight. Rising from a small pile of rags next to her mattress was a thin, acrid cloud of smoke—right where the Tanner boy had dropped his spent book of matches.

She backed away from the choking fumes, sat on the far edge of the mattress and watched. It was nearly an hour later before the first flames appeared.

They popped up in several places almost simultaneously, busily joined together into a crooked triangle of fire that stretched to a corner of her mattress. She stared mesmerized as loose wads of stuffing ignited, flared up into brilliant yellow-orange ribbons.

For a moment she debated alerting the household, jumping up and dashing to the stairs, climbing them and pounding on the door. She debated crying out, shrieking, filling the basement with her newfound voice. She didn't move, continued staring.

The heat finally forced her to retreat to a damp corner behind the furnace. She stood there and watched her mattress become a roaring blaze, watched as the flames spread to the stacks of egg cartons, the piles of rubbish and old furniture, then leaped upward until they were curling about the rafters and ceiling joists.

For the first time since her ordeal in the afternoon, she let her eyes return to the floor by the back wall. The snake still lay there, the stick jammed down its gullet. As the fire began to sweep over it, she thought she saw the creature come alive. For a brief moment she glimpsed it twisting and writhing anew, saw its charred, smoldering body uncoil and regurgitate the stick. She saw it shrink away, into the swirling flames.

Overhead she heard a scream. It rose high above the crackling tumult, wavered, was lost in a crash of collapsing timbers. She crouched in her corner and felt the heat blistering the skin of her back.

Suddenly it was raining on her—a downpour of water from the cracks in the living-room floor overhead. She raised up to see part of the kitchen cave in on what was left of the stairs. A torrent of water cascaded into the basement through the yawning gap. Thick mists of hissing steam rose all around her.

Voices. Outside.

She stood on her tiptoes, peered out the window at flashing red lights, people moving about in the yard. A man approached. She was showered with broken glass. Strong arms seized her, hoisted her whimpering out into the night.

Before she was wrapped in a blanket and carried away, she saw the naked body of her aunt lying nearby in the grass, her dull, rust-brown hair burnt black as coal and smoldering.

Bleary, swollen eyes peered at her. Her eyes. She was back in the white-tiled bathroom at Marina Towers, years later. She was Libby again, lost and found, clutching the rim of the sink and staring into the mirror.

Her eyes and not her eyes. The eyes of a stranger. Quick, darting. Frightened—

She jerked back, gave a hoarse cry. They were the eyes of the serpent —and her throat was burning, her head split open with pain. . . .

"Libby! Libby! What's the matter?" cried Debbie Turner, finding her sitting on the bathroom floor, halfway out of her clothes and staring blankly at a wall. She was babbling strange, unintelligible noises.

81

"Are you okay, honey? Tell me what's wrong!" Debbie dropped to her knees beside her, put an arm around her shoulder. Libby stared straight ahead, mouthing gibberish.

Several onlookers crowded at the doorway.

"Sounds like a goddamn zoo in there."

"I told you that was primo grass!"

Debbie told the others to close the door. Then she and a girl friend removed the rest of Libby's clothes and helped her into the shower. After holding her under the cold spray for a good ten minutes, they brought her out and dried her. Debbie called outside for her boy friend to put on a pot of coffee. When Libby was dressed, her head wrapped in a towel, they led her out to the kitchen.

No longer was she babbling. Though she still appeared somewhat disoriented, the shower had calmed her. Sitting in silence at a small breakfast-nook table, she allowed her roommate to pour three cups of hot, black coffee down her.

It was after two-thirty when they finally returned to the dorm—over an hour past lockout. At the front door Debbie gave a feeble excuse about car trouble to the night monitor as she let them in. The girl smirked and handed her the late register. Fearful that Libby might not be able to write her name, Debbie quickly signed in for both of them. Monday they would have to go before Miss Bernstick and give a full accounting. Libby probably would get off with a light lecture; it was her first offense. She, Debbie, wouldn't be so lucky. It was her third lockout since January.

Two girls were still up in the commons. They called to Debbie as she and Libby stepped from the elevator, but Debbie ignored them. She took Libby straight to their room, helped her undress and got her into bed.

Later in the night Debbie was awakened by her roommate talking in her sleep. Only it really wasn't talking—it was the same gibberish she'd heard her mumbling on the bathroom floor: whistles and hisses, deep-throated moans and growls.

The sounds frightened her. She'd never seen anyone get so freaked before on grass, on so few hits. Maybe her roommate had permanently flipped. She tried not to think about it, climbed from her bed and shook Libby vigorously to shut her up. Thank God it was Sunday. Neither of them was on duty, and they could sleep as late as they wanted.

Debbie awoke around noon. She felt awful. Then she remembered Libby. She rolled over, discovered the bed next to her was empty and sat up abruptly. Libby was nowhere in the room. Fighting her hangover, Debbie tried to clear her thoughts. Where could she have wandered off to in her wigged-out condition? She had a sudden vision of Libby sprawled on the floor of Miss Bernstick's office, babbling her crazy noises. Debbie leaped out of bed and threw on her robe.

She checked the lavatory first, heard water running and peered in the shower. It was Frances Taylor.

"Have you seen Libby?"

Frances shook her head. "Not since breakfast."

"Breakfast!" exclaimed Debbie. "Libby was at breakfast?"

"Has she ever missed a meal?" said Frances, laughing, and bent over to soap her calves.

Debbie found her in the commons. Libby was sitting on a couch reading a newspaper. She looked up as her roommate sat down beside her and greeted her with a smile. "I . . . I was going to wake you for breakfast, but you looked so peaceful I decided to let you sleep. Was that okay?"

"Ya . . . sure," answered Debbie. "Er . . . how do you feel?"

"Fine. Breakfast did wonders. I was really hungry."

"Do you remember anything from last night?" Though they sat alone in the room, Debbie had lowered her voice.

"Not much."

"You were pretty stoned."

"Stoned?"

"High from smoking all that dope."

"I guess I did get sort of sick. I must have acted pretty stupid."

Debbie laughed, shook her head. "That's okay. You should have seen me the first time I really got stoned. It was with David last summer. When he tried to make out with me I thought he was my father! Anyway, it's great you're feeling better," she said, standing up. "You're sure you're okay now?"

"Fine," Libby repeated, reached out and patted her roommate's hand.

After Debbie left the room Libby put down the paper. She shut her eyes and placed her stout fingers to her head, slowly began kneading her temples and brow.

That night when Debbie returned from a date with David, she found Libby still up at midnight.

"Thought you'd be asleep for sure after the sack time you got last night."

Libby sat at her desk, peering down, her head propped in her hands. Debbie failed to notice there was no book beneath her gaze.

"Which reminds me, Miss Bernstick's sure to call us on the carpet Monday," she said, pulling off her sweater. "Now, I know you hate to fib . . ."

"Don't worry, Debbie. I won't tell her about what we done—about smoking the marijuana and everything."

Debbie breathed a sigh of relief. She finished undressing and scrambled into bed.

"Hey, you coming to bed soon?"

"Uh-huh. I'll just be here a little longer."

Much later Debbie woke up. She was surprised to find a light still on. Libby was still sitting at her desk. Debbie rolled over and glanced at the clock: four-fifteen. Krikeez!

"Libby, what are you doing? When are you coming to bed?"

"Huh?"

"I said, when are you going to turn that light off and come to bed? It's after four!"

Libby mumbled something, then switched off the light. Debbie waited to hear her get up from her chair. The room was still. Finally she propped herself up on one elbow and looked hard through the darkness.

"Hey, what are you doing? Why are you sitting there in the dark?"

"Huh? . . . oh, nothing . . . just resting my eyes."

"You sure you're feeling okay?"

"Sure. I just had some things to catch up on."

"What's so important it can't wait till tomorrow?"

"Nothing. Just some things." She got up slowly, crossed the room and stood by her bed.

"Well for God's sake, turn in and get some sleep!" Debbie yawned, rolled over on her pillow. When she didn't hear Libby's bed creak, she rolled back.

"Well?"

Libby hesitated, lowered herself into bed.

"Good night."

"G'night."

Less than an hour later Debbie again was awake. This time it was Libby's noises—more of the same gibberish from the night before. Debbie listened for only a few moments. The hissing and growling seemed louder than ever.

"Libby! Libby!" she called sharply. No response. She got out of bed to shake her.

She put a hand on her shoulder, then jerked it away. In the thin, eerie light of dawn she was able to see her face—jaw clenched, lips drawn tightly back, baring her teeth in an ugly grimace. Her eyes were rolled up white, twitching. It was a face from a nightmare. It barely resembled a face at all.

Debbie gathered her nerve, again grabbed Libby's shoulder and shook her frantically. "Hey! . . . Libby! . . . Hey! Snap out of it! You're having a bad dream. It's okay. Everything's okay!"

The noises stopped. Libby's face relaxed. Her eyes closed as she slowly awakened.

"Miss O'Leary, are you feeling all right?"

Nurse Irma Bussey, the matronly floor supervisor, stood by the door watching Libby take a patient's temperature. Libby had just removed the thermometer from the patient's mouth. Libby had been about to read it when she'd been hit with a dizzy spell. She braced herself momentarily against the bed railing. When her head cleared again she lifted the thermometer to read it, found her right hand shaking so badly she was forced to hold the thermometer in both hands.

The sound of Nurse Bussey's voice startled her. The thermometer jumped from her fingers, fell to the hard tile floor and shattered.

"Sorry!" she blurted, bending over to pick up the pieces.

"Never mind that, child, I asked if you were feeling all right."

"Oh . . . uh . . . yes, fine."

"You're sure?"

Libby nodded.

"Well, I'm not so sure. There's a lot of flu going around now. You look white as a sheet—a wonder nobody's thrown you in the laundry hamper. I think you better finish up in here and then go to the infirmary."

Libby started to protest.

"I haven't time to argue, Miss O'Leary," interrupted Nurse Bussey. She glanced at her watch. "If you hurry you can catch Dr. Evans before he leaves for lunch—so run along now."

Libby took the elevator down. She got off at the ground floor, but she did not go to the infirmary. She crossed the street to the residence hall, went up to her room instead. There was no need to see a doctor; she knew she did not have the flu.

In her room she glanced at her bed, went directly to her desk and sat down, propped her head in her hands and began massaging her temples.

Almost a week had gone by since the party at Marina Towers. Almost a week now that she'd suffered from terrible headaches. Her old migraines. It had been years since they'd last plagued her—not since her early teens, when she was living her new life at the home, after the fire. Somehow the marijuana had brought them on again, her old memories. The O'Learys —Kevin, Lloyd, Eudora—had all died in the fire. Only she had survived, confined in the basement where the blaze had begun. That was the night she had had her first period. She had been more bewildered and frightened by the changes within her than by the flames themselves. It also was the night of her first migraine.

The attacks had continued off and on for several years after that, striking most severely during her periods. Gradually, however, she'd seemed to outgrow them. By the time she was sixteen, they were only a bad memory.

Now they were back, worse than ever. The piercing throb was unrelenting. She couldn't study, couldn't concentrate. Her nerves were shot. Jagged arcs crossed her field of vision. Sounds exploded in her ears—doors slamming, trays clattering, buzzers ringing, people shouting. She barely could carry out the simplest routines at work. Yesterday she'd bungled on her charting, mixing up two patients' intake and output records. Today she couldn't even read a thermometer.

She was exhausted, badly needed sleep, but doggedly refused to lie down. The last place she wanted to be was in bed, the last thing she wanted to do was fall asleep, because worse than the migraines, worse than all the throbbing pain and tension, were the nightmares.

They stalked her round the clock, crept up on her, invaded her mind the moment she let down her guard, nodded her head and drifted into unconsciousness. Tormenting voices and visions filled her with dread.

85

She found herself fighting to stay awake through each day. Through each night.

"Libby, how you feeling? Sheila told me Bussey sent you home." Debbie entered the room, a load of books under her arms.

"Uh?" Libby looked up. It was late in the afternoon. She hadn't moved from her desk. "I'm okay. Fine now."

Debbie set her books down on her own desk, turned to face her roommate squarely.

"Libby, what is it? What's bothering you?"

"Nothing . . . uh, I don't know—maybe a touch of the flu."

"Is that what Dr. Evans told you?"

Libby was silent.

"Did you even go to the infirmary?"

Libby looked away.

"I thought as much. Look, maybe you can play games with everybody else, but you can't fool me. I know something's bothering you. So why don't you level with me for once. What's going on?"

"Oh, Debbie, please . . . Just leave me be! It's nobody's business . . . nobody else's but my own!"

Debbie was taken aback. It was the first time Libby ever had spoken sharply to her, the first time she'd ever heard her speak sharply to anyone.

"Sorry. I didn't mean to pry," she finally responded in an injured voice. She walked stiffly over to her bureau, began rummaging through a drawer.

"I . . . I'm sorry, Debbie. I'm not trying to be ornery. Honest."

"Look, no problem."

"I guess I'm just sort of run-down lately. It's hardly nothing—really. I'll be okay."

"Look, I understand. I promise not to bug you about it anymore. Okay?"

Libby managed a smile.

Debbie closed the drawer, sat down on her bed to remove her shoes. "Hey, guess who I bumped into in the hall downstairs?"

Libby was silent, appeared not to have heard her.

"Guess who I bumped into in the hall downstairs?"

"Um? . . . Who?"

"Miss Bernstick! And can you believe it? She didn't even mention our lockout last Friday."

Libby tried to show interest.

"She even asked if you had a good time at the party. I told you you did —that we both did. Boy, if she only knew . . . Hey, you feeling well enough to go eat or you want me to bring you something?"

She said she was feeling well enough.

Debbie started to say something, thought better of it. She slipped into a pair of casual pumps and got up to leave instead.

Around ten-thirty that evening Libby went to bed. She lay awake, eyes wide, staring out the window, until Debbie was sound asleep. Then she slipped out of bed, tiptoed from the room and spent the rest of the night in the lounge—as she'd been doing almost every night for the past week.

She watched TV until it went off the air at two forty-five. Sometime after three she felt herself going under, her eyelids sticking closed when she blinked, then becoming harder and harder to reopen. She struggled to her feet and took a shower. First hot, then cold. That did the trick. Revitalized —at least for the moment—she returned to the lounge and continued her strange vigil. At six she took another shower and grimly prepared to face the new day.

She did not last long in her morning duties. While changing her second patient's bedding, she removed the dirty sheets and pillowcases only to turn around minutes later and put them right back on again. She made up her mind then and there she'd had enough, saw no reason to hang around for Nurse Bussey's critical eye. She had gone too many hours, too many days without sleep. It was better she quit now before she really did something stupid.

Back in her room, exhausted as she was, she still fought to stay awake. The only way was to keep on her feet. She would take a long walk.

Outside she found the bright, hot sun unbearable. It drove her indoors again. She began walking through one department store after another, up and down the aisles, never stopping at the counters, never even glancing at the merchandise. She moved like some frenzied shopper, lost, disillusioned, searching out the perfect gift at some special sale just around the next counter, just beyond the next display.

The important thing was to keep moving. She found herself starting to doze when she stood still. She maneuvered around aisles that were clogged with people, took to the stairs, avoiding elevators and escalators. Of course, sooner or later she would have to stop. She knew it. Sooner or later she would have to give in, collapse into a terrible, bottomless slumber from which—she grew more and more convinced—she would never awaken. But in the meantime . . . she'd just keep walking.

By noon she'd worked her way west to the Merchandise Mart. An entire city in one massive hulking building—she was able to hike down its endless corridors, expansive lobbies and exhaustless rows of shops for the rest of the afternoon.

It was early evening when she finally got back to the residence hall. Though she hadn't eaten all day, she skipped dinner, instead going directly up to her room.

Two things now had become apparent to her even in her present stupor. One, she was quitting school and quitting the profession. She had no idea what she was going to do after that—though it really didn't matter because she knew she was losing her mind. During the second month of school, her class had made a trip to the state mental institution at Manteno. Touring the security ward she'd seen patients screaming, flailing about, had seen several strapped to their beds, blubbering like little children. She was told they were given heavy sedation to keep from injuring themselves. Maybe she was going to end up like them. Maybe they too were fleeing from horrible dreams.

The second thing apparent to her was that she was through walking, through trying to stay awake. She had no strength, no will, nothing left to fight with. She was going straight to bed.

The room was empty. Debbie already had gone out for the evening. She'd left a note on her desk. Libby tried to read it. The words swam in her mind. She gave up. It took all her remaining concentration to undress. Resigned to whatever fate awaited her, she climbed into bed, pulled up the covers. If she didn't wake again, at least they'd find her in a clean gown. That was her last thought before sleep came crushing down.

She did wake again. The room was dark. She was damp with sweat and lay with both sheets twisted around her like a rope. Another nightmare. She stared at the luminous hands of the clock on the nightstand in disbelief. It was only a little after nine. She'd been asleep all of forty-five minutes!

She remade the bed, tried to go back to sleep. She tossed; she rolled about. Her migraine had let up, but not her anxiety. The nightmare had been a strange one, different from the others, though no less horrible:

She was back once more on that balcony of Marina Towers, overlooking the city, filled once again with that vague, threatening presence of the night. She stared down at the river, became frightened by its dark, coursing waters. Suddenly she saw it as a great tributary of evil, as though the whole malevolent animus of the city somehow had poured into it, seeped through the concrete and steel of the towering buildings, the vast enclosures of space, washed down the streets, gutters, and spewed through the sewers —all that was hostile and alien, all that was violent and ugly run off like so much rainwater into those shadowy depths.

Then she was no longer staring at the river, she was immersed in it, fighting its savage current, struggling through a thick gray scum, a great foul web of refuse that spread across its surface. The harder she struggled in it the more tangled she became. Filth clung to her hair, burned her face. In an effort to free herself, she dove, swam for a distance with the current underwater. When she came up for air, she found she was trapped beneath the surface, that the scum had hardened, solidified like a sheet of ice. She beat it, clawed and kicked it. It refused to yield. Heart pounding, lungs ready to burst, she plunged again into the inky gloom, churned downward until she struck the bottom. There she thrashed about in mud—soft, black and oozing—watched herself thrash about as though she were something strange, separate, outside herself, some crazed, amphibious creature from another age.

At last she closed her eyes, opened her mouth in a scream. She drank in the river, felt its dark waters pumping through her veins, mingling with her blood, flooding her heart, the highest, driest recess of her soul.

Only in death did she escape from the river; only in death did she escape from her dream. She awoke.

It was no use; she couldn't go back to sleep. Abruptly she got out of bed, put on her clothes. The room had become stifling; she couldn't bear to be cooped up in it a minute longer. She had to get out into the night air. She had to be on her feet again, walking.

For over an hour she wandered aimlessly through the streets, the sights and sounds of the city bombarding her senses with the real world. The Near North Side was bustling with nighttime activity. Neon signs and marquees glittered. Music overflowed into the streets. Crowds of gaudy people shouldered by, laughing, shouting. The din of traffic was incessant: engines revving, horns blaring, tires screeching.

She tramped down deserted side streets past dingy hollow buildings, dark alleys and lots strewn with rubble and garbage. Passing headlights occasionally revealed a figure slumped in the shadows: legs sticking out of a doorway, a head propped against a gated storefront, reeking of alcohol, of vomit and urine. In the distance a siren wailed. It was answered by another nearby. They echoed off into the night, chasing in different directions, faded away.

A fist fight broke out among several youths in front of a corner liquor store. She was barely noticed as she made her way through the scuffle. In the middle of the next block a man kicked a beer can into the side of a passing bus. The bus stopped. The driver got out, shoved the man to the pavement. A burglar alarm went off from an alley across the street. She still could hear it ringing several blocks away when she turned the corner at Ohio and Clark, headed south toward the Loop. Toward the river.

Halfway across the Clark Street Bridge she stopped, leaned against the railing. The river where it was not in shadow flowed a mottled brown and sickly green. It smelled like garlic, harsh and stale. The surface was littered with debris—empty bottles, bits of wood, bright slicks of oil. The current was slow, barely perceptible. Nothing like the swift waters of her dream.

A car rumbled across the bridge, its wheels droning noisily over the waffled steel roadway. She turned briefly, watched its red taillights disappear into the downtown caverns of the Loop.

Farther upriver beyond the next bridge, which she absently noticed was rising, she could see the Marina Towers. She gazed at their high, scalloped balconies, thought grimly of the night of the party. Which one had she stood upon? She couldn't begin to guess. There were so many and they all looked alike.

Someone was standing behind her! She glanced over her shoulder and spun around in the same motion. No one was there. She searched both ends of the bridge. Nobody. She couldn't believe it—the feeling had been so real, so intense. It persisted even now, though she did her best to ignore it. She gazed back down at the water.

The river suddenly took on the sinister, unsettling aspect of her dream. Its mottled, smooth surface seemed almost membranous—like some great sheath of skin. Oil slicks turned to glistening scales, a thing alive slithering beneath her, winding through the city. . . .

Her breath caught in her throat. She became dizzy, clutched at the railing with both hands, closed her eyes. In the back of her mind she knew why she'd come here. She only wondered now if she had the nerve.

Two more cars sped by. The driver of one honked his horn, yelled an obscenity as he passed. She could feel the hum of the tires through her body, her hips pressed hard against the steel railing. She could feel the vibration of the span.

A bell rang out. She yanked her head up, opened her eyes. Road barriers with flashing red lights were lowering at either end of the bridge. She heard a deep-throated blast sound across the water, saw a barge and pilot ship slowly approaching from upriver. There was still time to get off, but she would have to hurry.

She stood firmly planted by the railing and didn't move.

In the control house of the bridge the lone operator sat working a crossword puzzle. He cleared the ship's approach over his radio without looking up. Seven down: a celestial blackout . . . ending in "e"? He thought for a moment, tried another tack. Four across: an S-shaped arch . . . starting with "o"? Ogee! That was a snap—a crossword regular.

Before engaging the lift mechanism, he gave a perfunctory glance out his window at the roadway. Satisfied there were no stalled cars, no last-minute speeders, he threw the big red-handled lever at the control console by his side. Again, seven down: a celestial blackout . . . this time starting with "e" and ending in "e."

She felt the walkway quivering beneath her. The night air was filled with the creak and groan of straining metal. The bridge broke apart with a sudden jerk not two steps from where she was standing, almost throwing her down. The quaking structure halted momentarily. She regripped the railing tightly. The walkway jerked beneath her feet again. It shook with a grating throb; then the whole span commenced to swing slowly upward. She held on for dear life.

The walkway steepened. Soon she could no longer keep her footing. She clung to the railing, managed to place her feet on one of the balusters that were leveling like the rungs of a ladder. Not until the span was almost perpendicular did it stop its upward swing. She now towered above the streets, the waiting line of traffic at the gates. The river flowed some eighty feet below.

As the barge and pilot ship plied their way toward the bridge, its two spotlights scanned the channel and shore, occasionally jumping up to illuminate the walls and windows of surrounding buildings. One beam swept a high arc across the structure of the bridge. The other beam criss-crossed it.

"Jules, sving dot light up again," called the captain to one of his crew beside the wheelhouse. Though the captain was busy at the wheel, his eyes had caught something where it shouldn't be—a flash, a flutter of white, he wasn't sure.

The crewman played the light back on the south shore buttress, swung it up the span.

"Other side," said the captain, without taking his eyes off the channel.

The crewman corrected over to the opposite buttress, tracked slowly upward.

She looked down at the barge approaching—less than a hundred yards away now. In the moonlight its cargo of sulphur piled in rows resembled mounds of dirty snow. She was no longer terrified, instead felt strangely at ease. Her perch was secure; her instinctual fear of falling had given way to something quite the opposite: a sense of exhilaration similar to what she'd first felt that night on the balcony. She was soaring—not simply on this drawbridge, high above the city streets, but high above herself as well —liberated from her sadness, the anxiety and dread that had hounded her for so long.

An explosion of light hit her. She gave a startled cry, rocked backward, nearly slipping from the railing. The ship's spotlight had found her and set her ablaze in its blinding beam.

"Ach!" muttered the captain at the helm, fumbled at the radio to alert the bridge operator.

"Eclipse!" announced the bridge operator triumphantly to himself. He began to pencil in the squares, heard the captain's voice suddenly squawk over the receiver.

A moment later he'd thrown down his pencil and sprung up from his chair. He wrenched open the observation window, thrust his head and shoulders out as far as he dared. Damn! She was up there, all right! Nothing he could do about it either—not until the barge passed clear. She better have a good grip. He pulled himself back inside. Nobody ever used them walkways at night. Still, he should've checked. . . . Who said he didn't? Maybe she was a jumper. Maybe she was hiding, didn't come running out till after he threw the lever. Sure as hell couldn't blame him for that. . . . He debated for a moment, then called the police.

"Vot you think you doing up there, you?" yelled the captain. He'd turned the wheel over to his mate, stood outside the wheelhouse clutching a bullhorn. When he got no response he softened his tone. "Vee get you down, miss. Don't you vorry. Just you keep a holdt on tight, ya?"

A man waiting in the line of cars at the gate spotted her. He climbed out of his car and pointed high above. Others climbed out of their cars to join him.

She didn't open her eyes again until the barge had slid beneath her, until she was once more embraced in darkness. The ship's spotlights now were blocked out by the trusswork of the span. Though the captain had passed from view, she still could hear the bullhorn, his guttural voice booming out encouragement.

Directly beneath her the water swirled and foamed in the ship's wake. She watched an oil slick, shattered by the waves, come together again, reform, smooth out the choppy surface. Oval at one end, jagged and strung out at the other, it resembled some huge, exotic jungle flower. It shone iridescent in the light from the street, its leaves and petals rolling and twisting almost to the far shore.

"I've been waiting . . ."

Startled, she reeled back, lost her balance. Her feet slipped from the smooth metal baluster, left her dangling, holding on with just her hands.

Below, the small crowd of onlookers at the barrier waved and whistled, shouted advice. Car horns blared. A siren whooped loudly on a nearby street.

She struggled to pull herself up. Her arms were tiring rapidly. Kicking and scraping her feet, she managed to regain her stance.

"You and I . . . waiting so long . . ." The voice—her voice! Felt the words forming, breathless, on her lips.

"Who are you?"

The span suddenly gave a jerk. It wavered like a tree in the wind. Then started slowly down.

"Who am I?" came her own wavering reply.

A squad car turned the corner at Wacker Drive, sped up to the bridge, blue lights flashing, wailing shrill concern.

In the next instant she knew what she had to do. Before the bridge had lowered ten feet, she slid around the railing, hung poised over the water. The oil slick, the glistening flower, still rippled beneath her. She let go, for dear life.

Leaped into the night.

6

Debbie Turner had just climbed out of a cab and was walking up the front steps to the residence hall when she heard her name being called in a hissing whisper. She looked quickly around but saw no one. A moment later, a figure stepped out from a darkened recess of the building across the street.

"Libby . . . good God! Is that you?" She rushed across the street to greet her.

"Look at you! Krikeez! You're a mess! What on earth happened?"

Libby hung her head but failed to speak. She was soaking wet. Her clothes looked like dishrags—ripped and stretched out of shape, filthy with smudges of oil and grime. Clots of gray scum still clung to them. Her arms and legs were caked with mud and covered with cuts and bruises.

"Your hair!" Debbie reached out and touched it, felt its strands, slimy, gritty, draped with mung. "Uhgg!" She jerked her hand away.

"Your shoes! Where are your shoes?"

Libby looked down, as if to verify she was standing barefoot. She shook her head, sidled out of a small black puddle that had formed beneath the torn, dripping hem of her dress.

"Are . . . are you all right?"

She managed to shrug, even smile.

"Well, what happened? Tell me, for godsakes!"

"I . . . fell into the lake."

"You *what?*"

Debbie listened with amazement as her roommate proceeded to recount how she'd become bored sitting around the room, how she'd gone for a walk and ended up over by Navy Pier. The night being so beautiful and everything, she'd decided to go on one of the harbor sightseeing cruises. Stepping ashore from the boat, she'd slipped on the landing, had fallen into Lake Michigan.

"So how did you get out? Didn't anybody help you?"

She nodded, went on to explain how she'd been fished from the water, that when her rescuers had left her lying on the dock for a moment to go fetch a blanket and call a doctor, she'd gotten up and run away. She had been embarrassed, she explained. She'd been waiting here in the darkness ever since.

Debbie giggled with relief. She'd really been worried. Now that she'd learned nothing really horrible had happened, she could see the funny side; her big silly goose of a roommate taking a pratfall into the drink, then dashing off without a word, leaving everyone up in the air. Poor Libby— she was really something else!

"God, you smell awful! You smell like a sewer!"

Libby broke into tears. Debbie, taken by surprise, started to put a consoling arm around her but thought better of it. She gave her a light pat on the cheek instead.

"I forgot to sign out," Libby finally sobbed, her head bowed. "How can I go in looking like this?"

"No problem," said Debbie. "You wait here. I'll go sign in first. Then I'll let you in through the fire exit in the alley. Over there," she pointed. "Old reliable."

Before Debbie trotted off, she lifted Libby's chin. "Come on, silly, smile. You could have drowned, you know. Then think how bad you'd feel. . . ." Her voice trailed off as she stared at her roommate's mouth. Her teeth were black and smeared, dripping filth. It looked as though she'd been eating mud.

The next morning Libby awoke feeling wonderful. As a matter of fact, she never could remember feeling better—so totally refreshed, so alive! It seemed incredible to her that only yesterday she'd been considering quitting Windhaven. Now she felt more determined than ever to pursue her calling. She would become a nurse; there was no doubt in her mind. She was brimming with positive energy. Yesterday seemed so long ago, like another lifetime.

On the evening TV news, mention was made of an unidentified girl who the night before had jumped from the top of the raised Clark Street Bridge, narrowly missing a barge passing beneath. Libby sat watching with several girls in the lounge, listening attentively as a jowly newscaster recounted in dramatic rhetoric her apparent suicide.

"The Chicago River—yehk! What a way to go," commented Frances Taylor, sitting next to Libby.

"Bet they never find her," responded another girl.

"Probably buried under ten feet of crud."

"Like drowning in a giant bedpan."

Libby quietly excused herself and returned to her room to study. On her way she stopped in the bathroom and surveyed herself in the mirror. Her skin shone clean and white. Not a smudge remained. She'd spent the better part of an hour in the shower after coming in last night: rinsing and scrubbing, scrubbing and rinsing.

"Krikeez—look at the water!" Debbie had exclaimed, peering into the stall to see how she was progressing. Libby had glanced down, watched it swirling black as coffee grounds into the drain. Later when she'd stepped out, Debbie was waiting with two towels to help dry her off.

"Hey, have you been dieting lately?" her roommate asked, vigorously rubbing her back.

Libby shook her head.

"No kidding, you look like you've lost some weight. You ought to fall into the lake more often. I think it agrees with you."

Looking at herself in the mirror now, the rich, golden luster of her hair, Libby thought so too.

During the days that followed, a number of other girls began commenting on how well Libby was doing with her diet. She was, of course, still stout—a sow's ear and all that—yet as Babs Anderson put it, at least she wasn't "such a lump anymore."

Libby continued to lose weight. One month went by; then another. By the end of the summer, she and her diet were the talk of the school. Her weight loss was phenomenal, and it had radically altered her overall appearance. Not a trace of her former "lumpishness" remained. She was no longer even pleasingly plump. Her bovine frame had shrunk away to a shapely ghost of itself.

Each new day when the other girls encountered her in the classrooms and halls, they would swarm over her with incredulous eyes, buzz among themselves the moment she walked away. Not only was she on a crash diet, she also must be secretly enrolled in some miracle Michigan Avenue beauty cure. Granted she'd lost weight in her face, but not only was the puffiness gone, so too were all the blemishes, all those ruddy streaks and blotches. Her skin seemed almost to glow now, milk white, and its tautness revealed the delicate underlying features, the finely chiseled bone structure of a classic beauty. Her eyes were stunning and her hair . . . she'd let it grow: The thin, scraggly strands that once had looked as faded as pulled weeds now cascaded to her shoulders in thick, golden tresses.

Royal jelly, honey and egg, shark oil, peacock grease, mink sweat, cell therapy, protein massage, hormone injections, plastic surgery ... How else could you explain it? It had to be the result of some exotic glamour treatment. Debbie's great klutz of a roommate was becoming an absolute silk purse!

They pried Debbie for information in an effort to get the real lowdown. She could tell them nothing. As far as she knew, Libby wasn't involved in any beauty program—exotic or otherwise. She didn't wear makeup, didn't even bother to cream her face at night. Come to think of it, Debbie had never seen her brush her hair—not even now, grown longer. And as for a crash diet, Debbie asked her classmates how many of them had ever seen Libby miss a meal, or skip a dessert, or pass up a piece of late-night pizza. The girls looked at one another. No one said a word.

It was amazing what better posture could do for a person, absolutely amazing! Stella Bernstick watched Libby walking through the lower lobby one day on her way to the wards. Oh, she'd let her hair grow and she'd lost a lot of weight, but that didn't spell the difference. No, sir. It was her posture—that straight back and high carriage of her shoulders—that's what did the trick! Miss Bernstick recalled the slouching, homely girl she'd watched plodding down the corridors only a few months ago. Months? It seemed more like weeks! Where had the summer gone? She had to admit that in all her years at the school she'd never witnessed a more abrupt, a more remarkable transformation. It was hard to believe Libby was the same girl. Of course, inside she was undoubtedly still her same old, slow and toilsome self. Still ... having a lovely appearance, it did so give her every advantage. Miss Bernstick watched after her for several moments as she proceeded through the foyer and out the front door. When the director turned and walked back into her office, she made a conscious effort to carry herself as straight as her troublesome back would allow.

"Now, what do we call a drug that will dilate the pupils of the eyes?"

Nurse Frieda Torkle stood before her class lecturing on pharmacology, waited a practiced moment, then swelled to answer the question herself. It was her habit to question her students on material they hadn't yet read. She delighted in intimidating them, felt it kept them from becoming too complacent and cocksure. She was surprised when she saw a hand go up in the back row. The chapter relating to local-acting drugs and specific remedies would not be assigned until the end of the week.

She was doubly surprised when she saw it was Libby O'Leary, her slowest student. She had a mind like a bowl of pudding, had never spoken so much as a word in class—even when called upon. She probably wanted to be excused.

"Yes, Miss O'Leary?" The rest of the class turned in their seats, tittered.

"A mydriatic?"

Nurse Torkle stared in silence. "That's . . . yes . . . uh, exactly right. A mydriatic." Astonished whispers filled the room.

Nurse Torkle cleared her throat. She was a small, defensive woman with a pouchy face and close-set, humorless eyes. "Perhaps you could further enlighten the class with an example?"

"Atropine. From the belladonna. It also can serve as an antispasmodic, an anhidrotic and . . . uh, a temporary stimulant."

The whispers grew louder.

"Quiet, class!" snapped Nurse Torkle. "All right, Miss O'Leary, suppose I were a doctor and I wanted to slow a patient's pulse and reduce his body temperature. Name a drug I might consider."

"Aconite. Extracted from wolfsbane. It acts as both an antipyretic and a nerve paralytic depressant."

"Suppose I wanted to relieve a patient's pain—"

"You'd give him aspirin or morphine," broke in Miriam Arp, raising her hand and answering at the same time. Miriam was the acknowledged class scholar.

"Wrong! Now let me finish," rebuked Nurse Torkle. "Suppose I wanted to relieve a patient's pain . . . *and* he was suffering from a rheumatic condition."

Miriam fell silent with the rest of the class. Libby's hand went up.

"Miss O'Leary?"

"I think you'd prescribe strontium salicylate."

Nurse Torkle nodded quietly. She was stunned. When she spoke again there was mounting agitation in her voice. "And why would I give a patient ferrous sulfate?"

"As a hematinic."

"Chrysarobin?"

"An antiparasitic."

"Chlorobutanol?"

"An inhalation anesthetic."

"Oleum juniperi?"

"A diuretic."

"Cascara sagrada?"

"A laxative."

"Lobelia?"

"An expectorant."

"Benzyl benzoate?"

"An antiscabietic."

"Well!" Nurse Torkle finally conceded, slightly out of breath. "Well, well, well . . . I must say, Miss O'Leary, you certainly seem to have a firm grasp on next week's lesson." She stalked around behind her desk, glanced at the wall clock, noting the hour was nearly up. "Maybe the rest of us are moving too slowly. Ummm . . . Yes, I think we'll just include Chapter Six in tomorrow's assignment."

There were groans.

"I think that will be quite enough for today, class."

The students continued to grumble as they rose from their chairs.

"Nice going, Libby," said Connie Petry as they filed through the doorway.

"Ya, thanks a lot, smart-ass!" added Babs Anderson.

A few nights later Debbie and Libby were lying in their beds still awake talking for a while before turning off the light. Debbie had just been telling about a recent run-in between Sheila Klein, a friend of theirs from the second floor, and Gaylord Radzim, Jr., the orderly who'd goosed Libby a few months earlier in a hallway. He'd done the same thing (using his own hand this time) to Sheila yesterday while she was stepping from an elevator on her way to the lab with a urine specimen. Sheila, diminutive, feisty as a Boston terrier, had flown into a rage and hurled the specimen at him. The floor supervisor had called them both in. Radzim had gotten off with a lecture, but Sheila had been sent before the disciplinary board and put on strict probation.

"I know they're hurting for orderlies, but I still think they ought to give that roach the boot."

Libby stared at the ceiling and nodded.

"Hey, cheerfully changing the subject, I heard about your performance in old lady Torkle's class. Sounds like you really got those gray cells humming."

"I sure didn't make any friends."

"Jerks. What do they know? I also heard you got the highest score on yesterday's pop quiz in physiology. Babs said you didn't miss a one."

"Oh, it wasn't a very hard test."

"Dr. Stylar's? Are you kidding? I know what his tests are like."

Libby smiled.

"I guess all that studying, it must be starting to pay off for you, huh?"

"I do seem to be understanding things better. Remembering them better too."

Debbie suddenly chuckled to herself, then said, "Hey, Libby, maybe that's where all your weight's going. Maybe you're burning it up thinking so hard."

They both laughed. Then they said good night. Debbie switched off the light.

"Say, I meant to tell you," she said in the dark, "I really liked that new, blue blouse dress you were wearing today. Is that from Fields?"

"No, it's from Belscot's back in Carthage. I've been wearing it for years."

"Sure fooled me. You must've taken it in a couple of yards. Did you have it altered or do it yourself?"

"Neither. It's just the same old dress. Actually it needs to be re-hemmed."

Debbie shook her head. "I don't believe it. I guess it's just you, though. I mean, everything you wear now looks so great on you—looks like it's brand new."

A few minutes later, Debbie spoke again. "Crescent . . . Cres . . . cent . . ." She pronounced the name slowly, softly. "How come you never use your real name?"

"I don't know. Everybody's always called me Libby. You know, from my middle name, Elizabeth."

"Well, maybe you can get by wearing your old clothes, but I sure don't think Libby fits you—not anymore. There's just nothing Libbyish about you." Debbie paused for a moment. "Cres . . . cent . . ." she pronounced the name again. "Kind of different . . . makes me think of the moon. I like it, though. Do you like it?"

Libby was silent. Crescent smiled.

The next day she was asked by her Nursing II teacher, Mrs. Kreeley, to stay after class. Mrs. Kreeley had gone over a paper of Libby's the night before, and she was unhappy. She did not expect her nursing students to write like budding journalists, but she did demand that they do their own work, at least organize and express things in their own words. It was obvious Libby had copied her entire paper verbatim from some outside source.

"Uh . . . Miss O'Leary, I read your paper," she began in a stern voice. She held up the title page and read it to Libby, who sat alone in the classroom before her. " 'The Dying Patient: Theoretical Considerations in Nursing.' I must say, a rather different sort of topic for this class. It's quite good, though. . . ." She studied Libby's face carefully, then added: "Perhaps a little too good?"

Libby, who was smiling, continued to smile. Mrs. Kreeley could discern no betrayal in her face, not so much as a blink. Before Mrs. Kreeley could repeat the insinuation, Libby spoke up:

"I only wish I could have gone into more detail on the inherent psychosocial problems related to the dying trajectory, you know, discussed the behavioral consequences of things like prejudice, stereotyping and selective perception. I wanted to include case studies of a few wrongheaded attitudes—I think it would have led to a more balanced treatment of my subject, but you'd, uh, set the limit at two thousand words, and I didn't want to ramble."

"Yes, well, uh . . . I mean, your paper certainly was adequate as it was," Mrs. Kreeley heard herself replying.

"Anyway, I focused mainly on the positive aspects of congruent death. Those theorized by Weisman and Hackett. It seemed like the most relevant and informative approach. The most fascinating too. I mean, it's incredible when you consider the concept of the caregiver shaping a patient's dying trajectory—the idea of making his death compatible with his sense of himself, the life he's led, his present needs and desires . . . that he can be molded to see there's a time for death and a time to face it . . . that conflicting fears and frustration—even pain—can give way to an inner harmony of resignation, of personal relief. . . ."

Mrs. Kreeley found herself staring dumbly and nodding. She'd completely misjudged this girl. Such alert, bright eyes. She probably was just awakening intellectually; some students took longer than others. Longer? More like never.

"Who?" blurted Babs Anderson.

The girls were standing in the vending room on the first floor. Frances Taylor put a quarter into the Coke machine. She got no Coke, punched the coin return, got no coin back, slammed the machine with her hand.

"It won't take quarters," said Debbie, inserting two dimes and a nickel. A can rattled down the chute. She handed Frances the Coke, searched her purse for more change.

"Who?" repeated Babs.

Moments earlier they'd been discussing Libby, who was not present. Connie Petry had just asked Debbie if her roommate used a rinse. "Afraid not," she'd replied, then added, "You might as well learn to live with it, gang, Crescent's just a natural-born knockout—granted one hell of a late bloomer, but a knockout nonetheless."

"Cres-who? What did you call her?"

"Crescent. Why?"

"Crescent?"

"That's right. It just happens to be her real name, dumbo."

There were clucks of surprise.

"Well la-tee-da," responded Babs. "What kind of a name is that? Crescent . . ."

"I don't know, but it's hers and that's good enough for me."

"Well, you can call her what you want," Babs persisted. "As far as I'm concerned she's still Libby—rinse or no rinse."

Later the same day in the ward, Babs left her patient for a moment and stuck her head into the room next door.

"Libby, how's about running to the pharmacy and picking up some stat medication for me? I'm really snowed under right now. . . ." Her voice trailed off.

Crescent herself was on a tight schedule, had a patient yet to feed and another one due back from surgery any minute. She gave Babs a brief, quizzical smile. Then before Babs could utter another word, Crescent nodded, set down the pitcher she was carrying and left the room.

Babs had trouble forgetting that smile. It made her uneasy for the rest of the day. The very next morning, when the two girls met in the report room, she felt compelled to say something.

"Hey, um . . . uh . . . Crescent, thanks much for helping me out yesterday. Maybe I can make some beds or something for you this morning?"

Crescent smiled politely. "Thanks. I'll call you if I need you."

"Promise?"

"Promise."

It was the first time Babs ever had offered to return a favor.

One day early in September, Debbie and Crescent ran into Alan Farber while shopping at Marshall Field's. He struck up a conversation on the escalator between the sixth and fifth floors, rode down with them all the way to street level. It soon was apparent that he had no idea Crescent was the same girl he'd ditched at the party of Carla Boswell's fiancé. It also was apparent that he couldn't take his eyes off her. Debbie treated him icily. He persisted, offering them a ride back to the dorm. She told him outright that she would rather take the bus. Crescent, however, seemed amused and accepted the offer.

"How could you?" demanded Debbie while they stood at a Wabash exit waiting for Farber to bring his car around.

Crescent clicked her tongue and smiled. "Oh, Debbie, he's not all that bad; probably just a little insecure."

"About as insecure as a virus! You may have lost tons of weight and gained oodles of charm, but in here"—she rapped her chest with a fist—"you haven't changed one bit. You've still got your old martyr complex; you're still bucking for sainthood."

Crescent laughed.

"I thought you were going to take the bus," said Farber, smirking, when Debbie climbed into the car, a bright orange Corvette with pumpkin leather interior.

"I changed my mind. Besides, the buses are packed at this hour. This isn't much of an improvement, though," she grumbled as she and Crescent were forced to share a single bucket seat.

"Sorry, but these wheels aren't exactly meant for three," he said pointedly, then gave a short, smug laugh, accelerated into traffic with a flourish of burning rubber. He spent the rest of the ride talking about his car, his apartment, his stereo, etc.

When they turned up Windhaven Drive he finally got around to Crescent. "Haven't I seen you somewhere before? You look awfully familiar."

"Do I?"

"Ya, and it's not just a line. There's something about you . . . I don't know. . . . I do know one thing, though: You sure don't look like any student nurse I've ever seen before."

"Have you seen very many?"

Farber snorted. "You should have seen the one your friend there tried to saddle me with a few months ago."

"Oh?"

"Ya, on a blind date. I mean, she could have played middle linebacker for the Bears. Hey, what was her name? I can't remember."

Debbie looked at Crescent.

101

"Libby," she finally replied. "Libby O'Leary."

"Ya, Libby. That was it." He snorted again. "Hut one, hut two, move over, Butkus, big Libby's coming through!"

By the time they'd reached the residence hall, he was telling Crescent how difficult it was living in the city, especially when it came to meeting nice girls. He parked the car and started to climb out. Debbie, opening her own door, told him not to bother.

"How's about you and me going out some night this week?" he asked Crescent as she slid toward the door.

"Mmmm . . . I guess I'd better not."

Farber leaned across the seat as she climbed from the car. "Why not? You busy?"

"Not really."

"Why not, then? Give me one good reason."

"You need a reason?"

He nodded vigorously.

Crescent thought for a moment, closed the door.

"Come on," Farber pressured, "I'll pick you up eight o'clock, tomorrow night. Whadaya say?"

"Well . . . I don't know. . . ."

Debbie gave her a sharp poke in the ribs from behind.

"I'll tell you what," she continued. "Why don't you give Libby a call? I'm sure she's free, and I . . . I promise she'll go out with you."

Farber snorted. "Thanks loads, but no thanks."

Crescent shrugged, turned to follow her roommate, who was walking away with a big grin on her face.

"Hey, what about us?" he called after her. "Have we got a date or not?"

"Thanks, I guess, loads," she said, waving back, "but no thanks."

Farber pulled his head in and watched her stroll up the front steps. Before entering the building, her roommate turned around. She smiled at him and gave him the finger.

"And I continue to hear nothing but wonderful things about you, Libby —or, excuse me, it's Crescent now, isn't it?"

Crescent sat in Miss Bernstick's office having tea with the director. The summer semester grades were in, and she'd been informed that she no longer was on academic probation.

"Oh, drats! I should never pour with my bifocals on." Miss Bernstick wiped off the desk where she'd dribbled tea over the edge of a saucer. After handing Crescent a cup, she lifted her own and inhaled the steaming fragrance.

"Mmmm . . . jasmine tea. I just love the aroma. I don't know what I'd do without my afternoon cup."

Crescent sniffed. She took a sip. "It's very nice."

"You know, I have to confess that not so very long ago I had my doubts."

Miss Bernstick sipped from her cup again, then set it down. "Quite frankly, I wasn't sure you'd be able to handle the requirements here. Not that I ever doubted your sincerity or sense of dedication, but you must admit your performance in the classroom . . . it was certainly something less than reassuring."

Crescent smiled, nodded.

"Now the only question in my mind is whether or not you'll finish at the top of your class."

"I guess I'm learning to cope."

A very accurate guess, indeed, mused Miss Bernstick. She sipped again from her cup, held it up, staring at the delicate green flowers etched around its thin rim of eggshell china. "So many girls . . . they never find themselves, stay locked up inside, never give themselves a chance. I . . . I marvel at you. How you've blossomed."

"Finding oneself . . ." Crescent offered softly, "or being found by others? I think I've been very fortunate in that respect, Miss Bernstick. I'm very grateful for all that you and the school have done for me."

"Oh, now, tut," clucked Miss Bernstick, beaming. Then she chided herself for positively gloating. After all, she, Miss Bernstick, really hadn't done that much. Granted, she'd made an exception in Libby's—Crescent's —case, had given her special treatment when she was having her problems. But certainly it was her roommate, Debbie Turner, who deserved the most credit. She was the one who'd really taken her under her wing. She was the one who'd performed the miracle.

"Good Lord," Miss Bernstick had said to Debbie, sitting in this same room just the other day, enjoying a cup of tea, "I've never seen such a dramatic turnaround . . . such a complete metamorphosis. I've a good mind to assign you as a roommate to half the girls in the school!"

Debbie had laughed but refused to take the credit. And she was right, of course, because if there was any miracle involved, it was Crescent herself who'd really accomplished it. An ugly duckling—at twenty-two, no less— she was the one who'd finally quit slouching, both in her posture and her schoolwork; she was the one who'd finally made the effort, finally chosen to stand straight and realize the full height of her surprising potential.

And even now the director smiled, noticing how well Crescent sat in her chair, drinking tea, how relaxed and yet how poised and attentive she looked. And how decidedly feminine. Miss Bernstick smiled a moment longer, then became pensive.

"It occurs to me, Crescent, that you may have to face a new obstacle in your career, one that didn't exist before."

Crescent gave her a look of earnest surprise.

"Here inside," the director added, lightly tapping the middle of her bosom.

"How do you mean?"

Miss Bernstick hesitated, then chose to be direct. "I mean you've become beautiful without ever having been pretty. You've grown in so many different ways so quickly; you've become a very different person. Maybe the desires of your heart have changed as well, or will change. What you want to be and what you want out of life. Nursing is a fine and rewarding profession, but it isn't for everyone. The motivation has to be there. And it has to be strong and enduring."

Crescent looked relieved. "Don't worry, Miss Bernstick," she said and smiled, giving the middle of her own bosom a light tap. "Mine is chiseled in stone."

A day later, to celebrate the end of the summer semester, Crescent joined Debbie and two other classmates for an evening of fun at Riverview. Sheila Klein, whose folks lived nearby in Skokie, borrowed the family Buick just for the occasion.

"See that tower over there?" said Sheila, pointing as she steered aggressively through the northbound traffic of the Kennedy Expressway.

Crescent, Debbie and Frances Taylor turned to see what resembled a giant Erector Set rising high above the rooftops and power lines on their right.

"That's the parachute ride. You can see the roller coaster just beyond —Damn, I'm in the wrong lane!" She tried to swerve over, but a semi blocking her path refused to yield and blasted her with its horn.

"Son-of-a-bitch!" she snarled, wriggling on her driving pillow. She was barely five feet tall and needed the added boost both to reach the pedals and to see over the steering wheel. They had to continue north another mile and a half before she could exit from the expressway and double back. Chattering away about the great time they were going to have, she also missed the park entrance off Western Avenue and had to pull a sharp U-turn. Horns blared.

"Up yours!" she shouted out the window, then at her passengers, "Any fuzz on our tails?" The girls, giggling, shook their heads.

They paid admission at the main gate and drove into a large, sparsely filled parking lot. An attendant signaled them with a flashlight and directed them to a space.

"That'll be fifty cents, please, ma'am," the attendant mumbled, opening the door for Sheila. He was an elderly black, small and wizened. A blue streetcar conductor's cap tilted lopsidedly across his brow, a tiny American flag pinned on its bill. He wore no uniform.

"What?" snorted Sheila. "Fifty cents for what? We already paid at the gate, fella. The sign said, 'Free Parking.' "

"Fo' the service, ma'am," he persisted, holding up his flashlight to remind her.

"I'll bet he doesn't even work here," she said, turning to the other girls. "Come on, let's go."

"Ah's working," he called after her as she walked away.

104

She stopped in her tracks. "I better make sure all the doors are locked."

She returned to circle the car, trying all the handles, including the trunk. While she did this, Crescent stepped forward and gave the old man two quarters.

"Thank you kindly, ma'am." He pulled a whisk broom from his hip pocket, quickly brushed off her dress. "You ladies have fun now, but be mos' careful. There's bogos out there."

"Crescent, why'd you do that? I could have paid him if I'd wanted to," Sheila said as they walked across the lot. "He was just panhandling, for godsakes. I mean, it was so obvious."

"I know, Sheila, I'm sorry. He just looked like he could really use it, that's all."

"Oh, I suppose you're right. I guess I just can't stand the idea of being hustled."

"What was all that about being careful? What's a bogo?" asked Frances.

"Who knows? Who cares?" snapped Sheila.

"I thought there'd be more people," commented Debbie when they entered the brightly lit main grounds. Sheila eyed the thin crowds scattered along the midway and explained that the park had been doing poorly in recent years, that there even was talk of tearing it down.

"I suppose I should warn you," she added, "they've had a lot of trouble with crime out here."

"What kind of crime?"

"You know—robbings, stabbings . . . rapes. I guess the place sort of attracts a lot of weirdos and undesirables."

"Now she tells us," said Frances, laughing. "I'm surprised you didn't take us to the Dunes for some real excitement." Debbie almost kicked her, but Crescent, walking on, already had turned her attention to the glittering rides and arcades. Gradually they were all drawn into the carnival spirit. Frances bought a swirl of cotton candy. Sheila hurled baseballs at a stack of wooden milk bottles on a stool. They bet on racing turtles, mechanical horses, plastic fish. Frances won a compact; Debbie a rattail comb; Sheila a pack of Camels, a pocket knife, a stuffed poodle and a straw hat with a large button that read: *I did it at Riverview.* Crescent came away empty-handed, though she almost won a wristwatch.

"You'd have won it, too," consoled Sheila, "if that lousy bastard hadn't snatched your hoop away. It was just hanging on the winder. You *know* it was going to fall."

Crescent separated herself for a moment from the others to buy a sno-cone. The night air was hot and sticky, and the crushed ice tasted good. When she rejoined her companions, they were in the process of being weighed.

A man dressed like a cowboy in a white Stetson, boots and a big silver belt buckle claimed he could guess each girl's weight correctly to within plus or minus five pounds. So far he'd been right on target.

"Come on, Crescent, your turn."

Crescent handed the man a quarter, and he carefully looked her over. He had a friendly face with fast, playful eyes, sported a small, brindled goatee that was stained brown along the corners of his mouth. The belt he wore hung so that the big silver buckle was almost buried under the fold of his hanging potbelly.

"Lift your arms and turn around, honey-child," he drawled, then spat a wad of tobacco accurately off to one side in the dirt. "See, I've saved me the best for last. What are we doin' later on tonight, sweet darlin'?"

The other girls giggled.

"All righty, let's see if Texas Bub Baker can make it four in a row. How does a hunnert-un-seventeen sound?"

She shrugged, had no idea what she weighed.

"Yessir, they say you can't never figure out a woman, but they don't fool ol' Texas Bub Baker none. Been married six times. Never paid a dime in alimony. Ain't bragging, but I just about know you ladies better'n you know yourselves."

Crescent climbed into the swing seat that hung suspended beneath the scales. The needle bounced once, twice and came to rest. Texas Bub stared.

"I don't believe it!" he sputtered. He made her get out of the swing and reseat herself. The needle bounced once, twice and read the same. One hundred and seventy-five pounds.

"Well, I'll be a dog-eared coon!" he finally exclaimed. "Gol-durned scale must be broke! 'Scuse my language, miss, but there ain't no way in hell's half acre you can weigh that much." He fiddled with the scales, then told her she could climb down.

"You got your choice of anything hanging on the wall there," he said, pointing to a dozen stuffed animals. "You're only the second one I missed this year. The other—that was last week—he was one of them smart-ass college jokers. Had on a money belt filled with birdshot—say, you ain't wearing one of them, are you?" He looked at Crescent's figure again, dismissed the idea with a shake of his head.

"Fifty-eight pounds—Texas Bub Baker ain't never missed by fifty-eight pounds before! You just don't look it no way—not in the wrists or the ankles. The neck either. Them are the giveaways. Scale's just got to be plumb loco."

Crescent grinned. She pointed with her empty sno-cone at the display in his booth. "I'd like the one on the end."

"You want the snake?" he asked, amazed again.

Crescent nodded that she did.

"You don't want the snake. How's about one of them cute teddy bears there? That pink one'd go real purty with your dress." He looked quickly around, nodding at the other girls. They agreed.

"No, I like the snake."

"You're sure."

"I'm sure."

He spit another wad over his shoulder, ran a finger across his beard and went to fetch a stepladder.

When he climbed down with her prize and handed it to her, he confessed she'd chosen the most expensive stuffed animal he had.

"Them bears and poodles I can pick up for peanuts. This snake here, he cost me some bucks. I just bought him for display . . . never figured anybody'd pick him."

Crescent offered to exchange him, but he shook his head.

"Nope, wouldn't hear of it. You won him fair and square—the only way Texas Bub plays the game."

"He *is* sort of cute," said Debbie as they once again were strolling down the midway. She gave the snake a pat on its curled green tail. It had big, black tiddleywink eyes, short, tufted ears and a black, buttoned snout. Its pink mouth hung partly open exposing white flannel teeth and a red, forked tongue. "And look at that smile. You don't know whether he wants to snuggle up or take a bite out of you."

"Ugh," said Sheila. "I'll take my poodle any day. Hey—what'd you do to that poor guy's scale, anyway?"

"Ya," chimed in Frances. "If you weigh a hundred and seventy-five then I'm Kate Smith's double!"

Crescent shrugged.

"Must have been me," said the snake; she held up its head, spoke in a low, throaty voice. "I crawled down when nobody was looking and sat on her lap."

The other three girls laughed.

"Pretty sneaky," said Sheila. "Not that I blame you, though. I can think of a lot of places I'd rather be than hanging in Texas Bub's booth." She relented, reached out and gave the snake a pat.

They walked by the freak-show tent.

"Bet he could perform his own gastrotomy," quipped one of the girls, staring up at a giant poster of a Gypsy sword swallower gargling a saber.

"Right out of an ab-phiz textbook," commented another on the alligator man.

"Can you imagine trying to lift her onto a bedpan?" They were standing before a portrait of the fat lady, Lona Evers. She was billed as the world's largest woman, weighing in at a "petite" 817 pounds. Her great glandular bulk was offset and humanized by a sad, weary smile.

"You ought to let her in on your reducing secrets, Crescent," said Sheila as they walked away. "You'd probably have her on the cover of *Vogue* within a year."

"Why not let us all in on your secrets," said Frances. "So we all could make the cover of *Vogue.*"

The girls finally went on a number of rides. After a spin on the Bobs, Frances said she was starting to feel woozy.

"Okay, okay," ceded Sheila, "we'll ride the Bumper Cars. They're nice and slow. They don't spin or go upside down or anything. Real tame."

Frances and Debbie rode in one car—neither of them would ride with Sheila; Crescent and Sheila rode in another. The moment the power was turned on, Sheila took command, grabbing the steering wheel and maneuvering fearlessly around the track, bashing into all cars that got in her way. Frances and Debbie meanwhile skirted the main flow of traffic, avoiding as many collisions as possible.

Halfway through the ride, a purple car driven by a lone man began hounding Sheila and Crescent's car, smashing into it at every opportunity. Sheila weaved elaborately through traffic to avoid the man, but whenever she stopped to look about he was there, relentlessly preparing to run them down.

Just before the ride ended, the purple car cornered them between another car and the barrier wall. It was able to get up a long run, and it slammed into them with surprising force. Crescent was thrown across the seat into the steering wheel; Sheila halfway out of the car. By the time she was seated again, sputtering and cursing, raring to go, the power went dead and the ride was over.

The man jumped out of the purple car. Neither smiling nor looking at the girls, he walked briskly across the oval drive to the opposite exit and disappeared into the crowd.

"That son-of-a-bitch!" Sheila shouted after him. "I wish he'd stayed for another ride. I'd knock his keester through the roof! Come on, let's get out of here."

"Haven't we had enough fun for one evening?" said Frances wearily. Seated on a fire engine, they were getting their picture taken rushing toward the great Chicago conflagration of 1871, and Sheila had just suggested they move on to the fun house.

"Enough fun? Hell, no, we haven't had enough fun!" Sheila glanced at her watch. "It's not even nine-thirty yet."

Frances groaned. Debbie started to speak, but Sheila interrupted: "Besides, we have to kill some time while the pictures are being developed."

The fun house was called the Sultan's Castle; its onetime exotic façade, however, looked more like the target for a slum-clearance project than a palace out of the *Arabian Nights.* Its paint was faded and peeling; panels were torn loose and filled with holes; windows were broken.

They entered through the main portal, the enormous gaping mouth of the sultan himself. Hysterical laughter burbled continuously from a speaker in his nose. Inside was a crooked corridor of mirrors, swinging doors, culs-de-sac, haunting screams and flashing monsters.

They became separated negotiating a dark maze. Crescent was the first to find her way out into the castle's large central chamber. She was soon followed by Frances. After a lapse of several minutes, Sheila and Debbie emerged. Both were visibly shaken.

Red-faced, struggling for words, they told Crescent and Frances how they'd been molested in the section of dark tunnels. Debbie had had her arm twisted behind her and her breasts roughly grabbed. Her clothes were mussed; the right-shoulder sleeve to her blouse was torn. Sheila had been choked and felt up. Her clothes also were mussed. There were red marks on her neck and thighs.

"Huh?" said a guard stationed at an exit turnstile when they told him what had happened. He sat in a chair with his feet propped up on the turnstile rail, a small transistor radio glued to his ear.

"Aren't you going to do anything?" steamed Sheila.

The guard suddenly held up his free hand to silence her. A roar sounding like static came from his radio followed by excited chatter. He was listening to a ball game. Ernie Banks had just hit for extra bases. One run was scoring, two runs . . .

"I don't believe this!" Sheila stamped her foot.

The guard, satisfied with the progress of the game, returned his attention to the girls. He was young, probably still in his twenties.

"Look, be realistic: You don't know who did it. It could be anyone in here"—he waved his hand to include all the people, men, women and children wandering about the main room—"anyone. You don't even know if he come through the tunnel. There's an exit in there, ya know. I'm sure your friend's long gone by now."

"He's not my fucking friend!" screamed Sheila.

"Come on, Sheila," said Debbie, putting her arm around her. "You're just wasting your time with him."

"Look, don't take it so hard. Happens every day." The guard swung his legs down from the railing; the billy club belted to his waist banged on the floor. "Be glad he didn't kill you—or worse!" He raised his eyebrows and gave a knowing smile.

"Oh, shit!" said Sheila.

"If you want I'll go search the tunnel."

"Don't bother."

"No bother," he said, getting to his feet.

The girls watched him saunter off, one hand resting on the butt of his billy club, the other holding the radio tightly to his ear.

While he was gone, a number of other people emerged from the tunnel. The girls stood off to one side and closely scrutinized them. There were several couples, a group of children with their parents, three or four teenagers. One of the teenagers, his patched jeans stuffed in cycle boots, a soiled Schlitz T-shirt with a chain wrapped around his waist, certainly looked the part. But if he was the mugger he skillfully concealed it, gazing coolly about the room and walking past Sheila and Debbie without a second glance.

The guard returned in a few minutes, radio still pressed to his ear. Everything was okay now, he told them; their assailant obviously had fled; there was nothing more to worry about. They could fill out a complaint if they wanted, but he added that it would accomplish absolutely nothing.

"What do we do now?" asked Debbie after the guard had left.

Frances wanted to forget about the photographs and go to the car. Debbie agreed, though she thought they should wait for the pictures— after all, they'd already paid for them. Then she added that she wished David had come along, that they'd brought dates instead of making it a night out on their own.

The remark made Sheila furious.

"Why do we have to have guys with us every time we want to go somewhere? What are we, prisoners?"

The other girls were silent.

"Well, I for one am not going to let some pervo-creepo spoil my evening. I'm not leaving here till I'm good and ready. If you all want to go now, I'll give you the keys to the car and I'll take the bus." She turned and marched off toward the trampoline pit.

Crescent, Debbie and Frances shrugged and walked after her.

Frances finally threw up in the revolving barrels. Crescent led her to a rest room. Debbie and Sheila already had passed through the barrels and were navigating the rocking escalators. When Crescent and Frances returned, they were gone. Frances, still ashen-white, had to sit down and rest. Crescent walked her to a bench by the escalators, then went off to find the others.

She searched the topsy-turvy rooms without success, came to a narrow corridor with a sign on its wall that read: *This way to the Huge Fuge.* She followed the sign, came to another room, smaller, just large enough, in fact, to contain a strange-looking silver dome. Igloo-shaped, the dome had a door in its side: Several people were entering through it. Crescent followed them inside.

She looked quickly around the brightly lit interior for her missing companions. They were not there. She was about to leave when an attendant standing in the middle of the dome directed her to keep moving, to take a place against the surrounding circular wall, which was almost completely ringed with people. She did as she was told.

Almost immediately the attendant stepped outside the chamber and slammed the door behind him, securing it with a chain. The lights dimmed.

The wall was heavily padded, as was the floor. Crescent leaned back and glanced at the people standing next to her: a mother with two giggling children on her right, a young high school couple on her left. She exchanged smiles with the couple.

The room started turning. Slowly at first, then gradually building speed. She spread her arms against the wall to keep her balance, scanned the remaining circle of laughing, excited faces. Her gaze drifted lazily—then abruptly froze. Standing directly across from her and staring icily back was the man from the bumper cars.

The chamber continued spinning faster and faster. She felt herself being pushed—pressed deeper and deeper into the padding of the wall. Suddenly the bottom dropped out. There were shrieks and gasps as the entire floor sank from view. She, with everyone else, was left suspended in midair over darkness, squashed against the spinning wall by centrifugal force.

She tried to move, but it was all she could do to turn her head. Her neck seemed weak as a baby's; her arms and legs made of lead. She was Lona Evers, the fat lady, imprisoned, mashed to the wall by her own immense weight.

She closed her eyes. In her mind another centrifuge whirled, hurling deep, dark thoughts against the hard outer walls of her consciousness. She saw herself . . . saw the man from the bumper cars: He was tall, lean; his hair, brown and scraggly; his face, tightly drawn with narrow, shallow eyes —cruel eyes—and little more than a fleshless slit for a mouth. He wore a bright green fishnet shirt, and his thin white body showed through it like a cold, embittered threat.

And they were spinning round and round each other—she and he— diametrically opposed, chasing each other, never gaining, never losing ground, remaining always apart, until suddenly at the very limit of that reeling vortex, they merged, became one. . . .

Crescent opened her eyes. The dome was slowing down. The mother of the children next to her had begun to sag. A large, dumpy woman, she slid down the wall inch by inch until she was several feet below everyone else. Convinced she was doomed, that something had gone horribly wrong with the apparatus, she filled the chamber with frightened squeals. Her children giggled above her.

The dome continued to decelerate. Soon everyone was sliding down. As Crescent descended, her skirt clung to the wall, dragging behind her. The lower she sank, the higher it worked its way up. She tried to wriggle free and pull it down, but it was pinned by her own weight and wouldn't budge. The heavyset woman on her right, the only other person wearing a dress, had encountered the same problem, but her bulging hips and thighs had kept her hem from rising above her support hose.

Crescent was not so fortunate. Her skirt already was hauled above her waist, her pink nylon-tricot panties already in full view. Worse yet, as she continued down, her panties themselves clung to the wall, drawn so tightly against the contours of her body that she might as well have not been wearing them.

The lights inside brightened. People were grinning, laughing at her. She looked across the chamber. The man in the green fishnet shirt had slid several feet below her, was staring up.

In the instant she met his eyes—the cold, brutal assessment in their gaze —she knew: It was he who'd attacked the girls in the tunnel.

111

When the dome finally came to a jerky halt, everyone was down, standing on the floor again. A lower-level door opened and the attendant reentered and motioned the way out. Crescent bunched up with everyone else waiting to exit. She kept her eyes lowered. While she followed the woman with the two children through the doorway, a foot stamped down from behind on her heel and almost wedged her out of her shoe. She stumbled forward but did not turn around—she knew whose foot it was. She continued walking swiftly away.

Sheila and Debbie had joined Frances, who still was waiting on the bench by the escalators.

"The wanderer returns," greeted Sheila. "Just where the hell have you been?"

When Crescent told her, she wanted to go immediately for a ride on the Huge Fuge herself.

"Oh, no you don't!" protested Frances. "We're leaving right now. I'm not sitting here another minute!"

Sheila argued, but this time Frances would not be bullied, and both Crescent and Debbie sided with her.

On the way out, the guard at the turnstile lowered his radio. "Good night, girls," he offered with a smile bordering on a smirk.

Sheila smiled back at him, then gave him the finger, twice, with both hands.

Their prints were ready at the photographer's booth. They picked them up, had a big laugh over their hammy poses as they headed for the car.

The way out led by the Parachute Jumps. Sheila had forgotten all about them.

"But we have to!" she implored. "It's . . . it's the big ride—the most famous ride in the park!"

"Count me out," snorted Frances, staring up at the huge steel tower.

"Me too," seconded Debbie with a whistle. "I'm afraid of heights."

Crescent craned her neck. She watched a chute in its collapsed state slowly rising under one of the two great arms that cantilevered from the tower several hundred feet above. When it finally reached the arm, it plummeted earthward—its two occupants, dangling from a swing beneath, rent the night with their screams. She watched the chute blossom open.

"You've got to be crazy," said Frances, gazing at the same chute. It glided down four guy wires and slammed into a set of braking springs; its two riders were brought to a wild, bouncing halt a dozen feet above the ground.

"What a bunch of chickens."

"Look, if you want to go, nobody's stopping you."

"It's no fun alone."

"I'll go with you."

Sheila looked at Crescent, then grinned and clapped her hands.

"You're both nuts," said Frances. "How 'bout the keys to the car so we don't have to stick around and pick up the pieces."

Sheila and Crescent purchased their tickets and proceeded through a gateway to a large, circular boarding area.

Before the worker rolled away the boarding stairway and signaled for the lift, he removed Sheila's loafers. "Might as well lose 'em here as up there," he told her. Moments later the seat gave a jerk, and they held on tightly as the ascent began.

The ground fell away rapidly. Above them the collapsed canopy fluttered like a sail in the breeze. It seemed to Crescent they were rising much faster than it had appeared from the ground. Though she'd experienced nervousness while waiting below, now, oddly, she felt herself entering a great calm. Sheila, on the other hand, seemed to be growing more tense. She was fidgeting about in the seat, chattering incessantly.

". . . hang on, it won't be long now, ooh! God, the suspense is killing me!"

They *were* getting up there, high above the park—the crowds, the tents and buildings, the other glittering rides. Crescent looked eastward, could see over a multitude of rooftops to the towering skyscrapers of the Loop. She felt she could reach out, graze them with her fingertips. It was as though she had transcended the park, as though she were no longer part of it but now belonged to the city.

Suddenly there was a loud, metallic click overhead. The seat shuddered beneath them. In the next instant they were plunging earthward.

Sheila screamed. Crescent fell silently within herself, felt time expand, stretching out like a length of surgical tubing: microseconds lapsing into minutes . . . hours . . . years. . . .

How long had she been falling? . . . Down through the centuries, millennia . . . suspended between the ages . . . waiting to be reborn. . . .

"Who are you?" It was Libby's voice echoing, reechoing for one last time above the warped vibrato of Sheila's scream. Her mind reeled under the weight of histories long since spent. Strange odors, exotic fragrances cloyed her nostrils. Her eyes watered in the bitter mists, the loneliness of dank, low places. Her lips burned with the salt of distant seas.

"Who am I?"

She felt the touch of gold shimmering against her belly, writhed in the embrace of a thousand strangers.

And in that instant—that aeon—high above the park, above the city, still fixed in free fall, she understood . . . hunted him down with fierce eyes, plucked his image from the crowd below—the man in the green fishnet shirt—his face, frozen, predatory, gazing upward. Though he stood far away, she saw the beads of sweat glistening in the squint lines of his eyes, the stubble of beard shading his drawn, pitted cheeks. She could feel his lips, cracked and fleshless, pressed against her own. She could smell his breath, the fetid rancor of his soul. . . .

The chute opened. The surgical tubing snapped back as the rush of time reasserted itself. She was yanked upright, the billowing canopy above checking her fall. Sheila no longer was screaming. The metal grommets of the chute whirred down the guy wires. Crescent watched the ground surge up to meet them.

The chute hit the braking springs thirty feet above the landing area. Crescent and Sheila were brought to a bouncing halt, danced and twisted in their seat like a Yo-Yo.

"Wow! Terrific!" exclaimed Sheila as the attendant unstrapped them, helped them down to the ground. "Wasn't that the most terrific ride you've ever been on!?"

Sheila slipped into her shoes again; then she and Crescent quickly walked back out onto the midway and headed for the north exit, where they'd entered.

"How about the free fall—I almost peed my pants! Didn't that really grab you—you know—just before the chute opened?"

Crescent smiled, nodded. She was barely listening.

"I mean, it really got me. I couldn't stop screaming."

Halfway across the parking lot, Crescent began to tremble. She didn't have to turn around; she knew he was there, following them, the green fishnet shirt darting and ducking through the rows of parked cars behind them.

When they turned down the last row that led to their car, Crescent fell a few steps behind. She let her purse slip from her shoulder, drop softly to the ground. Then she quickly caught up again. At the car she announced she'd lost it.

"I thought I saw you carrying it," said Sheila, who'd already climbed behind the wheel and begun babbling to Debbie and Frances. "I know you had it when you got off the jumps."

"I must have set it down by the gate while you were putting your shoes on. Anyway, I'd better run back and find it. Wait here—I'll be back in a jiffy."

Both Sheila and Debbie offered to go with her, but she waved them to sit still and trotted off before they could climb out. She was relieved to hear Sheila resume her babbling, recounting the ride, taunting the other girls for missing the "thrill of a lifetime."

Crescent picked up her purse where she'd dropped it, continued on her way. She cut back through the rows of parked cars until she'd reached the darkest, most remote corner of the lot. There she entered a small grove of catalpa trees that grew beneath the trestle of a roller coaster. She stood by the trestle in the darkest shadow of the trees. Fumes of oil and grease from the track mingled with the sour smell of the catalpa leaves, filling the air with a heavy, rancid odor.

Suddenly the trestle began to shake. Moments later the Blue Streak roared by overhead. Its gleaming coach showered down sparks on Crescent, hurtled into a sharp curve and disappeared as abruptly as it had come. The trestle continued to shake for several more seconds.

In the imperfect silence that followed, Crescent could hear the muffled clamor of the midway in the distance, the sound of traffic on Western Avenue. Presently she heard different sounds. Closer sounds. She stood there gently stroking the head of her stuffed snake. She did not have long to wait.

—PART THREE—

7

Sunday afternoon. Valjohn sat in his small cubicle office—assigned to him when he was given the case—and stared at the city map hanging on the wall in front of his desk. The surface of the map was decorated with nineteen neat little red pins—three of which he'd just stuck up there an hour ago. The Reaper's victims, the murder sites . . .

The first body—the control MO—had turned up at Riverview Amusement Park in a clump of weeds under the trestle of a ride: Richard Spate, an acquitted rape defendant who was being sought at the time for questioning in connection with the slaying of a Berwyn waitress. When they'd first found Spate's body, it was thought he'd been run over and mangled by a roller coaster, thrown from the tracks. That was back in the late summer of '65. They had a lot to learn. Now the red pins were spread so widely they made it look as though the city had a bad case of prickly heat or a touch of St. Anthony's fire. There were six stuck in the North Side, five in the South, five more in the West, three downtown in the Loop itself. He studied them all carefully, separately and together . . . grouping and regrouping . . . and regrouping. . . .

The Reaper had received his name from the press. He was, of course, grim. More importantly, however, the last four digits in the referral code of the case, C-65-1834 (denoting the 1,834th murder committed in the city during 1965), happened to form the year Cyrus McCormick invented his famous corn reaping machine (later to be manufactured in Chicago). Chick Screed of the *Trib* had been the first to make the association—no doubt in tribute to the heralded lineage of his former employer, benefactor and editor-in-chief, the late, renowned Colonel "Dewey Wins" Bob himself. In any event, the name caught on, and the Reaper soon was thrilling a city full of readers with his brutal, baffling harvest.

And the harvest continued, thought Valjohn, shaking his head deject-edly. The three new pins on the map failed to provide any intelligible sense of order to the overall scattered pattern. It appeared as always, random and unpredictable, leaving him no starting point, nothing solid to pursue.

He returned to busily organizing the notes on his desk for his prelimi-nary report of yesterday's triple homicide. Twenty minutes later the phone rang. Annoyed at the interruption, he picked it up and punched the flash-ing intercom button.

He'd hoped to deposit the final draft of his report on Captain Howland's desk before he went home that evening.

It was Moe.

A few minutes later Valjohn was making hasty steps down the north wing corridor to the lab.

On his way he mulled over Moe's message with guarded optimism: "The ancient one" had just informed him of finding some interesting new trace evidence. Maybe the old law of transference finally was going to deliver. Whenever two objects came in contact with one another, there was a transfer of material, however slight; generally it was from the softer object to the harder one, though sometimes the displacement was mutual. The more forceful the contact, the greater the degree of transference. This law served as the very cornerstone of the crime lab.

So far in the case there was phenomenally little trace evidence, especially when one considered the violent nature of the murders. The little there was, however, did seem to substantiate the single, common-killer theory —by no means a foregone conclusion, despite the Reaper's considerable following.

Three separate blood types, for instance, had been found at the murder site in Pullman Hill Cemetery. Two belonged to Dix and Varner. The third and most intriguing sample—found in extremely minuscule amounts, a few dried flecks, in Dix's pubic region—matched that of Jimmy Lee Cook. If the same individual had committed all three murders, then it was reason-able to assume that he might have the blood of all three victims on his person. It also was possible that some of the blood from one victim on the murderer might be transferred or rubbed off onto another victim. Valjohn felt it was reasonable, possible and, in this instance, very highly probable.

Unlike fingerprints, blood types were not unique, and comparisons of samples could ultimately only prove things in the negative. All Chihuahuas were dogs, but not all dogs were Chihuahuas. Moe's forensic serologist,

120

however, had matched the sample in question not only with Cook's ABO grouping but with his red-cell isoenzyme types as well. The number of people sharing the resultant matching combination was estimated at something like twenty-one in ten thousand. Maybe that left a shadow of doubt in a courtroom, but as far as Valjohn was concerned, those weren't bad numbers to substantiate a working theory.

Foreign hairs were discovered in the pubic regions of both Cook and Dix. Curly and short, only a few centimeters long, with very light pigmentation, these hairs also proved to be pubic. Analysis of their medulla, cortex and cuticle composition further proved them to be similar to extrinsic samples found in the pubic regions of other 1834 victims. Again the single, common-killer theory was corroborated, though hair, like blood, could be used only to eliminate, not to identify, people.

The elements of time and distance in yesterday's slayings initially tended to contradict the single, common-killer theory, but a few quick calculations demonstrated otherwise. The alley off Cottage Grove and the Pullman Hill Cemetery were 15.7 miles apart. The affixed probable times of death allowed a leeway of three hours between the first and last murders. Plenty of time for the killer to be in both places, even in heavy rush-hour traffic —absent that time of night. The fact that the killer never had struck more than once on a given day or night in the past certainly didn't preclude the possibility.

Evidence found of a much more perplexing nature was that of semen residue. There were gobs of it on all the victims, past and present—with the lone exception of Varner, who hadn't been sexually assaulted, and appeared to have been dispatched merely for being in the way. It clung to their private parts, their legs, their stomachs. The ultraviolet light had detected its white luminescence on articles of clothing, and the telltale brown rhombic crystals of the Florence test even verified its presence spattering the surrounding areas: pavement, floors, walls—in yesterday's mayhem, the Chevy's rear-seat upholstery. The quantity suggested more than one source. Even more than two. A gang bang. A train ride. This inference—kinky though not farfetched—did not hold up under closer scrutiny in the lab, however. As nearly as could be determined through chemical analysis—that is, identifying certain genetic markers in the seminal plasma—the semen present at each murder was the discharge solely of the victim.

Though the amount seemed incredible, it was found that in every victim examined, the spermatozoa reservoirs—the vas deferens, the tubules and retia of the testes—were totally depleted. It was as though the body's ejaculatory mechanism had jammed in the "on" position, as though each man could not stop coming until the entire contents of his gonads were spent. Until there was literally nothing left.

Bert Carlson met him at the door in a white technician's smock and saved him the effort of fumbling with its digital security lock.

"How'd you end up yesterday?"

"Terrible," laughed Carlson. "Had to par the last hole to break a hundred. That course oughta be plowed under and planted with corn."

"How about Glad and his storm trooper?"

"Glad had an 83 or 84. Satucci sort of fell apart after you left. He started spraying his tee shots. Parred the front side but he took a fat 45 on the back.

"Wish I'd stayed," said Valjohn, chuckling.

Moe, also in a white smock, sat on a stool by a large table cluttered with apparatus in the middle of the room. Without looking up from the notebook he was reading, he pointed to a couple of microscopes set up at the other end of the table. Valjohn walked over to them. He chose the one on the left to look through first. There he saw magnified several hundred times a faint sepia substance, cloudy, broken with occasional clusters of tiny, bubblelike spheres. The cross section of a cheese soufflé, he thought. He peered through the other microscope. More cheese soufflé.

"Very pretty. Now, just what the hell am I looking at?"

"A very common glandular secretion. Chemically it belongs to a viscous group called glycoproteins. Essentially it's mucoid. The specimen on your left was taken from the hair at the base of Dix's scrotum. The other came from Cook's ventral pubic region."

Valjohn studied Moe in silence.

"I have to admit, I almost skipped over it myself," continued Moe. "Happened to catch some of it under the glass during a routine sperm check on Luchione last week."

Up until yesterday's bloodbath, Rico "Hunch-Hunch" Luchione had been the most recent addition to the hapless fraternity of 1834 victims. His typically mutilated body had been found on the first day of spring behind the bleachers of a West Side bocce ball court. He still was wearing the tool of his trade, a .22 automatic with a silencer snugly holstered under his left arm.

"It was mixed in with all that blood and semen and matted hair. I rechecked the medical examiner's report: He simply explained it away as tissue fluid, suppurations from some of the vicinal wounds."

"Explained it away?"

"Right. I guess nobody was really considering it. Nobody had their eyes open. A gross oversight. Anyway, I was still fighting that summer cold," he cleared his throat, "and I just sort of let my suspicions slide—that is, until yesterday, when my nose pointed the way. The first time my smeller's worked in over two weeks, I might add." He ran a finger down his prominent, convex bridge and gave it a tap.

"Wait a minute. Explained what away? I'm still not sure what the hell you're talking about. A glandular secretion? What gland?"

Moe glanced at Carlson, who had a silly smirk on his face.

"The Bartholin's gland," he said, scratching his grizzled beard.

Valjohn drew a blank, screwed his face.

"The Bartholin's gland," repeated Moe, "located in the labia minora."
That rang a bell.

"The labia minora? . . . a vagina?"

"Only one I know."

"You mean—"

"Correct. What we have on those slides is none other than the discharge of a woman having, or at least anticipating, sexual intercourse. To put it more crudely, if I may slip into the colorful vernacular of our patrolmen: cunt cream . . . joy jelly—"

"V-jam . . . crack wax . . . miracle whip," Carlson expanded.

"What's in a name? Take your pick."

Valjohn was back fumbling at a microscope. He felt as though he should be putting a quarter into it, as though he were hunched over an X-rated viewer in one of the smut parlors on South Wabash Avenue. But there was no sultry stripper wriggling out of her clothes on the slide. Only the same clouded sepia smear, the same cut of cheese soufflé.

"As I said, the gland is neuroactivated during sexual stimulation. The secretion acts as a lubricant to the vaginal introitus, the meaty protective folds of the labias. A similar substance is transuded through the vaginal wall itself and forms there during the sex act. Like sweat on your forehead."

Valjohn looked up again from the microscope. He could well understand the oversight. Everyone in the lab, the coroner's office, his predecessor, the other detectives—himself included—all were guilty of the same blind spot, the same preconception, namely: In the investigation of sex crimes, semen was the Holy Grail. One always was searching for it—whether the victims were male or female—and once detected, the search was considered over. Of course, there were other things like blood and hair to consider. Even traces of saliva. But semen was the real find; semen ruled supreme.

Now it seemed to have a rival.

"Normally the secretion carries a sweet, musky odor; a natural, erotic scent."

Valjohn smiled in a moment of reminiscence.

"In today's cover-up world of deodorants, a vestigial service, I suppose," Moe offered with a note of wistful cynicism. He stood up and hobbled stiffly over to another pair of microscopes set up on a nearby bench, peered into one and adjusted its focus. He lapsed into another coughing siege, waved Valjohn over and stepped aside.

"Anyway, what I'm telling you is, whoever left us these specimens . . . ahem . . . she has something of what's known as a little problem."

"A problem?"

"As in the initials VD. Take a look."

"Spirochetes?" asked Valjohn when he raised his head. He was referring to a motionless swarm of spermlike organisms under the glass.

"Nothing that serious. They're trichomonads. 'Tricks' for short. A very

123

common form of vaginitis. Unlike syphilis and gonorrhea, tricks is more of a nuisance than a disease. It causes a lot of itching and burning, but it doesn't spread beyond the vagina or do any real damage. It does, however, produce a very foul-smelling, yellow discharge. Back when I was young and a real *shaygets* with the ladies, I had a girl friend from Winnetka. Her name I forget, but she was a beaut. Very *zaftig*. She also had tricks. Had it so bad if you put your head under the sheets you'd have thought somebody'd unplugged the refrigerator. In August, no less."

"Gefilte fish?"

Moe grinned. "I would have told you yesterday, but I wanted to make sure first. I was up all last night researching the subject. Pretty spicy stuff, actually. Some of those old med books read like best sellers."

"Glad to see you're enjoying yourself. How do men figure in this?"

"They can carry it in their prostate. Fortunately or unfortunately— depending on whether you're a man or a woman, I guess—the symptoms are so slight it's rarely detected or treated. The result is a man continues passing it on to his sex partners—one of the main reasons it's so wide-spread. I'm surprised you've never run across it, Valjohnny. Either you're not playing enough of the field, or you're going out with all the right kind of girls."

Valjohn reflected on Mona for a moment. "All the right kind of girls," he barely murmured. "What's in the other scope?"

"More vaginitis. Monilial, or more commonly known as a yeast infection. It's also fairly benign—itches a lot, produces a thick, white discharge, but not much odor."

"Hold on a second. Now, all this gunk—it was found on yesterday's bodies? Dix and Cook's?"

Moe nodded. "But there's no evidence of similar morbid discharge on any of the earlier victims—at least not in the reports, as you well know. Luchione's the only one we've been able to reexamine. He's still in the cooler; nobody's claimed him. A hit man's remains—they're not exactly a big mover in the grief department. As I indicated earlier, we found traces of Bartholin's secretion on him but no sign of vaginitis."

Valjohn mused for a moment in silence. If the female source of this new evidence was a common denominator in all the murders, maybe she'd only recently contracted the vaginitis. That would help explain why her presence hadn't been detected before now. No gefilte fish. And the Reaper? He'd obviously become a carrier. He'd obviously become . . . Valjohn's thoughts came to a skidding halt. *He?* Was it that hard to imagine? *He'd obviously become—*

"Jacqueline," Moe pronounced slowly, then broke into a grin. "Jacqueline the Reaper—not bad, eh?"

Valjohn stared at him. *A woman.* Carlson hooted.

"Jacqueline the Reaper?" Valjohn finally repeated, grimacing.

"So you can do better?" challenged Moe, clearly pleased with himself.

Valjohn shook his head. "I'm not even going to try. I'm still having trouble digesting all this."

"How about Madame Defarge at large?"

Both Valjohn and Moe stared at Carlson.

"Sorry," he said.

"See what you started?"

Moe hung his head.

"I will say this," Valjohn offered after several moments of silence, "there must be one very strange lady walking around out there—whatever you call her."

"A *wilder meshuggeneh,*" nodded Moe, lapsing into Yiddish. "A real *malech hamovesteh.*"

"*Meshuggeneh* I can handle. What's the rest?"

Moe pulled at his beard, looked beyond Valjohn to the pile of notes on his table. "A *malech hamovesteh,*" he repeated, "a real angel of death."

Valjohn nodded. "At least."

"There is one baffling detail," Moe announced, hobbling back to his stool.

"One baffling detail," Valjohn spoke slowly. His mind was reeling with what seemed like countless thousands.

"Yes. The amount of Bartholin's secretion we've found on the victims —it doesn't jibe. You see, normally a nulliparous woman—that's one who hasn't had children—she'll only secrete a drop or two of the solution during intercourse. A multiparous woman may secrete a drop or two more. But the amounts we've found, they're a hell of a lot more than a few drops. It's more like a deluge. Certainly several centiliters."

Valjohn, who'd just removed his glasses to wipe them clean, shoved them on again dirty. He took several steps toward the door, then spun around.

"Now, let me get this straight: First you're telling me that our killer may be a woman, and now you're trying to suggest that 'she' may be 'they'? That the victims are not simply being raped, murdered and mutilated— that they're being gang-banged as well by . . . by what? A sewing circle gone berserk? A sorority of Amazon degenerates?"

Moe sucked in his cheeks. His bony fingers pulled at his beard again. He shrugged.

"You can draw your own conclusions, Valjohnny. All I know is what I see in the slide show."

Valjohn started to say something, let it pass.

"One thing I am going to do, though," Moe continued. "Since this is a special assignment for me, I'm only going to write up one report. No copy. For your eyes and your eyes only."

"I take it you foresee complications?"

Moe smiled noncommittally. "Let's just say I've been working around here a few years. Anyway, I don't know how you're going to handle this, but if I were you, I'd move cautiously. Take it to your friend upstairs. I'm sure he'll have a few words to offer on the matter."

Valjohn reflected on what Moe was telling him. He didn't like the sound of it, but it might not hurt to play it safe. At least for a day or so, till he'd had some time to really mull things over. "How many people know about this?"

"You, Bert, me, a serologist over in the coroner's office named Mark Dietz. I've already told him to discuss it with no one—either in or outside his office."

Valjohn nodded.

"Moe, I think you missed your calling," he observed, patting the old ex-lab chief on the back as they walked to the door.

"What's that?"

"You would have made a great gynecologist."

Superintendent Estes Merriwether Gordon, the great reformer, the visionary, sat behind his desk, Moe's lab report spread out before him. It was Monday and Valjohn had just delivered it. He sat attentive, watching Gordon read. The emblem of the Chicago Police Department, with its motto, "We Serve and Protect," hung on the wall behind the superintendent between two gilt-framed portraits: one of the president, the other of the mayor.

While Gordon read he attempted to fill his pipe, a white pressed meerschaum, from a leather-cased humidor which sat beside a picture of his six grandchildren. He would absently dip a crooked index finger into the humidor, start to lift out a pinch of tobacco and then, coming across some new detail in the report, would shake his head and straighten his finger, dumping the tobacco, a particularly aromatic blend—apricot brandy? Bourbon musket?—back into the container. He repeated this several times. When he'd finished the report, the bowl of his pipe still was half empty.

He shuffled the pages back in order, lifted them a few inches off the desk and held them there delicately balanced on the tips of his fingers. Finally he let them drop to the desk.

"Fascinating," he whispered to himself. Then without another word he stood up and began walking back and forth across the room.

Valjohn waited calmly. Gordon's pacing was nothing new to him. He'd had ample occasion to witness it years ago when he was a student at the University of California and the superintendent was then dean of the Criminology Department. Later Valjohn had become his TA, even helping him research his last book, *Police Department Communication Systems: A Treatise on Computerized Dispatching.* In those days Gordon would measure the pace of his lectures by his stride on the hardwood floor of his classrooms. Now the hardwood had been replaced by a plush executive carpet, and although relatively new, it already was showing signs of wear along some of the more well-traveled routes. Valjohn wondered what the superintendent would have done if his office were something less than the spacious domain it was,

126

something, say, on the order of his own closet cubicle. Run in place? Isometrics? But then, he supposed, a man like Gordon always ended up in a big office. He was a problem solver; problem solvers rose to the top, and people at the top had big offices. A simple matter of natural selection.

What was not so natural was Gordon's image as the "chief" of the CCPD. No potbelly, no hulking shoulders or bull neck, never blustering or red-faced, loudmouthed or crude; he completely defied the popular stereotype. Indeed, he was even ascetic in appearance, so tall and lean he looked undernourished. His eyes were gray, deep-set and sad. When he spoke it was with slow, almost painful deliberation. His dress was tweedish, academic, complete with leather elbow patches. And, of course, there was the pipe.

At one point in his pacing, Gordon stopped by a large bookcase where another pipe was resting on a shelf in front of an imposing collection of black, clothbound copies of the annual revised criminal statutes from the Illinois General Assembly (dating back to 1897). There also was another humidor. He picked up the pipe, this one a bulldog briar, filled it, carefully tamping down the tobacco with his little finger. From his coat pocket he took out a lighter, directed its small, horizontal flame into the bowl and drew through the stem—"thwuk, thwuk, thwuk"—until the entire surface of the tobacco was burning evenly. Then he set the pipe back down in a small wooden holder and resumed pacing.

His next stop was at the window overlooking State Street. There he lit and left smoldering on the sill a Canadian stemmed pot-bowl.

Valjohn watched undismayed. He'd seen the show before: Gordon and his pipes, his old mentor deep in thought, lighting them up en masse without smoking them—just banking and leaving them to slow-burn . . . and eventually turning the air of his office into the fusty miasma of a staid men's club lounge.

Valjohn swiveled in his chair to see if he could spot any more cached about the room. He could find none, but Gordon surprised him, stopping beside a large, black filing cabinet and rolling open a drawer to withdraw yet another, an ornate applewood free hand.

"Thwuk, thwuk, thwuk . . ."

He crisscrossed the room two more times, mumbled "fascinating" again and returned to his desk. He sat down, lit the meerschaum and peered through the rising smoke at Valjohn.

"—and preposterous. How many people know about this?"

When Valjohn told him, he nodded his approval.

"So what's your conclusion, John? Does this mean our back-alley avenger is a woman?"

"No conclusions yet, sir. It does become a distinct possibility, though."

"I suppose nothing in this day and age should surprise me." Gordon shook his head and rapped the report with his knuckles. "I don't have to tell you we could do very nicely without this."

Valjohn nodded. With its macabre MO and its rogue's gallery of victims, the case already was steeped in notoriety. There also was the scandal surrounding the dismissal of his predecessor, Joseph Blear. And now this latest tidbit of information—he could just imagine what the local tabloids would do with it. Jacqueline the Reaper?

The superintendent suddenly stood up.

"For the time being, John, I want you to sit tight on this matter."

"For the time being?"

"That's right," he said, picking up the report and filing it away in a drawer. "I'll get back to you as soon as possible. I . . . uh . . . just need some more time to think it through."

"Uh . . ."

"Yes?"

"Nothing." Valjohn rose to his feet, walked to the door.

"John?"

"Yes?"

"I'm not sure I did you any favor handing you this one."

On the way back to his own office, Valjohn reflected on the superintendent. Valjohn could readily understand Gordon's preoccupation with publicity. It was essentially "bad press" that had brought him to Chicago five years ago in the first place. The department—already considered one of the worst big-city police forces in the nation—had just been rocked to its foundations by several new and particularly shocking scandals. The most notable involved an elaborate burglary ring of officers who were using their patrol cars brazenly, while on duty, to haul away loot. The public was outraged.

Not the least outraged was Mayor Robert J. Dooley. Not by the deeds themselves—"Show me a city where larcenous acts don't rear their ugly heads." Nor with the police—"Cops is human beans—just like the next guy." What outraged Mayor Dooley was the amount of print and fervor devoted to the scandal itself. He found it "typically blown way out of its proportion by a bunch of your mud-slinging hack journalists—and why don't they ever write about any of the good, positive things happening in this city?" Clearly something had to be done to redeem the public's faith in its police department. That something was Estes Merriwether Gordon.

Gordon was an academician with practical experience—as chief of police in Omaha, as army colonel and chief public liaison officer of the military government in occupied Germany—and his advice was continually being sought by city and state police departments across the land and abroad. He'd authored fourteen books, one of which, *Corporate Practices and the Police Administrator,* had become a modern classic.

The mayor was convinced he'd found a savior. As a pretext he initially obtained the dean to head a highly publicized committee investigating police reform. Shortly thereafter he announced with a bold flourish surprising everyone—Gordon and the committee included—that the committee's handpicked choice to succeed as Chicago's new chief of police was none other than the committee chairman himself, E.M.G. Reluctant at first, Gordon finally had accepted the challenge—along with a sizable salary and a promised "free hand" in his administration. He exercised his free hand the very first day he took office, becoming "Superintendent" Gordon rather than "Chief," an archaic title, he felt, loaded with militaristic overtones.

This concern for language later was demonstrated when he undertook to clean up the jargon in the ranks. Officers were taught to say "We apprehended a suspect" or "subdued a perpetrator with necessary force" instead of "We collared an asshole" or "Beat the living shit out of a scrote."

During his years at the helm, Gordon had done his best, but he was no miracle worker. The expectations and proclamations of the politicians were unrealistic. The patient was too far gone; the complications too numerous and severe. There could be no overnight panacea for the CCPD.

The superintendent did, however, pare away at the cumbersome administrative superstructure, compressed thirty-eight districts into twenty-one, demolishing the ancient ward boundaries and the political patronage that went with them. He renovated the old headquarters and moved his own office out of City Hall and into the new Police Headquarters, where it belonged. He substantially raised patrolmen's salaries and attempted to unplug the bottleneck in promotion caused by an encrusted system of seniority and nepotism by promising to advance the better-educated, the paltry 2 percent of college graduates on the force, just as far and fast as their capabilities would allow.

Valjohn's own rise, however, had not gone unchallenged. The FPOP had sent a formal letter of protest, on behalf of those veteran officers who'd been "tragically overlooked," to the City Council and the Civil Service Commission, and Chick Screed had even run it in the *Trib*. The mayor, however, let it be known that he was backing the superintendent 100 percent, and Valjohn's promotion stood firm.

"Brown-noser" and "suck-butt" were two of the more delicate epithets Valjohn heard muttered behind his back. While he hadn't joined the CCPD to win a popularity contest, he hadn't expected to become a social leper, either. There were times when he longed for the relative serenity of his academic life.

It was Gordon who'd persuaded him to leave the university. Though his former professor brought no key personnel with him to Chicago, he did suggest that Valjohn join the Force after earning his degree in grad school, offering to instate him as a detective lieutenant. The position would afford him invaluable field experience, allow him to test all the theories he'd learned from books—whether he chose to remain or return at some later date to an academic career. Valjohn had leaped at the opportunity. He'd become bored with the academic scene. He wanted a taste of the real world, to see and experience things firsthand. And there also was another motive, a rumbling deeper inside. There was the ghost of his father. . . .

"Hey, Lieutenant!"

Walking through the central office of Homicide, Valjohn stopped and turned toward a familiar rasping voice. Max Howland stood by a stenographer's desk, an open folder in his hands.

"Yes?"

"Where's your report?"

"Not done yet."

The captain smiled at the steno as though he were sharing a joke, set down the folder on her desk and walked over to him.

"How come? Everybody else's in."

"No reason." Valjohn shrugged. The deadline wasn't until tomorrow.

"That ain't what I hear."

Valjohn was silent.

"Like maybe we're interfering with your golf game?"

"I don't think so."

"I mean, we sure don't want this case to inconvenience your life of leisure."

"Don't worry about it."

"Worry? I ain't worried, Lieutenant. But you better be! This ain't no picnic on the quad. This is Homicide! Now, suppose you tell me what you've got going in that report."

"You can read it when you read it." Valjohn studied Howland's ugly box of a head. When he puffed up red his freckles looked like a rash. Hogarth would have done the captain an excellent likeness.

"Ya, I'll read it when I read it—only I don't want to hafta spend half the day fumblin' through no goddamn dictionary like last time." Howland reached up with a forefinger and drilled out a hard kernel of snot from his right nostril. He removed the stubby black cigar from his mouth, inserted the kernel between his teeth and cracked it, then spit the pieces on the floor between them.

"Nothing over one syllable, Captain, I promise." Scratch Hogarth, he thought; make that George Grosz.

"Ya, sure. Now lemme see your piece."

Valjohn feigned surprise. He mockingly frisked himself, shook his head and turned up both palms. Then, as if an afterthought, he suddenly patted his belt line and smiled. He lifted his shirt partway to reveal the basket stamp of his hip-hugger holster.

Howland grumbled something that sounded like "Now see that it stays there" and stalked off.

Valjohn breathed a sigh of relief. The holster was empty; his gun still home in his bureau drawer.

"Hey, Lieutenant!" Howland called from the door to his office.

Valjohn swallowed, turned.

"Get a haircut. You look like a goddamn clown!"

Valjohn nodded. He walked briskly back to his own office, tucking in his shirt.

In his apartment that evening he spent several hours working on his art project, an elaborate collage rendering of C-65-1834. Since taking over the investigation in February, he'd constructed a separate panel for each new victim, an abstraction or overall impression of each murder. Before last weekend the number stood at three. Now it had doubled. That put the grand total of victims at nineteen—no piddling mass murder.

He'd condensed the earlier murders, a baker's dozen committed while Joseph Blear was heading the case, into one large composite on a six-foot-by-six-foot pegboard. One day when he had more time, he'd go back and devote individual panels to these victims also. Maybe one to Billy Pivot as well.

William "Billy" Pivot had not been killed by the Reaper, but he was, nevertheless, one of the case's bona fide victims. A twenty-two-year-old hippie from New York, he'd come to Chicago a year ago last August to visit his sister and had had the misfortune, while walking across the University of Chicago's Midway Plaisance one evening, to stumble over a dead body. On acid, Pivot had tried to help the corpse, still warm, to its feet. When he'd finally got a good look at his newfound friend under a streetlight, he'd panicked and dashed into the eastbound lanes of the drive, where he was hit by a car. Though he'd managed to escape with minor injuries, he was not so lucky when it came time for him to explain just what he'd been doing with the mutilated remains of an 1834 victim. Several witnesses had seen him fleeing from the body; one actually claimed to have seen him wrestling with it. Clothes torn, covered with cuts and bruises from the accident, he looked as though he'd just been in a fight. He also was covered with the victim's blood.

Joseph Blear had had no doubts. A drug-crazed, long-haired freako, a high school drop-out; a section 8 army reject; an out-of-towner and New Yorker to boot—Billy Pivot was made to order. The evidence was overwhelming. Only Pivot wouldn't confess, and Blear wanted a confession in the worst way, to tie up neatly all the Reaper's crimes and allow them to be filed away and forgotten.

After nineteen hours of questioning Pivot finally did "unburden his guilty conscience" (Blear's words), signing several sworn statements admitting to the Midway Plaisance murder and eight other slayings. The following morning he was found lying comatose on the floor of his cell. He died in the county hospital a day later. Cause of death was attributed to his run-in with the car, drug overdose and epilepsy (he had no previous history of the disease).

Open and shut. The matter might have ended there except for two events. First, a young man came forward and identified himself as a student whom Pivot had claimed he'd been with only a short time before his alleged discovery of the body. Pivot had been unable to remember his name, had only just met him in a nearby gay bar. They'd returned to the student's dorm, popped a couple of pinks and had sex. It left Pivot little time, little motive as well, to commit the murder. Particularly *that* kind of murder.

Secondly, another Reaper murder took place near Washington Lagoon. Two days after Pivot's body had been shipped back to Brooklyn.

As more evidence turned up, it became increasingly obvious that Pivot had been merely a victim of circumstance and police brutality. Under pressure Superintendent Gordon had called for an immediate IID inquest. Joseph Blear had subsequently been dropped from the case, and then from the Force.

Valjohn took a six-foot-by-four-foot sheet of Masonite and sawed it diagonally into two congruent triangles. Since Skip Varner and Jeffrey Dix, Jr. had been snuffed together at one site, it seemed appropriate to mount their panels together, which he did, fastening the two triangles complementing one another on a common, wood-frame backing. For Jimmy Lee Cook he found a three-foot-by-four-foot panel already cut.

He cleared an area in the center of his studio and laid the panels on the floor, using chalk to block them out. Then working with scissors, he began arranging and rearranging bits and scraps of material: newspaper clippings, Xerox copies of his notes and sketches, photos and make-sheets on all three of the deceased. He played with the different sizes and shapes for over an hour, satisfied himself with several compositional effects, then called it a night. He would not start gluing things in place until he knew the extent of the evidence at his disposal.

Later, in bed, he awoke from a nightmare, shivering and disoriented. He got up and went to the kitchen, made himself a cup of winterberry tea— an old reliable brew, it never failed to soothe his nerves.

The nightmare was a frightening variation of a dream he had had off and on ever since his early childhood. The dream involved his mother, and in it she was always trying to come back to him.

Which she could never do, because one hot and dusty afternoon in the fall of 1941, Laura Dean Valjohn had dropped off her young son with a neighborhood friend while she ostensibly went to get her hair done. She had in fact returned to their small apartment in Kimberley, Indiana, there to put the barrel of her late husband's service pistol to her stomach and pull the trigger. She had then bled to death calmly seated at the kitchen table, smoking a cigarette. "Sorry," read a one-word note found wadded in her purse.

The consensus was his mother could no longer bear the grief she'd suffered following the death of his father four years earlier. It was also believed, however, that her sad fate was just another example of what

132

happened to those who "played around with mixed marriage." Her attempts to regain acceptance into the white community—particularly with a child—had ended in anger and frustration; her own father, living nearby in Coal Bluff, would have nothing to do with her. There was rumor of a recent, unhappy love affair.

Valjohn's immediate fate had been no less exemplary to the Fabian citizens of Kimberley. The friend he'd been left with while his mother went to have her "hair done," a divorcee living in a trailer park with five children of her own, was in no position to take him in. She tried with the help of authorities to locate relatives; failed. Valjohn's father, like himself, had been an orphan with no record of kin. On his mother's side, Valjohn's grandfather refused to acknowledge his existence. Consequently, a month after his mother's death, Valjohn had been sent to the Kimberley County Foster Home, and there he'd remained for the next thirteen years.

Valjohn's recurring dream came in several versions, each with its own variations. The most common of these usually began with him awakening in his bed in the orphanage dormitory. There would be a sound at the window, a gentle tapping, and he would get up to investigate. He would go to the window and raise the shade. Outside in the dead of night, his mother would be standing there, peering in at him. She would be knocking on the glass with a small, delicate fist, her skin glowing pale in the moonlight. Overjoyed to find that she somehow was miraculously still alive, he would try to open the window and let her in. The window wouldn't budge. While he struggled with it she would smile in at him, her eyes dark and gentle with love.

The window would remain stuck. Tiring, sweating profusely, he would signal for her to go around to the door. He would start out running across the room to meet her, eager to be held once again in her arms and feel her kisses. Across the room . . . across the universe—it was the same thing. He could never reach that distant door. On the journey, he would stumble over furniture, lose his way, slip into other, unrelated dreams. Once he refused to even try, knelt down behind his bed and hid. More often than not he would simply wake up.

It had been years since he'd had the dream. Tonight's version was the first since coming to Chicago, and it was by far the most horrifying. It began, as it had so many times in the past, with him in bed, awakening in the middle of the night. There was a tapping at the window. He got up, hurried across the room—he was in his present apartment—threw open a curtain. She was there, waiting for him as always. This time her face, inches from the windowpane, was not quite at eye level. She was looking up, her head just above the sill. There was something wrong about her smile . . . something strangely twisted.

As he struggled with the window, it dawned on him his bedroom was on the second floor. He leaned over closer to see if she were clinging to the building or balanced on a ladder. . . . She was standing on the dark street twenty feet below, her neck somehow stretched out grotesquely. Suddenly he felt the window give, and struck with horror, he leaped back. Her head soared higher, swaying to and fro on that elongated stalk of her neck like a great snake. He saw her thin lips move and heard her whisper, "Johnny, let me in."

He stood rooted to the floor, torn between love and revulsion. He heard his roommates stirring in their beds behind him, and he knew he was back in the orphanage dormitory.

"Johnny, oh, Johnny . . ."

He sprang forward, panicked that the others might see the hideous image that his mother had become. He yanked the curtain closed. It came down in his hands.

"Johnny, you be a good little pickaninny . . . you let your mama in!"

The next morning Valjohn got a haircut.

"Thwuk, thwuk, thwuk."

He was back seated in Gordon's office. It was Tuesday afternoon. The pipes already were ablaze. A blue-gray haze hung in near-cumulous proportions about the ceiling and drapes. He felt his eyes watering. It wasn't the sweet aroma of apricot brandy or Bourbon musket today. The smoke was stale, rancid—a smoldering funk of cornsilk, toilet paper and horse balls. The superintendent must have spent the whole morning pacing.

He was only partly right: Gordon had spent half the morning on the phone with City Hall.

"We simply can't ignore or be completely unresponsive to those outside the department—those who, I'm convinced, are as deeply dedicated to the principles of law enforcement as we. Not to mention the well-being of this city." The superintendent stood up from his desk. He walked over to the window and stared out at the street below. When he spoke again it seemed to be as much to himself as to Valjohn.

"We can't be insensitive to their . . . their views. We do share common goals. We have to make certain capitulations—to realize those goals." He glanced over at Valjohn as though he were making sure he was still there.

Valjohn coughed. He could sympathize with Gordon's distress. They were leaning on him to put the lid on Moe's lab report.

"There's more to gaining back the community's confidence and respect than merely solving crimes," continued the superintendent, again gazing out the window. "That's a fact, unfortunate or otherwise, we in the department have to live with. Even at the University . . . there are concessions to be made. The ivory tower was never that high. Or that ivory." He moved his face closer to the window, almost as if he were looking for it among the row of dingy, flat-roofed office buildings across South Wabash.

"In any event, the city leadership (he rarely referred to the mayor directly) feels it important that we accede to its wishes. I argued, but they remained adamant. I must admit I'm skeptical. Their premise seems tinged with a certain irrationality. On the other hand, Mr. Glad, who spent most of the morning at City Hall, shares their position."

"That figures."

"Excuse me?"

"Nothing, sir."

"Perhaps you and I, John—being outsiders—we don't quite see things in the same light as native Chicagoans. Perhaps our sensibilities are not tuned in on certain local nuances of feeling. . . ."

"Hog butcher of the world," recited Valjohn. "Brawling city of the big shoulders?"

"Precisely," smiled the superintendent. Then he sighed. "City Hall is convinced it's all some sort of conspiracy. 'An unholy plot to humiliate a great American city' I think is how they phrased it."

"A conspiracy?"

"Don't ask me, John. All I can tell you is how it was explained to me over the phone. Draw your own conclusions."

He listened with fascination while Gordon proceeded to give him a lengthy account of his morning conversation with that most prominent spokesman for local sensibilities Mayor Robert J. Dooley. Valjohn envisioned the mayor seated behind his massive mahogany desk in his great office complex, assiduously running the business of the city. He was puffed, red-faced and resolute with the glory of his own boundless and paternal civic pride. This was his city. He loved it, doted upon it, slaved for it with all his energies. When it prospered and sang for joy, he too prospered and sang for joy. When it suffered and cried out in agony, he too suffered and cried out. Early in the year a fire had destroyed a grandiose civic auditorium newly built on the lakefront. For the mayor it was like a death in the family. He wept. The opening of a super crosstown expressway dried his eyes. It was the birth of a son. He handed out cigars.

His reaction to Moe's report was one of blustering confusion waxing into purple-faced rage.

Oh, there was crime in his city. He could admit that. He didn't wear your rose-colored glasses like a lot of hoity-toity mayors from the East. There were murders, rapes, kidnapings, muggings. Sure, and there were syndicates for gambling, prostitution, drugs, juice loans, extortion. What the hell, there might even be a little rake and take now and then among certain elected public officials. But what city didn't have all this? Who could answer him that one?

Every city had its crime. That's why you had police. If you didn't have crime you wouldn't need them. He wasn't trying to endorse crime or stick up for it or nothing like that.

"But . . . but this latest iniquity, this . . . this . . . utterly detestable . . ."

Valjohn almost could hear that familiar droning baritone begin to shake and splutter over the phone.

"Estes, this ain't—isn't—your acceptable everyday crime I was talking about. I mean, a woman? Raping? Murdering? Mutilating? A female, for chrissakes! It's indecent. It's unnatural and unnormal and totally uncalled-for. What're they trying to turn this city into? What do they take us for? Lying down? Are we supposed to be your laughingstocks? I'd like to know."

Valjohn could see Gordon cringing at the other end of the line, holding the phone gingerly away from his ear.

"And if they think we're going to play their slutty little game, they got a bunch of things coming—never mind who, Estes, it's beneath our indignity. Yours, mine, the indignity of this great American city!"

The superintendent emptied the bowl of his meerschaum into the ashtray on his desk, refilled it.

"Be that as it may, however, I've decided to go along with City Hall in this matter, at least for the time being, while things are still in such a highly speculative stage. For the sake of harmony," he added with a shrug.

Gordon's words roused Valjohn abruptly from his bemusement. He felt a touch of disappointment but no great surprise.

"Of course, I realize it's going to put some added pressure on your investigation, John." He engaged him firmly with his tired, moon-sad eyes. "But nothing I'm sure you can't handle."

Valjohn nodded.

"Thwuk, thwuk, thwuk."

On his way through Gordon's outer office, Valjohn met Hans Glad. The PR director had just returned from lunch. The two of them stepped out into the hallway.

"How about a game tonight, super-stick? We could get in a quick nine at Columbus Park."

"You have to be kidding."

"No, I was just thinking it'd be the last time for you and Sergeant Satucci to play together. He's leaving town tomorrow."

"That breaks my heart. Now, if I might change the subject for a moment, what's all this nonsense coming down from City Hall?"

"What nonsense?" Glad knitted his brow, his slack, doughy features conveying a look of eroded innocence. The face of a Van Eyck Christchild.

"Come off it, Hans, I happen to know you spent the morning in the mayor's office. The lab report?"

"Okay, okay—but it's not nonsense as far as I'm concerned."

"A conspiracy? Against what? The city's masculinity?"

"So maybe they went a little overboard. But I'm still in agreement with their, uh, recommendation."

"A cover-up."

"Call it what you like. Let's face it—forget the city's image—this case is a real millstone for the department. Until we solve it, it means nothing but

136

bad press. And the disclosures in that report—Jesus! Believe me, the less said the better. You ought to be grateful. Hell, it's your investigation that's in the frying pan. We're just trying to keep you out of the fire."

"No favors, please."

"I can understand your feelings."

"Terrific. There's just been a triple murder. The press is all over my back, and you're telling me to squelch the only solid new lead we've managed to come up with since I took over? And why? Because some paranoid politician finds the facts offensive to his . . . his cockamamy sense of civic pride!"

The Christchild frowned. "I'll pretend I didn't hear that, Lieutenant."

Valjohn put his hands on his hips, felt his empty holster. "It's not just me, you know. What about the public? Don't they have a right to know? They're the ones ending up in the morgue."

"Oh, Jesus Christ, some public! As far as I'm concerned if we ever do catch the killer we ought to waive prosecution and pin a medal on the son-of-a-bitch."

"Daughter," corrected Valjohn. "Pin your medal on the daughter-of-a-bitch."

Joseph M. Blear awoke. It was morning. Or early afternoon. He wasn't sure which—his watch had stopped. More likely early afternoon, he thought, approximating the time by the amount of sunlight that seeped through the grimy window shade of his cheap hotel room. "Oh, shit! Oh, God!" he greeted the new day. He had to urinate so badly he debated pissing his bed, chose to endure the discomfort until he could stumble across the room to the wall sink.

"Oshitogod," he groaned again after relieving himself. He splashed cold water over his haggard face, rinsed down the traces of urine from the yellowed porcelain bowl. A wave of nausea swept through him. He stumbled back to the bed and flopped down. He ran a hand under the bed and groped for a moment. He felt a large leather valise; next to it, his fingers found what he was after. A bottle of Kentucky Gentleman. He lifted it and surveyed the damage. Still alive.

"Oshitogod!" He drained the bottle, rolling his tongue around the inside of his burning mouth. Then he lay back, closed his eyes and let the eighty-proof whiskey go to work. He could feel it spreading through his veins, regenerating his arms, legs. Frayed and cut nerves fused together. Injured, bleeding tissue rehealed. Splintered bones mended. Miraculously. And in his head . . . in that dismal, aching morass behind his eyes . . .

He reopened those eyes. He was ready to face the day now, ready once more to deal with his life and the piled garbage of the world around him. Nothing like the hair of the dog.

At the sink again, he splashed more cold water on his face, stared at

137

himself in the small, round shaving mirror. His bloodshot gaze no longer startled him. Nor did the haggard lines, the red-blotched pallor of his skin, the heavy growth that stubbled his sizable jaw. He was never hounded by self-rebuke or criticism, felt no remorse, no hint of contrition. When he looked in the mirror he saw only the face of a man betrayed. He thrust a hand to the seat of his pants, dug his fingers vigorously.

So he'd wasted a drug-freak hippie by mistake. Some big catastrophe! Everybody makes mistakes. He was a cop doing his job: Why wasn't he entitled to a cop's mistake? The bitterness quickly grew into a well-rehearsed and consuming hatred. It filled his head like the sweet stench of whiskey in his nostrils.

Before leaving the room he brought out the large leather valise from under his bed. He took it with him.

Outside walking on the street, he was hit with a racking cough. Here it was summer already, and he still had January in his lungs. By God, he'd never spend another winter in this frozen-ass town. Vegas! That's where he belonged. Plenty of sun, booze, money and snatch. He had connections there too. He hawked a wad of phlegm on the sidewalk and entered a corner lunch counter.

He was pleased with himself after he'd eaten—coffee, steak and eggs—hadn't had an appetite like that in weeks. Yessir, a little unfinished business and he'd be on his way. When he got up to leave, he felt the urge to defecate. He cursed, dug his fingers. Not here. Needed cotton for his piles. Goddamn grapes of wrath! A major operation just to take a crap.

He started to cross the street to his car and stepped quickly back on the curb as a white '55 Cadillac with four blacks sped past him, hurrying to make a light.

"Fuckin' load a' coal!" He coughed after them, fingering a pocketed revolver. "Oughta pump a slug up their tailpipe."

He drove out of the Loop on a westbound lane of the Eisenhower, swung north when he reached Elmhurst. There he stopped at a supermarket and bought a pound of hamburger.

While he was picking up another fifth at a liquor store, he noticed a young couple shopping by the wine racks. The girl was a strawberry blonde, tall and lanky, legs like a giraffe. She reminded him of a rape victim he'd interrogated several years ago when he was back working sexual assaults. Same freckled face, pouty mouth . . . Christ, how he wished he'd never left that detail. The bitches, they'd come to him with their oh-so-sad stories—all meek and woozy and shamefaced. Jesus, what a show; made him want to laugh and puke at the same time. Well, he'd straightened them stupid scrunts out fast. He had his technique down pat: He'd always start out all fatherly and indulgent. When did it happen? Where? Lots of general questions and plenty of nodding and "Oh, geez, that's too bad." Then he'd slowly work into the good stuff. When he hit on what embarrassed them the most, he'd really go after them. They'd look away and say something like, ". . . then he knocked me to the ground and did it."

"Did what?" he would ask, picking his nose.

"You know, did it. Raped me."

"No, I don't know. Raped you? How? What with?"

"While I was lying on the ground," they'd snivel. "His thing—he took it out."

"His thing? What? His fist? His foot? A broom handle? What?"

"His thing, you know!"

"No, I don't know."

"His c-c . . . his penis."

"All right, he took out his cock. What did he do then?"

"I told you. He raped me." More snuffling.

"No, you didn't tell me. Did you pull down your pants for him?"

"No, he did!"

"Did you spread your legs for him?"

"No! He made me spread them!"

"Made you?"

When they became too upset to continue—either too angry to speak or completely unraveled, blubbering—he'd usually shake his head with contempt and say a few words about enticement.

Minnelli, his commander, hated to see him go. Said his record for dropped charges was positively unbeatable.

As he watched the girl in the liquor store saunter over to the beer cooler, he thought about his interview with her look-alike. Stacy was her name—he couldn't recall her last name, but he remembered she'd got nailed while she was jogging along the lakefront, over by Jackson Park. Some big boogie had grabbed her in broad daylight and dragged her back in the bushes. After he fucked her, he'd made her blow him off.

Blear grinned to himself remembering their meeting at headquarters. He'd really made her squirm.

"What do you mean, he did other things?" he'd asked her. His partner sat nearby taking notes.

"Like oral sex. Fell-fellatio." Oh, she was an educated little bitch, a college student. But he knew he had her number, winked at his partner. This was going to be good.

"He made you put it in your mouth?" he asked with feigned disbelief.

"I told you he had a knife, had it pressed against my throat." She showed him for the third or fourth time a bruised cut under her chin.

"Yes, yes. Now, what can you remember about his, uh, organ? Was it black?"

"I already told you he was black."

"I know. I'm just checking. He could have been a white man wearing a disguise."

"It . . . he was black."

"Was it big?"

She didn't answer.

"It was big, wasn't it?"

"It was huge," she finally admitted.

"You've seen a few, have you?"

"I . . . uh," she wavered, "I have a boy friend."

"I see. It was bigger than your boy friend's, then?"

She nodded.

"Is he black?"

"No."

"Was it circumcised?"

"I don't know," she whispered.

"You don't know? You had it in your mouth, didn't you?"

"I . . . I just don't know."

"Think back—it could be important." His partner had started to snicker and had to look away.

She finally said she thought maybe he'd been circumcised.

"Did he say anything?"

She'd lowered her face in her hands, looked up questioningly.

"While you were having oral sex—did he say anything?"

"He told me not to bite."

"What were his exact words?"

"Uh . . . 'Don't bite.' I think he said, 'Baby . . . Don't bite, baby.' "

"Uh-huh. So, did he have an orgasm?"

She was silent, mumbled something.

"I didn't hear you," he said, staring at her pouty mouth.

"I guess so."

"What do you mean, you guess so? Did he come? Did he ejaculate sperm in your mouth or didn't he?"

"All right, yes, yes, he did!"

Tears welled in her eyes.

"Did you swallow it?"

She looked at the floor. The tears were flowing.

"You swallowed it, didn't you?"

"He made me!" She broke down. "He made me!"

"Oh, sure. You said he had a knife, right?" he asked, looking at his partner with unveiled disgust.

His parting words to her had been that she was crazy as hell to go jogging in that area and ought to be thankful she was still alive; she ought to forget the whole thing.

She hadn't taken his advice. Stacy Templeton. That was her name. He remembered it now because she was largely responsible for him being moved into Homicide. She'd told her old man about the interview. He was some big-shot professor at the University of Chicago, and he'd raised holy hell.

The girl walked up to the sales counter with her boy friend to purchase their beer. Blear moved up behind them with his bottle. He let the back of his hand brush up against the cheeks of her ass, held it there. She turned

140

around to scowl at him, then stepped on the other side of her boy friend. She didn't say a word. Smart, he thought; didn't want her scrawny twerp of a boy friend getting his head busted. Blear smiled.

He came across the dog on a country road over near Aurora. He sat upright on his foam donut pillow the moment he spied it, and slowly braked the dark blue '62 Tempest to a halt. He whistled to the animal as it trotted by, nose to the ground, along a fence line. He brought out the hamburger. The dog looked up, a black Lab—too small to be a purebred—and sniffed the air. A few minutes later it was inside the car, tail wagging, wolfing down the meat.

Blear undid its collar and tossed it out the window. Then from his valise, he took out his own special "collar" and slipped it over the dog's head. The "collar," acquired from a friend in the mob, was woven from soft-spun silk with braided handles. Sheathed inside the silk was a piano-wire noose. While the dog sat wagging its tail and sniffing for more hamburger, he yanked it off the seat and hung it, legs thrashing, eyes bulging, over the open door.

Heading north, he turned at the end of Insull Road onto a cinder drive posted with "No Trespassing" signs. He parked by a complex of abandoned buildings, an old brick foundry that had folded long ago; it was also the site for many clandestine meetings he'd had over the years, mostly with informers and syndicate figures.

He carried the dog by its hind legs into a dingy gray warehouse. In an area of the building that was well lit under a broken skylight, he set the animal down and cleared a pile of debris off a long, narrow shipping bench. He slung the dog up on the bench and went back out to the car, returning with the valise and his bottle.

He set the valise down by the dog and opened it. Its contents were wrapped in a towel. He removed his coat and took a stiff swig of whiskey. Another. Then he opened the towel.

A strange array of tools and cutlery lay before him. There were pliers and wrenches, a file, a banding clamp, hand clippers, a magnifying glass. There were scissors, a straight razor, a fishing knife with a serrated scaling edge, an assortment of scalpels, a bone saw, a small wood planer with shaping blades, pruning shears and a hand cultivator—its normally blunt tines had been filed into a razor-edged claw. There was also a coil of 3/16-inch steel cable.

He'd collected the various items over a period of several weeks. Now the time had come to see what they could do.

First he shaved one whole side of the dog's torso, using the clippers and the straight razor. He shaved part of a foreleg and a haunch. He then proceeded to laboriously mutilate the exposed carcass. He cut, stabbed, whittled and rived—examining with care, under the glass, each and every wound inflicted. For more than three hours he hunched over, totally engrossed in his task.

His final act of mutilation was to encircle the thorax with the steel cable wrapped in the towel. Using a special clamp and a wrench, he began tightening the cable like his silk noose. He continued tightening until he could hear ribs splintering, the sternum crack. He grunted with satisfaction.

Gathering up his instruments, he stuffed them back into the valise, then from his overcoat he took out a copy of *Hustle* magazine. He opened it to the centerfold, glanced at it briefly, flipped through some other pages. One depicting a nude French starlet bound in chains particularly caught his eye. Reaching down to unzip his fly, he found it was stuck. Careful not to lose his place, he set the magazine on the bench beside the carcass of the dog and undid the zipper with both hands.

When he emerged at last from the warehouse, coughing badly again, the sun was starting to set. On an impulse he drew his gun and aimed at it, a great red balloon balanced on a horizon of distant trees and power lines. He squinted through the sights until his eyes watered.

8

John Valjohn swung off the main highway five miles north of Kankakee and drove east on Route 114 until he came to a large complex of buildings sprawled in the countryside. The surrounding fields of corn, wind-riffled and shimmering in the bright afternoon sun, were a rich chrome green. Intense, unmixed—right off Van Gogh's palette, he thought as he slowed and turned at the entrance, a high wrought-iron gate with a sign that read: *Mengert's State Psychiatric Center.* He parked his Volks in front of the administration building, a rambling, two-story affair of dull yellow brick, and climbed out.

"May I help you?" asked a receptionist in the small outer lobby of the building.

He introduced himself, displayed his shield with a brief, self-conscious flip of the wrist.

The receptionist nodded, said she was expecting him. She pressed a buzzer, allowing him passage through an electronic door behind her. He was met in the narrow inner corridor by a young man in a gray suit who introduced himself as Dr. Culp.

Valjohn had come to the center to interview a patient named Ernly Chard. In November of the previous year, a man by the name of Ted Fulton, a paroled wife-slayer and a solid 1834, had met his brutal demise

143

late at night in a small storefront alcove on a skid-row side street. Chard had been found lying nearby in the gutter, drunk and raving incoherently. There was a strong possibility that he may have seen the murderer, may even have seen the murder taking place. Whatever he saw, however, it remained his secret, because he never stopped raving. Days went by in the psychiatric ward of Cook County Hospital, weeks; there was no improvement. Finally he was transferred to Mengert's, where he'd been ever since.

The Fulton murder had taken place several months before Valjohn had been assigned to the case. Recently, when he'd learned of a possible eyewitness existing, he'd decided to make an attempt at interrogating Chard himself. Dr. Breslin, the department's psychiatric consultant, had set up the meeting through Dr. Culp. Valjohn came armed with a tape recorder and Dr. Breslin's briefing on paranoid and reactive schizophrenic behavior.

Dr. Culp led Valjohn through a series of hallways and locked doors to an observation cubicle next to a large connecting ward. He asked Valjohn to please be seated and then excused himself. Valjohn set up his tape recorder on a table in the center of the room, gave it a quick test. A few minutes later the doctor returned with Mr. Chard.

"Ernly, I'd like you to meet Lieutenant John Valjohn from the Chicago Police Department. He's here on a friendly little visit to ask you a few questions."

Valjohn rose, offered to shake hands, but Chard ignored him, walking instead into the nearest corner of the room and standing there.

"Lieutenant, I wish I could stay and help you with this, but I'm ten minutes late for a consultation as it is," the doctor said, glancing at his watch. "If you need anything, call an orderly; there's a buzzer on the wall there."

Valjohn studied the solitary figure in the corner. Though still in his fifties, Chard was an old man, white-haired, stooped and withered. He looked a little bit like an underfed Charlie Ruggles with bad teeth. Valjohn could see clearly the crooked brown nubs as Chard made a series of grimaces and began vigorously rubbing his hands together. He wore slippers, pajamas and an institutional green robe which blended right into the pastel walls of the corner.

Chard had been a graduate student and TA at the University of Michigan back in the forties. He'd had his first breakdown working on his thesis in English literature and had to spend four months recovering in a private sanitarium near Ann Arbor. After he got out, he abandoned his academic career and came to Chicago where he worked at a variety of menial jobs from bellhopping to washing dishes and mopping floors. In 1958 he became the manager of a magazine concession stand in the lobby of the La Salle Street Station. He suffered another breakdown in 1962—brought on by job-related stress, a drinking problem and the Cuban missile crisis—and was briefly hospitalized at St. Luke's. A year later he lost the concession stand and dropped out of sight, eventually surfacing on skid row, a seasoned derelict.

Valjohn was about to speak when Chard took a sudden step forward.

"You don't know. You don't think you don't, but you want to. I know plenty, but either way if you didn't have a mother it wouldn't matter. Who could tell? Not me. Not by a long shot, a potshot, a snot pot—"

Valjohn took a deep breath and sat down.

"Uh, Mr. Chard, would you like to sit down here? Relax. Take a load off your feet. How about a smoke?" Valjohn reached into his pocket and pulled out a pack of Marlboros he'd bought just for the occasion. "Can I offer you a cigarette?"

Chard stared at the pack of Marlboros. "Take a load off my node. I don't think I won't. Not enough time. A smoke's a joke. And a joke won't hurt. Will it?"

"Uh, Mr. Chard, can you remember anything about the night of November 14 last year?" Valjohn set the cigarettes down on the table, tried not to think how ridiculous the question sounded at the moment. He turned on the tape recorder. "Did anything at all unusual happen that night? The night they found you, uh, lying in the street?"

Chard ignored the questions, walked over to the table and nudged the pack of cigarettes with an elbow.

"Do you remember a scuffle? A man being killed in front of a store? Yerkes' Pawnshop?"

Chard abruptly dropped to his knees, tilted his head against the tabletop and slid it forward until his nose was only inches away from the cigarettes.

"Now I lay me down to sleep, down to weep, pray the gourd my soul is cheap. If I should die before I cry, before I try . . . pry . . . fly . . . before I lie . . ."

The old man put a small, gnarled hand on Valjohn's leg to steady himself. The sagging skin of his face was pulled back where he'd slid it across the table, drawn so tight and thin it looked as though the sharp bones of his skull were going to push through. Valjohn stared down at a snarl of white hairs, some of them several inches long, growing out of an upturned ear.

"Now I lay me down to creep. Lay me down. Lay me, baby, lay me! Lay me a . . . lay me a . . . daughter of the dark! Come cunt cocksucker! Begone foul dream ream suck! Shriek, shriek nothing but sad echo shrieks. Hair. Snare! You think you won't? A smoke's no joke. You want to get laid? You want to get paid? Beauty twists her braid. Think twice. Think vice. Stink nice. 'That's not nice,' said little old we. I don't care. Don't swear. Don't cuss, you old cuss. Do you feel the terror in your hair?"

With surprising nimbleness Chard sprang to his feet. He was off pacing frantically around the room, clasping and reclasping his hands, a steady torrent of words spewing from his lips. Valjohn continued throwing out questions, tried to prompt the old man into a few calm moments of coher-

145

ence. He failed miserably. Chard grew more and more excited, delirious. When he started kicking the wall and pulling his hair, tearing it out in thick, white tufts, Valjohn threw in the towel. He rang the buzzer for an aide. Chard was sedated. The interview was over.

Some eyewitness, mused Valjohn, once again on the interstate, driving back to the city. And, according to the doctor, chances of recovery were practically nil. The short circuit was too deep-rooted and the wiring too old and abused. Too many miles and too many bottles of stinko red wine. Whatever had precipitated this last breakdown, whatever Chard had seen in the shadows of the streetlights that November night—it had been enough, fixed his clock for good. He might just as well have had his head bashed in with a brick.

It was after four when Valjohn reached the city. Feeling a little flat from his trek south, he decided not to return to headquarters, drove instead out to Capone Memorial Park for a round of golf. His clubs and shoes were still in the back seat from his short-lived match with Glad and company a few weeks earlier.

Out on the course, he had difficulty concentrating on his game. He bogied the first hole, double-bogied the second, tripled the third. At this torrid pace, he told himself, slinging his bag over his shoulder and plodding on to the next tee, he'd be an arithmetic 45 over par by the end of nine. He then popped up another drive, barely clearing a creek that crossed the fairway all of a hundred and fifty yards away. Walking to his ball, he paused on a narrow wooden bridge over the creek and stared down at the water.

"I'm not sure I did you any favor handing you this one." The words of Superintendent Gordon echoed in his thoughts. Well, Valjohn wasn't sure either; in fact, he was becoming less sure every day. Following Moe's discovery in the lab, the pressure from City Hall, the cover-up, Hans Glad's manipulations behind the scenes—he was beginning to feel more and more removed from his own investigation, confused and totally ineffectual. He was starting to doubt himself, his energies and capabilities, his choice of profession. As if the recurring dreams of his mother weren't enough, he now was beginning to ponder the ghost of his father. . . .

Talbot Tyler Valjohn. A career cop: an eighteen-year veteran on the municipal force of Kimberley, Indiana and the first black police officer in the whole state south of Gary; before that, a decorated war hero and at fifteen the youngest private in the famous, black 369th Infantry Regiment during World War I. The heroism didn't stop there. Talbot Valjohn had died in the first month of his young wife's pregnancy, killed in the line of duty while investigating a reported burglary in progress.

It had happened one evening in 1937 at a lumberyard on the outskirts of Kimberley. He'd been blown away by a part-time deputy sheriff also responding to the same 10-31. The deputy, later testifying that his gun accidentally discharged, was acquitted, though the general feeling of the town was that he'd opened fire in the dark without bothering to identify the other officer. The man had a reputation for a nervous trigger finger, had once shot a farmer's prize trotter while hunting deer in Michigan. Valjohn's father had died from a neck wound. The burglary call proved to be a false alarm.

A brief footnote was added to the episode years later: When Valjohn was fifteen he vowed to avenge his father's death. By that time Skip Burkhardt —the deputy with the nervous trigger finger—no longer was a law officer. He was a part-time general handyman around the town and a full-time drunk. One night Valjohn slipped away from the county foster home, an eight-inch hunting knife tucked under his shirt, and followed Burkhardt home from his favorite tavern. Stumbling drunk, his intended victim made it easy for him, passed out on the front lawn of his rooming house. Valjohn stood over the slobbering, wheezing figure sprawled in the grass . . . and shook with tears. He could not even bring himself to draw the knife from under his shirt, let alone plunge its hard steel blade into a living person. Learning at an early age that he had no heart for revenge, he had turned and run away.

Curious, he thought as he resumed walking down the fairway, how he'd ended up a career cop himself. Obviously no coincidence—yet he'd felt no driving impulse to follow in his father's footsteps. It had just happened. On a lark he'd taken a course in police ethics while an undergraduate at Indiana, had eventually earned a minor in law enforcement to go with another minor in art history and his major in U.S. history. He'd ended up in the graduate school of criminology under Gordon at Berkeley only after an unsatisfying year at Bloomington in the History Department, his move West being precipitated more by an unhappy love affair than anything else. Then Gordon had come to Chicago, and Valjohn followed.

In any event, it seemed to him his choice of profession would have made more sense if he'd at least come to know and love his father. But what could he feel for a stranger? For a man who'd been laid to rest like some distant ancestor before he was born? Even his lame attempt to do in Burkhardt had been an act not so much of hatred as of frustration: He was not avenging the loss of a loved one, only the lost chance to love. There were no memories. No dreams. Only one snapshot, old and fading, a couple of letters addressed to his mother, a few ribbons and medals. And a silver shield from the Kimberley City Police Department.

Now he wore his own shield tucked away in his wallet like a hidden birthmark.

Valjohn played his next shot strategically, using an iron instead of a wood to lay up short of the green and its defending bunkers, followed with a delicate wedge six feet from the pin. As he lined up the putt, his thoughts returned to the case.

Valjohn's predecessor, Joseph Blear, had been convinced, along with everyone else, that the Reaper was a deranged homosexual—in Blear's own words, "one of your faggoty cocksuckers getting his jollies off icing and dicing his connections." Dr. Breslin had elaborated on the theory, suggesting that the killer's violent deeds were performed not out of sadistic pleasure, but on the contrary, grew out of intense feelings of shame and self-loathing. After engaging in homosexual acts with his victims, the killer was psychically overwhelmed: Each victim became in his guilt-crazed mind an extension of himself, a vile alter ego who needed to be punished, and he was driven in a rage to kill and mutilate. Dr. Breslin further surmised that the killer was highly suicidal, might even kill himself before he ever was apprehended. The newspapers, picking up on this diagnosis, had run personal, front-page messages to the killer after each new murder, pleading with him to give himself up, to seek psychiatric help before it was too late, before—horror of horrors—he took his own life. The city's homosexual community also had been alerted (much to the chagrin of City Hall): Individuals so inclined were constantly reminded to be wary of any strangers making deviate sexual advances. Following these warnings, it was interesting to note, business in the gay bars had practically tripled.

Moe's slide show now had abruptly put an end to this line of speculation —at least within the department. The media and general public still were in the dark—thanks to Hans Glad's press releases—though Valjohn did not feel he was much better off. He simply could not get a handle on the perpetrator's newly projected profile, could not generate any sort of satisfactory mental picture of the Reaper as a woman. Motivation was no problem: Women were killing men all the time, shooting them, stabbing them, running over them with cars—as one irate housewife out in Villa Park had done to her drunken husband just the other day. But how could he reconcile the MO? The strength factor? The ferocity? All he could come up with was some sort of demented, comic-book vigilante—a Wonder Woman gone berserk, a psychotic Sheena of the Jungle.

Well, whether he could visualize her or not, first thing Monday morning he was going to start rounding up all those women in the metropolitan area with criminal records that were heavily into violence. First on the list would be the paroled murderers and rehabilitated psychopaths. Then he'd focus on hetero-assaults; that would include a number of tough prostitutes who were on the sheets for strong-arming their johns. After them, who? He wasn't sure. Maybe a list of belligerent bull dykes.

Valjohn sank the putt . . . in spite of himself. He misread the green breaking left, then mishit the ball, pushing it off his intended line, one mistake canceling out the other. Not very satisfying, but at least his bogie progression had ended with a par. As he plucked the ball out of the hole with the blade of his putter, he noted with passing interest that two wrongs on occasion could indeed make a right.

She really had to be something else—the killer, whoever she was. A *malech hamovesteh*—that's what Moe had dubbed her. An angel of death.

148

He'd also once called her a *zeltenkeit*—an anomaly, a real nondescript. Well, *zeltenkeit* or not, he'd better find her and find her soon or . . . or what? He wasn't sure; he had a bad feeling, though. Maybe the case would break him like it had his predecessor? No way. He and Blear were as different as night and day. And besides, Blear got what was coming to him. At any rate, he thought with a grin, if he didn't find her pretty soon, there wouldn't be a decent rapist-murderer drawing breath within a hundred miles of this old "toddlin' town." That much seemed certain.

He glanced at his watch and quickened his stride. Moe had invited him over to his mother's for dinner tonight at eight-thirty. If he didn't get his mind back on golf and hurry up, he wouldn't get off the course before dark. His mouth watered at the thought of dinner; he hadn't eaten since breakfast. He loved *kreplach*—Moe's mother, Rose Frank, was making them specially for him. And his date. Moe told him she'd been very explicit about that. She wanted him to bring a girl. Every time he came to dinner he was alone. She felt guilty, was afraid her cooking might be keeping him out of circulation, sitting around with a couple of old fogies when he might be out meeting someone special. It was bad enough that Moe, her own flesh and blood, never had married (she'd given up on him long ago); she wasn't going to sit idly by and watch Valjohn follow in his footsteps.

"Like it or not," Moe had informed him solemnly, "you've been adopted. You are now the property of one authentic, slightly ancient Jewish mother."

Valjohn birdied the next four holes, suddenly could do no wrong. A crazy round—as many birdies as he'd ever strung together. He hit a big downwind drive on the ninth hole—a short par-five, the easiest hole on the course—and strode confidently in pursuit. A birdie here and he'd finish the round one over par. Not bad considering his rocky start.

He put a good swing on a three-iron. The ball flew straight on line toward the green, and for a moment he thought he'd be putting for an eagle. The wind gusted, however, and he watched the ball bounce over the green into a bordering rough. He was undismayed. No eagle putt, but the rough was short, and he'd still be chipping for a putt at a bird.

Valjohn hated to disappoint Rose, but he'd be showing up tonight, same as usual, by himself. It was too late to call anybody—even if there was anybody, which there wasn't. His last date had been with Mona Cobb, and he was not about to give her another go.

He almost walked by his ball. Short rough or not, he'd managed a lousy lie, the ball coming to rest right in the middle of someone's divot hole. Damn! Before playing his next shot he bent over to make sure the ball was his. This particular rough was shared with another fairway. He could see through a group of evenly spaced alders a foursome on the tenth tee. One of them could easily have hooked it over here.

Red Dot. Maxfli six. Satisfied, he stepped back and sighted a line to the pin. He visualized the shot, a short pitch to the elevated green fifteen yards away, the ball floating softly to the green, biting when it hit with plenty of backspin—difficult to achieve from this lie, but not impossible—so it wouldn't run too far past the hole. He flipped the clubhead a few times through the grass, then took his stance.

Hands ahead, a nice, easy take-away . . . a demented Mary Marvel, Dracula's daughter, the bride of Frankenstein . . .

He struck the ball badly, his concentration broken by a new parade of distaff anomalies. It zinged out of the rough like a bullet, hit once into the side of the green, bounded over the embankment, streaked across the putting surface. On perfect line. Amazed, he watched it slam into the flagstick, jump three feet up the pole, drop straight back down into the cup.

The club awkwardly held in his hands, he stared at the empty green and burst out laughing. That had to be the most bullshit eagle of all time. If it hadn't hit the pin, the ball would've run all the way into the next county. At least into the trap on the other side of the green. He would have been lucky to salvage par. He'd finished the nine in thirty-six, even par. As they say: not how, but how many.

He reached down, picked up his bag, took a step toward the green.

He heard a loud, resounding crash.

His first thought was that there'd been a wreck, a collision on the main road that ran by the parking lot. He turned his head in that direction, discovered with some surprise that it was already night. Had he been playing that long? It was much too dark to see the main road, even to see the parking lot or the trees . . . or the grass which he now felt pressing against his face, pressing prickly and bitter into his mouth.

Something was very wrong. He'd played golf in the dark before—back in college: He and his teammates would putt out on the final hole in the moonlight, would wait in the shadows and listen for the "clunk" of the ball as it dropped into the cup. But this was different. There was no moonlight; there were no shadows. He could not remember the sunset.

And why should he be tasting grass? Unless, of course, he wasn't standing . . . which he wasn't. He was lying flat on the ground—he was sure of it! He tried to raise himself, to crawl, but his arms and legs were cast in concrete; he couldn't budge them. He became angry. What the hell was going on? Was this somebody's idea of a joke?

It was still too dark to see anything. It was almost too dark to think.

Then it grew even darker.

9

Valjohn opened his eyes slowly, blinked at the flood of burning light. Then he closed them again, wanting the night to return. His head throbbed with pain. He reopened his eyes, fought the brightness. . . .

He was in a room. He was in a bed. Not his room. The walls were green . . . soft pastel . . . the bed had railings. Someone was standing over him, peering down at him—no, it wasn't a person. It was glass, a bottle. His vision cleared, and he saw that it was an IV bottle, hanging upside down. A tube ran from its stoppered neck to his taped left forearm. Glucose clear as water was dribbling into his veins.

What the hell was he doing in a hospital?

He struggled against the pain, tried to think back. His mind was mushy. He'd been playing golf. That's right—out at Capone Park. He'd just shot a thirty-six, even par. He'd mishit a pitch shot—no . . . yes—he'd bladed it but sunk it anyway, for an eagle. . . . What after that? His mind was gumbo again. He was walking toward the green; he was going to retrieve the ball—but somehow he never got there. Why not? The crash, of course! There'd been a collision! Then he remembered the darkness. He remembered crawling on the ground, the taste of grass. Something had happened to him. Maybe he'd had a stroke? Maybe he'd been shot?

She was standing across the room with her back to him. He could see her through the chrome railings of the bed. A nurse. White uniform. She was arranging some flowers on a table by the window; her long blond hair caught the sunlight through the glass, poured down her back like molten gold. Dazzled, he closed his eyes and saw the afterimage of her hair blazing inside his head.

He rose up slightly and tried to speak. No words came, only a guttural croak. His head reeled inside. When he fell back on his pillow, a sharp pain pierced his left temple.

She turned around. Through the railing he watched her walk to the bed. She leaned over him, touched his forehead with cool fingers and smiled. Then she was gone.

He dozed, then awoke from a strange dream to find a man and a nurse standing over him. The nurse was not the one he'd seen earlier; she was older, heavyset. The man introduced himself as Dr. Tabor, a neurosurgeon, and began examining him. Dr. Tabor recounted what had happened. Valjohn had trouble listening as confusion spread in his mind.

". . . lucky to be alive . . . concussion at the temporal bone . . . a fraction of an inch lower . . . the cranial crease . . . the coronal and sphenoid suture . . ."

It was as though he were preoccupied with a single thought or idea. Only he couldn't remember what it was. He only knew it was there, as vague and unrevealing as it was compelling.

". . . weighs less than three ounces . . . hard to believe the force . . . must have dropped in your tracks . . . a duck hook . . . never know when . . . play a little golf myself . . ."

A golf ball! He'd been hit by a goddamn golf ball! The crash, the collision he'd been looking for—no wonder he couldn't find it: It was his own head being dented in! He instinctively reached for his left temple, felt gauze. The doctor pulled his hand away, told him it would be best to leave the wrap alone for another day or so. It was then Valjohn realized his entire head above his eyes was swathed in bandages . . . or was this too part of his strange dream?

Because at that moment he was having the dream again, the distinct impression that he was at sea. The doctor, the nurse, himself lying there awake in bed—they were all on the deck of a ship, and he could feel the waves heaving and rolling beneath them. Impertinently, absurdly, he felt a tensing in his loins.

". . . After the ambulance arrived . . . excessive bleeding . . . petechial hemorrhages . . ."

The room had filled with mist. He could smell the salt air, and a sea breeze moaned softly in his ear.

". . . debated emergency surgery . . . relieve pressure . . . contracoup effect . . ."

As suddenly as it had come, the mist cleared away. The breeze and salt spray with it. The deck became a floor again. He lay back in his sheets, becalmed, and managed to uncross his legs. Dr. Tabor was leaning over his chest and listening to his heartbeat through a stethoscope.

". . . possible hematoma . . . take more X rays Monday . . ."

Monday? Valjohn suddenly was attentive.

"Of course, if you hadn't come around by tomorrow, we were going in there anyway," the doctor was saying, and he pointed his forefinger at Valjohn's temple like a pistol, snapped the hammer down with his thumb.

By tomorrow? What day was that? How long had he been lying here? A couple of days? Weeks? Months? He jerked his head up and tried to speak. Again his best effort was a croak. He knew the words he wanted to say, saw them clearly in his mind—but they wouldn't come out. They lodged in his vocal cords, his throat and tongue rusted shut. Red-faced, rising up on the tips of his elbows, he tried again, but only sputtered and slurred like a lunatic. Not a single word.

"Now, now, Mr. Valjohn." The older nurse was at the doctor's side helping ease him back down on his pillow. "Nothing to get all lathered up about. You're going to be just fine."

"Nurse McGlocklin is quite right," assured Dr. Tabor. "Aphasia is very common with this type of injury, but most of the time it's only a temporary thing, an inconvenience. When you heal up inside, it should disappear. Like a scab on a cut."

Valjohn continued to stammer.

"Don't even try to speak now. Just lie back and take things easy. Your vision appears to be okay, and you can be thankful for that. You could very easily have been blinded." Dr. Tabor made some quick notations on a card, spoke a few words to Nurse McGlocklin, then coughing, cleared his throat for his bedside windup.

"Well then, I'll be checking back in on you later. In the meantime, lie still, get plenty of rest and be nice to your nurses . . . that shouldn't be too difficult," he added with a wink, then strode from the room.

Nurse McGlocklin immediately took charge. Like everyone's favorite Irish aunt, she bustled about, setting things in order, chattering all the while. She changed his sheets, cranked his bed, fluffed his pillow, sent an aide for a fresh pitcher of water.

"Poor old Mr. Sleepyhead," she cooed, slipping into a blithe brogue. "You had everyone worried silly, you did. But not me. You didn't fool me for a tinker's wink. I knew you were playing possum all the time. Sure, it would take more than a little knock on the noggin to do in the likes of a fine, strapping fellow such as yourself."

While she rattled on, Valjohn tried to patch together the remnants of his speech mechanism, at least on some makeshift, interim level. The lines were down; nothing but static. Somehow he had to get through.

"Oo-lawn?" he finally managed to garble aloud. He wanted to know what day it was, "how long" he'd been unconscious.

Nurse McGlocklin was wheeling away the IV apparatus; Dr. Tabor had disconnected it from his arm during the examination. She'd just finished telling him how much he reminded her of her husband twenty years ago when he too had been a "darlin' young man." Hearing him, she stopped at the door and looked at him uncertainly.

Valjohn gathered momentum. Concentrating with all his might, he momentarily broke through the static.

"Huh . . . how long?" he blurted triumphantly.

"Oh, very good, Mr. Valjohn!" she exclaimed. "How long, indeed! I married sweet Jimmy McGlocklin twenty-three years ago come this fall. Of course," she added with a sigh, "I've not laid eyes on the man for twelve years—me living here in the States and his lordship back in Dublin."

She paused for reflection. Valjohn lay in helpless silence.

"T'was the only way," she continued. "At each other's throat from morning till night, we were. T'was the only way to save the marriage."

The aide returned with the water, placed it on the bed stand. Nurse McGlocklin donated a few more insights into the mysterious workings of her marriage, then informed him she had to get back to her real chores, that she couldn't spend the whole day "lollygagging about," much as she enjoyed his "charming company."

"I'm leaving you in the tender hands of an angel, though," she declared as another nurse entered the room. "Miss O'Leary here has been assigned your continuity nurse. And sad as it is to say, I'll not be missed, I'm sure."

Valjohn turned his head.

The next day he discovered he was able to speak, or at least stammer out a number of words. Miss O'Leary, as if reading his mind, had brought in a calendar first thing in the morning. He'd learned that he'd been unconscious for nearly forty-five hours and that it was now Monday of the following week. It was a relief to know he hadn't been out weeks or even months, as he'd feared. Still, forty-five hours was hardly a nap. He'd been hit once before by a golf ball when he was a boy caddying. It had raised an ugly lump right between his eyes, but it hadn't KO'd him. Somewhere over the years he must have developed a glass jaw. Or more accurately, he thought, tenderly feeling his bandaged temple, a glass head.

"Who?" Valjohn asked, looking up from his half-eaten cup of raspberry Jell-O. He was sitting in bed, two pillows propped behind his back, had just finished a lunch of Swiss steak, mashed potatoes and cauliflower. The steak and potatoes had tasted more like cauliflower than the cauliflower.

"Carl Freetlock."

"Don't know an . . . ee . . . know . . . know any C-C-C-Carl Free . . ."
Nurse O'Leary had read the name on a card accompanying a bouquet of flaming red gladiolus on the table by the window. He'd received flowers from Moe and Rose, from Superintendent Gordon, from McTague, from Lieutenants Harris and Gillian, from Carlson in the lab, from Erwin Kaufman, his art agent, even from Mona Cobb—white roses, no less. He had

no problem remembering any of them. But Carl Freetlock? He drew a complete blank. Great! As if aphasia weren't bad enough. Now amnesia . . . God knows who and what else he'd forgotten.

"Mr. Freetlock is the man who hit you with the golf ball," Nurse O'Leary said with a little laugh. She walked over and handed him the card. "I doubt if you had much of an opportunity to be introduced."

He breathed a sigh of relief.

"Comes to the hospital every day to see how you're doing. Since he can't see you, he contacted me at the front desk, told me to tell you that if there's anything he can do for you, anything you need, don't hesitate letting him know. Poor man, I'm sure he feels terrible."

Up until this moment Valjohn hadn't really thought about someone else being involved. The golf ball had been an entity unto itself, an isolated, random molecule that had run amok. But, of course, someone had to hit it; someone had to send it on its way. Good old Carl Freetlock. No wonder the man was feeling terrible: He undoubtedly assumed he was going to get slapped with a big lawsuit. Come to think of it, Valjohn couldn't remember hearing anyone yell "Fore!" Good luck, Carl.

Valjohn was visited daily by a speech therapist—the only visitor Dr. Tabor would allow. Friends and relatives, if he'd had any of the latter, were *verboten*. The doctor didn't want to complicate his recovery with any psychological blocks that might build up out of strain and frustration. For the first week anyway, Valjohn was to remain essentially isolated, relaxed and free from all tensions and worries of the outside world. The sessions with the therapist rarely lasted more than twenty minutes and consisted basically of a series of vocal exercises. No pressure was put on him to converse.

Wednesday afternoon he was caught trying to call headquarters.

"Doesn't pay to pick a scab," said Dr. Tabor. He had the phone removed from the room.

Valjohn's only chance for conversation came through his day-to-day intercourse with the attendant staff—primarily his CN.

"C-C-Cres . . . cent. Crescent O . . . Lear . . . ry." He sounded out her name slowly, emphasizing each syllable. "That's a c-c-curious name. D-D-Do your f-f-friends call you Fertile for sh-sh-short?"

She looked puzzled at first, then grinned.

"No, just Tigris and Euphrates—for long." There was a certain quality to her voice . . . a familiarity, a melodic after-ring. The echo of her words seemed to hold back the rush of silence.

"Did your p-p-parents name you a . . . a . . . fff . . . fter the moo . . . con . . . the moon?" Damn! How could he make light, witty banter with all this stammering and stuttering?

"I really don't know," she said. "I never knew my father. I guess I never knew my mother either." She'd just finished changing his bedding, was wadding up the old sheets for the hamper.

"N-n-no kidding—that's grrr . . . great," he blurted, then quickly tried to apologize. "I mean—I did . . . didn't m-m-mean it was grrr . . . great. I mean . . . I m-m-meant it was grrr . . . great . . ." his voice trailed off, his mind clogging.

She smiled, forgiving him for whatever he might have meant, left the room with his dirty linen.

When she returned, his mind had cleared.

"What I meant to . . . to say was w-w-welcome to the cl . . . club." He held out his hand. "I nev . . . never knew my f-f-father, either. He d-d-died before I was b-born. My mother, sh . . . she d-d-died when I was four. I grrr . . . grew up in a . . . a . . . an orphan . . . phanage."

Crescent came forward and took his hand. "I had an aunt, my mother's sister. She and her husband took me in."

"You l-l-lucked out. No . . . nobody adopted m-m-me. I was t-t-too old, too ugly," he said, laughing, "and the wrong c-c-color."

She playfully patted his cheek. "I would have adopted you . . . Mr. Valjohn."

In the days that followed, she tended to his needs, fussed over him and conversed freely, coaxing words out of him and encouraging his efforts when he failed. He found himself basking in the aura of her care. She was exactly what the doctor ordered: In her presence the problems of the outside world seemed to dwindle, lose their significance, like so many pesky insects shut outdoors in the night. He missed her when she was gone, and when she returned, waking him in the morning, thermometer in hand, delicate fingers at his wrist, the sound of her voice . . . he actually felt himself yearning less and less for a speedy recovery.

One day after receiving a hypo, he accused her of giving him a "Hertz doughnut."

"What's a Hertz doughnut?" she asked.

"You n-n-never had a H-H-Hertz doughnut?"

She shook her head.

Rubbing his arm where she'd stuck the needle, he explained to her what she'd missed growing up a girl: *Want a Hertz doughnut?* any one of a dozen older, bigger boys would ask. And no matter what he answered, he would get one anyway—the sharp blow of a fist made with a raised middle knuckle and served high on his upper arm, where the meat was thinnest. Compliments of the pecking order at the Kimberley County Foster Home. If the bone were caught just right, the whole arm would go so numb it felt as though it were going to drop off. *"Hurts, don't it?"* then came the endless refrain of bleating laughter. Undersized, the only child of mixed parentage in an all-white school, Valjohn still could remember the bruises—little bouquets of violets—that blossomed on his arms through most of his childhood.

While she gave him his bath one morning, he told her how much he used to dread the occasion as a boy. How he and the rest of the children would form a line every Saturday night outside the lavatory, then take their turn

156

squatting two at a time in a great, gray zinc tub—its water always tepid, always hard and murky; how they cowered and waited for the ominous Mrs. Weiss and her brutal scrub brush. "Remove the skin, you remove the dirt," she would bray out, and the onslaught would begin. Valjohn was sure she spared no soap when his turn came. Sleeves rolled up to her armpits, she scoured his skin till it glistened. It was almost as if she were trying to find out which color he really was under that ambiguous veneer. A white boy trapped in black skin, or a black boy hiding in white?

"Which did she find?" asked Crescent.

"You t-t-tell me," he said, then wished he hadn't. It was not like him to angle for self-pity.

"I don't think she found either one. Just a boy. And he wasn't trapped and he wasn't hiding—here, catch!" she said, throwing him a towel to dry his face. Then she began washing his feet.

"Hey, watch it! I'm t-t-ticklish," he giggled as she plied the washcloth between his toes, scrubbed the bottoms.

"Remove the skin, you remove the dirt." She laughed and scrubbed even harder.

Later she told him how she too had spent a number of years as a ward of the state. She told him that the O'Learys had died in a fire; how she alone had managed to survive. He asked her questions. She remained vague. She was too young, she said; there were few memories.

To encourage him, she did tell of her own early speech problems, of how she'd finally learned to overcome them.

"Anything like your w-w-weight problems?" he asked skeptically. The day before, she'd confided that at one time she'd been tons overweight. She claimed to have been a nonstop eater as a teenager. He'd had trouble keeping a straight face. Beautiful women and their imagined woes. To hear her tell it, you'd have thought she was big as a cow.

"I'm serious," she exhorted, then went on to speak of Nancy Haas, her teacher, counselor and friend from Macomb. It was she who'd taken a special interest in her when she'd first come to the home, who'd given so much of her own time and effort—including driving Crescent eighty miles twice a week to a new speech-therapy clinic in Galesburg.

"She s-s-sounds great. Maybe you'd bet . . . better send me to her."

"Nancy's in Viet Nam now. She joined the Peace Corps last August."

"The P-P-Peace Corps's in Viet Nam? What are they d-d-doing—giving aid to poor, backward m-m-military advisers?"

Crescent smiled and shook her head. "Anyway, I think you're doing well enough here without her."

Valjohn thought so too.

A week and a day after the accident, he was allowed his first visitors.

"Poor *bubeleh!*" cried Rose Frank as she and Moe stood in the doorway, catching their first glimpse of him. "All those bandages—some *tsatske* you must have!"

Valjohn grinned, waving them in. "It's not as bad as it looks. Th-they . . . they're having a big sale on g-g-gauze this week."

Predictably, Moe was less sympathetic than his mother.

"Did I tell you about that golf? Now you believe me?"

"I know, a game for *sh* . . . *shleppers* and *shlemiels*."

"And *shlimazls* too. You know what a *shlimazl* is?"

"I can guess."

"A born loser. A *nebech*. A man who ruins a nice walk, chasing after a little white ball all day, then gets hit on the head for his efforts. A man who gets punished for punishing himself in the first place. Now, that's a *shlimazl!*"

"*Oy*, Moe, shut your *pisk*. He needs a visit from you? Is that what you learn all those hours in your laboratory—how to insult your friend?"

Moe handed her two sacks he was carrying, and she came forward to set them on his bed stand. Valjohn had to marvel at the resiliency in her walk. There was nothing stooped about her tiny, lively figure. Her eyes were sharp and bright; her hair that coarse, iron red that refused to gray even at the temples, let alone turn white.

"*Kichels* and strudel—I baked them special today for only you." She opened one of the sacks, handed him a small, puffed-up cookie sprinkled with sugar. "I think you need to catch up on some *noshing*. Look how skinny you are, how *milchedig*."

"*Milchedig?*" snorted Moe. "How can you tell?"

"I can tell is how I can tell."

"Never looked better to me."

"Hospital food!" she said, ignoring her froward son. "Who can eat such *chozzerai?* When you get out I'll fatten you up again. *Kreplach*. A feast! You can make up for the one you missed."

He'd forgotten about that dinner and reflected wistfully on it while he took a bite. He downed two more cookies, assured her that when he got out he'd ravenously devour all the *kreplach* she could set before him.

But seeing Moe again also reminded him of his problems in the outside world. He asked about the case.

Moe cleared his throat. "No *new* slayings."

"I guess that's something to be th-th-thankful for."

"I said *new*."

"What's that s-s-sup . . . supposed to mean?"

"They dragged a corpse out of the lake five days ago. Advanced state of decomposition. Probably been sloshing around for weeks . . ." Moe hesitated.

"And?"

"Okay, the remains . . . revealed certain wounds . . ."

"Yes?"

"Not here," said Moe, scratching his grizzled chin. "Let me just say they were of a highly suspicious nature. Of course, as I said, the remains were

158

in pretty bad shape—fish nibbling and everything—it's difficult to be certain."

"ID?"

"A Harold Bledsoe, thirty-six, lived alone in a flat on the West Side. Worked in a supermarket."

"Any make?"

"Next to zero. Ran a couple of red lights once."

Valjohn was silent for a moment. When he tried to pump Moe for more information, his old friend shook his head. Valjohn persisted.

"Enough is enough, Valjohnny. Your Dr. Tabor warned me before the visit not to talk shop." Then he added, changing the subject, "And anyway, I thought your speech was supposed to be suffering?"

"It's much better now," said Valjohn, sighing. "When I f-f-first came around, it was all I could do to grunt my name."

"Shall we test his Yiddish, *baba?*"

"*Oy,* Moe, leave him be *noch!*"

"*Chachem.* That's a tough one. If you can pronounce *chachem,* then we'll know you're recovered."

"Caa..." Valjohn started and stopped. He cleared his throat and started again.

"Khhakhhem." This time he succeeded in dropping the two "ch's" deep in his throat and gargled them out.

"Can he speak the *mama-loshen? Hoo-ha!*" said Rose, laughing. "That'll show you, Mr. *Chachem,* yourself."

"Dip your finger in honey and swab it around the inside of the bowl. The tobacco will stick to it and form a cake. That's the secret to cool flavor: You have to build a good cake."

Valjohn was sitting in a chair by the window in his room, listening to no less an authority on the finer points of breaking in a new pipe than Superintendent Estes Meriwether Gordon. Valjohn held in his hands a handsome Dublin briar, which the superintendent had presented him a few minutes earlier. He felt honored by the visit, though he had mixed feelings about the pipe.

Sensing his ex-professor and adviser was about to leave without offering any information concerning the case, Valjohn hurriedly asked him how things were going at headquarters. Gordon was silent for a moment, then began pacing.

He expounded on his own problems. He was concerned about mounting racial tensions in the black and Puerto Rican ghettos and told of issuing a new general order banning the firing of live rounds in riot situations. He dwelled briefly on the subject of juvenile gangs, then voiced his dismay with the Justice Department's apparent inability to cope with the work load. The courts were glutted, cases were backlogged for half a year or more—and the numbers kept growing. He was disgusted with the state's attorney's office and its continuing failure to meet prosecution deadlines. Defendants were set free on technicalities. Known felons were returned to society untried.

When Gordon finally had finished his ramblings, Valjohn asked about C-65-1834.

The superintendent stared absently out the window for a moment. "I must confess, John, I'm not really up on it. Sorry."

Valjohn considered pressing the matter, but nodded silently instead.

Gordon glanced at his watch and shook his head.

"Well, I have a meeting at three in the mayor's office with the ACLU's legal counsel, so I'd best be on my way."

Valjohn thanked him again for the pipe.

"Remember: Half full at first and keep your cake thin."

Valjohn was visited later in the day by Lieutenants Gillian and Harris. Valjohn questioned them at length, learned among other things that Bledsoe had been retrieved from the lake near the Davis Breakwater, that after some preliminary investigation, the word had come down to cool it, that Bledsoe was not to be regarded as a possible Reaper victim.

Alone again, Valjohn sat fondling his new briar. He rattled its black stem between his teeth and contemplated this new information.

Was Bledsoe No. 20 on the select list, or wasn't he? Was City Hall's paranoia spreading farther down into the investigation with another cover-up, or had Bledsoe's corpse been legitimately ruled out? For one thing, there was no make on him. Was that reason enough?

The Davis Breakwater.

He could imagine a red pin stuck beside the water's edge on the wall map in his office. The jetty had been named after Jefferson Davis, who in 1833, as a young lieutenant in the U.S. Army engineers, petitioned that the city's harbor be built at the mouth of the Chicago River. The city wisely chose his argument over that of Stephen A. Douglas, who wanted the harbor located fourteen miles to the south. For generations however, Davis's service—along with his memory—had been ignored by Chicago, and only recently had his name been assigned to the breakwater.

Valjohn repeated the name slowly under his breath, then outloud: "the Davis Breakwater." It rang a bell somewhere, but he couldn't make the connection. Finally he shook his head and gave up.

He had one last visitor in the evening: Grady McTague from the *Times*.

"I won't ask about your golf game, V.J., old scout," greeted the big Irishman, a wide grin on his face, his ever-present tam cocked down to his shaggy brow.

"There's a name for that de . . . device," responded Valjohn.

"Not bad for a cop—an invalid to boot. Apophasis. The art of insinuation through polite decline. Politicians thrive on it."

"What about rag reporters?"

McTague turned up his palms.

160

Valjohn never failed to marvel at the size of the man's hands, the thickness of his fingers. Could he really fit those huge cucumbers to typewriter keys?

"So how are things down at the old c-c-cop shop, Mac? Getting plenty of scratch?"

"You know better than that. But believe it or not, I didn't come here to bellyache—I actually wanted to see how you were coming along. I'm getting sentimental in my old age. A softening of the heart—or maybe it's my brain."

"I'm deeply moved, but I'm coming along just great, so why don't you unsoften your heart or brain or whatever, and clue me in on what's hap . . . happening in the outside world."

"Well, we're still in Viet Nam, Castro's still in Cuba and the Arabs still hate the Jews."

"What about the case?"

"Oh, I meant to tell you—it's been solved. The Reaper turned out to be Martin Bormann. He escaped Hitler's bunker after all. . . . Come on, V.J., you're asking me? A lowly rag reporter? Surely you jest."

"No jest. I'm being held here incommunicado."

"That's a switch. I think they call it poetic justice."

Valjohn shrugged, got up from a chair where he'd been resting by the window and hobbled over to his bed. He was stiff from sitting too long in one position.

"You don't move so hot."

"It's my golfer's back. I need a hot shower to loosen it up. All I get in this place are bed baths."

"Not the worst fate that can befall a young chap," said McTague with a wistful smile. "Did I ever tell you about my hospital experiences during the war?"

"Many times."

"The nurse on the hospital ship off Iwo?"

"Every other week."

"I mean when we got it on, I thought the Japs had sunk the ship! A direct hit! All hands lost at sea."

Valjohn yawned.

McTague stared at the floor for a moment in fond reminiscence, then added, "So how're those dear sweet angels of mercy treating you? Any wild baths?"

"My baths have all been strictly platonic."

McTague shook his head in commiseration. He removed his hat, ran a hand through his great shock of tawny hair, strode over to the bed and placed a foot on the bottom railing. He spoke again, this time in a low, earnest voice.

"I'll make a deal with you, V.J. I'll bring you up to date . . . if you tell me what's going on. What I mean is, why the cover-up?"

161

Friend or not, McTague leaning over him was an intimidating presence. Without a doubt, the man was miscast as a reporter; *he* was the one who should be the cop. Valjohn could see him clearly as a nineteenth-century street bull, or a southern sheriff, extracting confessions from some low-life felon. He wouldn't even need a rubber hose. Just the sight of those ham fists.

"Cover-up? What cover-up?"

"Come on, V.J., I've been around long enough to recognize the lid when I see it. The old bung—somebody's hammered it right up the pipe, only I can't for the life of me figure out why."

"You know the reasons as well as everybody else—"

McTague laughed, removed his foot from the railing and stepped back.

"Spare me the excerpts from Glad's PR manual, okay? Maybe some of my colleagues are buying, but not me."

Valjohn shrugged.

"Look, old scout, it's your neck, not mine. I know there was a lot of ballyhoo when you took this case over—the 'cubist cop' to the rescue and all that—but there've been six new murders since then, and so far you haven't come up with diddly-squat."

Valjohn was silent. McTague poured himself a glass of water.

"You need all the support you can get from the press. And I don't think all this tight-lipped bullshit is the way to win it."

"I'm a homicide detective, not a politician. I'm not trying to win a pop . . . popularity contest; I'm just trying to solve a few murders now and then. Twenty of them, to be exact."

"Twenty?"

"Make that n-n-nineteen."

McTague eyed him slowly. He became the southern sheriff again, put his foot on the railing, leaned forward.

"You're a public servant and I'll tell you right now, Chick Screed and at least two other good-old-boy reporters are after your black ass. I might add the APAD is hardly in your corner either."

"So what else is new?" An inveterate nonjoiner, Valjohn had been branded a Tom by the Association of Policemen of African Descent ages ago.

"I don't suppose you've had a chance to read his latest blurb in the *Trib.*"

"Whose?"

"Screed's. It seems he has serious doubts about your commitment to your job. Not to mention your credentials—his apophasis, not mine. He wants to know how you can possibly find the time to wander around a golf course when the city is being besieged by a murderous fiend whose number of victims already exceeds the combined total of Jack the Ripper's and the Boston Strangler's."

"How many is that?"

"Beats me, but he intimates that maybe with all your other activities, your exhibits and everything, you're more interested in advancing your career as an artist than as a cop."

"I haven't taken a dime yet for a painting."

"You're safe there, but don't think he isn't checking. Anyway, he thinks the guy who beaned you with the golf ball deserves a medal."

Nurse McGlocklin suddenly entered the room with her tray of evening medication. Visiting hours had been over for twenty minutes, she announced.

McTague informed her that he was a member of the press.

Nurse McGlocklin gave a snort and *informed him* that here in *her* hospital, he would abide by her rules—as would Valjohn, even if he was such a "darlin' young man" and important too—what with visits from the superintendent of police and flowers from the mayor. Then she clucked her tongue. "I'll give you no more than five minutes longer," and was gone with a rustle of her starched uniform.

"Flowers from the mayor?" McTague gave Valjohn a long, curious smile. There was a glint in McTague's eye.

Valjohn did his best to return the smile.

"Gordon's visit comes as no surprise, you being his former student and all—but flowers from the mayor . . . ?"

"So?"

"I mean, when did you get so chummy 'wid hizzonah'?"

"I've only met him once and th . . . that was on the St. Patrick's Day parade stand."

"Very interesting."

"So he knows every sparrow that falls. Jesus Christ, Mac! You're acting like it's an offering from the Mafia."

"Mmm," conceded McTague in a tone that indicated he'd conceded nothing.

Before McTague departed, Valjohn asked him if the Davis Breakwater meant anything to him.

"They pulled a stiff out of the lake near there just a few days ago."

"Right. Harold Bledsoe. Anything else?"

McTague thought for a moment, then shook his head. "Like what?"

"I don't know—that's why I'm asking. What do you know about Harold Bledsoe?"

"He's dead. What do you know about him? Wait! Is he No. 20?"

Valjohn hesitated, then decided to level with him. He repeated what Moe had said about the wounds.

McTague listened quietly. He was appreciative, promised not to move on the story until Valjohn had substantiated the facts himself.

"Now get the hell out of here and let me get some rest—or do I have to buzz Nurse McGlocklin to throw you out bodily?"

"I believe she could do it," he acknowledged, sauntering toward the door. "I'll say hello to Screed and the boys for you."

"Do that."

"Any messages?"

"Sure. Tell him I didn't say he had pigeon shit for brains."

"You learn fast, V.J."

"I know, apophasis. Rag reporters thrive on it."

McTague paused in the doorway, cocked his hat forward at a jaunty angle and replied, "Not to mention politicians and an occasional fallen sparrow." He gave a wry little smile, then broke into a grin. He waved and was gone.

"Never."

"Never?"

"Never."

"That doesn't sound very encouraging. Does that mean you never have or never will?"

"Never have, I suppose," replied Nurse O'Leary.

"Well, that's a little better," sighed Valjohn. He'd just asked her whether she ever dated any of her former patients. Dr. Tabor had advised him Monday that he probably would be released in another day or so. His headaches had cleared up for the most part and the soreness at his temple had started to itch—the bandages had been removed Friday. His speech had normalized to the point where he only stuttered when excited or upset.

He looked into her eyes—astonishingly a different shade of green each time he noticed them. Now they were viridescent, dark and brilliant beryl. Moments ago they'd been warm, lambent jade.

"After I leave here . . . will I ever s-s-see you again?"

She seemed surprised by the question. Finally she managed to smile and shrug her shoulders.

He felt deflated.

"If you don't say yes, I think I may have a relapse. Then you'll have to put up with me all over again."

She laughed, but her eyes were noncommittal . . . they had clouded, becoming as soft and light as serpentine.

Later in the afternoon Moe dropped by. Rose had not been up to making the trip, but she'd sent more *noshes* from her oven. This time Nurse O'Leary was on duty.

"A real *krassavitseh,*" observed Moe, staring after her when she left the room to return to her duties.

"*Krassavitseh?*"

"You know . . ." and Moe described her with a familiar curving sweep of both hands.

"And such eyes—I have never seen such eyes! If I were twenty years younger—all right, thirty years younger—look out! It's no wonder you're a little *farchadat* in the head. I would be so myself. Believe me, there were no nurses around like Miss O'Leary when I was in the hospital." He slapped his stiff knee disdainfully, as if somehow it were responsible. "You, Valjohnny, you're the detective. Always the right place, always the right time."

By the time Valjohn got around to mentioning McTague's visit, Moe was getting ready to leave.

He winced when he learned Valjohn had spoken of Bledsoe's wounds to the reporter. "You put your neck in a little noose there."

"Since when are we withholding that kind of information?"

"Since last week," said Moe, pulling at his goatee.

"Who issued the directive?"

"Howland spoke to me about it. But I'm sure the *kibosh* came down from Glad's office."

"Old Plastic Face himself. Why don't they just turn the investigation over to City Hall and forget about it?"

Moe smiled, shrugged.

"What about Bledsoe?"

"Have a free horror show on me. I talked the coroner into keeping him on ice for you. NKK."

Valjohn nodded. At least he'd still have the chance to judge for himself. "And what was your own learned opinion again?"

"Put it this way," smiled Moe. "If he's not a candidate for our little club, there are some very nasty fish swimming in Lake Michigan."

Before Moe left, Valjohn asked him about the Davis Breakwater, but Moe could come up with nothing.

That night Valjohn once more was struck with the eerie sensation of being at sea. He awoke from a troubling dream he couldn't remember, found the floor a deck again rolling beneath him. He could hear timbers creaking and groaning, the sound of canvas flapping in a stiff wind. He rang for the night nurse and she gave him a sleeping pill.

He was discharged from the hospital at one-thirty on Wednesday afternoon. Nurse O'Leary was nowhere to be seen. When he'd finished dressing —Moe had delivered his clothes in the morning—he walked out to the nurses' station and inquired about her. Nurse McGlocklin told him Crescent hadn't shown up for work all day. She also told him to go back to his room and wait for a wheelchair. No discharged patients were allowed to leave the hospital on their own two feet. Insurance regulations.

"And now, *mavournin*," said Nurse McGlocklin, pushing a wheelchair into his room, "lovelorn as I'm sure you are without your pretty colleen at your side, I've decided to escort you out myself. It's a rare privilege, indeed, and I hope you properly appreciate it."

Valjohn climbed into the chair, feeling a little ridiculous—he was quite capable of walking out on his own—but he assured Nurse McGlocklin that he not only appreciated it, he felt honored. She said she knew now he'd fully recovered, or he wouldn't be flaunting such blarney.

In the elevator Nurse McGlocklin spotted the plastic ID bracelet still encircling his left wrist and made a move to unfasten it. Valjohn pulled his arm away. He told her that he wanted to keep it as a memento.

"More blarney," she protested and reached for his arm again.

He shook his head.

"You're too late. I've already signed out. My regulations now, Mrs. McGlocklin."

She sighed, her tyranny of tidiness clearly at an end. The door opened. She contented herself to scold him as she rolled him out through the first-floor lobby.

Parting at a side-street exit, he handed her a note for Crescent that he'd hastily written in his room while waiting for the wheelchair. He also planted a kiss on her florid cheek.

"You take care of yourself now, Lieutenant—it's a wicked city out there," she called after him. Climbing into a cab, he grinned and waved. "Don't let the bad ones do you in, you devil of a darlin' man . . . or the good ones either!"

10

That night in his apartment Valjohn warmed a can of beefstock soup, downed a few spoonfuls and set it aside. He had no appetite.

Lovelorn. That's what Nurse McGlocklin had called him. In jest? Or was he that transparent? He opened a can of beer.

Now, what about this Nurse O'Leary? Why hadn't she been there to see him off? Granted, he was hurt—crushed, as a matter of fact. Puzzled too, though . . . yes, definitely puzzled. Even if she didn't care a lick for him, she still should have been there. A matter of common courtesy. What the hell—she was his continuity nurse, wasn't she? That meant from beginning to end; hello and good-bye. He felt deprived of his rights as a patient.

He dumped the soup in the sink, rinsed out the bowl, sat down on a kitchen counter stool and had another swig of beer.

His whole attitude was too defeatist. It simply wasn't like her not to be there. There had to be some other explanation, some other reason that made it impossible for her to show up. Poor kid, maybe she was sick or even injured. He was so damn quick to be hurt himself, he hadn't even considered that possibility.

He chugged the last of his beer, crushed the soft aluminum can in his hand and scored two points in the corner wastebasket; got up from the stool and roamed through the apartment searching for the phone book.

He found it in the bathroom on top of the toilet. He carried it into his study and sat down by the phone. Under Windhaven General Hospital, he located School of Nursing.

He hesitated before picking up the phone. Well? he asked himself. He downed his beer and began dialing.

He reached the receptionist at the residence hall. She buzzed Nurse O'Leary's room. There was no answer. She asked if he wanted to leave a message. He said no and hung up.

She wasn't home sick in bed; he could rule that one out. Still, something could have happened to her. A car wreck or a fall. She said she liked to go for long walks . . . a girl that attractive alone in this city—he shuddered. It was nine o'clock. He'd call again at ten.

At ten there still was no answer. None at ten-thirty either. He called at eleven and then every fifteen minutes after that. A few minutes before midnight he got an answer.

"Hello, Crescent?"

"No, I'm Debbie, her roommate. She isn't here now. May I take a message?"

"When do you expect her?"

"I don't know. I just got in myself. I haven't seen her all day. May I ask who's calling?"

"Is she usually out this late?" Always the interrogator.

"Not on weekdays. Say, who is this, anyway?"

He started to give his name, then stopped.

"Just a . . . a friend," he finally answered and hung up.

He paced through the apartment. He avoided his studio. He did not want to face his artwork yet. In the living room he picked through a pile of magazines on the floor, looking for something to read. Nothing interested him. He went back into the kitchen, opened the refrigerator, then closed it again, remembering he wasn't hungry. He stood for several minutes, drumming on a counter top with his fingers.

He was being ridiculous and he knew it. She was more than likely out on a date. Just because she'd never mentioned a boy friend didn't mean there wasn't any. A girl like her? She probably had dozens of them. More probably still, just one very special one. In any case, he could rest assured she was being well taken care of. . . . Thoughts of her in the back seat of a car with some studly young intern forced their way into his mind. Her golden hair: He saw it again—let down, long and shimmering—as it was that first time he'd laid eyes on it, awakening from the accident . . . cascading down her shoulders, blazing in sunlight. . . . He hadn't been sure at that moment whether she was real or some kind of stunning vision, a fantasy of his own bruised mind. Now, at least, he knew she was real, but somehow that had made her no less alluring. He couldn't get her out of his mind, no matter how he tried.

There were times she reminded him of a Renaissance Madonna, all purity and light; then again, one of Botticelli's pagan lovelies—not so much Venus on the half shell as Primavera or Flora or even the sword-wielding Judith, with the head of Holofernes firmly in her grasp. More often than not, though, she was pure Gustav Klimt, her beauty highly idealized, ethereal—an anemic angel, her skin so wan it seemed to glow —yet transcending all this spirituality, a hint of something quite different, something strange, hauntingly erotic . . . almost barbaric.

His thoughts returned to the studly intern and he grew angry with himself. The intensity of his jealousy—it was ridiculous! Coming on like a cuckold over his ex-nurse. He kicked off his shoes and went to bed.

Got up and took a shower. Went back to bed.

The next day he replunged into the thick of things at headquarters. After catching up on some of the routine paperwork that had accumulated on his desk, he made a trip to the city morgue.

"Bledsoe, Harold," he told the attendant, flashing his badge and ID. The attendant ran a finger down his desk chart.

"D-36." He got up from his chair, led Valjohn through the double, swinging metal doors to the lockers. From a wall resembling a huge stain-less-steel filing cabinet, he located D-36, grabbed the drawer's dull brass handle and rolled out Bledsoe's refrigerated remains.

"You want him on the table?"

Valjohn looked down at the white-sheeted lump lying on the pallet of the drawer. He nodded yes.

The attendant retrieved a litter from across the room, expertly slid the remains onto it and wheeled it through a short passageway that led to the inner chamber of the examining room.

The room was high-ceilinged, brightly lit, the walls and floor tiled in glaucous green ceramic.

The attendant lowered the autopsy table to facilitate sliding the body off the litter. He raised the table again with a pneumatic foot pump, then switched on a bright cluster of overhead lights and reached forward to remove the sheet.

Valjohn set his jaw and prepared himself. The formula was simple: cosmic objectivity. What he was about to see was nothing more than the rearrangement of molecules and atoms transforming themselves into dif-ferent compositions.

The sheet proved to be only an outer shroud. Under it Bledsoe's remains were contained in a black, rubber body bag. The attendant unzipped the bag.

Cosmic objectivity . . .

"He ain't no matinee idol," said the attendant, folding the sides of the bag down out of the way. "Might as well leave him in the bag. He's liable to come apart if we shift him around on the table."

Visibly shaken, grimacing, Valjohn pumped his head. By all means leave him in the bag.

"You want a mask?" There was a note of disdain in the attendant's voice.

"He is a . . . a bit r-r-ripe." His voice had become a hoarse whisper. The stench emitted from the bag was overpowering—an eye-watering blend of formaldehyde and rank putrescence.

"Seen 'em worse," snuffed the attendant, allowing him nothing. "So you want a mask or not?"

"Okay . . . yes, yes," he continued to whisper. If he spoke out loud, he was sure he'd jettison the entire contents of his stomach.

While the attendant walked over to a large metal cabinet in a corner of the room, Valjohn stepped back, wiped the tears from his eyes, studied the deceased from a distance.

The flesh corrupt.

He was reminded of the *Picture of Dorian Gray*—not the book, but the painting, the one done by Chicago's own master of the macabre, Ivan Le Lorraine Albright. He'd seen it in a Hollywood version of Wilde's classic back in the late forties. The film had been shot in black and white; Albright's painting, however, was diabolically flashed across the screen in Technicolor, its ghastly allegory of Victorian sin and physical decay revolting cinema audiences everywhere. Valjohn remembered his own reaction as a boy of ten, how he'd hit his head trying to duck behind the seat in front of him. Now there was no seat to duck behind.

And if, as in the case of Dorian Gray, sin and high living were responsible for reducing the body to a gangrenous mass of offal, then Harold Bledsoe must have rivaled Lucifer for the throne of evil. He was that hideous: waterlogged, wave-battered, cankered, bloated, shriveled, flyblown, rotten. . . .

"Yes, sir," continued the attendant, returning with the mask, "seen 'em a lot worse, I'll tell you." He handed the mask to Valjohn, who hastily slipped it on, the molded contours of the cotton filter covering his nose and mouth.

"You should see 'em after a few weeks in the river. Meat's so soft you can blow it off the bone."

Valjohn felt his stomach churn. The attendant opened a drawer in one of the two small, portable cabinets that stood by the table and brought out a pair of surgical gloves.

Valjohn watched him move to the other side of the table, noting a slight swagger in his walk. A photo nameplate pinned to his smock read: Elton Meeker. He was like an artist at his own private show, wheeling out his work, unveiling it, standing back to relish the reaction of his audience. Even now he probably was gloating over every ripple of nausea Valjohn felt. And Bledsoe . . . he was nothing more than another Meeker masterpiece—not to compare, of course, with his superlative river period, but a masterpiece nonetheless.

The gloves snapped tightly in place, Valjohn made a determined effort to gain at least a semblance of professional poise. The mask helped.

170

Fifteen minutes later he stepped back, wiping the perspiration from his forehead, satisfied. For one last philosophical moment he pondered the Reaper's work: If there was a fate worse than death, he'd like to know what it was. No, take that back. He wouldn't even like to guess.

He pulled off his gloves. He flung them down on the table and strode from the room.

Back in his office he picked up the phone and called McTague.

His thoughts returned to Nurse O'Leary late in the afternoon. He gave her a call at the hospital. She had not shown up for work again today. He called the residence hall. Her room didn't answer. He started worrying all over again. This time he wasn't thinking about late dates and boy friends.

He called her in the evening from his apartment, recognized the voice of her roommate.

"Is Crescent there?"

"No, she isn't. Are you the guy who called last night?"

Valjohn told her he was.

"Hi, this is Debbie again," she reintroduced herself, then proceeded to tell him that Crescent had gone home to attend a funeral in Macomb, that she wouldn't be returning until Monday.

Despite the underlying note of tragedy, Valjohn felt a surge of relief. She hadn't just ditched him. There had been a reason. And she was all right, safe and sound and not stretched out on some slab with the likes of Elton Meeker tending to her chilled remains.

"Would you care to leave a message?"

"Er . . . no, that's all right."

"May I ask who's calling?"

"Uh . . . John—Valjohn, that is." He hadn't intended leaving his name. "I'm not really . . . uh . . . I was a p-p-patient of hers at the hospital."

"Oh, the cute detective! She told me all about you. Playing any more golf these days?"

Friday morning Valjohn was summoned to Superintendent Gordon's office. Having seen the morning papers, he had more than a rough idea what was brewing. Bledsoe was smeared all over the headlines: The Reaper had struck again. Screed in the *Trib* made it sound as though the victim had been murdered just to celebrate Valjohn's return!

Entering the smoke-filled chamber, he nodded to Gordon, who sat solemnly behind his desk, then noticed Hans Glad sitting off in a corner. The PR director's usually doughy face flushed with anger:

"Why, Lieutenant? That's what I want to know. Why did you blatantly disobey a directive from your superiors and . . . and take it upon yourself to release this Bledsoe story?"

Valjohn took a few moments to gather himself.

171

"You know damn good and well the . . . the delicate ramifications attached to this case."

Gordon leaned back in his chair, chewing absently on a pipe, his gaze fixed on a section of carpet halfway between the wastebasket and Glad's shiny alligator shoes.

"First of all, I didn't blatantly disobey a d-d-directive," began Valjohn slowly. "Nobody ordered me not to examine Bledsoe. I did-did-didn't find any note to that effect on my desk either."

"Nothing was issued in writing."

"Secondly, I t-t-took it upon myself, as you put it, because I just ha-happen to be heading this investigation—that is, I still th-think I am. I do believe that entitles me to show . . . to show more than a passing interest in the R-r-reaper's victims."

"Reaper's victims! That's just the point. Says who? It doesn't give you the right to go around this city claiming every damn cast-off corpse that turns up! It doesn't give you the right to inflame the press and upset the public—not to mention certain other factions—"

"Oh, go ahead, mention him," said Valjohn, smiling.

Glad shot a quick glance at Gordon. The superintendent still was staring at the carpet.

"As I was saying," Glad went on, trying to control his voice, "it doesn't give you the right to go off half-cocked—with wild-ass conjecture."

"Wild-ass conjecture?"

"You heard me. The coroner's already gone on record. Bledsoe's body was too decomposed to determine the cause of death accurately. And too decomposed to assess any relevant disfigurement."

"Did you examine him?"

"Certainly not."

"Well, I did." Valjohn still could see Harold Bledsoe laid out before him . . . the arms and legs shriveled; the torso, bloated and lumpy. The features of the face were swollen, run together, almost like a visage smeared against a windowpane—except for the mouth, a large, shredded hole that exposed the man's teeth—exceptionally white—all the way back to his molars.

"For one thing, his lips were chewed away."

"By fish!"

"Possibly. So were his genitals. . . . And what about his heart?" There seemed to be evidence of myocardial rupture even in the organ's admittedly decomposed state.

"Fish, Lieutenant. The coroner's report specifies evidence of feeding fish."

Valjohn couldn't deny that. He'd seen the signs. He'd also seen other signs, such as a number of what might have once been long, deep lacerations running across the lower back and buttocks. The wounds now were indistinct, had blended in with the general disintegration of the surrounding tissue. Their outline remained, however, and the overall pattern looked all too familiar.

"There were broken ribs. A broken arm too."

"So? Nobody's claiming the man died in his sleep. So he got mangled. People get mangled all the time."

Valjohn shook his head. "The point I'm trying to make is that if you take all these wounds and mutilations—which g-g-granted are highly contestable by themselves—if you take them all and add them up together, you get a total picture, a pattern that becomes a whole lot less contestable. In fact, in my opinion, it becomes d-d-damn right convincing."

Glad scoffed, then added, "What about Bledsoe's profile? He's clean. Just an average, law-abiding citizen."

"I know," Valjohn said quietly. "That bothers me."

"Well, I'm glad to hear something bothers you, Lieutenant."

Valjohn was silent for a moment. He was in good spirits today and decided not to back off.

"I'll tell you something else that bothers me: It's how you people expect this case to be solved by pretending it doesn't exist. That is, if you even want it solved; I'm not too sure anymore."

It was Glad's turn to be silent.

"You're not going to get rid of it by just wishing it away. You can get rid of me, though. Because I'll tell you, right here and now, I don't want to be a part of any halfhearted dummy-up investigation."

Glad started to speak, but Valjohn held him off with a raised hand.

"Let me finish, please." There was no stuttering now. *The cute detective* —that's what she'd called him. And she'd told her roommate about him, too. "If my work or this position is judged unsatisfactory, then I suggest you replace me. The sooner the better." He directed this last sentiment to Gordon.

Glad started to speak again. This time it was the superintendent who cut him off.

"Simmer down, John," said Gordon, looking up with a long, weary sigh. "Nobody wants you replaced."

Glad managed to stifle a laugh, which Gordon ignored.

"Hans, thank you for your attentions in this matter. I think it's fairly obvious, though, we have a misunderstanding here. John didn't receive the directive. An oversight, but hardly his fault. Whether he agrees or disagrees with it in principle is neither here nor there at this juncture in time. The Bledsoe thing is out. So much spilled milk. I think any further discussion is rather counterproductive."

Glad stared straight ahead, pouting silently.

"I want to thank you too, John, for your frankness. I do hope, however, in the future you will try to be more sensitive to all the issues at stake here."

The meeting ended on a note of congeniality. Gordon was pleased to see Valjohn up and at it again. In good voice too.

On the way out of the office Valjohn asked Glad about his golf game. He actually felt a little sorry for the man; after all, it was he who had to face the wrath of City Hall.

"I haven't much time for golf these days, Lieutenant," he replied, his face still puffed and petulant as a Rubens cherub. "Neither, I would hopefully presume, do you."

"You're back!"
"Yes?"
"I mean, it's good to hear your voice again."
"John?"
"First guess. Wow! I'm flattered."
"My roommate said you'd called last week. I'm sorry I wasn't able to say good-bye at the hospital—I got your note. It . . . it was very sweet."
"I was sorry to hear about your loss. A friend?"
"Yes. Nancy Haas. I think I told you about her. She was one of the teachers and counselors at the home."
"Wasn't she the one in Viet Nam? The Peace Corps?"
"Yes."
"I remember. How . . . how did it happen?"
"She was hit in an air attack. Napalm."
"An air attack?" Valjohn was surprised to hear the Viet Cong had an air force.
"One of ours. They bombed the wrong sector. Six American soldiers and a number of villagers were also killed."
God, thought Valjohn, everything about that war was a mess. He steered the conversation away from the tragedy, talked to her instead about how hard it was to return to the drudgery of his job after his little vacation in the hospital.
"I meant what I said in the note."
She was silent.
"Anyway, I was hoping we could see each other again—maybe have dinner together some evening?"
More silence.
"Hello, are you still there?"
"Yes . . . sorry . . ."
"Sorry you're still there, or sorry you can't have dinner with me?"
No answer.
"Or both?"
"Don't be silly."
"Well?"
"I don't know—really. I don't think it would work out."
"What's to work out? You know how to eat. I know how to eat. I don't see how we can miss."
He detected a faint laugh at the other end of the line, felt encouraged.
"Just a simple dinner. I promise to brighten your evening. It'll do you good, get your mind off funerals and wars."
"That would be nice."

"Of course it would. Tomorrow night."

"If you say so."

"I say so. Patient's orders."

It came to him the next day while he was about to have lunch at Mr. Dick's. He was making his way through the crowded restaurant to join some old friends he'd worked with during his first year on the Force when he spotted Milton Stephansky sitting at a nearby table. The squat, bald-headed sergeant's rasping voice cut through the drone of surrounding conversations.

That's where he'd heard of the Davis Breakwater! It was Stephansky's phone call—the one he'd received while he was out on the golf course being steamrollered by Glad and company. And what had the sergeant said? . . . Something about a fisherman being shot. And they'd pulled his body out of the lake the same day the bodies of Jimmy Lee Cook, Skip Varner and Jeffrey Dix, Jr., had been discovered. Then two weeks later, in washes Harold Bledsoe. . . . Valjohn spun around in midstride and walked out of the restaurant.

The fisherman's name was Nels Torgelson. A seventy-four-year-old retired brakeman with the Rock Island Railroad. Cause of death: a gunshot wound to the head; .45 caliber. Time of death affixed between 6:00 P.M. and midnight on June 6. The two fishermen had discovered the body wedged against the pilings of the breakwater on the morning of June 7. There were no other significant wounds, no signs of a struggle. Unlike Bledsoe's body, Torgelson's had been found in relatively good condition, having been immersed only for several hours.

The follow-up reports on Torgelson were not very encouraging. He was a widower, had a daughter living in Alton. For the past six years he'd roomed alone in the old Woods Hotel. The main scope of his activities seemed to be fishing in the lake and playing euchre every evening with a bunch of his cronies at the Woods.

Valjohn theorized that if Torgelson were connected to the case, more than likely it was in the role of innocent bystander. Perhaps he'd stumbled onto Bledsoe's murder and been snuffed as a potential witness. Ernly Chard came to mind. Of course, the bullet in the head didn't figure, but the overall coincidence of time and place was too enticing to be ignored.

He called Gillian to his office and assigned him to check out Torgelson all over again, starting with a visit to the daughter in Alton.

"What are you doing still wearing that?"

Valjohn had just pulled back a coat sleeve revealing to Crescent his hospital ID bracelet. They were sitting at an intimate, dimly lit table for two, upstairs at Big Bill the Builder's Steak House on Grand Avenue.

"I've been waiting for my continuity nurse to discharge me properly.

Nurse McGlocklin almost broke my arm when I refused to let her remove it."

Valjohn handed Crescent his steak knife and proffered his banded wrist. She grinned and shook her head. "You're crazy. Did you know that?"

"Probably true but irrelevant. Do your duty."

"What if I slip and cut your wrist?"

"I'll bleed all over you."

She hesitated.

"You don't want me to go through life wearing this thing, do you? Besides, it's already starting to turn my arm green."

"All right—but you have to promise to hold very still."

"I promise."

She took his wrist in her left hand, paused for a moment, then slipped the knife blade underneath the band and drew it back, severing the plastic loop with ease.

"A masterful incision," he observed, rubbing his naked wrist gingerly. "What are you doing in nursing? You should be a surgeon."

She laughed, handed over his steak knife and the severed bracelet. He took the knife but refused the bracelet.

"No, no, that's yours. A keepsake. Consider it a small token of my deep appreciation for your . . . your many hours of noble service and always remember that . . . that diamonds are f-f-forever, but plastic is . . . is . . . uh . . ." He'd hit a snag, wanted to say something terribly clever. Nothing came.

"But plastic is easily disposed of," she said and laughed, gave the bracelet a twirl, dropped it into her purse and announced the arrival of their steaks.

"That was quite a cut of meat you put away, young lady. I wasn't sure you could manage it." Valjohn nodded toward her empty plate after they'd finished.

"You didn't do badly yourself."

"I skipped lunch. What's your excuse?"

She thought for a moment. "How about an exhausting operation between the shrimp cocktail and the main course?"

"Touché," he said with a grin.

"It really was marvelous. Thank you. They don't serve anything like that at the Windy Cafe."

When the waiter returned after clearing the table, Valjohn listened amazed as she ordered a slice of cherry cheesecake for dessert.

"No guilts about your waistline?" he chided.

"Maybe tomorrow. Tonight I'm too busy enjoying myself."

On the way out, Valjohn took special notice of that waistline. He was not alone. She wore a very simple, conservative summer dress, azure-blue with a high, white-collared bodice. Nevertheless, heads turned, even of other women.

Most of the men also glanced at Valjohn. He was not immune to their

176

stares, and found himself walking a little more erect, his brow tilted slightly back past perpendicular. As they stepped outside, the black doorman gave him a wink.

He took her for an after-dinner drink at the Top of the Rock, high above the city in the Prudential Building. They were lucky and found a cozy table by a window with a sweeping southern view. After ordering drinks they both sat staring out the window. Directly below was Grant Park, its broad, dark rectangles outlined by intersecting rows of streetlights, while Buckingham Fountain pulsed tons of rainbow-colored water high into the air. The Art Institute glowed faintly on the park's perimeter, while at the other end they could see the lights of the Field Museum, the Shedd Aquarium, Soldier Field, McCormick Place, Meigs Field. . . . A plane was taking off; they watched its flashing beacon rise and separate from the distant string of lights along the South Shore.

"So how does a small-town country girl like living in all this?" He gestured to the scene below.

"Oh, it's okay," replied Crescent thoughtfully. "I didn't care much for it at first. It sort of frightened me. I guess I've grown used to it, though."

"Not always an easy thing to do," said Valjohn, still staring out the window. "I mean, there's a lot out there that *is* pretty frightening. Believe me, I'm in a position to know."

"Do you . . . see many awful things in your work?" she asked softly.

"Enough," he said, shaking his head slowly, "enough to know things do go bump in the night." He suddenly became aware that she'd placed her hand over his, resting on the table, that she was gently stroking his fingers. He dared not breathe lest she take it away.

The waitress returned with their drinks.

"Let's make a toast," said Valjohn when they were alone again. Crescent agreed, lifted her glass.

"Here's to Carl Freetlock. . . ."

"To Carl Freetlock?"

"To Carl Freetlock and his unerring aim on the golf course—without which this entire evening would never have been possible." He took a drink of his Harvey's Bristol Cream and let it roll around his tongue, savoring it.

"To Carl Freetlock," she said and laughed, pressed her own glass to her lips, sipped slowly, never lowering her eyes from his gaze.

"Umm!" she exclaimed. "I like it!"

"What?" he mumbled.

"The drink. It's quite good. What did you call it?"

"I'm glad you like it," he echoed.

"What did you call it?"

"Umm? . . . Oh, Benedictine. A Benedictine frappé." Her eyes were like dancing emeralds now, trapping the candlelight that flickered between them.

"Before I forget," she said, looking away, breaking his trance, "I brought you something." She rummaged for a moment through her purse, then handed him his pipe. "You left it behind in the room."

"Gee, thanks, I've really been lost without it. Actually, if I want to keep my job, I'd better learn to smoke it."

"I didn't know detectives had to smoke pipes."

"Only this detective." He shook his head, put the pipe away in his coat pocket.

While they finished their drinks, she asked questions about his work. It was the first time she'd ever shown much interest. Some doctors at the hospital had been filling her in on his celebrated accomplishments as an artist. Just what was a "cubist cop," she wanted to know.

"It's a long story," he said.

"I love long stories."

Valjohn had been interested in art since his teens, but it wasn't until after he'd joined the Force that he began doing his own collages. He had taken a number of art appreciation courses at the University of Indiana, and later during grad school at Berkeley he'd even tried his hand at some sketching and painting—mainly through the coaxing of a girl friend who was an art major. The results had been mediocre. Then one day a few years back while working on a case, sorting through all the various pieces of evidence spread out before him, he'd gotten the idea of organizing them into a design. He'd fooled around with the idea for a couple of days, and a week later he'd created his first collage—an assemblage of debris, throwaway scraps of material evidence from several cases mounted on a backing of three-sixteenth-inch Masonite. He'd been pleased with the outcome. Since that time he'd constructed a collage of every significant or interesting case he'd worked on, a sort of visual log or artist's journal of his investigative career.

He had no grand ambitions, harbored no illusions of becoming another Miró or Picasso. He saw himself clearly as a dilettante, a weekend painter who pursued art as a means of personal amusement and relaxation, nothing more. Therefore it came as no small surprise to him when a little over a year ago, his modest pastime suddenly catapulted him into the limelight. Overnight he became a celebrity, the CCPD's own "artist in residence," his collages the rage of at least the Chicago art world.

The whole bizarre turn of events had been brought about by his performance on the case C-65-2117—Chicago's mad bomber—though two earlier cases had helped set the stage. The first had been Valjohn's successful solution of an assault case involving a "who's who"—one Wendel Gilbert, the weatherman for a local TV station, who had been accosted and badly beaten by two strangers on his way home one night after the late news wrap-up. Valjohn felt his performance in the case had been fairly routine, but because Gilbert was a TV personality the media build-up had been excessive. Valjohn earned considerable ink as a shining example of the city's "promising new breed of cop"—a term that did not particularly endear him to some of his older fellow officers. He also earned his gold badge.

Less than a month later, Valjohn had cracked what turned out to be the largest car theft ring ever uncovered in the state, a sprawling syndicate operation that trafficked mainly in Corvettes, by identifying the chalky clay substance caked in the grooves of the brake pedal pads of two different cannibalized vehicles. The substance proved to have an exceptionally high concentration of $CaCO_3$, calcium carbonate, a surface marl found only in one area of the city where there were a large number of material service excavations. A two-day reconnoitering of the suburb produced a junkyard and an abandoned farm whose two large barns had both been fitted with new, heavily padlocked sliding doors.

Round the clock surveillance disclosed enough incriminating activity for a search warrant. The barns were entered and a dismantling operation was found that rivaled the industrial efficiency of a GM plant. Once again Valjohn had been singled out for publicity.

But the most extraordinary coup had come a year later. For a period of thirteen months the city had been disrupted by a number of bombings— nothing to do with the usual crime syndicate squabblings, but apparently the work of a single deranged individual who seemed bent upon reducing everyone and everything related to the insurance industry to a pile of smoldering rubble. Half a dozen agencies had been bombed as well as several private residences. Salesmen, adjusters, upper echelon execs found their cars exploding in parking lots. A thirty-five-foot pleasure craft used for entertaining business associates of one of the nation's largest mutual firms sank to the bottom of the marina, a gaping three-foot hole blown in its hull.

Miraculously, in all the explosions only three people had been killed, though three more had been seriously injured including a bystander who'd lost a leg.

In late January Valjohn, assisting at the investigation of a bombed parked car in the 600 block of northern Dearborn, had noticed someone in the crowd of onlookers he thought he recognized. The man was wearing a light drab Ulster and maroon earmuffs. Valjohn stared at him for a moment but couldn't place him, returned his attention to the auto's twisted wreckage. When Valjohn again looked up and into the crowd, he spotted the man in the maroon earmuffs lingering on the sidewalk across the street, chatting with other spectators. The man was tall and thin with a round knob of a nose that didn't quite go with the rest of his narrow face. Though it was a young face, thinning, curly hair starting to gray at the temples suggested a man closer to forty than thirty. The more Valjohn studied him the more convinced he became that at least he'd seen him before. But where? And when? Usually he was very good with names and faces. Not this time. He was almost ready to go over and introduce himself, just to

179

satisfy his curiosity, when the man turned and walked away. Valjohn hesitated for a moment, then on an impulse followed him. He tailed him for a few blocks until the man climbed into a parked '59 Chevy station wagon and drove off, but not before Valjohn had memorized his license number.

He had not gotten around to checking with Springfield until the following day. The station wagon belonged to one Michael Murphy, 1011 West Olympic Road, Palatine. The name didn't ring a bell, and he'd never even been in Palatine. As a matter of routine, he ran the name through "Polifax" for a possible "make." When it came out clean he let the matter drop. He must have been mistaken. More than likely Murphy had reminded him of someone else.

A week and a half later he'd found there was no mistake. The realization came to him one evening in the quiet solitude of his study. He'd been writing up a progress report on the bombing investigation. His presentation was clear, accurate and concise. It also led nowhere. He was about to call it a day and turn in early, when his attention wandered across the room and settled on his collage of the mad-bomber case. The most interesting feature of this work was its overall shape. All his others had been mounted on square or rectangular backings. This one was circular, a four-foot diameter cut from one-half-inch plywood. Radiating from its center, which was still bare, was a conglomeration of data—police reports, photographs, newspaper clippings—all attesting to the bomber's busy schedule over the past year. Also scattered about the layout was testimony of a more direct nature: pieces of windshield glass and a chunk of torn metal that had once been part of a starter housing. The chunk had been blown through the dash of a Chrysler Imperial with the velocity of a high-powered rifle slug. Dangling near the top of the board was the remnant of a victim's shoe— the scorched tongue and part of a shredded heel.

He had felt his gaze drifting downward to a sector a little right of center near the bottom. At first he thought it was something in the design, some basic imbalance in the various shapes within the composition that caused him to focus there. Try as he might, however, he could not detect the source of the imbalance. Nevertheless, whenever he took his eyes from the composition and then returned them, they were drawn down as if by gravity to this same area in the lower right quadrant.

The area was dominated by a large newsphoto of the aftermath of a bombing that had taken place eleven months earlier in Lincoln Park. A vice-president of Motorman's Life and Casualty had been blasted through the roof of his Coup de Ville into a nearby duck pond. He was the bomber's first fatality. Included in the photo was the wreckage of the car, the pond and an embankment in between where a small group of onlookers stood. A dotted line arching over the embankment from the car and ending in the pond with an "x" diagramed the flight of the body like a golf shot in the sports section. Valjohn had cut off the top portion of the picture to fit it in between his own sketch of the scene and a Xeroxed copy of the victim's autopsy report. Snipping away the sky and the tops of trees, his scissors had swung an arc to include the flight of the body and the outlined heads of the spectators.

Suddenly Valjohn had leaped out of his chair and dropped to his knees in front of the picture. There, near the center of the crowd of spectators on the highest point of ground, wearing his maroon earmuffs against a chilling lakeshore breeze and a smile on his face that looked positively exultant, stood Michael Murphy. Five minutes later Valjohn was on his way to headquarters. He didn't come home for two days.

Further investigation of Murphy had turned up the following: He'd spent part of an eight-year hitch in the Navy in UDT (underwater demolitions); he'd also had a bitter experience involving a number of insurance firms. It had started when his automobile coverage had been dropped after he'd received six moving violations in a period of three years. After that he was turned down as a bad risk by several other companies—all having free access to his driving record. Two more gave him the run-around, agreed to cover him but ended up jacking the rate so high he couldn't afford it. In the interim, driving without coverage, he had an accident, was adjudged to be the cause of a four car pile-up on an expressway and was sued into bankruptcy. Subsequently he suffered a nervous breakdown and was hospitalized for three months. During that time he lost his job, his home and his wife (who took their two small children with her). While he was in the hospital he sent a letter—rambling but not totally incoherent —to the Secretary of State at Springfield, denouncing the conspiracy of the insurance industry, which was plotting to destroy him. He promised "to even the score." The letter had been filed away and forgotten.

On the weight of Valjohn's evidence Murphy was placed under twenty-four-hour surveillance. Eight days later he was caught red-handed wiring explosives behind a toilet in an executive rest room of the Prudential Building.

When the press learned the unusual manner in which Valjohn had discovered Murphy's identity they played it for all it was worth. Every *cause célèbre* had to have its hero, and Valjohn was tailor-made for the part. Naturally, Murphy still received star billing: He was, of course, the mad bomber. For once, however, the American criminal had to share the spotlight with his captor, Lieutenant John Valjohn, artist and police officer— a Renaissance man who used his creative gifts to battle crime in the city, who solved his cases, palette in hand, sighting down a raised thumb. Valjohn was terrific copy. Overnight he became "the cubist cop," "Picasso of the Police Department"—in his "blue period," no less. The epithets continued to fly: "Homer of Homicide," "the surrealistic sleuth," "the dabbling detective," "Grandma Moses of M Squad," "the gumshoe Gainsborough"—every reporter, columnist and newcaster in the city seeming to take his turn in the alliterative name-coining.

Even *Time* magazine had run a two-column piece on the case complete with a picture of "the futurist fuzz" standing in front of his artwork like an aspiring master. It was also *Time* that originated the phrase "cop art" and half-seriously proclaimed him a new pretender to modern art's trendy and fickle throne.

Valjohn had made several guest appearances on TV talk shows, including "Kup's Corner" and "Cromie's Circle," where he discussed law and order and the harmony of composition in the company of such personages as Thomas Hart Benton, Vincent Price, John Wayne and Jack Webb. On St. Patrick's Day, Valjohn was invited to don a green derby and parade down Michigan Avenue, then join the mayor and a select group of dignitaries on a stand in Soldier Field.

Valjohn viewed all this with healthy skepticism. He knew that tailing Murphy to his car and later recognizing him in a photograph was something considerably less than "the cool ratiocinations of a twentieth-century supersleuth"—as one paper had so effusively put it. Flattery that he did accept with fewer reservations, however, was the attention showered on his collages. Suddenly they were in great demand, almost universally celebrated for their "bold, imaginative design," their "rich provocative texture"—not to mention the sensational authenticity of their subject matter. Like closet children, he brought them out of his studio, gratefully allowed them to bask in the sunlight of popular praise. Though he refused to sell them—he felt it unethical—he did offer them for exhibition. And they were readily snatched up, displayed across the country in a tour not only of museums and galleries, but of a number of bank and corporation lobbies, municipal buildings, shopping malls, American Legion and V.F.W. halls as well.

"Guess I'm not doing so well on this one, though," said Valjohn and he lapsed into a brief lament over the way things were going with his current investigation.

"You can't be expected to solve all your cases. Doctors don't save all their patients."

"I know, but twenty murders? And who knows how many more?"

He felt her touch once again as she reached out, took his hand in her own.

"Think I got something for you, V.J.," said Greg Harris, walking into his office early Friday morning.

Valjohn looked up from Gillian's new report on Torgelson—every bit as barren as the earlier report—and raised his brows.

"Last night over in the Foster District, they picked up a couple of fuzzballs joyriding in a stolen car. The 500 block of Lawrence Avenue. One of the kids was packing iron. The arresting officers are sure it's stolen, but the kid claims he found it. Guess where?"

Valjohn shook his head. He leaned back in his chair, propped up one foot on an open drawer in his desk.

"The Davis Breakwater."

"What?" The foot slammed down to the floor. Before Harris could repeat himself, Valjohn, leaning forward, spoke again.

"What caliber?"

"You guessed it: a .45."

Valjohn was out of his chair, reaching for his coat.

"They still got 'em at the precinct?"

"Until nine-thirty. Then they're running 'em over to Juvenile for arraignment."

Valjohn was halfway out the door.

They were back at headquarters by noon, appropriating the gun for the firearms lab. Valjohn was confident Philip Armour and John Tilbury, both thirteen, were telling the truth. He'd questioned them separately and their story seemed to hold up: They'd found the gun while scavenging the beach for full beer cans left by bathers, a Saturday-morning ritual with them. Both claimed to have seen nothing else unusual—no dead bodies, for instance.

That afternoon, while the gun was being checked for ballistics, Valjohn started a trace. He had the magic four: make, caliber, model and serial number. Now all he needed was a little luck.

The gun was an import, a Hammerli replica of the old Colt Single-action Frontier Model. It was manufactured in Lenzburg, Switzerland, and sold in the States through a firm by the name of Interarms in Alexandria, Virginia. The sales manager of Interarms informed him over the phone that the gun with serial number 23-54214 had been shipped to a dealer in Denver on October 15, 1962. Wrangler Bob's Gun Mart.

Valjohn talked over the phone to Wrangler Bob himself, learned the gun had been sold the following December to Everett Lovecraft, a collector from Durango who'd died in '63. Lovecraft's extensive gun collection had been auctioned off to help settle claims against the estate, and an old gun broker by the unlikely name of James Jesse had handled the sales.

Valjohn called Jesse's number in Durango all afternoon but could get no answer. Finally around seven o'clock Mountain Time, Jesse's niece picked up the phone. Her answers were diappointing. Jesse had gone to the mountains for the weekend fishing and wouldn't be back until Monday or Tuesday; and no, he didn't keep records of his gun transactions.

At eight-thirty Valjohn took a short break for a cheeseburger and onion rings at Mr. Dick's. He was back in his office when Jim Delano down in Firearms called at nine-fifteen.

"We got a match, V.J. Every nick and groove. Old man's slug was in mint condition."

"All right!"

"That gray matter stops 'em better than cotton. Still got 'em in the comparator if you want to take a gander."

Valjohn thanked the technician for pushing him through—he knew the lab was really backlogged, and he said he'd be right down.

Just what it all meant yet, he wasn't sure . . . but he had a real gut feeling going. The old slot machine was spinning; two plums had come up: Torgelson's body and the gun. Now if he could just get lucky one more time, one more big, fat plum: a name to go with that gun . . . and jackpot!

Valjohn shuffled the papers on his desk into some semblance of order. He grabbed his coat and switched off the light. In the big outer office he nodded to a couple of scruffy undercover dicks pouring themselves coffee; then he was hotfooting it down to the lab. Damn, he was half tempted to hop on a plane and fly to Colorado that night, track down old James Jesse to the banks of his favorite trout stream.

Sunday afternoon he took Crescent O'Leary to the Art Institute. At their dinner she had confessed to knowing very little about the art world and expressed genuine interest in seeing his paintings. Valjohn was pleased, though he chose to spare her that particular experience, opting instead for a visit to the museum.

They started out with medieval paintings on the lower floor. Abandoning his usual leisurely perusals, he proceeded to give her in one afternoon a crash course on art in Western civilization. They flew from one room to the next, surging through the slower-moving crowds and spanning the centuries in record time. Crescent was a model student: She seldom lagged behind, never complained or asked to stop to rest. She remained bright and attentive, sprinkling his feverish, running commentary with a steady patter of pertinent questions.

Somewhere in the middle of the 1800s, in a small room, surrounded by Pre-Raphaelite canvases, he asked her how she was holding up. Did she want to sit down to rest for a while? Had she had enough for one day?

"Heavens, no!" she exclaimed. Had he forgotten that she spent the better part of a day on her feet, five and sometimes six days a week?

On their way through the postimpressionists, Crescent stopped by a Toulouse-Lautrec. Valjohn was several canvases ahead before he noticed her lingering. He came back, curious to see what had held her attention.

The painting was *The Ringmaster.* Done in 1888, it depicted a girl riding on a horse in a circus ring. The ringmaster stood by with a whip in his hand and a watchful eye. An orange-haired clown danced in the background, while several members of the audience looked on.

"You like it?" Crescent, who seemed totally absorbed in the picture, did not answer.

"I don't think they're the best of friends," she said at last.

Valjohn looked closely at the two central figures, the girl on horseback and the ringmaster. They were glaring at one another across the ring. He'd never really noticed before the outright ferocity of those looks. The longer he studied it, the more aware he became of the painting as a portrayal of man and woman locked in some sort of cosmic confrontation. Lautrec had managed to capture in that brief meeting of their eyes all the enmity that existed between the sexes. The ringmaster was a caricature of male chauvinism. Dressed in formal tails, he seemed to be strutting forward, aggressive, arrogant, his whip arm extended, ready to flail at any given moment. The jutting of his face gave him the predatory appearance of some voracious gamefish. The horse, a powerful, dappled stallion complete with big piston hooves and exposed scrotum, became an extension of the ringmaster's sexual tyranny. The girl, perching delicately sidesaddle on the prancing beast, appeared vulnerable and strikingly feminine, her gaudy orange hair offset by lilac leotards, soft-green crinoline and pink ballet slippers.

Her glance back at the ringmaster was a study in contempt. Her eyes burned defiance. Her mouth, a slash of red lipstick, was fleered in a surly snarl—as though she'd just been cracked with the whip. Yet she continued her ride. And all the women of the world rode with her.

"No . . . not exactly the best of friends," Valjohn finally echoed. He felt as if he were seeing the painting for the first time. "Looks like she's ready to jump off and tell him where to go."

Crescent smiled, but her gaze remained riveted on the picture.

"I think she's too afraid to jump off. Too afraid of the whip."

"Well then, she just might run him over next time around."

"Do you really think she could do that?" asked Crescent, still staring at the painting.

"Sure. Look at her. Hell, she could trample him into the ground without batting an eyelash." He said it, but he didn't really believe it. She'd been riding the horse for too long.

"Maybe she could at that," mused Crescent. She turned from the painting, favored Valjohn with a smile. "She might bat an eyelash, though."

Much of the modern art in the Morton Wing left her bewildered. Occasionally she would respond to a particular painting: "I think I like that one, but I don't know why," she said of a Tanguy dreamscape; or "That's nice, I guess," referring to a Braque still life. She remarked that a woman with a potted plant in a Grant Wood portrait looked just like the director of her nursing school, while a Bolen *gran tache* reminded her of a brain tumor she'd seen removed her last stint in OR.

"Before we leave I want you to meet someone."

Valjohn took her hand and led her through a series of rooms and corridors until they were in the west end of the main gallery for American artists.

"Miss O'Leary, allow me to introduce you to my mother, the Honorable Mrs. George Swinton. Mrs. Swinton, meet Miss O'Leary."

Crescent gazed up at the portrait towering before her. The regal figure of Mrs. Swinton looked nothing like the mother she might have imagined for Valjohn. Not from his descriptions, anyway. In fact the woman looked every inch like one of those courtly ladies depicted in the paintings of the eighteenth century—a duchess or a baroness, or maybe even a queen.

Valjohn had grown up with few actual memories of his mother, their vagueness lessened only by a couple of tattered photographs. Then one day in his middle twenties, he'd wandered into this room and had discovered the handsome lady now staring down at him from the gilded confines of her John Singer Sargent portrait. He'd blinked and done a double take. He'd stared back, struck with wonder.

Not for one instant did he really believe he was standing in the presence of his mother, her image, large as life, captured in the magic, lambent oils of a master's palette, swathed in regal satin, bedecked in a tortoiseshell tiara, her posture formal—even stiff—a gentle hand resting awkwardly on the back of a richly upholstered salon chair. Not for one instant did he really believe . . . and yet the feeling was there, remarkably intense, overpowering; he could not deny it.

The resemblance between this elegant nineteenth-century matron and the memory of his mother was uncanny. To be sure, the dress and pose were wrong, but that was really no more distracting than seeing one's favorite actress in a foreign role: Katharine Hepburn as Mary, Queen of Scots—was there any doubt who played the part? Laura Dean Valjohn, daughter of a poor, southern Indiana coal miner, wife to a black man, widow, mother to a dust-skinned boy—her features and those of the Honorable Mrs. Swinton, both in detail and effect, were hauntingly similar. The same fair skin and auburn hair. The same countenance: chin, mouth, nose, cheekbones and eyes. Most definitely the eyes: alert, dark, bright onyx—his eyes—but never too warm, never too caring, in a mother's face. Gazing into them he was filled with wistful remembrances and the pain of early loss.

It was seldom he visited the museum that he didn't walk by here, pause to pay his filial respects . . . and tell her that it was all right now, that he'd long since forgiven her.

"Is . . . is that really your mother?"

"Now, would I lie about a thing like that?"

"Tell me: Do mothers always dress that formally in Indiana?"

"Only in the evening," Valjohn said with a grin. He finally confessed she was only his dream mother. He told her about the remarkable resemblance and then spoke of the frustrating visits his mother paid him in recurring dreams. He did not mention the terrible nightmare version he'd suffered through only weeks before the accident.

Crescent listened in rapt silence. When he'd finished she squeezed his arm. "I think she's very beautiful. I think you're very lucky to have such a beautiful dream mother."

On the way to the ground floor, they passed another painting that caught Crescent's eye. She stopped to look at it.

Full Orbed Moon by Arthur Davies, 1901. A bright orange moon illuminated an eerie, nocturnal countryside. In the foreground a woman stood alone on a narrow road. She was stark-naked, her pale skin reflecting the brilliance of the moonlight.

"Now that's an interesting little landscape," commented Valjohn, joining her by the painting. "Tell me, is that your dream mother?"

Crescent laughed. Then she said, "Allow me to introduce you. Dream mother, meet Mr. Valjohn."

Valjohn nodded respectfully to the figure in the painting.

"And do dream mothers always dress so formally in Illinois?"

"Only in the moonlight," she replied.

Monday morning Valjohn called Colorado. James Jesse hadn't returned. When he hadn't returned by Wednesday, Valjohn suggested to Jesse's niece that maybe something had happened to her uncle. Not likely, she responded. He was a tough old coot—probably just ran into some good fishing. He'd be back tomorrow for sure, though—had his weekly appointment with his chiropractor then, and he hadn't missed one of those in years.

One more day, thought Valjohn, hanging up. If Jesse didn't show by then, he'd send the Colorado State Police looking for him. The Colorado National Guard, if necessary.

"And how do you pronounce them again?" asked Crescent O'Leary, her fork hovering over a plateful of tiny square, sauce-laden dumplings.

"*Kreplach,*" said Rose Frank, beaming. "I usually serve them in a soup."

"A traditional Jewish food," added Moe, refilling Crescent's crystal goblet with a light plum wine from a matching crystal carafe. "If I had a penny for every *kreplach* I've eaten in my life I could pay off the national debt and still have enough left to retire on."

"*Oy,* Moe—always a lump. So go out and eat a Big Mac."

It was Wednesday evening and Valjohn and Crescent were seated at the dinner table partaking of the sizable feast Rose had promised Valjohn when he got out of the hospital. Not surprisingly, Rose had taken immediately to Crescent.

"*Hoo-ha!* This is some girl, *Johneleh. Mazel tov!*" she exclaimed, lifting her goblet of wine in a toast, then turning to Moe. "What do you think about golf now, Mr. *Gonster Macher?* Some waste of time—ha! Look what it did for your friend there. Why can't you get off your *tochis* and meet such a girl?"

Then, before Moe could grumble a reply, she'd turned back to Valjohn. "Such a bride she'll make. Such eyes! Such a figure!"

Valjohn flushed and glanced at his date, who took the remark with an amused smile.

"Shame on you, *baba,*" broke in Moe. "Stop embarrassing our guests."

Later, retiring to the living room, Valjohn noticed Moe's limp and commented on the apparent improvement of his knee.

Moe scoffed. The knee still was stiff as a poker. He did confess, however, that he'd learned to sashay his hips to give the illusion of a more normal gait. "According to someone, I can't remember who, you can be cured of every folly but vanity."

"Unless you're mad," said Valjohn. "Rousseau said it. I had that one thrown at me in a philosophy final."

"I feel encouraged," said Moe with an oddly nervous laugh.

While the women were in the kitchen, Valjohn brought up developments surrounding the Davis Breakwater, his gut feeling he was onto something and his inability to reach James Jesse. "Be my luck, he's fallen off a mountain."

Moe seemed barely to be listening.

Valjohn asked if there was something bothering him.

He looked away for a moment, scratched his goatee. Finally he shrugged his shoulders and sighed.

"I need someone to confide in. Might as well be you, Valjohnny."

Valjohn was silent.

"Maybe I'm acting like an old woman. It's probably nothing."

Valjohn took a sip of sherry.

"It's probably all in my head. I've even thought about seeing a shrink. . . . But then haven't I still got my vanity?"

"Spit it out, Moe. What the hell is it?"

The old man lifted his glass of sherry, drained the remaining portion. "I think I'm being followed."

While Valjohn drove Crescent back to her dorm, he pondered his friend's strange divulgence. He didn't know what to make of it. As yet, Moe had no concrete evidence to support his suspicion, only a premonition. He'd felt it for the past few weeks now—riding home on the el, marketing at Midland Plaza or just strolling about the neighborhood in the evening —a distinct and disquieting feeling that someone was lurking in his shadow, watching every move he made. He had absolutely no idea who it might be.

"Been fooling with the money boys lately?" Valjohn had asked. "The horses? Your precious White Sox?"

Moe snorted, then admitted dryly he still owed four hundred dollars for his knee operation. Hospitals were getting pretty hard-nose; maybe they were letting out juice contracts.

When Crescent and Valjohn were leaving, Moe had told him to forget about the matter. All in his head, he'd repeated, laughing; a little touch of ethnic paranoia.

Valjohn wasn't about to speculate on ethnic paranoia, but Moe's occupation was something else. All those years in the lab submerged in all the sordid details of crime; what the hell, a little paranoia at Moe's stage of the game seemed almost healthy.

"Why so quiet?" asked Crescent as they swung onto Windhaven Drive and pulled into the parking zone in front of the residence hall. He apologized; just wrestling with problems from work, he said.

He climbed from the car, went around and let her out and walked her to the front door. Another couple stood in the vestibule, locked in a heated embrace.

Valjohn and Crescent faced one another. Hard as it was to believe, he had yet to hold her in his arms and kiss her. Now was the perfect opportunity . . . if he would just lean forward, draw her to him . . .

He couldn't move. He felt timid, as skittish as a schoolboy.

"Uh . . . Friday night then?" Damn! The moment had passed.

She nodded. Was there a look of amusement in her eyes?

"What time?"

"The second feature's at nine thirty-five. Make it seven-thirty for dinner?"

"Fine," she said.

He watched her walk away, his gaze lingering on the couple in the vestibule. They still were going at it. He turned and traipsed back to the car.

Thursday morning Valjohn managed to contact James Jesse. The niece had been right. "Trout were really hitting. Would've stayed up another week, but I had me an appointment with my local backbreaker. You ever tried one of them characters?"

Valjohn said no.

"Leave well enough alone, let me tell you," advised Jesse, his voice a reedy, nasal twang. "Threw a disc catawampus in the national fast-draw regionals back in '58. Been going to Doc Leuchre ever since. Back's not one lick better, but the way that man listens to you complain—it's plumb to downright habit-forming. What can I do you for, Lieutenant?"

Valjohn told him. Jesse remembered the Lovecraft collection—"lots of fine old Sharps and Whitneys"—and some of the buyers, but he couldn't remember whom he'd sold specific guns to. He was against keeping records. "Don't want to chance that kind of information gettin' into the wrong hands, if you know what I mean." Valjohn had only a vague notion.

He spent the rest of the day tracking down six names. By seven-thirty he was ready to close up shop. He'd talked to all but one and learned nothing.

Friday he reached the remaining individual and struck out again.

That night he and Crescent ate at the Ichi Ban, a small Japanese restaurant on Broadway, within walking distance of their intended movie. And of Valjohn's apartment on Oakdale Avenue as well. They enjoyed a splendid dinner of *sashimi*, chicken *teriyaki* and *tempura*, washing it down with cups of hot *sake*.

"I've got a great idea," announced Valjohn later as they emerged from the Biograph Theater. "It's still early—let's go over to my place for a nightcap." They were both in good spirits, having just laughed their way through a British comedy.

189

"Only if you promise to show me your paintings."

"Do I have to?"

She smiled, nodding obstinately.

He reached out and took her hand. "Okay, I promise—but don't say I didn't warn you."

As they stepped from the curb to cross the street, Valjohn glanced down where the bullet-riddled body of John Dillinger, Public Enemy No. 1, had fallen thirty-odd years ago. He too had just come out of the Biograph Theater, had then walked straight into an ambush of waiting police and federal agents. A big crowd had gathered for the occasion. Valjohn remembered the account of a woman bystander who, eager to take home a souvenir, had dipped the hem of her dress in the gutter where Dillinger's blood ran thick as crankcase oil. Valjohn continued walking in silence, choosing to keep this bit of Chicago nostalgia to himself.

His sense of expectation mounted the closer they approached Oakdale Avenue. By the time they reached his apartment building and were climbing the narrow stairway to his flat, he was positively giddy. He longed to reach out, to touch the graceful figure ascending the steps before him. He longed to hold her in his arms, feel her body warm and close to him—finally caress her with more than just his longing eyes. Was this to be the night?

He spent a full twenty seconds fumbling at his door, trying to open the lock with his office key. Crescent stood patiently at his side. He wondered if she could see his hands tremble, if she were mocking him with a smile.

The living room was a mess. Newspapers, magazines, books and clothes were scattered everywhere. Dirty dishes were piled on the coffee table and chairs. A putter lay on the sofa.

"Sorry, maid's night out," he said, and began picking up clothes off the floor. He'd had ample time last evening to straighten things up, but had purposely left them as they were. A clean, well-ordered apartment might have appeared calculating.

"Don't apologize," she said, laughing. "It all looks very masculine and lived in. I'd have been disappointed with anything less."

He smiled to himself. Feeling guilty for only the briefest of moments, he cleared the divan of debris, dumping the various articles along with an armful of shirts into a hallway closet.

"Do you like Kahlua?" he asked casually, returning from the hallway. He remembered her mentioning it when telling him about a dinner at Trader Vic's.

"Yes. Fine."

"Great! I'll make us a couple of black Russians." He was glad she didn't follow him to the kitchen. She might have found it curious that the only alcohol on the premises were two unopened bottles of vodka and Kahlua he'd purchased on the way home from work that afternoon. Two days earlier he'd made a more substantial purchase: a big brass four-poster to replace the lone, ascetic twin in his bedroom.

He returned with the drinks. She took a sip, then gave him a questioning look.

"It's the vodka. You probably had Kahlua straight before. A black Russian has a jigger of vodka in it."

She took another sip, then grinned and fanned her breath. She asked to see his paintings.

"I was hoping you'd forget."

"No chance of that."

"Okay, okay, but first I advise you to down your drink. It'll help prepare you for the worst."

She shook her head and took another drink. Then she lifted her hand, and he led her back to his study, where he'd lined eight of his works against the wall.

Not quite sure what she would think of them, he was relieved and pleased by her response. And finally, impressed, she did not stammer politely, nor gush. She said she liked them very much, then went on to explain. She spoke of things like surface harmony, of balances achieved through relationships of texture, of color and form. He found it hard to believe that she could have learned so much from their single visit to the museum. He was genuinely flattered.

When she'd finished looking at each collage, he asked her which was her favorite. She thoughtfully scanned the lot and finally pointed to one standing in a corner.

"MV-64-9665. The suburban car-theft ring." He could not fault her critical eye.

He too contemplated for a few moments his rendering of case MV-64-9665. It was artistically his most successful work. This was due, he felt, to the inherent aesthetic quality of a blown-up police photo—a picture of the farmsite—which served as the work's dominant motif. Black and white, grainy textured and tilted off-center in the layout, the photo depicted the abandoned, ramshackle farmhouse, its yard overgrown with weeds and inundated by the tangled wreckage of junked autos. In the background, ominous, hulking against a bleak winter sky, were the two huge converted barns, the dismantling centers for the stolen vehicles. It was an expressive portrait of rural decay and obsolescence in America. Set against this scene were the portents of the city, its corruption and malevolence conveyed in a periphery of police reports, photostats, accumulated bits of evidence, operational sketches and mug shots. He'd outlined the edges in black and added a number of cryptic arrows and what looked like ancient hieroglyphics in bold red acrylic to further balance and hold the composition together. Fastened in the lower left-hand corner like a signature was the shiny chrome-plated emblem of a Corvette.

"But they're all so good, so rich," she was saying, swinging her hand around to include the whole wall. "I think . . ." She paused for a moment. "Braque? Yes, Braque would have been very proud of you."

Well, perhaps she was a bit too generous.

"Where do you work?"

"I converted the back bedroom into a studio," he said, pointing to a door behind her.

"Oh, could I see it? I've never seen an artist's studio."

Valjohn was hesitant. "It's really an awful mess," he said, uncomfortably recalling Mona Cobb's visit.

"Please?"

He shrugged, walked to the door, opened it. He switched on the overhead light.

She barely seemed to notice the chaos. Handing him her drink, she immediately began picking her way along an obstacle path strewn with cans of paint, jars with brushes, boxes and piles of debris—until she was bending over a number of panels scattered about a huge, paint-spattered tarp in the center of the floor.

"As you can see, I have several works in progress. Actually, one work."

She studied the panels in silence.

"The case I'm working. C-65-1834. A little more elaborate undertaking than the others. Each panel there represents a victim. Sort of an overall montage of his demise. I've only finished five so far. Really running behind."

She moved to another panel, didn't look up.

"When I get done I plan to assemble them all into one huge, cohesive structure. A sculpture. Maybe mounted on welded metal or papier-mâché and chicken wire—I'm not sure yet."

He waited for some comment, but none came. Instead she knelt lower over a panel to get a closer look.

"At least that was my original idea. Lately I've even been toying with the idea of making a mobile out of them. Having them dangle about in a cluster. Sort of a giant Japanese ghost-trap effect."

She was down on all fours now. A sudden breeze from the window tugged at her long golden hair, made it swirl and flounce for a moment about her shoulders.

"I don't know. Maybe I've gotten . . . gotten a little carried away . . . with the project . . ." His voice trailed off. He was watching her crawl from panel to panel and was struck by the intensity of her inspection. She seemed engrossed in the minutest details, at times lowering her head until she was only inches away. The breeze continued to whip her hair.

He'd forgotten how morbidly fascinating murder could be, even abstracted in his collages. Certainly he'd tried to tone them down: the horror, the ghastliness . . .

As she made her way across the room to his latest panels—the ones of Cook and Dix and Varner, leaning partially completed against the far wall —he decided she'd seen enough. Explicit in the motif of those panels were the confidential revelations of Moe's lab report, and he saw no reason to burden her mind with any more gruesome particulars.

"Come on, I think I've bored you long enough with all this . . ." He couldn't think of a fitting word, and held out her drink instead.

Seeming not to hear him, she rose from the last panel on the tarp and moved toward the far wall, stepping gingerly over a tray of hardened gesso.

"Crescent? Hey, come on—let's go."

"But I'm not bored. Really," she replied, turning to face him for the first time since they'd entered the room.

"Well then, I am. Come on. I . . . I insist," he smiled, his hand still extended. "You have to humor temperamental artists. Especially when they're showing their unfinished work. Besides, your drink needs replenishing."

She looked at him evenly for a moment.

"I'm sorry," she suddenly said brightly and began picking her way back across the room to join him.

Before leaving the room, he went to close the window and discovered it wasn't open. Odd, he mused to himself, returning to switch off the light: not that the window was closed—he rarely opened it—but rather that he'd had such a distinct impression it needed to be closed.

When they were again in the front room, he flipped on the hi-fi. A record already poised above the turntable plopped down and moments later released the wandering, gentle phrasing of Miles Davis's "Nefertiti."

Valjohn sat down on the divan, slid over, hoping she would sit down beside him. Tonight he would not let her beauty intimidate him. He was in his own apartment, ensconced on his own low-slung Dansk (the most expensive stick of furniture he possessed). He felt secure, self-assured, positively dauntless.

She did not sit down beside him, but remained standing in the center of the room, her back to him. She appeared to be studying a Chagall print, *The Artist and His Model,* which hung over the stereo.

He patted the cushion next to him, called to her.

She turned around slowly and looked at him. It was a look he'd never seen on her face—unsmiling, her mouth parted, her eyes out of focus, drained of expression, almost as if she were in a daze.

"Are . . . are you all right?"

She said nothing but swayed slightly on her feet.

He was scrambling up from the divan, trying to get to her before she fainted, before she keeled over on the coffee table. . . .

As he reached out to clutch her shoulders, she backed away. Her eyes suddenly focused. Her face flushed with color.

"I . . . I thought you were going to replenish my drink." She held up her empty glass.

Thoroughly confused, he stared at her, started to speak, didn't know what to say. He took her glass instead.

He picked up his own glass from the coffee table, turned to look at her again. She dazzled him with a smile. He shrugged inwardly and walked to the kitchen.

She didn't finish her second drink. She politely sipped from it once, then excused herself to the bathroom. When she returned, she told him that she suddenly was very tired and would he mind very much taking her home.

Damn! he thought later that evening when he came back to the apartment alone. If only he hadn't shown her his studio; she'd been in great spirits before going in there. Those damn grisly Reaper panels! Hardly mood pieces for a romantic evening. Nice going, he told himself.

After his shower, a very long and cold one, he picked up Gordon's pipe and chewed on its stem. He actually felt like smoking it, and he made a mental note to buy himself some tobacco on his way to work in the morning.

11

Monday afternoon Valjohn brought Rebecca Anne Fulfner into headquarters for questioning.

"Well, uh, Rebecca, how've things been going for you these days?" he asked after she'd taken a seat across from him at his desk. "I've talked to your parole officer, Mr. . . . Mr. . . . uh . . . ?"

"Mr. Pervins."

"Pervins, right. He tells me you're doing very well. A real credit to the system."

Rebecca Anne Fulfner grinned and clucked her tongue. Rebecca Anne Fulfner, better known as "Dildo" Donna Dorsett, had been released five years ago from the state correctional facility at Dwight, where she'd served eight years of a ten to twenty for voluntary manslaughter.

"Let's see . . . you're a beauty operator now?" he asked, glancing at her folder.

"A technician."

"Excuse me?"

"Electrolysis. I'm an electrolysis technician. You know, hair removal."

"Oh." Back in the early fifties her specialty had been robbery and assault. Sexual assault. Her victims were almost always old men. She would entice them up to hotel rooms or waylay them in back alleys. There she would overcome them—at six feet, five inches and 250 pounds she was a raven-haired giant of a woman—and take their money, usually knocking them unconscious in the process. Then stretching them out on their backs and strapping to their foreheads a large rubber "dildo," the recorded dimensions of which were staggering, she would thrust herself upon their faces and proceed, from this somewhat immodest perch, to vigorously relieve the passions of her troubled mind.

Unfortunately one of her victims, an old wino with an acute asthmatic condition, suffocated during one such session. She was apprehended hanging him out a window upside down, trying to revive him.

Sitting across from Valjohn now in a bright pink pantsuit, with sequined black horn-rimmed glasses and a matching spangled snood, she looked considerably older than he'd imagined her, older than she appeared in the mug shots in her folder. Her raven hair had turned to steel wool. She was almost fifty.

"Bernie and me—that's my business partner, Bernie Fulfner. He's my fiancé too. He already give me his name," she said, holding up a diamond ring that was all but lost in the folds of her massive hand.

"Ah. Very nice," Valjohn admired. The hand still looked capable of throttling an ox.

"We set up shop on Randolph Street two years ago come September."

"Electrolysis. It sounds . . . like an interesting field."

"You bet," she said with enthusiasm. "And it's plenty rewarding too. You'd be surprised all the different people got hair they don't want. Not just women with moustaches either. Guys too. Take yourself, for instance. Them scrub-brush eyebrows. Makes you look grumpy. I could thin 'em out in one sitting."

Valjohn reached for his brows, rubbed them self-consciously with a forefinger over his glasses.

"Never really thought about it, did you? And you'd be surprised all the different places people got UH."

"UH?"

"Unwanted hair. Not just facial hair I'm talking about. Not just the nose and ears. Like just yesterday I had to zap some babe's boobs. I mean her nipples, they looked like big spiders! Try picturing yourself chewing down on them hairy devils," she added, filling Valjohn's tiny office with a loud, boisterous guffaw.

Valjohn found his mind doing just that and lowered his eyes.

"Why, we had a guy last month—"

"Er . . . look, Donna—I mean Rebecca—excuse me," he broke in. "What I really asked you here today for was to establish a few facts. I . . . uh . . . If you could—"

"If you mean am I foolin' around anymore, you know, like I used to do, well, the answer is capital N, capital O. I served my time, Lieutenant; I learned my lesson. Besides, Bernie told me if he ever caught me on some other guy's face, he'd zap all my hair off. He'd do it too," she said, her pink

196

suit shaking with another rumble of laughter. "You oughta meet him. He's really something. You know, real scientific and everything."

"I'd like to," said Valjohn, smiling. He started to hand her a sheet of paper, a short Xerox copy of a questionnaire he'd prepared.

"And besides that, I got my balls too."

"Excuse me?"

"My *ben wa* balls," she chortled. She reached into her purse and delivered him a pair of marble-sized, shiny brass spheres.

"*Ben wa* balls?" Valjohn puzzled. He weighed them in the palm of his hand, rolled them with his fingers.

"From Japan. Them Jap men, I guess they didn't want their wives getting too lonely while they was away. So they invented these little devils to keep 'em satisfied. When you feel an attack of the hot and hornies coming on, you just pop 'em in and go about your business."

"Pop them in?"

"Sure, just shove 'em up the old honeycomb and let 'em shake, rattle and roll. Keeps me grinning all day like a mule eating thistles."

Valjohn stared at them in his hand. He set them gently down on the desk.

"That's . . . uh . . . very resourceful, Rebecca," he said, then handed her the questionnaire. "Now, I wonder if you could look at a few dates I've got listed here. I'd like you to tell me your whereabouts and what you were doing during these particular times."

"Hey, Jesus, Lieutenant, some of these go back a couple of years!"

"Don't worry. I don't expect you to remember them all. Just try to pin down as many as you can. Take your time. Take the sheet home with you and fill in as much as you can. Be sure to include the names of any witnesses who can corroborate your story—that is, back up what you say. Mail it back to me in a few days. No need for you to make another trip down here."

"Can I ask what's it for?"

"Nothing to worry about. Just a little routine check."

"If maybe it should get lost in the mail?" She smiled, uncrossed her legs.

"You can count on a visit," he reassured her, trying not to look at her mammoth thighs or the *ben wa* balls lying on his desk. Before she got up to leave, she gave him one of her cards.

BERNIE AND BECKY'S HAIR REMOVAL STUDIO
SCIENTIFIC SHORT WAVE FOR PERMANENT RESULTS.
MEMBER OF THE ILLINOIS ELECTROLYSIS ASSOCIATION.
BY APPOINTMENT ONLY.
HAIR TODAY—GONE TOMORROW!

"In case you change your mind about those eyebrows." She winked, stood up and started to leave.

"Uh, Rebecca, didn't you forget something?" he asked, pointing to the two shiny orbs on his desk.

"Oh, Jesus, yes!" She snatched them up, shaking them loudly in her fist.

"Say, where's the powder room?" She gave him another wink. "It's a long ride home, if you know what I mean."

Valjohn led her to the door and pointed. He watched her walk through the outer office, still shaking her fist, heard the metallic clacking of her balls mingle with the surrounding murmurs and chatter of busy police work. Heard it mingle with his thoughts for the rest of the day.

July passed; the first two weeks in August. He continued to issue more of his questionnaires. Again and again he came up empty-handed.

Rebecca Anne Fulfner easily cleared herself. As did all the other women on the blotter: the paroled murderers, rehabilitated psychopaths, repudiated gun molls, the tough, strong-arm prostitutes. They all had solid, unshakable alibis. Crescent had none. Could only offer lame excuses: She didn't feel well—was tired, had a headache, felt a cold coming on—or people were watching; she didn't want to get her clothes mussed, or couldn't they just sit and talk for a while? Enjoy the scenery? the music? the anything else but . . .

What made it so confusing was that they got on so well together otherwise. The chemistry of their personalities. Doing all the things they did together: eating out, going to the museums and galleries, to the movies, to concerts in the park, walking along the beaches, conversing hours on end, confiding—sometimes giggling like children—or not saying a word, just looking at one another, just being together.

In so many ways they seemed like lovers. . . .

He reasoned she had to be of considerable size and strength, physically aggressive, agile, in excellent shape.

"Which one is Gertrude Gunterhausen?" he asked Harris, who'd spent the week poking around the female wrestling circuit.

"She's the one on top, the big one in the leopard skin."

Valjohn looked up from their front-row seats at Marigold Arena as Gertrude Gunterhausen—better known as Dirty Gertie the Grapevine Queen—jabbed a thumb into her opponent's eye, then picked her up and drop-kicked her into the corner turnbuckles. A modern-day Valkyrie, Dirty Gertie stood 6 feet, 7 inches and weighed 357 pounds. She had a head like an anvil (she wore her blond hair in a boot-camp butch), and serpents and daggers were tattooed on both her stovepipe arms. What appeared to be a large dragon had been etched across her voluminous bosom: The top of its head and a wing could be seen arching above her leopard-skin top, a couple of taloned feet clawing down her exposed midriff all the way to her navel.

The fact remained he'd been going with her for nearly two months now, was seeing her almost every other night, and yet aside from little greeting and parting pecks, he'd only kissed her once. Really locked on, dead-center, no-nonsense mashed lips. And even that one time, parked on Northern Island by the Adler Planetarium, watching a post-Fourth rain-delayed fireworks display over Lake Michigan, her lips had been taut and tentative, her mouth closed, unyielding to any further intimacies. He'd silently cursed the separate seats in the Volks, the gearshift lever rising stiffly between them.

Initially he'd assumed the problem was strictly his: a lack of nerve—that he found her beauty too forbidding. Now he realized that it wasn't only her beauty that was forbidding. It was her turn of mind, a provincial, puritan temperament as well. She seemed totally unresponsive to physical contact. She refused to tolerate any form of sexual dalliance and thwarted every attempt at serious embrace. She was cold. She was an iceberg, a veritable glacier of mid-Victorian restraint.

The anvil head lowered, slammed into the other woman, a short, chunky Gypsy with a curly mop of black hair, caught her in the stomach, sent her groaning and sprawling to the canvas. The crowd booed and hissed. Though Gertrude Gunterhausen was undefeated in the ring—she'd beaten a host of challengers, including a number of men—she was obviously no favorite with the fans. A natural heavy—awesome, overpowering, Nazi mean—she used every foul tactic in the trade to inflict maximum pain as well as to win.

But what Valjohn found most interesting was that her wrestling person-ality was something more than mere show-business façade. A notorious barroom brawler, Gertrude had been 86'd out of practically every night-club on the West Side. Harris also had uncovered the fact that she'd bribed and bullied her way out of five felonious-assault charges in three different states. The victims all were ex-boy friends.

Begrudgingly he had to admire the way she dealt with his passion, the way she was continually able to ward off his most heated advances. Her sense of timing and poise were incredible. It was as though she could read his mind, knew which hand was going where almost before he did. She would deftly parry his moves with her own, rarely becoming angry or upset. She would arrest him in a long, sweet smile, disable him with sympathy and martyred forbearance. Often he would leave these encoun-ters convinced she'd even saved him from some great wickedness.

The moment of truth had arrived. She sprang off the top rope, landed with a resounding thud on her opponent, both knees driving into the woman's back as she lay writhing face down on the mat.

"Grapevine! Grapevine! Grapevine!" the crowd began to chant. No longer were they booing. They had lost interest in the plight of the Gypsy. Now they only wanted to witness Dirtie Gertie administer the quietus—her dreaded figure-4 grapevine. She obliged them, yanking her dazed opponent upright by the hair, wrapping her arms and legs about the woman's limbs with practiced ease like an old salt tying knots. The two combatants formed for a brief moment a grotesque tableau of the number 4. Then the Grapevine Queen began bouncing on a foot, twisting the tangle of limbs like a human rack until the short, chunky woman in her grasp seemed to stretch before everyone's eyes as she filled the arena with her agonizing screams.

The referee leaped in, tried to separate the two women. He was forced to clout Gertrude Gunterhausen on the side of the head repeatedly with a fist before she would release the hold. Her opponent fell to the canvas in a crumpled heap.

Valjohn and Harris looked at one another as the referee raised one of Dirty Gertie's arms over her head in victory.

He vividly recalled the one time she had lost her temper. They'd played tennis in Lincoln Park one particularly muggy August night. When they'd finished, he'd suggested they go to his apartment for a quick shower. They had. Afterward, drying herself—they'd showered separately—she put on his bathrobe. In an unguarded moment while she stood in the hall, he crept up from behind and embraced her. He pressed her close to him, intoxicated with her fresh-washed scent, reached around to the loose front folds of the robe, plunged a hand inside and grabbed for all he was worth.

She lurched forward with a gasp, stumbling into a wall. When she turned to face him, there was such an animal fierceness blazing in her eyes that his heart froze. He stood before her with only a towel wrapped around him and dared not breathe.

For several moments the silence crashed between them. Slowly her anger dissipated. Her eyes softened. He found his voice, stuttered apologies: a moment of weakness, a stupid impulse. He assured her it would never happen again . . . never happen again. She said simply that she believed him.

They would play tennis several more times that summer, continue to take showers in his apartment. He would never forget the fierce look in her eyes. Nor the touch of her cool, damp breasts beneath that robe.

"Line up by the wall there. Don't block the corridor. Cost you ten bucks a head, gentlemen. Interview'll be in a couple of minutes."

Valjohn and Harris stood with a group of people outside Gertrude Gunterhausen's dressing room, where she was about to hold audience with some of her more ardent fans. Her manager, a large man with shoulder-length blond hair and pink shades, made his way through the group, collecting the money in a gym bag.

"An interview? What's the ten bucks for?" asked Harris.

Valjohn shrugged. A man standing next to them replied, "To see the dragon." He winked. "Ole Gertie's dragon puts on quite a show."

As the manager approached, Harris was about to flash his shield. Val-john caught his arm.

"Ten-forty," he whispered—no siren, no flashing light. He pulled out his wallet, being careful to cover his own shield with his hand. He paid for them both with a twenty.

When everybody's money was collected, the manager disappeared into the dressing room. A few moments later he opened the door and signaled for them to enter.

Gertrude Gunterhausen lay face down in the center of the room on a training table. An old, slick-bald man in a tank top was energetically massaging the muscles of her shoulders and neck.

"Great match, Gertie!"

"Sent her back to the body shop."

"The morgue."

"Beat the living shit out of her!"

After a few minutes she finally rolled over and acknowledged the presence of her audience. She swung her great tree-trunk legs down to the floor and stood up. The old, slick-bald man came around the table behind her and unzipped the back of her leopard skin. She reached up and peeled it down. Then she fumbled with the front hooks of a heavily staved corset bra. When it released, she spilled out to the oohs and ahs of her fans, setting the dragon free. . . . Disproportionately outsized even from her Amazonian torso, her mammaries made the women of Rubens look like prepubescent schoolgirls. Sprawled across them, the dragon—sinuous, green-scaled and red-eyed—breathed a raging fire, its long, lizard tongue slithering down the incline of her right breast, its forked tip pricking the outer rim of a nipple, her areolas as big as hub-caps.

With all the aplomb of a stripper, she flung the bra over her shoulder and leaned forward, placing her hands on her knees so that her breasts hung down like twin blockbusters. Slowly she began rocking from side to side.

"One, two, three, four—" several women in the audience started counting in unison. The men joined in.

As her breasts gained momentum, she rocked faster and faster. Soon they were a whirling centrifuge of flesh.

"—twenty-seven, twenty-eight, twenty-nine, thirty—"

The dragon writhed, its great neck and trunk stretching and contracting, its coiled tail pulsating. It beat its wings. Fire belched from its nostrils, leaped and crackled.

At the count of fifty she straightened up. Her breasts slammed together, coming to a joggling halt. She lifted them in both hands, buried her face in them. Then she pulled up her front and lay back down on the table. The interview was over.

When the last of the other onlookers had filed out through the doorway,

Valjohn and Harris stepped forward. Valjohn introduced himself and presented his badge.

"Shit!" growled the Grapevine Queen. "A nigger cop—just what I need to make my day."

"I hope so, Miss Gunterhausen," said Valjohn, adjusting his glasses. He reached into the small portfolio he was carrying and produced his questionnaire. "I sincerely hope so."

Gertrude Gunterhausen emerged as a prime suspect. For two days. On the third of September not quite a year ago, an 1834 had taken place in a parking lot a block from the Marigold Arena. The victim was Robert Etter, a man who'd randomly murdered a family picnicking in La Bagh Woods. He'd shot the parents, raping the mother first, then drowned their two children, holding them underwater in the North Branch of the Chicago River. Etter had been ruled incompetent to stand trial, had been remanded to a mental institution. Exactly twenty-one months later he'd been pronounced cured and released. He'd never been retried. Valjohn discovered that on the evening of the third, Miss Gunterhausen was on the card to wrestle at the arena in a tag-team match—paired with Thunder Thelma Faulk against the Siberian Sisters—and that Gertrude had failed to show, calling in sick half an hour after the match was scheduled to take place, about the same time affixed to the murder. She claimed she was home with a bad case of the "drizzling shits." There was no one to verify her story.

What she soon could verify, however, was that on the night of June 7, the night Cook, Dix, and Varner had been snuffed, she was out of state—out of the country, as a matter of fact—wrestling in Regina, Saskatchewan.

The search continued. The city abounded with aggressive, brawny women. There were the hoydens from the roller rinks, the stock-car-racing circuits, the bike gangs, the pool halls, the bowling alleys. There were two women's football leagues to scrutinize and a rugby league as well. There were the androgynes of industry: the women welders, stockflyers, stevedores, truck drivers, heavy-equipment operators. . . . What the hell, thought Valjohn, there were some pretty tough babes right upstairs in the Vice Squad.

Still, when Valjohn reflected on the carnage—the destructive level, the ferocity manifested in the murders—he found it difficult to suspect any of them. And that included the likes of Rebecca Anne Fulfner and Gertrude Gunterhausen.

At times he leaned toward the gang-bang theory—by far the most popular one with the rest of his men—despite certain contradictory evidence offered by the lab. Sweeney was convinced the Reaper was a rat pack: "a drug-crazed teenage girl-gang." Shoplifting, glue-sniffing, stealing hubcaps, tricking, even bum burning—all the old kicks were passé. Today's liberated pubettes had come up with their own new game, namely gang-fucking degenerates to death and mutilating their remains. Valjohn's mind boggled at the thought: a multitude of little hands grasping, pummeling, clawing; sweaters lifting; jeans dropping; a dozen or so saucy bottoms glistening, churning in the moonlight; the screams of the victim mingling and being drowned out by a chorus of giggling squeals; the padded thuds of tennies and penny loafers fading away down some dark, deserted alley.

And maybe it wasn't a rat pack at all; maybe it was a mature group of social reformers, a latter-day chapter of suffragettes. . . .

Maybe he was willing to believe anything at this point.

"So where do we go from here?"

Valjohn sat on the divan. Crescent stood nearby, straightening her dress. She had just disengaged herself from the tangle of his arms and abruptly scrambled to her feet. She looked at him quizzically.

"I mean, where do we go from here?" he repeated wearily. "We can't keep this up forever. I know I can't, anyway."

She looked away.

"I'm sorry," she said finally.

He wondered how many times he'd heard her say that lately.

"I'm just not cut out for a platonic relationship. Not with you, anyway. I mean, you know how I feel about you." He started to tell her, then shrugged. What was the use? She'd heard it all a dozen times—how much he loved her; how right things were between them; how much better they could be if only she would let it happen. . . .

But of course she wouldn't let it happen. Not even begin to happen. Oh, she would listen to him trying to explain things. She would patiently hear out his arguments, would even end up agreeing with him. Wholeheartedly. In theory. In practice, nothing changed between them. Mentally, spiritually, they mated like the final pieces of a puzzle. Physically . . . they were bust. She was driving him up the wall.

"Anyway, I can't go on like this," he heard himself saying. "I can't," he said and shrugged again.

A long silence followed. At any moment he expected to hear organ music in the background and watch this whole little scene fade into a detergent commercial.

"I can't," he added yet again.

"I think maybe I ought to leave."

"Now, what does that mean?" he snapped, not at all sure he wanted her to tell him.

"I don't know." She hesitated, looked away. "We just don't seem to be getting on."

And whose fault is that? he wanted to yell back at her but remained silent instead, wrestling for better lines.

"Maybe we shouldn't see each other for a while."

She'd said it. Not he.

"There's someone else, isn't there?" Banal script or not, he had to mount some sort of offense.

"No." She shook her head.

203

"Is it this?" he said, pointing to his arm. He couldn't help himself.

"Your arm?"

"Not my arm—my skin! The color of my skin."

She laughed, actually laughed.

"What's so goddamn funny? It has been known to make a difference, you know."

"Really, I think I should go now. We'll talk when you're in a better mood."

"By all means!" he exclaimed, jumping to his feet as if on cue. "If that's the way you want it."

She looked at him sadly.

"It's not the way I want it."

Two weeks went by. He didn't see her. He didn't call her. He was miserable. It was impossible to concentrate at work. He couldn't sleep at night. Nothing seemed to interest him. Nothing gave him pleasure. Food was tasteless; exercise, boring. On a beautiful, late-summer afternoon he tried to play golf again, walked off the course after four holes. A trip to the Art Institute only reminded him of visits shared with her. He stood before the Honorable Mrs. Swinton, complaining bitterly. He lingered in front of Davies' *Full Orbed Moon.*

"How come your daughter's such a snow queen?" he asked.

"Says who?" the naked lady in the foreground replied.

He reintroduced himself.

"Do I look like the dream mother of a snow queen?"

He admitted she did not.

"Then don't be so quick to blame others. Maybe it's you. Maybe she's only frigid with you."

"I asked her. She said there was no one else."

The woman in the painting fell silent. He looked at her closely, inspected Davies' short, hurried stroke. Was she smirking now, or was he just imagining it? A play of moonlight on her small, shadowed face?

He dated other girls, managed to ask out the Puerto Rican hostess at Mr. Dick's, the redhead from Osco's. They were nice, companionable. Made out of cardboard. Desperate, he took out Mona Cobb. He had to get rid of hormones, relieve the building pressures of his pent-up libido. In the grip of her powerful, thrusting thighs—she demanded to be on top—he lost his manhood, however, dwindling into putty.

"Fairy, fairy!" she screamed at him from the bedroom as he headed for the door to leave her apartment. "Here, you forgot your goddamn glasses!" She hurled them after him. "Since when did they start hiring fairy four-eyed nigger cops?"

Valjohn lunged back in the semidarkness to catch them, but the glasses came sailing through two rooms and struck the front door. He picked them up and hurriedly let himself out. Halfway down the hallway stairs, he discovered one of the shatterproof lenses had cracked in a perfect V. An act of providence? His eyes weren't really all that bad—20/30—just some fuzziness on distant edges. He needed a little change; he'd go without specs for a while.

He hadn't felt so forsaken since his early days at the home. He reflected on the other great love affairs of his life. There'd been two of them: Both had occurred while he was in school; both times he'd gone down in flames.

The first was a stunning black cheerleader from Terre Haute whom he'd met the end of his sophomore year at Indiana. Yvonne White. Voluptuous, with dark walnut skin and black, olive eyes, she was the first steady girl friend he'd ever had. He went with her for almost two years. It was Yvonne who'd first taught him the many splendors of sex. She'd stolen his heart. Then she'd dumped him, homecoming weekend of their senior year, for an all-conference wide receiver with epoxy hands and 9.4 speed in the hundred.

It had taken Valjohn a year to get over Yvonne. Two years . . . maybe he'd never gotten over her. On the rebound, while at Berkeley, he met Beth Midlenstein. Fiery, intense, relentlessly attractive with an explosion of auburn hair, she was an art major and a student activist. Their paths had first crossed in the San Francisco Museum of Fine Arts at a visiting exhibit of American painters. "God and wow!" she had said, stepping back from an immense Jackson Pollock canvas, "he comes to such, you know, positive conclusions!"—directing her comment as much to Valjohn, who also happened to be looking at the Pollock, as to the rather gawky-looking boy she was standing with. Valjohn, unsure, lonely—looking for even a hint of female companionship—had smiled. She, confident, bored—eager for an affair with a minority student—had returned his smile. Two days later she'd moved in with him.

When he'd first told her he was in police sciences, she was charmed by his drollery. Later, learning the truth, she made up her mind to convert him. Because of his interest in art, she decided he should become a painter. It was during the eight months of this tempestuous romance that he'd learned many of the techniques he would later employ as the "cubist cop." She introduced him to all her artsy-dissident friends. He got along surprisingly well, took part in a number of early civil-rights rallies and antiwar demonstrations. Yet doggedly he persisted in his chosen field.

Then one day her picture had appeared in the papers alongside Mario Savio, who was spouting obscenities from the campus steps. A day later, Valjohn came home from classes in the evening and found her gone. All her clothes were missing, her paints and brushes—and most of his too. She did leave him one of her sepia nudes—it hung now in his bedroom. She also left him a note pinned to the fly of a pair of his trousers. It read simply, "Oink-oink."

The old one-two punch. Yvonne and Beth. But they were just jabs

205

setting him up for what was coming. Mere love taps compared to Crescent's KO roundhouser. He thought he'd had the blues before? Nothing. Sky-dyed pastels. Now he was immersed in cobalt, down and drowning in pure, uncut ultramarine.

The next day, after returning to his office from a routine interrogation, Valjohn found a note on his desk from Moe telling him he wanted to talk to him. Valjohn called the lab, but Moe had already left for the afternoon.

Wednesday after work Valjohn met with him in the basement of Bathhouse John's, a small deli-bar off State Street that served bock beer plus the best roast beef sandwiches in town.

"So how're you feeling now?"

"For an old man in the fall, who's complaining?" said Moe. He'd been down with the flu earlier in the week. "It's the spring and fall that get you when you're my age. Not the summer or dead of winter. It's the change: Your old plumbing really starts banging around—all the pipes expanding and contracting." Then he added, "But you don't look so hot yourself, Valjohnny. You been sick?"

Valjohn knew he looked like hell; an accumulation of sleepless nights was beginning to drag him down. He couldn't blame it on the changing seasons, either. He debated burdening his old friend with a tedious account, decided to spare him.

"A lovers' quarrel," he said simply.

For a moment Moe acted as though he hadn't heard him, then abruptly he became concerned. "Oh . . . nothing serious, I hope?"

Valjohn was slow to reply.

"*Nu,*" said Moe, sighing, "every age has its problems. Yours . . ." his thoughts seemed to trail off and return, "I wish I had. Maybe you should start wearing your glasses, though—at least they'd hide the circles."

While Valjohn smiled and rubbed his eyes, Moe grew earnest. He asked if he remembered a certain conversation shared by them in private a few months ago, one concerning him, Moe, being followed—or, at any rate, thinking he was being followed.

Valjohn nodded. "Is that what the note in my office was about?"

Moe took a sip of beer, then gulped. He had almost chugged it down before he set the big stein, half drained, on the table again and wiped a ring of foam from his beard.

"You may recall I didn't rule out the distinct possibility I might be . . ." he tapped his temple, circled it with a bony forefinger.

"Well, before delivering myself—or selves, as the case might be—into the rigors of psychoanalysis, I decided first to give my premonitions the benefit of the doubt. Humor my paranoia, if you will."

He paused, downed the remainder of his beer.

"And?"

"Ah, *noch,* allow an old man the pleasure of telling a story. The sand-

206

wiches, I think they're ready," he interrupted, starting to get up from their booth.

"Keep your seat—it's my turn to buy." Valjohn picked up Moe's empty stein and walked over to the counter to pick up their orders.

"To continue," Moe said after washing down the first bite of his sandwich with fresh beer, "I replaced little furtive glances over my shoulder with more subtle devices. On the el I punched tiny holes in my newspaper so that I could watch other people observing me while I read. I varied my routes home from the el, sometimes taking a bus or a cab, sometimes walking. I studied reflections in store windows and mirrors. I frequently reversed my direction walking, stopped short going around corners to witness the reactions of people passing by. I even got on and off the train once just before it pulled out of the station to see if anyone else did the same."

Valjohn smiled. The image of Moe limping about the city playing cloak-and-dagger games was hard to take seriously.

Moe ignored his smile. All his cunning little maneuvers, he conceded, had revealed nothing. He could uncover not one shred of evidence that might support his suspicions.

Valjohn suggested that he might have used the services of a "convoy." Valjohn easily could have assigned him a man from his department. Hell, he'd have been glad to do the job himself.

Moe shook his head. "Proving to myself I'm senile is bad enough without having to prove it to everyone else. Anyway, after a few weeks of these shenanigans, I gave them up. Not that I was totally convinced, you understand. There was always the possibility that whoever might be following me was more expert in surveillance than I in countersurveillance."

"Maybe you were being ABC'd," offered Valjohn. "You know, three men rotating positions. Detection is very difficult."

Unimpressed, Moe took another bite from his sandwich and continued.

"For the next month or so I ignored my premonitions. I tried to forget the whole matter. I must admit it seemed to work. I became less and less suspicious, less jumpy. Soon I grew satisfied that I wasn't being followed, that most probably I'd never been followed."

He paused to take another bite, another swig of beer. Valjohn had to marvel at Moe's ability to consume food while talking. The old man had almost downed his sandwich and second glass of beer while Valjohn, who was doing most of the listening, had barely begun to eat.

"That is, up until a couple of weeks ago."

"What happened then?" asked Valjohn, about to chew off a bulging corner of his own sandwich.

"I think I've found out who it is."

"Who?" A slice of tomato slipped from between the black slices of pumpernickel, fell onto his lap.

"*Ai-yi-yi!* You tell me!"

"You mean there really is somebody?" He set the sandwich down, re-gripped it.

"Am I telling you?"

Valjohn started to press him with questions. Who and why, for God's sake? Then he realized the futility of rushing Moe with his story, lifted his sandwich and took another bite.

Moe proceeded to recount the details step by step in lab-report fashion.

"During my attempts at countersurveillance I became very aware of the people around me. I memorized faces. I suddenly began recognizing people I'd never noticed before—regular commuters like myself. I've probably been riding with them to and from the Loop for years. I'm sure they've never bothered to notice me either. I guess that's the way life is in the city. Everyone is too busy with their own problems, too locked up inside or too afraid. It's strange . . . all the hours spent traveling together, all the sad, empty stares.

"But then this is neither here nor there. What is important is that on Sunday before last, I was out for a stroll with Rose in the Clayton Smith Reserve—the trees are beautiful, exceptionally beautiful, this time of year —though I doubt you ever get a chance to notice them, thrashing about a golf course. Except maybe when they get in the way."

"Actually I haven't been playing much golf lately."

"Congratulations. Anyway, it was while I was at the reserve that I discov-ered somebody, or at least thought I did, because at that time I wasn't sure." He stuffed the last corner crust of his sandwich in his mouth.

"I was wandering along a path near the south grove picnic area, search-ing for a lavatory. I'd left Rose seated on a bench in the main clearing. Heading the wrong way, I turned around and was in the process of retrac-ing my steps when I saw a woman coming from the opposite direction, the clearing. When she saw me, she seemed almost startled. She left the path at a fast walk before we got any closer, and I lost sight of her in the woods.

"For some reason I felt suddenly apprehensive about Rose. The woman was coming from where I'd left her. I hobbled back as fast as I could on this old outrigger of mine and was greatly relieved to find her still seated on the bench, feeding *noshes* to some blue jays. I asked her if she'd seen the woman. She said no one had come through the clearing since I'd been gone."

"That's it? I mean, what'd she look like?"

"I only saw her from a distance. She was wearing dark glasses and a gray trench coat—though the temperature had to be in the seventies. Her hair was light brown, maybe blond."

"Umm . . ." Valjohn withheld comment, chewing on another bite.

"Anyway, three days later I saw her on the el and I'm pretty sure now your friend Rousseau was right. I've still got my vanity. I haven't lost my marbles either," he added with a wink.

"You're saying the woman in the woods—you think she's the one who's been following you?"

Moe nodded. He also said he was ready for another beer. Valjohn drained his own stein and started to get up, but Moe insisted on making the trip himself. Sitting in the booth had made his left hip ache. He needed to get up and walk it out.

"The train was crowded—five o'clock rush," he continued, returning with their refills. "I spotted her when some people got off. She was standing by a door. Apparently had followed me on."

"Just because she had no seat and maybe got on after you—that hardly proves she was following you."

Moe was silent. He stared into his beer.

"And how do you know it was the same person? You said before you saw her only from a distance."

Moe didn't look up from his beer. "When she caught me looking at her, she acted like she'd forgot her stop, hurried off the train just before the doors shut. I went after her, but it was too late; we were already moving. Even lost my seat."

"But how do you know—"

"Dark glasses, the gray trench coat. She was wearing a blue scarf this time, but I caught a glimpse of the same light-colored hair. I'm sure it was her, all right. . . . There was something else too."

"Something else?"

"Something peculiar. And not just peculiar, something familiar. The more I thought about it the more certain I became. There definitely was something familiar about her. Vaguely but definitely familiar."

"Vaguely but definitely? Peculiar and familiar?"

"More than anything," Moe went on, disregarding the comments, "I think it was the glasses that threw me. More than even the scarf."

"Threw you?"

"They were big, hid so much of the face. Then day before yesterday it just came to me out of the blue. If I'm right . . . well, I must admit it becomes no less bewildering—crazy, even."

"Hold on a second. You know this person?"

Moe nodded. "In a million years you'd never guess."

"No argument there. So who is it, for God's sake?"

Moe paused, sipped his beer. "Let me hedge a bit and say I *think* I know who it is. Until I'm absolutely certain, though, I'd rather keep it to myself. Better for everyone concerned." He glanced at his watch and howled, "*Ai-yi-yi!* After six already. Enough of this *megillah.* I promised Rose I'd take her out tonight."

"You're not going to leave me hanging?"

"Sorry, Valjohnny, no more time. Believe me, you'll be the first to know when I'm certain. Just be prepared for a shock."

Moe slid from the booth and stiffly hoisted himself to his feet. He announced that he was taking Rose to the Second City.

Valjohn remained seated, his thoughts still sorting through the mystery of Moe's earlier words.

"Coming?"

"Oh . . ." He stood up, absently commented that he didn't know Rose was into social satire.

Moe shrugged. "One of the neighbors' kids, he's in the cast. Who could talk her out of going?" He paused. "It's a new show this fall. Rave reviews. Maybe you should take Crescent?"

Valjohn didn't answer. Hearing Crescent's name jarred him back to the problems of his own life. It was the longest he'd gone in days without brooding over her.

"So what do you think?" asked Moe as he made his way up the steep, narrow stairway to the street.

"I'm not sure," deliberated Valjohn. He climbed slowly behind Moe, who had to hobble up one step at a time. "I don't like it, though. I mean, if this person is following you, did it ever occur to you that you could be in real danger?"

"Danger, shmanger—forget all that! I'm talking about Crescent. The girl of your dreams. Mine too. Take her out, Valjohnny. Patch things up. Quarrels are a waste of time. Besides," he said, turning back to eye Valjohn's haggard face, "from this one you may not survive."

Valjohn told him he'd think about it.

Later that evening, meditating in the shower, he tried to make some sense out of Moe's story. There was something terribly unsettling about it . . . the fact that a woman was implicated. Did it tie into the case? But how? My God, he couldn't imagine anyone farther from the victim profile than Moe. And despite his old friend's certainty that the woman was tailing him, that the person in the woods and the one on the train were the same individual—it really hadn't sounded all that convincing. His imagination could very well be working overtime. The case was enough to spook anyone. Hell, there were times he felt like looking over his shoulder himself.

Still, the whole matter was nothing to dismiss lightly. Damn it! He wished Moe had told him whom he suspected.

Valjohn slowly eased back on the hot water. Soon he was grimacing and dancing about in a frigid, bracing jet. Crescent . . . he wondered if she were going through anything that even closely resembled his limbo.

The next day he prodded Moe again to name the woman of his suspicions. When he refused, Valjohn tried to impress upon him the seriousness of the situation. Maybe it did somehow tie into the case. Maybe he actually was being stalked by the Reaper.

Moe had laughed. Then, not meaning to scoff at Valjohn's concern, he quickly did his best to assure him that he was way off base on that account. Again Moe faithfully promised to reveal the person's identity just as soon as he was positive himself.

On the way out of the building together in the evening, Moe stuffed a small envelope in Valjohn's coat pocket. "Oh, by the way . . ."

Valjohn looked at him.

"Rose told me to give you that," he said, adjusting his coat lapels in a brisk, tugging wind off the lake. "We had a couple left over. Enjoy!" He waved and hurried off into the flow of pedestrians along State Street.

Valjohn opened the envelope. Two tickets. The Second City. Saturday night's performance.

12

"I enjoyed that very much," said Crescent as they walked out of the Second City Theater Saturday night after watching the ten o'clock performance.

Valjohn bobbed his head vigorously. He admitted to himself, however, that tonight he was turned on to every positive tremor in the universe. He'd taken Moe's advice and given her a call.

"Even the third skit?" she asked with a faint smile.

"Even the third skit," he said and laughed, recalling a series of short sketches satirizing the CCPD. The skit had ended with Diogenes, lantern in hand, wandering through the streets in search of an honest man. He was summarily mugged—even his lantern stolen—by a Chicago cop.

They followed several people downstairs to the crowded theater bar, where they were able to find a small table just vacated. Ordering drinks, they continued to discuss the performance. Crescent, sitting across from him in a plain black dress, no jewelry, no makeup, looked stunning as ever. Yesterday when he'd called her he'd been afraid she'd refuse his invitation. Maybe she'd picked up with someone else. Maybe he'd lost her forever. . . . *I'd love to go,* she'd responded, relaxed, cheerful—as if they'd never been apart.

After he'd hung up he felt absolutely ecstatic, danced about his apartment, sang in the shower. While he was dressing he took his service revolver out of its drawer, practiced his fast draw for a good ten minutes in front of the mirror.

And now together again, there was nothing forced or awkward between them. They spoke and laughed with spirited ease, bouncing from one topic to the next—from politics and the war to art and civil rights; from the Beatles, heart transplants and satellites to movies, Zen and their own lives —the past few weeks spent away from each other. They refused to become bogged down, to dwell on any one subject longer than it amused them and sustained the gaiety of the evening. Nor did they struggle to fill the silences, were content instead to sit there sharing each other's eyes and the moment.

When their second round of drinks arrived, they turned their attention to a silent movie that was being projected on a screen against a far wall. It was an old Mack Sennett comedy with the Keystone Kops.

Valjohn turned from the film for a moment to watch Crescent. She was totally absorbed in the drama of the chase. She giggled, laughed, put a hand at her throat. He was struck by the childlike exuberance of her expressions. She was a kid at a Punch and Judy show. He continued watching her, felt a deep glow radiate within him as the soft candlelight from their table lamp flickered across her lively features. At one point she looked away from the screen and caught him staring at her. She started to say something, then saw the look in his eyes. She reached forward, squeezed his hand. Neither spoke.

A loud gasp from the audience drew their attention back to the movie. The Kops were chasing a man dressed in a striped convict's uniform across the rooftops of high buildings. One of them, following his peers up a wobbly ladder to a still higher roof, started to fall over backward, the ladder rocking loose on a broken shingle. He flailed his arms in the air, managed to keep his balance tottering back and forth several feet from the building's edge, the outstretched hands of his fellow officers. Just as he was about to plunge to the street far below, another Kop threw him a rope from a barrel nearby where some roofing construction was being done. He caught the rope, began frantically hauling himself forward to safety. The other Kops congratulated themselves, patted one another on the back. They failed to notice that the other end of the rope wasn't attached to anything, but simply coiled in the barrel. Still teetering at the brink, the Kop on the ladder continued hauling in rope as fast as his arms could haul in rope. But it was only a matter of time until the barrel emptied. . . .

And somewhere amid the surrounding swell of snickers and guffaws Valjohn heard a voice, strangely like his own, and it was murmuring—or was it shouting? He couldn't tell. The words hung in the air, seeds unto themselves.

"Crescent O'Leary . . . will you marry me?"

Valjohn kept very busy for the next few weeks, having chosen to bury his disappointment under the bulk of a heavy work load. The investigation continued to wallow in the doldrums, every lead either petering out or abruptly dead-ending. The profile dragnet continued to come up empty-handed. Computer tactics failed to make any operative projections. Despite all this, however, he'd actually begun to entertain a certain optimism: It had been five months since the Reaper had struck last, since Cook, Dix and Varner had been "offed." So far that was the killer's longest period of dormancy—more than twice the length of the previous longest period, seventy-one days from the middle of November to the end of January of the year before. Maybe the Reaper had tired of her sport or moved away. Maybe she was seriously ill or even dead. If the latter were true the case then could be allowed to die its own slow death, quietly buried in the vast and dusky archives of the city's great unsolved crimes. There it would lie to excite and confound scholars of crime in the future, but it would no longer plague his sleepless nights.

In the meantime, while he still had the case to brood over, he expanded the scope of his activities. With approval from his superiors, he took on other work—several routine investigations, shootings and stabbings, a bludgeoning here and there. He found dealing with motives like robbery, jealousy and drunken anger oddly refreshing. The old values endured.

On the first Thursday of November, snow fell. Nothing very dramatic or pretty, just a cold, sleety drizzle that turned into gray, wet flakes after the sun went down. Most of it melted the moment it hit the ground. Thin, gray webs of slush collected in the cracks of the pavement and the edges of buildings. It was the kind of evening not to venture out in, and Valjohn decided to spend it home at the apartment working on his long-neglected art project.

Sorting through a box of news clippings and photos relating to the Dix/Varner murder, he thought about giving Crescent a call. Maybe he could take her out for a quick snack later on, a hot toddy. Then he remembered she was working the night shift at Windhaven and resigned himself to his creative toils. It probably was just as well. He had gone out with her only a couple of times since their evening at the Second City. If he was unhappy being away from her at least he was not in pain; at least her beauty was not there to taunt him, to remind him of his rejection.

He placed a large blown-up police photo of the victims' car, Dix's raised leg just visible through a reflection of trees and headstones in a rear window, on the board of Masonite and moved it about, experimenting with different positions and angles. Then he began mixing a bowl of megilp with the handle of an old paintbrush. Though disastrous as a medium for bonding pigment (a multitude of cracked and blistered paintings from the nineteenth century could attest to that), Valjohn found the mixture of mastic and linseed oil excellent for holding and blending various materials and textures to Masonite. While he gobbed on the thick, amber goo, he thought about Crescent.

He hadn't planned on asking her to marry him. The idea and the voicing of that idea had occurred simultaneously. At first he couldn't believe he'd

214

said it. Then he couldn't believe he couldn't believe it. Asking her to marry him seemed the most natural thing he'd ever done. He loved her—had no doubts. He knew he'd been forming that question in his mind from the first moment he'd laid eyes on her—back in his hospital room, waking from his deep sleep. He also was convinced that her marrying him was what she needed—that is, if she really did love him, as she professed. What better way for him to allay her guilts and fears, her sexual hang-ups, than to make an honest woman of her?

But she'd turned him down. Not immediately, not right then and there with a point-blank no. Engrossed in the perils of the Keystone Kops, she hadn't even heard his first entreaty—or pretended not to hear it. He'd been obliged to repeat himself, and even then she wouldn't voice a reply. Instead she'd given him such a long, earnest look of sympathy and sorrow he'd needed no words.

Later that night in the car parked in front of her dorm, he'd asked again. The look had returned. "Why would you want to marry me?" she'd finally responded with a question of her own.

He gave her all the reasons and then gave them all again. As he listened to himself speak of love and need, and need and love, he suddenly wished that for once he could be more like the sneering, grim-lipped stereotype of his profession. Then he wouldn't have to be on his knees now bleating like a wounded calf. Hell, he was a homicide dick! He should be grabbing her by the hair, goddamnit, yanking her to him and growling, "Okay, babe, this is the way it is. You and me or nothing!"

". . . can't go on like this . . . living without . . . knowing that you'd never . . . more than anything in the world . . ." The words that followed fit his fantasy—only she wasn't speaking them, he was.

"But you know how I am," she reasoned. "You know my . . . my problems—how little I can truly give. It wouldn't be fair to you."

"Fair? Who know's what's fair? I'm willing to take my chances. I know it could work out between us. I'll make it work. I'll . . . I . . . I only know . . ." he faltered, empty with the realization of what he did know—that she'd already made up her mind.

"Is it someone else?" he started in again.

"We've been through this."

"Is it?"

"No, no, no!"

"You don't love me?"

"It's not that either."

"Then what the hell is it? Just tell me, for godsakes!"

"I've tried."

"I know, you're a female impersonator, right?"

She smiled.

"Not good enough because even if it were true I'd still want you, rather have you than the real thing."

She shook her head. "I can't explain it. Try to understand."

"My eyebrows. Is it because of my eyebrows?"

"Your eyebrows?"

"Yes, my goddamn bushy eyebrows. Somebody once told me I ought to get them plucked." If she gave the word he'd let "Dildo" Donna zap his brows tomorrow.

"Now you know," she said and laughed, reached out and gently teased them with her fingertips. He brushed her hand away.

A long moment of silence followed.

"I don't know what else I can say." His voice was drained of all emotion. He stared out the window at the passing cars, while she told him how much she hated hurting him but that she only wanted to avoid greater pain in the future.

He felt her lips on his cheek when she kissed him good night. He heard the car door close behind her and her footsteps fade away.

He still was sitting there staring minutes later when she came back and asked if he was all right.

"Oh, sure, sure." Then mumbling mostly to himself he added, "It's just that I don't know what else I can say. . . ."

The sight of her standing there in the drive outside the window, shivering without a coat, the worried expression on her face suddenly became too much for him. He had to go lick his wounds somewhere in solitude. He managed to smile, to wave, to drive off into the loneliest of nights.

Now hunched on his knees, sifting gravel and grass over the sticky, prepared surface of his collage, he realized that he'd be licking those wounds for quite some time. At least keeping busy spared him from OD-ing on self-pity. For that he was thankful.

It was after one in the morning when he got the phone call. He still was busy with the collage, had mixed another batch of megilp and was about to infuse it with fragments of bloodstained upholstery. Wiping his hands on his shirttail, he got up stiffly, made his way across the littered floor of his studio to the study. He answered the phone, cursed under his breath the moment he heard on the other end of the line Sergeant Milton Stephansky's rasping voice.

Gaylord Radzim had shown up for his midnight shift in a bad mood. He'd had an accident on his way to the hospital, had slid his new fire-red Malibu into the back end of a city sanitation truck stopped at an alley. The roads were wet and slick, but his mind also had been preoccupied with an argument he'd had earlier in the evening with his mother. She'd been going through his closet again, had found the girl's undergarments stuffed in an old suitcase. After dinner while he was sprawled on the sofa watching TV, she'd confronted him with them. He'd grabbed them from her, told her if she didn't stay the hell out of his things he was going to move out and this time he meant it.

After punching in, Radzim went to his locker, exchanged his overcoat for a light blue orderly tunic. He hoped the old bitch would keep her mouth shut about what she'd found. . . . God, how he hated her! Always snooping around. He should have moved out long ago.

Before going upstairs he decided to get a quick cup of coffee in the employees' lounge. He needed something to settle his nerves. In the hallway he was met by a black aide. She informed him that Nurse Comstock wanted him in Emergency. There'd been an expiration.

"How's about a cup of coffee?" She was young with a real set of knockers, and he knew it wouldn't rub off.

The aide shook her head. "She want you now."

"What's the rush? That stiff sure ain't going nowhere."

"They needs the room cleared, Jack—'sides, I got better things to do be drinkin' coffee with yo' ass."

He gave her the finger behind her back but followed her down the corridor to Emergency.

Radzim wheeled the litter into the ancient service elevator, pulled the doors closed and pushed the bottom button. The elevator groaned, gave a rattle and shuddered into motion. On the way down he inspected himself in the polished brass plate of the control panel. The reflection made his forehead bulge and flattened his nose. It softened his eyes, though. He liked that. He didn't like his eyes. Too tiny and quick. He didn't like to look into them for very long. He ran a hand through the oily black curls of his hair; wiped his fingers on a corner of linen hanging from the litter just as the car reached the basement level, jerking to a halt. He swung open the heavy doors and rolled his transport into a wide, dimly lit corridor which, winding by several storage and maintenance rooms, led to the morgue.

At the receiving desk he stopped and removed the spec sheets from the litter's clipboard. The desk stood in a small, lighted alcove at the end of the hall. He had to process the entry himself. There was no regular attendant on duty after five.

Cleona Wiggins. Female. Caucasian. Thirty-two. Time of death: 11:10 P.M. Cause of death: acute loss of blood resulting from self-inflicted wounds.

A smile formed on Radzim's full, even lips. His eyes flickered. He sat down and slowly typed out an ID tag, tore off the stub and stapled it to the other pages, filing them away in a desk drawer. Then he got up and pushed the litter into the PM room, noisily banging through its large, metal bumper doors.

He lifted the body, which was concealed under the litter's dummy pallet, and slung it draped in its sheet onto the bare metal pan of one of the cooler's massive, stainless-steel drawers. After he'd straightened the corpse's still, limp form onto its backside, he pulled away the sheet to look at the face.

Cleona Wiggins.

His smile screwed into a tight smirk. The loss of blood had drained her face, leaving her skin prematurely waxen—she looked as if she'd been dead for days instead of an hour or so. But he remembered her, all right. Hard to forget that face. A real clock stopper. What a nose! She looked like an anteater. He wondered how she'd lasted thirty-two years, how she'd kept from doing herself in every time she looked in a mirror.

It was a month ago, maybe longer. She'd come into Emergency, her wrists slit. The hospital had been shorthanded that night and also short of rooms. He'd brought a spare bed down from Maternity and she'd had to sleep in a hallway. In the absence of available nurses, he'd been assigned to make sure she slept soundly, didn't roll over or rip off her IV hookups. The extra duty pissed him off. It meant he'd have to forgo his usual late-night snooze down in the seclusion of the PM room. While he was tending to one of her wraps, she'd awakened. He remembered those big eyes of hers opening up wide as saucers, pale blue, almost colorless, staring at him and then at herself and the bed and the rest of her surroundings. She was doped up and in shock, but she'd managed to ask him where she was and what had happened to her. He didn't need a second invitation. He laid it on the line. "Here," he said, grabbing her arm that was free of tubes and lifting it, "you want to do the job right? You don't slit your wrist like that," he indicated, moving his finger like a razor across her bandaged veins. "You do it this way next time, lengthwise, up and down—that way the doctors can't clamp 'em off! You got that?" He grabbed her chin and scowled into those big, dumb, washed-out eyes. Then he let go with disgust. "Your kind . . . you're never serious."

Now standing over her corpse, he pulled up the sheet, looked at the wounds on her wrists. She hadn't taken his advice. The gashes, already morbidly blue, were conventional. They ran right along her previous scars. He'd been wrong about one thing, though: She'd been serious, all right —he gave a little laugh—dead serious!

He slipped the arms back under the sheet and then tied the ID tag with its wire to the big toe of her right foot. Before rolling the drawer back into the locker, he ran his hands under the sheet again, felt her breasts. Not a half-bad pair. He pulled at them roughly, poked and slapped them about. Suddenly he felt a twitching in his pants.

He walked quickly over to the swinging doors and glanced out one of the two small porthole windows. There was no one outside: no janitors on their way to the maintenance rooms, nobody wandering in the lower corridor. Satisfied, he returned to his charge.

"Okay, Cleona, you asked for it. . . ." He unzipped his fly, leaned forward and let his erection fall squarely across the bridge of her anteater nose. He proceeded to curse and abuse her, whipped the stem of his excitement about her face, flogged her small chin, her sunken cheeks, her high, pale, unlined forehead. He prodded her eyes, which were closed; her ears. He ravished the drab tangles of her ash-brown hair.

With both hands he grabbed excitedly at her mouth and pried it open, his high school ring clicking and scraping against her teeth. He tried to open her eyes, succeeded in propping up one lid. The other drooped halfway closed. The eyes themselves had rolled back: Only the whites and the lower rim of an iris showed.

Placing his knee in the narrow metal gutter beside her head, he raised himself until he was kneeling over her, hovered there for several seconds. Her expression resembled that of someone deep in the agonizing throes of some convulsive seizure—her face frozen in a scream of deafening silence. "Now you're going to get it, bitch," he said in a fierce whisper and thrust his member directly into the gaping abyss of that scream.

"Cleo-no-no-no-no-no-no-nona!"

At the very brink of his climax, he suddenly leaped from his perch, frantically began jamming his swollen organ back into his pants. He'd heard something. He was sure of it. A scuffling noise out in the hall. Painfully he zipped up his fly, replaced the sheet over the deceased and, trying his best to regain a semblance of composure, hobbled calmly over to the doorway. There, his face flushed and covered with beads of sweat, he peered out the window.

An aide! She was standing in the outer alcove, her back to him, leaning over the desk. No . . . no, it wasn't an aide. It was a student nurse—that luscious number from the West Wing. She'd moved slightly and he was able to make out her profile. But what the fuck was she doing down here? And more importantly, had she seen him? His ass was up for grabs if she had.

He watched her closely. She appeared to be thumbing through the files in one of the drawers, was sorting through death certificates. She hadn't seen him—he was certain. She wouldn't still be standing there if she had: She'd be halfway to the night supervisor's office by now, yelling her god-damn head off.

He continued watching her, found himself becoming more and more aware of her sexually. She leaned over the desk, her long, golden hair spilling off her shoulders. He eyed the taut material of her uniform stretching across her shapely ass. Christ! She was really put together. He felt his erection throbbing in his pants—the tantrums of an angry child confined against its will . . . begging to be let out again. . . .

All at once she straightened up, turned and caught him staring at her through the small window of the door. Too startled to look away, Radzim watched in amazement as a smile slowly crept across her face. It was a smile the likes of which he'd never seen, a strangely wicked smile that told him of such wonders it made his head swim. He knew instantly that she knew, that she'd seen everything.

And she hadn't run away.

He wet his lips and swallowed. Why, the gorgeous little nympho-bitch —she was turned on! She'd seen it all and she dug it!

As he watched her walk slowly toward him, the smile still there—so tantalizing and incongruous on that angelic face—he stepped away from the window, ran a trembling hand hurriedly through his hair and swung open the door wide to receive her.

"Sorry to bother you, Lieutenant," came Stephansky's rasping voice—sounding not the least bit sorry—over the phone. "Vacation's over. Got a you-know-who waiting for you over at Windhaven Hospital. An orderly, name of Gaylord Rad—"

"Where?" blurted Valjohn, the pit of his stomach feeling as though it had dropped somewhere below his knees.

"Windhaven Hospital. An orderly, Radzim—he was published in the morgue. Real accommodating of him, I'd say."

Valjohn drove to the hospital in record time. Crescent was working nights, and the thought of her being in the same building—albeit a very large building—was extremely disquieting. The first thing he did on arriving at Windhaven was to try to contact her through the receptionist at the main desk. When she couldn't be reached, he left word for her to get in touch with him as soon as possible.

In the basement hallway, he was met by Harris, neat as ever in a charcoal-brown button-down. Valjohn decided to keep his overcoat on. He hadn't taken time to change clothes. At least the coat would hide the paint rag of a shirt he was wearing. Most of the stains on his trousers too. Harris informed him that a janitor had discovered the body and that Radzim, the deceased, had turned up negative on a preliminary Polifax make. Valjohn nodded, took a deep breath, swung through the double metal doors of the morgue and proceeded to discover the body for himself.

When he stood up again, he had few doubts. Clothed only in a light blue, blood-spattered tunic, the contorted figure lay spread-eagle on the cold cement floor at his feet, hands twisted and groping outward like those of an anguished Christ in a Grünewald crucifixion.

There was one curious disparity: The victim's genitals were missing. They'd been torn off—not unusual in itself—but they were nowhere to be seen, neither wedged between clutching fingers nor stuffed in a gaping mouth.

"Artillery's over there." Harris tipped his head, anticipating Valjohn's puzzled expression.

Valjohn walked across the room to the autopsy table. Beside it stood a scale for weighing organs during dissection. He stared into the instrument's large, oval weighing pan, winced inwardly, shifted his stance uncomfortably, bringing his legs closer together. While he stood there trying to be a reasonable man, trying to make some sort of evaluation of the grim gesture, he absently read the dial. Eighty-seven one hundredths of a pound. He'd often wondered. . . .

"A sense of humor?" queried Harris.

"A sense of something," Valjohn replied. "Who's that?" He was pointing now to the cooler vaults, the sheeted figure lying in the open drawer.

"It's a woman. Died in Emergency just a few hours ago. A suicide.
Radzim brought her down here sometime after midnight. Evidently he was
interrupted before he could get her stowed away."

Valjohn walked over, read the ID tag dangling from her toe. Cleona
Wiggins. He pulled back the sheet to take a look at her, then wished he
hadn't. God, what an expression! It was almost as though she'd witnessed
what had happened to the orderly. He covered her again and walked out
of the room.

In the hallway by the receiving desk he interrogated the janitor who'd
discovered the body. Lester Colmes, hairless and sunken-cheeked, a man
rapidly approaching his pension, had found Radzim around 1:30 A.M.
Nope, he hadn't seen or heard anything suspicious beforehand, had simply
entered the PM room to mop the floor. His first reaction when he saw the
corpse lying there was that some med students had been playing pranks
with a cadaver.

Valjohn asked him again if he'd seen anyone suspicious in the basement
earlier, anybody who didn't belong there. The answer was "Nope." Valjohn asked him if he'd seen anyone at all in the basement.

"Just Pat Corbin—he's a custodian, another old-timer like myself,"
Colmes said and grinned, dentureless. He looked like Andy Gump, his lips
flapping in a distracting way, though his speech was surprisingly unaffected.

"What was he doing down here?"

"What was he doing down here?" Colmes repeated the question as
though it were the stupidest thing he'd heard in weeks. "He was working
—that's what he was doing. Same as me. Repairing soap dispensers over
in the shop. The plungers, they get to sticking real bad an'—"

"Where is he now?"

"Pat? Upstairs, I s'pose, putting them dispensers back in the lavatories.
Fifth floor, if I'm recollectin' rightly."

Valjohn sent a patrolman to find him.

"Did you see anyone else?"

"Nope."

"Nobody at all, you're sure?"

"Sure I'm sure—wait," the old man added thoughtfully rubbing the
loose wattle of skin beneath the stubbled knob of his chin. "I did see
somebody else. She wasn't exactly in the basement, though."

"She?" Valjohn pursued with sudden alertness.

"Yep, a nurse."

"What do you mean, 'She wasn't exactly in the basement'?"

"She was in the elevator coming up from the basement. I was on the
main floor waiting to go down."

"Did she get off?"

"Nope. The doors open automatically on the main floor. That's when I seen her—when the doors opened automatically. They closed and she went on up."

"What time was this?"

"Oh, I'd say one-fifteen or so. Not long before I went into the morgue."

"You didn't happen to notice which floor she stopped on?"

"Nope, can't say that I did, didn't have to wait that long, anyway. Caught another ride real quick."

"Then it wasn't the service elevator over there?" asked Valjohn, pointing to the single unit he'd ridden down.

"That's right," the old man replied. He thumbed in the opposite direction. "It was the main ones over by the West Wing."

Valjohn nodded. "Do you think you could recognize the nurse if you saw her again?"

The old man grinned and gave a wink. "Wouldn't have no trouble on that account. She was a real looker, I'll tell you."

Valjohn asked him if he'd mind going up to the night supervisor's office with him and try to identify her. Colmes said he'd be happy to, but wondered if he first might have a moment or two to finish up some chores. Valjohn told him fine, that they could meet in the supervisor's office in fifteen minutes.

Stopping in Emergency, Valjohn talked with Nurse Comstock. She was able to supply him with the approximate times of Radzim's whereabouts and activities immediately prior to his ill-fated trip down to the morgue. She also shed some light on the orderly's character. He was no Prince Charming. She described him as a troublesome employee: irresponsible, insolent and "a very nasty person." He asked her what she meant by nasty. She was hesitant, finally alluded to his crude behavior—particularly with the younger student nurses. She refused to be more specific, would only say that he'd been reprimanded on more than one occasion. Unfortunately, she added, the hospital was very short of male help.

On his way to the supervisor's office, Valjohn spotted Crescent in one of the long, angular connecting corridors of the ground floor. She waved. He waved back, greatly relieved. He felt a strong impulse to run forward and embrace her.

When they met he reached for her hands instead. "Glad to see you're safe and sound."

"I just now got your message." She smiled, then added, "I guess you're here on business."

They stood there talking for several minutes, Valjohn voicing concern over her safety. It was entirely possible the killer was still lurking in the building. He wanted her to take the rest of the night off and leave the premises. She told him that was impossible. She did promise to be careful, to stay out of dark corners and isolated areas.

"Hey, I see you found her!"

Valjohn and Crescent turned to see Lester Colmes approaching them.

222

"Found her?" Valjohn puzzled as the old man sidled up to them, grinning. He was wearing his dentures now and no longer resembled Andy Gump.

"The nurse. This is her—the one I was telling you about."

"She . . . you mean the one you saw in the elevator?"

"Yep."

Valjohn looked to Crescent, who was smiling at Colmes, then turned back to Colmes. "You're sure?"

"Uh-huh. I may be old but not so old I couldn't remember something as purty as she looks. Go ahead, ask her."

Before Valjohn had a chance to do that, he was interrupted by the supervisor, who at that moment emerged from his office. Valjohn introduced himself, and the supervisor, Mr. Hodgekiss, who seemed very anxious to meet with him, led him by the arm back into his office. At the door Valjohn told Crescent to wait there for him, that he had some questions. She nodded.

Bewildered by the janitor's disclosure, he tried to hurry his talk with the supervisor, a short, stocky, humorless man who seemed most concerned with all the impending bad publicity. He wondered if, perhaps, Lieutenant Valjohn might not be able to tone down some of the grim details for the press. Valjohn responded with sympathy but suggested that perhaps Mr. Hodgekiss might have better luck dealing directly with the press himself.

Before leaving the supervisor's office, Valjohn was able to substantiate Nurse Comstock's appraisal of Radzim's character and made a mental note to have the victim fingerprinted. He also was able to satisfy himself that the hospital's security was sufficiently lax to allow anyone off the street fairly easy access to the basement and morgue.

Crescent wasn't in the hall, where he'd asked her to wait for him. Momentarily perturbed, he went to the main desk to summon her, was told she'd left word for him to meet her in the lounge.

"I was on break," she explained as he joined her at a table where she was drinking a cup of coffee. "I didn't know how long you'd be tied up, and I really needed something to wake me up."

Valjohn asked her in a quiet, even voice if she'd seen anyone in the basement.

"In the basement?"

"Colmes, the janitor . . . did . . . didn't he see you in the elevator coming up from the basement?"

"Oh, that," she said and laughed. "Yes, he saw me in the elevator, but I hadn't been in the basement, not really."

"Not really?"

"No," she explained, "I got on the elevator at the main floor. I wanted to go up to the fourth—that's where I'm working. I pushed the button, but the car took me down to the basement instead. I guess someone else must have pushed the basement button before me."

"You didn't get off?"

223

She shook her head. "No. Why should I? I just stayed till the doors closed again and rode back up."

"Did you see anyone waiting at the basement level?"

She shook her head no.

Valjohn sighed. He thought of how many times he himself had been kidnaped in an automated elevator.

"I think you can consider yourself very lucky," he finally commented. "According to Colmes, he saw you coming up from the basement around one-fifteen. As I figure it, that's right about the time the murderer would have been fleeing the scene of the crime. There's a good chance that whoever pushed that elevator button—the one that brought you down to the basement—"

"Oh, I wish I could help you," broke in Crescent, reaching for his hand. "I really do."

He nodded. "More than likely whoever it was chose not to risk being seen and came up the stairs instead. A break for you, I might add, because nobody's ever seen the killer and lived to tell about it."

Crescent seemed genuinely startled.

He placed his hand on top of hers. They sat for several moments in silence.

"I guess I'd better be getting back to work," she said at last.

"I've got a few things to do myself," sighed Valjohn with a thin smile.

Before they went their separate ways, Valjohn expressed a desire to see her sometime during the week. She looked at him intently and told him she'd like that very much.

They went out the very next evening, Crescent's night off. They missed a nine o'clock movie and wound up instead among a horde of excited, gyrating bodies dancing at "The Cheetah," the old Aragon Ballroom of the big-band days renovated to psychedelic. Plastic plasmic forms enveloped the enormous dance floor while exotic lights pulsed to the beat of "Baby Huey and the Baby-sitters," a local blues-rock band led by a huge, three-hundred-pound black man sporting bibbed short pants and a top hat. A mountainous assemblage of speakers and amplifiers wailed refrain after throbbing refrain.

Valjohn and Crescent danced through an entire set, Valjohn venting all his recent frustrations in the vigorous exertions of the "jerk" and the "boogaloo." Crescent matched his frenzy with a cool exuberance of her own. They seemed to complement each other perfectly—he flinging himself about the gleaming hardwood with wild, often gymnastic, moves; she floating around him with an effortless, provocative grace. When the band took its break, Valjohn and Crescent returned to collapse in the gaudy confines of their free-form polystyrene booth.

"Some workout," said Valjohn, mopping his brow with a handkerchief. His shirt was soaking wet. "How do you manage to keep so dry?"

"Willpower," she said and laughed, looking as cool and refreshed as she did when he'd picked her up at her dorm. "I just pretend I'm dancing in a sunbaked desert."

"I'll have to try that next time. Right now I feel like a steamed clam."

While they sat there waiting for the band to return, Valjohn mentioned a few of the latest developments in the case, including a conversation he'd had with Pat Corbin, the other janitor working with Lester Colmes in the basement. Corbin claimed he'd seen, or thought he'd seen, a nurse walking in the lower corridor around the time of the murder. Valjohn paused for a moment, then asked Crescent again if she'd gotten off the elevator in the basement.

She shook her head.

"You're sure?" Corbin hadn't seen enough of whoever it was to make any sort of identification. He'd only glimpsed the individual passing by the open door of the maintenance room while he was working—had only the vague impression of a woman in uniform, nothing more.

"Positive," came her relaxed answer.

He shrugged, let the matter drop.

When Baby Huey and the band resumed their music, Valjohn asked her if she'd like to dance again. She said she'd rather not.

"I know," he said, "dancing in the desert—it must be very tiring. All that hot, blowing sand. All those scorpions and rattlesnakes you have to keep stepping over." He meant to be amusing, but even though she'd smiled he knew the words had sounded petulant. He was too damn thin-skinned around her now.

"Why so sad?" she asked as he sat staring glumly at their table's flickering candle.

"No reason," he lied, forcing a smile. "Just tired, I guess." They both fell silent.

At the end of another number, the miracle occurred.

"What would you think," she asked, "if I told you that I'd changed my mind?"

He started to get up, offered his hand to lead her out on the dance floor.

She shook her head. "That's not what I'm talking about."

He dropped back down in his seat, looked puzzledly at her. Now it was she who was staring at the candle.

"You did get off the elevator in the basement. You did see someone else?"

"No, not that either."

"What then?" he asked, his breath catching in his throat.

I got my mojo workin', got my mojo workin', Baby Huey's lusty voice howled into the mike.

Got my mojo workin', got my mojo workin'.

Strobe lights pulsed overhead, froze the writhing figures on the dance floor into tiny segments of time and light, an album of action snapshots.

225

Got my mojo workin'... but it jus' don' work on you.

Without looking up, her stare still fixed intently on the flame, she answered him.

"About us, John. I'm talking about us."

part four

13

Valjohn and Crescent were married in the first week of December. The wedding was a simple affair held in a chapel of a rural Presbyterian church near Debbie Turner's hometown, Morris. Moe was best man and Debbie, maid of honor. Afterward there was a small reception at the home of Debbie's parents. Present were several friends of Debbie's family; Stella Bernstick; Nurse McGlocklin; a few of Crescent's classmates, including Frances Taylor and Sheila Klein; Gillian and Harris from Homicide, Valjohn's art agent, Erwin Kaufman; Grady McTague and Moe's mother, Rose. Superintendent Gordon, home in bed with strep throat, had been unable to make it. Because of their work schedules, the newlyweds had ruled out an elaborate honeymoon, settling instead for a weekend at Starved Rock Park, a short drive west, and its scenic old Indian lodge.

Crescent slept most of the trip, her sleeping hours still jumbled from working nights. Valjohn, who hadn't been getting all that much sleep himself lately, started to doze at the wheel and was forced to pull in at a truck stop near Ottawa for a quick cup of coffee. He also was feeling the effects of the reception punch: pineapple-strawberry delight, a fairly innocuous libation prepared by Debbie's mother which had soon taken on a more potent personality—thanks to McTague, who had smuggled in two hip flasks of rum under his baggy tweed sport coat. It was the best the boisterous newsman could do after being forced to renege on loaning the couple his XKE for the honeymoon. Two days earlier a snowplow had backed over the sleek machine and nearly totaled it.

At the truck stop Valjohn went inside alone. Crescent had looked up bleary-eyed from her blanket and asked if they were there yet. He told her no, and mercifully left her to sleep it off.

Inside a large, belligerent waitress routed him from a "truckers only" booth and then slammed down a cup of lukewarm coffee before him at the counter nearly drenching his coat sleeve. He smiled and thanked her. There was no way she could get under his skin. Not today. What the hell —he'd just married the girl of his dreams! He was soaring high. All he had to do was think of Crescent waiting for him out there in the car . . . his wife! . . . remember her eyes, her smile—realize that she belonged to him, was part of his life now and . . . he could hardly believe it. Had it really happened?

The coffee cut through his drowsiness if not his blissful daze. Feeling alert enough to drive, he walked back out to the Volks and climbed inside.

"Are we there yet?" whispered Crescent, this time not bothering to look up from the blanketed folds of her cocoon. Valjohn leaned over, kissed an exposed ear and heard a muffled purr of affection. It had happened, all right.

It was almost seven-thirty when they arrived at the park. A light snow was falling. Valjohn unloaded the luggage with Crescent at the stone-stepped main entrance of the lodge, a large, rambling log construction situated high on the edge of a bluff overlooking the Illinois River. He parked the car nearby and rejoined her at the front desk. Informed that the dining room closed promptly at eight, they had to hurry to check into their room.

The accommodations of the honeymoon suite were rustic and cozy, the rooms all in knotty pine and cedar, the furniture Early American. The bed was an immense cherrywood four-poster complete with a thick-quilted down comforter folded at its foot. A large picture window provided them with an expansive view of the river, the northern bluffs and Starved Rock itself.

Splashing water on their faces to freshen up, they made it down to the dining room with minutes to spare. The specialty of the evening was "locally caught" channel catfish croquettes. Though neither of them was overly fond of fish, they were not disappointed. The croquettes, broiled to a tasty brown and served in a delicate white wine sauce, proved to be a gourmet treat.

During the meal they amused themselves trying to guess the occupations of some of the other guests. The park was basically a summer attraction for picnickers and campers. What sort of people came here in December? There were no ski slopes or toboggan runs, no fancy shops or discotheques. Nor were there the bustling throngs that flocked to the big-name resorts. No more than twenty or thirty people now were staying at the lodge.

Valjohn tended to be somewhat suspicious of his fellow guests. From the small group of people seated around them, he discerned no less than one husband-and-wife team of international jewel thieves, one kidnaper, one fugitive high-ranking German SS officer, two embezzlers, two double agents and three members of a smuggling ring responsible for shipping tons of heroin, cocaine and LSD up the river in barges. Crescent saw only retired doctors and X-ray technicians, clandestine lovers and one tragic young woman slowly dying of an incurable disease.

"What about those two at the corner table by the window?"

Valjohn finished off the last of his broccoli au gratin and glanced across the room. "Ummm . . . I'd say a couple of movie stars traveling incognito. Yes, of course, it's Liz and Dick. How silly of me not to recognize them. They must be here pricing Starved Rock. Liz wants it set in a ring so she can wear it on her pinky."

Crescent eyed the couple again. Liz was playing the part of a tiny, white-haired dowager complete with hearing aid and walking cane. Dick was impersonating her adolescent grandson. He had freckles, a red crew cut and braces.

"I'm not at all convinced," said Crescent.

"All right," continued Valjohn, "how about that guy behind you to your right? The one seated by the totem pole."

She turned to see a well-dressed, middle-aged man, very trim and distinguished-looking with a handsome, tanned face and thickly tufted white yet boyish hair.

"Well?" prompted Valjohn when she failed to speak. She was sitting motionless, twisted around in her seat, staring.

"It's obvious, isn't it?" he pursued, becoming a little uncomfortable with the intensity of her scrutiny. He was afraid the man would look up at any moment and notice her. "He's a bunko artist, a con man. He's here now posing as an archaeologist—trying to foist off rare old Indian artifacts made in Hong Kong."

She didn't respond, continued staring as if she hadn't heard him. As if she were locked in some sort of trance.

He was about to nudge her under the table with his foot when she finally looked away. She took a drink from her glass of water. Then she said simply, "He's a rapist and a murderer. Now what sounds good for dessert?"

After they left the dining room, Valjohn stopped at the front desk and picked up several park brochures. One of them included a map to the various hiking trails. From the lobby they walked up a few stairs and entered the main lounge or Powwow Room: a great cavernous chamber whose high, open-beamed ceiling showed off a grid of giant structural logs.

Indian tapestries decorated the walls with bright colors and sharp geometric patterns. In the center of the room stood a massive stone hearth with double walk-in fireplaces. Both were filled with roaring blazes. A group of fifteen or twenty people had gathered around one side. Valjohn recognized a number of faces from the dining room.

"You're just in time. Move in here close and grab a seat," a man standing on the hearthstone in front of the group called to them. Valjohn and Crescent looked at one another, shrugged and did as they were told—Liz and Dick making room for them on a buckskin divan.

The man who'd spoken to them introduced himself. He was a park ranger, and he was about to give one of his weekly fireside talks on some of the history and legends surrounding the local area. He also was a Winnebago Indian and his name was Always-Where-the-Wind-Blows. "You can call me Al, for short," he added.

Al proved to be a skilled raconteur, entertaining his small audience for almost an hour with anecdotes and dramatic tales about the early explorers, Marquette and Joliet, the confrontations and skirmishes between the settlers and the various Indian tribes—and also, of course, between "those two great paleface tribes," the French and the English.

He told of how Starved Rock, once known as Le Rocher, the French Gibraltar of the New World, later earned its somber name. It was during the mid-1700s when Pontiac, the great Ottawa chief and leader of the mighty Iroquois and Algonquin alliance, had been murdered during a heavy drinking bout to celebrate his growing number of victories against the invading settlers. A crazed young brave had set upon him while he slept, caved in his head with a pogamoggan.

A cry of vengeance rose up in the camps of his followers. The Peorias were blamed, a small tribe of Illini known to be unsympathetic to Pontiac's crusade against the whites. They were hunted like animals by an exterminating war party of Ottawas, Potawatomis, Miamis and Kickapoos. A final remnant of the Peorias fled north to the abandoned fortress rock of the French, Le Rocher. High atop that natural bastion, they were better able to defend themselves, but Pontiac's avengers, repulsed after several attacks, contented themselves to surround their quarry and wait. There was no water on the rock, and the Peorias had few provisions. During the night they would try to lower buckets into the river, but the enemy waiting below would cut the dangling vines.

Before they became too weak to fight, the warriors of the beleaguered Peorias came down from the rock to engage their enemies in one last desperate battle. Hopelessly outnumbered, they were annihilated. The slaughter continued into the night as the women and children left alone atop the rock were unable to defend it. To escape rape and tortured death, many of them took their own lives, flinging themselves off the high cliffs into the shallow rapids below. When the ordeal finally ended, not a single Peoria survived, and Starved Rock was legend.

At the conclusion of the talk, the small audience was served hot chocolate and hot, buttered rum. While Valjohn and Crescent stood around the fireplace sipping rum from their steaming mugs, they were able to meet a number of the guests who'd been the objects of their speculations in the dining room.

"Some judge of character you are," chided Crescent after they learned his gang of embezzlers and smugglers were members of a chapter of the Illinois State Historical Society meeting for an annual seminar on Indian lore. His fugitive Nazi war criminal turned out to be a university geologist on a rock hunt, and his husband-and-wife team of international jewel thieves weren't even married.

"What about your languishing Camille over there?" said Valjohn, nodding toward a girl in a lavender turtleneck sweater. "Lung cancer, right? How much longer did you give her to live?"

Crescent giggled. Not five minutes earlier the girl had been introduced to them as Helga Murley, a sensational, new cross-country ski champion.

"Looks like it's really getting serious out there."

Valjohn glanced over his shoulder to see the man whom Crescent had stared at so intently in the dining room, her rapist-murderer. The man was smiling at him and pointing toward the terrace windows. Valjohn looked outside. The glowing yellow gas lanterns that illuminated the terrace walk flickered and vanished and reappeared through swirling clouds of white.

"A full-scale blizzard," Valjohn agreed, listening for the first time to the rising wind as it rattled the windowpanes.

"Name's Wheeler Fairchild," the man said, stepping forward with an outstretched hand. He had startling, burnished turquoise eyes and exuded charisma with an energetic smile.

Valjohn reached out, shook his hand and introduced himself. When he let go—the man's handshake was firm as a Dale Carnegie *magna cum laude*'s —and turned to introduce his bride, he discovered she no longer was standing by his side. He looked around, spotted her making her way through several small groups of people across the room.

"Er . . . that's my wife over there," he gestured with his mug, which was almost empty. "I guess she went back for a refill," he added as he watched her join a couple of people standing in front of the refreshment table. Curious she hadn't asked him if he wanted one too. Nervous as a new bride, he thought and smiled, allowing himself to forget for the moment the stipulations of their marriage.

"Very lovely," said Wheeler Fairchild, staring after her with an appreciative eye.

Once again Valjohn had to pinch himself mentally. No dream. The lovely woman standing across the room was his wife. The lovely Crescent O'Leary . . . the lovely Mrs. John Valjohn . . . It really had happened.

"Thank you," he managed from incredible heights.

"Myself—I have to batch it this weekend," Fairchild confided. He pulled out his wallet and showed Valjohn a picture of his own wife, Tooter.

"Very lovely also," said Valjohn, returning the compliment. He did not have to lie. The young, raven-haired woman in the photo was unquestionably beautiful.

"Of course, that picture was taken over twenty years ago," said Fairchild, grinning. He showed Valjohn another picture of his two grown children, then handed him a business card declaring that he was a real-estate broker and consultant from Chicago who specialized in housing developments, shopping centers and high-rises.

"How about yourself, John, what do you do?"

Valjohn told him he was a detective with the CCPD.

Fairchild knitted his brow in a show of deep concentration. "Valjohn . . . Detective Valjohn . . . wait, now I remember!" he exclaimed triumphantly. "You're the 'cubist cop'—the guy who solves crimes by painting pictures!"

Valjohn nodded, amazed every time someone recognized him.

"I thought you looked familiar," continued Fairchild. "I'll bet you don't remember me, though, do you?" Before Valjohn could answer, Fairchild told him.

"I was up there on that bandstand with you—you know—a couple of years ago when the mayor pinned a medal on your chest. The St. Patrick's Day parade, right?"

Valjohn smiled. "Right."

"I forgot to mention I dabble in politics. I'm an alderman—or was. I resigned my seat a few months back. I'm planning to run for state Senate next term." He announced this last piece of information loudly enough to include in his audience nearly everyone on their side of the fireplace. "Anyway, I sat a few rows in front of you. Right behind the governor and the mayor."

Valjohn continued smiling and nodded. Though he couldn't remember Fairchild, he did remember the platform had been overflowing with bigwigs.

"So what brings you down here to Starved Rock, Lieutenant? It is 'Lieutenant,' isn't it?"

Valjohn started to tell him he was on his honeymoon, then thought better of it.

"Bring your paints with you, or is this a pleasure trip?"

"A pleasure trip," said Valjohn. "Just taking a little weekend vacation."

"Wonderful," said Wheeler Fairchild with resounding sincerity. He reached up, patted one side of his carefully fluffed hair, then launched into a long-winded discourse on his own weekend activities. He was returning from a business confab in the Quad Cities—very important—had stopped off here at the lodge to look over the park, to size up the neighboring farm acreage in terms of possible recreation development.

"This place could really take off, you know."

234

What was taking Crescent so long to get her drink? While Valjohn listened to Fairchild's scheme for turning the modest historical park into a major tourist funland, he scanned the room to see where she'd gotten sidetracked.

"—nothing like it downstate and only a few hours away from one of the major population centers in the country."

She was nowhere to be seen.

"You've already got the water—so there's your boating and water skiing and what-have-you. All you need to do is put in a shopping mall, maybe a miniature golf course, some go-cart racetracks, kiddie rides . . ."

Concerned, he decided he'd better go looking for her. He set down his mug on a nearby table.

"—room for a dozen condominiums around the rock. Hell—a whole damn village across the river!"

Valjohn excused himself. He found her shortly afterward in the hallway outside the ladies' rest room.

"Hey, I missed you. Are you all right?"

"Yes, yes, I'm sorry. I just felt a little dizzy in there."

"You're sure you're all right?"

"Yes, I'm fine now. Just a little too much good cheer, that's all."

"You missed meeting our rapist-murderer-dealer-in-phony-Indian-artifacts. He may not be a bunko artist, but he's the next best thing."

"What's that?"

"A Chicago alderman. Come on, I'll introduce you to him. He's dying to meet you."

"I . . . I'd rather not. I'm really tired. Would you mind terribly if we went up to our room now?"

Valjohn didn't mind at all.

The blizzard was still raging. He sat on the edge of the bed in a pair of blue pinstripe pajamas, brand-new, staring out the window. The dense swarm of flakes made his eyes swim. He could barely discern the outline of tree branches a few feet beyond the frosted pane.

He glanced at the bed, the big, honeymoon four-poster he was sitting on. Its top sheet, blanket and comforter all were turned back, ready and waiting. He gave it a sudden commiserating slap and reflected on the conditions of his marriage.

"I still think it would be very unfair to you," her words echoed. "Marriage wouldn't change anything between us—I mean—I'd still be the way I am."

"And I'd still be willing to take my chances." Those had been his words. He loved her. Life was miserable without her, wasn't worth living. He'd accept her on any terms.

He often wondered after that night dancing at The Cheetah just what it was that had made her change her mind. He never asked her, though, fearful she might change it again. Now as he sat here on their honeymoon bed, he only hoped he possessed the strength to honor the fine print of their agreement.

Crescent emerged from the bathroom wearing a modest, pastel green nightie. She stored some toiletries in her overnight bag, walked to the window and looked out, commenting on the fury of the storm. Valjohn looked at her, then diverted his eyes to the floor, trying not to gaze on her beauty too long or too intently. Seeming to sense his discomfort, she climbed quickly into bed and slid under the covers.

He started to speak, stopped, started to speak and stopped again.

He climbed into bed beside her. Turned away from one another, they exchanged "good nights." He smiled bravely, stared at the wall. Nothing had changed between them. But time was on his side now. He was sure of it. He could wait. He had all the patience in the world. Sooner or later . . .

Right now he was content simply to lie there, feel her warm, breathing presence next to him in the same bed. That was enough. Before he fell asleep he realized for the last time that day he was a married man. He felt gloriously happy.

They were up early the next morning playing in the fresh snow like a couple of kids. The blizzard had subsided, but the clouds continued to hang low and swollen.

After a hearty breakfast of sourdough pancakes, grits and bacon, they went ice skating on a nearby pond. Valjohn was not overly fond of the sport: His ankles sagged and his knees wobbled, but he managed to survive the ordeal with only half a dozen minor spills.

"All right, hotdog, where did you learn to skate?" he growled as he watched his bride slash the ice in sweeping, graceful arcs and sharp, cutting pirouettes.

"I'm really not that good," she said, laughing back at him. "It's just that you're so terrible."

For lunch they had bowls of hot chili, sitting with red faces by the fireplace in the Powwow Room and warming their feet. Before going out again in the afternoon, they both bundled up in extra sweaters and stockings.

They climbed Starved Rock, following a snow-covered trail with icy stone steps that led them up the back side to the summit. There they found a bare flagpole and, imbedded in a large boulder, a bronze plaque commemorating the rock's history. They dutifully read the inscription, then ventured out as close as they dared to the icy edge of the sandstone cliffs.

"That's a long way down to lower a bucket," said Valjohn, peering cautiously over the precipice.

Crescent took a step closer and stared down in silence. Valjohn, not normally bothered by heights, found his legs starting to tremble, grabbed hold of her arm and made her step back.

"Let's not re-create history here—I mean, we're not even under attack."

Crescent didn't speak, continued looking down at the rocks and river below.

"It is kind of spooky up here," said Valjohn after a long silence. It was as if the ghosts of the ill-fated Peorias still were there—all those poor women and children. He looked at Crescent, imagined her for a moment as a young squaw, babe in arms, getting ready to leap to her doom. . . .

He looked down again, felt dizzy, closed his eyes. When he reopened them he shifted his gaze upriver. A dam stretched across the water to the east with a lock and pilot channel on the far shore. Above the dam the river was frozen over, streaked with patches of snow and broken ice. Below it the water churned through open gates, flowing downriver in a swift, rolling current. He lifted his eyes to include the vast white panorama of the valley to the north—the wooded bluffs, the open fields and bordering rim of prairie. He cringed when he thought of Wheeler Fairchild's plans, of what he and his high-powered developers might do someday to this picture-book landscape. The rock was under siege again, he mused—twentieth-century style.

"Come on, let's go down. I'm starting to get cold up here." He turned to go, then looked back to see if she was coming. She wasn't. Instead when he'd moved away, she took another step forward and once more was standing inches from the edge.

"Jesus, Crescent, be careful!"

She seemed not to hear him. It was as if she were completely mesmerized by the churning flow of the river below. The wind surged behind them, making her stance even more precarious. At any instant she appeared as though she might lean too far, lose her balance, slip on the icy edge.

"Crescent!"

She failed to respond.

"What in hell are you trying to prove?"

She swung around, her face with that appalling look he'd seen before—strangely devoid of expression, her eyes disoriented, slightly out of focus.

He made a lunge forward, grabbed at her arm. She recoiled from his touch, jerked away. For one awful moment as she wavered on the brink, the wind tugging at them both, he thought she was going over.

In the next instant her eyes cleared; they seemed to recognize him for the first time. She fell forward into his arms.

"I'm sorry," she apologized when they'd climbed down from the rock and stood at last along the main trail on level ground. "I guess I'm still dizzy from all that's happened."

Valjohn tried to help her shrug off the incident with a few jokes, but inside he still was badly shaken.

"Maybe we should go back to the lodge," he suggested.

"No, really, I feel fine now. Let's go see some more sights."

They continued climbing around the bluffs for another hour, enjoying the higher promontories—Lover's Leap, Eagle Cliff and Pulpit Rock—however, from the lower trails. Leaving the bluffs, they hiked in an easterly direction through a heavily thicketed woods, eventually joining a trail that flanked the river. Along this trail they came across a succession of small canyons that cut back deep into the ridge above. They explored a number of these, each one seeming more beautiful and intriguing than the last. The sheer walls of erosion-carved earth and stone towered over them as they wound their way through the narrow corridors. There were countless caves and rocky caldrons. At the end of Tonti Canyon they discovered a spectacular frozen waterfall. A huge pillar of ice, rising from the canyon floor, attached itself to a horseshoe rim of stone sixty feet above. They were able to climb behind it into a deep grotto hollowed from the rock by time and beating water. From within the grotto the great wall of translucent hanging ice bathed them in a deep emerald light.

"It's like being in a cathedral," marveled Crescent, her words resounding off the silent, crystal cataract with a sepulchral ring.

"Look," Valjohn said, holding up his hand to Crescent's face. "We're the same color: green."

"I guess the marriage took."

They both laughed.

They'd lost all track of time exploring the canyons. When they were again out on the river trail, Valjohn began to worry. It had started to snow. The overcast sky was already darkening in the east, and a frigid breeze swept across the river. They hadn't seen anyone else on the trails for over an hour now. The last one had been Helga Murley at Sandstone Point. She was speedily high-toeing it back to the lodge on her cross-country skis.

"We'd better make tracks," he exhorted, picking up the pace. "We've got two or three miles to cover at least."

Following the river trail gave them no trouble. Though the sky in front of them grew darker by the minute, the path itself was wide and easy to see, and the river offered a constant bearing. Things worsened considerably, however, when they had to leave the river and head south through the woods. The snowfall had increased steadily until it now was approaching the blizzard proportions of the night before. What little daylight remained was blotted out by the trees.

Valjohn lowered his head and did his best to trace the path through the stinging, wind-driven darkness. He soon learned he was no Nanook of the North. Less than five minutes after they'd left the river trail, he lost the way and floundered in a snowdrift up to his waist.

He felt Crescent tugging on his arm. He heard her shout something; her scarf muffled the words. She pointed in another direction. He followed her, found the path again.

Resuming the lead, it was only a matter of time before he was once more floundering. His concern rapidly approached panic. If they kept stumbling blindly about, they might fall into one of a number of deep ravines. Yet

238

they had to keep moving or they'd freeze. Tomorrow's headlines flashed in his mind as he struggled to free his legs from the deep snow.

SEVERE WINTER STORM CONTINUES
ICY GRIP ON MIDWEST:
TWO DIE IN STATE PARK

She was tugging on his arm again, pointing a different way. The path led off behind them. He made another attempt to stay on it, squinted in the swirling gloom. His face was sliced raw by the wind-driven flakes. His eyes watered, blurred. He crashed into snagging thickets, wallowed once again into waist-deep drifts. Christ, they were goners!

The frozen bodies of a honeymoon couple were discovered today at the bottom of an icy cliff only ten yards from the main trail. It is not known at this time whether the victims were killed outright by the fall or whether lying injured in the snow they succumbed to freezing temperatures. . . .

When he felt her pulling his arm, beckoning him back in another direction, he decided it was time to swallow his male pride and let her do the leading. What the hell, he admitted to himself, plodding along behind, she seemed to be having no trouble staying on the path, while he could barely see beyond his own stumbling feet. She must be part polar bear. . . .

Make that *all* polar bear, he decided twenty minutes later when they emerged from the woods, trudged halfway across the parking lot before the lights of the lodge at last became visible, glowing faintly—gloriously orange—through the blinding storm.

"Well, if it isn't the intrepid explorers, Marquette and Joliet. We'd about given up on you."

Valjohn and Crescent, busily shaking off snow in the vestibule of the lobby, turned to see Always-Where-the-Wind-Blows. Helga Murley had told him that she'd seen them heading east near Sandstone Point as late as four o'clock. He'd already phoned for a rescue detail.

Soon they were out of their cold, wet clothes and sitting by an enormous crackling fire in the Powwow Room, sipping hot, buttered rum.

"You're lucky you married a real woodsman there," said the ranger to Crescent as he worked on the fire with a poker. "Not many men could find their way back in this kind of blow."

"Not many women either," said Valjohn with a grin. Crescent smiled back a young bride's smile. They reached out and held each other's hand tightly.

Monday morning they decided to stay over a couple of extra days. They were having too much fun to face the reality of the city so soon. Miss Bernstick granted Crescent's request over the phone with her blessing,

239

even said laughingly that she'd fill in for her herself if the need arose. Howland didn't care if Valjohn ever came back. When Valjohn talked to Greg Harris, however, he learned that James Jesse had called Saturday and wanted Valjohn to call him back. Moe also had left a message first thing in the morning. He hadn't elaborated, just said it was important.

"Damn!" muttered Valjohn to himself in the phone booth. He knew it was too good to last. He debated walking away and rejoining Crescent in the Powwow Room, where he'd left her writing postcards. Instead he sighed and placed a call to Durango, Colorado.

"Got to thinking again about that gun of yours, Lieutenant," twanged Jesse's voice. "Only foreign-made piece in the collection. A replica besides. Then just t'other day while I was on old Doc Leuchre's table, getting my back knuckle-popped, it come to me. Donald Strunt, a dealer back there in your own town—he's your man. Reason I remember is 'cuz he was interested in buying a package, half a dozen guns or so. I threw in yours just to sweeten the pot. He went for it, but said he'd prob'ly never move the Hammerli—not in Chicago. Claimed nobody never bought nothing over a three-inch barrel there. Strictly snub-nose territory. That just kind of stuck in my mind. Hope you still can use it. . . ."

Valjohn was back on the line to headquarters. He relayed Strunt's name to Harris and set him in motion; then he called through to the lab, but Moe had stepped out. Bert Carlson had no idea what was on the old man's mind.

After Valjohn hung up, he sat for a moment with his thoughts. His gut feeling that the case was about to break had returned, and he could only lament the lousy timing. He wondered if Moe's message had anything more to do with that crazy matter regarding the woman in the woods.

He warned Crescent when he returned to the Powwow Room that the honeymoon had been put on hold.

Harris didn't call until after lunch. He'd located Donald Strunt. He was still a gun dealer but had moved his business from Chicago to East St. Louis over a year ago. Harris had called him, and Strunt had acknowledged selling the Hammerli in Chicago. He refused to divulge the name of the buyer over the phone, though. Greg had a ten o'clock appointment at the dentist's tomorrow but he was planning to fly down afterward.

"No need," said Valjohn. "I'm halfway there."

Crescent was disappointed but understanding. They drove to Joliet—snowplows had the roads in fairly good shape—where she was able to take a commuter back to the city. Two hours later Valjohn caught an Ozark flight to St. Louis.

Early Tuesday morning he stepped out of a waiting taxi in a small East St. Louis shopping center and entered a store called Guns, Guns, Guns. He introduced himself to Donald Strunt, who stood solemn-faced behind a display counter filled with Saturday-night specials. A short, slight man with ferret eyes, he made a show of carefully scrutinizing Valjohn's identification. Finally he shrugged and walked away.

240

While Strunt searched his files in a back room, a salesman standing nearby tried to engage Valjohn in gun talk.

"Got some great buys in Smith and Wessons. Take a trade too."

"Could never part with old Betsy here," said Valjohn, slapping the hollow holster under his coat. "Not for love or money."

Strunt returned with a yellow sales slip and let it drop on the counter. Valjohn read the name beneath a down-payment entry. Then read it again. He swore under his breath.

The proprietor smiled faintly. "Anything else I can do for you, Lieutenant?"

Flying back under heavy clouds that seemed to merge with the white landscape below, Valjohn stared out the plane's oval window and contemplated the name on the sales slip. Another dead end. About as dead as they come, he sighed, recalling yet again the remains of Harold Bledsoe. So much for a major breakthrough.

It was snowing when he landed at Joliet. In the car heading for Chicago, he tried looking on the positive side. At least Bledsoe's ownership of the gun that had killed the old fisherman corroborated his findings in the autopsy. Bledsoe now was a prime murder suspect. And that made his profile compute. Valjohn scoffed. Some detective he was. To hell with tracking down the murderer. It took all his time and effort just to prove who the victims were!

"I wasn't sure you'd be able to make it home today," greeted Crescent at the apartment with an affectionate kiss, "but I started dinner anyway. It's been snowing solid since noon."

"Roads weren't too bad," Valjohn said, shaking off his coat. "Plane was delayed, though. Spent an hour and a half sitting on the runway."

She told him headquarters had been trying to reach him all afternoon. First thing tomorrow, he told himself as he strode to the phone, get that damn radio in the Volks repaired!

After he'd hung up, he walked to the hall and put his coat back on.

"Duty calls again so soon?" asked Crescent. The disappointment brimmed in her eyes.

"It's not that," he said. He started to repeat himself, fell silent. "It's . . . it's not that," he finally did repeat himself. "It's not that at all."

Sweeney, Gillian and Harris met him in his office. They gave verbal summaries of their written reports. Moe's body had been found last night in an alley a couple of blocks from his home. Apparently he was returning from a neighborhood deli where he'd just bought groceries.

Murdered. Sexually molested. Mutilated. Moe, they were telling him, was being tabbed a C-65-1834 victim.

"For chrissakes, he was an old man! A cripple! What about the profile?" Valjohn was shouting, but not at the three men in his office.

"I know how you feel, V.J.," said Harris softly. "The evidence, though . . . the MO . . ."

Sweeney shrugged.

"See for yourself. Draw your own conclusions."

Valjohn wasn't sure he was up to it. Not while he was still in shock. He swallowed air, then decided there was no way he could put it off. He had to get it over with, to find out what was what while he still possessed some semblance of sanity.

Late in the evening he took a break to call Crescent. He told her he was not coming home. He tried to apologize—not just for deserting her two nights in a row, but for everything—the way their honeymoon had ended, the way their new life was beginning. She cut him short. The honeymoon had been wonderful, she said. Its memory never could be marred or taken away from her. The other—it was nothing he could have prevented, and now at least they could share and endure their grief together.

As he worked through the night, he was vexed with the nagging thought that he damn straight could have prevented it. He'd certainly been fore-warned. Why hadn't he been more emphatic? Why had he let Moe talk him out of his worst fears? It was as though the only thing his old friend were afraid of was losing his mind. Once he'd proved to himself there really was someone following him, he was too relieved to see the danger. And if only he'd confided the woman's name. But, damnit, he, Valjohn, should have called Moe back Monday afternoon! There'd still been time. . . . Now all he could do was renew his efforts to nail the killer. Renew them with a vengeance and try somehow to live with his guilts.

He drove to the murder site as soon as it was daylight. In the middle of the morning he returned to catch an hour's sleep on a cot at headquarters. It was night before he once more went home.

They ate dinner in the kitchen. Though Valjohn hadn't eaten since a hurried breakfast, he wasn't hungry. Out of deference to his young bride, he did manage to down a few mouthfuls of a tasty rice dish with stewed lentils and chunks of lamb.

When he'd finished, Crescent handed him a newspaper.

"You didn't tell me about this," she said, turning to clear the dishes from the table.

It was yesterday's final edition of the *Times*. The morning lead story—a bombing run into Cambodia—had been dropped to a short hanger halfway down the second page. The front page was all Moe. *Reaper Strikes Again!* There were pictures of the alley, bloodstained snow, his sheeted remains being rolled away on an ambulance litter. Inserted to one side was his recent retirement photo—an unbecoming likeness that made him look morbidly underweight and at least ninety years old. The caption read: "Moe Frank. Victim No. 22."

"I didn't know myself until I went to headquarters."

"Don't you find it hard to believe?"

Valjohn looked at Crescent staring at him across the kitchen. There was an edge to her voice that surprised him.

He shrugged. Examining the remains of strangers was bad enough. Seeing Moe stretched out on the gleaming PM table had been almost more than he could bear. But the wounds had been there, more grisly than ever, looking pathetically grotesque on the broken body of an old man.

"Don't you?"

Of course there were discrepancies. Bruises around his neck suggested strangulation, yet he'd bled to death. The telltale residue of evidence that Moe himself had discovered was missing. There was also his heart—in bad shape, ischemic, somewhat enlarged—but nothing like the ruptured, blown-out organs of the other victims. Most other victims. There were exceptions. Skip Varner, for instance. A postmortem had revealed nothing unusual about his heart; like Moe, he too had died from loss of blood. Varner's body also lacked any trace of the telltale residue. Then Moe's story about the woman in the woods and on the train—that left even less room for doubt. The fact that he thought he recognized her certainly supplied a motive. The Reaper had already proved deadly efficient in keeping her identity a secret . . . though why she was tailing him in the first place was still a complete mystery. Perhaps there were other particulars Moe hadn't confided.

"I . . . I guess I really don't feel up to discussing it, love, not tonight," he finally replied in a voice emphasizing his exhaustion. The least he could do was spare her the details. They would only upset her further.

For an instant he was startled; he thought he detected a flash of anger in her eyes. "I mean, it's pretty awful," he added quickly, wondering if he'd somehow offended her.

"I understand," she yielded softly. "I didn't mean to pry. Forgive me?"

He reached for her hand. It had been a long day, and they both were feeling the strain. Whatever look he'd thought he'd seen in her eyes was gone. In its place he could see only warmth, love, a reflection of their mutual sorrow.

Thursday presented no new startling revelations, only another curiosity to add to the growing list. A single black hair had been found in a wound, one of the lacerations across the buttocks. It did not appear to be human, proved instead to be that of a dog. Valjohn mused over it, at last dismissed it as stray debris picked up in the alley.

The funeral was set for Friday. Valjohn and Crescent both spent as much time as possible with Rose, staying overnight with her until her younger sister, Marla—a mere child of seventy-nine—arrived from California on Friday morning. Rose held up surprisingly well. She managed to keep busy, shuffled about the house, occupying herself with an endless succession of time-consuming tasks. In conversation she refused to dwell on Moe's death, would speak only about her happy memories and good fortune for being blessed with such a son. She did complain about the newspapers running his retirement picture. "Poor Moey—like I never fed him he looked."

After the funeral, Rose announced she was accepting an invitation to go live on the West Coast in Carmel Valley with her sister. She admitted that she'd had more than enough of the Windy City for one lifetime.

Rose and her sister left Monday. Crescent had to work, but Valjohn was able to drive them to O'Hare and to see them safely aboard their plane. Standing by a concourse observation window, he stayed to watch the giant silver 707 lumber down the runway and rotate skyward with almost supernatural defiance. He continued to stand there until the plane was nothing more than a glint in the fading afternoon light.

As he walked back down the long concourse, then across the crowded lobby and out to his car, he couldn't explain it, but he had the undeniable feeling he was being followed.

The feeling persisted through the holidays and on into the new year. It remained a premonition, nothing more; yet there were moments when it loomed every bit as distinct and disquieting as the experience described by Moe. Valjohn did not take it lightly—particularly after what had happened to Moe and the alarming possibility that the Reaper was now somehow bent on turning the tables and hunting her pursuers. But for the same reasons, he also could not rule out his imagination. Moe's fate had shaken him profoundly. He did take consolation in the knowledge, however, that if it was all in his mind, it hardly gainsaid his sanity. What might only be a bad case of jitters seemed, as a matter of self-preservation, perfectly reasonable.

14

Frigidity: Its Causes and Cures, by Dr. Cronus C. Striddler. The young librarian, her face made up like Elizabeth Taylor made up like Cleopatra, stamped the inside cover and slid the book across her desk.

"Good luck," she said with a smirk.

Valjohn almost thanked her as he picked up the book, a medium-thick gold volume, and hastily retreated, his footsteps echoing soulfully down an empty marble corridor of the main public library. He paused at the door before going outside and spun quickly around.

For the next few days he kept the copy in his desk at headquarters, reading it in his spare time and after work. He told himself he wasn't panicking, just calmly researching a logical avenue of consideration. They'd been married now for nearly three months.

It came as no great surprise to find out that frigidity was an extremely complex condition. He learned its causes could range all the way from religious guilts and fear of unwanted pregnancy to deficient thyroid output and tumors on the spine. The cures, whenever possible, were just as varied and complex.

Striddler dwelled on one particular cause of frigidity most common in the American marriage: namely, clitoral bypass. Clitoral bypass—or "clit-b," as Striddler referred to it in the incisive economy of his clinical vernacular—was the failure of a woman to become sexually aroused stemming from a lack of physical stimulation: Her clitoris simply was not being adequately manipulated. Consequently sex became drudgery for her. Striddler's remedy was obvious. The blame rested squarely on the shoulders—or more accurately, the fingertips—of the American male who, impatient as he was arrogant, had to learn "how to prime the pump."

"Clit-b," Valjohn scoffed, setting the book aside. A lot of good it did him to contemplate his digital dexterity. Crescent might very well be suffering from penis envy or a castration complex, but she could never be regarded the victim of his impatient fumblings. She wouldn't so much as allow him to stroke her derriere, fully clothed, no less. She was not about to let him trespass the hallowed breach. If Striddler's patients were frigid, then Crescent was cryogenic, her passion never rising above the temperature of liquid nitrogen.

At night in their apartment, after dinner, watching TV or listening to the stereo, she would allow him to rest his head on her lap. He would lie stretched out on the divan, and she would hold his head, gently teasing his springy, cinnamon hair. There were times when he felt complete serenity, basking in the luxury of her nearness, her touch. He felt intoxicated—wonderfully insulated from all loneliness, the cold and fears of the outside world.

It was not always such a pleasant experience. Sometimes lying there he would become suddenly aroused. He would concentrate on the feel of her thighs beneath his head . . . longed to roll over . . . bury his face in the folds of her clothing. When the desire became more than he could bear, when his body began to tremble and his mouth run dry, he would jump up, extricate himself from her. He would change a record or pour himself a drink, go to the bathroom, to the study, smoke his pipe—anything that would give him time to simmer down, regain a handle on his heroic equanimity.

"I can't believe you said that!" he exclaimed one evening, lifting his head from her lap and giving her a look of shocked reproach.

"Oh, come now, I don't think it's that awful," she replied, deftly massaging his temples. She pressed his head gently down until it was again resting on her lap. "Considering the circumstances . . ."

Valjohn closed his eyes. Debussy was playing on the stereo. Earlier in the evening they'd been out to see a movie, a spicy Italian comedy starring Marcello Mastroianni. That obviously was where she'd gotten the idea, and he still found it hard to believe—she, his own wife, suggesting that he take a mistress!

"I mean, it seems only fair. And logical too. Our marriage has to be difficult for you. The strain you must be under—"

"I can handle it," he snapped, his head popping up again.

"I know you can," she said softly. This time her fingers worked the muscles of his neck. "I just thought it might . . . might relieve some of your tension. I feel so guilty."

246

He lowered his head and closed his eyes again, concentrated on the pulsing orchestral strains of *La Mer*. He wasn't trying to play the martyr's role. From the moment he'd first met Crescent, his interest in other women had waned. Now it was nonexistent. The idea of a mistress was repugnant to him. That Crescent had suggested it made it even worse. He heard it as a declaration of her own dispassion. She either couldn't or wouldn't feel jealousy because she ultimately didn't love. It seemed as though she herself were committing the infidelity.

"You're angry with me for bringing it up, aren't you?"

"Let's just drop it, okay?"

She leaned over and kissed him on the mouth—hardly a seductive smooch but not exactly a sisterly peck either. God, she was driving him crazy! For an instant he glimpsed the incredible power she had over him. His head lying like a sacrificial offering on the altar of her lap . . . and his manhood . . . withering away in his pants like a cloistered monk.

If he had any balls he'd roll over right now and tear off her clothes. To hell with the fine print of their arrangement and to hell with mistresses and being fair—he'd take her right now, with *La Mer* flooding in their ears!

If he had any balls.

In the next instant he was on his feet. He strode to the record player, rejected Debussy. He thumbed through a pile of albums, flung on a Bach concerto in its place. He stalked into the kitchen and poured himself a glass of water. He took a drink, took another, emptied the glass in the sink and slammed it upside down on the counter. Then he walked out of the kitchen, being careful not to glance back into the living room—he didn't want her to see the turmoil in his eyes—and proceeded to his study. There he packed his pipe with an acrid burley blend. He lit it and feverishly continued sucking on the stem long after the fire had turned to ashes. Finally he set it down. He took a cold shower. He went to bed.

On his way home from work one evening he stopped off at the library to return the Striddler book. This time he'd exited the building and was halfway down the block before he spun around. Startled, he stood rooted to the pavement. She was there! Or someone was—he'd just seen the person duck back quickly into the entranceway.

Dodging pedestrians, he ran up the sidewalk, the front steps and reentered the building. Again he spotted a figure just disappearing through a doorway at the end of the corridor. It was a woman, he was sure; he'd caught a glimpse of her blue scarf and long blond hair.

He pursued her into a periodical reference room. A dozen people sat around reading at tables or hunched over microfilm projectors. He took a quick scan. Nobody fit. Across the room stood another doorway. He hurried through it. He arrived at the main entrance to the stacks, halted at a turnstile and asked the attendant seated there if anyone had just passed through.

"Like how long ago?" the attendant asked without looking up. Books and papers were spread before him. He was busily writing notes.

"Like right now—moments ago!"

The attendant shook his head.

"Is this the only way into the stacks?"

"Uh huh."

"What about that door over there—the one marked 'Library Personnel Only'—is it locked?"

"Not while I'm on duty."

Valjohn loosely whistled air. He started through the turnstile.

"You got a stack permit?" said the attendant, looking up from his work for the first time.

Hopeless, thought Valjohn as he made his way along the lower tier of the stacks. Endless rows of books. A labyrinth of aisles. And there were seven levels! He came to a small elevator. He paused and reached inside, pushing the button to the top floor. He pulled his arm out as the door rolled shut. Then he positioned himself behind a nearby stairway and waited.

Shortly, he heard footsteps coming down the metal stairs. They stopped at what sounded to be the next level above him. Several seconds elapsed. Suddenly he heard them again, louder this time, rushing back upstairs. He chased after them.

On the fourth level, he stopped to catch his breath and listen. No sound from above. He ran heavy-footed a short distance, then abruptly halted. The footsteps returned, ran a short distance and also halted. In the following silence, he almost could hear her listening.

The Reaper. Was she trying to escape or lure him into a trap? He'd find out soon enough. He lunged up the stairs again and dashed all the way to the top.

The seventh level, unlike the lower ones, stretched before him dark and deserted. He walked cautiously over to the first row and turned on a light switch. The aisle was filled with shadows, less than half its string of lights working. It appeared empty. He checked three more aisles, then found the lights to the next two completely burned out. Damn! He stared into the gloom and shook his head. He walked back to the first row, where a skylight window pole stood in a corner. He picked it up and swung it.

He moved slowly in the darkness, jabbing the metal tip of the pole ahead of him like a spear. Near the end of the second unlit aisle, he thought he heard something. He stopped, listened.

And his skin began to crawl—a ridiculous hyperbole, he'd always thought—but now he actually felt it: little dermal patches slithering up his backside, the insides of his arms; his entire scalp migrating . . . because out of the corner of his left eye, he detected something moving! One of the books on a shelf, head high, across from him—he could barely discern it in the darkness—but it was slowly sliding inward. . . .

He turned his head slightly and watched as an adjacent book also began to slip away softly. Then another—each disappearing as if being swallowed by the shelf itself. He leaned forward, heart pounding, and peered into the widening gap. Something brushed by his hair. He met the faintest glimmer of eyes peering back.

Recoiling, he lurched to one side, lashed the pole upward at the shelf, scattering musty books and ancient dust. He continued beating at the shelf until he heard footsteps retreating on the other side—running down the aisle. He stood there soaked in sweat and gasping, momentarily drained by his frenzied outburst. Then he resumed the chase. A stool hidden in the shadows sent him sprawling.

By the time he was on his feet again and had picked up his pole, the footsteps were long gone. If she'd doubled back, she probably was halfway out of the building by now. Just in case, though, he decided to search the remaining four rows.

None of the lights worked. Once more he was about to venture into the darkness when he heard a scuffling sound beyond the last row where several study carrels lined the wall. He approached them, both hands locked and trembling on the pole. The door to the second one hung ajar. He could hear strained breathing just inside. Inching forward, holding his own breath, he ran a hand across the outer partition and felt a light switch. In one swift motion, pole uplifted to strike, he switched on the light and kicked open the door.

Two teenagers screwing on the floor rolled apart. They shielded their eyes and scrambled for their clothes.

In the first week of April, following the assassination of Dr. Martin Luther King in Memphis, rioting broke out in the West Side ghetto, one of the most squalid and heavily populated areas in the city. Mayor Dooley, viewing the torched and looted buildings from a helicopter, was stunned. After landing from his apocalyptic flight all he could say was, "It's beyond me . . . a thing like this happening here . . . in our city." His dismay turned quickly into anger, and he went on television to demand that the police be instructed to shoot to kill arsonists, and to shoot to maim or cripple looters. Children were only to be sprayed with Mace and detained.

When Superintendent Gordon ignored his directives, the mayor reiterated them in person. Gordon remained unbending. Aggrieved by such insubordination, the mayor called a press conference and let it be known that he was *very* disappointed with his police department.

"I assumed they (the police) would want to shoot an arsonist on sight, anyone with a Molotov cocktail in his hand. This type of person is a potential murderer or worse. He is trying to burn down our city for which it stands. I assumed looters running from stores would also want to be shot. Not killed, just maimed. I learned today I was sadly mistaken. This was not the case at all. . . ."

Gordon was forced to defend his position publicly. He stated that nearly a year ago he'd delivered a general order banning the use of weapon fire during riot situations. He felt it was his duty to remind the mayor that the police still were dealing with suspects, not convicted felons; he suggested that it might be difficult at times to determine whether a man was preparing to throw a bottle of suspected flammable liquid or merely preparing to take a drink. The superintendent stressed the importance of "minimum force" and leaving life-and-death decision making to the discretion of the individual officers on the scene.

The mayor fumed, but backed off as strong criticism mounted against him. He was astonished by the furor his rash statements had touched off across the nation. For the first time in his political career there was mention of his age, whisperings of being out of touch. . . .

After the riots began to die down, Mayor Dooley let it be known that his controversial stance had all been a big misunderstanding. He claimed that his shoot-to-kill order had been nothing more than a bluff to help preserve the peace.

"Sometimes talking tough is just what's needed. Maybe those very words were actually out there working to save lives and property while the rest of you were home sleeping safely in our beds. Who is to say? People don't know you have to say unpopular things sometimes for their own good! Somebody once said to be great is to be misquoted. Probably F.D.R. or maybe Mayor Cermak. Anyway, whoever said it—you can be damn sure he was a Democrat."

Two weeks before the riots the Reaper had chalked up victim No. 23, an ex-star junior college basketball player by the name of Calvin Thomas. A few years back Thomas and the rest of the basketball squad had been implicated in the gang-rape of a coed in a college dormitory. The school, battling for national recognition in the basketball polls, had tried to hush up the matter, even threatening the coed with expulsion. She wouldn't drop the charges, however, and the whole thing went to court. A skilled defense attorney managed to sell enticement to an all-male jury, and Thomas, who with the rest of his teammates was acquitted, went on to finish the season with a fourth-place finish in the NJCAA. The coed dropped out of school and never returned.

Six days after Thomas's body had been found in the back of his van parked in a secluded turnaround under a towering exit ramp of the Dan Ryan Expressway, Captain Maxwell Howland called Valjohn into his office.

"Lieutenant, I'd like you to meet Lieutenant Egil Heintz." The captain sat at his desk without looking up. He was eating an order of carry-out chicken.

Valjohn nodded to a man in shoulder-length blond hair, tennis sneakers, patched dungarees and a faded Army fatigue jacket. The man was standing beside Howland's desk, also gnawing on a chicken leg. Valjohn recognized him and felt himself instinctively grow tense.

Lieutenant Heintz appeared to be about his age. He stood a couple of inches taller and probably outweighed him by fifty or sixty pounds—all sinew and whipcord muscle. He was an awesome physical specimen, and it wasn't just a matter of size; there was something else about him, an animal quality . . . instinctual and uncompromising, predatory, wolf-like . . .

"I'm assigning Egil here to the case."

"The case?"

"C-65-1834."

Valjohn was silent. He stared at Howland and then at Heintz as Howland began to elaborate.

Heintz would be heading a special team of five men from TUF, the department's elite Technical Undercover Force. They were going to operate stakeouts in computer-designated prime-target areas. "They'll also be answering," Howland emphasized, shoveling a forkful of coleslaw into his mouth, "directly back to me."

"You're taking over the investigation?"

"I didn't say that."

"Might I ask whose idea this is?"

"Consider it my own, Lieutenant. Consider this sort of a parallel maneuver."

Heintz smiled.

Valjohn wasn't about to consider it anything less than it was: an obvious encroachment on his assignment. Howland had pulled rank, and now he was moving in. Valjohn started to speak, thought better of it. He better cool down first and gather his thoughts.

Egil "Magnum" Heintz—the notorious tiger cop. Valjohn watched him flip a chicken bone into the wastebasket, wipe his hands on his jacket and sit down on the edge of Howland's desk. Stories of Heintz's exploits—dramatic vice collars, flamboyant drug busts—were continually circulating around the department. Always people were getting hurt in his wake, often ending up maimed or dead. Several years ago he'd helped form a controversial "jack-in-the-box" squad, a robbery ambush unit patterned after similar units operating in a number of southern cities. Heintz and two or three other "crack" officers would plant themselves at night in high-crime target areas, usually stores or warehouses. From their hiding places they would spring out on hapless burglars, shredding them in shotgun crossfire. Superintendent Gordon had eliminated the operation during his second year of command.

As far as Valjohn was concerned, Heintz represented all the worst aspects of overly aggressive law enforcement. He was ruthless, sadistic—a real throwback. He also supplied plenty of ammunition for the critics who claimed today's police were no different from those of the past. Valjohn wanted nothing to do with the man. Still he listened as Howland requested his cooperation.

A long, tension-filled silence followed. Valjohn and Heintz stared at one another across the captain's desk. The lieutenant from TUF blinked, his eyelids moving so slowly they appeared to be sticking to his eyeballs.

Finally Valjohn turned to Howland.

"May I speak with you in private, sir?"

Once Heintz had stepped out of the room, Howland waved rank aside with a half-devoured chicken breast, and Valjohn proceeded to argue strenuously over the intrusion into his case.

Howland sat eating his chicken. When Valjohn was through talking, he continued eating. After he'd finished the last piece, he wiped his greasy hands on a paper napkin. He tossed the paper napkin along with the chicken bones into his wastebasket. Then he leaned back in his chair and studied Valjohn thoughtfully.

"You finished, Lieutenant?"

Valjohn shrugged, nodded.

"Then lemme see your piece."

Beautiful, thought Valjohn. He took a step forward and patted the bulge of his empty hip-hugger hidden beneath his sweater.

The captain suddenly lifted his blocky head, his face screwed enigmatically. He made a noise closely resembling a muffled snarl.

"Shit," muttered Valjohn under his breath. Now he was really going to catch it.

"Hhgyaaaghhh!" The office resounded with the captain's angry yell.

"Jesus," muttered Valjohn, feeling at least his mother's half of him blanching. Then suddenly he realized Howland's angry yell hadn't been a yell at all. It had been a sneeze.

"Gesundheit," he offered.

Howland nodded, eyes watering, leaned forward to search the desk, the carry-out chicken box, for another napkin. Finding none he looked about, finally settling for an unbuttered roll. He picked it up, broke it open and commenced to blow his nose in it.

"I'm going to tell you something, Lieutenant," he said, refolding the roll and dabbing it at his reddened beak. "I'm going to tell you that I personally don't give a fart in church what you think, Lieutenant. I'll tell you something else: I also happen to think Officer Heintz and his men from TUF are just what this case needs. I don't think it'll hurt one shitty little bit to shake up your precious goddamn investigation. Not one shitty little bit! And I also too likewise don't think it'll fucking hurt to shake up this fucking city a little bit either. . . . So you might as well go crying to Superintendent Gordon right now about it," he added, flinging the roll into the wastebasket, "cuz my mind's goddamn well made up."

Valjohn considered doing just that, then rejected it. Things were strained enough for him around here without defying Howland head-on. Besides, Valjohn had a sudden sinking feeling that maybe Howland wasn't all that wrong. So far his own investigation sure as hell wasn't setting the world on fire. Maybe deep down that's what was bothering him: the idea that Howland and Heintz might actually come up with something.

"Whatever you say, sir."

"You're goddamn right, Lieutenant!" snarled Howland. Then he sneezed again.

Crescent was gone when Valjohn arrived home that evening. Probably taking one of her late-night walks. Damn! Those really bothered him. Before they were married, she'd told him how every now and then she had to go off, spend time by herself just walking and thinking things over. She claimed she'd been taking these strolls all her life and made him promise that if they married he'd allow her to continue them. He'd promised. Now, however, he tried to talk her out of the practice every chance he got. He was appalled at the risk involved. She wasn't back in some little hick town traipsing through the cow pastures. She insisted she only walked along well-lit streets and main thoroughfares, but he responded with just as much insistence that no streets were well-lit or well-traveled enough to make them safe—not in this city, not for a woman alone after dark. And he was in a position to know. She remained adamant.

He found a Rock Cornish game hen cooked and waiting for him in the broiler. There also was a tossed salad in the refrigerator. He put his dinner on a tray and went into the living room to watch the ten o'clock news.

There was another aspect about her walks which bothered him. He had to admit he'd never been able totally to dismiss suspicions of another man. If there was someone else, certainly her late-night strolls were perfect for clandestine rendezvous. Valjohn even tortured himself by conjuring up a vision of the man: He was married; his wife was stricken with some terminal illness, and both he and Crescent chose to spare her the cruelty of divorce. Either that or the man was a Catholic priest. In any case he was someone Crescent loved deeply but from whom she was destined to live apart. She could, however, remain faithful, give herself to him and no one else— including her husband.

He caught the tail end of the news, then switched to a movie, to a talk show, then to another movie, another talk show and finally back to the first movie. He sat staring listlessly as Steve Reeves wrestled a lion.

He got up, went out to the kitchen and opened himself a can of beer. Returning to the living room, he glanced again at the TV, Steve Reeves now standing atop a sandy hummock flexing his pectorals in the sunset. Instead of sitting down again, Valjohn wandered back to his study and workroom.

He hadn't labored on his art project since before his marriage. The bowl of megilp he'd mixed had hardened and cracked and still sat on the floor where he'd left it to answer Stephansky's call informing him of Radzim's murder at the hospital. That had been in November. Well, he wasn't up to resuming work tonight. Not the way he felt. Too unsettled and restless. Too harried by the events of the day.

He took a swig of beer, walked out into the hallway, closing the door to the study behind him. From the front room the TV blared, "But Hercules, what if the Amazons surround the temple?"

He entered the bedroom, glanced about. The bed was neatly made. Oh, she was great at that. Her uniform lay folded over the back of a chair. He walked across the room, lifted up the uniform by its hanger, imagined her in it. He draped it carefully back over the chair and turned to face the dresser.

Her dresser. He took another swig of beer and set the can down on top of it. He opened the top drawer, gazed at its contents, an assortment of personal effects: There were gloves, a small wooden jewelry box, a coiled belt, some pencils, a bottle of perfume, a barrette, a small sewing kit, an extra hospital nameplate and her nursing school memo book with several envelopes protruding from its cover.

He'd never gone through her things before. The prospect of doing so now became suddenly disconcerting. What was he looking for? What did he hope to find? Love letters? Snapshots of a secret lover?

He withstood temptation, closed the drawer and felt instantly better for it. With a sort of absentminded curiosity he opened the other drawers. He glanced at their stacks of neatly folded clothing and quickly slid them shut. All except the last one: the bottom drawer, filled with dirty laundry. There were jeans and blouses piled together; stockings wadded up and thrown on top. There also were undergarments stuffed in a corner.

He stood there motionless, staring. Had it come to this? . . . He reached down and lifted out a brassiere. He pondered it, holding it dangling before him between a thumb and forefinger. He thought of the privileges denied him and yet afforded this simple article of clothing, contemplated the intimacy of its function—how closely it held her, cupped her lovely flesh hours on end. Envious, he pressed the garment to his face, felt the halter's silken fabric, cool and smooth against his cheek . . . against his lips. He tasted her salt on the elastic straps, inhaled the scent of her body—bitter-sweet, tantalizing, mingling with just the faintest fragrance of perfume.

So it had come to this. . . . The sexual deprivation of his marriage had driven him to a new low. He'd become a fetishist! He dropped the brassiere back into the open drawer and hovered there, deliberating. Finally he sighed, straightened up, grabbed his beer and drained it. He supposed there were worse fates, uglier perversions available to him. At least he was harming no one.

As he reached down again into the open drawer, to pluck a pair of her flowered silk panties from its midst, he was amazed at how swiftly he'd resigned himself to the humiliations of this new sexual aberrancy, the untroubled ease with which he now pursued it.

He didn't question Crescent when she returned—it was after midnight. He didn't ask her, as was his usual custom, where she'd walked and whom she might have seen along the way. He avoided her eyes, feigning preoccupation with some case-related papers he'd brought home from headquarters.

She asked him if his dinner had been all right, if the game hen had stayed warm and not dried out too much in the oven. She asked him how his day had gone.

"Fine, fine," came his noncommittal response. He had no desire to discuss with her his latest flare-up with Howland.

"I'm really bushed," she announced, tugging off a white turtleneck sweater and heading for the bedroom. "I don't know about you, but I'm ready to turn in."

Valjohn wasn't ready. He waited until she'd fallen fast asleep, then slid into bed beside her. He lay awake brooding for quite some time—not about the problems at headquarters, not about the case or Crescent's walk or even his newfound perversion. What upset him now was something else, something he'd inadvertently come across while indulging that perversion.

Crescent had vaginitis. He was sure of it, thanks to Moe's informative lab lectures. He had encountered the unmistakable telltale crust on the inner V seam of her flowered silk panties. She had tricks or a yeast infection—maybe both; he couldn't be positive without a lab check.

And it blew his mind.

He knew from his follow-up readings that vaginitis wasn't necessarily contracted through sexual intercourse. Lots of other things could cause it. Faulty body chemistry, poor personal hygiene, nervous tension and anxiety—hell, she could've even picked it up from the old proverbial toilet seat. *Ha!*

Crescent with vaginitis . . . Her beauty, her vitality and radiance—it seemed too incongruous. He was appalled at the thought of the flower of his desire infected—desecrated—by a foul horde of microorganisms. It was an outrage . . . a sacrilege.

Ridiculous for him to carry on like this. Was it her fault that he idolized her so, put her on such a lofty pedestal? If pubescent virgins could have the infection, then why couldn't she? He was willing to give her the benefit of the doubt—even with her late-night meanderings. Besides, she never said she was a virgin—and who was he to be sitting in judgment, anyway? She should be judging him, his snooping through her undergarments like some disgusting degenerate.

Well, there was no way he was going to confront her with the matter. It would only serve to embarrass and humiliate both of them. Her infection was her own business, and he was quite sure she would rather he didn't know about it.

Would rather he didn't know about it—the phrase stuck in his mind. Suddenly he raised up on an elbow in bed, his eyes wide open.

Would rather he didn't know about it.

Of course! Epiphany! Maybe some pieces in the puzzle were finally going to fit. Before he settled back down and tried to fall asleep, he congratulated himself with a big, mental pat on the back.

The first thing he did on his way to work the next morning was again borrow Cronus Striddler's book on frigidity from the library. In his office he thumbed through the pages, scanning several sections he'd already read. His eyes halted abruptly when they skimmed across the word he was searching for.

"Vulvaphobia."

He paused for a moment, reflected on his thoughts from the night before. Then he read on. Striddler defined "vulvaphobia" as a woman's abnormal dread of her own sexual apparatus. Following the onset of puberty and the menstrual cycle, almost every woman developed a certain degree of emotional sensitivity or self-consciousness regarding her sex. In some women, however, this normal sense of modesty grew to neurotic proportions. Individuals subjected to strong puritanical upbringings were particularly susceptible to this neurosis. They were inculcated with a confusion of overzealous attitudes associating their bodily functions with the sins of the flesh. The shared proximity of the genital and excretory organs did little to help matters. In the economizing of parts, nature had done no favor to the human psyche. Striddler quoted Yeats:

> A woman can be proud and stiff
> When on love intent;
> But Love has pitched his mansion in
> The place of excrement;
> For nothing can be sole or whole
> That has not been rent.

A woman suffering from vulvaphobia was deeply ashamed of her body. She saw her vulva as a wound, a gaping slash—not only rending her flesh but her mind as well. It was a stigma, a biological scarlet letter, and it served as a constant reminder of her primal squalor, her baseness; it continually reinforced her feelings of guilt and inadequacy.

To the vulvaphobic the idea of sexual intercourse was naturally repugnant. An intolerable act. The source of her shame was to be kept hidden away like an ugly scar. It never should be exposed to the desires of a lover, least of all a man.

Lieutenant Harris dropped by his desk, and Valjohn set the book aside. They chatted for a few minutes; then Captain Howland also stopped by. He told Valjohn he wanted to see him in his office at ten-thirty to meet some of the men who'd be working with Lieutenant Heintz. Alone again at his desk, Valjohn eagerly resumed his train of thought.

Would rather he didn't know . . .

It just might be that Crescent had a touch of vulvaphobia. And it just might be that her vaginitis was partly to blame. He remembered learning from case-related research that many women who had vaginitis didn't know they were infected; they had had it for so many years they just assumed it was the natural state of things, like the menses. Maybe Crescent was one of them. With such a condition it certainly was understandable how she could develop anguish over the plight of her sex. The discharge was foul-smelling and odious. It also was incessant. Her anguish easily could have turned into a deep-seated sense of shame—shame that would in turn lead most logically to frigidity.

It also just might be that if Crescent were rid of the odious discharge, of her vaginitis, she just might also rid herself of her maddening sexual suppression. Hell—they might even get around to consummating their marriage!

He realized how grossly he was oversimplifying, how much of his reasoning was pure wishful thinking. Nevertheless, it was an inroad, the first idea that suggested any sort of positive resolution to their problem. His mind reeled with hope.

When he walked into Howland's office later that morning and met Heintz's teammates—three more Neanderthals from TUF—he even managed to smile.

"Perhaps you'd be interested in something more elaborate—a bit more ostent, as they say?"

Valjohn grunted, wondered who "they" might be. He stood before a vanity counter at one of the numerous smart shops for women that lined North Michigan Avenue. The clerk waiting on him, a particularly sleek-wristed young man with lightly mascaraed eyes, returned an assortment of aerosol deodorants to a shelf behind him. He was the only male sales-person on the floor. Valjohn had sought him out for assistance and still was experiencing difficulty explaining what he wanted.

"Something . . . uh . . . more in the line of hygiene, I guess, but . . . but . . . uh . . ." he tried again.

"But not too blatant?" the clerk offered.

Valjohn nodded.

"Aha!" the clerk said, his face brightening with understanding. "Does your lady friend have, shall we say, a problem?"

Valjohn nodded again, vigorously.

"I think I have just what you're looking for."

The clerk crossed over to a nearby display rack, returned with a large, heart-shaped case and set it down on the glass counter between them.

"Madame Pristianna's Elixir Feminique!" he announced grandly. He opened a robin's-egg-blue velvet lid and Valjohn peered into the case's plush, satin-ruffled interior at a wide assortment of cosmetics: eye makeup, facial creams, perfumes, powders, lipsticks, nail polish.

"The lipsticks include natural peach, plum and glacier," the clerk was telling him. "Of course, all the creams and powders contain Lady Pristianna's own secret formulas." He picked up a green hourglass-shaped bottle, shook it and unscrewed the cap. "Here's a special cactus-bloom shampoo. Smell it," he said, first smelling it himself, then handing the bottle to Valjohn. "I can personally recommend it—use it all the time," he added, giving his head an effeminate little bob to show off the luster and bounce of his own carefully coiffed locks. "Doesn't it have a delicious fragrance?"

Valjohn took a dutiful sniff. "Uh . . . very nice, but . . . uh . . ."

"But not what you're after, right? Be patient," he said with a grin, "you'll find the case is a veritable Trojan horse of tactfulness." He pulled at a small gold ring attached to the front of the display, then lifted out the cosmetics in a removable tray, revealing what proved to be a sizable bottom compartment.

"Voilà! The more intimate effects and unmentionables." He reached down and picked up a plastic atomizer.

" 'Magic Maiden Mist'—it's a dry powder spray for the nitty-gritty, if you know what I mean," he grinned coyly. " 'Contains no hexachlorophene or chloroxylenol,' " he read from the label. He tucked back the cuff of his lavender shirt, sprayed some of the magic mist on his wrist, extended his arm across the counter.

Valjohn hesitated, not sure what was expected of him.

"Come now, don't be a bashful boy—take a whiff. If you don't like it on my arm you'll hardly like it you know where." He winked and bit his tongue.

Valjohn glanced around the store to see if anyone was watching. He leaned forward.

"Very nice."

"It's jasmine—don't you just adore jasmine?" The clerk lifted his wrist to his own nose and inhaled rapturously.

"They say jasmine is the most erotic of all herbal fragrances. I would agree. Wouldn't you?" He delivered these last words in a very slow *sotto voce.* He sniffed his wrist again and gave Valjohn a most disconcerting gaze with his shadowed, hazel eyes.

"I . . . it's very nice, all right . . . er, what's that?" asked Valjohn, doing his best to divert the clerk's attention back to the case on the counter. He pointed to a long pink box tucked behind several yellow bars of beauty soap.

"Oh . . . yes," responded the clerk absently, then his voice took on a harder tone, all business. "That is, of course, your vaginal applicator and folding syringe. The case comes with three dozen packets of medicated douche concentrate and twenty-four germicidal suppositories. All jasmine-scented, I might add."

He set the upper tray back into the case and finished the rest of his sales spiel with an air of boredom.

Valjohn asked the price.

"The Elixir Feminique represents the ultimate in Madame Pristianna's *'soixante-neuf'* line. All of the items included can be refilled or replaced at this counter. It's an absolute steal at one twenty-nine, ninety-five."

Valjohn strode down Michigan Avenue to the lot where he'd parked his car, the case gift-wrapped in an explosion of red ribbon under his arm. A hundred and thirty bucks! He felt as though he'd been mugged. He realized he probably could have bought comparable articles of feminine hygiene at a discount drugstore for less than a tenth of what he'd just spent. But then how could he just up and give Crescent a vaginal deodorant or a douche kit? Not too subtle. Much better to hide them in a big fancy vanity case and let her figure things out for herself. What had the clerk called it? A Trojan horse of tactfulness. Well . . . if it helped him win the Battle of Troy, it was well worth every penny.

Too bad Valentine's Day was gone, he reflected after he'd paid the parking attendant and climbed into his car. The first day of spring would have made a good excuse too. Her birthday was months away. He could give her her present on Easter, but that still was two weeks off. He didn't want to wait two more weeks. He didn't want to wait two more minutes.

"Passion Sunday?" exclaimed Crescent. "I didn't know people gave presents on Passion Sunday."

"Oh, a lot of people don't," conceded Valjohn. "I . . . uh . . . guess it's an old Indiana custom."

"Why didn't you tell me ahead of time? I could have gotten you something too. Now I feel bad."

"It's no big deal—just a little something I picked up on the way home from work the other day. Go ahead, open it."

She shook her head reprovingly, then sat down on the arm of an easy chair, weighing the gift he'd just given her in both hands. She carefully began undoing the ribbons.

"Another valentine?" she said when she'd removed the case from its box.

Valjohn nervously pulled at his nose.

She set the case on her lap and opened the lid, gazed in at the profusion of cosmetics. "It's . . . it's very nice," she finally managed, looking somewhat puzzled.

"I . . . uh, know you don't use much makeup. But there're all sorts of other things in there—you know, perfume, shampoo, soap. And it's really an attractive case. Hell, if you want, you can throw everything out and just use it to store jewelry and things."

He opened the bottle of cactus-bloom shampoo, sniffed it and handed it to her.

"Umm . . . I like it," she said and smiled.

He watched her open several jars of facial creams and moisturizers, dab a finger in them and rub them on the back of her hand. He watched her sample a couple of vials of perfume. He watched her fumble with the gold ring that lifted out the upper tray—

At which point he chose to retreat quickly to the kitchen and pour himself another cup of tea.

When he returned, she'd removed the tray from the case and was staring at the inner contents.

"Oh, what's that?" asked Valjohn with what he hoped would pass for curious surprise. "I didn't know there was a lower level."

Monday afternoon at work, Valjohn received a call from Grady McTague. They exchanged small talk for a few minutes: How was married life treating Valjohn? How was McTague bearing up under his most recent car woes? (His XKE was in the shop again; this time a tree limb had fallen on it.) Finally Valjohn asked him what was on his mind.

"I guess I'd like to know when the Police Department decided to reinstate your ignominious predecessor."

"My who?"

"Joseph Blear."

"Are you putting me on?"

"No joke. He's not working undercover?"

"Not to my knowledge. Why?"

"Nothing important. Just that the man must be more screwed up than even I imagined."

Valjohn listened enthralled as McTague explained. Last night he'd received an anonymous call from a woman asking him to meet her in a dive called Gacy's Tap over on West Madison. She claimed she had information of interest to him. He tried to question her, but she said she'd be the only blonde sitting at the bar, and then hung up. He'd showed at Gacy's and sure enough there was a blonde at the bar, but when he'd sat down beside her and introduced himself, she'd practically dropped her teeth. He'd realized almost immediately that she was a he; then he'd practically dropped his own teeth, recognizing who it was.

"Blear!?"

"Big as life. Queen for a day. Offered to buy him a drink, but he was so shook seeing me there he took off like a shot for the john."

"He didn't phone you?"

"No way. That voice was too soft and sexy sounding. About as feminine as they come. Anyway, I followed Blear to the ladies' room, but he'd locked the door. Time I worked it open, he'd made leg bail out an alley window. . . . So what do you make of that?"

So what do you make of that? Valjohn repeated McTague's question to himself after he'd hung up. Blear in drag! And wearing a blond wig, no less. Valjohn paced in his office—two and a half steps forward, two and a half steps back. Could the man possibly be Moe's woman in the woods? The train? Hell, what about his own little hide-and-seek playmate in the library?

His mind raced back to the events surrounding Blear's dismissal. Following the death of Billy Pivot, the IID inquest had begun as a routine whitewashing. While the coroner had been satisfied to uphold a police medical examiner's original report, Moe, in a separate postmortem, had come up with findings of his own. He'd detected tiny fragments of leather in a number of wounds about Pivot's head and body. Particles which came not from the fender of a car or the pavement, but, as was later confirmed by the testimony of another detective present during Pivot's interrogation, from a curious—though hardly quaint—tool of the trade known as the "muffin." A remnant from the dark ages of police coercion, the muffin was a large, leather-bound pillow of a club used on uncooperative suspects to refreshen memories and loosen tongues. It could be wielded in both hands and had the distinct advantage of leaving its victims unscathed—at least on the surface—their skin unbroken and relatively unmarked. It was considered far superior to the Chicago Telephone Directory, which had almost universally replaced it. Unfortunately for Blear, the instrument had been too long in service and the leather not properly cared for. Like an old, discarded catcher's mitt, the muffin had dried and cracked. It could no longer keep a secret.

Moe also had found suspicious bruises around Pivot's wrists; torn muscles in his arms, plus a shoulder dislocation, suggested the victim might have been subjected to strappado. This too was later confirmed by testimony. The suspect's wrists had been bound behind him, one end of the rope slung over a heating pipe. Arms and shoulders painfully inverted, he'd been hoisted and lowered repeatedly through the night.

"Blear and Captain Howland tried to pressure me into keeping hush-hush on the matter," Moe had told Valjohn shortly after the proceedings. "I even had a tear-jerking visit from your golfing cohort, Hans Glad. They should have known better. I sent a full report to the IID and then made sure a copy found its way to Gordon's desk as well. You know the rest."

He knew the rest, all right: Moe was dead and buried and Blear had a motive. For a moment Valjohn was stirred by the memory of his friend.

"I felt bad about it; all the bad publicity for the department. But what could I do?" Moe had confided. "A man like Blear—he doesn't belong on the Force. . . . But I can sympathize . . ."

"Sympathize? What about Billy Pivot?"

"I know, I know—but a policeman's job is no bed of roses. Being married to violence. It's a terrible burden. Can do terrible things to a man."

"Who's married to violence?"

"The old ball and chain—you can't deny it, Valjohnny. Even you. You have to live with it, day in and day out. Not just the violence out there in the street, but the violence in here." Moe tapped his chest. "A policeman has to fight it and love it at the same time. And hope it doesn't destroy him."

"I'm not so sure about that."

"I know you're not, Valjohnny, and it's one of the things I cherish about you. But I worry."

On a hunch Valjohn left his office in search of George Sweeney. He couldn't be found. Valjohn spent the remainder of the morning digging up all the info he could on his predecessor's activities after he'd left the Force. He found Blear had been given a job by a ward boss within a week of his discharge. A building-code inspector with the City Public Works Department. He'd held the job for less than a month. It was not made clear whether he'd quit or been canned. There were rumors of a drinking problem. After this, little was known about him—where he was living (he'd sold his house in Bridgeport) or what he was doing. It was known that he had an ex-wife living in Rantoul and that he'd stopped sending her alimony checks about the same time he'd dropped out of sight.

Sweeney returned shortly after lunch—he'd been out running errands for Howland—and met with Valjohn in his office. The lieutenant had worked under Blear for years, had been a close friend. Valjohn talked over some minor details on one of Sweeney's ancillary reports, then casually asked him if he'd kept in touch with his former boss. Sweeney said that he'd seen him a few times but not lately. At that point Valjohn put it to him directly: Did he know of any reason why Blear would be going around the city these days in drag? Sweeney reacted with genuine astonishment. There must be some mistake. Valjohn assured him the source of his information was reliable.

The lieutenant sat down, shaking his head. He confessed that he'd run into Blear about a month ago over on West Van Buren. He added, almost under his breath, that he wished he hadn't.

"Why is that?"

Sweeney hesitated for a moment, then spoke candidly. Blear had hit the skids, turned into a real alchy-bum. Sweeney could barely recognize him. His clothes were a mess. He was dirty, unshaven, had lost a lot of weight. He was drinking from a bottle in a paper sack.

"Did you talk to him?"

"Only for a minute or so. It was clear he wanted to be left alone. He wanted nothing to do with me—nothing to do with anything, I guess, that reminded him of the past."

Valjohn asked about his wife. Sweeney told him that he'd never met her, that Blear had been divorced for a long time, ten years or more.

Suddenly he looked hard at Valjohn with his steely-gray eyes.

"He was married to the Force, Lieutenant. He was married to this," he said, waving a hand to include Valjohn's office. "This here was his life."

What the hell was with the marriage metaphor? thought Valjohn. He'd just recalled Moe's words earlier tying the knot between Blear and violence —along with everybody else on the Force. Now it was Sweeney's turn.

After Sweeney left his office, Valjohn assigned a detail of men to comb the squalid district of flophouses and bars, including a stakeout of Gacy's Tap, on the Loop's west side.

It was almost nine by the time he and Greg Harris walked into the old Prendergast Hotel off Madison Avenue. So far they'd been to half a dozen rooming houses and a couple of missions. Again the name of Joseph Blear failed to appear in a register, but when they showed the manager at the desk photographs, he identified the ex-detective as one George Claybaugh, a resident for the past eight months in a room on the second floor.

Valjohn asked for a key.

Earlier that same day, Joseph Blear watched the long black limo creep into the cindered lot, swing a slow semicircle and park across from him in the shadows of the old warehouse. He flashed his lights once and got out, tugging at the seat of his pants.

Twenty minutes later he was driving back to the city, feeling flush. The bastards had finally come through. He had a name and address in his pocket, a bankroll to tide him over. At last he could blow this burg. Not tonight, though. Just a little more unfinished business.

It was dark when he reached the hotel.

He pulled the blond wig over his head, his dusty crew cut grown out scruffy, and carefully straightened it before the mirror in his room. The wig, the dress—they made him look like an old Polack stew from Packing Town. He'd had the outfit for years. Since his undercover days. Didn't know why he'd kept it. . . . He broke into a fitful cough, gulped down a swallow of whiskey to clear his throat.

So why wasn't he entitled to a cop's mistake?

When he felt the old hatred welling up inside him, he lit a cigarette. He hated the city, the vermin and lowlife it spawned in its gutters. He hated Billy Pivot for being innocent, for being puny and dying on him. He hated the press and all those upper-echelon sob-sisters who'd raised such a stink. And he hated the Force and Superintendent Gordon for not standing behind him, for throwing him to the dogs. But most of all he'd hated the Jew.

He took another drink. Part of the gutter—the niggers, the spics, the hunkies—you name them. All garbage stunk the same. Only the Jew, he'd wormed his way inside. Like a Commie, a cancer. The Force was as vulnerable as the next place to his kind. He'd wormed his way inside, and then who was out on his ass? Who was dumped in the street after twenty-three years of service, a distinguished record and a handful of decorations including two Purple Hearts—he'd been shot once and knifed once, both in the same arm?

Well, yours truly was nobody's patsy. You stuck it to Joseph Blear, you paid the price. He was smiling now.

When he'd first started following Frank, he wasn't sure what he was going to do. Then the plan had hit him all at once, and he'd pulled it off to perfection. Almost perfection. He'd meant to do him in and be long gone the same day, preferably before winter, but that part hadn't worked out. Last fall he'd spent a waiting game, had to hang around until his connections panned out—which they hadn't until today. In the meantime, he'd kept on the old Hebe's tail, learning his habits, just for the hell of it. Relishing it—like a cat playing with a tired old mouse. And finally the mouse had forced his hand.

That last day back in December he'd been shading him along Midland Avenue after work. Frank had entered a phone booth by a gas station. He'd appeared to make a call, then scribbled a note and dropped it outside the booth. He'd walked on across the street and entered a drugstore. Browsing at a nearby newsstand, Blear had proceeded to the booth, picked up the wadded note and gone inside, pretending to make a call.

"Keep up the good work, Josephine," the note had read. "The Gestapo would be proud of you. Best Regards always, your pal, Moe Frank."

There was also a P.S. that said only a fifth-rate flatfoot would fall for such a trick and pick up the note. And only a first-rate *putz* would read it.

When he'd looked up, there was Frank standing across the street, smiling and waving at him. Oh, he was a real smart-ass, that old Hebe. Had half a mind to blow him away right there. He'd managed to control himself, however, and walk away. With Frank onto him, though, he knew he'd have to act fast.

Later that night he'd ambushed him while he was out shopping. He'd noosed him real good and drug him back still squirming into an alley. Then he'd opened his valise and gone to work.

Now it was the cubist cop's turn. He was pretty much an afterthought, a little diversion to keep him amused while he spent another frigging winter here, waiting for things to break. He smiled at the choice: his own hot-shot successor, Gordon's suck-butt protégé—a nigger to boot. Icing him would be a pleasure.

Blear glanced at the black valise under his bed, decided against taking it. That spade dick was spookier than a pet coon—particularly after the run-in at the library. That's where he'd blown it—a perfect Reaper setup —almost got the noose over his head, too. Then the bastard had spotted him through the stacks and gone crazy. Lucky he didn't start shooting. Anyway, nothing fancy tonight. Just a straight hit and he'd be on his way. He left the room, stuffing his revolver into his purse.

In his car, centering himself behind the wheel on his foam doughnut, he realized he needed to take a crap bad. He returned to the hotel and spent a labored fifteen minutes relieving himself in the toilet at the end of the hall. On his way out again, he stopped off at his room to pick up the valise. What the shit—he might just get lucky. . . .

He started down the stairs to the lobby and froze. The nigger cop— Lieutenant Valjohn! He was there—on the stairs—coming up with another man!

Incredibly they hadn't seen him, for some reason were stopped, both looking away. Oshitogod! He stepped back and ducked to his left. How could they be onto him so soon? That goddamn reporter at Gacy's! He could hear them coming up now. No time to make a dash to the fire escape. His gun was in his purse in the car. He shrank back into the shadow of a doorway and lifted the valise.

"I can't do that," said the manager, refusing them the key.

"It's your door." Valjohn and Harris headed for the stairs. They climbed a couple of steps. When the manager called after them, they both turned.

"Here," he grumbled.

Harris caught the key, and they continued on up.

At the second floor, Harris turned right, checking the number on the key. Valjohn glanced warily down the hall in both directions. He had just enough time to raise an arm and blurt a warning cry before the figure of a woman, leaping from a dimly lit doorway, brought a weighted valise forcefully down on his head and fending forearm. The blow sent him crashing against a wall. Stepping past Valjohn and swinging the valise upward, the woman caught Harris, startled and fumbling for his gun, squarely on the jaw. He hit the floor lengthwise like a felled tree.

Valjohn, staggering off the wall, lunged forward, trying to seize the attacker in a headlock. He succeeded momentarily; then he felt the valise being driven sharply into his stomach. He gasped as an elbow and a powerful hand broke his hold. He was shoved backward, sent tumbling down the stairs, his right hand clutching a blond wig.

For several seconds he lay stunned in a heap on the lobby landing. His head felt as though it had bounced off every step on the way down. He struggled to his feet, the wig still in his grasp. Satisfied nothing was broken, he gingerly started up the stairs. He was running by the time he reached the top.

"Greg, you all right?"

Harris, who sat propped against a wall, nodded groggily. He pointed down the hall to a yawning fire exit.

Running along Wacker Drive, Blear glanced over his shoulder and saw the nigger cop starting down the fire escape in pursuit. He continued north for another block and a half, then circled back down an alley to the vacant lot where his car was parked. He opened it and got his purse. The Tempest couldn't be traced, but it was too risky to drive off now. Another minute and the place would be swarming with units.

He walked around to the rear of the car. He unlocked the trunk and climbed inside.

Angry with himself, sweating and winded after a futile chase, Valjohn returned to help Harris search Blear's room. In a closet cluttered with dirty clothes and empty whiskey bottles, they found a pair of dark blue gabardine trousers that appeared to be spattered with bloodstains.

The morning report from the lab was anything but encouraging. The trousers were bloodstained, all right; the only hitch was the blood wasn't human. It belonged to a canine. Later in the day, however, in a cuff of one of the pantlegs, dog hairs were found. Short, black—probably from a Labrador or some related breed—they proved identical on the OC to the one found on Moe's body.

The hair of the dog, mused Valjohn. Nothing like it. Only the reporters at the cop shop leaped at the sensational implications. Valjohn voiced skepticism, but Blear as the Reaper was much too enticing a proposition. Foot-dragging facts could be examined later. Right now the press and the public alike were captivated by the idea of the city's most prolific and fiendish killer turning out to be the very detective once in charge of the case. The murderer investigating his own murders! And where else but Chicago?

Even City Hall seemed to buy the idea. Blear made a sufferable scapegoat. Sure, he'd been a cop—but was he a cop now? Hadn't he already been booted off the force? And, it might be added, long before this latest exposé. Every police department had its share of rotten apples. . . .

The speculation of Blear as the Reaper lasted less than a week. It sold a lot of newspapers, a lot of TV time, then quickly died away: All the hasty assumptions failed to hold up under scrutiny. Even disregarding what Valjohn considered major inconsistencies in Moe's case—the trace evidence, for instance: no vaginal mucosa, the ABO grouping of the semen present ruling out Moe as its origin—it became more and more obvious that Blear was not the Reaper, that just by record of his whereabouts, he could not possibly have committed a large number of the murders. The mystery of Blear masquerading as a woman diminished when Lieutenant Sweeney admitted leaking information about the Reaper's suspected sex to his ex-boss shortly after learning it himself.

To the public, Blear became just another sordid nonentity, a run-of-the-mill grudge killer whose gruesome crime finally was nothing but a sham, a ghastly counterfeit. As he remained at large, his notoriety continued to fizzle.

To Valjohn, however, the man remained true: a constant source of hatred, frustration and bitter self-criticism.

15

Egil "Magnum" Heintz stood at the corner of Fifty-third and Torrio Avenue and stared across the street into Daley Park. Beyond the pools of light from the bordering streetlamps, the park's wooded interior loomed black and forbidding. Heintz took a bite from a Baby Ruth candy bar and crossed the deserted street.

Once on the other side, he walked along the park perimeter, padding stealthily. When he came to a drive that entered the park, he paused at the curb. A sign standing in the middle of the entrance announced with silver reflectors:

PARK CLOSED AFTER SUNDOWN

He let his eyes follow the drive, tried to penetrate the surrounding gloom of trees and shrubbery. No-man's-land now that the sun was down.

He debated walking the drive, decided against it. Not that he was afraid: He felt confident he was more lethal, more ruthless, than anyone who might be lurking in the darkness. But tonight he was after different quarry.

Half a block from the drive he came to several benches by a drinking fountain. He looked around, was satisfied with the spot and sat down.

At first he slouched across one of the benches, lifted a leg up, and leaned

267

forward in his rumpled fatigue jacket, feigning sleep. Then he straightened up. The pose was all wrong. He wasn't trying to bait muggers and bum burners. He reflected on the information he'd received from his briefing with Lieutenant Valjohn. The projected profile of the killer was a real shocker. He found it hard to believe, though evidence made a damn strong argument. But there was no mystery about the victims. And he didn't have to slouch in a drunken stupor to fit their profile. They weren't rummies and wasted derelicts; they were for the most part predators, prowlers and peddlers of violence themselves.

He glanced at a line of steel-gated storefronts across the street, looked farther down the block at a large fenced-in auto graveyard. While he absently watched three figures standing on the corner of the next block, he smiled, thinking just how well suited he was for playing this new role.

The smile turned bitter on his lips as he reflected on his career in the military. Five years ago, after leaving a fizzling football career in the semi-pros, he'd become a member of Special Forces, a Green Beret, one of ten thousand American "advisers" in Nam, slogging through the rice paddies trying to teach a bunch of slopes how to defend themselves, their country and democracy against another bunch of slopes who happened to be Commie gooks besides. Shit! What a crock. Best thing they could've done over there was nuke the whole fucking rat's nest off the map.

The three figures he'd spotted standing on the corner of the next block had sidled across the street. He watched with mild interest as they approached him along the park walkway.

It was the incident at Tuy Son which had finally led to his undoing. Cleaning up that small hamlet near the Laotian border had been no small chore: a two-day siege, he and his men pinned down most of that time, suffering heavy casualties, before an air strike had turned the tide, reducing the village to a cinder.

The few guerrillas still alive were rounded up and marched to a clearing outside the perimeter of smoldering hootches. They were "interrogated" and left to rot. One of them was a woman, young and pregnant, and he'd interrogated her himself. He'd clubbed her to the ground with the butt of his AR-15, then repeating a ritual he'd seen his native counterparts from CIDG perform more than once, he proceeded to disembowel her with a wide-bladed parang. He also performed an impromptu Caesarean, flinging the fetus at his startled advisees. Grinning, they'd flung it back—the little slope bastards loved having him on their side!

Unfortunately, there'd been another American adviser present during the incident. A green NCO who'd joined the company a few days earlier. The wimpy little fucker'd been in Nam less than two weeks, and he turned in a detailed report when they shuttled back to Saigon. Heintz was quietly called in by his commanding officers and reprimanded—not for allowing the "interrogations" to take place, but for "overtly participating." He clearly lacked the basic ingredient of a Special Forces adviser: namely, detachment. A week later, he was sent home.

Back in the States he served out the remainder of his hitch as a recruiter. He didn't re-enlist, chose instead to hang up his green beret and try on a blue CCPD hat for size. So far he liked the fit. Maybe the streets of Chicago weren't exactly a football gridiron or the jungles of Nam . . . and then again, maybe they weren't all that different either.

They were muggers. He was sure of it. The three figures who'd crossed the street now stopped twenty yards away, stood just out of sight behind a large clump of bushes fringing the park. He heard whispers, complaining mumbles. He knew they were sizing him up for a quick touch.

Finally one of them slowly sauntered into view. He was black, slender, maybe seventeen, wore a "Y" sweatshirt, and gym shoes. When he reached a point on the walk even with the benches, he turned and registered surprise, as though he'd just noticed Heintz sitting there.

"Say hey, man—you got a light?"

It was all Heintz could do to suppress a snort of laughter. Normally he'd set the scrote up, slur a drunken response, loll his head and fumble for matches. Not tonight. He wasn't about to diddle away the evening at a precinct station processing some two-bit street collars.

The youth misread Heintz's silence, took a step closer.

"Hey, muthafucka, I said, 'You got a light?' "

In the next instant Heintz was up from the bench, had jammed his snub-nose .38 into the youth's mouth all the way to the rear sight and driven his knee like a battering ram into his groin. A cry of pain barely escaped from the youth's throat as he choked on blood, broken teeth and gunmetal.

His two accomplices sprang from the bushes. One held a knife; the other, a piece of pipe. Heintz spun around, let the youth he was holding crumple to the ground and faced his new adversaries with glee. His eyes danced, begging them to attack.

They wanted no part of him. Even before they saw the gun they were stumbling backward. He drew a bead on the back of one of them as they fled across the street.

"Bang!" he said out loud, but his finger rested on the trigger. Not tonight.

He slipped the revolver into his shoulder holster and looked down at the figure groveling and moaning beneath him. He reached down, grabbed a handful of wool, hoisted the youth to his feet. With his other hand he clenched the stricken face, held it inches from his own.

"Listen good, nigger-shit—I wanta kill you so bad I can taste it, but I ain't got time. So get the fuck outa my sight before I make time!"

He let go and gave him a shove on his way with his foot. The youth tripped and fell to the pavement again. Sobbing, spitting blood, he painfully struggled to his feet. Then, clutching himself in both hands, he limped off after his companions.

Heintz moved on, continuing around the park. He arrived back at the benches by the drinking fountain an hour and a half later. Aside from shaking up a couple of winos he'd found sleeping in a rain shelter, he'd seen no one who aroused suspicion.

He sat down again, rummaged through his coat pocket, retrieved an unfinished portion of candy bar. While he ate it he tried to come to terms with his impatience. Granted, the computer had designated this park as a prime target area: It was one of the few spots where the Reaper had struck twice, and both those murders, not a month apart, had occurred approximately this same time last spring. Nevertheless, the stakeout had to be considered at best a long shot. Getting antsy wouldn't help matters. He might as well resign himself to a lengthy, drawn-out vigil. It might take months.

It was after 2:00 A.M. when he first saw her. He was still resting on the bench, his attention fixed on a car that had double-parked across the street in front of the auto graveyard. Two men had gotten out, opened the gate to the lot and entered it. He couldn't tell from where he sat whether they'd used a key or whether they'd forced the lock.

Suddenly a woman was walking by him on the sidewalk. He hadn't heard her approach and was momentarily startled. She glanced back at him, went on for several steps, then came back.

Standing before him was an enormous black woman. She was no more than five feet, eight inches, but must have weighed close to three hundred pounds. She wore a bright green scarf around her head, a black windbreaker—awning-sized—and under that a purple dress that hung halfway down to two swollen tree knots for knees. Her calves and ankles looked stouter than any lineman's he'd ever played against. She was wearing orange sneakers.

"How you like a place to stay, honey?"

Heintz stared up into a great, round, animated face—a smile that flashed gold and pure, black-magic soul.

"You juiced up or junked out?"

He continued to stare open-mouthed.

"Tha's okay, honey. It don't matter none. You gonna be okay now. . . . You got any bread?"

He finally managed to mutter a few syllables.

"Wha's that you sayin'?"

"I said, 'Yah, I got some . . . enough.' "

She clapped her meaty hands together, the full expanse of her mighty bosom shaking with laughter.

"Well, jes' you let ole Hermadine take care you. She gonna do you fine. Come on now, this here park ain't no fit place be spen' the night. Not fo' my most mister man, no, sir." She took a step closer, loomed over him like some great nimbus cloud blotting out the streetlight.

Was it possible? He eyed her huge, quaking arms. Fat or solid muscle? "Think you kin walk good 'nuff to follow old Hermadine home?"

A giant niggeress! Of course. What else? She was perfect—King Kong's sister! Who would have guessed it? He couldn't believe his luck.

The Reaper leaned over, pressed her bosom in his face and took hold of his arm.

"Come on, sugar, let ole Hermadine he'p you up."

Heintz let her haul him to his feet, ready at a moment's notice to defend himself. She hugged him once to her elephantine hips, and he was sure D-Day had arrived. He drew back his right arm in karate readiness, stiffened his fingers into lethal cudgels. Before he could strike, Hermadine had turned away, humming gospel and beckoning him to follow her into the night.

They crossed the street together, Heintz matching her thick-thighed waddle with his own slow, uneasy shuffle.

"How . . . uh, far we going?" he asked, trying to sound as nonchalant as possible. Why hadn't she made her move in the park? Maybe there was too much light from the street. Or then again, he thought, reflecting on the profile of her victims, maybe she was waiting for him to make the first move.

"Not far, sugar. Ain't goin' far at all."

A grisly montage of police photos ran vividly through Heintz's mind—pictures Lieutenant Valjohn had shown him of her handiwork. As he felt her great mass lumbering alongside him, sensed her horrendous strength, he felt a tightening chill in the pit of his stomach. For the first time he began to wonder if he might be overmatched.

Well, he wasn't about to be led off to the slaughter. Ahead of them he spotted the auto graveyard, its gate still yawning open. Damn right he'd make the first move—he needed every advantage he could get! He'd force her to play her hand right now.

Sweating, trembling, he watched the gate approach, felt a burst of adrenaline surging through his veins. Four steps away . . . three . . . two . . . one . . .

Geronimo!

In one lightning move he wrenched back her arm that he'd been holding, pivoted his body and flung her past him through the entranceway. She lurched across the cinder drive, staggering awkwardly to keep her balance.

"You crazy! . . . What you doing?" she half bawled, half squealed.

He didn't stop to explain but charged into her midsection with a lowered shoulder. She expelled a loud grunt, crashed backward into the front fender of a junked Edsel and toppled to the ground beneath its rusted grill. She lay there stunned, heaving and gasping for air, a stricken behemoth amid a pile of broken glass, cinders and discarded head gaskets. Her scarf was gone, revealing a tangled mass of stiff, straightened hair. Her dress was hiked up above her waist. She tried to rise.

Heintz, reeling himself from the impact, took a step back and paused to

271

discern her outstretched form lying in the shadows. Then with all the abandon of recovering a fumble in the end zone, he hurled himself on top of her.

Valjohn didn't learn of Heintz's exploits until the next evening. He'd had been out of town all day pursuing a possible lead on some new tangential evidence that had turned up. Gaylord Radzim's fingerprints had been found in a girl's apartment in Milwaukee; the girl, a stewardess, had been reported missing since last August. A week ago her skeletal remains had been exhumed from a shallow grave in a woods near Lake Geneva. Valjohn had driven up to Milwaukee to interview local investigators there as well as the girl's roommate, who still was living in the same apartment. Hoping as always to stumble across the big breakthrough, he'd only succeeded in adding another grim footnote to the case's growing reams of sordid data.

"He did what?" said Valjohn over the phone at home that night.

Greg Harris repeated the news.

"He assaulted a black prostitute in Daley Park. She also claims he tried to rape her."

"You're putting me on."

"No put-on, Lieutenant. Actually, the assault didn't take place in the park. He picked her up there on a stakeout. It all happened in a junkyard across Torrio Avenue."

"Beautiful."

"Right, the department's been in a turmoil all day. Howland's been running around like a chicken with his head off."

"Hey, that sounds like an improvement. How's the prostitute?"

"He roughed her up pretty bad. Cracked some ribs, broke an arm—"

"Jesus!"

"She's in Cook County Hospital now. Name's Hermadine Turpin. She owns her own house over on Railroad Avenue, a cheap crash for derelicts. Evidently she free-lances the park now and then when business is slow. She sure hit the jackpot with supercop, huh?"

Valjohn laughed grimly. "So what's his story?"

"I guess he was convinced she was the Reaper. Said he came on at her to get her to make a move—you know, attack him and give herself away."

Brilliant strategy, thought Valjohn. Just beat up and rape every suspicious, brawny woman in the city and you were bound to collar the perpetrator.

"Claims he lost his head and didn't know what he was doing. Can't blame him—not for being scared, anyway. I saw the prostitute, and, believe me, no racial slur intended, but she's nothing you'd want to meet in a dark alley. A well-lit one, for that matter."

Valjohn was silent for a moment; then he said, "I'm surprised he didn't just split—I mean, after he realized his mistake."

"Didn't get the chance. One of the owners of the junkyard was working in a back shed. He called the police. They got there about the same time Heintz was pulling up his pants."

Valjohn hung the phone on his shoulder for a second, bit his lip. "So how do things stand now?" he asked again.

"Well, she was pretty hot for a while there—particularly when she found out Heintz was a cop. She's cooled off now, though. They brought in Hans Glad to talk to her. She's agreed to drop charges."

Valjohn speculated on how much it must have cost Glad to shut her up: medical expenses, a hundred bucks or so tucked under her G-string and probably a firm promise of *laissez faire* when she was well enough to resume her trade. Plenty cheap. If the media ever got hold of this one the shit would really hit the fan.

"Anything wrong?" asked Crescent, clearing away dishes from the coffee table where they'd eaten dinner. Valjohn still was seated on the barstool by the phone, shaking his head.

He nodded, then reflected that at least the mess hadn't been his fault.

"Anything you want to talk about?"

He thought for a moment, decided what the hell. . . .

She listened to Heintz's exploits in the park while she scraped the dishes, washed and rinsed them. She did not seem to find the story particularly amusing.

"I didn't know you suspected a woman," she commented when he'd finished.

"It's a . . . a strong possibility—it's also very confidential," he added quickly. "But the point I'm trying to make is that I warned Howland something like this might happen if he turned Heintz loose on the case."

"He should have listened to you."

"Ya, he should have listened to me: My investigation's been such a whirlwind of productivity."

Crescent stared at him.

He closed his eyes, rubbed them. It had been a long day. He helped her finish drying the dishes; then they both walked into the living room, an arm around each other's waist. He told her about his sojourn to Milwaukee, his inability to come up with any new leads.

"Well, you learned something about Radzim, anyway," she said, trying to cheer him up. "He must have been an awful person. Doesn't it make you feel a little better knowing that he was a murderer—that maybe he really got what he deserved?"

"Let's just say that's an attitude a police officer can't afford," he answered with unintended stuffiness.

She looked away. For a moment he wondered if she was hiding a smile.

The next day at work, Valjohn learned that Heintz and the rest of his men from TUF had been taken off the case. Gillian told him the news.

Howland wouldn't speak to him. They passed each other a couple of times in the hallway. On both occasions the captain refused even to look at him, stared straight ahead, chewing furiously on his stubby black cigar.

Egil "Magnum" Heintz stood up. He'd been crouched for over an hour in a small grove of evergreens by McDonald Lagoon. The lagoon was situated in the southeastern corner of Daley Park. He glanced at his watch: The luminous hands pointed after three.

He picked up a stone from the gravel bank and hurled it, listened for the answering splash moments later out in the deep, absorbing gloom of stagnant water and lily pads. Then he shuffled onto a path that led to Fifty-third Street.

Not a good night for predators, he thought. Too dark. No shadows. The moon was a clipped thumbnail of light hanging on the rim of a blackened, starry sky. What he needed was a full moon. That's what brought the real prowlers out. Plenty of light to spot their prey; plenty of long, dark shadows to lurk in. He wondered if Lieutenant Valjohn had checked that out —a possible correlation between the murders and the phases of the moon. Hell, Heintz grinned to himself, maybe he should trade in his magnum loads for silver bullets!

He wouldn't need them tonight, though. There was nothing doing; the park was dead. He left it on Fifty-third, headed south for two blocks to the el station. No sense hanging around any longer. He might as well call it a night, catch a train back downtown and pick up his car.

While he sauntered along the deserted street he reflected on his recent woes. What galled him the most was not just being removed from the case —so he'd assaulted a whore; you'd think she was the Queen of England the way everyone was carrying on. What really rankled him was the fear he'd been made to feel: the cold grip that had seized his guts while he was walking arm in arm with that big black tub of lard . . . convinced *she was* the Reaper.

Oh, he'd known fear before—he wasn't crazy. Certainly in Nam it was common as sweat. But what he felt the other night was different . . . more personal . . . as though what he feared were something within himself, something he couldn't run from. After the panic had left him, the adrenaline all worn off, it still was there, a small residue that remained locked deep inside. It stayed with him like a bad taste, a foul odor. The humiliation he endured on the Force was nothing compared to this, the knowledge that he was still afraid.

And so he had come to hunt the Reaper on his own time. Neutralize her Nam style, for good.

While he bought his token at the el station, he heard a train clatter on the tracks overhead and come to a screeching halt. He thrust his change into his pocket, stuffed the token into the turnstile and raced up the dingy metal stairway, two steps at a time. As he reached the upper level, he heard the train's doors bang shut, the loud hiss of air escaping from its released brakes. He slowed to a walk on the boarding platform, stared down the tracks at the receding ring of taillights. Northbound. Shit! At this time of night he'd have to wait a half hour for another one—maybe longer.

Resignedly he glanced up and down the long platform. Deserted. So was the southbound across the way. He spotted a candy-bar machine in the next bay, strolled over to it. He sorted through his change and inserted a dime into the coin slot. He pulled the red knob of his choice. It jammed. He tried the other knobs. None of them worked. He flipped the coin return, but his dime didn't drop out. He flipped the lever again, violently wrenched it. No coin.

"Son-of-a-bitch!" he swore and kicked the machine's base. The "clunk" of his foot against solid metal incensed him all the more. He looked quickly up and down the platform to make sure he still was alone. Then he leaped at the machine, smashing into it with his powerful shoulder, kicking and kneeing it, hammering it with his fists.

When his anger was spent, he took a step back and surveyed the damage. The machine was covered with dents. Its steel-paneled front was caved in, and the delivery tray was buckled. The shatterproof plastic display window was cracked in two: One piece still hung loosely from its frame; the other lay at his feet.

A trickle of blood seeped from the knuckles of his left hand. He smiled, licked clean his wound. He kicked the piece of plastic lying at his feet out onto the tracks and walked away.

He sat down on a bench, fidgeted for a few moments and then got up again. When he'd left the park he was starting to feel drowsy. Now he was wide awake. His little outburst had really gotten the blood pumping.

He paced back and forth for a while at the edge of the platform. One thing was for sure: The next time he jumped a suspect he better not hang around and get caught—not unless he was damn well positive she was the killer. He couldn't count on Howland going to bat for him again. Shit. Way things were going lately he'd be lucky that fucking candy machine didn't report him. . . .

He stopped pacing and stared down at the far end of the platform. Something had moved over there, he was sure of it. He took a few steps to his left, removing a row of posts from his field of vision. Yes, he could see someone now. The area was dimly lit, but he could just make out the form of someone standing by the exit stairway, someone—he couldn't tell if it was a man or a woman—pressed back in the shadows as if in hiding. He wondered how long whoever it was had been standing there and why the person didn't want to be seen. Hell, he was probably the reason. Probably thought he was a crazy man, all the racket he made pounding that fucking machine.

Well, mused Heintz, sucking again on the knuckles of his left hand, he had some time to kill. He'd just wander on down there and say hello.

275

16

He is in the Kimberley County Foster Home again. He is upstairs standing in his dormitory bedroom, looking out the window. It is not nighttime; it is the middle of the day. The sun is brilliant. The lawn is Technicolor green and the surrounding trees shimmer in light and shadow. She is out there in all that brilliance waiting for him. His mother. She sits in a swing beneath his favorite tree, a great dappled sycamore. She is smiling. She waves to him.

He waves and dashes to the hallway door. He starts to open the door and stops. Then he dashes back to a bed in the corner of the room where Crescent lies sleeping. He wakes her, tells her that they are going to meet his mother. Crescent seems delighted, and he feels his own joy swell larger within him. She is dressed in her uniform. Her smile is brilliant as sunlight. Eagerly he takes her hand.

He reaches to open the hallway door. It slides away from him and opens by itself. The hallway has become an elevator—a bright, gleaming, stainless-steel cubicle like the ones at headquarters. On the ride down they stop at Crescent's childhood farm in Carthage. Mr. O'Leary is out working in a field of corn. When he sees Crescent he turns his tractor and cuts right across the rows to meet them. He leaves a flattened path of crushed stalks behind him. The elevator door closes in his face.

The door rolls open again on the ground floor. Still holding Crescent's hand, Valjohn leads her quickly outside. He knows they are too late, that his mother will be gone.

She is not gone. She still is sitting there in the swing beneath the sycamore. She sees them and rises immediately from the swing, walks across the lawn to meet them. She is the Honorable Mrs. George Swinton, lovely, stately, dressed in regal satin.

Valjohn is flushed with joy. He steps forward to embrace her, whirls in the next instant to include Crescent in the greeting. It is then he discovers he is no longer holding his wife's hand. He is holding the hand of Ernly Chard—the old derelict psycho he'd interviewed at the state institution. Chard is drunk, unshaven, dressed in soiled, baggy pajamas. He breaks into a racking cough, spits strings of gray phlegm onto the lush Technicolor grass at his feet. He grins, revealing a mouthful of brown and broken teeth. Valjohn tries to pull his hand away, but the old row bum refuses to let go, instead tightening his grip, which feels crusted and scaly. Valjohn looks about frantically for Crescent. She is nowhere to be seen.

The smile has left his mother's face. He is sure she too will disappear. But only if he looks away. He stares at her intently, refuses even to blink. Suddenly she steps forward and embraces Chard. They kiss passionately, sloppily, mouths wide open. He watches horrified as Chard lewdly shoves a knee between his mother's legs—and she responds, gripping him between her satin thighs, hunching slightly, undulating her hips against him—

Valjohn awoke with a start. He rolled over, tried to get his bearings in the dark. He slowly recognized his bedroom in the dim illumination of an amber night-light. He felt Crescent lying asleep beside him.

The telephone rang again.

He sat upright, looked at the clock on the bed stand: four twenty-five! Christ, he hoped it was a wrong number. He let it continue ringing. Good to see Crescent home safe and sound, anyway. She'd gone out for one of her late-night strolls—after midnight. She still wasn't home yet when he'd fallen asleep reading. That was after two.

The phone.

Damn! He struggled out of bed, stumbled into the study, rubbing his face in a hasty effort to clear the cobwebs. God, what an awful dream! Hadn't had one of his oedipal nightmares for ages. Not since before his marriage. Hoped this wasn't a sneak preview of the coming season.

He picked up the phone; a voice rasped in his ear. Stephansky! Jesus, didn't that bastard ever sleep? No, it was not Stephansky; just another CS. They all sounded the same.

Valjohn listened dumbly to the message, finally muttered an *"Oy vay."* Before hanging up he asked the sergeant to repeat the address. Then he shuffled back into the bedroom, tried to assimilate what he'd just heard while he looked for his clothes.

Heintz had been killed. Old tiger cop himself. In the Fourth Sector. A possible you-know-who. That really ought to stir things up. One of the old home team. He could already hear the nightsticks cracking heads. Maybe his own would get cracked in the process.

When he'd finished dressing he glanced over at Crescent. She was sleeping like a rock. No sense waking her. He grabbed his car keys off the top of the dresser and plodded out the door.

Twenty minutes later he was climbing the dingy metal stairs of a South Side el station.

"Body's over here, Lieutenant."

Valjohn was met on the upper level by a young patrolman who introduced himself as Officer Finneman. Finneman explained that he'd been on the scene of another 1834 slaying a year ago. Same sector, Daley Park. It was he who'd called in the tentative code identification.

"Anyone else here from Homicide?"

"Negative, sir. You're the first."

Well, that was something new for a change, thought Valjohn as he followed the young patrolman down the northbound platform to view the carnage.

Egil "Magnum" Heintz had been gibbeted. He hung twisted like a pretzel from an exit turnstile, one of the large barrier types with rows of meshing spokes that made it virtually impossible to back up or squeeze through. His limbs had been broken and jammed between the thick spokes. His great muscular torso, naked, sagging outward, partly entwined the turnstile's tall, vertical axle. In the dim yellow light of the station, the scene resembled something from a medieval dungeon.

Valjohn stood a few feet away staring at the deceased. His initial revulsion quickly turned into disbelief, then into awe, then back into revulsion. He kept remembering the man he'd seen only weeks ago in Howland's office, the arrogant, menacing cop from TUF. Like him or not, Heintz had been one very imposing figure of a man. He was big, strong as a horse and an expert in combatives. He also was mean as hell—

Jesus! It had never hit him so hard before. He'd always managed to lose himself in the details before. But now somehow having known Heintz . . . He suddenly realized they'd all made a serious mistake—he and everybody else connected with the case. They hadn't really noticed what was going down here . . . the force . . . the incredible expenditure of destructive energy. . . .

"Do you ever get the feeling," he'd once asked Moe, "that what we're dealing with isn't human?"

"An animal?"

"No, I mean . . . well . . . something that isn't natural. As far as we know, anyway."

278

"Oh, 'Creature Features' time," said Moe, laughing. "How about a homosexual werewolf?"

Valjohn smiled but remained silent.

Moe had thought for a moment, removed his glasses, rubbed his eyes. "Correction," he said. "Considering the assortment of wounds, make that a werezoo."

They'd both laughed. The conversation had been interrupted at that point, and the subject never had arisen again.

Now standing here staring at Heintz, Valjohn contemplated boundaries. The world he knew was changing. Moe was dead. There was serious talk of landing on the moon.

"Excuse me, Lieutenant . . . that gun there . . ." Officer Finneman was standing by his side pointing to a revolver that lay on the iron walkway beneath the victim.

"What about it?"

"Smith and Wesson Combat Masterpiece; .357 magnum. Checked it out already. It's registered to the deceased."

Valjohn looked sharply at the officer.

"Oh, I didn't touch it, sir. I could read the numbers right off the frame there."

Valjohn nodded.

"When we first got here . . . uh . . ."

"Yes?"

"Uh . . . Officer Heintz—that is, the gun . . . well, it was shoved up his ass, his rectum, sir. Fell out, oh . . . fifteen or twenty minutes ago."

Valjohn sighed, knelt down to inspect the weapon. He could see the tips of the bullets in the cylinder. It probably hadn't been fired; the hammer still was on safety.

"Who discovered the body?"

"Some passenger. Nobody got his name. Evidently he spotted it when his train was pulling out of the station."

Must have been something of an eye-opener, thought Valjohn, standing up again.

"He notified the conductor at the next stop. That's when we were called in."

"Mind doing me a favor, Officer?"

"What, sir?"

"Go down to the guy selling tokens, see if he remembers selling one to Lieutenant Heintz. See if you can pinpoint what time he came up here."

Eager to assist in the investigation, the young patrolman hurried off. He was likable, seemed competent and alert, but Valjohn was glad to be rid of him.

He satisfied himself with a close examination of the wounds: the sizes, the shapes, the overall configurations. He was about to step back again when he remembered Moe and his bloodhound nose. The final verification, he thought. He leaned slightly forward and sniffed.

He recoiled, stumbling backward as though he'd been struck in the face. He stood there for a moment stunned, then stepped forward. He sniffed again.

The fetor of dead fish—the telltale odor of vaginitis—wasn't there. In its place was the poignant, scented aroma of jasmine. Jasmine! There was no mistaking it. It cloyed in his nostrils, made his head swim. Heintz's exposed and mutilated privates were a reeking bed of flowers. . . .

"Well, Lieutenant?"

He jumped back, spun around.

Captain Howland, grim-faced, cigar in mouth, was stalking up the exit ramp on the other side of the turnstile. Lieutenant Sweeney accompanied him. As Valjohn watched them approach, he tried to clear the chaos in his mind.

Howland stopped at the barrier, gaped at Heintz through the blood-smeared spokes of the turnstile.

"Goddamn sickening!" he snorted. To Valjohn's recollection it was the captain's first appearance at one of the murder sites. Valjohn's superior took a step backward, noticeably shaken, and muttered something to Sweeney. Then Howland turned to look for a way to gain entrance onto the boarding platform.

"I . . . uh, think you'll have to go around, Captain. The gate's locked," Valjohn said in a voice he barely recognized as his own. He still was miles away, his mind reeling with a dozen thoughts.

Howland ignored him, walked over to a maintenance gate and yanked at it. A padlocked chain rattled. "Son-of-a-bitch," he growled, kicked it. Then he walked back to the turnstile partition and abruptly confronted Valjohn.

"Well, Lieutenant, you sure as fuck better come up with something." Valjohn stared at him.

"What have you found so far? Anything? Have you found one fucking clue, one solitary shred of evidence that'll bring us that much closer to nailing down the perpetrator?" Howland was holding up a stubby thumb and forefinger to measure the proposed distance.

Valjohn was momentarily silent. "I just got here, sir," he finally mumbled.

"Well, I'm telling you right now, the Chicago fucking Police Department isn't going to sit around with its thumb up its ass waiting for you to pussyfoot through this one—not when one of its own ends up like this poor bastard!"

Howland removed his cigar from his mouth. He gestured toward the body with it. "As far as I'm concerned we've already got our suspect and we're bringing her in first thing this morning."

Valjohn felt a sinking sensation in the pit of his stomach. The odor of jasmine hung like a fog in the deepest corners of his brain.

280

"Bring . . . b-b-bringing in who?" he managed barely above a whisper.

"Who? Who do you think, for chrissakes? Who lives less than three blocks from here—over on Railroad Avenue? And who just got out of the hospital yesterday?"

"Herm-Hermadine Turpin?" he asked incredulously.

"Who the fuck else? Old Aunt Jemima herself!" Howland blurted, bit at his cigar, jerked it out of his mouth again in a show of exasperation. "I mean, look what he done to her. She couldn't wait to get even—it's your airtight motive, plain and simple. You know, I think that's the main problem with you hot-shit college boys: You spend all your fucking time trying to make things complicated."

Valjohn suddenly felt relieved. He could not believe what he'd been thinking.

"Airtight motive?" he responded absently. "I always thought it was alibis that were airtight. Aren't motives supposed to be plausible?"

Howland, pretending not to hear him, returned his attention to the body.

"Maybe if we'd listened to this cop, trusted his God-given instincts . . . maybe if we hadn't been so quick to condemn him—maybe he'd still be alive. Instead he had to go it alone. Come out here in this jungle on his own time. Jesus! She had us all fooled, goddamnit—me included."

Valjohn could hear no more.

"Do me a favor, Captain: Take a good look at the deceased. That's no slaughtered innocent there. That happens to be Magnum Heintz—two hundred plus pounds of very mean mesomorph. You're trying to tell me some overweight over-the-hill hooker could do him in like that? And just out of the hospital besides with her ribs bandaged and both arms in a sling? There's no way—I mean, look at him. He hasn't been offed, he's been obliterated!" Valjohn was surprised to find he was shouting.

"One arm," Howland corrected lamely, "she only had one arm in a sling."

"Go ahead, Lieutenant Sweeney, you tell me otherwise. Try to visualize the force it must have taken to bend back that right elbow, to pop the joint like that."

"Maybe she had help."

"Ya, and maybe you ought to think twice about harassing that poor hooker again. She might just decide to remember how she ended up in the hospital in the first place."

Sweeney stared down at the walkway and scraped the edge of the grating with his shoe. Howland and Valjohn glared through the turnstile at one another, Heintz's mangled body between them.

Howland finally shrugged, bit down on his cigar, spit to one side.

"All right, Lieutenant. Okay, we'll hold off on the Turpin woman—but this time you do me a favor. This time you take a good look and remember that that's a cop hanging there—not some degenerate asshole off the street. Then get your fucking ass in gear and come up with something solid fast—because . . . because this is war!"

He whirled around and stomped off. Halfway down the exit ramp he turned and called back. "And for chrissakes throw a goddamn tarp or something up to screen the body from the tracks. The fucking commuters are gonna start running any time now."

Valjohn nodded. There were cover-ups and there were cover-ups.

Valjohn spent the next few weeks in a state of perpetual mental turmoil. The lab verified the accuracy of his olfactory sense—not that he'd had much doubt. One whiff and he was back at the counter of that posh boutique on Michigan Avenue, the exotic contents of Madame Pristianna's Elixir Feminique spread before him.

"They say jasmine is the most erotic of all herbal fragrances. I would agree. Wouldn't you?"

He could still hear the sultry, fey voice of the clerk, see him spraying his sleek wrist and holding it out to be sniffed. . . .

There probably were tens of thousands of women in the city using flower-scented douches. And thousands of these using jasmine. It also was probably reasonable to assume that a large percentage of them had one form of vaginitis or another.

Plenty of room for coincidence, and yet . . . he couldn't shut his mind off.

Crescent's late-night walks, for one thing. She'd been out the very night of Heintz's murder. And then there was that matter at Windhaven Hospital during Radzim's murder. Her presence in the basement elevator and the confusion surrounding her story: Had she gotten off, or not gotten off?

But it was preposterous to think she was somehow connected with the murders. So what did it all mean? Where could it possibly lead?

Was it Heintz? Was that the connection? Was she having an affair with the victim? She could have been with him that fateful night. She could have left his arms only an hour or so—maybe even minutes—before he got blitzed. The idea of Crescent and old Tigercop was ludicrous. But he couldn't let it drop. The longer he mulled over the notion, the fonder he became of it. It seemed to feed off the frustrations of his marriage, to satisfy some deep, masochistic hunger within. He readily overlooked inconsistencies, torturing himself instead by recalling past conversations with the deceased and trying to discover hidden innuendoes. He remembered the smirk Heintz had greeted him with the first time they'd met in Howland's office. Now he felt sure he understood it. He wondered if Howland knew. Maybe everyone in the department knew. The husband always was the last to find out. Even if he was a detective.

"It'll be hard to replace a man like Heintz," he mentioned casually one evening while he and Crescent were having dinner at home. He'd had a couple of beers.

"Watch out, it's still hot," she said, setting down a steaming casserole of baked lasagne on the table before him. She made no other comment, walked over to a kitchen cabinet, returned with a cup of grated Parmesan.

"They'll really miss him in undercover." He continued dishing out a large portion for himself. "He was . . . something else, I guess."

"Who?" she finally responded, sitting down. She spooned out a large portion for herself—larger than his.

"Heintz. Lieutenant Egil Heintz. I was just thinking what a tough job it'll be to find someone to fill his shoes." She was playing it a bit too cool. He knew damn well she knew whom he was talking about.

"Oh, the policeman who died."

"Yes. Supercop. Tigercop—that's what they called him."

"Was he very special?"

Valjohn paused, a forkful of crumbling ricotta cheese and noodles poised halfway to his mouth.

"I don't know, was he?" He answered her question with one of his own, studied her expression, intently trying to discern some betrayal of feeling.

She looked up blankly from her salad.

"Was he?"

"Was he what?"

"Very special."

Her face filled with puzzlement. "You're asking me?"

Valjohn lost his nerve. He shoveled the forkful of food into his mouth. "You're asking me?"

A faint touch of hardness had crept into her voice, her eyes. He looked quickly away, angry with himself for having put it there.

"No, no . . . sorry, I guess I was just thinking out loud," he stumbled, hoping she'd let the matter drop.

"Oh," she said.

Valjohn did his best to enjoy the rest of the meal, which was not difficult. The lasagne—her first attempt—was delicious. There seemed to be no dish she could not master instantly. That included an assortment of entrees from delicate soufflés to broiled meats with a variety of exotic, tasty sauces and his favorite dish, Romanian smothered chicken. Her shrimp *teriyaki* was better than any he'd had in a Japanese restaurant, and her *kreplach* rivaled Rose Frank's. If Crescent had been having an affair with Heintz, at least she was doing her best to keep it from him.

While Valjohn wrestled with his own problems, the department reacted to Heintz's murder in typical fashion. They flooded the Grand Crossing and South Chicago districts with manpower. Squadrons of blue and whites patrolled the area. An army of tactical units roamed the streets. All known sex offenders were run in and grilled along with anyone else who looked halfway suspicious. The street people—pimps and prostitutes, deadbeats, drunks, junkies and hustlers—were jostled around and generally made miserable. This calculated show of force was meant to display the awesome wrath of the department when one of its own was struck down, but Valjohn was unimpressed. He knew it would bring him not one step closer to the Reaper.

He was unimpressed but not unaffected. Howland inserted himself more and more into the case, demanding meetings with him as often as two or three times a day. Patrick Maloney, the deputy chief for violent crimes, demanded a daily written progress report, as did James Shroeder, the deputy superintendent.

Two days after Heintz's murder, Gordon had called Valjohn into his office for a personal accounting. A few weeks later he summoned him again. During this second visit Gordon spoke of the growing antagonism within the department directed at Valjohn. Demands for his removal from the case were becoming increasingly insistent.

While he sat listening to Gordon ramble on, his mind kept slipping back to Crescent. Last evening she'd taken another late-night walk.

"I trust I'm not boring you?"

Valjohn sat in a reflective trance, his eyes fastened on a thin wisp of smoke that curled up from a bulldog briar on Gordon's desk.

"I said I trust I'm not boring you, John?"

"No, no . . . sorry." He looked up quickly from the smoldering pipe. "I . . . I was thinking about something else for a moment. Please go on."

The superintendent studied him long and hard with his deep-set, tired, gray eyes. Then he continued.

"As I was saying, I feel we have to come up with something rather quickly. We need to give the media—the public—something solid, some definite sign of headway. We have to let them know we're not just out there writing parking tickets."

"What about Moe Frank's lab report—the disclosure of the Reaper's sex?"

Gordon fell silent. Valjohn watched him as he reached across the desk, picked up the bulldog briar and actually began smoking it.

When Valjohn left Gordon's office, he didn't return to his desk but went downstairs and across the street to Mr. Dick's, where he ordered a cold beer. He should have complained to Gordon about all the bureaucratic harassment he was getting, but he hadn't. Just another sign of his waning self-confidence, he supposed.

He drained his glass and ordered another beer. Crescent's walks were having a very demoralizing effect on him. Of course, he'd dismissed the ridiculous idea of her and Heintz as lovers. . . . Still, all those late-night walks . . . They festered in his mind, filling his head with ugly, jaundiced fantasies. In the worst of these, he saw her as totally wanton, nymphomaniacal in her wanderings. She lusted after and became available to all men. He was cuckolded a thousand times over, by any and all comers —a teeming army of bawdy, sneering strangers. He envisioned her with them, yielding to their lewd advances, to their dirty, groping fingers. He saw her smile, her flesh trembling, her knees turning slowly outward. . . .

He slammed his fist down on the counter of the bar. Two customers standing at the other end looked at him. He recognized them from the department. Vice dicks. He glared back until they looked away.

His mind was made up. He was tired of all this crazy conjecture. Maybe he couldn't solve the case, but he could damn well find out if his wife was having an affair!

He got up and paid his bill. The two men at the end of the bar watched him leave.

On Friday Valjohn announced to Crescent that he'd be going to Pittsburgh Tuesday. He was planning to attend a special seminar at the Police Institute there and would be gone for several days. When Tuesday arrived he packed a bag and kissed her good-bye. She made him promise to call her faithfully every day.

Later that afternoon, after arranging for all his incoming calls to be transferred to a detective who had agreed to cover for him, he rented a car from an agency in the Loop, did some shopping, then drove to the Holiday Manor Inn on the Outer Drive and checked in.

Surveillance was not exactly his forte. He probably should have hired a private eye, enlisted the services of one of the supershadows from the department. Certainly a stranger would have a much easier time maintaining cover. He was bound and determined, however, to do his own laundry.

He ate dinner that evening at the inn, then drove over to the apartment in the rented car around seven. There he was forced to circle the block for half an hour before finding a parking place, one that afforded him an unobstructed view through the lush parkway trees of both the apartment's front window and its street entrance.

After parking the green two-door Fairlane—still pungent with the smell of newness—he adjusted the outside rearview mirror to cover the front steps, spread the evening newspaper over the steering wheel and settled back in the driver's seat to wait.

The clothes he was wearing he'd bought today. Black peg trousers and a gaudy, green satin shirt with sequins. He'd picked up sunglasses, the sneaky kind with one-way reflector lenses—all he needed to go with them was a phony moustache and a plastic nose. He'd also picked up a hat: a wide-brimmed pimp's fedora, black felt with an orange feather. He tried it on, glanced at himself in a mirror hanging from the visor. Not bad. Maybe he'd missed his true calling.

He sat at his vigil for the next hour, not sure whether she was home yet. He amused himself keeping track of the number of dogs that went by on leashes. Twenty-six of them: ten poodles, two Afghans, three German shepherds, one Chihuahua, a Great Dane, three collies, a schnauzer, and five unknowns. In less than an hour. Jesus! No wonder he was stepping in dog shit every day.

A light went on in the apartment around eight-thirty. The sun was just going down. A few minutes later he saw Crescent draw the living room curtains closed. At nine-fifteen, the light went off. The faint blue glow of the TV showed around the outer edges of the curtains. Shortly before eleven, the TV went off. Other lights went on and off. After that nothing but darkness. He was certain she'd turned in. Nevertheless, he didn't drive away until after three.

The next morning he awoke feeling rotten. He was so hounded by guilt he could barely abide looking at himself in the mirror while he shaved. He was tempted to go to the phone to call Crescent then and there, confess everything and beg for forgiveness. Well . . . maybe not everything. He would simply tell her the seminar had ended early, that he hated Pittsburgh, and he was on his way home just as soon as he could pack his bag.

He was tempted, but he didn't call. By noon he'd regained his sense of determination.

Later, after he'd returned from work, he did call her. Sitting up on the end of his bed with the phone in his lap, he tuned to an empty channel on the TV, turned the volume of static way up, and dialed. When Crescent answered, he held the receiver a full twenty inches from his mouth and spoke in a loud, strained voice.

She was happy to hear from him, chided him for not calling her last night. He apologized, moving the phone back and forth as he alternated listening and speaking. He told her he'd been tied up in meetings and that when he finally did get free it was too late to do anything but fall asleep.

She asked about his plane trip.

He answered that his flight had been bumpy but on time.

"Are you finding out anything interesting?"

He was silent.

She repeated the question. "At the Police Institute," she added, "are you learning anything new?"

"Oh . . . sure, sure. I mean you have to keep up with the times." He proceeded to elaborate on several new technological advances in police work involving computer-dispatching methods.

Crescent interrupted him. "I can hardly hear you. What did you say?"

"Nothing important," he said, moving the receiver a few inches closer to his mouth. "I guess we've got a bad connection."

He sat with the phone on his lap several minutes after he'd hung up, the static from the TV still flooding in his ears. Never had he felt so small, so contemptible. At last he stood up and turned off the set.

Instead of dinner, he rode the elevator up to the inn's famous, revolving, rooftop bar and had a beer. Then another. After the second beer he felt bloated, switched to Scotch and sodas. He had three of them while he sat watching the panorama of Lake Michigan swing slowly around him. The water was somber gray under an overcast sky. He watched its surface harden to anthracite as the evening light faded from the sky behind him.

By the time he was again strategically parked across from the apartment, it was well after nine. There were no lights on. He cursed himself for being late, for having drunk so much on an empty stomach. He debated leaving. No, at least he might learn what time she got in. If she did get in.

Readjusting the rearview mirror, he saw he'd forgotten to put on his hat. He reached down under the seat and picked up the fedora, flipped it on his head. He settled back into the seat. Thunder rumbled in the distance.

A light was on in the living room! She must have slipped in when he wasn't looking, while his mind wandered in alcoholic reverie. He checked his watch. It was going on eleven. He must have dozed. How long had the light been on? Five minutes? Half an hour? He wasn't sure, couldn't even be sure she'd been out. She'd told him over the phone it had been a tiring day at the hospital. She could very well have been inside all this time, napping.

He lurched upright in his seat. She'd just come out through the front doorway, skipped down the steps wearing her light blue raincoat. She headed west toward Broadway at a brisk walk.

He waited until she disappeared around the corner before wheeling out of the parking space. He swung into a U-turn, came up short, nearly hitting the fender of a parked Porsche, had to back up, recramp his wheels and tighten the arc to complete the turn. When he reached Broadway he steered left and slowed down, scanning the sidewalks for her. She was nowhere to be seen. A car behind him honked. He pulled over, double-parking to let it by. Maybe she'd gone into one of the boutiques. No, it was too late. The corner drugstore was closed also.

He spotted a green commuter bus pulling away from the curb at Wellington. It was the only explanation. She had to be on it.

He started to make another U-turn, changed his mind. Too much traffic. He turned down the first side street, wheels squealing. Intent on circling the block, he turned right again on the next street, then noticed he was going the wrong way down a one-way. He looked to the end of the street. No one was coming. He decided to chance it, kept his foot planted on the gas.

Too late. A pair of headlights swerved around the next corner and approached him head-on. He hit the brakes, came to a screeching halt. The other car, a checkered taxi, also came to a halt. Barely three feet separated them. The taxi proceeded to inch forward with flashing brights and blaring horn until it nudged him bumper to bumper. The cabbie stuck his head out the window, shouted obscenities.

There was nowhere to pull over. The street lined with cars was too narrow. One of them would have to back up and give ground. Valjohn was in the wrong, but he had practically the whole block behind him. The cabbie had only a dozen or so yards to the corner.

"Come on, move it, bonehead! Learn how to drive or get your goddamn ass off the streets!"

It was senseless to argue.

Valjohn waved acquiescence. He prepared to put it in reverse, craned to look out the rear window. No way. Almost before he knew what he was doing, he spun around, slammed into low and floored it. The Fairlane lunged forward, plowed into the cab and propelled it and its astonished driver—his hat sent flying as he jerked his head inside—backwards out the lane, across the intersecting street and up over the far curb onto the sidewalk.

Valjohn then backed off, wrenched a sharp right, accelerating away, tires squealing. At Broadway again, he shot the intersection, causing two cars to slam on their brakes, and nearly broadsided a motorcyclist coming out of a Burger King.

Jesus! What was he doing? He couldn't believe he was this drunk. He felt as if he were watching himself on TV. Lucky he'd spent the extra dollar a day for collision coverage.

With the bus still not in sight, he ran two red lights, swinging around the stopped cars and nosing his way, horn blaring, through the flow of bewildered cross traffic.

One of the cars, a blue and white cruiser, was less than bewildered. It came after him, lights flashing. He slammed the steering wheel with both hands and pulled over.

A young patrolman got out, warily approached him, hand on gun.

"Aw-right, mister, out and spread 'em."

By the time he'd overtaken the bus, it was halfway to Evanston. He followed it to the end of the line, then passed it on Sheridan Road heading south to the Loop. All its passengers had gotten off. She'd either exited before he'd caught up with it or never gotten on in the first place.

Back at the apartment, which was dark, he couldn't find a parking space. He circled the block for twenty minutes without luck and ended up double-parking.

Two hours later a policeman shook him awake, hunched over the wheel. It was pouring rain. For the second time that night he was forced to flash his gold. When he finally drove off at five, hung over and back aching, the apartment was still dark.

Thursday night he resumed his vigil by seven o'clock. He donned his fedora, sat parked across the street, sipping a strawberry shake—the strongest thing he'd had to drink all day. He was ready. He was alert. He was not about to repeat last evening's performance.

His little jousting match with the taxi had knocked out a headlight and punched a baseball-sized hole in the Fairlane's grill. It had also given him a black eye. Probably hit it on the steering wheel when the cab flew over the curb, though he couldn't remember in all the excitement. To add insult to injury, it had dawned on him, as he stumbled drowsily through work today, that when Crescent had left the apartment last night the living room light had been on—not off. Consequently he needn't have hung around waiting for her return. She was already home.

Well . . . he'd give himself one more chance tonight, then throw in the towel.

He kept his attention glued to the rearview mirror, ignoring a Frisbee game in the street, the dogs squatting on the sidewalk. He did watch one enormous St. Bernard in the mirror hunch its back directly in front of the apartment, its harried master glancing nervously about like a sneak thief in a supermarket. Valjohn almost yelled out the window.

Crescent emerged from the building at a quarter after eight, stood at the door for a moment staring up at the sky. He almost didn't recognize her. She was wearing an outfit he'd never seen before, a light green corduroy jacket and red plaid culottes. Her hair was braided into pigtails. She looked all of fourteen years old.

She skipped down to the sidewalk, stepping squarely in the middle of the fresh pile of dog shit. He watched in amazement as she didn't slip or jerk her foot away. Indeed, she seemed to glide through the pile as though it were some kind of mirage.

Valjohn had no time to ponder the phenomenon. He wheeled out of his parking place and cut a well-practiced U-turn. She was walking fast, but this time he managed to overtake her before she reached the corner. He swung left on Broadway, pulled into a loading zone. At the corner she crossed the street, walked directly to the bus stop and stood there. She opened her purse and fished out change.

He sped off again. At the next side street he made another U-turn and reentered Broadway heading north. Then he parked by a fire hydrant and waited for the bus. It came by a few minutes later. He watched Crescent climb aboard. When it swung back into traffic, he could see her walking down the aisle, taking a seat near the rear exit. He still could see the back of her head, her pigtails swaying.

He eased in behind the lumbering vehicle and calmly followed it through a yellow light.

17

Wheeler Fairchild, preparing to go out for the evening, slipped into a tweed sport coat with leather elbow patches and told his wife, Tooter, that he was taking Colonel, their miniature schnauzer, over to the park for a walk.

"You're bleeding," she said, looking up from a piece of furniture she was refinishing on the kitchen floor.

Fairchild, opening a closet door, stopped abruptly. He touched his lower lip, inspected his finger.

"Must have cut myself shaving."

His wife resumed her work without comment; she was busily sanding an old bentwood rocker for her daughter's room at college.

Fairchild put the dog in its special tote bag—Chandler Arms house rules required dogs to be carried in the elevator—and slung it over his shoulder. He strode from the kitchen. At the front door he hesitated, glanced back at his wife. She didn't look up. He might be back in fifteen minutes or gone for the entire weekend. It was all the same to her.

He closed the front door softly behind him, rode down to the garage, dumped the dog into the back seat of his carmine Cadillac Seville. He drove across Lake Shore Drive to Montrose Beach; there he watched the dog urinate on a park bench. He hauled the animal back to the car. Before getting in he rubbed himself vigorously between the legs.

He did not drive back to the apartment, instead swinging south on Lake Shore Drive. He had other plans tonight. He was on fire tonight.

A half hour later in a back-alley parking lot off Grand Avenue near the Loop, he exchanged cars. Leaving behind the dog and his jacket with the elbow patches in the Seville, he drove off in a beat-up cream '61 Chevy. The Chevy had a walleyed headlight and a caved-in passenger door. It also bore out-of-state plates. He headed north.

Things were not going well for him lately. He needed this little diversion. His Starved Rock development schemes had hit a real snag. He'd underestimated the opposition—the local residents and river ecologists as well as the Bureau of Illinois State Parks. The project was doomed at least for the immediate future and might be hung up in court battles for years. It wasn't like the city. He simply didn't have the clout downstate to steamroller it through.

To make matters worse, two weeks ago a three-story fire escape had collapsed on one of his South Side tenements, killing a woman and critically injuring two of her children. Investigators had revealed that the building's fire escape had been cited as unsafe three years earlier by a city building inspector, but nothing had ever been done to repair it.

The newspapers had run their usual tedious sermons against slumlords. One of them, the *Times,* had even started a probe. Of course, Fairchild had taken standard precautions: His name was submerged in a trust title, held in the strictest confidence by one of the most reputable banks in the city. Nevertheless, he felt uneasy with reporters nosing around. There always was the danger of a court order. Certainly a disclosure of this nature would do little to enhance his election prospects.

As he leisurely followed the flow of outgoing traffic on Sheridan Road, he reflected on another disclosure that would do little to enhance his political career. His right hand dropped from the steering wheel to his lap. He rubbed hard with his knuckles. His eyes began to water.

It had been the better part of a year since he'd set himself on fire. Last September 14, to be exact. He leaned forward, glanced at himself in the rearview mirror. The headlights of oncoming cars illuminated a grimace on his square-set, handsome face, a face still sporting its winter Florida tan. The grimace turned into a grin.

He suddenly thought of his wife, the image of her there in the kitchen where he'd left her tonight working on her knees, her brassy dyed hair up in curlers, her flabby arms quivering while she rubbed away endlessly on her antique furniture. Too bad she couldn't use the sandpaper on herself, rub away the years like so much old varnish.

Tooter. His childhood sweetheart. For better or for worse. He'd had the better—the bouncy, cute girl he'd grown up with, all grins and good times. She'd given him two fine children: a son and a daughter, both in college now. She'd given him the image his political ambitions required. Now after twenty-four years of marriage he was stuck with the worse. Oh, he still had his stable political image, all right. But the grins and good times had faded

291

into lumpish frowns and sullen pouts, into a travail of dull, tiresome to-getherness.

Yet he could admit to himself he didn't hate his wife—not her swollen thighs, her surfaced veins, her bulging hips and sagging breasts, not even her voice, which had sunk to a throaty cackle—though she never nagged him with it. She was like an old garment to him, a favorite coat he'd worn faithfully years ago. It still hung in the closet; he saw it every day, but he never put it on. Or almost never. He simply slid it aside and reached for other things to wear.

How long had it been since they'd shared the same bed? Eight years? Ten? They hadn't had sex since . . . not since nearly a year ago. September 14. No trouble remembering that date. Maybe tonight she'd get lucky again.

"Shit! Christ—oh, fucker!" He was gripping the wheel fiercely, his knuckles white, his fingers slippery with sweat on the smooth plastic. A paroxysm hit him. He shuddered. His mouth went dry. His ears plugged. He fought to gain control of himself. He reduced his speed.

At the next light he exited Sheridan Road and headed west on Morrison Avenue. A few blocks later he turned right off Morrison, continued north again until he came to a corner with a large, stone Presbyterian church on the left. He turned left, slowed to a crawl, lit a cigarette.

He was on Mudgett Drive. He was calmer now, though he was almost there. Though he was going up in flames.

He'd set himself on fire earlier in the evening after dinner. He excused himself from the table around seven, passing up one of Tooter's calorie-crammed desserts, and went to his study, bolting the door behind him.

With a small brass key he kept in a compartment of his wallet, he unlocked his desk, a colonial rolltop his wife had picked up in Galena, and slid back its squeaky canopy of walnut slats. From its dark, polished interior he withdrew a large fruit jar. A piece of cheesecloth, secured with rubber bands, sealed the top.

He shook the jar and lifted it to the light. A dusky black cloud swirled up inside the glass.

Mosquitoes. Hundreds, maybe thousands of them.

He pressed the jar to his ear, listened to the microcosmic din of angry, droning wings. He set it back down, walked over to the window, pulled the shade. Before taking off his trousers he removed a small penknife from one of the pockets.

He laid his trousers and boxer shorts neatly over an arm of his favorite reading chair, an overstuffed Victorian wingback complete with matching gout rest, picked up the jar and stood there in the center of the room, white shirt and tie, naked from the waist down to his black stockings.

He was excited by the thought of what he was about to do.

Opening his penknife, he proceeded to cut a slit in the cheesecloth seal. He lowered the jar, again shook it. Then he inserted his penis—which had

292

grown erect—through the slit, and thrust its entire length into the jar.

He did not have long to wait. Almost instantly he felt the first bite—the tiniest of pinpricks near the rim of the glans. He felt two more along the shaft, on top, and then a fourth puncture in the sensitive meatus of the urethra. After that the bites were too numerous to distinguish. The insects swarmed over his offering and riddled his burning flesh.

"Holy God!" he'd grunted, biting his lip. He'd forgotten how starved and angry they could be.

When he could stand it no longer—when he was dancing around the room, bouncing off walls, knocking over furniture—he yanked his throbbing organ from the jar.

A large number of mosquitoes still were feasting on him. He slapped and grabbed at them with his free hand. Few bothered to fly away. Weak and bloated, they allowed themselves to be squashed; his penis was smeared red with his own ingested blood. He took a handkerchief from a drawer and wiped himself off.

"Wheeler? Are you all right?" His wife had knocked lightly at the door.

"Yes, yes—of course!" he'd snarled. He stood motionless, holding himself in his handkerchief. He heard her footsteps retreat down the hallway.

Making sure his wife had vacated the hallway, he'd slipped into his trousers, carried the jar into the bathroom. He filled it with water, removed the cheesecloth and inspected the drowned insects. They formed a thick scum floating on the surface. He dumped the contents into the toilet, then inspected himself. His penis was partially limp though still throbbing. The siege had left it swollen and misshapen. The glans and foreskin were distended and bulging with lumps. The shaft also was covered with lumps, the skin highly discolored by white and ruddy blotches. New lumps were still forming.

He hadn't dared scratch his tormented flesh, instead brushing it lightly with a dry washcloth. He watched and winced with satisfaction as it sprang once more to life. It rose up, disfigured, grotesque, engorged with blood until it was livid and poker stiff. He ran cold water over it, laved it gently, almost crying aloud. Then he worked it back into his trousers—he wasn't wearing shorts now—and rezipped his fly. Glancing at himself in the vanity mirror, he managed a look of triumph. The fire was lit, blazing. Tonight he would see that it raged.

Three years ago he and Tooter had taken a winter Caribbean cruise. Sailing with Charon Lines out of New Orleans on the S.S. *Eudaimonia,* they'd made the grand tour: Puerto Rico, the Virgin Islands, Barbados, Trinidad, the Dominican Republic . . . Haiti.

The ship lay anchored in Port-au-Prince for three and a half days while it unloaded a cargo of automobiles—all old clunkers—took on sacks of coffee beans and boxes of handstitched baseballs. The Fairchilds went ashore together their first afternoon in port. They returned to the ship a few hours later, arms laden with pottery, handcarved wooden sculptures, native jewelry and several bottles of duty-free rum. A dollar went a long way under "Papa Doc."

Though "good buys" had abounded in the markets, Tooter announced she would never set foot ashore there again. She'd not been feeling well for several days, and the squalor of Port-au-Prince had completely overwhelmed her. She could not stand the fetid smell of its streets, the sight of its destitute people—particularly the children.

So that evening, when another excursion ashore was scheduled, a visit to an authentic voodoo rite, Tooter would not budge from their stateroom. Fairchild went ashore alone.

He found the voodoo rite entertaining, an elaborate spectacle with a throng of colorfully dressed dancers, lots of chanting and wild hypnotic drumming. Not quite what he'd hoped for, however. There were no naked dancing girls, no wax dolls stuck with pins, no zombies, no human sacrifices.

During the performance Fairchild met another passenger from the ship, a bachelor lawyer from Atlanta by the name of George Quast. Quast, professing to be well read on the subject of voodoo, informed him that the version they were watching was strictly for the tourists. Pin-sticking, zombies and human sacrifices also had little to do with the real thing. They were just minor aspects of what was in truth a very staid and meaningful religion.

"The same thing could be done to Christianity," Quast maintained while they sat on their folding seats during intermission.

"Take Lazarus, for instance, rising from the dead—there's your zombie. And how about the Holy Ghost? A sensationalist could have a field day with the cannibalism of Communion rites!"

Fairchild didn't feel he had to comment. The man was obviously an atheist. . . .

When the performance ended, Quast invited him to share a cab back to the ship.

A young black man approached them on their way to the street and asked if they were interested in some female companionship. He wore a threadbare pinstriped suit, a T-shirt and black dress shoes without socks. Both Fairchild and Quast ignored him, joking with one another, and climbed into a waiting taxi. But the black man also climbed into the taxi. He introduced himself as Charles and continued his pitch from the front seat as they drove back to the docks.

"Oh, what the hell," said Quast, finally giving in. He agreed at least to go take a look at the girls—that is, after they'd first dropped his married friend off at the ship.

"No need," said Fairchild. "I'll come along . . . for the ride."

They spent over an hour in a bordello drinking rum, but rejected the whores as unpalatable.

294

On the way back to the ship, Charles made new overtures. This time he promised young, beautiful girls. Virgins. Of course, he added, it would cost more. Much more. Fairchild and Quast, both fairly drunk by now, exclaimed they didn't care how much it cost; they wanted to get laid!

This time their quest took them back into the hills behind the city. For nearly an hour they bounced and swerved along tortuous, rock-strewn roads, finally turning off on a narrow lane which ended, a mile or so later, in a clearing surrounded by shacks and dilapidated mud huts.

Fairchild surveyed the dwellings with a scornful sigh. Too bad some of those bleeding-heart liberals from Better Housing couldn't be here to see this. Hell, compared to these dumps his tenants lived in castles.

After a fifteen-minute wait in the cab, Charles waved them into a shack. Inside, several sleeping mats lay scattered about on a dirt floor. A bed and table stood in a corner on a torn sheet of linoleum. These were separated from the rest of the room—there was only one room—by a faded yellow blanket hanging from a section of corrugated metal roofing. A kerosene lamp cast its dim light over the interior.

Charles stepped out a rear doorway and returned shortly with three native girls. They were very pretty, but only children—the oldest couldn't have been more than twelve, the youngest seven or eight.

Fairchild and Quast looked at one another. Quast muttered something about having a niece their age. Fairchild reflected on his own college-age daughter. Both of them walked out of the shack. Charles followed, pleading. The girls were very nice girls. They also were orphans, destitute, *"qui n'ont pas le sou."* Fairchild and Quast could buy them cheap—and do anything they wanted with them.

As they drove back to town Quast lectured Charles on the depravity of the offer. Even a pimp should have some pangs of conscience. Fairchild tried to match his fellow American's indignation with sober silence. At one point he thought he was going to have to restrain Quast from taking a swing at Charles. Eventually Quast calmed down. They settled the fare at the dock without incident and went aboard just in time to catch "last call" at the ship's bar. They never discussed the episode again.

But all the next day Fairchild dwelled on it. In the evening, he returned to the voodoo rite. He spotted Charles in his pinstripe suit lounging on the grass near the entrance to the theater and nodded. The black pimp sprang to his feet grinning. He shook Fairchild's hand like an old and long lost friend.

Fairchild sat on the small bed, its wire springs sagging like a hammock. He stared at his shadow dimly cast against the room's pale yellow blanket partition, and tried to convince himself that he was actually going through with it.

Charles returned with a girl. She was one of the native children from the night before. Fairchild rose nervously from the bed, too embarrassed to look at her. Charles informed him that because he was alone, the price had gone up: It would cost him a hundred dollars instead of seventy-five.

Fairchild protested, entering eagerly into a bartering dispute. Talking dollars and cents made him feel more at home. He even glanced at the girl, carefully sizing her up as she stood now in the center of the room, staring down at her small brown feet. She looked to be about ten and was prettier than he remembered, with saffron skin and wide, oval, nut-brown eyes. He sensed her innocence, her fear. She looked as if she were ready at any moment to turn and bolt from the shack.

Charles would not lower the price. He did offer to throw in some extras: ganja, more rum and a secret trick—one that was guaranteed to enhance Fairchild's sexual performance and pleasure. Fairchild finally agreed. He would have paid twice as much to satisfy his growing desire.

It was after he'd gotten high smoking ganja that he was introduced to *les flammes du paradis.* A withered old crone with a black patch where her nose should have been brought him the mosquitoes in an earthen jar. She showed him what to do, cackled at his timidity. This first time he could endure the insects' voracious attack for only a few seconds. Nevertheless, it worked its magic. He was gifted with the erection of a lifetime.

The old woman stripped the little girl of her clothes and made her lie on the bed. She told Fairchild to give her a good poke if she gave him any trouble. Then she hobbled away, taking her earthen jar with her.

As he climbed onto the bed alongside his new acquisition, he tried to be gentle. He apologized, soothed her with words, though she spoke only Creole. He reached out and softly caressed her. She was small, pubescent, her breasts just starting to swell, her petals faintly glowing. He gathered her in his arms, felt her tremble beneath him, wince as he began to enter her.

Slowly . . . gently . . . begging her forgiveness, he patiently worked his throbbing size into her tender, underdeveloped folds. Her eyes were sealed shut, squeezing out tears. She struggled on the mattress to endure him, gripped at the bedding with both hands.

His penis burning, hypersensitive and prurient with dozens of bites . . . he came in a matter of moments, with such intensity it left him gasping, mindless, spinning off in radiating waves. . . .

He was lying on the floor, a lumpy sheet of green, paint-spattered linoleum. The girl sat on a far corner of the bed, her legs drawn up, her arms encircling her knees. She was whimpering softly.

He got up, stood over her in his nakedness. She looked at him in silence, suddenly reached out and touched him.

He lifted his right hand and slapped her. She drew back startled, confused, her eyes flashing white. He slapped her again, harder, feeding on her bewilderment, her terror.

Even as he continued slapping her, clouting her with a loosely made fist, he couldn't explain the impulse, the wild, sweet sense of exhilaration that followed each blow. He glanced down at himself, discovered with amazement that he had another erection. Perhaps he'd never lost the first.

When his arms grew tired and his hands numb, he threw her sobbing form across the bed. She groaned under his weight as he fell on top of her. Now there was no patience, no gentleness in his demands. There were no soothing words. He grabbed at her flesh, pulled her apart, thrust himself brutally into her galled, budding wound. . . . His hands found their way to her throat.

It was early morning when he returned to the ship. His wife was sound asleep in their stateroom. She asked him the next day where he'd been all night. He invented a story, told her the Ton Tons had arrested him by mistake, had taken him to the police station and held him there for hours. They'd worked him over—that was how he explained away the scratches and bruises on his face, his arms and shoulders.

He didn't go ashore again, nervously pacing the decks, expecting at any moment to see the authorities come marching up the gangplank.

They never came. The authorities or Charles. The girl was, after all, a stray. More than likely Charles had found her body stuffed under the bed and not wanting to get involved had secretly buried her himself. He'd lost a source of future income, but it was hardly a staggering blow. The hills were full of little girls. And they were all hungry in Haiti.

Fairchild didn't start relaxing until the ship had weighed anchor the next day. Until the land crest had slid away and finally sunk from sight in a glistening, busy sea.

Back in Chicago he tried to erase from his memory what had happened in Haiti. Not from any sufferings of remorse, but rather from fear. He'd allowed his darkest dreams to surface, become real. He'd given them life and now could he simply walk away?

In the fall he drove down to Champaign to visit his daughter, Allison, at the University of Illinois. Tooter was off visiting her mother in Denver. It was Dad's Day weekend, and he spent Saturday touring the campus, attended an afternoon football game and dined in the evening at his daughter's sorority house. Allison had entered his name in the nomination for "King Dad," and during halftime at the game he learned that he was one of four finalists still in the running. He was summoned onto the field along with the other three to be honored in front of the Block I homestand while the winner was announced over the public-address system. Though the judges had been impressed with his credentials—an alderman and committee chairman on Mayor Dooley's powerful City Council—they chose another, a portly dentist and high-ranking Rotarian from Peoria.

Still, that evening at dinner the girls at the sorority house proclaimed him "Emperor Dad" and presented him with a cardboard crown all his own. Everyone toasted and cheered him. His daughter's friends treated him like a celebrity. They cooed and fussed over him, Allison's handsome dad. Fairchild looked around at his bald-headed, potbellied contemporaries. He smiled at himself in a hallway mirror, adjusted his crown.

Later in his motel room, all he could think about was the pretty young coeds flirting and bubbling around him. They were so fresh and enticing. So inaccessible. Poor Allison, pink-faced and overweight—she was the plainest girl in sight. He'd been forced to pull a few strings to get her in the house. One of the girls, a particularly attractive blonde named Betty, had needed a ride home Sunday. She asked him if Bloomington was on his way. It wasn't, but he was half tempted to lie and offer her a ride anyway. With Allison standing right there—she already had something of her mother's untimeliness about her—he abstained. He wondered, though, what might have been.

He had tossed about in his bed for a couple of hours, unable to fall asleep. Eventually his hand found himself and resignedly he began to fumble. When he grew hard in his grasp his mind became alive with fantasy. At first he saw only the faces of the girls he'd met that day, tried to imagine their expressions as he made each one spread for his pleasure. Betty, the blonde going to Bloomington—he'd give her a ride now, one she'd never forget. He saw her cry out, her pretty blue eyes brimming with tears. . . .

And then the eyes turned brown and it wasn't Betty anymore. He was back in Haiti.

While he masturbated with his right hand, he caressed himself with his left, excitedly massaging his chest and shoulders. Familiar, sordid details glittered in his mind. He felt her smallness squirming beneath him, felt the kinky nap of her hair against his cheeks, breathed in the pungent fragrance of her smooth, callow body. Once more he heard her cries and moans, mimicked them softly with his voice, his fingers gently measuring his own throat.

He'd taken a life, desecrated another human being, a child. The realization hit him anew for the thousandth time. And for the thousandth time he savored the memory of those last vivid moments: the fear and the pain and the ecstasy. He thought of her, all of life's sunny options denied her. He tried to visualize her body decomposing in some shallow grave. He was intoxicated with sadness. She emerged somehow more innocent, more vulnerable from the dust, and he used her now to again excite his flesh, exalting in his wickedness.

When he ejaculated, he kissed the tears from her lifeless eyes. He'd taken the ultimate advantage. She was his slave forever.

He had lunch with Allison the next day, met her pink-faced, overweight boy friend, spent some more time with her driving about campus. In the middle of the afternoon back at the sorority house they said their good-byes. He drove off honking his horn. Several girls from an upstairs open window waved and hollered, "Later, Emperor Dad . . ."

On the way out of town, he turned off University at Lincoln Avenue and noticed a girl standing beyond the intersection pumping her thumb. Times had changed. No girl would've been caught dead hitchhiking back in his college days. He glimpsed blond hair as he sped by, pulled over to the shoulder thinking it might be Allison's friend Betty. The girl ran to the car, opened the door, smiled and climbed in. It wasn't Betty.

The hitchhiker's name was Judy Connors and she wasn't nearly as pretty as Betty. She had a stubby nose and wide-set Pekinese eyes. She wore faded blue jeans and at least three sweaters. Her cheeks were puffy red from standing in the wind.

She didn't go to the university but was headed back to Kankakee. She'd been down for the weekend visiting her boy friend.

On the other side of Paxton, Fairchild swung off Route 45 onto a gravel country road. She asked him where he was going. He told her the main highway detoured ahead and that he was taking a shortcut. A tense silence crystallized between them.

"Why are we stopping here?" she demanded when he pulled off the road and parked on a deserted tractor lane by a cornfield. He told her there was something wrong with the motor. He got out and raised the hood.

He stood in front of the car staring at the radiator cap, not knowing what to do next. After a couple of minutes he called to her, asked if she could come give him some assistance. She refused, said she wasn't budging from the car till he'd driven her to Kankakee as he said he would. He heard her locking the car doors.

Stalling for a few minutes, flustered, he fiddled with the fan belt, slammed the hood closed again. He opened his door with a key from the set he'd removed from the ignition.

"Everything's okay now," he assured her and backed out onto the road.

She sat pressed against the door, her hands gripping her knees. He acted nonchalant, laid the problem to a loose battery cable. He could see she wanted to believe him. She tried to smile but didn't speak all the way to Kankakee. He offered to drive her home but she shook her head, getting out at the first overpass and slamming the door behind her.

Fairchild was angry with himself for weeks after the incident. His rashness was unforgivable. If he was determined to pursue such risky amusement he'd better start exercising some forethought. He wasn't in Haiti now. He could not afford to be impulsive.

Still, the prospect was not all that forbidding. Just pick up a newspaper. Murders were being committed every day in the city. And a big percentage —if not the majority—went unsolved. No, there was no reason to deny himself. If he moved with caution, applied his good old American know-how, it shouldn't be much more difficult than, say, taking an occasional bribe.

The first thing Fairchild did was get another car, something untraceable and a little less conspicuous than his Caddy. Dealing through a business associate, a building contractor with mob connections, he was able to obtain a '59 Valiant, registered with Montana plates under a fictitious name. A set of bogus ID's came with the car.

Rather than plunge immediately into anything serious, Fairchild contented himself to play an elaborate game of cat and mouse. He would cruise about the city and suburbs for hours reconnoitering parks, playgrounds, secluded residential areas. When he spotted a likely victim, usually a teenage girl, though sometimes younger or older, he would park and keep her under surveillance, then follow her home if he was able. Frequently he would continue the little game off and on for several days, learning her name, her habits and constructing the most viable plan of assault, fantasizing its execution to the last detail.

He amused himself in this manner through the winter and most of the spring.

In early May he was sidetracked from his diversion by a number of pressing business obligations. Along with a new condo development near O'Hare, he was involved in a land-speculation deal west of the city where, he'd learned from his aldermanic post, the government was planning to put up a large research facility. It was not until the end of the summer that he had time once more to devote to his darker desires. And by then he'd decided he'd had enough of fantasy and game-playing. He was ready for *les flammes du paradis.*

He set himself on fire on Thursday, September 14, then drove southwest from the city on Archer Avenue until the sprawling suburban homes and shopping centers gave way to open countryside. Just north of Lemont he turned onto a gravel county road and drove east for several miles, finally coming to a small country schoolhouse. He'd discovered the picturesque brick one-roomer while out inspecting real estate during the summer. He'd been intrigued by its isolation—nothing but trees, cornfields and an occasional farmhouse for miles around. A week earlier when he'd returned again, he hadn't had real estate on his mind.

Cindy was her name. Cindy Bossert. He'd followed her home Monday, and learned her name the next day by phoning the school and posing as a county health official. It bothered him that he'd never learned the name of the girl in Haiti. He felt genuinely deprived. Cindy was a pert, red-headed fourth-grader, an only child, big for her age. She rode to and from school every day on a bicycle.

Tuesday and Wednesday he drove by her several times as she and her friends, two girls and a smaller towheaded boy, pedaled east along the country road. After the two girls pulled into neighboring farmhouses set close to the main road, Cindy and the boy would go on together until they came to the next intersection. There she would leave her companion and turn down another, narrower, gravel road, which crossed a creek on an old rusted iron bridge and wound through several acres of woods before coming to her farmhouse. A distance of nearly a mile from the main road.

The school was just letting out when he drove by Thursday. He was

300

careful not to look for her among the dispersing children as he drove by.

At the intersection he turned left down the narrow lane, drove over the iron bridge that rattled and shook under the weight of his car, parked on the other side in a bend that was partially concealed in either direction by overhanging trees.

He got out, raised the Valiant's hood and waited.

As the minutes passed, he grew more and more nervous. At last he decided to walk up the road a short distance to see if she was coming.

"Damn!" he muttered, staring through parted branches when she finally appeared. She wasn't alone. The towheaded boy hadn't left her at the turnoff.

The two children stopped on the bridge, got off their bikes and began throwing stones into the creek. As Fairchild listened to their giggling bursts of laughter, his nervousness quickly turned to angry frustration. He'd denied himself for so long, now had gone to such lengths. . . . What happened next? Certainly it would be too risky attacking them both.

He leaned against the tree he was hiding behind, rubbed his burning crotch against its shaggy bark. All he could do was watch and wait. And go up in smoke.

Resigned to disappointment, ready to return to the car and masturbate, he suddenly heard Cindy's companion announce that he had to get home. The boy jumped on his bike and pedaled away. Cindy shouted something after him, then picked up her own bike. She leisurely restacked some schoolbooks in her handlebar basket, got on and once again headed for home.

Fairchild dashed back to the car. Breathing hard, he took his position under the hood. He shook with anticipation. In his right hand he clenched the smooth, wooden handle of a rubber-headed mallet.

He could hear the crunch of her wheels on the gravel growing louder. He didn't step out from behind the hood until she was nearly even with the rear bumper. When he did, he moved abruptly, at the same time disarming her with a cheerful smile.

Startled, she veered slightly, then smiled back. She was wearing a bright yellow dress and white knee socks. She started to raise her right hand in a wave—

He lunged out, grabbed at her, shoved her sideways.

Bike and rider went down, school books flying. In two strides he was standing over her. She lay sprawled in the middle of the road, one leg hooked under the bike's frame. Raising herself on her left arm, she looked up at him dazedly. There was no fear in her wide blue eyes, only confusion.

He hit her on the head with the mallet.

The blow failed to knock her unconscious, instead jarring her from her stupor. She cried out, frantically pulled her leg from under the bike and tried to scramble to her feet.

He hit her again, this time harder. The mallet struck the side of her head and glanced off. She cried out louder than ever, began crawling across the road on her hands and knees.

Fairchild felt a rush of panic. He was afraid someone might happen along the road at any moment. He lifted the mallet a third time, brought it down still harder. The blow caught her squarely on the back of her head, just below the crown. She plopped forward into the gravel, still.

He stood there for a moment staring at her crumpled form. Her yellow dress was torn and covered with dust; her knees bloody. He hoped he hadn't killed her.

He drove north for forty miles. During the drive the strain of the abduction dissipated. He congratulated himself on his performance. Granted, the girl wasn't in the best of shape—he'd hit her much too hard that last time—but at least she was alive. Lying in the seat beside him, she made faint gurgling noises every now and then, her breathing loud and labored. He was giddy with expectation.

In the vicinity of Wauconda he turned down the private work road of an old, abandoned strip mine. He came to a gate, opened it, drove in, closed it behind him, slipping his own padlock through the chain latch.

She was still unconscious. Parking on a secluded cinder path, he leaned over her and picked away some tiny pebbles that were caught in a corner of her crusted mouth. He stroked her head with tenderness, avoiding the gash in her scalp over her left temple where her hair was matted with blood. A thin red trickle had seeped down and dried on her cheek. For ten full minutes he did nothing, just sat there staring. At last he unbuckled his belt, reached over and tried to get her to open her eyes.

An hour before sunset he buried her naked body in the soft clay of a shallow grave he'd dug the day before. He removed his padlock from the gate when he left and drove directly back to the city. After thoroughly wiping the Valiant for fingerprints and stripping the plates, he abandoned it in one of the cavernous parking lots under Grant Park. Two aisles away from his waiting Cadillac Seville. He changed clothes in a rest-room stall, enjoyed a leisurely dinner at the Playboy Club, then drove home.

Later that evening he came to his wife in her bedroom. He awakened her. She balked, irritably protested his cold, groping hands. It had been months since they'd slept together; years since she'd enjoyed it. Her husband was selfish, totally indifferent to her needs.

She weakened, finally gave in. She never could stand up to his persistence. Sulking, humiliated, she opened one more time to endure the immemorial duty of her marriage.

Unwashed, Fairchild entered her. He found himself wildly titillated by the day's juxtaposition—the thought of mingling the residue of the girl's fresh sex with Tooter's tired juices; it was as though she were secretly sharing his wicked exploit. He was amazed at how exciting his wife's flaccid, unresponsive body became in the process.

And she too was no less amazed when she felt his lips upon her flesh, heard him whimpering softly as he kissed her eyes, her breasts. She rose to his sudden display of affection, reached out, contained his back in her arms, passionately searched for his lips with her own.

The pain and soreness would come later, he mused. It would take weeks to heal. In the meantime he leaped into the flames, filled his wife, the room, the whole city with his soul-searing conflagration.

This time Valjohn saw Crescent get off the bus. She stood up and waited by the rear door a block before she exited. Not wanting to risk losing her, he stopped in the middle of traffic, ignoring the blaring horns to keep her plainly in front of him.

She skipped diagonally across Clark Street, her red culottes and dangling pigtails disappearing around the corner as she headed west on Morrison Avenue. He hesitated a few moments longer, let a couple of cars behind swing by, then eased up to the intersection and took a left, resuming his pursuit.

He passed her, drove on and parked. When she walked by, he waited, keeping her in sight as long as he dared, then sped off after her again. He repeated this process several times, implementing a number of minor variations to remain inconspicuous.

He left his car in front of a large stone Presbyterian church on a quiet, dimly lit residential street and followed her on foot. A block later he glanced up at a street sign: Mudgett Drive.

She wasn't just out for one of her nightly strolls. Her walk seemed too brisk and deliberate. She seemed headed for some definite place. If he could manage to hang back and not blow his cover, there was a good chance he might find out tonight what he wanted to know.

He lagged behind her almost a block and a half, watching her distant figure vanish and reappear as she strode through the alternate shadows and pools of light spilling from a long row of antiquated globe streetlamps that had just come on.

Far ahead he saw her disappear to his right. He squinted in the growing darkness and picked up his pace. When she failed to show again in the next pool of light, he broke into a run. A car drove slowly by him. He couldn't see her in the car's headlights when it passed farther up the street.

At the end of the next block, he came to a school. He heard children's laughter coming from its playground. He turned, saw Crescent sitting in a swing. She was watching a small boy and girl playing on a slide. The girl climbed a ladder to the top, waited for the boy to join her, inching his way up the slick metal chute, holding on to the sides. When he reached the top, the girl shoved him; they both slid down giggling and tumbling in a tangle of arms and legs.

Valjohn stepped back in the shadows, then proceeded to sneak around the edge of the school yard until he'd maneuvered behind her. He made his way closer, crouching, finally scrambling forward into a large clump of shoulder-high junipers not twenty yards from the swings.

He dropped to his knees and rested for a moment. He was in lousy shape, he thought, gasping for breath from his short sprint. He shifted his weight on his knees and was swatted in the face by a prickly branch of juniper needles. He slowly eased the branch aside. A car drove slowly by the playground. The same one that had passed him earlier: a cream-colored '61 Chevy. He recognized its walleyed headlight.

A minute later the car came back. It must have made a U-turn farther up the road. This time it swung around the corner. Valjohn watched its misaligned headlight send a high, stray beam cutting through the upper branches of the trees bordering the narrow side street. It was an out-of-state vehicle. He glimpsed a plate, couldn't make out the state or numbers, but it definitely wasn't *Land of Lincoln* white.

The car turned left at the next corner, continued out of sight behind the school building. He returned his attention to Crescent.

What was she up to? Had she really come all this way to swing herself in a school yard and watch a couple of kids play?

For a while he thought she might know the two kids. The longer he observed them playing, however, the more unlikely he sensed this to be. Not only didn't they seem to know her, they also seemed totally unaware of her presence. There was a certain spontaneity in their play that suggested they had the entire playground to themselves. Though they frolicked directly in front of her now, they never once smiled or glanced in her direction.

The children moved to a teeterboard a few feet away. They rode it, pretending they were on bucking broncos, hollering and vigorously slamming the board to the ground, thumping each other high off the seat at the opposite ends. Crescent began swinging, leaning back and pumping her legs, slowly adding momentum to her ascending arc. She looked innocent and alone, wistful—a child herself off in a child's world of dreams.

Again he felt foolish, guilty. He wanted to step out from his hiding place, go over to her and become her playground companion. He wanted to stand behind her, feel his hands upon her back, push her skyward until her toes touched the moon.

He remained crouching in the bushes, unmoving.

After a while the girl jumped off the teeterboard and ran home. The boy straddled the crossbar, shifted his weight back and forth, banging the ends of the board to the ground by himself. Tiring quickly of playing alone, he started to wander off across the school yard toward the street.

Near the sidewalk he picked up a stick: sword-sized. He waved it in the air a few times, then looked around. His eyes came to rest on the clump of junipers in which Valjohn was hiding. He began stalking it. A few yards away he gave a battle cry, charged forward and wildly began hacking at the branches.

304

Startled, Valjohn straightened up. For a moment he thought the boy was attacking him and raised his arms to ward off the blows. Only one actually struck him: a sharp, glancing whack just above his left elbow.

If Valjohn was startled, the boy was dumbstruck. He halted the stick in midair, jumped backward. The two of them stood there staring at one another in the bright moonlight for several seconds. Then the boy dropped the stick, dashed from the playground and disappeared across the street.

Valjohn hurriedly recrouched among the branches. Had she seen him?

Apparently not. She still was on the swing—quite high now. She had quit pumping and was leaning way back, coasting, her outstretched legs held tightly together, toes pointed.

He listened to the rhythmic creaking of the chains as her arc slowly dwindled back to perpendicular. Dragging her heels in the gravel for the last few feet, she brought herself to an abrupt stop. She stood up.

He wondered if she was getting ready to leave. She took a couple of steps, suddenly turned around.

He held his breath, motionless. Was she looking at him?

He heard footsteps crunching in the gravel behind him. Turning his head slightly, he saw a figure approaching from the corner of the school building on his left. It was a man.

A few minutes earlier Wheeler Fairchild had slowed the beat-up, cream Chevy to fifteen miles an hour. He was cruising west on Mudgett Drive. There was a man jogging along the sidewalk on his right. A black man. He looked like one of those pimps that hung around downtown State Street. What was he doing in this neighborhood?

Fairchild sped up. He came to the Deerpath Elementary School in the next block, slowed again. His new target area. He'd surveyed the playground and vicinity for several weeks now. Children played here after dark almost every evening; the school yard itself was partially hidden from the row of neighboring houses by a wooded parkway that divided Mudgett Drive.

He scanned the school yard, observing a couple of kids wrestling by the slide. A lone, larger figure sat in a nearby swing. He hoped it was she.

He continued driving for a couple of blocks, then turned around and came back. The figure was still on the swing. He searched the sidewalk for the black man he'd seen jogging a few minutes earlier. Nowhere in sight. Must have turned down the intersecting street or gone into a house.

Fairchild wheeled around and came by the school yard one more time. He swung up the adjacent street, entered an alley behind the school and parked in an empty lot.

He got out of the car and donned a dark blue knit sweater. From the trunk he took out the rubber mallet. He ran the handle under his belt and down his pants, pulled his sweater over the protruding head. Then he walked to the far end of the school building fronting the playground and peered around the corner.

It was she; he was sure of it. She still was some distance away, but he could easily make out the long blond pigtails trailing behind her in the moonlight. The other two children had moved from the slide and were loudly bouncing each other on the teeterboard. All he had to do was wait.

She came here every Wednesday and Thursday night, regular as clockwork. And she always was the last to leave. She must live in the neighborhood, though he hadn't been able to follow her home. He hadn't even been able to learn her name. She was too old for this school, looked to be around high school age—probably a well-developed ninth-grader who hadn't yet discovered boys. Otherwise she wouldn't be spending her evenings here alone on the swings.

Well, she'd discover boys tonight—just as soon as those other two kids got tired of banging around on that teeterboard and toddled off to their little beds. He smiled and reached down, rubbed the head of the mallet. He could feel the flames shooting right up the handle.

So at last, thought Valjohn, the rendezvous—the liaison—here in a deserted school playground . . .

He felt a hunter's surge of satisfaction. The surveillance, the arduous stalk, had ended; he'd flushed his quarry. The surge was only momentary. It ebbed abruptly as his heart sank with the realization that his worst suspicion now was being confirmed. He had no marriage. There was indeed another man.

He caught only a quartering glimpse of the man as he walked by the junipers. He was older than he'd expected and had a full head of shaggy white hair. Valjohn had the feeling he'd seen the man before somewhere.

Something was wrong. As the man came closer to Crescent, Valjohn sensed it: a change in his manner, a certain inaptness in his movement. His walk, a relaxed saunter, now grew tense, measured. His shoulders tilted forward until he was almost crouching.

Crescent stood where she'd turned around. She hadn't taken a step. She looked oddly detached, impassive; her face offered no more than a bland smile.

When only a few steps separated them, the man's right hand went to his waist, withdrew an object from under his belt. Valjohn looked on in horror as the man sprang at her, brandishing a hammer over his head.

"Dear God!" He tried to leap up from his squatting position, to bound forward out of the bushes—all in one frantic move. He came up short, tripped on a limb, tumbled back down through a tangle of branches. He fought to free himself from the clawing junipers, raised his head again as he scrambled to his hands and knees.

She was still standing. She had not yet been felled by the man. Nor had she made any attempt to scream, to run away or defend herself. The man just stood there, the hammer still raised—though lower, less threatening.

Had he struck her? Was she stunned? Out on her feet? What the hell was happening?

The hammer lifted higher, wavered—

Valjohn was struggling to rise again, cursing himself for not carrying a gun. If anything happened to her while he was sneaking around in these goddamn bushes!

Halfway up he could rise no farther. His arms and legs, seeming to lose all capacity for motion, turned to stone. His breath became something solid, lodged immobile and chalky in his throat, his lungs.

Crescent's hair . . . had come alive. Her long, dangling pigtails unraveled themselves, swirled up and burst over her head like a swarm of angry insects.

part five

18

The phone was ringing.

He gave a cry, emerged sweating profusely from a turbulent sleep. He opened his eyes, stared up blankly for several moments at an expanse of white, textured ceiling. His head ached fiercely. He felt as if he'd been clubbed with a hammer. His mind struggled to surface from the chaotic welter of unremembered dream.

The phone continued ringing.

He sat upright in bed, waiting patiently for the room to encircle him with meaning, for his own thoughts to gather into some recognizable continuum.

The room was glaring. Every light in it was on. A TV flickered images without sound. Sunlight burned around the edges of closed drapes.

His eyes remained bleary, refused to focus sharply.

The phone stopped ringing. He was startled, seemed to hear it now for the first time. Responding to the exigency of silence and innuendo, he lurched over on his side, grabbed across a nightstand to answer it. The line buzzed in his ear.

He hung up, started to straighten out of bed, was hit with an attack of nausea, dizziness. He lay back flat, closed his eyes, waited for it to pass.

Christ, was he polluted! He must have really tied one on! He couldn't remember anything: where he'd been, whom he'd been with—actually couldn't remember taking one goddamn drink!

When he began to feel a little better, he reopened his eyes, searched about his surroundings again.

Finally he managed to recognize it: He was in a motel room, the formula layout and furniture, the two tiresome paintings hanging on the wall. Bargain-basement Buffet copies. His opened suitcase rested on the luggage rack at the foot of the bed.

Now, if he could only figure out what he was doing here, why he was lying in bed, fully clothed, suspended in limbo.

He sat up once more, slowly this time, his eyes settling on a hat lying on a chair near the dressing alcove. He stared at it—its wide black brim, the orange feather in its high band. Nothing he'd wear—yet it looked uncomfortably familiar.

The phone rang again.

He reached over and calmly picked it up on the second ring. Lieutenant Harris was on the other end.

"Where the hell have you been? I been trying to reach you for two days!"

Valjohn was silent. He flipped again through the diary of his mind. No luck. The ink had run, the pages of his last entry were stuck together. Spilled booze? He wasn't so sure now: There was no old sweat sock wrapped around his tongue.

"I been calling your room every hour since eight."

Valjohn eased the receiver away from his throbbing temple. Maybe he'd been hit on the head, beaned broadside by another golf ball.

"Did you say *two days?*" The sound of his own voice boxed his ears.

"Two days!" Harris repeated vehemently. "Howland's screaming for your ass. And I think he's got the old man listening to him. They spent all morning in conference—Hans Glad was there and so were a couple of men from the mayor's office. I don't have to tell you, you picked a dilly to duck out on."

"A dilly?"

Now it was Harris who fell silent.

"The murder, V.J.," he finally said. "You *do* know about the murder?"

Valjohn felt himself growing cold.

"Jesus," muttered Harris. "You gotta be the only one in town who doesn't. It's been front-page headlines ever since it broke."

Valjohn started to tremble.

"No. 24, V.J.—and this time the victim's no scrote. This time the Reaper croaked a Who's Who. Wheeler Fairchild. Maybe you heard of him: big-shot land developer, ex-alderman—machine's choice in the next state Senate race. He's a personal friend of the mayor's—or was."

Harris paused. No comment from Valjohn, not even a heavy-laden sigh. He began filling in details about the murder.

"Where . . . where did you say?" Valjohn struggled to hold the phone. It had become so incredibly heavy.

"A school playground," Harris answered with some relief. "Deerpath Elementary on West Mudgett Drive. Around the thirty-three-hundred block—"

Valjohn had difficulty hearing the rest. The pages of his diary came unstuck, flew wide open as if caught in an icy draft from a broken window. He read bits and pieces. . . .

The school yard. He was there again crouching in the prickly bushes. He couldn't move. It was as if he were chiseled out of granite. And he couldn't look away, close his eyes, shut out the horror taking place before him—so close, so far away—on that bright, moonlit playground. . . .

"I don't have to tell you the cop shop's been buzzing like a hornet's nest," droned Harris's voice. "They want to know where the hell you are, why you're unavailable for comment. Howland's already intimated to them there's been a shake-up in the investigation."

Couldn't look away—even now in the safety of his Holiday Manor room . . . watched the man beat her to the ground with his hammer, tear at her clothes. . . . He saw himself trying to move, trying to scream—no sound from his throat—as if he were in the hospital once more: the words forming in his mind, refusing to form on his lips.

"Your friend McTague's all worked up. He's convinced you've been bumped off. I was beginning to wonder myself."

It glistened in the moonlight. The man's erection. He hunched down over her still form, parted her legs, arranged them like the lifeless limbs of a doll. He entered her.

". . . was all I could do to keep from calling your wife."

She stirred beneath the man's hunkering weight, came alive from the touch of his intruding flesh.

"Figured I'd hold off another day, though. No sense upsetting her till I absolutely had to."

Disbelief. Revulsion. Valjohn watched her embrace her assailant, gather him in trembling arms. Her hands swept across his back, fingers lightly encouraging his naked, straining buttocks. He watched the man shudder, groan. She clasped him, sharing in his climax, lifted his face to soft, angelic eyes, kissed him.

"Anyway, I think you better get down here to headquarters—"

The man continued to shudder, to groan, was swept away in multiple orgasms. She continued to hold him, rocking him gently in her arms. In the depth of his seizure, he seemed to be struggling, wriggling to free himself. His groans grew louder, sharpened into cries.

"—I mean like right away, V.J., pronto."

The man was dancing wildly about in her arms now, his body jerking, arching in great violent spasms. His muscles bunched and knotted, tearing against one another; his bones, his joints, deflected to unnatural angles, skewing and quivering, popping and groaning in protest. She encircled his waist with her legs, scissored him to her, seemed to ride him in the dust, the gravel, as if he were some frenzied, bucking steed. Yet all the while she

313

appeared hopelessly fragile, submissive. She caressed him, fondled him with delicate, fluttering hands. She nuzzled him. She comforted him, her voice a soothing echo of soft whispers.

"Lieutenant?"

Her hair . . . her mantle of long, golden tresses silken silver in the moonlight. It rustled over them, billowed up, crackled and whipped about like a raging fire, consumed them both. The air was rancid with the sweet stench of jasmine.

Blood was flowing—black and shiny as gunmetal. The man was writhing, breaking up, coming apart in her arms. In one final effort to free himself he straightened to his knees, lifted his head. Valjohn could see his face, the bleeding, lipless hole that was his mouth.

And then she was forcing his head down, gently but firmly, forcing it lower and lower, between her legs—lower still. Beyond the ringent, dripping petals of her sex . . . The man was doubled at the waist, his spine bent like a circus contortionist's. She was forcing his head down between his own legs! Down until he was savagely mouthing his own flesh.

Valjohn felt his scrotum ascend, a hard, leather knot shriveling all the way up into his stomach. His eyes lost their focus, blurred in the crackling fury of her hair. He was mesmerized, the whirling strands casting monstrous shadows in his mind: A serpent formed, slithered in endless coils, fangs bared. Scales shimmered in silver light. A low, sibilant hiss rose, pierced the darkness, scattered into angry whispers. The strands whirled; the serpent became a host of phantom creatures, a shifting montage of stabbing beaks, gnashing teeth, raking talons and claws. Thorny shoulders bowed upward into giant scapular wings, opened and filled the sky— blotted out the moon, the stars, in stormy clouds of beating plumage.

"Are you there, Lieutenant?"

Valjohn held the phone in both hands. He hadn't dropped it.

"Lieutenant? V.J., are you still there?"

He was.

Valjohn didn't leave the room for two more days. After his phone conversation with Harris, he managed to make a short trip to the bathroom, where he spent nearly an hour doubled over the toilet in a hacking fit of dry heaves. Stomach knotted with cramps, head spinning, he returned to bed and remained there flat on his back staring at the ceiling for the rest of the day, the night, most of the next morning. He left all lights burning, refused to close his eyes. The phone rang several times. He made no move to answer it.

A little before noon, Monday, he turned on the sound to the TV. He watched the tail end of a morning talk show, then a long string of soap operas that stretched halfway through the afternoon. He watched with a fierce intensity, his eyes never leaving the screen.

During the six o'clock news, Mayor Dooley was interviewed leaving the chapel of a stately, North Side funeral home, following the memorial services for Wheeler Fairchild. Valjohn made a move to change the station, held up, fascinated as the Mayor's thick, halting voice resounded off the bedroom walls with somber words of mourning.

". . . was an outstanding dedicated servant to his community and the great people of Chicago everywhere. It's a contemptible thing to see our young, promising leaders getting nipped in their buds like this. And he was a fine, respectable family man also."

The mayor, faultlessly tailored in a dark blue suit, stood on a sidewalk flanked by the fire chief, sanitation commissioner, and an alderman. All four were honorary pallbearers. The reporter asked the mayor if the police were any closer to apprehending the Reaper. Had this latest slaying, coupled with the April riots, jeopardized Chicago's role as host for the upcoming Democratic National Convention? Was there anything to the rumor that L.A. was being considered as a possible alternate site?

For a moment the mayor's face matched the color of the brick funeral home behind him. His lower lip quivered; his jowls seemed to pulsate. Half clearing his throat, half muttering under his breath, he wrenched the mike so sharply from the interviewer's grasp that the man stumbled off balance, dropping a clipboard to the pavement. The mayor, strangling the mike in a meaty fist, faced the camera:

"That rumor is nothing but a damned insinuendo, and I think it speaks for itself! So let's not beat the bushes here—there's enough of that going around. There's always rumors. Anybody could tell you a rumor. You could make one up, for instance. But what I will tell you is not a rumor and it is not made up and it is there will be a Democratic National Convention to elect the next President of the United States and that convention will be held right here in Chicago, the greatest convention city in the world, and nowhere else! And you can beat around the bushes with that for a while till you're blue in the faces! . . . Here—"

He thrust the mike back at the interviewer and stomped off, his everpresent retinue stomping off behind him.

Valjohn watched the same interview three more times: on the ten o'-clock, the midnight, the 3:00 A.M. final news wrap-up. He made no move to change the station or turn it off. Nevertheless, when the six o'clock news came on in the morning, he was relieved not to hear Wheeler Fairchild's name mentioned once.

At 10:00 A.M. he called room service and had a breakfast tray delivered. Poached eggs, toast and tea. Though he had no appetite, he knew he was badly in need of nourishment—that is, if he was to continue to exist. By no means in his mind a settled point.

He was amazed after forcing down the food how much better he felt. His insides no longer ached. Some of the light-headedness had left him. A half hour later he ordered another tray. This time he had an appetite. He proceeded to down a stack of pancakes, orange juice, sausage, more toast and another cup of tea. He felt better still. Strong enough to venture outside. He left the room at noon.

On the way down to the garage, a middle-aged couple joined him in the elevator a floor below his. They glanced at him, then at each other, stepped quickly back outside just as the doors slid shut.

Bigots, thought Valjohn, yet he found their actions oddly reassuring.

"What you lookin' fo'?" a black attendant in white coveralls asked him as he wandered up and down the rows of parked cars.

"My car. I . . . uh, forgot where I parked it."

"What you drivin'?"

Valjohn thought for a moment, couldn't remember. "I . . . I'm not too sure."

The attendant gave him a hard look. "What you mean, you 'not too sure'?"

"I . . . I'm trying to think. . . ." Valjohn closed his eyes, grimaced with effort. "It was a rent-a-car."

"You a guest here?"

Valjohn nodded.

The attendant looked him over carefully, scoffed his disbelief. "You a guest here, show me yo' room key."

Valjohn fumbled through his pockets, not sure where it was or whether he even had it on him. His fingers finally discovered the plastic tag deep in his left front pocket. He pulled it out, read it dutifully—"room 407."

The attendant continued to eye him in disdainful silence. Finally he shrugged and walked off.

"Maybe you stayin' here; maybe you ain't," he called back over his shoulder, "but I ain't got no time be wastin' helpin' no fool find what he don't even know he lookin' fo'."

It seemed as hopeless to Valjohn. He had no recollection of parking the vehicle, was not even sure he'd left it here. He continued to search.

Five minutes later he recognized it when he came upon it: a green two-door Fairlane, complete with hole in grill and knocked out left headlight.

He drove aimlessly about the city for over an hour. It was a beautiful spring day, no clouds, a stiff but warm breeze sweeping steadily off the lake. The sun was dazzling on the pavement. He hunted for his dark glasses. They weren't in the car. He must have left them back in the room. Following the flow of traffic from one street to the next, he swung east off Ogden Avenue onto Division Street, headed north again on Lake Shore Drive. At North Avenue Beach, he pulled over and parked.

The sunbathers were out in force—not anything to match the throngs on summer weekends; but even so, groups of brightly clad bathers could be seen scattered along the entire mile-long strand to Simmons Island.

Valjohn studied the lake. Whitecaps danced beyond the harbor. A moderate surf bound the shoreline with lacy webs of foam. He watched the

316

waves building in close, rolling forward, rising, cresting, toppling over and shattering against the sand. Wave after wave. An ordered procession.

Wave
    after
        wave
           after
               wave
                   after
                       wave
                           after
                               wave . . .

Damn! He slammed the steering wheel with the heel of a hand. So what happens now? The world as he knew it no longer existed. A lifetime of empirical evidence turned topsy-turvy—to say nothing of his dreams, his ambitions, his love. . . . Reality and reason had collapsed, broken apart like so many waves down there on the beach. Was he insane? Was everyone else insane? Did it really matter?

Another wave formed, curled over, burst. He watched the shattering remnants gather, a thin sheet of bubbling froth and flashing sunlight, watched it suck back into the building blue-green water.

Wave
    after
        wave
           after
               wave
                   after
                       wave
                           after
                               wave . . .

Damn! He slammed the wheel again. He reached down and turned the key.

"Hey, look the fuck where you're going!" a voice yelled out as he backed from his parking space. He braked, turned his head to see two joggers trot by, both giving him the finger.

"Fuck you, too!" he called after them under his breath. He resumed backing out, wheeled around and this time drove for the heart of the city.

He parked in his assigned space at headquarters but didn't enter the building. Instead he walked across Eleventh Street to Mr. Dick's for a bite to eat. It didn't seem that long ago he'd devoured two breakfasts; yet he felt famished.

The hostess, a tall and aloof woman whom he'd never seen working there before, met him without a smile. She led him to an isolated booth in the rear of the main dining room. Averting her eyes, she laid down his menu on the table and walked off briskly.

"You had me fooled too, Lieutenant," greeted the waitress when she came to take his order. She was a cheery, buxom redhead who'd been waiting tables at Mr. Dick's for at least a decade longer than Valjohn had been with the department.

"If I didn't know you I'd have hid you back here myself," she clucked. Her name was Rita Pearl and her husband was on the Force, a patrolman out of the Wentworth Station. "I just hope my Carmen never has to work undercover."

For the first time that day, Valjohn became aware that he still was wearing his surveillance clothes—in fact, he had never taken them off. He glanced quickly down at himself. The gaudy green sequined shirt was gaudy no longer. It was covered with smudges, wrinkled and frayed. A number of sequins were torn off. His kneecap stared back at him through a rip in the right pantleg of his black peg trousers.

"I think it's lousy enough you guys get badmouthed and shot at without having to look like bums besides," she offered, patting his arm. "What'll it be today?"

Valjohn debated getting up and leaving. He had a change of clothes in his locker at headquarters. He shifted in his seat, ordered the veal parmigiana instead, the corn au gratin, a tossed salad with Roquefort dressing and a baked potato with sour cream and chives.

He paused at the glass doorway before entering the massive edifice at 1121 South State Street, gaped upward at its imposing, white marble façade against which CHICAGO POLICE DEPARTMENT was boldly spelled out in big, blue letters. It seemed as if he'd been away for years. No. More than that: It seemed as if he'd never been there at all. He had the sudden eerie feeling that when he entered the building he would find only dark, unfamiliar corridors and strange gray rooms; busy, impatient strangers who had never seen him or heard his name.

He wished it were true.

Lowering his eyes, he sucked in his breath, belched up the syrupy taste of a Boston soda he'd just consumed to top off his lunch. Then walked inside.

He crossed the brightly lit lobby filled with its many public exhibits and stood at the elevators. A moment or two later one of the gleaming stainless-steel doors popped open. He was about to step into the elevator when he heard someone call his name. He turned to see Greg Harris standing with a couple of patrolmen across the hall to his left.

The elevator dinged. Valjohn reached out automatically to catch the door as it started to roll shut.

"V.J.?" Harris called again, taking a step in his direction.

Valjohn shrugged, let the door go and walked over to join him.

"Jesus, V.J., what's going on? What the hell happened to you? You look
. . . terrible," the detective's voice trailed off in dismay.

Valjohn nodded, smiled, tried his best to appear in control. No words
came.

Harris turned his head and glared at the two patrolmen gawking over
his shoulder. They exchanged looks and walked away.

"Okay, now tell me what happened. Where the hell have you been?"

Valjohn kept smiling, nodding.

"Howland's been on my back ever since I talked to you on the phone.
I told him you'd be here two days ago."

Valjohn cleared his throat, quit nodding, smiling, shook his head. Then
started nodding and smiling all over again.

Harris broke the silence with nervous laughter. "Well, Jesus, say something—anything!"

Poor Greg. He looked upset, ruffled, positively unbuttoned in his burnt-
brown, three-piece pebble-stitch. Valjohn wanted to put him at ease.

"Uh, Greg . . . uh, look, believe me . . ." he tried, then broke off. He tried
again. "It . . . uh . . . it's a long story—too long and involved, uh, to go
into right now. I'll tell you later. Promise. Right now, do me a favor and,
uh, bring me up to date."

"But—"

"Okay?"

Harris shook his head, whistled exasperation, even mussed his neatly
trimmed black hair, running a hand through it at an off angle.

"I don't know where to begin," he began.

"Anywhere, Greg, anywhere'll be just fine."

"All right, I'll start with the good and hit you with the bad later."

While Harris talked, first recounting what he'd said over the phone,
Valjohn struggled not to listen. He had little need for a secondhand rehash
of Fairchild's demise. He glanced up at the huge bronze-cast figure of
Captain William Ward that towered directly before them in the center of
the lobby. Though he knew the words already, he let his eyes scan the
inscription at the base of the statue:

In the name of the people of Illinois
I command peace.

Ward's historic utterance had been followed promptly by the Haymarket
Massacre: a bomb blast and gunfire that left seventy-two people wounded
and eight dead. Almost all of them police.

Valjohn's attention suddenly was yanked back to the lieutenant's voice,
now pumped with enthusiasm.

". . . actually the boy found them. He was showing me where he'd seen
the man standing in the bushes—that's when he spotted them. They were
hanging from a branch about a foot or so off the ground."

319

"Found what? What boy?"

"The dark glasses. Scotty Conlisk—the boy I've been telling you about. I just now got back from talking to him over at the Deerpath school yard. If these glasses belong to whoever was hiding in those bushes—and plus the kid's description . . ." He paused, trying to curb his mounting excitement. "I mean, it's got to be the biggest break we've had yet!"

Valjohn's head was swimming. So that's what happened to his dark glasses! He'd dropped them out of his shirt pocket while he was falling all over himself in those goddamn bushes! He closed his eyes for an instant, saw the boy once again coming at him in the night, wildly swinging his stick, hacking the branches he was hiding behind. He could feel one of the blows hitting his arm again, looked down, saw a tear in the sleeve of his shirt, a scratch scabbed over just above his left elbow. Then his eyes were closed again and he was once more in the bushes, the boy jumping back startled, the look of fright vividly illuminated in his little round face by bright moonlight as the two of them stared at one another only a few feet apart.

"V.J.?"

"What?" He reopened his eyes.

"You feeling okay?"

"Huh? Sure. Sure. Nothing—go on."

Harris studied him thoughtfully, then continued. "Anyway, I can't wait to run them through the lab." He hoisted a small black briefcase he was carrying.

"They haven't been dusted yet?"

"Nope. That's what I'm trying to tell you. We just now found them. I just got back here a few minutes before you did."

"Does anybody else know about them?"

"Sweeney. I called him right away. I talked to a patrolman too. Why?"

"Uh, no reason, I guess." Valjohn was amazed at how well his mind suddenly was functioning. "Just, you know, considering everything involved, it might be wise not to sound off too much yet, that's all."

Harris nodded, but Valjohn detected his subordinate's face taking on a slight pout.

"I think you're right, though," he said quickly, "this could be a big break, maybe the one we've been looking for. Hey, you've been doing a hell of a job in my absence!"

Harris smiled. Then his face quickly darkened. He looked away. Something else was eating him, but Valjohn ignored it.

"What kind of description did the kid give you on the, uh . . . suspect in the bushes?"

"Oh, great," said Harris, his enthusiasm taking over again. "You'll have to hear it."

"I'd like to."

Harris debated for a moment, opened his briefcase, removed a small cassette recorder. He handed the cassette to Valjohn. "Be my guest."

Valjohn thanked him, then, as if moved by an afterthought, asked if he could see the glasses.

Harris shrugged, searched into the briefcase again, came out with a manila field envelope.

Valjohn unwound the string seal and peered inside. He could see his own fish-eyed reflection in one of the lenses.

"Spy shades," grinned Harris. "One-way peekaboos."

Valjohn shut the envelope, rewound the string carefully but made no move to hand it back. Instead he glanced at his watch, gave a sigh. He informed Harris that he was on his way to the lab at that very moment himself.

"Look, I might as well drop these off with Carlson and get him going on them right away."

Harris's face clouded with hesitancy. "I . . . uh . . . I don't know, V.J. . . ."

"Don't worry, Greg, I'm not going to steal the credit." He laughed and gave him a good-natured slap on the shoulder.

"Come on, it's not that . . ."

"What then?"

Harris shrugged. "Okay, I told you the good news. Here comes the bad: You're off the case. Howland's dumped you. He's turned the whole thing over to Sweeney."

Valjohn received the information without batting an eyelash. It seemed redundant and irrelevant, something that had happened to him in the distant past, something he'd learned to accept and deal with ages ago.

"Don't count on it," he bluffed with a wink.

Harris looked painfully unconvinced. "I warned you over the phone, V.J.—"

"All right, I'll concede it: Officially you're not under me anymore—for the moment, that is."

"For the moment?"

"Look, I can't go into it at this point—it's still very hush-hush—but for chrissakes I'm talking about cracking this case wide open! You think Sweeney's going to pull it off? Be serious."

Harris was silent.

"Believe me, everything'll be straightened out in a day or so. Just bear with me a little longer."

His ex-subordinate still looked unconvinced but at least he wasn't reaching for the envelope anymore.

"Hey, I'm not worried," Valjohn called back, already striding toward an open elevator, "so why should you be?"

As the door closed he was giving him a thumb's-up gesture and beaming hearty confidence.

The elevator ascended. He breathed a sigh of relief. He felt bad about Greg—the way he'd buffaloed him into relinquishing the glasses, the way he'd traded on his friendship, his loyalty. Not much choice in the matter. He had to get them back; they were plastered with his prints. He could just imagine the wild-eyed speculation following such a disclosure. No way could he have endured the ensuing third degree. But now that he had the glasses, just what did he intend to do with them? He couldn't simply destroy them. They were going to be sorely missed. And soon.

The elevator stopped at the next floor and a group of schoolchildren crowded in, followed by a teacher who eyed Valjohn warily. Shrewish, middle-aged, not much taller than her charges, she snipped and snarled at them for the next two floors, then herded them out on Valjohn's floor. When he stepped out, she fixed him with a classroom scowl. He nodded, feeling indebted to her: He'd better spruce up a bit before waltzing into Homicide.

He could not remember the last time he'd bothered to look at himself in a mirror. On the way to his locker he stopped in the washroom. He was shocked at what he saw. His face was gaunt, grimy, stubbled with beard. Dried spittle ran from his crusted lower lip to the dimpled tip of his chin. There were scratches on his right cheek and more on his forehead. His black eye had passed from blue into a sickly shade of yellowish-green. His eyes themselves appeared bloodshot, burned out, almost ghostly.

He changed clothes, returned to the washroom with his shaving kit. After cleaning up he stepped back and again examined himself in the mirror. His face still looked gaunt. He still had his black eye, his scratches. It was a big improvement, though. All things considered, he could have looked a lot worse.

He leaned forward, steadying himself with both hands on the sink and staring into his bloodshot, burned-out eyes. He felt like the lone survivor of a nuclear holocaust. The world lay in shambles all around him. Rules, values, goals had gone up in smoke. Nothing remained except his own battered, shellshocked self.

He asked himself the question again: Was he insane? The answer hadn't changed: Yes, of course he was insane. But that offered no satisfactory solution, nor did it mitigate the horror one little bit. The circumstances, the absurdity of events had become too outsized. Insanity was nothing more than copping a plea. It no longer mattered whether this nightmare was illusion or not. What did matter was that it was real to him, that it had happened to him. And deep down he was convinced that if none of it existed, then neither did he.

So what happened next? How did one deal with one's nightmare after accepting it as gospel? His return to headquarters suddenly struck him as ludicrous. What was he doing here? What did he hope to accomplish? Certainly he couldn't expect to pick up where he'd left off.

He'd driven here in a daze—was probably still in a daze. At least now, though, he was aware of it. The incident with the dark glasses had jolted him. Here standing safely ensconced in the men's room of the Chicago

Police Department, he felt the will to survive spreading through him like some newly acquired guilt.

On his desk he found a stack of papers awaiting his attention. There was a note from Superintendent Gordon requesting him to report to his office immediately. There was also a note from his wife. She wanted him to call her as soon as he returned, either at home or the hospital.

Valjohn's legs went rubbery. He felt all the air being sucked from his lungs. He sat down hard in his chair, struggled to catch his breath. The dizziness returned, the nausea. He was only a shudder or two away from complete hysteria. For a moment he contemplated running out of the room, hurling himself through the nearest plate-glass window. But he lacked whatever it took: the determination, the courage—hell, the intelligence. Instead he reached over and punched his intercom key.

Gordon's private secretary answered. He asked if he could see the superintendent. She told him he was attending a conference out of town and wouldn't be back until tomorrow. Could she take a message?

He flipped off the intercom and swayed back in his chair. A temporary reprieve. Though he was hardly looking forward to a meeting with his old mentor, his spirit sagged. He felt the urgent need to talk to somebody, anybody. Sitting there musing alone was bad; he was slipping fast. He needed to be drawn out of himself right now.

He got to his feet and marched shakily into the outer office. Anybody. Even Howland would do.

"Just a minute, Lieutenant," a secretary from one of the front desks called as he was about to enter the captain's chamber. "He left word he don't want to be disturbed."

"Uh . . . I think he probably wants to see me."

"Just a minute," she repeated, rose from her desk, removed a huge wad of gum from her mouth, scurried through the doorway.

"He's tied up with Lieutenant Sweeney," she announced, emerging moments later, closing the door behind her. She popped the wad of gum, which she'd deftly palmed, back into her mouth.

"He . . . they don't want to see me?"

She nodded. "Especially you, Lieutenant." Another girl working up front caught her eye, snickered.

"How long is he going to be tied up?"

"I'm afraid all afternoon," she said with no embarrassment.

"Oh."

Valjohn watched her walk back and sit down. He started to turn away, changed his mind, went over to her desk. She pretended not to notice him standing there as she rustled through her notebook. She inserted a fresh sheet of paper into her typewriter.

"Ya, Lieutenant?" She finally looked up. The wad of gum made a busy lump in what was otherwise a young, pretty, if somewhat sharply featured face.

323

"Uh," he coughed, watched the lump in her cheek move, "I guess I just wanted to ask your name."

She looked at him for a full five seconds. "Eunice," she replied, went back to setting her margins.

"Eunice . . . that's a nice name."

"Ain't it, though," she snorted. She glanced over at her friend, shook her head, then returned her attention to her notebook.

"Uh, Eunice?"

"Ya?" She didn't bother to look up.

"Don't . . . don't be afraid."

The lump in her cheek came to a halt. Her eyes flashed at him.

"What?"

"Don't be afraid."

"What? Who's afraid?"

"You—you said you were afraid."

She stared at him dumbly, shot a bewildered glance at her friend to make sure she was taking all this in.

"I asked you how long Captain Howland would be tied up. I asked you and you said you were afraid all afternoon. I just don't want you to be afraid."

She looked at him long and hard.

Valjohn stood there nodding, smiling, trying to think of something else to say. There was a long, awkward silence.

"Shit!" the girl finally muttered. She rapidly began typing—*Clackety-clack-clack-clackety-clack-clack-clack* . . .

"Are you new here?" he said at last, thinking of something to say.

She ignored him. *Clackety-clack-clack-clack-clackety-clack. Ding. Bang. Clackety-clackety—*

"Are you new here?"

"Shit!" she muttered again. She stopped typing and looked up. "I been here almost a year. Okay?"

"Ah. I guess I never noticed you."

"I guess not. Look, Lieutenant, I'm kind of busy right now. Real busy." She glanced once again at her friend, rolled her eyes. Then she resumed her typing, made a mistake, swore, the lump in her cheek working furiously.

"Right. Well, it's been nice talking with you, Eunice."

She didn't look up.

In the hallway, he ran into Mona Cobb. Actively avoiding her in the past, he now tried to strike up a conversation. She responded coolly. She didn't have time to talk. She did mention that she was engaged to be married, though. "To a cop, a real cop," she added pointedly, flashing a gaudy ring and starting to walk away.

"That's great, Mona. Really."

"Maybe you know him," she looked back still walking. "Milton Stephansky. Special dispatcher over in Communications."

"Sure, sure. I mean I don't know him well, but we've conversed. Often. Plenty of times. He's . . . he's probably a heckofa guy"—she was gone around a corner—"when you get to know him," he mumbled on.

Back at his desk he sat down again and shuffled through the papers. Mostly Xerox copies of the Fairchild investigation: detective reports, lab sheets and photos. He was surprised Howland hadn't ordered them removed. He was more surprised he could now ponder the horror of what had happened that night without becoming dizzy or nauseated.

He picked up one of the reports, read it, didn't have to look at the signature to know whose it was. Slovenly written, disorganized, thick-headedly dogmatic. Unmistakably the effort of his successor, Lieutenant George Sweeney. All was right with the world. . . .

He did avoid looking at photos of the victim—still too graphic a trip down old memory lane. He was able to study a sketch of the scene, though: the body oriented in the school yard with the swings, a sidewalk and the juniper bushes. He noted the hammer lying several feet away from the victim's feet. Scanning one of the lab sheets, he saw that the hammer was actually a rubber mallet, the kind used in auto body shops to pound out dented fenders. All of the prints on it belonged to the victim. Some dried flecks of blood, very old, were discovered on the mallet's hard rubber head. Interestingly they did not belong to the victim, were typed AB positive.

Halfway through another report, he started to laugh. A couple of detectives walking by peered into his cubicle. He shrugged, tried to stop himself, but that only made matters worse and he ended up whooping louder than ever. Eyes watering, feeling weak, he got to his feet. He caught sight of Greg Harris in an outer hallway. Probably coming from the lab to ask him about the glasses.

Valjohn sobered quickly. He ran back to his desk, grabbed the envelope containing the glasses and fled from his office. He made a hasty retreat out a rear corridor through Rape and Aggravated Battery.

Doubling back along another hallway, he took the elevator to street level. He walked fast out of the building and climbed into his car again. He drove north on State Street for two blocks, headed west on Polk. When he came to the south branch of the Chicago River, he stopped in the middle of the bridge, got out, raised the hood. Leaning over the radiator as if he were examining the motor, he removed the dark glasses from the envelope, snapped them in half. He sauntered over to the railing and dropped the pieces into the river.

That was that. Now all he had to do was buy another pair, be careful not to touch them, and get them to the lab. If Harris questioned him about the delay, he'd just say he forgot about them. Too shook up over his removal from the case. He walked back to the car, lowered the hood. He drove away.

He drove and he drove. Once again, nowhere in particular. He reflected on his earlier outburst of laughter: Back in his office reading through those reports, it suddenly had dawned on him for the first time that he'd solved the case. No more sorting through all that voluminous bulk of tiresome data and evidence. No more groveling for clues and doggedly pursuing skimpy, dead-end leads. He was his own eyewitness. The Reaper . . . had been delivered to his doorstep, tucked right into his own bed! Once again the cubist cop had cracked the case wide open. . . .

So wide, in fact, that in the process he'd split himself right down the middle.

He thought about the note on his desk—the one from Crescent asking him to call her. He started shaking so badly he couldn't trust himself in traffic. He pulled over to the shoulder and parked. He sat there staring straight ahead, the steering wheel tightly clenched in both hands. The terror slowly seeped away, as if grounded by his vise-like grip on the wheel. A few minutes later he swung back in the flow of cars on the Eisenhower Expressway. He sped under the post office, over the river, into the heart of downtown.

Heading north on Wabash Avenue, slowly weaving through the big steel girders of the el, he made up his mind. If he didn't have it in him to commit suicide, couldn't kill himself outright, he could damn well do the next best thing: He could go home and confront his loving wife.

Tying up loose ends to steady himself, he drove to the car rental agency and returned the Fairlane, picked up his trusty old Volks in a lot across the street. From there he headed north to New Town.

He got cold feet when he saw the apartment, sped off intent on never coming back. He'd drive to O'Hare, take a jet to the coast. Any coast. Make it the Ivory. He'd start at square one. Back to Africa. He'd live in the bush, the desert . . . anywhere but Chicago.

He got as far as a Burger King on the other side of Belden Avenue.

He had a cheese Whopper, fries and a vanilla shake. The fast food gave him courage.

He returned to Oakdale Avenue just in time to spot a car pulling away from the curb in the middle of the block. He eased into the sizable vacated space, took a deep breath, grabbed his suitcase, climbed out. He paused at the front steps to scrape dog shit from a shoe—had anything truly changed?—then entered the building.

He inserted his key into the lock of the apartment, started to open the door, stopped. A story he'd once heard about the Indians on Kodiak Island suddenly came to mind, how when walking through the tall grass they'd carry cans full of pebbles, shaking them loudly so they wouldn't come up on the island's great brown bears and startle them into a charge.

Valjohn knocked, softly at first, then louder, shaking his own can of pebbles for all they were worth. There was no answer. Cautiously he opened the door.

He went through all the rooms, checked the closets, double-checked the bathroom, pulling back the shower curtain. Everything looked the same. Disconcertingly, he felt nostalgia replacing fear.

326

Satisfied he was alone, he returned to the kitchen and looked in the refrigerator. He finished off a bottle of dill pickles—there were only three left—made himself a lunch-meat sandwich with lettuce and tomato. He opened a can of beer, thought for a moment, then poured it down the drain. He might not be able to stop with one, and much as he could use a drink right now, he felt he'd better stay cold sober for this particular homecoming. He boiled some water, poured himself a cup of winterberry tea.

He ate standing at the kitchen counter. It was almost six. Crescent should have been home by now. Unless she went shopping with her girl friends. After downing a second cup of tea, he resumed his wait, pacing through the rooms. It wasn't too late to change his mind; he could bolt right now, still catch that jet. . . .

A little after six he turned on the TV and watched the news. The plight of the world failed to hold his interest, and he got up again, searched the cupboards for something more to eat. He found two cans of soup: one of minestrone, the other clam chowder, Manhattan style. He couldn't make up his mind; they both sounded good. He resolved the dilemma by opening both, setting a pan on the stove and pouring them together.

He crumbled a handful of crackers into a bowl of the steaming concoction and went back to the divan in the living room. This time he ate sitting down.

An inane game show had replaced the news. While he watched its grinning, oily-tongued emcee cajole wild exuberance from the studio audience, he thought about Wheeler Fairchild. Now he remembered him! The man from Starved Rock! He remembered his no-nonsense handshake, the charisma of his handsome smile. His high-powered plans to turn the park into Disneyland. Fairchild might be "Mr. Prominent Citizen" in the eyes of the public, but Valjohn had a feeling the man's past wasn't all that solid sterling. He kept seeing him in the playground brandishing that mallet, kept reliving his own panic and frustration as he sprawled in the bushes, helpless to save his wife from an imminent death by bludgeoning.

Poor Fairchild. Though he probably got what he deserved. What was it Crescent had called him when she first saw him? A rapist and a murderer? Yes, it came back to him clearly—they were in the lodge dining room playing their silly guessing game. He remembered the way she'd said it, the somber, odd tone to her voice.

Considering the profile of her other victims, she probably had him accurately pegged. There was the lab report, the little matter of someone else's blood on that mallet head. More than likely she wasn't the first person he'd ever taken a swing at.

He finished the soup, surprised at how good it had tasted.

At seven a movie came on. Spencer Tracy and Elizabeth Taylor in *Father of the Bride*. His mind wandered, but he felt too exhausted to move. The soup had made him suddenly very sleepy. He settled back on the couch.

Crescent O'Leary . . . Valjohn.

Who—what had he married? What preposterous interloper from God knows what dark, Stygian pit? His thoughts raced back to a freshman survey course in English lit where he'd read Dante: Was she some terrible avenging angel from the inferno? Maybe she was possessed? He had to admit he knew very little about such things—until a few days ago he considered all such matters ignorant fears and superstitions. Now the lock was broken. Hell hags of every size and shape overran his mind: harpies, banshees, ogresses. . . .

He began trembling and soon broke into a chilling sweat. He tried to get hold of himself but couldn't do it. He jumped up from the couch, a cry forming in his throat.

Any minute now! She'd be home! She'd be coming through the front doorway!

He dashed for the door—he had to get the hell out of there—yanked it open and fled into the hallway. He bounded down the stairway two, three steps at a time.

In the vestibule he came to a sudden halt. He could see someone coming up the steps outside, approaching through the thinly curtained oval glass of the big, Victorian front door. A woman.

Too late. He'd had it. The door was opening. He felt his heart stop pumping, brain cells dying. . . .

It wasn't she. Another tenant: one of the stewardesses from down the hall. He brushed by her and was out of the building before she had time to close the door behind her.

He raced down the street, crossed it to his car, climbed in. He jammed the key into the ignition, started the engine, grabbed the gearshift knob, shoved it into low. He cramped the wheels to swing out of the parking space. He didn't move.

His right foot gunned the engine several times; his left refused to disengage the clutch. After a few more moments, he turned off the engine and just sat there.

He wasn't going anywhere. Not to the airport, not to the Ivory Coast . . . points unknown. It had become too late to run a long time ago. Years too late. He could no more run away than he could do himself in.

He was back in the apartment, slouched on the divan again, watching the movie. The panic had subsided. He felt relaxed, even drowsy.

What was keeping her? It was almost eight. Maybe she wasn't coming. Maybe she knew he was in those bushes—that he'd seen her in action. Maybe she was too embarrassed to face him. *Ha!* More than likely she was just waiting for the sun to go down. Then she could come bursting through the doorway and have done with him right here in the comfort of their own living room.

The gun. He supposed he should get it out of the dresser, for protection. Ridiculous. There was no way he could use it on her. Besides, he probably needed silver bullets. No, that was for werewolves. Crucifixes, garlic cloves and wooden stakes were for vampires; for mummies you couldn't beat fire and collapsing buildings.

He yawned. How could he be expected to deal with his wife when he had no idea what she was? He yawned again, sank lower in the cushions. He watched Elizabeth Taylor run off to her room in some sort of postadolescent snit. He was just thinking what it would have been like to grow up in middle America with Spencer Tracy and Joan Bennett for parents, whether all that paternal befuddlement and decorative motherly charm could possibly have delivered him from the terrible scheme of his present life. He was just thinking—and then his eyes were closed and he was not thinking at all.

19

For a brief moment when he reopened his eyes, he felt confused, lost. It all came back to him soon enough. He'd fallen asleep sprawled on the living-room divan. He was waiting for his wife to come home from work.

It surprised him how easily he'd dozed off. No light nap, either; he'd really been under. He glanced at his watch. Only nine twenty-five.

He sat abruptly upright. The TV set was turned off. He was sure he'd fallen asleep with it on. Almost simultaneously he smelled something cooking. Seafood.

He heard noises in the kitchen: a cupboard door banging shut; water running in the sink.

"Greetings to the weary traveler. Welcome home."

The voice. He could not force himself to turn to face its source.

"I'd come and give you a big hug, but as you can see . . ."

He refused to turn. The words were left hanging. An unbearable silence built. He could feel her gaze a solid object crashing against the back of his head.

"As you can see," she repeated, "I'm right in the middle of a sauce."

Almost against his will, his head rotated. Slowly, toward the kitchen. She stood in the entryway, wearing her red calico apron, a spoon and saucepan

330

in her hands. Her hair was backlit, a streaming golden nimbus against the bright kitchen light.

"You looked so peaceful I couldn't bring myself to disturb you." She spooned the sauce.

He tried not to meet her eyes but failed. They drew him in with hopeless ease. Awakened from one dream, he felt himself plunging into another.

It was she who looked away. She walked back into the kitchen.

"I was going to be mad at you," she said, opening the oven door. "You promised to call me every night, if I remember correctly. I didn't know whether you were living or dead."

Their eyes had fused for only a few moments, but it was enough. He understood fully what he'd perhaps known all along—

"I even called headquarters but I couldn't get a straight answer. They seemed to know less than I did."

—that he was still in love with her. Irredeemably.

"Anyway," she said, smiling at him and reappearing at the counter, "I just had a feeling you'd be home tonight. Think I'm psychic?"

He felt like an addict doomed on heroin. He could not imagine a world bearable without that smile; yet in its magic he saw his own destruction.

"Debbie and I went out shopping. That's why I got home so late." She'd again disappeared into the kitchen and was rattling about in the pantry. "I brought you a surprise from that little market on West Elm Street. Can you smell it cooking? I hope you didn't lose your appetite in Pittsburgh."

Valjohn became aware at that moment of how much appetite he definitely had not lost in Pittsburgh. He stared at the empty soup bowl on the coffee table and thought about all the food he'd put away today; two breakfasts at the Holiday, a big lunch at Mr. Dick's topped off with a Boston soda, a stop at Burger King on the way home, a lunchmeat sandwich, three dill pickles—the clam chowder-minestrone gumbo—more food than he'd normally eat in a couple of days. He glanced down at his belly. Already it was straining against his belt. Yet he felt as though he hadn't eaten in a week. And the aroma coming from the kitchen . . .

"What's for dinner?" His first words to her. Hard to believe after all that had transpired.

"I told you—a surprise," came the cheerful response from the kitchen. "Just be patient, love. It won't be much longer."

It proved to be lobster, exquisitely prepared: simmered in white wine and imbued with a sauce made from the entrails of the lobster itself, the tomalley and coral, liver and ovaries thickened with chopped tarragon and chervil.

They ate in candlelight. Crescent brought the deep-dish casserole to the table and placed it before him. She poured from a small silver cruet what she claimed to be absinthe over the succulent entree and set it aflame.

Lobster was one of his favorite foods and though he enjoyed it as often as he could afford—which was about once every two years—never had he

331

tasted the equal of what he'd now been served. It would have humbled the palate of Dionysus himself.

"I guess I sort of splurged. They were on sale. Two would have been plenty—they're so big."

She'd bought four and cooked them all. One was all she could eat herself, but there were no leftovers to worry about. Valjohn with his new-found appetite cleaned the casserole, ingesting his own and the two left over as if they'd been little more than crayfish appetizers.

"What happened to your eye?" she asked as if noticing it for the first time.

He paused, a fork laden with a chunk of tender claw meat halfway to his mouth. Was this it? The confrontation. Did he dump it all right now on the table between them?

"It's . . . nothing. A little accident—wasn't watching where I was going," he said, backing off. Then he shoveled the dripping forkful into his mouth.

"I know all about you detectives. A doorknob, right? Staring through too many keyholes." Incredibly, she was laughing.

"Something like that," he mumbled in a voice that was barely audible. He tried to absorb himself with his chewing.

"It's good to have you home again. You look exhausted. I don't think Pittsburgh agreed with you."

Chewing really was a simple matter. You kept your mouth working, your jaw moving up and down. Occasionally you even swallowed.

"I didn't have time to fix a dessert," she said as she began to clear the table. "You'll have to settle for some French pastries I picked up at Jacques'.

And settle he did. He unbuckled his belt, wolfed down éclairs, Napoleons and cream horns until the sluggishness of his body reduced him to a state of bloated stupefaction.

He awoke the next morning alone in bed. He could not remember undressing or putting on his pajamas. He could not remember coming to bed. For that matter he could not remember finishing dinner. It seemed as though he should still be seated at the table, stuffing his face with lobster and pastries.

Crescent was gone. He could see the imprint of her form on the bedding where she'd lain beside him. He found a note on the nightstand saying she'd had to get up early to attend a special ANA meeting but that she'd try to get home in the evening before six.

Everything the same as usual. Nothing had happened.

While he dressed he thought about the ease with which she'd handled things last night. She owned him. The moment he'd met her eyes it was all over. Love bound him fast in ever-tightening coils of despair.

Once more he pondered the breadth of her powers. Did she know he was hiding in those bushes or not? Of course she did—even if she wasn't letting on. He wondered about their relationship: patient/nurse, man/wife, cop/-killer—wondered how much chance was involved in that fateful first meeting, the errant flight of a golf ball. . . .

In the kitchen he found she'd fixed him breakfast. A tiny mountain of scrambled eggs, mushrooms, diced ham and melted cheddar cheese rose from a platter keeping warm in the oven. Beside it was another, smaller platter stacked with link sausage and bacon. On the counter was a bowl filled with dry cereal—Cheerios—a dish of croissants, each gobbed with butter, and a couple of tumblers brimming with marmalade and honey. His orange juice was already poured in a glass in the refrigerator alongside half a cantaloupe that had been deseeded.

Hardly his usual skimpy breakfast! After last night's feed he doubted he could manage much more than a meager sampling. Once he started eating, however, his appetite returned with a vengeance. When his meager sampling came to an end, there was nothing left but cantaloupe rind and grease on a platter.

On his way to headquarters, he drove all the way to the Loop before he remembered the dark glasses. He made a U-turn and headed back twelve blocks to Chicago Avenue, parked in a bus zone and went into the corner drugstore where he'd purchased the originals.

He searched the racks, two large revolving drums, for several minutes. There was no similar pair. The assortment was vast: lenses and frames of all sizes, shapes and colors. The combinations seemed endless, yet the only ones he could find with one-way reflector glass had small lenses and wire rims.

The longer he hunted, the angrier he became with himself. It had been impulsive, stupid to throw them away. He could just as easily have wiped them clean. Not thinking too clearly yesterday. Spots on his hands; he would've made a great Lady Macbeth.

Turning the drums for the umpteenth time, he spied a pair on the bottom tier. Big fisheye reflectors in a black plastic frame! He carefully removed them from the rack with a handkerchief, took them to the checkout counter. He paid for them, refusing to let the cashier touch them or put them in a sack.

Estes Merriwether Gordon sat at his desk solemnly staring down at his thin, sensitive, crossed hands. Valjohn sat before him, coughed once, the smoke swirling up around him. All but one pipe, the bulldog briar on the bookcase, were acridly smoldering away.

"It's not the end of the world," the superintendent began again. "I . . . I sometimes feel a setback like this often can be the best thing to happen to a young man. I know once when I was a callow patrolman . . ."

Valjohn listened with patient deference as Gordon recounted one of his own early setbacks.

"But as you can see, I managed to bounce back. I'm sure you'll bounce back too, John. I still entertain the highest hopes for your future here."

Valjohn did his best to look properly moved. It was not easy. His mind was miles away.

"If it's personal problems you're having"—Gordon scanned the room, his moon-sad eyes coming to rest on the smokeless briar—"perhaps you'd like some time off." He was up pacing across the room. He picked up the pipe on the bookcase; from a small humidor nearby he pinched out a brimming bowlful of tobacco, lit it.

"I've already told you, I'm not going to pry into your unaccountable absence."

"Thwuk, thwuk," his gaunt, narrow face pulled even tighter as he drew on the stem. "If you don't feel like talking about it . . ." Now his moon-sad eyes fixed intently on Valjohn. They neither accused nor condemned, only questioned.

Valjohn could not hold their gaze and glanced down at the tips of his shoes.

"Thwuk, thwuk, thwuk." A fresh plume of smoke billowed up between them.

"If you don't feel like talking about it," the superintendent spoke at last, his shoulders sagging wearily, "I'll simply take your word for it. That it was unavoidable and leave it at that."

He set the well-stoked briar back in its holder and returned to his chair.

"I only hope that you realize your removal from the case at this time is equally unavoidable. I'm sorry."

Valjohn wanted to put an arm around those narrow, beleaguered shoulders, wanted to say: *Look, Estes, it's okay, really, don't sweat it. It's just that something's come up and . . .*

"I understand, sir."

"If you're not feeling well . . . in any way—that was a nasty head injury you received last summer. It might be a good idea to take some time off and have a complete checkup. Go on up to Mayo's for a week. Do some fishing.

"What do you think? John? Are you with me?"

Valjohn was with him. He knew exactly what Gordon was suggesting— that it might look better if he took a little leave of absence now and blamed the setback on his injury.

"John, how does that sound?"

"It sounds good, sir. May I have some time to think it over?"

Back at his desk, he absently opened his top drawer, still reflecting on Gordon's proposal. The tape Harris had given him of the Conlisk boy caught his attention and he decided to listen to it. From another drawer he withdrew a recorder and set it on top of the desk. He snapped in the cassette.

"My name is Scotty Conlisk."

334

"And how old are you, Scotty?"

"I'm eight—but I'll be nine next week."

"Very good. And where do you live?"

"I live in a big yellow house next door to Ricky Peterson."

"Do you know the address?"

"Sure. 1223 Wampler Drive."

"Good. And where do you go to school?"

"I use to go to St. Francis Parochial, but now I go here."

"Uh-huh. Now, why don't you tell me everything you did last Thursday night again. Start with after supper."

Valjohn listened to the boy recount his adventures of the evening, winding up at the school playground where he met the little girl Valjohn had seen him playing with on the teeterboard.

"So after Nancy left," broke in Greg Harris's hoarse baritone, "you picked up the stick. You pretended it was a sword and you attacked the bushes—you pretended they were . . . ?"

"Nuns. A bunch of nuns. Mainly Sister Conti."

Cute kid, thought Valjohn, remembering the fury of the attack.

"Uh, yes. So what happened then?"

"Well, like I told you, I was hacking them branches real good and this man all of a sudden he stands up in the middle of them."

"Did you actually strike the man?"

"I . . . I don't know. I don't think so. I was awful scared—I couldn't hardly move."

"And what did the man do?"

"Nothing. He didn't do nothing. He just stood there."

"Did you get a good look at him?"

"Sure."

"What did he look like?"

There was a long pause.

"Can you remember?"

"Uh . . . I guess he was real big."

"Would you say he was my size?"

"Oh, bigger. He was real ugly too and awful mean-looking."

"How was he mean-looking?"

"Oh, I don't know, maybe he had these big teeth and everything."

"Big teeth?"

"You know, like fangs."

"The man had fangs?"

"Oh, I don't know, it was awful dark."

"But you're sure it was a man."

"Uh-huh. It wasn't that dark."

"Was he wearing glasses? Dark glasses?"

"Nope. I could see his eyes. They were real spooky-looking."

"Spooky how?"

"Spooky he was getting ready to kill me dead! Tear me into pieces like he done that other guy! I took off running fast as I could run."

"Do you remember anything else about him? Take your time and think real hard."

There was a pause.

"Oh, I think he was a nigger."

"A nigger? I mean, a black? You're sure?"

"I think so. Not real niggery, but, you know, kind of a nigger."

"Scotty, do you think you could recognize him if you ever saw him again?"

"Uh-huh . . . but I don't want to see him again. Do I have to?"

Valjohn switched off the playback and smiled. He could just imagine the little bastard picking him out of a lineup: *There he is! That's him—the big ugly mean kind of niggery one with the fangs!* Curious, he thought, as he removed the cassette from the recorder, the boy did not once mention Crescent, though she was sitting there in a swing the whole time. Harris should have questioned him more thoroughly.

Putting the recorder away, he noticed another tape cartridge lying in the bottom of the drawer. His interview at the state mental hospital with Ernly Chard, the potential eyewitness who'd flipped out at the scene of the Fulton murder. Valjohn, suddenly feeling an affinity for the old wino, put the cassette in the recorder and played it.

He leaned back in his chair and listened, hands behind his head, staring at the tiny holes of his acoustic ceiling. When it was over, he ran it back and dug in the files for his notes on Chard. He found them, read quickly through them.

Yes . . . now he remembered: Before the straitjackets, the booze and the shattered life, Chard had been an aspiring scholar, a graduate student in English lit. He'd cracked under the pressures of writing a thesis.

Valjohn took out a pencil and blank sheet of paper, started the tape over again. Words and phrases from the old man's ravings suddenly had come alive. Unclear, abstruse, mad—but now there was a hint of meaning in them. He was sure of it—some sort of sense in the garbled nonsense! He copied them down, worked slowly, playing, rewinding and replaying again and again, listening intently to distinguish between coherent syllables and wild gibberish.

It was the middle of the afternoon before he'd finished. He edited his longhand copy on the typewriter and filled three full pages, single-spaced. He leaned back in his chair for a moment's rest. He felt exhausted. A belated sense of accomplishment.

He reached for the phone.

Thirty minutes later he was on the University of Chicago's campus, strolling briskly across the humanities quadrangle. The afternoon sky had become heavily overcast, and the Gothic, soot-gray limestone buildings that rose up around him looked particularly foreboding. At the west end of Harper Library he entered a building inscribed Wieboldt Hall and made his way into the brightly lit main office of the graduate English Department.

"May I help you?" asked a dour-looking woman sorting through papers by a filing cabinet. She had long, flowing brindled hair and wore black horn-rimmed glasses.

"Miss Samuels?"

"Yes?" She tilted her head forward and stared at him over the top of her glasses.

"I just spoke with you a little while ago over the phone—"

"Ah, you must be Mr. Brown?"

"Yes," Valjohn said. In a moment of prickling paranoia he'd decided to use an alias.

"The man in search of learned opinion?"

"Yes."

"I'm not sure if anyone's still here," she said, smiling and picking up her intercom phone, then blurted, "Oh, there's Professor Stone!"

She waved and called out to a man who stood in the hallway by a rack of mailing cubicles, collecting his correspondence.

"Will a Shakespearean scholar do?"

Valjohn shrugged.

The man waved back to her and entered the office, shuffling several letters in his hands. The secretary cheerfully introduced them, then returned to her filing cabinet.

Valjohn explained the nature of his visit with an elaborate story. He, Mr. Brown, was a private investigator working on a case. A client had come to him with a tape recording of the last words of a dying father. The client had been away on a trip at the time of the old man's death, and being a devoted son he wished to know if there was any thread of meaning that could be deciphered from these last words or whether they simply were as they seemed: the senseless babblings of a senile mind. He added that the father had once been an English professor and that a number of his recorded words struck a decidedly literary note. If Professor Stone could perhaps identify some of them as quotations . . .

"Do you have the recording with you?" the professor asked, glancing at his watch. A brusque little man, he flicked a finger at his tight black moustache all in the same motion.

"No, but I have a transcript," said Valjohn, producing from a folder the three pages he'd typed.

The professor took them, made a great show of looking at his watch again, scanned a couple of the pages.

"Nothing of Shakespeare here," he finally commented.

Valjohn nodded with disappointment.

"But I think I do see some Keats . . . and maybe some Coleridge. Look, I hate to be abrupt but I really must be off. I have a meeting across campus and I'm already late."

He handed the sheets back to Valjohn. "I'm sorry. Why don't you talk

337

to Professor Whittier. He's still upstairs in his office. He'll be happy to help you. He loves puzzles—however improbable," he added with a pointed smile, "and the romantics are his *pièce de résistance.*"

The first impression Valjohn had when he walked into room 207, the office of Yvor Whittier, was that he'd entered a cave—a dark, musty grotto with books for walls. A huge oaken desk occupied one side of the room, its surface awash with papers and books. More books lay scattered like stepping-stones on the hardwood floor.

In a far corner to his right near a stepladder, a man was seated in a large, overstuffed leather chair. He had slouched to one side and appeared to be napping. Valjohn advanced to the center of the room. The man did not look up.

Valjohn glanced uncomfortably about. There was no one else. He was ready to go back outside and knock again when the man growled, still not moving:

"Well?"

"Professor Whittier?"

No answer.

"Excuse me, sir, my name is J . . . George Brown, and I'm a private investigator. Professor Stone, whom I met downstairs, suggested—"

"You're not a student?"

"No, sir."

The professor raised his head, straightened in the chair. He held a book tucked in his lap and had, in the feeble light, actually been reading.

"I thought you were a student. I've seen my limit for the day. If I have to bandy grade points with one more whining would-be scholar, I might be driven to a rash and violent act. What can I do for you?"

Valjohn repeated his story. He found his invention growing more believable with each telling. He could almost see the father now, pale, withered, El Greco features, stretched out on his bed slavering his last words into the tape recorder.

"I realize it all sounds a little strange," he said, handing the transcript to the professor. The professor waved off his apology, settled back in his chair and began reading.

He read slowly with great concentration, his lips forming every word. Occasionally he would mumble something to himself and shake his head. When he'd finished, he shuffled the pages together and began again. He finished a second time, reshuffled the pages and seemed on the verge of reading through a third time.

Valjohn shifted his weight uneasily from one leg to the other.

The professor looked up, almost as if surprised to see him still standing there. "Odd," he finally said. "I find nothing that would seem to console your client. Nothing that appears even remotely relevant to a father-son relationship."

"Professor Stone—he mentioned some lines from Keats and Coleridge."

"Mmm . . . quite right. Some fragments, badly mangled, chopped up, but still easily recognizable. Here, for instance"—he marked a page with a pencil—"and here and here again." He handed the sheet to Valjohn.

Valjohn held the sheet close to his face, squinted.

"By Jove, it *is* becoming somewhat crepuscular in here!" The professor reached up behind his chair, switched on a wrought-iron floor lamp. "Much better," he said. "More than enough obscurity in the world without adding to it, eh?"

Valjohn read where the professor had penciled.

Bracy, bard Bracy does thou loiter? My kind of town? Ha! Her kind of town! Your music is sweet, louder than your horses' feet listen Lord Roland loud loud loud the call, the squall. Who is safe at Langdale Hall?

He looked up. "Is that Keats?"

"No, that's some fractured Coleridge. From his unfinished poem, *Christabel.*"

Valjohn shook his head. "I'm a little weak in English literature."

"No need for apology, Mr. Brown. I have a host of students who wouldn't know the difference either."

In the light Professor Whittier now appeared older than Valjohn's first impression of him. Closer to seventy than sixty. He had a round face, wrinkled like a walnut. His white hair was thin and unkempt, a fringe of wispy elflocks that failed to cover a bulging, freckled pate. His eyes brimmed with boyish energy, strangely out of place in his hoary countenance.

"The other two places I marked are Keats."

Valjohn glanced down at the page again.

Don't pass the city gates shit who goes to Corinth? That old toddling town. The time of your life. The time of your wife. Beauty twists its braid. Beauty twists its maid. Fuck fuck fuck fuck fuck senseless lizzy us asshole lizzy us.

"As for 'lizzy us'—I think that's spelled capital L-y-c-i-u-s: Lycius, a man's name," the professor corrected, then closed his eyes and recited:

" 'Ah, happy Lycius—for she was a maid more beautiful than ever twisted braid.' "

Valjohn read on.

Now I lay me down to creep. Lay me down. Lay me, baby, lay me! Lay me a . . . lay me a . . . daughter of the dark! Come cunt cocksucker! Begone foul dream ream suck! Shriek, shriek nothing but sad echo shrieks.

"I think 'lay me a' is written wrong there," the professor interjected again. "It should read as one word, Lamia: capital L-a-m-i-a." He proceeded once more to recount from memory:

" ' "Lamia!" he shriek'd; and nothing but the shriek with its sad echo did the silence break.' "

Valjohn nodded, read some more.

Hair. Snare! You think you won't? A smoke's no joke. You want to get laid? You want to get paid? Beauty twists her braid. Think twice. Think vice. Stink nice. "That's not nice," said little old we. I don't care. Don't swear. Don't cuss, you old cuss. Do you feel the terror in your hair?

The words brought back vivid memories of his interview with Ernly Chard. He still could see him dressed in his green robe, an anemic Charlie Ruggles, ranting and raving as he stumbled about that small observation room at Mengerts. He still could hear the strident, tortured voice:

Gordian shape of dazzling hue; foul-mouthed crusty cunt full of silver moons, I'll tell you, and sometimes into cities she'd send her dreams . . . sure, the gritty spitty shitty city—yagh!

At that point Chard had spit on the floor and sobbed, lunged forward, grabbed Valjohn's arm, almost knocking the tape recorder off the table. "Don't look! For God's sake, don't look!" he'd cried out. In the next instant he'd calmed down; his wild eyes had become small and crafty. "My elfin blood in madness runs," he'd whispered in Valjohn's ear. "My mouth foams—" he'd opened his mouth, revealing a lifetime of dental neglect. He'd spit on the floor, narrowly missing Valjohn's feet. "The grass besprent, withered at dew so virulent." Chard then had rubbed the toe of a slipper in a gob of his sputum. "Awful rainbow, awful rainbow, awful rainbow . . ." He had stared at Valjohn, finally bawling out again, "Do you feel the terror in your hair?" He reached up and pulled at his own hair, yanked at it until white tufts floated in the room like milkweed. It was then Valjohn had called an attendant.

Now it was Valjohn who felt the terror in his hair.

"What's the poem? Who was Lycius?" he struggled to ask.

Professor Whittier was deeply engrossed in another page. *"Lamia* is the name of the poem. Lycius was a beguiled lover, foolish and all too mortal," he added without looking up. "Mmm . . . this is curious." He proceeded to read aloud what he was puzzling over:

" 'Lycius . . . Mercutius—you'll end where you began. Mary mother sweet, oh, save me! Bark you mastiff bitch! Help me. I know the big-shouldered hog butcher, all celestial beauty blazes, stinkfinger sucker-cunt fuckhead'—need I tell you the expletives aren't Keats?" The professor smiled aside, continued, " 'She's got the only bleeding bleeding bastard mugger bugger plugger'—I'll skip over some of this . . . mmm . . . mmm . . . mmm . . . ah, yes, here again:

" 'Mercutius, dizzy, my brain is dizzy is Greece, in the midst of Greece. I grow gray in Corinth but my eyes never remember—come hither, you dumb fucking prickshit for brains, shit for change, we are a fit pair—charge upon the spikes! Only, please shut up that hissing, pissing, crawling spite —Jesus, God shut up! Shove it scumbag, hide your nether parts! Your feather parts, your leather farts, your jelly tarts, your heather garts' . . . mmm . . . yes and so on."

"More Keats?"

"No. I think there's some Spenser, though. A murmur of Carl Sandburg as well."

"Big-shouldered hog butcher," said Valjohn. "I caught that. Mercutius —isn't he from Shakespeare?"

"No, that's Mercutio, Romeo's ill-fated friend. However, the only Mercutius I can bring to mind also was a wild Italian gallant, much less renowned than Mercutio, less colorful and witty, I might add, though certainly no less ill-fated."

The professor with considerable effort hoisted himself from the sunken confines of his chair, began searching his bookshelves.

"Bring the stepladder here a moment," he ordered, scrutinizing the upper reaches of his library. Valjohn hauled the ladder across the room and set it down before him.

With remarkable agility the old man sprang up the steps. He stood balanced with both feet on the topmost tread and stretched almost to the ceiling.

"The works of Thomas Hood, 1799 to 1845." He withdrew a book from a set of a dozen or so green volumes on the highest shelf and examined its Table of Contents. The ladder creaked ominously as he shifted his weight. He replaced the book and withdrew another from the set.

Valjohn leaped forward and steadied the wobbly supports with both hands. The professor continued his inspection, oblivious of his own precarious stance.

"Ah, here we are," he announced, thumbing through the sixth volume. *Lamia: A Romance.* Instead of climbing down the ladder, he chose to peruse the text from his lofty perch.

"Of course, this is a far cry from Keats' version. I haven't read it in ages . . . but as I . . . as I remember . . . it's . . . it's somewhat trivial," he commented absently as he flipped through the pages. "The dialogue . . . for the most part . . . rather weak . . . the characters carelessly sketched."

"What does 'Lamia' mean?" asked Valjohn, staring up at the professor's baggy trousers.

"Voilà!" the professor suddenly exclaimed. "Listen to this:

" 'Go to, ye silly fools!—Lo! here's a palace!
I have grown grey in Corinth,
But my eyes never remember it?'

"That's the philosopher, the old Sophist Apollonius speaking. He's telling us that there's something fishy about Lamia's home. He's lived in

Corinth all his life. In a familiar neighborhood he suddenly comes upon a palace he's never seen before. You see, Mr. Brown, it's not 'What does Lamia mean?' but 'Who was Lamia?' Aha! Listen:

> " 'Here again? What folly led me hither?
> I thought I was proceeding homeward.
> Why, I've walked a circle
> And end where I began!'

"That's Mercutius speaking now. He's smitten with love, enchanted by Lamia, and he too finds something fishy about her house. Every time he tries to leave it, he keeps circling back. Apollonius tells him:

> " 'It's magic, it's vile magic brought you hither,
> And made you walk in a fog.
> There, think of that;—be wise, and save yourself!'

"Naturally, Mercutius is neither wise nor does he save himself. I'll turn to the final scene."

"Who . . . who was Lamia then?" Valjohn rephrased his question, more than a little confused.

"She was . . . mmm . . . mmm . . . here we go!" said the professor, glancing over the concluding lines. "Listen to this—this is Lamia speaking:

> " 'Thou ruthless devil!
> To bear him so bloody a will—Why then come hither,
> We are a fit pair.'

"She's telling Mercutius, whom she hates, that he's as dreadful as she is. She then proceeds to kill him—he was about to rape her at that point. Listen to his dying words:

> " 'O thou false witch!
> Thou hast pricked me to the heart! Ha! What a film
> Falls from my eyes!—or have the righteous gods
> Transformed you to a beast for this! Thou crawling spite,
> Thou hideous—venomous—'

"Mercutius dies. Obviously in the throes of death he is seeing her real self for the first time."

"Her real self?" asked Valjohn, his hands starting to tremble on the ladder. Beads of sweat were forming on his brow.

"A lamia, of course. Now she answers him:

> " 'I know what I am. Thou wilful desperate fool,
> To charge upon the spikes!—Thy death be upon thee!—

Why wouldst thou have me sting? Heavens knows I had spared thee
But for thy menace of a dearer life.'

"Here she accuses him of killing himself—thrusting himself on the stationary spikes of a battlement—his own wicked acts warranting his destruction."

Professor Whittier slammed the book shut and spun around as if the ladder he was standing on were wide as a classroom dais. "I must say the deceased, your client's father, seems to have been thoroughly obsessed with—"

In the next instant he'd stepped into space, apparently in his enthusiasm forgetting he was aloft. Down he plunged. Valjohn, who was almost directly under him, grabbed at him. They both tumbled to the floor.

"Uffgh . . . ooh . . . my, my, my!" groaned the professor as he clambered to his feet over Valjohn's prostrate body. "I haven't pulled that stunt in quite a while." He shuffled on his legs, felt his arms for broken bones. Miraculously he was unhurt. "Five years ago, to be exact. Stepped off with *Pepys' Diary*—only I wasn't fortunate enough to have you below to catch me. Spent half a sabbatical in traction mending a broken hip. Are you all right?"

Valjohn sat up on the floor. He rubbed his jaw where one of the professor's bony elbows had struck him.

"I . . . I think so."

"You're bleeding. Let me get you something."

Valjohn managed to stand up gingerly while the professor rummaged through a drawer in his desk.

"I'm intensely sorry, Mr. Brown," he said, offering Valjohn a handful of Kleenex. "Intensely sorry . . . You're sure you're all right?"

"Yes—fine. It's nothing . . . really." He wiped away the trickle of blood at a corner of his mouth. He could feel a tooth—one of his big front incisors—wiggling in its socket.

"Please, go on."

"Go on?"

"You were saying—before you fell—something about my client's father."

"Ah . . . yes . . . let me see. I mean, I realize he was on his deathbed—it's apparent he was quite out of his mind—but I was just saying that he certainly seemed to be obsessed with her."

"Who?"

"Why, Lamia, of course."

"Professor Whittier, you still haven't told me who she was."

"Not *who* she was, Mr. Brown, but *what* she was—still is."

Valjohn tried not to look cross-eyed.

"I don't mean to confuse you," the professor hastened. "It's simply that she has more than one identity. She exists on two different levels. Lamia

343

is, of course, her original self, a queen of ancient Libya. But she also is her generic self or selves; she is a spirit that takes on a multitude of identities down through history, all spawned from that original conceit. She becomes a sort of dark, pervasive, feminine force—one of the truly great distaff demons in all of literature. More than that. Hers is a spirit that perhaps lurks in all women, all members of the sexually oppressed. It is one of love and tragedy; of violent retribution."

They were both silent for several moments. Valjohn wondered if the professor heard him swallow.

"Would you join me in a cup of tea? I think my nerves could use a little settling after those acrobatics."

"Only," said Valjohn, trying to keep his voice slow and even, "only if you'll tell me more about her. Lamia. What she was . . . is."

"Done!"

From his desk the professor brought out a small copper samovar, went down the hall to fetch water. While they sat waiting for the water to boil, he spoke further:

"I should warn you, Mr. Brown, I can talk for hours about Lamia; she's long been a pet topic of mine."

Valjohn nodded. "I'm warned."

"Well, as I said, she was originally a queen of Libya. She was mortal then, a great beauty and the mother of two children. Her beauty proved to be her undoing, however, for she caught the roving eye of Zeus—that archetypal rapist and king of all lechers. He descended from the heavens and had his way with her. Naturally Hera, his wife, found out and, jealous bitch that she was, sought revenge. True to form, Zeus, all-powerful, went unpunished. Lamia, the innocent victim of his divine lust, suffered the full brunt of his wife's wrath. Under Hera's curse, she went temporarily insane and devoured her own children. Later, learning what she'd done, she retreated from civilization, taking abode in a lonely mountain cavern. It was there, tormented by grief and guilt, she was slowly twisted into the demon thing her name has come to mean.

"According to legend, she would venture from her lair at night and prey on lonely old men and young boys. She would embrace them, her touch afflicting them with wasting diseases. She would suck their blood, devour their souls. Do you take your tea sweet?"

Valjohn made an inaudible moan deep in his throat.

"Sugar?" pursued the professor, pouring a steaming cup of Earl Grey tea from the samovar.

"No . . . no, thank you." Valjohn found his voice.

The professor handed him his tea, the cup filled close to the brim. Valjohn, his hands trembling, spilled more than a few drops in his lap before he could set it down at the edge of the desk.

The professor, failing to notice, poured a packet of sugar into his own cup and continued his discourse.

"As I remember, she could pop her eyes out of her head and hold them in her hands. Thanks to Zeus. He felt sorry for her because she was so guilt-ridden she couldn't close her eyes at night. Ah . . . the charity of the gods."

Valjohn wriggled in his seat, the hot liquid seeping through his pants.

"Anyway, from this early myth, she emerges in subsequent literature as a full-fledged supernatural being. She's most frequently depicted as a serpent woman—the body of a snake and the head of a woman, or vice versa. Sometimes she's totally mongrel, like a chimera, a concoction of animal features—say, the head of a woman, the body of a lion, goat legs, the wings and talons of an eagle and so on. One version has Poseidon as her father and her living in the sea, mating with all sorts of monsters and dragons from the deep. She's almost always had the power of sorcery, the power to become a beautiful woman."

He took a sip of tea. "Tell me when all this starts to bore you. Surely none of it can be of much benefit to your client."

Valjohn stared into his cup.

"Mr. Brown?"

Valjohn continued to stare.

"Mr. Brown?"

"What? Oh . . ." Valjohn jerked his head up. "I . . . excuse me—I was lost for a moment in thought. Please go on."

"I was just saying surely none of this can be of much use to you or your client."

"That's all right. Please go on. I want to hear it all. I . . . I want to hear it all. Really."

The professor shrugged. "Well, as I said before, variations of her identity keep reappearing down through history. In *The Odyssey*, for instance, she ruled a cannibalistic kingdom in Sicily called Laestrygones. As I remember she sank the redoubtable Greek's ships and ate his men.

"And there was a time in later Greek and Roman literature when slovenly, ignorant housewives and mothers-in-law were called lamias. She'd become a subject of derision and satire, was regarded as a gigantic, coarse-looking woman with dissimilar feet—an utter frump, gluttonous and filthy. Much like Duessa in Spenser's *Faerie Queene.* He describes her in graphic detail, a hideous, foul hag from the waist up, but from the waist down, 'her nether parts,' he finds her too disgusting for words.

"During the thirteenth century, ecclesiastic authorities professed lamias preyed on unbaptized children. Milton in his *Paradise Lost* sat her on either side of the gates of hell, where she met Satan coming and going.

"The lamia was a popular motif in European literature through the Middle Ages and long after. Being a scholar of the nineteenth-century English Romantic movement, however, I'm most intrigued by her manifestation in the works of Coleridge and Keats, for example—as apparently was your client's father. How's your tea?"

345

Valjohn glanced down at his cup, discovered he hadn't yet taken a sip. He promptly did so. "Fine. Great."

"Not too strong?"

He shook his head no.

"I have a tendency to make it too strong. Anyway, they saw her in very contrasting light. Coleridge and Keats. Coleridge saw her as evil incarnate, a serpent transformed into a woman who used her beauty to cast spells and perform wicked deeds.

"Keats' Lamia was quite different. Though she too was a serpent woman, her intentions were never to do harm or evil. She was a sympathetic, tragic figure whose only sin was failing to accept her dismal fate, her serpent's lot, and loving a mortal. Lycius. Predictably she deceived him into believing she was a beautiful maiden. Surrounded by the wealth of illusion they lived together for a short time in total bliss."

"A short time?"

Professor Whittier nodded, pleased with the earnest attention of his audience. "Apollonius, the old philosopher, was able to see through her guise. He exposed her to Lycius on their wedding day.

" ' "Fool! Fool!" repeated he, while his eyes still
Relented not, nor mov'd; "from every ill
Of life have I preserv'd thee to this day,
And shall I see thee made a serpent's prey?" '

"Instantly the illusion was broken. Lamia vanished before their eyes, and Lycius was found lying lifeless where only moments earlier he'd been sitting with his intended bride. The loss of her love had felled him as surely as the loss of his own heartbeat.

"Naturally, Keats employed the lamia motif to express his own romantic precepts. Apollonius symbolizes reason and logic. He is ruthless, self-righteous, uncompromising in his effort to deliver Lycius from the illusion of bliss. He succeeds in disposing of Lamia, but he destroys the young man in the process.

"We are left to ponder whether the bliss shared by Lycius and Lamia was all that bad. True, it was based on illusion, but did that make the bliss itself any less real or good?

"Well!" The professor set down his empty cup on the desk with a punctuating bang. "How I've rambled. Now I would say you know more about Lamia than 99 9/10 percent of the population. . . . More, I dare say, than you probably care to know."

Valjohn made an effort at politeness. "I . . . your discourse—it was fascinating."

"She is fascinating," the professor agreed almost wistfully. "A marvelous creature. So many dimensions to her, such a wealth of metaphor. It's no wonder she has such range—both through time and space. And not just

European countries: Kipling wrote of finding her in the folklore of India. Then in China there was the white snake lady of Hangchow—Su Chen, I believe her name was. And in ancient rabbinic literature there's Lilith. She was Adam's first wife, a dark female spirit who eventually fled him on wings."

Valjohn sipped his tea. It was lukewarm. He gulped it.

"I've often wondered why Lamia hasn't enjoyed greater popularity in this day and age—particularly with the current monster craze that the movies and television seem to have augmented. Frankenstein, Dracula, the wolfman, the mummy . . . Godzilla, for godsakes! Surely she deserves her share of celebrity status. Ah, well, she never sought the limelight. Too shy; too retiring. Perhaps obscurity is a blessing."

Valjohn finished the remainder of his tea.

"I'm certain of one thing, though," the professor added, rising from his chair. "She'll turn up again sometime . . . somewhere. Maybe she'll even find her handsome young man, her Lycius. Oh, my," he fretted, taking a few hobbling steps around his desk. "I think I'm going to be just a wee bit stiff tomorrow."

When Valjohn finally departed he and the professor appeared to be the only ones left in the building. It was going on seven; outside the heavy, overcast sky made it look even later. If the Gothic structures of the quad had seemed solemn and foreboding earlier, they were now, in the eerie, premature twilight, totally ghostridden. In every shadowed arch and corner lurked menacing phantom figures. The buildings themselves seemed to hunch on their foundations, threatening at any moment to come tumbling down.

He quickened his pace to the car. He still was soggy in the crotch from the spilled tea. He carried several books Professor Whittier had loaned him. The professor also had jotted down a list for further reading.

He found a parking ticket on the windshield of his Volks. He opened the door, set the books down on the passenger seat, climbed in. Where to go? What to do? The library? But first a bite to eat. He had not eaten since grabbing a hurried lunch at Mr. Dick's, and he was starving. As he sped north on the outer drive, he watched the parking ticket, bright yellow pinned under a wiper blade, flutter and tug in the wind like a trapped butterfly.

He ate at O'Banion's, a small Wabash Avenue grill. Some chili, a ground sirloin steak, an order of fries. A second order of fries. For dessert he had a piece of deep-dish cherry pie à la mode washed down with a glass of milk. He'd risen to leave, was about to pay his check when he spied a slice of watermelon in a display cooler behind the counter. He sat back down and ordered it.

It was after eight by the time he entered the downtown library. He checked out several books on the professor's list and retired, along with the books the professor had given him, to a reading room. He remained there bent over a table in a state of morbid fascination until closing time.

He read about the lamia spirit in a published M.A. thesis by Edward Irwin. He learned still more identities; Lamia surfaced again and again in the various folklores of the world. She was Melusine in French literature during the Middle Ages. Her husband, Raymond, spying on her one day through a keyhole in the seclusion of her bedroom, discovered she was half woman, half serpent. She fled his scorn, leaving the impression of her foot where it still may be seen in the stone walkway at the palace of Lusignan. She appeared as Manto in Switzerland, Jomfruen in Denmark, the widow from the Vale of Taff in Wales. In Scotland she was known as the "Laidley Worm of Spindleston Houghs."

He read *The Lady of the Land* by the nineteenth-century poet William Morris, a familiar legend about a young Greek sailor falling in love with a beautiful maiden who lived alone in a castle, crumbling and overgrown, on a jungle island. She told him that because of a curse she was forced to live all but this one day each year as a hideous monster. She also told him that if he would kiss her after she'd changed into her loathsome alter ego, the curse would be broken. Her love, beauty, all her treasures would be his. He returned the next day, but coming face to face with the monster, he lost his nerve and ran away. Three days later he died a raving madman.

Valjohn felt a tap on his shoulder. He straightened with a start.

"Sorry, I didn't mean to frighten you, sir," said an elderly, stooped librarian. "Closing time was announced ten minutes ago. You'll have to be leaving now."

Outside the building he decided to continue his reading in a motel room. He got into his car again and drove north on Michigan Avenue bound for the Holiday Manor Inn. He simply didn't feel up to facing Crescent tonight.

He must have been daydreaming. He wasn't on Michigan Avenue anymore; he was making a right-hand turn off Broadway onto Oakdale, and the familiar graystone building with the wrought-iron steps on his left certainly wasn't the Holiday Manor. He'd driven home!

Nothing like being a creature of habit, he thought with a smile. No reason he couldn't turn around, though. The motel was only ten minutes away. He drove on to Sheridan Road. Heading south, he let his mind wander, reflecting again on the events of the day. . . .

Ten minutes later he suddenly discovered that he was making a right-hand turn off Broadway onto Oakdale Avenue.

Once more he'd found his way home! This time he was genuinely unnerved.

I'll try one more time, he thought, circling the block twice looking for a place to park. He found one around the corner on Pine Grove. He took it.

"I'll try one more time," he ordered himself aloud. He sat staring straight ahead, unmoving, the engine running. A few minutes passed. He sighed, turned off the ignition, removed the key, rolled up his window. Suddenly he felt very tired.

"Come on, Mercutius or Lycius or whoever the hell I'm supposed to be," he muttered as he climbed out of the car. "Let's not keep a legend waiting."

He shortly learned that he'd kept the legend's dinner waiting as well. For almost four hours.

"See that little white object hanging on the wall there?" Crescent said after greeting him with the briefest of smiles. "It's called a telephone. A marvel of communication. You pick it up and you put a finger in those silly little holes there and you dial a number—our number, for instance. You dial our number and then you speak in one end and say things like, 'Hello, dear, I'm sorry but I won't be home till late tonight,' or even 'I won't be home at all.' And then you'll hear an understanding voice answer at the other end, 'Fine. That's okay. I won't cook dinner at the usual time. I won't fix something fragile like a cheese herb soufflé and lamb patties in sauce au cari. We can have it another night. Thank you for calling. Thank you for being so kind and considerate.' Then all you have to do is hang up. It's really that simple."

"I . . . I'm sorry. I'm sorry," he mumbled lamely with downcast eyes. Even when she was angry with him, scolding him, her voice seemed to lull his gnawing dread. It was as though nothing terrible really had happened, ever could happen.

"It's . . . I've been under a lot of pressure lately," he blurted bravely, looked up. She hadn't heard him; she was back in the kitchen busily reheating food.

He thought to call out to her that it wasn't necessary to make dinner, that he'd already eaten. He thought, but he didn't speak. It probably would only upset her further. Besides, judging from the sounds his stomach was starting to make, his earlier repast was little more than a memory now.

"Need any help?"

She shook her head. "Go sit down—you look exhausted. I'll bring in a tray."

He was exhausted. Wearily he made his way to the living-room couch and plopped himself down among the soft, yielding cushions. It had been a long day. It almost felt good to be home. It did feel good.

"I'm sorry for being such a shrew," said Crescent as she entered the room, carrying a large tray of steaming food. Miraculously the soufflé had maintained its billowy peak.

"I forgive you for not calling. Will you forgive me for being so nasty?"

Valjohn gazed up at the incredible concentration of love, of loveliness smiling down at him.

Let the poets say whatever they please
Of the sweets of Faeries, Goddesses,

349

There is not such a treat among them all,
Haunters of cavern, lake, and waterfall,
As a real woman, lineal indeed
From Pyrrha's pebbles or old Adam's seed.

Keats' verse ran through his mind.
"Will you forgive me, John?"
"There's nothing to forgive," he said and he heard his stomach growl
like a wolf at some distant, unlocked door.

20

"So how do you explain it?"

He was sitting in Superintendent Gordon's office. On his left sat Lieutenant Harris, head tilted down, staring at his feet. On his right were Captain Howland, First Deputy Superintendent James Shroeder and Hans Glad—all of them staring at him. Gordon, leaning forward on both elbows, hunched behind his desk, a haggard face held motionless between his hands. The room's atmosphere, though heavy with tension, was remarkably breathable. There were no miasmic clouds of smoke hanging from the ceiling. The furnaces of the Ruhr had shut down; not a single pipe lay smoldering. Nor did Gordon make any move to light one. He too was staring at Valjohn.

"John, I think Captain Howland has asked you a fair question," the superintendent finally intervened in a slow, painful voice. "Do you have an explanation?"

Valjohn fought to keep from smiling at the guarded understatement: Howland's "fair question" referred to the pair of dark glasses lying on Gordon's desk. And the pair that was not there.

Harris, it seems, had initialed the originals in a corner of the frame. When the young detective visited the lab, he soon discovered that not only did the glasses lack prints of any kind—they lacked his identifying mark as well.

351

And Lady Macbeth was caught with her pants down.

Valjohn glanced over at Harris, who still sat with downcast eyes. The lieutenant held his hands together on his lap, the fingers of one hand nervously drumming on the knuckles of the other. He knew Greg felt bad about blowing the whistle on him. Valjohn felt bad himself for having dragged Greg into the mess. He could just imagine the ass-chewing Howland must have given him for releasing evidence to a *persona non grata*. And things could get a lot hotter for his ex-assistant if Valjohn chose to challenge his story.

He turned his gaze slowly to include the others. Howland was on the edge of his chair, leering—an attack dog straining at the leash, fangs bared, sensing the kill.

"John, are these the glasses Lieutenant Harris gave you or not?" Gordon asked sharply. His patience was beginning to wear thin.

Valjohn looked at them lying in the middle of Gordon's big leather blotter. The originals probably were halfway to the Mississippi by now, not that it mattered; they might just as well be there on the desk too, for all to see. Broken, wet and incriminating.

"No, sir, they're not."

"Are these the glasses you submitted to the lab?"

"Yes, sir."

"All right, I want you to weigh your words very carefully before you answer my next question, John," cautioned Gordon, apparently weighing his own words with great care. "This could be an extremely serious point, an extremely serious offense you'll be conceding.

"Did . . . you . . . switch . . . glasses? Did . . . you . . . willfully . . . break . . . the chain . . . of evidence?"

The chain of evidence. Valjohn's thoughts thumbed back through the pages of his textbooks:

An invisible linkage or chain stretches out . . . . the investigator must preserve the integrity of that linkage, that no evidence be adulterated by mutilation, pollution or alteration. . . . If the democratic processes of justice are to prevail, this chain must remain inviolable.

Amen.

"Yes," Valjohn said without so much as a flutter in his voice. "I switched the glasses; I willfully broke the chain."

"But why, for godsakes?" blurted Gordon.

Valjohn shrugged, stared up at the ceiling in silence.

"For what possible reason?" These last words were spoken as if from far away, as if the superintendent were peering down into the opening of a very deep well and calling to someone who'd just fallen in.

"Do you have the other glasses?" A tremor of hope had entered his voice. He was lowering a rope. Perhaps things still could be set aright. Now, if Valjohn would only grab hold and pull himself up, hand over hand . . .

"No, sir, I'm afraid I don't."

"Where are they? Wha'd you do with 'em?" growled Howland, trying to keep him at bay.

Gordon silenced the captain with a withering glance. "Where are the glasses now, John?"

Valjohn hesitated for a moment. Then he spoke, surprising himself with his answer. "I lost them."

Howland snorted. Glad smiled. Harris crossed his legs.

"Lost them? How did you do that? Where?"

"In the car, I guess."

"The car?"

"My car."

"What were they doing in your car? Lieutenant Harris has already told us that he gave them to you in the building. In the lobby. He says you were going to take them to the lab. He saw you enter the elevator."

"That's true," said Valjohn. "But I forgot about them. I guess I was upset—being taken off the case and everything." If he were going to be evasive, he might as well make it good. "Anyway, the folder they were in must have gotten mixed up with some other papers I took home that night."

"But how did you lose them in the car?"

"That part I don't know. I must have dropped them when I carried everything into the house. I left the car unlocked. Maybe they were stolen that night."

"Somebody stole 'em, all right—you did!"

Howland no longer could contain his anger.

This time there was no reproaching glance from Gordon. Instead he only heaved a loud sigh, took a moment to rub his moon-sad eyes, then proceeded.

"Am I to understand that you substituted these for the glasses Lieutenant Harris gave you because you lost them—because you were . . . embarrassed?"

Valjohn lowered his eyes. How far was he going to let this nonsense continue? Why didn't he just own up? Why didn't he just tell them the other glasses were crawling with his prints, and if they wanted, he'd be the Reaper for them? Full confession. Not that it would stick . . . Or should he announce that he'd already cracked the case? He could lead them to the killer right now, surround himself with blue uniforms, cordon off Oakdale Avenue and lay siege to his own apartment, bellow into a bullhorn: *Come on out with your hands on your head; we know you're in there!*

"I know it sounds stupid," he was telling them. "It *was* stupid. An idiotic thing to do. Moronic. Crazy. I just panicked. Thought I could get away with it, that's all."

353

"That's all, my ass!" exploded Howland. "I know goddamn well why you lost them glasses!"

Gordon turned. "Tell us what you know, Captain."

"Well, sir, as I see it, it's just your plain and simple case of professional jealousy. Hot-shit there—excuse me—Lieutenant Valjohn, the cubicle cop or whatever they call him, he couldn't stand the idea of a major break-through coming along right after he'd been dumped . . . uh, removed from the investigation, sir. He's always been scared of being upstaged by Lieutenant Sweeney. He's always been jealous of him."

"Jealous of Lieutenant Sweeney?"

"His experience in the field, sir. His popularity in the department too. Like I say, I think it sort of got to him an' he flipped. Even my secretary, she said he was coming on funny at her a couple of days ago—like a weirdo, she said."

Gordon cleared his throat. "You're suggesting he got rid of the glasses out of spite?"

Howland nodded vigorously. "You bet I am! And it wouldn't surprise me a bit if he dusted them glasses himself before he got rid of 'em. Probably knows right now who the killer is."

The room fell silent. Everyone was studying Valjohn.

Valjohn crossed his legs, wondering what weirdo things he'd said to Howland's secretary. He couldn't remember anything from that day.

"Well, I intend to get to the bottom of this," Gordon finally said. "Whatever the reasons. In the meantime—Jim, Max, Lieutenant Harris—I think that's all for now."

After the men had left the room, Gordon continued. "All right, John, would you care to go into this in a little more detail?"

"Respectfully not, sir."

"Would you speak more freely if Hans weren't here?"

Valjohn shrugged. "I'm sorry, sir."

"I see." Gordon set his pipe down beside the dark glasses. "I don't for one minute believe Captain Howland's interpretation of your actions—I think I know you better than that, John."

"Thank you, sir."

"Nor do I believe your own."

Glad smiled, cleared his throat.

The next step seemed perfectly obvious to Valjohn. "I think it might be best then if I tender my resignation."

"Under normal circumstances I'd demand it." Gordon exchanged glances with Glad. "However, at the present time both Hans and I feel that your resignation following so closely your removal from the case . . . well, it would only serve to draw more attention to you and this whole embarrassing mess."

Valjohn nodded.

"The offer I made you the other day, the leave of absence for health

354

reasons—I'm no longer asking you to consider it. I'm ordering you to take it."

It is night and he is lying beside her in bed. He has been asleep for some time, two, three hours, maybe longer. Crescent is asleep. She lies on her back motionless, except for her gentle, even breathing.

Suddenly he is aware of another presence in the room. It is too dark to see, but someone is there. He is sure of it, can sense whoever it is moving about.

A faint winnowing sound traverses the room—like the soft quiver of wings flying back and forth. And, of course, that must be it. A bird has trapped itself, flown in through the open window and can't find its way out again. A swallow or a nighthawk or maybe a bat. He tries to spot its fluttering shape as his eyes grow accustomed to the dark.

He will have to do something. He will have to get up and capture it, release it out the window before it injures itself—

And he is not moving, cannot move. He has once again been turned to stone! He can see now; his eyes have penetrated the gloom. And it is not a swallow or a nighthawk that has flown into the room. It is not a bat.

Crescent, his wife who is lying beside him . . . only even as she is lying there she is not there. It is she who is moving about the room—not on wings—but her head held aloft, gliding through the darkness on the great stalk of a serpent neck! She is the lamia: Melusine, Jomfruen, Manto, Su Chen, the Laidley Worm and all the rest! Her shoulders have dwindled to a memory. Her mythic soul has uncoiled, stretched out from the rest of her slumbering form, now sweeps across his field of vision, dipping and lifting from wall to wall, the rhythmic breathing of her sleep resounding from every corner of the room.

She lolls beneath the foot of the bed, arches to the ceiling, hovers directly above him. Her face is unrecognizable, monstrous: It is shrunken, wedged back into a snake's head—flat, adderlike. Her rhythmic breathing has slid into a pulsing hiss.

He waits, eyes wide open, beyond terror.

She swoops low, veers, strikes his pillow, narrowly missing him, and slithers away.

In the next instant her snake head has thrust itself through the open window, descends to the street below; her scaly neck runs over the sill, droning loudly as an anchor rope plunging over the gunnel of a boat.

Her coils extrude into the night. She fills the streets, absorbs them. Girdling the entire city, she tightens her grip. She is a constrictor, a colossal python flexing her cervical might. Pavement buckles; buildings crack and burst; people scream, are crushed like ants. Valjohn is screaming. . . .

"That was exciting."
"What?"

"You just ran two red lights in a row back there. I thought for a moment you were going to try for three," Crescent spoke as they came to a halt, a huge semi thundering across a busy intersection in front of them.

"Uhm . . . sorry," said Valjohn, nervously revving the motor, waiting for the light to change. "Daydreaming, I guess."

The light turned green. He continued to sit there revving the motor. A car behind him honked. He popped forward, wound through the gears keeping abreast of a big, beige Imperial that was attempting to pass on the right.

"What's that on the windshield?"

He glanced at the parking ticket still stuck under his wiper blade. Though it fluttered in his field of vision every day—a trapped butterfly still frantically beating its wings—he hadn't noticed it for weeks. "A parking ticket," he told her. The Imperial pulled away.

"I didn't know cops got parking tickets."

He was silent for several moments. "Only a chosen few," he finally mumbled, his eyes fixed straight ahead on the road.

Another silence followed.

"Is something bothering you?"

He didn't answer.

"Something bothering you, love?"

"What? No . . . nothing—you know, just the usual hassles at work."

"Anything you feel like talking about?"

"No. Really. Nothing like that." He flashed her a quick, reassuring smile, downshifted into third and cut in behind a bus. He sped by the great hulking, charred skeleton of McCormick Place—a vision out of a Peter Blume landscape—swung onto a tightly banked oval ramp and emerged into a heavy flow of traffic on the southbound expressway.

"Lot of people leaving the city tonight," he commented, eager to change the subject. "Maybe they know something we don't."

"Maybe," she said and smiled, "but don't forget, we're leaving too."

And she was right because it was late Friday afternoon and they were on their way to Starved Rock Park for the weekend.

The idea had come to him only a few days ago during dinner when Crescent had told him about her new job. They'd just finished another one of her gourmet entrees—chicken livers Annette—and were well into a particularly ethereal dessert of Charlotte Malakoff when she announced matter-of-factly that the hospital finally had managed to place her in maternity. Starting Monday she'd be working in postpartum and the nursery.

Ethereal or not, the dessert had lodged in his throat. Quietly choking, he washed down a glob of whipped cream and kirsch with Chablis and recalled a passage he'd read from one of Professor Whittier's books, how in England lamias were regarded at one time as witchlike midwives whose specialty was kidnaping newborn infants. And what about the original legend? Lamia, the twisted, demented queen who got her kicks preying on

356

young boys, sucking their blood, afflicting them with wasting diseases . . .

Slow down, he had told himself. He was overreacting. She was a terrific nurse—kind, responsible, dedicated, capable. The other . . . okay, so she had this quirk, this hang-up of hers; so she wasted assholes, degenerate, vicious people. That was no reason to assume she was automatically going to start slaughtering innocent children. My God, he knew her well enough by now. Or did he? Could he ever? And maybe he'd been suspended as a cop, but did that mean he'd been suspended as a human being as well? What gave him the right to gamble with the lives of newborn babes?

They arrived at the lodge at eight-o-four—exactly four minutes after the dining room had closed. Also, there were no rooms available. Not a very propitious beginning for their "spur-of-the-moment second honeymoon," but the ending was all that concerned Valjohn, because it was the only solution, the only way out, and he'd finally made up his mind. Just and honorable—there would be no betrayal. He would not call upon the Force. No police, no help or interference from others. It was a personal matter, a private thing to be settled between husband and wife. He would keep it that way. He would deal with it on his own. Simply. Conclusively.

They had to drive back across the Illinois River to a truck stop on Interstate 80, where they got a quick dinner and a motel room.

During the night Valjohn fought to stay awake. They sat up in twin beds watching television. Crescent said she was exhausted and fell soundly asleep before the first guest walked out on "The Johnny Carson Show." Later Valjohn went over to the truck stop for a midnight snack. He returned to the room with a couple of cheeseburgers, fries and a piece of strawberry cream pie.

He watched an Audie Murphy western followed by an evening meditation entitled "Five Minutes to Live By." He switched channels, watched a news wrap-up and the national anthem; switched again, got another news wrap-up, this one followed by a closing benediction recited against a backdrop of the Pacific Fleet steaming to victory, war planes flying in tight formation and a montage of ICBMs blasting heavenward.

He continued watching the set's bright, snowy screen long after the last station had gone off the air.

When he felt himself starting to doze, he got up and took a shower. The shower was wretched: a few scattered needles of lukewarm water that stung no matter where he directed the spray. Nonetheless, it served to wake him, and for that he was thankful. He did not want to fall asleep and face another one of his unsettling nightmares. Not now. Not after coming this far.

While he dried off he glanced at himself in a mirror. The shower had not been hot enough to steam it over, and he could see his reflection all too clearly. It was the first time in ages he'd really looked himself over. What he now saw shocked and embarrassed him.

He shook his head and grabbed at the slack flesh hanging over his hips. Christ, what a roll! He turned sideways, sadly contemplated the bulge.

Even his chest looked flabby—like some pubescent schoolgirl just starting to grow tits.

Well, what the hell did he expect? How could he hope to keep in shape the way he'd been stuffing food down his gullet lately? He shrugged, finished drying himself. Wrapping the towel around his waist, he paused before the mirror one last time.

"Oink, oink."

In the small dressing alcove, he opened his suitcase for a change of clothes. He started to close it, stopped. He glanced over his shoulder to make sure Crescent was still asleep, then ran his hands into the suitcase again. He found a heavy object wrapped in a towel, then slowly, stealthily, uncovered it. He stared at it for several minutes: his service revolver. Then he tucked it snugly away.

They were up bright and early the next day, drove to the lodge for breakfast. Valjohn had finally dozed off for a short time around dawn. He very much regretted it.

"There, there," Crescent had smiled gently, shaking him awake. "I have just the thing for bad dreams." And still smiling she'd crooked her index finger and popped out an eye—both eyes—as easily as if removing contacts. She offered them to him while she sang a strange lilting song that had no words.

He was neither astonished nor afraid.

Still smiling, still singing her strange song, she poured them, liquid, into his outstretched hand where they formed a gleaming pool, dipped her fingertips into the pool and caressed his brow. He stared into his hand, watching the residue of her sight become a dozen tiny beads rolling and scattering like quicksilver across his palm, run together, cleave, swell, solidify into her eyes again. He held them up and watched them refract light like brilliant gems. And then he was in the bathroom, holding them over the toilet, tilting his hand forward, letting them spill through his fingers, "ploop, ploop" into the bowl. They rose slowly in the water, two dead minnows, belly-up and pasty white beneath the surface. He flipped the bright chrome handle and flushed them down.

And he was lying in bed again, and she was asking him to give her back her eyes. And he could not bring himself to tell her what he'd done. He lay perfectly still, not daring to even breathe. And she was pleading with him, stumbling about the room, bumping into furniture. She knocked over a chair, then a lamp; its bulb struck the floor, exploding like a gunshot.

When he had looked into her face, into those two black hollow sockets, he was overcome with sorrow, shame. He was overcome with aching loneliness. More than anything in the world he wished he could give her back her eyes.

And once again he was in the bathroom on his knees by the toilet, moaning as if he were sick, only instead of puking he was plunging a hand into the bowl, jamming it down the narrow porcelain throat as far as his arm would go, his fingers groping, searching . . . desperately . . . blindly. . . .

And it was Crescent herself gently shaking him awake, mercifully delivering him from the anguish of his nightmare. He felt the soothing touch of her cool fingers on his damp, hot brow, waited for her to speak, waited for the haunting words: "There, there—I have just the thing for bad dreams." Only she said nothing, smiled, stroked his hair and looked quietly down at him with her lost, found, loving eyes.

Studying the menu at the lodge, he felt a moment of hesitancy as he recalled the sorry image of himself last night in the motel mirror. A moment—no longer. Then he ordered himself a sizable breakfast, ate it all and half of Crescent's as well.

On the way out, he slipped a small backpack over his shoulders and donned his white golf hat. They paused to study a map of the trails at the main desk, a clerk there asking if he could be of any assistance.

Valjohn explained they were looking for some of the more secluded hiking areas.

"East end of the park's your best bet," the clerk said pointing. "Not many people get up to Tonti Canyon either. They all take the cutoff here for Horseshoe and La Salle."

Tonti Canyon. Valjohn remembered it clearly—the frozen waterfall. He also remembered the bliss of that winter weekend, and he knew instantly that would be the place.

Outside they tramped down the steep west bluff to the campgrounds and the river. They were amazed at the number of people. The large, grassy fields that had been snow-covered and vacant last winter now were overrun with humanity: campers and picnickers, hikers, sunbathers and swimmers, Frisbee players, kite fliers, brawling beer drinkers, bird watchers, rock hounds. A city of tents had sprung up along the river. Paper scattered in the wind. Trash lay strewn about everywhere. A steady stream of cars and buses poured in and out of the parking lot.

At a picnic snack bar, they ordered some food to take on their hike—fried chicken, potato salad, a couple of candy bars. Valjohn produced a plastic canteen from his backpack and asked to have it filled with lemonade.

While they waited for their order, he watched half a dozen motorcycles rumble into the parking lot, followed by a battered green van. They all parked together in front of the snack bar, wheeling their machines to a halt and sit-walking them back against the curb. They appeared to be members of a gang. Most wore cut-off Levi's jackets with the insignia: "The God-fucks CHMC" stitched in spangles on their backs. Two men carrying six-packs climbed out of the van and joined the others. One had shoulder-length hair; the other's head was slick-shaved bald.

"That'll be five eighty-five, sir."

Valjohn returned his attention to the girl who was waiting on him.

Freckle-faced, maybe seventeen, she labored under an explosion of frizzy, carrot-red hair. He paid the check, tipped her generously for filling the canteen, and Crescent helped him slip the loaded backpack onto his shoulders.

One of the cyclists spotted Crescent as they walked across the parking lot, and soon he and his buddies were whistling and hooting. He even jumped off his Harley and pranced after them, howling and slavering. Crescent made the mistake of glancing at him. The man—a short, bearded clown wearing purple earmuffs and a Maltese cross dangling against an exposed, hairless chest—grabbed his crotch, leaped into the air and crumpled to the pavement. The other men roared with laughter.

"A lovely group," said Crescent when once again they were on a trail winding through the woods.

Valjohn grunted, said nothing. He'd already forgotten them.

They hiked for several miles on the main river trail, the number of people dwindling steadily along the way. East of Sandstone Point, they took a cutoff and headed south into the bluffs. After a short time they came to another fork: The main route continued straight ahead to Horseshoe and La Salle Canyon; a much narrower path, however, veered to the right and rose steeply into wooded hills.

A knocked-over signpost lay on its side several feet off the path in some bushes. It read:

TONTI CANYON

1.3 MILES

The sign's arrow pointed straight down in the dirt.

Valjohn led the way.

The clerk in the lodge had been right about the canyon's seclusion. They met no one on the trail now, nor saw any signs of recent use. A large section of the path was overgrown with weeds.

Farther on they came across a massive limb blocking their way. It proved to be half a tree, a giant oak, that had been split down the middle by lightning. They had difficulty pushing through the mesh of branches still thick with green foliage as they clambered over the great splintered trunk.

"I think we'd be better off going around it on the way back," said Crescent. She retucked her blouse in her jeans where it had pulled out and examined her arms for scratches.

Valjohn agreed in a voice so low he said nothing at all.

It seemed considerably hotter and muggier now. Though the high wall of trees on both sides of the path helped shade them from the sun, it also blocked out the cooling river breeze. By the time they climbed over the lower rim of the canyon and descended inside, Valjohn was sweating like a steamfitter. Crescent looked as fresh and cool as ever.

The waterfall was smaller than he remembered it—no less high, but less massive, the cascade of water now appearing but a fraction of last winter's towering pillar of ice.

"Look, a rainbow!" said Crescent, pointing to the base of the cliff where the plummeting stream crashed into jagged rocks. A miniature arc played across the prism of mist that hung in sunlight, fading high up into the waterfall. Failing to emerge on the other side, it appeared to be swept downward, its iridescence dashed against the jagged rocks.

They left the path and scrambled over a limestone shelf that took them closer. There was no way of entering the grotto behind the fall without getting drenched.

"No more icicles," said Crescent, gaily.

Valjohn peered into the recessed archway and remembered how their skin had turned green in the frozen, eerie light. He stared hypnotically now at the rivulets streaming down the rocks. His head was filled with the roar of the fall.

They retreated from the spray and climbed back onto the limestone shelf.

"That looks awfully inviting."

Valjohn turned to Crescent. She was eyeing the rocky basin beneath them, where the water that had welled out from under the cataract formed a wide, deep pool.

It did look inviting, he thought. Blue and crystal clear.

"Why don't we take a quick dip?"

Valjohn looked at her. He reminded her that they hadn't brought swimsuits.

"I'm game if you are," she said. She gave him a wink.

They worked down from the shelf to another ledge, followed it until they could cross a narrow stream, stepping on rocks and a sandbar below the lagoon. Then they climbed back up the other side to a broad rift in the steep rock walls which allowed some of the forest to edge down into the canyon. There they undressed and hung their clothes on the small, crooked limbs of a bordering Judas scrub.

Crescent led the way to the water's edge. He followed at a distance, his eyes riveted to her nakedness. It was not the first time he'd seen her without clothes: There always had been fleeting glimpses in the apartment —the shower, passing in the hallway, dressing in the bedroom. Always fleeting glimpses. Somehow this seemed different. It left him momentarily shaken.

At the sandstone rim of the pool, she stood on one foot and dangled the other into the water. She turned, smiled at him. He endured the exquisite profile of her beauty.

"It's wet," she said, laughing, and withdrew her foot, shaking droplets over the water.

Self-consciously he folded his arms across his middle.

She took a step back, then leaped forward, executing a standing ballet entrance—arms outstretched, legs scissored apart, so that plunging, she sank no lower than her shoulders. In that brief instant while she hung between land and water, legs apart, he saw from behind the faint tumescence where she came together, a hint of golden down: the glowing nimbus of her sex.

He was suddenly overcome with jealous rage. He envied all of them—the low-life vermin, the rapists and murderers—she'd given herself to. No matter their pleasures had cost them their lives. Would he not gladly give his own life to consummate that loveliness? He felt bitter, used, fatuous.

And then he felt excited. He glanced down to see the vestigial appendage of his forgotten manhood stirring, throbbing.

Crescent, treading water, waved at him. "Brrr . . . Come on in, the water's fine!"

He didn't need a second invitation. Setting his jaw, he hurtled headlong into her wake.

The shock of the cold water cleared his head with a jolt. His heart pounded; his chest was in a vise. He felt his whole system recoil from the chilling embrace. He remained submerged as long as he could bear it.

"There you are!" she exclaimed when at last he came up for air. "I was starting to worry—thought maybe you'd hit your head on a rock. Either that or grown gills."

They swam back and forth a few times across a small expanse of deep water. On the other side of the basin they discovered several underground springs; they could feel with their toes the icy currents rippling up through the rocks. The water was invigorating but too cold to withstand for long. About to call it quits, they ventured under the fall. A pleasant surprise: The water was much warmer coming off the cliff. "Rainbow heat," said Crescent. They gloried in the downpour, diving and kicking about, splashing at one another like children in a giant shower. They didn't come out until they were thoroughly exhausted.

Valjohn retrieved a towel from the backpack and they shared it. When Crescent had finished drying herself she handed it to him. He did his best to look away. She made no move to get dressed. She said she was sleepy, how good the sun felt and why didn't they just leave their clothes off for a while and do a little sunbathing? It was so peaceful here, and they had it all to themselves . . . ?

Why not, thought Valjohn, adjusting the towel around his waist. It wasn't in the script, but it might work out fine. At this point it was all ad lib anyway. . . . He was puzzled by her sudden loss of modesty. He had no idea what it meant, nor was he about to tie his mind in knots trying to figure it out. That's why he was here, he told himself—because he was through trying to figure things out. He had an answer, not an explanation. And the time had come to realize it.

While Crescent searched for a place to lie down, he slipped into his trousers. The towel had proven inadequate, failed to conceal his weak flesh, his manhood once more asserting itself, untimely and autonomous, between his legs.

She located a suitable spot, a large slab of sandstone at the edge of the copse. The slab rose from a tangled bed of bellworts and maidenhair, jack-in-the-pulpits. Its smooth surface tilted gently down toward the water. A thick canopy of bittersweet vines clung to several small trees nearby, shielding it from the trail.

She asked for the towel again. He handed it to her and she spread it out on the stone beneath her head. Lying on her back, she fanned out her long, wet hair.

"I guess we used up all the rainbow," she said, then shut her eyes.

Valjohn glanced at the fall. The same mist hung above the water and rocks, but the sun had shifted overhead, leaving the lower end of the canyon in shadow. Still avoiding her with his eyes, he lay down beside her.

He stared up at the sky, his head propped above the stone on his hands. He tried to keep his mind a blank, tried not to visualize what came next. If she could read his mind . . .

Not think, but do!

He rolled over on his right side and reached into the backpack that lay just off the slab. His fingers quickly found what they were searching for: the Colt Python. He felt its hard, bare steel lying wedged between the bag of chicken, which had torn open at the bottom, and a folded plastic poncho. The revolver had been rolled up in the towel Crescent now rested upon. Without hesitating he pulled the gun out, lay over on his back again, holding the weapon out of sight, pressed against his right thigh.

Not think, but do—

He froze. She was touching him. She had seized his left hand. He swallowed hard, gulped air. Then slowly, terrified, he turned his head to face her.

He swallowed again, took another deep breath and relaxed. She was lying there as before, still resting, eyes still closed, a blissful expression on her face. Her right hand, which held his left, squeezed it gently with parenthetical affection.

He stared at the sky again, the gun at his side.

Not think, but do.

Only he couldn't move. He lay there paralyzed, trembling. He could not *not think.* He lacked the necessary *sang-froid;* he lacked the self-command that would allow him to act swiftly on the impetus of the moment, to charge through to the conclusion of a feverish week's planning. . . .

Which was to place the muzzle of the gun he now held in his hand to his wife's temple and blow her brains out; then turn the gun on himself, shove the barrel in his mouth and follow her into oblivion!

Though his mind was already made up—totally and irrevocably—he would have to muster all his strength and determination, right down to the wire, if the deed were to be done . . . if the deed could be done. . . .

Which he had no way of knowing. Maybe she was illusion—pure as Lycius's intended bride; maybe the bullet would go through her like so much smoke. Or maybe she'd transform herself, absorbing the gunshot as if it were nothing more than a beesting.

In any event, he would shoot himself on the spot. And to him—he could be sure—the bullet would be no beesting. He was loaded for bear. Egil Heintz would be proud of him. He'd picked up a box of .357 magnums yesterday and stuffed six of the brutal cartridges into the cylinder last night.

Lying there for some time, afraid to look away from the sky, he felt her grip on his hand slowly relax. He paused, glanced at her. Her hand still was there resting on his, but limp and open. Her face was slightly turned away, her lips parted. Apparently she had dozed off.

He lifted the revolver and rolled over on his side facing her. The gun felt immense and obscene in his hand. He spied a glob of potato salad on the raised rib of the barrel, wiped it clean on his pantleg. Then he pointed it at Crescent's head, cringed at the thought of what those high-velocity hollow-points would do at such short range to flesh and blood.

And at this particular moment Crescent looked very much flesh and blood.

Still holding the gun to her head, he let his eyes finally take her in a slow, deliberate gaze. Her hair, still wet, flowed upon the towel like strands of raw buckwheat honey. He avoided her face, fearing his stare might somehow awake her. Panning down the length of her basking nakedness, he pondered what had never been his.

Her beauty had taken on a curious guise. In the bright sunlight her skin looked pale, almost translucent. Her breasts spilled flat and unassuming on her chest. At her nipples he could detect a delicate network of veins. The longer he stared the more minutely detailed he perceived her. It was if he were looking through some giant magnifying glass: Every pore became visible, every nevus, every pit and bump, every hint of blemish. No longer was her loveliness so dazzling and flawless, so assertive and absolute. Instead it had become poignant with imperfection, and he was filled with an overriding sense of her own mortality—her frailty, her vulnerability.

Eyes brimming with tears, he barely glanced at the tufted crest between her legs. Once more he fastened his attention on the gun and what he demanded of it. He felt himself weakening. He wrestled to withstand the sudden surge of countering emotion she'd unlocked within him.

Get on with it! he shouted to himself. Enough deliberation. Everything was going his way. What more could he ask for? Their second honeymoon —here in the park where they'd once known happiness . . . alone . . . she sleeping contentedly . . . waiting for deliverance . . . For God's sake give it to her!

He cocked the gun, avoiding the noisy click of its mechanism by depressing the trigger momentarily while he drew back the hammer with his thumb. He took aim—though the muzzle was only inches from her head —squinted down the sights to the soft-spun target of her right temple.

His index finger tightened on the wide-grooved trigger. A fraction of an inch and it would all be over; 1.6 pounds of pull according to the manual —a jerk, a flinch, a small beckoning waver. . . .

The explosion was deafening. But even as he felt his ears ringing, heard the magnum report echoing off the canyon walls, saw bits of bone, blood, hair and scalp spray the stone, he didn't believe—realized with gunshot clarity how futile was his scheme. That he could never pull the trigger—

A recoil of nerves jerked his hand away, the smokeless barrel pointing toward the sun, the hammer still pulled back, poised, waiting to strike. . . .

—that he could no more kill her than kill the love he felt.

Overhead a squirrel began a loud, squabbling chatter. He looked up. A blue jay flitted into view on a nearby limb, then flew off. The squirrel fell silent. Valjohn swung the gun around, pressed it to his own head.

She might be out of range, but there was no reason he couldn't blow himself away. He was a sitting duck: point-blank sick to death of himself!

"Mmm . . . mmm . . ."

His finger wilted on the trigger.

Crescent had awakened, was yawning, stretching her arms languorously over her head.

"Wow, that swim really did me in!"

He felt his hand with the gun drop to his side. He debated hurling the useless weapon into the lagoon, slid it instead out of sight beneath his leg.

"How long did I nap?"

Her eyes were open now, gazing at him with sleepy innocence. He was sure they were mocking him.

"Not long."

"Well, I don't know about you, but I think I've had enough sun for one day." She yawned again, feeling how dry her hair was. She reached for her clothing.

Again dressed, they ate their picnic lunch, then started the hike back down. It was a long, silent march. Valjohn felt as though he'd just climbed out of his own grave. How could he go on from here? He was an actor who'd missed his exit cue; now he was left stranded on center stage.

They joined a number of other people returning west on the main trail along the river. By the time the Devil's Nose came into view, the sun had slipped behind the ridge. A thin scud of clouds hung over the river's horizon. On the south side of Starved Rock, they discovered a branch trail that led up a steep bluff to the lodge via French Canyon. They decided it would be a shortcut back to the car and took it.

They'd plodded up the trail little more than a few hundred feet when they heard a commotion in the distance below: a woman's cries followed by several loud shouts. Muffled through the trees it seemed to be coming from the direction of the lower campground. Next they heard what sounded like a gunshot.

They stopped and looked at one another. A second shot rang out. There were several long moments of silence, a scream, then more shouting.

"Stay here," said Valjohn, and he started down the trail at a fast jog. He met people coming up; they made room for him to pass, shook their heads gravely, continued on their way.

When he reached the main trail, he turned left and headed toward the campground. Rounding a bend, he encountered a family standing by a narrow path which led to a lavatory shelter. The father pressed his two small children against his legs, shielding them from the direction of the lavatory. The mother stood nearby, holding a cocker spaniel on a leash.

"Over there," the man nodded to Valjohn. He offered no further explanation, then turned away.

Valjohn looked in the lavatory. Both doors swung open. No one was inside. He circled the small building, spied a figure lying on the ground some thirty yards away at the edge of heavy thickets. He ran to it, found a young man sprawled face down in the weeds. Valjohn carefully rolled the young man over.

Stabbed. There were numerous puncture wounds in his chest and abdominal cavity; the T-shirt he wore was a sopping rag of blood. His face had been slashed; so had his throat. Several deep cuts on his arms indicated a struggle with his attacker. A trail of blood and broken branches showed where he'd crawled along the ground for five or six yards.

None of the wounds spurted blood. There was no pulse.

"He's dead, isn't he?" a voice called out from deeper in the thickets.

Valjohn, kneeling, turned to see who'd spoken—instead saw Crescent making her way past him into the thickets.

"Crescent! Hey! Wait up!" he called to her. Scrambling to his feet, he went after her, shaking his head. An hour ago he was ready to blow her brains out; now he was yelling for her to be careful.

The thickets were slow going, dense with underbrush and fallen logs. After several yards, however, the scrubwood opened into a pocket clearing at the foot of a high, rocky bluff. A towheaded girl was bent over a young woman by a stump. The woman was nude except for one green knee sock collapsed around her ankle. Glassy-eyed with a large gash on the side of her head, she barely supported herself on all fours. Her lower lip was split, her nose bleeding. She also was bleeding between her legs. Bits of rotten bark and moss clung to the bare skin of her buttocks. The towheaded girl steadied her with both hands.

Crescent, immediately taking charge, succeeded in getting the woman to quit struggling and lie down. There was a stab wound in her chest. It foamed as she labored to breathe. The piercing instrument had missed her heart, apparently puncturing a lung. As she tossed her head about, choking and coughing on blood, she repeated the name "Roger" over and over in a low whisper.

Valjohn removed a poncho from the backpack and helped Crescent cover the woman with it. Crescent sat down on the ground and lifted the woman's head into her lap to ease her breathing. Meanwhile Valjohn learned from the girl what had happened.

Her name was Bobbie Talbert. It was her voice he'd heard from beyond the thickets. Thin and gawky, maybe twelve, she pointed to the rocky bluff across the clearing; she'd seen everything from up there, where she'd been climbing around taking pictures. A camera still dangled from her neck.

Two men had grabbed the young woman outside the lavatory where she was waiting for her boy friend and dragged her to the edge of the brush. Her boy friend, hearing her screams, came running to the rescue. One of the men went for him with a knife. That was her boy friend, Roger, lying dead in the weeds.

"Then they dragged her here; they tore off her clothes and started . . . you know . . . doing stuff to her."

Bobbie Talbert's eyes filled with tears, and Valjohn put an arm around her trembling shoulders, told her she didn't have to talk anymore.

"I couldn't move. I couldn't stop looking—they were so *mean* to her!"

She was sobbing and sniffling. Valjohn turned her from the sight of the woman in Crescent's lap and walked her slowly away.

She said one of the men had hit the woman over the head with a gun. Afterward, when they were pulling up their pants and laughing, the one with the knife stabbed her. Then they took off running.

"I was too scared to climb down right away. . . ."

Her words were interrupted by the loud report of another gunshot.

Valjohn spun around, looked at Crescent. She stared at him, her face gone strangely blank—so blank, in fact, so void of any expression that for one absolutely insane moment he thought it was no face at all.

"I . . . I think I better see what's going on."

She nodded. The woman in her lap closed her eyes, whimpered softly.

"You'll be all right here?"

Crescent continued nodding.

Her face was fading again—a picture with no detail, the roughed-in sketch of a portrait. He had to look away. He ran over, picked up his backpack where he'd dropped it in a clump of thistles. He handed Bobbie Talbert the canteen, gave her a hug, told her she was a brave girl. Then he was crashing back through the underbrush toward the main trail.

Not a hundred yards from the lavatory he came upon another body, this one sprawled along the trail. A park ranger with two gunshot wounds, one in the chest; another in the head, from very close range—execution style.

And he was running again, reaching into his backpack, fumbling for the revolver while he ran. He tossed the backpack away, tucked the gun under his belt, where it dug into his stomach. He pulled it out and carried it in his hand.

Chances are they were gone by now. . . . Maybe not, though . . .

He came over a small rise and could see the end of the woods ahead. The trail was deserted. Everyone must have fled up the ridge.

Not everyone. He spotted a small cluster of people off to his left by some picnic tables and loped across the grass to talk to them. Seeing him, they flushed like a covey of quail—several through the trees, one couple diving under a table.

The gun. He'd forgotten he was holding it in his hand.

"I'm a police officer!" he blurted, lowering the pistol to his side. "It's all right! It's okay! Police officer."

They slowly returned. "Thank God!" cried one woman. "It's about time," muttered another. A few men laughed uneasily. Most of them kept their eyes fixed on the gun.

Valjohn, fighting to catch his breath, asked if they'd seen a couple of men running by, acting suspicious.

"Suspicious?" snorted a large, burly man, straightening up from behind a trash barrel. "Is a bullet in the arm suspicious enough for you?" He wore a brightly flowered Hawaiian shirt open down the front, held a wadded T-shirt pressed against his right bicep. His lower arm was drenched with blood.

"Them sons-of-bitches shot me! We was eating here and they come running along the trail there just like you and one of them yells, 'Happy birthday, turkeys!' and he hauls off and shoots me just like that. They . . . we . . . he just hauls off and shoots me! He could as likely a killed me! Any of us—my wife, my kids . . ." He tried to raise his arm, made a face. "I never been shot before."

"What did they look like?"

"The one with the gun was bald. Not bald bald, but, you know, bald like his head was shaved. The other guy—"

Valjohn was off and running again. He left the trail where it emerged from the woods, staying hidden behind the tree line that bordered the east side of the parking lot.

He could see the top of the battered green van. It was still sitting in front of the snack bar. He climbed a small outcrop of rock to get a better view. The motorcycles were gone. He scanned up and down the rows of parked cars, but there was no sign of the two men. Maybe they'd abandoned the van, taken off with the rest of the gang on bikes. . . .

And maybe that was them standing by a sno-cone vendor between the lot and the river. No doubt about it. He could see the bald head gleaming in the sunlight. A woman stood next to them. There were children. . . .

Presently the woman screamed.

Valjohn leaped from the rock, pitched forward when he landed, jamming the gun into the ground. He scrambled to his feet, sprinted down the nearest row of parked cars, blowing dirt from the muzzle.

Too late. He arrived to find the vendor's shiny metal ice chest knocked over, the woman lying unconscious on the ground, surrounded by crying children. The vendor, a small teenage boy in a striped apron, knelt beside her. She had a nasty cut running down her forehead and across the bridge of her nose.

Valjohn swung around half hidden by the cars, saw the men sauntering off in the direction of their van. The bald-headed one carried a child—a tot—under his right arm. They didn't bother to look back.

Valjohn raised the gun, aimed at the man with the child. Then at his long-haired companion. The gun wavered in his hand. He was trembling all over, gasping for breath. His eyes stung, blurred with sweat. No way. Forget it. He was no Wyatt Earp. He couldn't risk hitting the kid. He would have to get a hell of a lot closer.

He lowered the gun, turned his attention back to the scene left in their wake. The boy, trying to revive the woman, had scooped up a handful of crushed ice that lay spilled in piles on the grass and was rubbing it gently against her cheeks. She started to moan. Two of the children, both pre-schoolers, were bawling their heads off. A third, older girl stood with her arms folded across her front, silent, staring down in a daze at the moaning woman.

"They snatched her kid," said the boy in the striped apron, looking up at Valjohn.

"I think they're on their way to rob the snack bar."

Valjohn started to speak, then realized he didn't have time.

Hunched over, threading his way through two rows of parked cars, he dashed down a lane paralleling the path taken by the suspects. He came to a halt by a red Dodge pickup, eased himself between it and a closely parked motor home. Peering over the bed of the pickup, he could see the two men standing in front of their van.

They seemed to be arguing. The long-haired one was nervous and wanted to split. He climbed into the driver's seat, slamming the door behind him and gesturing the other man to get in.

No-hair shook his head. He said something in a fit of anger and shoved the child, who was kicking and crying, up through the window to his grumbling companion. Then No-hair checked his gun, an automatic, and trotted around the van toward the snack bar.

As Valjohn stood motionless gripping the fender of the pickup with his free hand, he raced through his options. There was nothing he could do about the holdup. If he chased after No-hair now, he'd be spotted from the van and squander the element of surprise. And Long-hair held the child.

Valjohn backed his way out from between the two vehicles. Keeping very low, he scuttled like a crab to the far end of the lot. There he crossed over the one remaining lane and doubled back behind the same line of cars in which the van was parked.

A Ford Falcon stood between him and the van. An empty space where the motorcycles had been parked, maybe ten yards wide, separated the two vehicles. The pavement was strewn with beer cans. He barely had time to hunker down behind the Falcon's trunk before the screen door to the snack bar burst open.

No-hair appeared, gun in one hand, a girl in the other. Valjohn recognized her—the same girl who'd filled his canteen with lemonade earlier. Her captor had hold of her frizzy red hair and was dragging her outside behind him. A cashier's pouch bulged under his belt.

"Goddamnit, Denny, no! Leave her!" The man in the van was shouting out the window.

"We got a hostage, you ignorant numbnuts!"

No-hair, ignoring Long-hair's protests, led the girl around to the other side of the vehicle. She stumbled along, grimacing.

Valjohn tensed, flushed. If he was going to act, it would have to be soon. He rose slightly from his crouch, keeping them in view through the windows of the Falcon. He still had surprise going for him; a few steps carefully taken and he'd have position as well.

No-hair gave the girl's head a vicious yank downward when he reached the passenger door. She dropped to her knees, rattling the beer cans on the pavement.

"Ho, little piggy-bitch! Like to get down there and snort choad for old Denny? Sure you would."

He let go of her hair, pulled his arm away and she fell forward. With his hand free he turned to open the door.

Now or never, thought Valjohn. He sprang up, lurched around the rear of the car.

No-hair, opening the door, didn't hear Valjohn's movement behind him over the scrape of rusty hinges. He reached back down with his right hand, grabbed the girl by her hair and started to drag her up into the van. The gun in his other hand hung at his side.

Valjohn had his own gun raised, aimed. Once again it shook uncontrollably: The front sight danced across the entire breadth of the man's back. He steadied it with both hands, narrowed the waver to a span between the vowels, the "o" and the "u," of the spangled emblem stitched on the man's soiled denim vest.

Suddenly the gun became rigid, welded fast in his grasp. He felt as if his hands had been caught in some piece of enormous machinery. He could not let go, could not extricate his fingers from a vast mesh of unseen gears and pulleys. The front sight zeroed in on the irreverent "f."

"Free . . . freeze!" he bawled out, drawing back the hammer to punctuate his command.

The man let go of the girl's hair immediately; she pitched forward again at his feet. He remained motionless for several seconds, then turned to face his adversary. There was nothing jerky or abrupt in his movement, nothing frantic or aggressive. He swung around slowly, almost nonchalantly. His shoulders sagged. A submissive smile played at the corners of his mouth.

Valjohn understood in an instant what was expected of him; what was happening and what was going to happen.

He was a boy once again hovering over the drunken figure of his father's slayer, Skip Burkhardt. He was running away down an empty street, the fishing knife still tucked under his shirt where his fingers had refused to grasp it, draw it out and plunge it into another human being.

And even now as he watched the gun at the man's left side coming up, slowly, effortlessly, watched it leveling—he knew that he was helpless, that he could never pull the trigger—not on Crescent, not on himself, not on this demented animal who stood before him, preparing at this very moment to pull the trigger on him, that his strident mandate to "freeze" had been nothing more than a declaration of his own inability to act.

And when the deafening roar burst in his ears this time, he knew it was real, not imagined. And he heard it as the sound of his own death.

The slug was on its way. In slow motion. The jarring impact hit him in the wrists, and he waited the endless milliseconds for it to emerge from those splintered bones and crash homeward into his paralyzed body.

The crash never came. He looked on in a daze as the man standing before him caved in—flung back by some unseen force hammering on his chest, hurled against the open door where he bounced, limp, already dead, and came to rest jammed halfway inside the yawning cab of the van.

The jarring impact Valjohn had felt in his wrists had been the magnum's big kick! It had been he who'd fired, he who'd sent the devastating hollow-point on its way. It had been he who'd taken a life.

No time for soul-searching. Almost immediately the van shot forward, narrowly missing an arm of the girl who still lay outstretched and trembling on the pavement. It swerved up the parking lane in a shriek of burning rubber. No-hair's body tumbled out the open door.

Valjohn leaped over the girl and took off at a dead run across the lot after the fleeing vehicle. The only exit onto the main road lay straight ahead. The van would have to swing around the far end of the rows of parked cars, then come back. Which gave him a slim chance to head it off.

As the race unfolded, the chance became slimmer. Still three rows away from the exit, he could see the van making the final turn. Beaten, he eased up; then, amazed, he watched the vehicle suddenly screech to a halt. A moment later he heard the man slamming shut the passenger door. The act had taken only a few seconds, but it was enough. By the time the van was once more accelerating toward the exit, he was firmly planted in its path. He held up one hand like a traffic cop and aimed the gun with the other.

The van kept coming, then slowed abruptly to negotiate the corner. Through the windshield he could see the child in the man's arms. Valjohn lowered his aim, fired a gratuitous shot into the wide, blunt grill bearing down on him and threw himself clear of the swerving wheels.

He rolled in the gravel shoulder, scrambled to his feet. The van squealed onto the main road and headed out of the park in the opposite direction. Valjohn dashed several steps after it, dropped to one knee and sighted in on a rear tire. He held his fire.

The vehicle was slowing. It was sputtering, backfiring. He watched in disbelief as it coasted to a stop in the middle of the road not two hundred yards away.

He got up almost leisurely and trotted in pursuit. He could hear the starter grinding, could see the man frantically eyeballing him through the rear window.

A car appeared around a bend farther up the road. Long-hair jumped out of his stricken vehicle with his hostage and ran toward it. Valjohn quickened his pace. The man held up the child and waved the approaching motorist to a stop. In the next instant he had wrenched open the door and dragged the driver, a shrunken, elderly lady, out of the front seat. She clawed at him after he'd shoved her aside, yanking at his hair while he attempted to slide in behind the wheel. He fought her one-handed, hammering at her several times, but she held on like a feisty terrier. Stepping out of the car, he managed to kick her to the ground. When he spun around to climb back in, the car no longer was there.

The old woman had left it in gear. Fast idling, it had crept ahead and now was veering slowly off the road a dozen yards away. He gave chase, still holding the child, but could not overtake it before it had plowed through a clump of bushes and crunched to a complete stop against the forked trunk of a sapling.

The door still hung open, but a large branch that had wedged itself through the window into the driver's seat blocked entry. Valjohn came running up as the man was tugging at the branch. Hearing footsteps, Long-hair jerked around, whipped out his knife and thrust the blade to the child's throat.

"Take another step and the kid's hamburger."

Valjohn stumbled to a halt about five yards away. He was gasping for air, and his side ached. For the moment he just stood there, unable to speak, chest heaving. People gathered on the other side of the road, most of them coming from the lower campground, others from the parking lot and the ridge.

"Now, why don't you just drop that cannon there and let me get into this car and wheel on outta here. Cuz there ain't nothing you can do about it —dig?"

Mutterings and worried whispers issued from the crowd.

"Better do what he says, mister," a voice spoke out.

"Looks like he means business," another chimed in.

"You better believe I mean business! That's good advice you're getting, pig meat. You are a pig, ain't you?" the man asked, flicking his eyes from the gun to Valjohn's gaze.

Valjohn said nothing.

"I already wasted a bunch of people up that trail. One more don't mean shit to me."

Valjohn looked at the child. A little girl, two years old, maybe younger. Her blue bib overalls were pulled up tight on chubby, dangling legs. She no longer struggled in her captor's grasp. Her eyes were reddened, fitful and afraid.

"What's it gonna be, pig meat—the kid's neck or me driving outta here?"

Valjohn studied the man closely. Middle twenties. Middle of the Bertillon scale: 6 feet, 170—about his own height and weight. Cephalic index between 75 and 80. Orthognathous—square, handsome face. Couldn't classify his ears—couldn't see them under those long, wavy, chestnut locks. Eyes: slate gray, cruel, glazed over, hyped white.

The front of his vest and T-shirt were spattered with blood. So were his hands. Valjohn flashed on the body of the young man lying in the weeds by the lavatory. Some of the blood had smeared on the child's overalls.

What were her chances if he let them go? Pretty dismal. A high-speed chase. Might get shot by some trigger-happy deputy. A good chance she'd wind up a crash victim. Then again, if the man got away, he'd probably slit her throat for kicks.

"Come on, pig meat, I ain't got all day. Make up your mind: Which is it gonna be?" He regripped the knife to emphasize his impatience, creasing the baby fat of the child's double chin.

Valjohn had no idea what he was going to do next, yet he heard himself answer in a voice clear and even:

"Neither."

"Huh?" Long-hair's face puckered.

"That's right. You're not going anywhere, and you're not going to hurt the kid."

"You don't listen good, do you, pig meat? Your ears must be full a fuzz, or maybe you're just pork-dumb stupid. There ain't no way it can be *neither*. I go or the kid gets cut—simple as that."

"Not that simple."

"Look, I already told you I already wasted a couple of people today! You think one more's gonna make any difference?"

"One more *will* make a difference."

"Shee-yit!" The man spat angrily. He cast a quick glance at the driver's seat behind him. He appeared to be pondering a move. He could slide over to the door without saying another word, scramble his way under the branch and slip in behind the steering wheel in a matter of a second or two. Only the child was too small to make a good shield. And scrambling under the branch would leave him wide open.

"I ought to cut her head off right now just for the hell of it," he said and glowered.

"Before you do, may I say something?"

"Make it short. I'm getting tired standing here." He shifted the child's weight threateningly in his arms.

Valjohn leaned forward, thrust out his chin and roared:

"I AIN'T NO PIG, MOTHERFUGGER! YOU CALL ME 'PIG MEAT' ONE MORE TIME I'M GONNA START BLASTING RIGHT THROUGH THAT FUCKING KID!"

"Hey, man, hold on—"

"SHUT YOUR FUCKING MOUTH AND LISTEN—I AIN'T THROUGH YET!" Valjohn bellowed, took a menacing step forward. His words came automatically. They amazed him, seeming to form on his lips before he had the slightest notion of them in his mind.

"Take a look down this barrel, asswipe, and tell me what you see!"

The man was struggling to keep on top. His confusion grew.

"Go on, look! Wha'dya see?"

He stared deadpan into the black muzzle pointing at him.

"You're so fucking dumb, motherfugger, I'll tell you what you see: Magnum hollow-points! Dum-dums! Gut-rippers!"

There was no response.

"You know what else, asswipe?"

The man slowly shook his head. His eyes, still locked on the barrel of the gun, had taken on a flat glaze.

"I'm gonna do you a big favor. I'm gonna spell things out for you—like what's gonna happen, say, for instance, if that kid even gets her skin nicked." Valjohn paused, then lowered his voice. "You ain't going behind bars—I guarantee it. You ain't just gonna die either. It's important you understand that: I ain't just gonna shoot out your lights. Not like I done your cue-ball buddy back there. You ain't gonna be that lucky. . . ."

The man managed to wrench his gaze away from the gun. Valjohn, meeting his eyes, felt strangely inspired. When he spoke again, he barely could recognize his own voice.

"I'm gonna introduce you to Agony, asswipe. You're gonna go down on her; you're gonna make love to her right there in the dirt." He pointed to a patch of bare ground between them. "First I'm gonna stump-cut you, pop both your knees like walnuts. Then I'm gonna gut-shoot you. Blow your belly open like a watermelon, splatter your balls into jelly. You listening?"

Long-hair was listening.

"Right there!" Valjohn shouted pointing to the ground. "I can see you writhing, squirming, at my feet; you begging me to kill your ugly ass . . . only it ain't gonna happen. Not real quick, anyway. Cuz, Agony, she don't like it that way; no, sir, she likes to enjoy herself so good. SLOO-OOW good! I'm just gonna start whittling away. You're gonna hurt so bad, so long, so many different ways. . . ."

Valjohn paused to gulp air. The words continued to pour. "And I'm gonna be standing over you giggling and gawking. I'm gonna be giggling and gawking and when I think you can't take it no more, I'm gonna whip out my pecker and piss on you and drop my pants and shit all over you—"

"You . . . you're crazy!"

"—piss and shit all over you, all over your motherfuggin wounds till they're bubbling and burning and steaming and stinking—"

"He's crazy!" The man had turned to the crowd of onlookers across the road. He found no argument in their wide-eyed, dumbstruck faces.

Valjohn grinned, allowed a string of saliva to seep over his lower lip.

The man crumbled. There was nothing left of his fierce bravura. He shrank, hunched his spine, drew his legs close together. The child weighed like a stone in his arms. The knife still was at her throat, but it looked tired, unconvincing.

Valjohn asked the man to hand her over.

The man shook his head. "No . . . no, let's wait."

"Wait? Wait for what?"

"The cops. Let's wait for the cops. They'll be here any minute."

"WE AIN'T WAITING FOR NO FUCKING PIGS!" Valjohn roared. He tossed the gun back and forth between trembling hands, glared with hysterical eyes. "Come on, do something stupid! Gimme an excuse—any fucking excuse, motherfugger! Gimme, gimme, gimme—"

"Hey, cool it, man! Jesus! Look . . . if I did hand over the kid . . . how do I know you won't shoot me?"

A car suddenly came around the far bend into the park. A family. The driver slowed at the sight of the crowd. When he saw Valjohn holding the gun, he sped quickly by.

"I'm tired of talking. I'm gonna count to three," said Valjohn. He took slow, deliberate aim at the man's groin, counted quickly.

"One, two, three—"

"All right! All right!" The man lowered the knife from the child's throat and lowered the child to cover Valjohn's new target area. "I wasn't gonna hurt her anyway."

"Drop the knife!"

The man hesitated, shrugged, dropped it.

"Bring her here."

He nodded, walked cautiously forward, still slightly hunched over. When no more than a couple of steps separated them, he suddenly shouted, "Here, catch!" and pitched the child at Valjohn's gun. In the same motion, he pivoted, took off running down the road toward the main gate.

Valjohn lunged, caught the child with his free arm. He cradled her for several moments, watching the man dash away. She began to cry. He carried her over to the crowd. The people eyed him warily. Several nearest the road backed away. A few turned and ran. A young woman in bright yellow slacks held her ground. He handed her the child.

Then he was back running down the road.

When he stopped running, he was neither tired nor out of breath. He swung up the big Colt Python, sighted in on the center of the fleeing man's back. It would be a long shot. The man was almost to the bend. Valjohn yelled once.

"Stop in the name of the law!"

The man kept running.

Valjohn decided to leg-shoot him. The decision seemed clear in his mind; yet when he tried to lower his aim, he found he couldn't do it. The gun remained rigid, anchored in midair. He couldn't budge it, or even slightly swerve it from its deadly alignment. His hand, his whole arm, seemed but an extension of the weapon's cold, inflexible steel. He could feel his finger tightening on the trigger.

No! No, no, no no no—he would not give in! He brought up his other hand, grappled with the gun for control. The man had almost reached the far trees, would soon be out of sight.

The gun fired, jerked and fired again.

The man stopped in his tracks, thrust up his hands as one slug ricocheted off the pavement at his feet, another crashed nearby, over his head through the leaves and limbs of a towering oak.

In the distance, a siren wailed.

21

"Surprised hell out of me he was even packing one—off duty, no less!"

"I can remember the time—"

Captain Howland and Deputy Superintendent Shroeder, standing at the urinals, turned to see Valjohn walk into the men's room. He strode to the vacant fixture between them, unzipped his fly.

"Ah, Lieutenant—we were just talking about you." Shroeder greeted him with a smile. "Which reminds me, I haven't had an opportunity to . . . ahem, personally congratulate you." He reached out his right hand while he still stood there relieving himself.

Valjohn, fumbling with his privates, looked over at the proffered hand.

"I won't pretend I've been in your corner in the past, and I wouldn't make any promises about the future, either. But right now I'd like to shake your hand for a job well done—and I sincerely mean that."

Valjohn contemplated the hand a moment longer, shrugged. He ceased fumbling and grasped it.

"I was telling Jim about the time I come down on you in here," said Howland. "You know, back when you thought carrying a gun would give you warts or something."

Valjohn glanced at the captain, who was chomping his stubby black cigar.

"I ain't one to take any undue credit, but you got to admit that little ass-chewing didn't do you no harm."

Valjohn was experiencing difficulty pissing. His bladder felt full, bursting—but nothing was coming out. He strained to produce a few dribbles and farted loudly.

"Now you're talking," said Howland, grinning, and he replied with a thunderous volley of his own.

"Hey, you two virtuosos want to play a duet, let me out of here first!" Shroeder said and laughed, waved a hand to clear the air. He flushed his urinal and walked over to a sink.

Howland farted again, shook himself, zipped up. He stood looking at Valjohn as if there were something else he wanted to say. He rolled the cigar to the other side of his mouth, gave him a hearty slap on the shoulder instead and walked out. Shroeder finished washing and, ignoring the towel dispenser, withdrew a large handkerchief from an inside coat pocket and dried his hands. He exited waving.

Left alone, Valjohn soon was pissing like a fire hose. Several days had gone by now since the incident. Strange, puzzling days.

He'd returned to the city a conquering hero. The press had plastered the whole episode across its front pages: the gripping story of terror and death stalking the picturesque trails of a state park. Three people killed; a woman raped and knifed (she'd just been taken off the critical list Tuesday); picnickers assaulted, shot; several instances of armed robbery; a child wrenched from her mother's arms and held at knifepoint—it was an impressive box score relished by the media and the public alike.

And no ink had been spared recounting the bravery of one man—one among the multitude of stunned vacationers—who'd dared to become involved: an off-duty policeman enjoying his second honeymoon, trying to forget for a few days the demands of his job, the crime and violence of the big city . . . only to be thrust headlong once more into the arena. All the old alliterations were dredged up. "The cubist cop," "the dabbling detective," "the futurist fuzz" rode again. Only this time he'd traded in his "paintbrushes for a peacemaker," his "cool palette for hot lead." One columnist dubbed him the founder of "pistol pointilism," while another argued that his work was clearly rooted in Chicago's time-honored style of "can do" action art. A TV commentator, showing with questionable taste the body of Dennis "No-hair" Zebko being rolled away on a litter to a waiting hearse, referred to Valjohn simply as a "master of still life."

Valjohn's picture, his formal departmental portrait taken a few years ago, appeared in several papers along with mug shots of the killers. There was a picture in the *Trib* of the frizzy-haired waitress who'd been dragged out of the snack bar by Zebko. She was smiling up at a heavyset, middle-aged-looking man in a golf hat. Valjohn had looked at the picture for several moments before he finally realized the man was himself.

He'd returned to the city a conquering hero; he'd also returned to the

Force. Within the first hour after he and Crescent had arrived back at their apartment Sunday, he'd received a call from Gordon's office: He was to report to headquarters early Monday morning.

Which he did.

At 10:00 A.M. he met with Gordon and Hans Glad in the superintendent's office. The mood of that meeting was in sharp contrast to the last one he'd attended there. Now everyone was all smiles and hearty handshakes, Gordon's pipes smoldering in the background with an acrid vengeance.

It was obvious the superintendent's pride had been rekindled in his former student. He lauded at length Valjohn's valorous conduct over the past weekend, his moon-sad eyes moist, bright, almost glittering. Valjohn learned he was being given a reprieve, his obligatory leave of absence terminated forthwith. His past improprieties were being dismissed as misunderstandings.

"Understandably, I'm not reassigning you to the case," the superintendent had concluded, repacking his meerschaum. "I think a fresh start is called for at this point. Therefore I'm transferring you out of Homicide to the Vice Squad."

When Valjohn emerged from the meeting his clothes reeked of mundungus and rich burley blend. He felt faintly amused, faintly embarrassed; he also felt more and more strangely detached—as though each day he were stepping a little farther outside himself.

What seemed as amazing to him as his official reinstatement was the general acceptance of his return to the fold by the rank and file. Zebko, it turned out, had been wanted: a cop-killer who'd gunned down a state trooper on the Pennsylvania Turnpike in 1966. Now officers who wouldn't normally give Valjohn the time of day were nodding to him, faces sober with respect. Complete strangers walked up to shake his hand.

Yesterday in the hallway Lieutenant Sweeney had called out to him.

"We sure coulda used you'n our gunnery crew back in the Pacific," joked the crusty lieutenant. He was referring to Valjohn's shot that had put the oncoming van out of commission. An inspection under the hood had revealed that the slug or a fragment of it had passed through the radiator, struck the carburetor and shattered its manifold. Gasoline, unable to vaporize, had poured into the cylinders, flooding out the engine, bringing the vehicle to a halt. "Been shittin' deadly behind an old Archie."

Even the blacks on the Force had warmed to him. Overnight he'd become a "brother" officer again, his Tom image another "misunderstanding" of the past. Theotis Ivory, president of the APAD, contacted him earlier in the day, asked him both to reconsider membership in the organization and to appear as a guest speaker at an APAD benefit being held on the South Side next month at the Woodlawn Association. Valjohn agreed at least to think it over.

Leaving the lavatory, he stopped off at his cubicle to see if he'd left

379

anything behind. He'd already transferred the bulk of his personal belongings to his new desk, which he'd be sharing with another detective on the fifth floor. He found an envelope with a paycheck waiting for him on top of his old desk: remuneration for his canceled leave of absence.

Later in the elevator at the end of the day, he met Howland's secretary, Eunice Mervin, getting on at the fourth floor. He half expected her to jump back off when she saw him. Instead she surprised him with a smile.

"Hi, Lieutenant."

"Hello, Eunice."

She beamed, seemed flattered he'd remembered her name. "I read all about you in the newspapers. . . ."

He allowed a modest smile, watched her trim jaw working hard on a wad of gum. Judging from the lump in her cheek, it had to be a whole pack. Maybe two.

"That was some weekend you sure had, huh?"

He continued smiling, continued watching her work her gum. They rode down the remaining floors in silence.

Just before the doors rolled open to the lobby, he yielded to a sudden impulse and farted loudly. Basso profundo. He winked.

It was going on eleven when Valjohn left Eunice's apartment. He let himself out, walked down a flight of carpeted stairs to the main door and strode out into the oval parking lot of the complex. His Volks was still double-parked behind Eunice's big Merk, where he'd left it. The lot had been full then. More than three hours ago. Now there were a number of empty spaces.

He drove aimlessly for several blocks trying to get his bearings. He knew he was somewhere out in the western suburbs—Arlington Heights or Mount Prospect—but his directions were jumbled. He recognized a small shopping center at Kirchoff Road, took a right and hoped he was heading east.

Poor Miss Mervin. If only she'd known what she was letting herself in for when she'd invited him over for a quick drink. But then he hadn't known either—or, for that matter, why he'd bothered to accept the invitation. But bothered he had.

Somehow the drinks never got poured. Almost before her front door had closed, they were in her bedroom groping.

While they were wrestling their clothes off on her bed—a huge, plush rookery of Titian pink sheets and satin pillows—she asked to see his gun.

"You'll be seeing it soon enough."

"Not that, silly." She slapped him playfully on a thigh. "I mean the one in your holster."

Jesus, she was as bad as her boss. He handed it to her.

She stared at it very carefully in her hands for a few moments, then brought it up to her face, pressed it against a cheek, her lips and sniffed it all over. He knew she was going to put the muzzle in her mouth and she did. Right out of a pop detective novel. Sucked and blew down the barrel. She unhooked her bra and held the gun to her small, pointed breasts, rubbed the trigger against her nipples. Even from where he sat he could see them swell, stiffen.

He watched her as he continued to undress. By the time he was naked, she was holding the big Colt between her legs, the front sight buried in the crease of her pastel blue panties.

"Can I have a bullet?"

Valjohn shrugged.

She expertly flipped open the cylinder, plucked out one of the two remaining live rounds—he hadn't reloaded since Saturday's fracas. She held the round up between her thumb and forefinger and examined it closely.

"A hollow-point! My favorite kind." She flicked out her tongue and Frenched the tiny hole in the nose of the slug. Then she sprang up from the bed and dropped the round into the top drawer of her bureau.

Damn! He'd just entered the city limits of Rolling Meadows. He was going the wrong way. He let two cars following him swing by, then pulled a U-turn.

It was not until her little charade with the gun that he'd felt himself swelling and stiffening. Past failures, his humiliating moments with Mona Cobb, were not easily laid to rest. Poor Miss Mervin . . . she'd hardly been prepared for what was to come.

She'd actually been disappointed in the beginning. Almost immediately upon their first earnest embrace he'd climaxed. "Jack be nimble, Jack be quick," she said and sighed, gave a little whistle through her teeth and rolled out from under him. No sooner had she sunk into a self-pitying sulk than he was nudging her from behind, ready to go again, his confidence gleaming between his legs.

She was positively exuberant and flung her spare young body at him with gymnastic abandon.

She applauded his third erection, marveled at his fourth.

At his fifth she was enthralled, though a faint, hollow ring had crept into her enthusiasm.

When they grappled yet a sixth time, the faint, hollow ring was faint no longer. She was weary and moaning loudly. Disbelief had given way to dismay; concupiscence to a grim battle of attrition.

Glassily surveying his seventh erection, she suggested he lie back and allow her to conclude the evening by paying him lip service.

He shrugged and did as he was told.

"Aren't you forgetting something?" he asked.

"What?"

"Your gum."

She smiled a wicked smile and shook her head. He should have known better.

In the descriptive patois of the patrol car, Eunice Mervin "played a mean flute." And the wad of gum proved to be anything but an impediment. Soft and pliant, it became another tongue trilling upon his vigilant flesh. At one point she removed him from her mouth to catch her breath, or show off —he was not sure which—for she'd flattened the gum into a thin sheet and molded it over the head of his phallus like a bishop's calotte. Gobbling him up again, she rolled the wad into a coil; when he next glimpsed himself he was sporting a sultan's turban. . . . Moments later he emerged yet again: This time she'd stretched out the coils of the turban into a helix, a constricting serpent that wound around the entire length of his erection.

Valjohn shut his eyes, gave a short warning cry. Whatever fears the last tableau might have evoked in him were quickly swept away in waves of turbulent orgasm. He was left momentarily dazed, spent. His eyelids fluttered and seemed to shake every bone in his body. When the tremors ceased, she still was there, looming above his loins, grinning at him.

"Watch," she mumbled, began blowing a bubble. It grew into a huge, diaphanous sphere, peachblow, swelling bigger and bigger until at last it burst, spattering everything in the immediate vicinity—Eunice, himself, the Titian pink sheets—with hot, sticky gum. And his own glistening seed.

"Bubble come!" she gasped triumphantly, collapsed and rested her head upon his thigh.

Her triumph was short-lived. No sooner had she wiped the mux from her face than he was starting to paw and snort like a bull. It was as though he'd been stockpiling all those orgasms denied him during the desolate continence of his marriage.

"Jeeze! My God, Johnny! You're the killer cop of all time, ain't you?"

A sign read Route 114 ahead. He definitely knew where he was now. He took a right at the next intersection and sped confidently toward the city.

She'd balked when he tried to mount her again, suggested they just lie there for a while and talk. For five minutes she chattered away about herself, about the trials and tribulations of growing up in an all-girl parochial school: the tyranny of tight-assed nuns, and learning how to masturbate in dark, secluded closets.

She also told him how great it was working for the Force. Her life had been so empty, so meaningless. She'd been such a goof-off and everything —like all the other assholes running around. And then bang! She was working for Howland and Homicide. It really turned her around. It was like she was a completely different person and everything. She felt so fulfilled and everything, so much more a part of everything. And everything.

He listened to her for as long as he could lie still. "Euny-baby," he interrupted her at last, "I know just what you mean." And he prodded her crossed legs with his eager truncheon.

"I can't. Jesus God, Killer, I'm whipped!"

"Aw, Euny-reuny, how's about just one more little old tumble for the road? For auld lang syne, whataya say, huh?"

There was no reply.

"We'll make it short and sweet. A little old quickie. For the Force."

"No."

"For Howland and Homicide."

"No."

"For Captain William Ward and all the gang down at the Haymarket."

"Who?"

"For Superintendent Gordon and the Big Blue Guy in the sky."

"No, no, no! Really, I mean it, goddamnit! I've had it. My battery's *kaput*. You'll have to take a rain check."

So much for cajolery.

"Whatyathink you're doing?"

He was climbing on top of her. She struggled, was much too tired to offer anything but token resistance. Apologetic, he overpowered her with ease.

He came again: No. 8. Instead of withdrawing and rolling off, he continued pumping away—resolutely, mechanically, hypnotically. His erection lost some of its broaching edge but refused to go flat. Minutes later it was tool steel.

So much for rain checks.

His partner lay beneath him, limp, almost comatose. Her moans and protests dwindled away into grunts and labored breathing.

As he came one, two, three more times, he had the peculiar feeling that he was in the midst of a great journey, tediously making his way toward some far-off destination where he was long overdue and much awaited. Only as he progressed he also had the distinct and disturbing sensation that he actually was receding, moving farther and farther away from himself, like a shadow stretching out at sunset and slowly fading. Each orgasm left him feeling more vague, disconnected, more extraneous.

Fearful he might vanish altogether, he finally dismounted—one shy of an even dozen—and began foraging about the floor for his discarded clothing. When he'd dressed he asked Eunice if she had anything to eat. She groaned and rolled over, silent.

On his way out of the room he paused by the dresser drawer where she'd deposited his bullet. He peered inside. It looked like a miniature munitions dump. There was a slew of regulation issue—.38 specials—forty or fifty rounds. Mixed with these were maybe half a dozen .357's (including his own), twice that many .32's and .45's. In addition, there were a couple of twelve-gauge-shotgun shells—he picked one up: 00 buck—riot load; a couple of .270's—sharpshooter's issue from TUF; and no less than three big tear-gas canisters.

A pretty fair cross section of the department's firepower, he mused, easing the drawer closed. Miss Mervin had had herself a busy year.

He entered her kitchen and switched on a light. He was famished. Without bothering to sit down he proceeded to eat from her refrigerator a dish of sliced peaches, a tomato, some leftover spaghetti and meatballs and a couple of uncooked wieners. He also consumed half a jar of mayonnaise and three raw eggs, washing them down with a carton of half and half. He debated thawing a steak from her freezer, but decided he wanted to get home before Crescent left for work. He departed the premises, finishing off a box of Waffle Cremes he'd scavenged from a cupboard.

A car in the opposite lane approached with its brights on. The exertions of the evening had left his eyes sensitive, sore and stinging with sweat. He testily flashed his own high beams. The car dimmed and they passed each other in an onrush of hasty détente.

So he'd finally gotten laid. Only it sure as hell hadn't done any great wonders for him. His scrotum still ached; his balls were still blue. He could feel his erection at that very moment painfully doubled over in the tight crotch of his pants.

A truck approached, flashing its lights. Valjohn realized he'd left his own brights on and quickly dimmed them. The truck followed suit.

Poor Miss Mervin, he reflected once again for the last time. So the dumb bitch got what she deserved. Those were the breaks. Tough titty city . . . no, that wasn't fair. Not fair at all . . .

Another car approached with brights. He dimmed while it was still far off, patiently waited for the other driver to reciprocate. When his eyes started to burn, the distance sufficiently closing between them, he flashed his high beams on and off, a quick reminder.

No response.

He flashed again.

No response.

His eyes were on fire now. The double banked headlights of the oncoming car glared at him like kliegs. In the last few seconds before they shot by one another, he angrily retaliated, slamming on his brights with his fist.

Momentarily blinded, he felt his right tires hit the gravel shoulder. He jerked the wheel, overcorrected as the tires caught a high edge of pavement. The Volks lurched back onto the road, across the median, right into the path of a high-balling semi.

He wrenched the wheel the other way. His brights were still on, but he was too busy to dim them. The truck gave him a dose of high beams and blew by him like a hurricane. Blinded again, he thought for an instant they'd collided. Then he found himself once more skidding on the gravel shoulder, fighting to keep out of the ditch.

Goddamn! No motherfugginassholesonofabitchinbastard was gonna get away with that!

Almost before he knew what he was doing, he jammed on the brakes, shoved it into low, spun around into the other lane. Eyes watering, he planted the accelerator to the floor, wound up through the gears. Soon, with the aid of a strong tailwind, the needle on his speedometer was trembling near the bottom line.

He overtook the truck in a matter of minutes, eased off to sixty-five and

384

tailgated it while he waited for a couple of cars to go by. Then he swung around it, high beams blazing, gave a finger in the rearview mirror and doggedly built his speed back up to eighty-five.

The red taillights glowing in the distance grew larger and larger. "Here I come, you motherfugginassholesonofabitchinbastard!" he shouted, could feel the heat of the chase further stoking his rage. The yellow parking ticket still trapped on his windshield thrashed fiercely. It suddenly worked free, flew across his vision and was gone.

The taillights continued to grow, then suddenly flared. The car was swinging off into a parking lot beside a large, brightly lit building. A bowling alley.

As Valjohn spun into the lot, he saw a man climbing out of the car near the front of the building. He appeared large, heavyset, wore a bright yellow shirt with lettering on the back. Valjohn pulled behind the car and rolled down his window.

"Hey! . . . you!" he called out. Too late. The man hadn't heard him. Valjohn got out of the Volks, chased up the steps after him. Overhead a swarm of bulbs illuminating a large sign flashed on and off:

ECHO LANES . . . ECHO LANES . . . ECHO LANES . . .

He entered a lobby, came upon half a dozen people milling about a cashier's counter. No yellow shirt. Valjohn walked past the counter to the rows of spectator seats overlooking the alleys. The air was thick with cigarette smoke; his eyes began watering again. He searched the teams of bowlers spread out below him. Red shirts, blue shirts, orange, black and green shirts—yellow shirts! On the farthest lane to his right. He spied the man he was looking for, disappearing through a doorway on the other side of a row of pinball machines. He hurried after him.

The doorway led to a large men's locker room. Valjohn searched up and down the narrow rows of lockers, found the man seated on a bench changing his shoes.

Valjohn adjusted the bulge in his pants. His hard-on, which refused to demobilize, had become uncomfortably wedged in the opening of his jockey shorts and he had to ease it to one side down a pantleg. He strode forward.

"Excuse me?"

The man looked up. His name was Wally—or so said a nametag stitched over his shirt pocket. The lettering on the back of his shirt read "Gene and Jean's Tap; City Scratch Champs, '63."

"Excuse me. Did you just now pull up in a maroon and white Buick, license plate DD-112?"

The man smiled. "What'd I do, leave my lights on?"

"In a manner of speaking."

"In a manner of speaking?" The man looked puzzled. He was still smiling.

"That's what I said," Valjohn replied icily.

The man's smile faded. He resumed tying his shoelaces. "What manner is that?" he asked without bothering to look up again.

"I'll tell you what manner is that," said Valjohn, keeping his voice slow and even. He paused, took a big, self-righteous suck of air . . . then bawled out: "IT'S WHY THE FUCK COULDN'T YOU DIM YOUR FUCKIN' HEADLIGHTS FIVE FUCKIN' MINUTES AGO OUT ON THAT FUCK-IN' HIGHWAY—THAT'S WHAT FUCKIN' KIND OF MANNER IS FUC-KIN' THAT!"

The man stared straight ahead at the lockers. Several seconds elapsed before he began retying his laces. He didn't look up, didn't say a word.

"I fuckin' dimmed twice for you, but, oh, no, you kept right on coming like a goddamn . . . a goddamn fuckin' searchlight!"

The man finished tying his shoes. He stood up. He put his street shoes in the locker and lifted out his bowling ball.

"What I want to know is: Which is it? Are you too fuckin' lazy to move your fuckin' big toe or just too goddamn fuckin' high and mighty to give a fuckin' fuck?"

The man shut his locker, turned and faced Valjohn.

"Fella, I don't know what your problem is, but I do know I'm in a heckuva hurry. My team's already out there rolling . . . so why don't you—"

Valjohn moved directly in front of him, blocked the aisle.

"—just step aside."

"Maybe that's your problem, mister." Valjohn held his ground, found his voice slowing into a drawl. "Maybe people jus' been stepping aside for you more'n a little too often."

The man swelled his chest and became for the moment Ernest Borgnine, a mean fatso version. He stammered something halfway between a growl and a curse, then swung a shoulder and hurled his bulk forward. Valjohn grunted, stumbled backward but didn't go down—he was not without considerable ballast of his own. Before the man could stride past, Valjohn charged blindly back, intent on ramming his adversary's midsection with a lowered head. He butted him squarely in the groin instead. The man crashed sidelong into the lockers and slumped to the floor.

Valjohn, breathing hard, stood over him. He seized the man by his collar, hoisted him to a sitting position against a locker. Then he reached under his own shirt and whipped out the big Python from his hip-hugger, shoved it into the man's contorted face.

"Five hundred feet! That's the goddamn minimum in this state, asshole! Five hundred feet!"

"Don't . . . don't shoot," the man gasped. He was stricken white-eyed.

Valjohn released his collar and stuffed the revolver back in his holster. The man slid down the locker to the floor again. He looked convinced.

"Rules of the road," Valjohn admonished in a softer voice, "they're for everyone . . . Wally."

On his way out of the building he eyed a display tray of candy at the front counter and asked for a Zagnut bar. He rifled his pockets for change, grinned sheepishly at the woman waiting on him and pulled out his wallet. Behind him the steady din of the alleys flooded his ears: the bang and drone of the heavy balls on hardwood, the explosive clatter of falling pins, the rattle and scraping of automatic machinery, relentless as Sisyphus, resetting the endless games.

"Aw, what the hell, miss," he said, handing her a ten, "gimme the whole box."

It was after midnight when Valjohn arrived home. The apartment was empty. Crescent had left for work nearly an hour ago. There was a note waiting for him on the kitchen counter. There were no words of reproach: She said simply that he'd find dinner in the fridge, that she was sorry they'd missed seeing each other. She signed the note, "Love, C."

Valjohn opened the refrigerator. An eggplant casserole. He sampled it before placing it in the oven. He decided it wasn't all that cold, sat down right there at the kitchen table and finished it off with the serving spoon.

He started to wander through the apartment, then went directly to his dresser in the bedroom and ferreted from its bottom drawer a key to the studio. He hadn't done any work there since the days of his bachelorhood.

Inserting the key in the lock, he felt a certain uneasiness—as though he were about to open the door on some new, harrowing revelation. He felt like Dorian Gray about to confront his odious portrait after keeping it hidden away for so many years. Would he find his 1834 collage changed? Maybe he'd find it completed—Crescent's likeness, the specter of her hellborn alter ego, grinning at him from the large main panel, the one he'd set aside, primed and waiting for the final rendering of the Reaper. . . .

He turned on the light. Oscar Wilde could rest in peace. Aside from an accumulation of dust and cobwebs, everything was as he'd left it—including the large main panel, still blank as the wall it leaned against. The floor was cluttered, just as he remembered it: Paint cans, brushes and assorted tools, jars, paper sacks and boxes lay strewn about everywhere. A bowl of megilp, hardened and cracked, rested on the green tarp where he'd mixed it the better part of a year ago.

He shuffled about the room surveying his work—the finished panels and the ones still in process, some upright against the wall, some flat on the tarp covering the floor—a rogues' gallery of victims, his assemblage of the bits and pieces of their demise. Several minutes later he was digging into a box of supplies.

He located a bottle of mastic, half a can of linseed oil, quickly mixed up a fresh bowl of megilp. He'd been hit with a sudden attack of inspiration. He grabbed an empty cardboard box and charged out of the room in search of new material.

He went no farther than the bedroom and Crescent's dresser. From the top drawer among her personal effects, he appropriated her Windhaven nameplate, an SNAI pin, a memento black stripe from her senior nurse cap. Tucked away in a corner of the drawer he found his own plastic ID band from the hospital. He also found the letter he'd written her the day he'd left the hospital. He opened it, read it again:

Dear Continuity,

Sorry you couldn't be here to see me off. Wanted the chance to thank you in person for all the time and TLC squandered on me. Guess this note will have to do—so thanks for everything.

I may as well confess right here and now that I have a terrible schoolboy crush on you. If you think I'm just infatuated with your uniform there's no better way to prove it than by letting me see you in a dinner dress. I know you never date former patients, but—

God, how long ago that all seemed! He could read no more, wadded up the letter and tossed it along with his severed ID band into the cardboard box.

When he returned to his studio, the box was full. Now dénouement. He faced the big blank panel that had waited so long, laid it flat on the floor and went to work.

He didn't bother to make a layout, plunged right in throwing things together as fast as he could fasten them down. He draped part of her white uniform in the lower right corner of the panel, stapled it to the Masonite, then built upward from there, combining grim police data with the sundry items he'd just collected, including pages torn from her school yearbook.

Using up everything he'd gathered in the box, he stood back and scrutinized his effort. Still had some empty spaces. He left the room again, returned shortly with a copy of their marriage license and a pair of jasmine-scented panties. He glued and laminated the license to the panel in the lower left corner with megilp, wired the panties near the middle, overlapping a torn portion of an official Penry facial ID chart. Once more he stood back.

The collage was a jumbled mess. It needed something. He continued to stare at it until he discerned a certain flow of line asserting itself among the various shapes. He squeezed out some ivory black on a palette, dabbed at it with a big, flat hog bristle. Then he traced the flow with ragged, bold, jabbing strokes.

Memento mori. He'd outlined a definite visage in the center of the panel. A death's-head. He brushed in two dark shadows suggesting eyes; then squeezed out more paint: this time, cadmium yellow, a dab of ocher and Indian red. He rapidly mixed them, cut them onto the collage in broad, slashing strokes with a palette knife and crowned the visage with a wild, twisting tangle of golden hair.

When he stepped back again, he was startled. The effect was grotesque, chilling. Complete. He tossed the palette knife to the floor, didn't bother cleaning his brushes. The frenzy of creative energy, along with the rest of the evening's activities, finally had caught up with him.

In the bedroom he started to unbutton his shirt, had trouble remembering how his fingers worked. He gave up on the project and flung himself fully clothed into bed.

He is standing on the deck of a ship, an ancient sailing vessel, a lateener. A strange sea surrounds him—gray, shrouded in mist, smooth as glass, yet the ship pitches and yaws as if floundering in heavy swells. It seems he has not seen land for years, and now suddenly there is an island before him. It parts the mist, appears verdant, drenched and glistening, as though it has risen from the water only moments earlier.

Alluring, forbidding, the island swells ambivalent as a Max Ernst landscape. Strange noises emanate from its jungled interior: the cries of eldritch birds; the roars of unknown beasts. He can hear the jungle itself, a din of vegetation tangling and scraping against itself, thickening into the sky, blotting out the light.

And he is over the side swimming. The sea is black, warm as sweat. To reach the island takes forever and takes no time at all. Exhausted, he crawls ashore. The beach is furrowed as an old man's brow. Between the furrows, the sand is covered with alewives rotting in the moonlight, rusty beer cans, the footprints of little cat feet.

"It's about time," says Yvor Whittier, seated on the middle of the beach in his overstuffed chair. He looks around and shakes his hoary head. "Now, where did she wander off to? . . . You really shouldn't keep a lady waiting."

"Who?"

"The Lady of the Land, of course. She was here just a moment ago."

Valjohn discerns a figure moving at the edge of the jungle. He catches only the faintest glimpse of clothing—a flash of regal satin—vanishing into the encroaching gloom.

"I wouldn't go in there if I were you," says the professor to Valjohn, who is already walking past him. "Not alone. Not without the Lady."

Valjohn trips on a large black lump writhing in the sand. It looks very much like a body bag.

"Let me out!" a muffled voice calls from within.

He bends over, yanks at the zipper. The bag shudders.

"Phwew!" Harold Bledsoe lifts his head through the opening, emits a fetid exhalation. "Thanks loads—it really gets stuffy in there. Say . . . where you headed?"

"The jungle," replies Valjohn, staring at the putrefaction that is Bledsoe.

"No kidding? Hey, mind if I come along?"

"You're in no shape to go hiking. You'll never be able to keep up."

"Who can't keep up? I can keep up. Just try me."

"A nasty place," calls Professor Whittier as Valjohn enters the undergrowth. "Much too crepuscular. But you suit yourself . . . Mr. Brown, I'm sure you've been here before." The professor reaches up and turns on the reading lamp by his chair. The jungle lights with an eerie glow.

Valjohn trudges deeper and deeper into the greening maze. It seems dense and impenetrable, yet he moves through it with unnatural ease. He turns and sees several people following him. He recognizes Chick Screed, other reporters from the cop shop. He sees Max Howland and Sweeney and Stephansky and Jim Shroeder. He sees Bert Carlson from the lab, Ernest Borgnine, Clint Eastwood and Charlie Ruggles. They are plodding along safari-style behind Captain William Ward, who looks every bit as imposing as his bronze likeness in the CCPD lobby.

When Valjohn looks back again, the safari has grown. He sees Elton Meeker in his white morgue apron. Hans Glad and Superintendent Gordon follow. Then Mayor Dooley himself, strutting along in a green hat to the pipes and drums of the Shamrock Rovers. They are followed by a throng of civil servants: clerks, administrators, street cleaners, attorneys, sanitation engineers, building inspectors, ward bosses and committeemen; their faces all form a giant composite of some long-forgotten childhood bully.

And suddenly everyone is scattering, fanning out into the underbrush. A couple of voting supervisors rush by him, almost knocking him down.

"Hey, what's the big hurry?" he shouts after them.

One glances over his shoulder, his face filled with horror.

A voice from nearby cries, "Run! Run for your life!"

"Run from what?" Valjohn shouts back.

"Head for the hills!"

"Feet, don't fail me now!"

The voices die out, and soon he is left behind, standing alone on the trail. A fierce hush has settled over the landscape. Presently he hears a distant stirring. Something is out there, moving, coming his way. Something big . . . heavy. He can hear branches snapping, vegetation being crushed and torn aside.

He retreats a step. Another. Then he too is running. When he trips and falls, he scrambles to his feet in an instant, starts to run again and freezes. A giant baboon, fifty feet tall, crouches ahead blocking his path through the jungle. It stares at him, unblinking down a long, tapered snout.

The beast vanishes as a gust of wind surges through the trees. When the branches settle, the baboon is still there—only it is not there. It has become the head of a woman: long faced, pinched lips, hair swept back high and symmetrical from a sharp widow's peak, and falling to the broad outline of her shoulders. Her eyes stare with the same close-set intensity of the baboon.

The Lady of the Land! She has found him. He waits, brittle with new fear, for the awesome crush of lips. . . .

The wind surges again; branches sway. When they resettle, she is gone, vanished with the beast. Her visage has become chunks and slabs of steel, welded joints and tie rods. It is the Picasso statue from the Civic Center

Plaza, its gaunt hulk now rusting in the jungle like some massive piece of abandoned machinery.

The noise behind him grows louder, closer. He dashes ahead without a backward glance. At the edge of a clearing he sees an ancient castle, a feudal barbican, rising above the trees. The old Chicago Water Tower. He heads for it, finds it overgrown with weeds and twisting vines, apparently gutted by recent fire. From atop its crenellated spire he looks out across the jungle below him all the way back to the beach, the storm-swept Aegean beyond. He can see the trail of his own fear: It is a giant midnight snake winding back and forth, cutting a deep swath through the lush canopy of green. And even now as he watches, it is gaining on him, relentlessly leveling the jungle in its path: Limbs splinter, trees topple, great masses of foliage are ground asunder. It is closing in on the tower.

He descends to escape. Too late. At the charred main portal, the stalking noises surge to crescendo. The sky turns blood red; a cold wind rushes past, scatters data, faded reams of Polifax print-outs, like withered autumn leaves. Suddenly the trembling wall of vegetation parts with a splintering crash.

Harold Bledsoe emerges. He wriggles forward in his black body bag resembling some huge variety of garden slug. "See! See! I told you I could keep up!" he shouts triumphantly. "Say, where are we, anyway?"

Valjohn shook his head, straightened up. He was lying in bed with his clothes still on. The phone was ringing. He didn't feel like talking to anyone; his mind was too scrambled. He glanced at the clock. Ten to three. When the phone quit ringing, he got out of bed anyway.

On the top of his dresser, he spotted the key to the studio. Right where he'd set it before collapsing a few hours earlier. He picked it up, started to put it in a drawer. He hesitated. A moment later he was on his way back to unlock the studio door.

He stood deliberating over the collage he'd just done. Startling. Doubtful it ever would replace the Mona Lisa, but it definitely was startling. He did feel confident his agent would like it. Probably start in all over again with his New York gallery pitch. That is, if he ever got the chance to see it . . .

In a burst of new energy Valjohn gathered it along with all the other panels, both finished and unfinished, and stacked them together into one big pile by the door. Then, making several trips, he carried them out of the apartment, down the stairs and into the back alley. He found a couple of empty trash barrels, stuffed the panels into them, breaking up a number of the larger boards to make them fit.

Upstairs again he loaded all the debris of case evidence, all the grim memorabilia scattered about the room, into boxes, hauled the boxes downstairs and dumped them into the barrels as well.

He made another trip to the apartment, returned with a book of matches.

He crumpled up part of an old newspaper, lit it, crammed it into one of the barrels.

The fire licked tentatively at the heap, appeared to like what it tasted, burst into hungry, crackling flames. He ignited the other barrel, stood back and watched both fires rage. The flames shot high up, filled the dark alley with fitful, leaping shadows.

So much for his masterpiece.

Valjohn took a shower and got dressed again, being careful to ease his hard-on down the opening of a pantleg. Incredibly it had refused to wither. Before leaving he scribbled a short note to Crescent.

It still was dark out. He drove aimlessly across the city, wandered on and off freeways, turned down side streets, back onto main thoroughfares, back down side streets. He drove as far south as the blockhouse tenements of Pullman Town. Then north again, he drove past the Moody Bible Institute, cruised around Bughouse Square. Later, angling back east on Lincoln Avenue, he came to the Biograph Theater, noted Fellini's *8 1/2* showing. The figure of a woman standing in the shadows under the marquee moved out onto the sidewalk as he drove past. Something about her made him turn his head. Her face, neither young nor old, seemed to be all rouge and creams with a slash of red lipstick; her hair, jet black, was coiled and knotted atop her head, reminiscent of a style from some vintage movie on late-night TV. She wore a tight-torsoed red dress with jutting, tailored shoulders . . . same movie.

Stopping at the corner for a red light, he framed her in his rearview mirror.

She was standing on the curb now, looking at him, grinning. He watched her step off the curb, never taking her eyes from him—there in the eerie half light of dawn, the fading yellow incandescence of the streetlights, watched her lower to her haunches in the gutter, almost as if she were genuflecting before some distant altar. She clutched the hem of her dress in both hands, dipped it into a dark, shallow pool glistening at her feet. She straightened, stood with her dripping hem slightly hoisted, just below her knees, still looking at him . . . still grinning. . . .

The light turned green. He shot forward across the intersection, then swerved abruptly down Racine Avenue. He circled the block.

When he drove by the Biograph again, the woman was gone. There was no sign of her anywhere. The sidewalks were deserted; the street empty. Along the gutter . . . where no more than a minute or two ago she'd been standing—squatting!—a few scraps of paper rattled in the dust.

At the corner he stopped for a yellow light, sat staring straight ahead, hands trembling on the wheel. Slowly he tilted his head, forced his eyes to look once more in the rearview mirror.

Twenty minutes later he was on the Dan Ryan Expressway, fleeing the city. When the sun came up, a big fried egg sizzling on a skillet over

Chicago Heights, he turned around and headed back. Dillinger's blood had dried up and blown away thirty years ago, and Valjohn felt as if he were ready to dry up and blow away himself. On Division, he spied the big golden griddle of a Universal Pancake Palace and pulled in to park for breakfast.

He ordered the first thing he read on the menu: Hawaiian pancakes. He finished them off before the coconut syrup had a chance to level on his plate, picked the menu up again and ordered the next dish that met his eyes.

And the next.

Returning to headquarters later in the morning, his belt tongue out, holding mightily on the first notch, Valjohn padded slowly to his new desk in Vice.

". . . hasn't regained consciousness. All indications are he probably never will." Vice Squad Captain Newton Aldrich stood before a number of officers assembled at the front of the room. "Realistically speaking, I think it's fair to say he's pretty much bought the old produce shelf."

"Any idea who's going to replace him, Newt?"

Aldrich shrugged.

"One of our own this time, huh, Captain?" There were several grunts of approval.

Barely listening, Valjohn sat down, then sprang to his feet again, the words finally filtering through.

"What's going on? Replace who?" he demanded of a detective seated on the edge of a nearby desk.

"You ain't heard? Gordon—he was in an accident last night."

A high-speed auto chase. The superintendent, returning home from a dinner engagement with the mayor and members of the central planning committee for the Democratic National Convention, witnessed a car striking down a pedestrian in Grant Park. The car failed to stop, pulled an abrupt U-turn, racing by Gordon's limousine instead. It sped onto the Outer Drive, running a red light, nearly downing two more pedestrians in the process.

The superintendent had uncharacteristically lost his temper. He was already in a bad humor from arguing with the mayor over mobilization of the National Guard. (Gordon considered the move premature and provocative, but the mayor seemed determined to fortify the city against "invading hundreds of thousands of your typical guerrilla hordes.") The spectacle of the blatant hit-and-run had been too much for Gordon to endure. "Go after the son-of-a-bitch!" he'd shouted at his driver. A wild pursuit had followed with both vehicles going out of control on the drive's infamous Z-curve at the mouth of the Chicago River. Gordon's limousine had slammed into a concrete retaining wall, throwing him sharply sideways, his head striking a custom-built smoking rack protruding from a panel in the rear seat. The blow, well placed and severe, had sent him into a deep coma from which he was not expected to recover.

Valjohn stood there, numb, listening as the detective elaborated. Two others joined in, eager to relate all the bizarre details.

When Valjohn had heard enough, he walked hurriedly out of the room and out of the building.

Gordon a vegetable . . . the somber, pensive voice gone . . . the moon-sad eyes . . . the warmth and understanding . . . the vision . . . the hope . . .

Valjohn walked around the block, circled it again. He stopped along the way, stared at his reflection in the window of a bail bond office.

Too much had happened. He was too weary, too wasted, too burned out inside to feel anything deeply anymore.

He detected a red smudge of syrup crusted on his chin, rubbed it clean.

He phoned Crescent from headquarters in the early afternoon. He apologized for not calling the previous evening, promised it wouldn't happen again. She sounded not the least bit upset, informed him that Greg Harris had called in the morning shortly after she'd arrived home from work, had told her about Superintendent Gordon.

"I know how much he meant to you, John. Your career."

Valjohn held the phone away from his head, stared at the tiny holes in the receiver. He was glad she wasn't there to see his face. He finally mumbled something about not being home for supper, that he'd been assigned again to night duty.

She was understanding but disappointed, observed they were rapidly becoming strangers.

He thought of a particularly sardonic reply, but kept it to himself. In an effort to change the subject, he asked how her work was going.

"Wonderfully," she said and proceeded to outline her new job in post-partum. She went on and on about how much she enjoyed working in the nursery.

A feeling of uneasiness crept into the pit of his stomach, seemed directly proportioned to the level of her enthusiasm. He lied that someone had just stepped into his office. He promised they would get together tomorrow.

"That would be nice," she said.

Valjohn got off the elevator at the second floor of Passavant Hospital, tramped down a hallway to a pair of red swinging doors lettered:

INTENSIVE CARE UNIT
RESTRICTED ADMITTANCE

He hesitated, entered. A heavyset nurse in a yellow cardigan looked up from her station. He asked her about the superintendent. She informed him the patient was "being maintained" in bed No. 3 of the first ward, that he'd spent a total of five hours in surgery during the night and early morning and that no visitors other than next of kin were being allowed to see him. She added cheerfully, though, if he wished to stay, there was a waiting room farther down the hall where he could register and keep vigil.

Valjohn proceeded to the waiting room, ignored signing the large register open on a table and took a seat. On his left sat a young couple with puffy red eyes. They were holding hands, grimly staring at the floor. A man sat across from him, impatiently thumbing through a religious magazine.

Valjohn grew tense. He got up and walked over to a table piled with reading material. A few moments later, looking up from a pamphlet entitled *Suffering As Message,* he saw Gordon's sister Agnes walk by, dabbing at her nose with a handkerchief. He followed her into the hallway and watched her leave in an elevator. He debated, then turned and marched off in the opposite direction.

The nurse's station in the center of the first ward was unattended. He entered and began peering around drawn curtains. He found the superintendent stretched out naked on the third bed. A nurse was in the process of closing his eyelids with her fingers. She reached for his IV tubes.

"Is he dead?"

She looked up, startled. "Heavens, no! I'm just checking his connections. The infusion pump's been acting up lately." She lifted his limp left arm, fiddled with a set of plastic tubes that ran to a small machine with a flashing blue light mounted beside the bed.

"Now, who are you?" she asked, laying his arm at rest again. Suddenly remembering her patient was nude, she picked up a fresh bed apron folded on a nearby chair.

"We're not allowing visitors, you know. Immediate family only." She covered Gordon with the apron, reached for a clean sheet.

"Son," said Valjohn softly. "I'm his son."

She looked up from the sheet she was unfolding, looked at him long and hard.

"Uh, that is . . . son-in-law," he added, defying her stare with a long, hard look of his own.

She nodded with some embarrassment and busily covered Gordon with the sheet.

"He's scheduled for another EEG session at four-thirty," she said, checking her watch. "That's in twenty minutes. You'll have to leave then."

Before leaving herself she reached over and gently closed his eyelids, which were slowly working their way open again.

"Poor old dear," she cooed, "he still thinks he can see."

Alone with the patient, Valjohn sat down in the chair by the bed. Ill at ease, he avoided looking at the superintendent, instead gazed around at the extensive battery of life-support and sensor systems engulfing the bed.

He listened to the rhythmic clicking and whirring of the respirator, a large apparatus partially hidden from view on the other side of the bed. A thick endotracheal tube ran from its bright chrome-trimmed panel to the patient's mouth. Gordon's chest rose and fell in perfect cadence to the mutterings of the machine. Hanging overhead from the wall, a long black console projected his vital signs on a cluster of small monitoring screens. A relentless series of jagged green lines measured and broadcast his heartbeats; his pulse rate was flashed in orange on a digital readout every sixty seconds. Mesmerized, Valjohn watched it holding steady at seventy-one.

Finally Valjohn allowed his gaze to fasten on Gordon's face . . . not a face. A mask, a death's-mask, made from the visage of some long dead pope or king. His cheeks were sunken, the skin tone of a Goya corpse. Mercifully the tape securing the respirator tube covered his mouth, concealing any hint of expression.

While Valjohn pondered the nose of his fallen leader—swollen, ruddy, the only spot of color in his face—Gordon's eyelids began to twitch, flutter. Valjohn watched fascinated as the left lid slowly crept up—a slit at first, then a gap. The gap continued to widen until the lid, still thick, drooping, had risen to reveal almost the full ring of the superintendent's dove-gray iris. The right lid followed, snapping open wide like a window shade with a broken catch.

Valjohn was leaning over the bed now. The respirator clicked and whirred; Gordon's chest rose and fell. The left eye . . . its pupil was fixed and dilated. Valjohn knew that empty stare.

"Only so much you could do, sir—so much you did . . . No one man . . ." he let his voice trail off. The right eye, its pupil a pinpoint even in the soft light of the ward, seemed to glare back, as though it were a thing alive itself. It jerked and bobbed, then roved by.

"I . . . I'm sorry about everything . . . the way I fell through . . ."

The clicking, whirring. Sheets swelling, settling. The eye roved back and continued past him.

Valjohn stepped away to leave, then lurched forward again, blurted out:

"The case! I solved the case, sir! C-65-1834 . . . Moe's report: He was right! The perpetrator—the Reaper—she's a woman! She . . . she's my wife, sir; I'm married to her. Crescent O'Leary . . . Valjohn."

The eye was back again. It stopped, centered on him, quivered. Was it seeing? Was Gordon somehow somewhere on the other side looking through?

"I had to tell you, sir. I had to tell you. . . ."

Click, whir, rustle, shhh . . .

"I had to tell you." He reached down, squeezed a thin, still wrist. "I knew you'd want to know."

Click, whir, rustle, shhh . . .

Then he was turning away, striding from the ward. The tears were falling now. He wiped his cheeks, his eyes, with the back of a hand. They were dry. It didn't matter. He knew the tears were falling. For Gordon, for himself, for just about everyone he cared to think of and maybe some he didn't.

22

Sergeant Burr Abrahamson swung the unmarked green Dodge sedan off North Wells and parked it on a side street.

"Better lock up. Last time I parked here I lost the aerial and four hubcaps."

Valjohn climbed out, slammed the door shut, tried the handle. He was wearing brushed denim bell-bottoms and a bright red Paisley shirt that was free at the waist and unbuttoned halfway down the front. A string of beads dangled around his neck.

Sergeant Abrahamson, late forties, balding, wore a wrinkled black suit, a narrow fifties tie, the knot pulled loose and his collar unbuttoned. A conventioner's nametag was pinned to his lapel. It read: "Hi! I'm Andy Bleckert; National Plastics; Flint, Mich." He and Valjohn were about to go busting hookers in Old Town.

"Uh, now, remember, Lieutenant, they got to commit themselves before you can cuff 'em. You know—they got to say they fuck for money. If you go putting words in their mouth . . . I don't have to tell you it's entrapment."

"That's right, Sergeant. You don't have to tell me."

The sergeant shrugged. He was used to breaking in rookies, loanies from patrol. Under his breath he cursed Captain Aldrich for sticking him with this black prima donna.

Walking back to Wells Street they turned right, continued south toward the Loop at a slow stroll. Prostitutes stood in groups by the bus stops and taxi stands; others walked the sidewalks in pairs. Bold ones stood out in the street flagging down traffic, while their more cautious sisters hung back in the shadows and entranceways.

"Time to slop the hogs!"

"Oink, oink!"

"Sooee, sooee, sooee!"

The sergeant and Valjohn were loudly hooted as they walked along. Whenever the sergeant tried to engage a particular girl in conversation, she would walk quickly away.

"Uh, Lieutenant, think we're gonna have to split up. They just ain't gonna buy our act together. My hippie wig's being dry-cleaned or I'd'a worn my beads and sandals too."

Valjohn nodded. He crossed the street at the next corner, headed back in the other direction. The catcalls followed.

"Hey, pig meat, you get that belly from eatin' poor-street pussy or what?"

Valjohn stared straight ahead, oblivious.

"No luck, huh?" asked Sergeant Abrahamson, who was waiting for him in the car when he returned an hour later. A hooker sat in the back seat. "Don't feel bad, Lieutenant. Takes a while to get the knack. Ain't that right, Wardine?"

"Up yours, Sergeant," the woman in the back seat replied. She was black, small and slender, wore pink hot pants and an orange wig.

The sergeant grinned. "Might as well run over to the station and book her. About time for the whore wagons anyway."

Valjohn got in and they drove off. The whore wagons rolled only when the mayor wanted his city looking its best. This time it was for the big convention. The mass arrests were illegal and rarely led to anything beyond overnight detention.

"Hey, there's Annette—that fat-ass cocksucker! How come you ain't bustin' her?"

"No reason," said Abrahamson. He was inching forward in the heavy Wells Street traffic.

"Bust her trashy-white ass! I squeeze down so she can't see me."

"She'll make the wheels."

"Shit! Then get out. She too dumb to make shit. Tell her Lamar sent you."

"Lamar?"

"Serve his ass right. He always braggin' her cuz she be bring in top dollar. Shit. She don't never get her fat ass busted, tha's why. If I gots to cool off in the cage so she gots t' too!"

Abrahamson nodded. "Seems only fair. You want to take her, Lieutenant?"

"Not him—you!" the woman objected, jerking her head up. "Even Annette ain't fool 'nuff to buy his pig Tom face."

Valjohn glanced over his shoulder at the prostitute crouching in the back seat. Eyes front again, he stared at his reflection in the windshield, the drooping outline of his double chin.

The sergeant pulled into an alley and got out. A few minutes later he returned with a big buxom white woman dressed in tight green slacks and a huge Afro. Abrahamson opened the car door. The moment she caught sight of Wardine she went berserk.

"You ugly black crack!" she screamed, hurling herself on top of the girl crouched in the back seat. The two of them went at it, screeching and tearing at one another. Wardine lost her orange wig beneath the seat. Annette's Afro wound up in the street. The sergeant and Valjohn finally pulled them apart.

"Wardine, pussy, yo' ass had it when Lamar he find out."

"Honky sack a' slush," Wardine spat back defiantly. Annette cursed, tried to take a swipe at her. Valjohn, sitting between them in the back seat, pinned her arm against her thigh.

"Tha's right," snarled the white prostitute, her speech surprisingly indistinguishable from the black hooker's. "You hides behind Mr. Pig-man Tom here. See how long that'll do you. Sooner later you be back on the street an' Lamar he g'na fix you fine. You be lucky you pee through it!"

"Shee-it!"

"When Lamar he through with you then I be stompin' you."

"Shee-it."

"Shee-it."

"Says you."

"Says yo'self."

"Shee-it."

By the time they'd booked the suspects and returned to Old Town, the whore wagons had come and gone. The brazen bands of women were nowhere to be seen. Those who'd eluded the roundup still were in hiding.

Abrahamson parked in the same spot. "Say, Lieutenant, we finish early here, maybe we can cruise on over to Grant Park and bust us some hippies."

They split up again, Valjohn following the same route he'd taken earlier. At North Avenue he hesitated, shrugged and continued on into the quieter residential neighborhood. He went no farther than Lincoln Avenue, crossed to the other side of the street and headed back.

"Hey, sugar, got the time?"

He turned, saw a black woman step out from the shadows of a nearby apartment building stairway. She was dressed in a black miniskirt and sporting a blond Betty Grable wig. Her smile quickly faded when she got a closer look at him.

"What?"

"Nothing. The time. I ask you got the time."

Valjohn glanced at his watch. "Twelve-fifteen," he replied, and started to walk away.

"You the fuzz?"

Valjohn looked at her.

"I guess you be too much like fuzz to be fuzz." She grinned, relaxing. "You wanna party?"

"What?"

"Party. You wanna party?"

Valjohn shrugged.

She stared at him.

"Do . . . do you?" he finally managed.

"Course I do, sugar," she said, putting both hands on her hips. "Why else I be askin' fo'?"

Valjohn gathered himself. He said the key question.

"How much?" she mocked him, strutted a few steps down the sidewalk, spun around. She had skinny legs, slightly bowed, and a flat ass; her breasts, very large, made her look top-heavy. She had a young, pretty face.

"How much you think I worth?"

Valjohn wondered what Sergeant Abrahamson would answer.

She cupped her hands under her breasts, lifted and pressed them together. He could see the pink lace of her bra through her unbuttoned blouse, the deep cleavage of her flesh.

"How much?"

"What's the going rate?" Sergeant Abrahamson couldn't do much better than that.

"Fifty dolla'."

"Fifty?"

"Twenty," she quickly amended. "Fo' you only."

"For what?" He spun the web tighter.

"Half 'n' half. Ten fo' head; ten fo' leg."

Done. She'd trapped herself all nice and legal. Now the sergeant could be proud of him.

"You're under arrest," he mumbled.

"What?"

"I said, 'You're under arrest.' "

"Shit! Shit! Shit! You *is* the fuzz. I knew it! Shit! I is *dumb*. This the second time this week I be busted. My main man—he gonna shoot me!"

Valjohn had taken hold of her wrist. He could feel her pulse, her anger and frustration beating beneath his fingertips. He could feel her despair.

He let go.

"I'm . . . I'm not a cop. I was only kidding."

"You ain't no cop?"

Valjohn shook his head.

For an instant she looked angry, fierce, then she grinned. "You sure some funny dude, all right. Come on, we gonna party yo' ass off." She grabbed his arm.

"I don't have a car."

"Don't needs no car."

"I . . . I can't go to a room."

"Don't needs no room."

She led him over to the nearest apartment building and down wrought-iron steps to a basement alcove. It reeked of garbage and urine. She guided him into a corner littered with discarded Kleenex and used condoms. He half expected to be jumped by a mugger, but no one was lurking in the shadows. He reached out, felt her shoulders.

"Got to see some bread first, sugar. House rules."

Valjohn pulled out his wallet, put a hand over his shield and thumbed out a twenty.

She took the bill, held it up to the light from the street above.

"You wants it lyin' down or standin' up?"

Valjohn didn't answer.

She dropped to her knees, groped for his zipper. "My, you is set to party, ain't you! All fit to be bustin' yo' britches cooped up in there! Jus' can't wait fo' Sandra show you some a' that good, sweet-street lovin'."

She had him out, placed him down the open front of her blouse and worked him deep into her cleavage.

"You like dat?"

Valjohn didn't hear her. He was listening to the rustle of satin, to angry voices shouting in the distance, the jungle closing in.

"Hey, sugar, you gots to stand still!" She was holding him now in her hands. He'd taken a step back. She moved forward on her knees, purred, lowered her head. He stared down at the top of her blond wig, recoiled from images within images.

At the touch of her lips, he exploded, jerking away. He stumbled past her, bolting up the stairway.

"Hey! What—you crazy! Where you goin'?"

He ran down the sidewalk and dashed across an intersection, causing a car to veer and slam on its brakes. He continued running until the images in his mind began to dim and he once more was in the midst of bright lights and Old Town.

Trembling, soaked with sweat, he came to a halt. A group of people emerging from Piper's Alley confronted him with startled faces. Gasping for breath, he looked down his front, discovered his fly was still unzipped and that he was still jutting out. Erect. Throbbing. Releasing seed on the sidewalk.

He took off, running again, jamming himself back in his pants without breaking stride. Behind him he could hear curses and embarrassed laughter. Someone was threatening to call a cop.

At Division Street he ran east for a few blocks, then headed south again, bypassing the crowded sidewalks on Wells Street. He soon slowed to a walk and got his wind back. Crossing West Wacker Drive, he stopped to hail a cab.

A yellow snubbed him; then a checker. Both vehicles slowed, sped up again when they got close. Another checker approached, slowed, sped up. He watched it zoom by him, then saw its taillights flare as it skidded to a sudden halt. He shuffled after it.

"Thought you was a hippie," apologized the driver as Valjohn wielded himself into the back seat. "Then I seen you was a Negro. Where to?"

"1121 South State Street," Valjohn mumbled.

"I knew it. I knew you was a cop," said the driver, triumphantly slapping down the meter flag. He was a short, stocky man with wrinkled folds in the back of his neck, wore a visor with a green shade. "Ain't no Negro hippies —leastwise, I never seen one. Not in this town. You're working under-cover, ain't you?"

Valjohn looked at the face staring, grinning at him in the rearview mirror. He nodded. The best way to stay awake was to talk. He tried to think of something to say.

"Look at 'em. Scruffy garbage," the cabbie said as he stopped for a light at Balbo Drive. There were several groups of hippies milling about the sidewalk in front of the Sheraton Blackstone. A number of them were crossing the street to join other groups gathering at the edge of Grant Park. "Already run 'em out of the park once tonight. Looks like they're headed back."

The light changed. The cab shot forward.

"Say, why don't you drive on for a while," Valjohn finally spoke up. "I . . . uh, I'm not ready to get out yet."

"Sure, sure. Want I should stay on Mich'gan Av'noo or cut over to State?"

"Doesn't matter."

The driver nodded, flipped off his turn signal, stayed on Michigan.

"Can't figure all this protestin' and marchin' bullshit anyway. I mean when I was back in Korea nobody give three shits on a paper plate about us. Nowadays . . ." the cabbie's voice grew weary, "who knows what the hell's going on."

They drove as far south as the 4300 block, swung west, then took State Street north again.

"Redwood forest." They were stopped at an intersection. Across the street a floodlighted area was filled with workmen. "They still got a ways to go there."

"Redwood forest?"

"The mayor's fence. For the convention. They been workin' night an' day on it the whole week. S'pose to run all the way from the Loop to the Amphitheatre."

Valjohn stared out at the workers, carpenters, hammering and sawing away. They were erecting large sections of picket fence in front of a shallow rubble-strewn lot.

"You know, spruce things up a little—the route the delegates'll be drivin' to their hotels. Course I personally feel Mayor Dooley—maybe he went a little bit overboard. I mean all that lumber's got to cost some bucks." He eased the cab forward through a light change. "But then you got to admit there're some real eyesores along here. I ain't meaning to bad-mouth . . . uh, your people, but you got to admit it. Things can get pretty crummy lookin' out here."

Valjohn continued staring out the window as they sped on. Block after block of dingy buildings, littered alleyways, more rubble-strewn lots. He had to admit it.

As they approached the Loop, the streets suddenly became alive with sirens, flashing blue lights. Squad cars, unmarked prowlers, paddy wagons seemed to be coming from all directions, going in all directions.

"Somebody must've declared war!" blurted the cabbie. "Maybe they got to the water supply. They said they was gonna dump a bunch of that LSD in it. Make everybody go crazy just like them."

"I've changed my mind," said Valjohn as they came to a stop in front of headquarters. "Take me to Windhaven Hospital instead."

He entered the hospital through the emergency walkway. After glancing at a directory, he rode an elevator to the maternity ward on the third floor.

The nurses' station was empty. He walked quickly past it, headed down the first corridor on his left. The floor seemed deserted. He glanced into several rooms with open doors, found a couple of nurses tending a patient. Neither of them knew Crescent.

Farther down the corridor he heard the moans of a woman in labor, walked by another open door, glanced inside. A curtain blocked his view. More moans sounded from behind the curtain; then a woman's calming voice in the background.

"Won't be long now, Mrs. Speck. You're almost four fingers."

Not Crescent's voice. He continued on down the corridor.

In the anteroom of the nursery, he walked over to a large viewing window and edged out slowly in front of the glass. The nursery was brightly lit, a big, robin's-egg-blue room filled with cribs and sleeping infants. The infants came in a wide assortment: There were white ones; black ones; brown and blotchy red ones; ones with hair and ones without; hefty ones; tiny ones; short, plump ones; long, scrawny ones. . . .

He scanned the room from corner to corner. There were no nurses present. A small card taped to the window read:

If you wish to see a baby, please ring the buzzer. The nurse on duty will be glad to assist you.

He walked past the window to a door, rang the buzzer. There was no response. He rang it again. Still no response. He started to leave, turned back, tried the door. It was open.

He hesitated, entered. He had to find Crescent. He had to see her, talk to her. He had to be reassured. The evening had so jumbled his mind he couldn't bear to think anymore. He was desperate to be overwhelmed by her, yearned like Lycius for even an illusion of bliss.

There was nobody in the room. A faucet was running in a sink in a small kitchen area to his left. A thin vapor of steam rose from a stainless-steel cabinet on a nearby counter lined with formula bottles.

He went over to a desk, recognized Crescent's handwriting on what appeared to be a recent work sheet. She must have stepped out for a few minutes. He fidgeted with some papers, then walked past a pair of swinging doors of the nursery to a solitary door at the far end of the room. He peered through its small, rectangular window.

The room on the other side proved to be an addition to the nursery. There were more cribs; two walls lined with incubators. Crescent sat off to one side in a rocking chair. She was giving a bottle to an infant. She held the infant in her lap, gently rocking.

Presently she took the bottle away. The baby objected, its newborn voice a tight, high-pitched squall. Crescent increased the tempo of her rocking. She sang a lullaby. Valjohn lifted a hand to tap on the window. His fist poised inches from the window. It never struck the glass.

He watched fascinated as Crescent, supporting the baby with one hand, began unbuttoning the front of her uniform. Moments later she was guiding the infant to her proffered breast, kneading herself until milk glistened on the roseate disc of her nipple and ran in droplets down the curve of her tumid flesh.

While she nursed the infant, her lullaby changed. The words died away and were replaced by a gentle soughing from deep in her throat. The soughing rose and fell, then broke off abruptly into a strange mixture of animal and birdlike noises—clicking whistles; pips and chirks; purrs; long, lilting warbles; short guttural cries; grunts.

And her hair . . . had come undone. Her nurse's cap fell to the floor; her long golden tresses tumbled to her shoulders, then swirled upward, as if caught in some wild, buffeting wind. They whirled and crackled above her head, each strand somehow alive and glowing with dancing, static fury.

Valjohn's fascination turned to horror. He stumbled backward away from the window, banging into the desk and sending the tray of bottles clattering to the floor. Then he was fleeing from one room into another; down one corridor, down another—stopping only long enough to punch the button at the elevator, then not waiting but bounding down the stairway and out of the building.

And for the second time that night he was running through the streets of the city. He still could hear Crescent's strange utterances; they filled his head, merged into one long, drawn-out susurrant hiss. And suddenly the hiss no longer was coming from just Crescent, but from the lips of the suckling infant as well.

When he finally stopped running, he had no idea where he was or how long he'd been running. All he knew for sure was that he could run no farther.

He staggered along a sidewalk for some distance like a drunk, doubled over, chest heaving, trying to get his breath. Cramps stabbed at his sides. His legs barely supported him.

He jerked his head up to keep from passing out, blinked as he saw a giant figure hulking over him. The Picasso statue! He took a step back and glanced around, convinced he was once more immured in dream. There was no surrounding jungle. Only buildings. His marathon flight had taken him into the heart of the Loop. He was standing in the middle of the Civic Center Plaza.

"Oh-ow-oommmmm . . ."

A strange sound rose up from the plaza not far from where he stood. He turned, saw several people gathered by the "eternal flame," a large, circular burner embedded in concrete memorializing the country's war dead. The people were sitting on the pavement, legs bent up under them yoga style surrounding a guru figure dressed in a loose-fitting white robe, sandals, beads. They were all staring at the "eternal flame" and loudly intoning the same deep resonant syllable, over and over, individual voices blending in an eerie, almost mechanical droning harmony.

"Oh-ow-oommmmm . . ."

The guru figure looked familiar: the top of a balding head, egg-shaped, emerging from a thick bird's nest of black hair, black beard. Thick glasses. The face unmistakably Jewish; its expression beatific. A famous personage, a celebrity—Valjohn was sure of it, but he couldn't recall the name.

Valjohn was breathing a little easier now. He turned from them, made his way across the plaza to a nearby fountain.

"Oh-ow-oommmmm . . ." He found himself mouthing the incantation as he watched the fountain's twenty-five evenly spaced jets of water create a pulsing garden of spray and light. A cool breeze felt good against his brow, the clinging dampness of his shirt. There was a faint caustic edge to the breeze . . . the smell of rotten onions. The wind was blowing off the lake, sweeping through the park. He finally realized it was tear gas.

"Oh-ow-oommmmm . . ."

He gazed through the spray to the dark, massive columns of City Hall that rose behind it. A smile crept into his face. He spun around quickly to look again at the Picasso statue.

As in his dream, he saw the baboon: It sat crouched, waiting, shoulders hunched up behind its head, a gaunt rib cage all but trembling with hot breath. It looked subdued, complacent, as though it had just finished gorging itself. Its beady eyes stared straight ahead, fixed on nothing in particular, its long, tapered snout sniffing the night air.

Valjohn's smile broadened to a grin. The artist's intentions suddenly had become clear. Picasso was mocking the city, holding a mirror up to its inner soul for all to see, fifty feet high. One hundred sixty-two tons of steel. The giant baboon squatted in the midst of the plaza, a reflection of the city contemplating its own bestiality. Chicago . . . city of apes. Carnal, corrupt, debasing inhabitants to the level of their libidinal, brutish origins. He almost could see Picasso, his face painted like a clown's, shaking with hilarity when he learned the city fathers had not only accepted his gift but were actually going to enshrine it in the very heart of their twentieth-century Gomorrah.

Even in the depths of his fear and despair, Valjohn gave way to laughter. He laughed to himself and then out loud. A couple of late-night strollers cutting across the plaza nearby glanced nervously over their shoulders at him and quickened their pace. He continued laughing until his eyes watered and once more cramps stabbed at his sides.

When his laughter subsided and he'd wiped his eyes, he looked again at the sculpture. The baboon was gone. In its place stood the bust of a woman. The Lady of the Land, right out of his nightmare. The baboon's shoulders had become her parted mantle of swept back hair. It fell to two sharp points on her own shoulders, which rose smooth and curving from the pavement. It was as though her body were imprisoned beneath the plaza, encased in the concrete of the city. She stared straight ahead, grotesquely intent, close-set eyes directed across Washington Street to the soaring glass front of the Chicago Tokyo Bank. Valjohn wondered what she saw. Was it her own reflection? Or were her eyes riveted to the image of the beast?

He blinked. She was gone. The baboon was back again. They were one and the same—like the shifting sides of a necker cube—reversals.

Valjohn stepped over a loose span of restraining chain and climbed onto the wide, granite pedestal of the statue. He rubbed a hand across its base and felt the minutely pitted, oxidized surface of the steel. He gazed up at the towering structure and slowly made his way around it, continuing to explore it with his hands.

At the back side—behind the haunches of the baboon, beneath the shoulders of the lady—he discovered an opening, a large space, that ran the width of the base. He got down on all fours and crawled inside.

Dark. Cool. He inched forward up a low, inclined shelf. Crumpled newspapers slid beneath his hands and knees. The crevice proved shallow, V-shaped; he bumped his head on a steel plate slanting down above him. He turned around, felt his foot strike something soft, yielding. There was a groan.

He jerked his foot away, knelt motionless in the dark. A moment later there was coughing, the sound of someone scuffling down the shelf. He saw a figure rise silhouetted against the light of the opening and stumble off across the plaza. He remained motionless, listening intently for anyone else lurking in the crevice. There were no more sounds.

When he moved again, his foot kicked a bottle. It rolled down the incline with gathering speed, burst noisily on the granite pedestal below. Exhausted, he lay back and shut his eyes.

He slid down the shelf, gingerly scrambled over the broken glass of a whiskey bottle and stepped out into the morning sun. He rubbed his eyes, stretched. He was amazed at how soundly he'd slept. And for the first time in ages he hadn't been plagued by dreams. He felt cogent, decisive, strangely animated with positive energy. He reached down, adjusted his trousers, his hard-on apparently a permanent fixture.

He glanced up at the towering sculpture, saw only slabs of steel, welded joints and tie rods. Above it, three flags—the city, the county and Old Glory—fluttered on separate poles in a humid, late-summer breeze. He stared at them, shaking his head grimly. At that very moment, he perceived his duty clearly. As citizen and policeman; as husband and lover. It had become one and the same. He understood now what he had to do. He felt the pieces of himself coming together for one final act.

The plaza already was busy with people. Office workers and early shoppers hustled across its walkways; elderly pensioners sunned themselves on the stone benches. A group of hippies sat by the fountain; several dangled their feet in the water; a youth in a coonskin cap waded, picking up coins off the bottom of the pool with his toes. Valjohn had to urinate. He left the plaza, walked across Dearborn Street and entered Hinky Dink's Diner. He walked through to the rear of the establishment and used the lavatory.

On the way out, he was hit with the aroma of cooking food. It made him giddy with hunger, but he lowered his head and continued walking. He had too much to do and not much time to do it. He didn't want to lose his determination; a full stomach and he might see things differently.

A man stood with both feet planted in the front doorway, barring entrance to half a dozen hippies. They appeared to be hard-core guerrilla types. Some were barefoot; a couple of them in Indian headbands were naked to the waist and covered with Day Glo war paint.

"You can read, can't cha?"

The man standing in their way wore a white shirt and tie. His sleeves were rolled up to his elbows, revealing a stout pair of hairy forearms. He was pointing to a sign in the window.

NO SHOES

NO SHIRT

NO SERVICE

He turned, eyeing Valjohn warily as he approached him from behind. When he saw he only wanted out, he stepped aside.

"Like we're not going to eat with our feet, man, you know, so what's the big hang-up with shoes?"

"Look, do I gotta call a cop? Is that it?"

"Hey, man," one of the hippies in a headband spoke to Valjohn as he shouldered through them, "want to buy some superhoney? California home cookin'?"

Valjohn shook his head, hurried away. The arguing voices behind him were drowned out in a rush of traffic. At the corner he hailed a cab.

Sitting at his new desk at headquarters, Valjohn inserted a fresh sheet of paper into his typewriter. He began pecking out a letter to his immediate supervisor, Captain Newton Aldrich.

Dear Sir:
> *This is to inform you—*

He broke off, got up quickly and walked out of the office to the men's room. Minutes later he returned to his desk feeling a good deal less complicated. For all the eating he'd been doing lately, it'd been days since he'd taken a healthy crap. He resumed typing.

> *—that I am resigning from the Force as of today, Aug. 22, 10:30 A.M.*

> *Respectfully yours,*

> John Valjohn
> Badge No. 63-4811

He removed the sheet and signed it. Then he began cleaning out his desk. When he'd finished, throwing everything that belonged to him into the wastebasket, he took the letter into Aldrich's office. The captain was out with several other officers from command taking a strategic tour of Lincoln Park. Valjohn placed the letter on the captain's desk, thankful he wasn't there asking for an explanation. He'd learn the truth soon enough. They all would.

No sooner had he returned to his own desk, sat down for a moment to rethink the details of his hasty plan, than he had to make another trip to the men's room. *Pregame jitters,* he told himself.

He reentered the lavatory and sat in the same stall he'd occupied earlier. The door had a broken hinge and wouldn't close but at least the toilet wasn't clogged. When he was through, he flushed and stood up, rebuckling his pants. Then he sat back down again, deciding it was as good a place as any to think things over for a while.

He checked his watch; he'd give Crescent twenty more minutes, then make the call.

He heard someone enter the lavatory. He looked out the opening of the stall to see a man in a dark blue suit walk to the row of sinks across the room. A moment passed before he got a clear view of his heavily jowled face in the mirror. Of course, the big black limousine—he'd seen it parked out front on State Street. Not really all that surprising to find him here today—not when one considered all the sudden changes the department was going through: Gordon's condition, the threat of rebellion in the streets, the emergence of a police state . . . not really all that surprising.

The man suddenly turned and glanced quickly about the room as if he sensed he was being watched. Satisfied he was alone—apparently assuming the stalls were empty because of open doors—he took off his suit coat and hung it on a nearby wall hook.

Valjohn leaned slightly forward on the toilet seat to keep him in view. He watched him roll up his sleeves and splash water on his face. Without his coat, he looked conspicuously less imposing. The thickset, bullish appearance of a dynamic leader—last of the big city bosses, kingmaker, had abandoned him. Now he only looked fat and dumpy, his surprisingly narrow shoulders making his head look oddly immense.

He finished at the sink, walked over to the towel dispenser. Valjohn could no longer see him, but he could hear him trying to operate the dispenser. The advance lever rattled a number of times. There was cursing. The lever rattled again. More cursing. He heard cloth being yanked and torn; several moments of silence; then an outburst of loud banging.

When the mayor appeared again, he was drying his hands on his shirt-tail, breathing heavily, his face the color of boiled lobster. He put on his coat and started to exit, then hesitated. He walked to the urinals instead. Unzipping, he flushed the center fixture, shuffled in close and began to relieve himself.

Then took a step back.

Valjohn watched in fascination as the mayor, still relieving himself, continued backing away: slowly, a half step at a time. He directed his stream of water in a golden rainbow, arching it higher and higher as he opened the span several feet between himself and the fixture.

Valjohn shifted uncomfortably on his seat. The hinges groaned.

The mayor jerked his head around, discovering he had an audience. In the same instant the pressure in his bladder faltered; the rainbow collapsed. Hurriedly he tried to stem the flow, stumbling forward, wetting the floor, his gleaming cordovan wingtips with several broken, dying spurts.

After finishing at the urinal, he came storming back. He glared into the stall at Valjohn, who was sitting with his trousers raised and buckled.

"What're you doing in there, fella?" he demanded to know.

Valjohn thought for a moment. "Resting."

"Resting! Are you a police officer employed of this city?" His face was boiled lobster again.

"No," said Valjohn, reflecting on his letter on Aldrich's desk. "No, I'm not."

"Well, what're you doing here then? These facilities of toilets, they're for your police officers."

"I know," said Valjohn rising to his feet. "I was just leaving."

The mayor struggled to gain control of himself. For a moment he seemed intent on blocking Valjohn's exit from the stall; then he walked away to the mirror and began straightening his tie.

"Are you a Chicagoan resident?" he asked in a calmer voice.

Valjohn, on his way out, stopped, stared at the pale blue eyes fixing him in the mirror.

"You're from outta town, aren't you?"

Valjohn nodded.

The mayor scoffed. "What do you people hope to think you can get accomplished by coming into our midst like this? I'd really like to know."

Valjohn continued to nod. He had fleeting memories of meeting the man at the St. Patrick's Day parade—shaking his hand, walking beside him, sharing the same grandstand.

"All you protesters—it's easy to disrupt and tear things down and . . . criticize. But do you have any programs? Where are your programs?"

Hell, the man had even pinned a medal on his chest.

"I'd like to hear a constructive idea. You tell me one thing you could do to make things better."

Valjohn thought about it. "Die," he finally said.

The mayor turned from the mirror. He eyed Valjohn up and down warily. Then he exhaled loudly, dismissing what he saw with a seismic tremor of his jowls. He ran water in the sink and began washing his hands a second time.

Valjohn stood waiting, not sure what was expected of him. Presently the mayor looked up as if surprised to see him still there in the mirror.

"Something I can do for you, fella?"

Valjohn once more sat at his desk, staring at the phone. He glanced at his watch. Eleven-forty. *Time,* he told himself. He picked up the phone, hesitated, then dialed.

The phone rang seven times. No answer. It rang seven more times before a drowsy voice on the other end finally mumbled, "Hello."

"Hi! It's me. Good morning."

"John?" Crescent yawned. She yawned again. "Good morning—I guess. What time is it?"

"Almost noon, love. Look, I'm sorry I woke you up . . . I just had to do it. It's such a great day . . . a gorgeous day! Why don't you get up and meet me downtown and we'll go for a walk, feed the pigeons or something? We can have lunch together."

"Ummm . . . I'm so sleepy, John. Couldn't we do it later in the day? You know my new hours now—"

"I know, I know, but I have to be back on duty by two. Things are really

410

in an uproar down here. I'll be lucky to get off before midnight, and they've
. . . they've stuck me with a heavy weekend assignment. I'm afraid if we
don't get together now, we won't see each other for days."

Crescent was silent.

"You're the one who said we're becoming strangers," he persisted.
"Here's a chance to help remedy that. We can be together for a little while,
anyway. . . . But we've got to make the effort."

A few minutes later he hung up and sat back in his chair, quietly trembling. The stage was almost set. She'd agreed to make the effort. She was
meeting him in the Civic Center Plaza between twelve-thirty and one. So
far his performance had been flawless. He only hoped he was up for the
grand finale.

He spent the next five minutes trying to reach Grady McTague. No luck.
He wasn't at his desk at the cop shop and couldn't be located at the *Times;*
no answer at his home.

He hung up, checked his watch. He slapped the top of the desk decisively
with the palms of both hands and rose to his feet. No use hanging around
headquarters any longer. If he left now he'd have plenty of time to walk
to the plaza. And he felt like walking. It would help settle his nerves. He
was sure this time he had the willpower, the courage. Now all he had to
do was keep cool.

He started away from his desk, then came back. He reached under his
shirt, withdrew his revolver—hip-hugger holster and all. Almost forgot he
was wearing it, he mused. Didn't take long to get used to. He opened a
drawer, thought for a moment, then closed it. He dropped the weapon into
the wastebasket instead.

On his way out of the building, he paused by the statue of Captain
William Ward. For a moment it seemed as though the venerable magis-
trate's raised arm and imperative gaze were directed at him. He thought
wistfully of Superintendent Gordon. He thought wistfully of his father. He
reached out and gave the captain a pat on one of his stalwart bronze knees.
"It's been nice making your acquaintance, sir."

The lobby was crowded. Converging teams of undercover men made it
look like intermission at a Haight-Ashbury rock concert. Valjohn was halfway to the exit when he saw Greg Harris enter from the street. A boy was
with him. Valjohn slowed his walk. There was something disquietingly
familiar about the boy's small, round face—

Valjohn whirled 180 degrees, strode rapidly toward the elevators. He
remembered where he'd last seen that face—saw it again all too clearly in
the moonlight, wide-eyed with fright, staring at him while he hid in the
bushes of the Deerfield School playground. The boy was Scotty Conlisk.

Harris called to him. Valjohn cursed the rotten timing, quickened his
pace to an elevator just emptying. He ducked inside, jabbed a finger at the
buttons on the panel.

"Hey, Lieutenant! Wait up!"

411

The bell dinged. The doors rolled shut.

Almost.

A hand suddenly appeared, inserted itself between the closing doors, held them apart. The bell dinged again. The doors rolled open.

"Hiya, hotshot! What's your big hurry?"

The hand belonged to Mona Cobb.

"Boy, did I ever get the lowdown on you the other day!" She joined him inside.

His head swam. Lowdown? Had the Conlisk kid already fingered him? Did she know about Crescent?

"Hey, V.J., clean out your ears. Didn't you hear me yelling at you?" Harris laughed, hurrying to catch the elevator before the doors closed again. The boy trotted in behind him.

Valjohn smiled weakly.

"I've got somebody here I want you to meet. A very good friend of mine. V.J., shake hands with Scotty Conlisk."

Valjohn reached out and grasped the boy's small, extended hand, stared dumbly into his shy, smiling, upturned face. He waited . . .

Nothing happened. Not the least little hint of surprise or recognition.

Valjohn chided himself for panicking. Granted the moon had been bright that night, but night still was night. And besides, he thought, recalling the boy's taped interview—all that talk about fangs and monsters—the kid was too busy imagining things to know who or what he really saw.

"Scotty's going to try and help us out today. We've got some more pictures for him to look at, and then he's going to see his first lineup. Aren't you, son?"

The boy nodded.

The door rolled open on the second floor. Nobody was waiting to get on. Nobody got off. The door rolled closed.

"How come you're not out with everybody else cracking heads?" asked Valjohn, trying to divert the conversation.

"You know Homicide, V.J. Anyway, we all can't be out there playing stickball in the park. Somebody's got to mind the store. . . . Hey, tell the lieutenant what you want to be when you grow up, Scotty."

The boy blushed.

"Go on, tell him."

"A policeman."

Valjohn nodded, sensed that it wasn't enough. "Hey, that's . . . that's great!" He reached over and patted the boy on his shoulder.

"He's a brave kid, all right," said Harris, putting a hand on the boy's other shoulder.

"Maybe Lieutenant Valjohn could teach him how to be a big hero," spoke up Mona Cobb with a jagged smile. "He could learn how to handle himself in all sorts of tight and ticklish situations."

"Say, that's right," said Harris. "Scotty, do you know who that guy is you're standing next to there?"

412

Once again the boy looked up at Valjohn. He shook his head, but he continued focusing intently on Valjohn's face. Valjohn shifted his weight uneasily. The boy's face was clouding.

The elevator dinged. The doors rolled open.

"Oops, here's where we get off," broke in Harris. As he and the boy stepped out of the car, he began recounting Valjohn's exploits at Starved Rock. Valjohn watched the boy turn and gaze back in at him. His brows were knotted tightly. Cumulonimbus—the barometer was falling fast. . . .

"It's him!" blurted Scotty Conlisk in a squeaky, high-pitched whisper. He had just enough time to point an accusing finger before the elevator doors banged shut.

"So how are you and old Eunice getting on these days, Lieutenant?" said Mona when they were once more ascending. She'd taken no notice of the boy's send-off.

"Eunice?" Valjohn mumbled, frantically trying to determine his next move.

"Don't play dumb with me, lover boy! Eunice Mervin! She filled me in on *everything*."

He had to get out of the building fast.

"I'll admit I found some of the details hard to swallow."

He'd get off at Mona's floor and try to slip down the back stairs.

"But then I guess a lot of things about you are hard to swallow these days."

No, on second thought he'd better ride up another floor and be rid of her.

The elevator dinged. He nodded toward the opening doors. Mona didn't budge.

"For one thing, you oughta go on a diet."

"You're going to miss your floor, Mona."

"Screw my floor!" She stuck out a leg and blocked the door. "Seriously, have you looked at yourself in a mirror lately? You're turning into a real lardo. You know that?"

"Mona—"

"I can remember when you were a young, lean, good-looking stud . . . well, maybe not such a stud—"

"Mona, I'm kind of in a hurry right now."

"Sure, sure, only . . ." her voice fell off for a moment. Valjohn exhaled impatiently.

"Only why don'cha come over to my place for a drink tonight?"

"Mona—"

"No, it's okay. Milton's on vacation. Honest. He went to Disneyland."

"Mona—"

"Listen, maybe Eunice can't handle a real man, but I sure as hell can!" Still blocking the door with her leg, she glanced out to see if anyone was in the hallway, then reached down and grabbed him between the legs. She was surprised to find he had an erection.

413

"Oh, Jesus, tiger! . . ."

"Mona, I've really got to go. I mean it!" He tried to pull away, but she held fast.

"Promise you'll come over—I was only kidding about all that fairy-cop stuff." She was speaking in short gasps now. "And being fat too. I was only kidding—honest! I love men with beef on their bones! Like they say, you can't drive a spike with a tack hammer. So . . . promise you'll come over—take another crack at it—promise? Pretty please with Mona on top? . . ."

"Okay, Mona . . ." twisting to his left, "I'm sorry . . ." managing to pull free, "I have to do . . ." he spun her off balance, "this!" He gave her a solid shove out the door. She tripped over the edge of the landing and went down on all fours. As the doors rolled shut, she struggled to a sitting position, tugged at her rumpled dress and called back to him, "Remember, you promised!"

He left the elevator at the next floor, walked quickly to the stairs. He wondered how Harris was reacting to the Conlisk kid's discovery. Maybe he was laughing it off. . . . No, scratch that—not after all he'd been through with the dark glasses. Past loyalties were dead. He'd be putting things together fast now. Hero or not, Valjohn was going to have to do some very tall explaining.

But first they'd have to catch him.

He abandoned the stairs when he reached the second floor, made his way through the dispatching rooms to the rear of the building. More than likely Harris first would contact his superiors. Sweeney or Howland. Then they'd come looking for him. When they found he'd quit the Force, they'd really swing into high gear.

Doubtful the main exits were blocked yet, but he decided not to chance it.

He took a small service elevator down to the basement garages, then proceeded through several maintenance bays to an exit ramp that led up to an alley off Eleventh Street. Calmly waving to a mechanic he knew, he sauntered up the drive and out of the building.

He paused at street level. Dozens of cops in riot gear stood around in the back lot waiting for transportation to the front lines. They pushed and shoved each other around, joking, fencing with their clubs, banging helmets. Valjohn was reminded of a football team going through pregame warm-ups. He glanced at his watch. A few minutes after twelve—still plenty of time to make it to the plaza on foot. His car was probably staked out by now anyway.

He kept to back alleys until he emerged at Ninth Street. From there he headed to State Street, then north toward the Loop.

He stopped at the first phone booth he came to, gave McTague another ring. This time he was able to reach him at his desk.

"So what's up, V.J.? And make it fast—I'm just on my way over to Lincoln Park."

Valjohn told him that he wanted to talk.

"So talk."

"Not over the phone."

"Name a time and place."

"The Civic Center Plaza. In fifteen minutes."

"No can do. I just told you, I'm on my way out."

"Now or never, Grady. It's important. I . . . I resigned from the Force today."

McTague was silent for a moment. "I'm sorry to hear that," he said in a lowered voice. "Any reason in particular?"

"Not over the phone."

"It can't wait?"

"It can't wait. The Civic Center Plaza—in front of the Picasso statue. Be there between twelve-thirty and one."

McTague cleared his throat.

"One other thing," continued Valjohn. "Keep a low profile. No matter who you see there. Don't come forward until I give you a signal."

"Why the cloak and dagger? Tell me: Did you quit on your own or were you pressured?"

"It's not important. What is important is that you be there . . . that, that I . . . that is, that you . . . uh . . ."

"Ya, I what? Go on."

". . . know who the killer is."

"The Reaper?"

Valjohn was silent, couldn't believe he was finding the courage.

McTague cleared his throat again, gave a short whistle. "This do get dark. How long have you known? Before you got bumped off the case I'd be willing to bet?"

Valjohn regripped the phone. It was growing slippery in his hand.

"It's tied in with the department, isn't it? Somebody upstairs, a Who's Who—maybe even City Hall. Am I right? A real big fish for this kind of hanky-panky."

"The plaza. Twelve-thirty. Okay?"

"Right, right! And thanks, V.J. Oh, I almost forgot: What's the signal?"

"You'll know it when you see it." And Valjohn hung up.

He was walking north along State Street again. *That great street . . . he'd brought a friend; he'd brought his wife:* Soon he'd be in for the time of his life.

His legs all but cried out to run, but he didn't want to chance attracting any undue attention, so he held off, maintaining instead a brisk, even stride. He stared at the faces of the people he passed on the sidewalk. They all looked alike: drawn and anxious, alien and hostile. The indelible stamp of the city. He could see it in their eyes, the reflection of his own brooding paranoia.

He shifted his gaze to the buildings and storefronts, the sidewalk itself. In the windows of adult bookstores, naked women leered out at him from a spread of magazine covers, posters and calendars. Crossed strips of black tape dutifully censored the cracks and bulges. Passing an amusement arcade, he heard a sporadic din of buzzers and bells as sailors and gaunt young men in leather jackets bent over brightly lit machines.

From the window of a novelty shop, the eyes of a wily Christ opened and closed and opened again in a grotesque wink of resurrection and corrugated plastic. At another window of the same store, the slain Kennedy brothers stared out from a tapestry, their wan profiles woven against a glowing sunset of pinks and golds. Beneath the tapestry a combination Martin Luther King-Abraham Lincoln salt and pepper shaker stood amid an assortment of parlor tricks, rubber dog shit, windup teeth, whoopee cushions. . . .

He turned west on Van Buren Street under the shadow of the el. In the distance he heard a train approaching. When it was a block away, he felt his stomach tighten.

He stopped at a stairway entrance and glanced up at the platform. There still was time for escape, to dash up the steps, hurdle the turnstile and throw himself on the tracks. The roar of the onrushing commuter reverberated off the surrounding buildings. He stared at the steps, grabbed the railing, felt it trembling in his grip. He crouched. *Do it! Do it! Do it!* He shouted in his mind, but his legs refused to spring him forward.

The train rumbled to a halt overhead, blotting out patches of sunlight. The screeching wheels sent shivers to his bones. Then the train was moving again. He stood there crouching at the stairway long after it had ceased to shake.

He slowly straightened up. He'd been through all this before. Only this time it wasn't just fear holding him back. Now suicide seemed too easy. Too simple and solitary a deliverance. Strictly onanistic—the ultimate form of masturbation. He reached down, felt the sempiternal bulge in his pants. Not today. He had better things on the agenda than jerking off.

Determined, he set out again, walking west on Van Buren. At Dearborn he turned north, checked his watch. It was almost twelve-thirty. He picked up the pace, broke into a run in the middle of the next block to catch the walk light at Jackson Boulevard. The light changed, but he didn't stop running. He zigzagged through the traffic and kept right on running when he reached the other side.

The plaza was crowded with people on their lunch break, just as he'd anticipated. The majority had gathered by the fountain, where a band was playing and Bohemian dancers were performing a lively polka. A number of hippies carried antiwar signs. Some joined the dancers, reeling and kicking wildly about. A TV truck sat parked nearby on Clark Street. Toward the center of the square, the crowd began to thin out.

There were few people in the immediate vicinity of the Picasso statue. A small group of tourists stood off to one side taking pictures and reading brochures. Several young midinettes sat on the statue's broad pedestal, earnestly sunning themselves, aluminum-foil reflectors held dished out under their upthrust chins. A scattering of businessmen in white shirts and ties, some with coats slung over their shoulders, strolled leisurely about, smiling at girls, conversing among themselves, enjoying the open air.

Valjohn stood across the street at the corner of Dearborn and Washington, searching the throng of faces. She must be late, he told himself, then scoffed. Did he really think she was going to show? She'd probably read his mind like a billboard and was back home sacked out. Nothing left for him to do at this point but go over by the statue and wait . . . just in case.

He stepped off the curb. Quickly he stepped back onto it. She was there! He'd spotted her seated on a bench at the other side of the statue. How could he have missed her? That hair burning gold in the bright sunlight —she stood out like . . . wildfire on the prairie. She wore a light pink cotton dress, rested on the bench with her head tilted back—as though she actually were trying to tan that delicate cream illusion that was her skin.

Behind him he suddenly heard a police "wowie." He swung around to see a speeding squad car approaching on Dearborn. He cramped, motionless on the curb. As the blue-and-white bore down on him through the traffic, he was sure he'd been betrayed. McTague? . . . No. More likely Crescent herself. She'd phoned back and tipped them off to the meeting. Now the vehicle would slam to a halt. Sweeney and Howland would come piling out, guns leveled. They would slap the cuffs on him. They would haul him away. . . .

The squad car sped by, turned down another street, wowie fading.

He returned his attention to the plaza. Now Crescent was nearly blocked from view by an elderly couple carrying suitcases who had sat down on the bench beside her. He took a deep breath; another deep breath. Once more he stepped off the curb.

The "don't walk" sign was flashing. The light changed red. He ignored it, the oncoming traffic as well and marched resolutely across the street, his eyes fixed upon the Picasso. Cars veered, hit their brakes, honked horns. A fender brushed by him. He felt nothing, heard nothing. He saw only the brooding simian eyes, the beckoning gynic smile.

Safely on the other side, he paused at the edge of the square and again searched for Crescent. He could see her now: She'd risen from the bench and was walking toward the sculpture. As he made his own way through the people, a stillness seemed to settle over the plaza. The band quit playing. There was a temporary lull in traffic. Flags that had been flapping vigorously moments earlier hung limp from their poles. A flock of pigeons erupted from somewhere near the memorial flame, whirled overhead and vanished through a chink in the skyline.

He halted a dozen feet away. She stood with her back to him. She was gazing up at the statue that rose directly in front of them both. The episode at Starved Rock suddenly came back to him—his abortive attempt to destroy her in Tonti Canyon. . . . He saw himself holding the cocked revolver to her head, felt the paralysis of his finger on the trigger, the complete dissolution of his will! He remembered his sense of impotence, his shame; remembered turning the gun on himself—remembered failing, failing, failing. . . .

Not today. Not now. Not here. There would be no failure. His crippling inner conflict was resolved. This time she'd been outmaneuvered; he could sense it.

His hands went to his waist. No gun this time, they found, instead, the zipper to his fly. He yanked it down; open.

In the act that lay ahead she would be powerless to stop him. She would be powerless because he was not going to challenge her power. He was not going to contest it, the spell of her love. He would not fight another agonizing battle within his heart that he could never win. . . .

Gratification, not denial! He would yield to love, embrace it and turn it against her. He would surrender once and for all to the passions her spell engendered. Gratification, not denial! He would have her now—right here in the middle of the Civic Center Plaza, in the shadows of the Chicago temple, City Hall, the Picasso statue!

Here in front of everybody. He would consummate his marriage!

He strode forward, fearless, ever uxorious . . . and exposed. *Move over, Fairchild!* he wanted to shout. *Move over, Heintz and Radzim and Cook and Dix and Varner and Bledsoe and all the rest of you assholes! One more asshole's coming home!*

Two of the young women sunning themselves at the base of the statue —their eyes at waist level—were the first to notice Valjohn's approach. One of them dropped her foil reflector; the other emitted a short, startled cry. Both of them drew their knees together.

Crescent, lowering her gaze from the statue, saw their expressions and turned.

"Amor vincit omnia," he mumbled, his manhood glistening in the noon-day sun. He met her eyes without blinking. She looked genuinely sur-prised. He grabbed at her dress, felt the light summer fabric rend in his grasp. He thrust himself forward, an awkward, wanton lunge, probing her nakedness with his own, and braced himself for the terrible, terrible conse-quence.

Her hair, swirling up, billowing over her head, failed to confuse him. Though it blocked the sun, diffused light, exploded—dazzling, gold— though he was blinded, staggering in a swelter of unearthly anima, yet he wrestled on, triumphant in his dread. The gambit had worked: Her lamia rancor was aroused! She was incapable of stemming it, must let her rage run its savage course. For all to see. A city full of witnesses . . .

And he has thrown her down. He is on his knees, crawling forward and pinning her to the pavement beneath his trembling bulk. It is as though he has grown his broad belly for just this moment, so effortlessly does it hold her to him, contain her squirming hips. And now, as he always dreamed it might be, they are alone—the people, the plaza receding into mist—and she is struggling no longer. She is his, in his arms . . . opening. In her eyes he sees forbearance fierce as lust. He feels her hands upon his back, urging him on, her hips lifting almost imperceptibly to meet him.

He enters her. He does.

Blood rushes in his ears like piercing whispers; the shadow of massive wings beats the living daylight from his mind. Heart soaring, he is swept head over heels into darkness, ruthless orgasm. He writhes. He cries out. He ejaculates beyond his wildest dream.

EPILOGUE

23

"I try to get down every weekend. It isn't all that far and the bus connections are good. I must admit this is quite an improvement, though."

Grady McTague at the wheel of his XKE glanced over at his passenger. She was patting the car's posh leather interior and smiling at him.

"I wish I could drive you down here more often."

"You don't have to make excuses, Grady. You've done more than enough for me already," interrupted Crescent. She told him how much she appreciated his friendship during the past few months and that she was sure Valjohn shared her gratitude. Somehow.

"It's still all so hard to figure. I just can't get a handle on any of it." McTague sighed. He tilted his battered tam higher on his forehead and scratched his craggy face. "You know, my being at the Civic Center—it didn't just happen by chance. He called me that morning."

Crescent stared out the window at the passing landscape.

"He said he knew who the killer was, but he wouldn't—or couldn't—tell me over the phone. Some way, somehow, it's all connected with his quitting the Force."

They were out of the city now, heading south on Interstate 57. Crescent sat watching farm after farm slide swiftly by.

"He told me to meet him at the plaza around twelve-thirty. He told me to lay low and stay out of sight."

"Why was that?" asked Crescent without turning her head. The fields of corn had been cut to stubble. There still were a few scattered rows left standing. Faded and brown, they looked brittle in the wind.

"Must have thought he was being tailed. Anyway, he said he'd signal to me when the coast was clear. But . . . uh, as you know, he never got around to it."

"I'm glad you didn't wait."

"What?"

"For his signal—I'm glad you didn't wait for it." She turned and smiled at him.

McTague nodded, then shook his head as he reran the whole crazy scene through his mind one more time.

He'd been milling around the square a good five minutes before Valjohn finally showed. When he spotted him crossing Washington Street, his first impression was that his friend was drunk. He was walking against the light, oblivious to the traffic. Cars were honking and swerving to avoid hitting him.

Following Valjohn's instructions, McTague had stayed hidden behind a troupe of folk dancers, then sidled over to the fountain, waiting for the high sign, which never came. Instead Valjohn had walked across the square, paused a short distance away and suddenly exposed himself like some crackpot flasher. What happened after that was even more preposterous. He'd proceeded to march past several startled onlookers with his wang stuck out, then flung himself—literally flung himself—on a woman in front of the Picasso statue. Began tearing her clothes off and sexually assaulting her!

And what made it utterly insane was that the woman turned out to be none other than Valjohn's own wife!

Recognizing her almost immediately, McTague had rushed forward through the crowd. By the time he reached them, she was flat on the pavement with Valjohn plunked down on top of her like a fallen log. McTague had grabbed a foot and dragged him off her, everyone else just standing around too stunned to move.

McTague had taken one look at Valjohn lying there—all curled up and moaning in a fetal position—and then gone to help Crescent. On her feet again, she stood sobbing, clutching herself in her arms, her eyes dazed and wounded. He'd taken off his coat and draped it over her shoulders, doing his best to comfort her and cover her nakedness. He could feel her trembling in his arms.

In the meantime several people standing around had found their courage. They pressed forward, circling Valjohn's motionless body and began pummeling and kicking him. McTague yelled at them, but they wouldn't stop. He had to desert Crescent for the moment and physically fend them off. He yanked and shoved a few of them, threatened others with his fist. Two men retreated cursing. A woman hit him with her shoe.

"How's he been doing?" McTague asked her miles later down the high-way.

"Better, I think. He's painting now. They've given him an easel in his room. Some brushes and paint. Finger paints—they don't dare give him anything that might be toxic. I'm taking him some canvas boards." She nodded to a large sack she'd stowed behind her seat.

"Sounds encouraging."

An hour later Crescent and McTague arrived at Mengert's Psychiatric Center. They were led by an aide through the pale green dormitory of a high-security compound to a small private room where they found the ex-lieutenant on a bench, gazing out a small window reinforced by a heavy metal grill.

Crescent kissed his cheek and introduced McTague. McTague, hat in hand, stood back, stunned. He hadn't seen his friend for almost two months—in fact, not since Valjohn had been committed under the Sexually Dangerous Persons Act and transferred from St. Luke's in the city to Mengert's. The man he saw now bore little resemblance to the man he remembered.

Valjohn had lost much of his hair. It had come out in clumps, exposing broad patches of crusty scalp. His eyes were dull, glazed; his face was devoid of any personal expression. Yet it was neither his hair loss nor the specter of madness in his eyes that shocked McTague.

It was his size.

Certainly Valjohn had been putting on the pounds before his breakdown (McTague could not help noticing his sizable girth when he'd dragged him off Crescent at the plaza). But this was something different. He was not simply obese. He was . . . mountainesque. . . .

Four hundred pounds? Five, six hundred? McTague had no idea how much he must go on the scales, but it had to be staggering. It was as though his very features had been swept away in a rampant flood of swelling flesh. Moonfaced, bulbous-nosed, his chin little more than a wrinkle in his neck —he'd become a candidate for a sideshow exhibit. His back, his sagging, shapeless behind were broad as a side of beef. Giant blebs of cellulite hung from his chest and midriff and overlapped. He sat on the bench by necessity: It was obvious he could fit in neither of the room's two chairs.

Valjohn continued staring out the window.

Crescent read the look of astonishment on McTague's face.

"I'm sorry—I guess I forgot to tell you about his weight problem."

"Weight problem?" blurted McTague, trying to keep his voice down.

"Prader-Willi syndrome," answered a woman striding into the room to join them. She wore a white tunic with a stethoscope dangling from a pocket and carried a clipboard. "He'd eat himself to death if we let him."

"If you let him?" growled McTague. "Looks to me like he's been eating nonstop since he got here!"

"I assure you, Mr. . . . uh . . . ?"

"Dr. Warner, I'd like you to meet a close friend of ours, Grady McTague," said Crescent, stepping between them. "Grady, Dr. Elsa Warner."

The doctor, matronly with careful gray eyes, extended her hand brusquely.

"I assure you, Mr. McTague, such is not the case. We've had John on a restricted diet since we first diagnosed his ailment five weeks ago. Unfortunately, a person afflicted with Prader-Willi syndrome not only displays a ravenous appetite, but he gains weight at a phenomenally accelerated rate as well. Actually, he can fatten up on what would be for us bare subsistence eating. It's only been within the past few days or so that his weight has shown any sign of stabilizing."

"Prader-Willi . . . how do you spell that?" asked McTague, whipping out his ever-present notebook and pen. He moved past the doctor several steps to a corner of the room. It made him uncomfortable to talk in front of Valjohn as though he weren't there.

The doctor smiled at Crescent, politely followed him. The doctor spelled the name.

"It's a rare disease—though maybe not so rare: just undiagnosed. At least in less severe cases. We know very little about what causes it. We do know it's not metabolic or chromosomal in origin. We're fairly certain it's something gone haywire in the central nervous system, but otherwise we're still pretty much in the dark. The disease is especially serious in children because it affects development. It can lead to anything from soft teeth and stunted genitals to mental retardation. I'm sure it's responsible for John's hair loss there." She nodded toward Valjohn's blotchy scalp. "I'm also of the opinion that it's all tied in some way with his basic underlying psychosis."

"Which is?"

"Catatonic schizophrenia, of course."

"Of course," echoed McTague.

While they stood there, Crescent fussed over the patient. She cooed in his ear, patted his flaky forehead and straightened his robe.

The doctor admitted classification of Valjohn's illness was inexact. Basically he seemed to be running away from something. His subsequent deep withdrawal, his mutism, his overall loss of animation and the apparent breakdown of his perceptual powers—these were all typically catatonic symptoms. Strangely, she noted, he did lack schizophrenia's telltale antibody—there was no taxarein in his bloodstream.

"The Prader-Willi syndrome fits so nicely in the schizophrenic framework," Dr. Warner added with a touch of professional enthusiasm. "It's classic conversion-reaction hysteria."

"Come again?" asked McTague.

"A defensive subconscious maneuver to avoid stress. In other words, the patient's obsession with eating is just another form of running away, of trying to elude some situation—real or imagined—in his life that he finds intolerable."

At that point in the conversation, Valjohn's condition suddenly changed. He entered what Dr. Warner would later describe as his manic state. He became tense and fidgety. Color flooded into his face and massive neck (his skin had become remarkably pasty considering his bloodlines). He began slapping his legs repeatedly in a manner of great impatience, beating on his huge thighs, which looked like beer kegs stuffed up his pajama pant-legs. Then he labored to his feet, grunting and groaning, and lumbered across the room to an opposite corner, where he started swaying back and forth from one foot to the other like some huge beast chained in a cage.

Dr. Warner sent an aide for Valjohn's paints and brushes (which couldn't be left in his room because he ate the paint and chewed the bristles off the brushes). Crescent set up one of the canvas boards she'd brought him on his easel. When the aide returned with a tray of art supplies, Valjohn wasted no time putting them to use.

McTague watched in fascination as the ex-lieutenant, still swaying, jabbed and daubed at the canvas in a furious barrage of jerky strokes. Crescent held his tray of paints, making sure things stayed out of his mouth.

Valjohn painted nothing recognizable. He used only one pigment—blue —and seemed intent on nothing other than covering the white of the canvas. When he'd accomplished this, he continued, adding layer after layer of the same pigment.

"Is it background?" McTague asked Dr. Warner, who'd just returned to the room from answering a call.

"Perhaps. He's painted close to a dozen of them now. All the same color. He never goes any farther."

While they talked for some time about Valjohn's notable artistic accomplishments of the past, his outburst of creative energy began to wane. The frenzy of his stroke subsided. He moved the brush slower and slower, his furious daubs becoming tentative nudges. At times he didn't move the brush at all, just held it glued to the canvas and stared off into space. Finally the brush fell from his fingers.

He stood there teetering, shoulders slumping, head hanging to one side. He looked as though he no longer could bear his great weight, as though at any moment he suddenly might topple to the floor. With the aide's assistance Crescent steered him back to his bench and sat him down. She stayed at his side, gently tidying his scant wisps of frizzled cinnamon hair with her fingers.

Dr. Warner glanced at her watch, noting that Valjohn's period of excitation had run its normal course—not quite half an hour. The stupor he was in now could last for several hours, days or even weeks; there was no way of predicting.

Valjohn's arms hung down, turned out awkwardly at his bulging sides.

Grasping a huge wrist in both hands, Crescent in turn lifted both arms and set them on his knees. Then she changed her mind, rearranging them across his lap.

"Another symptom of his new state," commented the doctor. "*Cerea flexibilitas.* The patient will hold his limbs in whatever position they're placed. He's like a wax doll."

McTague asked what Valjohn's chances of recovery were.

The doctor shook her head. She offered little in the way of encouragement. So far he'd not responded to any form of treatment. All forms of chemotherapy had failed. So had electroshock therapy and microcircuitry implant. Any psychological approach to his disorder was, of course, an exercise in futility: His withdrawal was too severe and too prolonged.

"There's always the chance of a new cure coming along, though," she concluded with a ray of hope. "Great strides have been made in the past two decades. We'll just have to wait and see."

On the drive back to the city, McTague spoke bluntly to Crescent about getting hung up on lost causes. He reminded her that she still was a young, beautiful woman with most of her life before her. She should be trying to separate herself from the past, meeting new people.

"You're saying I should abandon him?"

" 'Abandon' is a rather harsh word."

"Yes, it is."

The subject was dropped. They drove the rest of the way in silence.

When he let her off at the apartment, he made a promise that he would continue probing into the circumstances surrounding Valjohn's resignation and breakdown. So far, he admitted, he hadn't made much headway. Valjohn's case had been all but forgotten in the great wake of the convention riots. He wasn't forgetting, though, and he had his suspicions. The Police Department, City Hall—they were all hiding something, he was sure of it. And somehow he was going to get to the bottom of things, if it took him the rest of his journalistic career.

"Now who's hung up on lost causes?" said Crescent as she climbed out of the car.

McTague smiled and shrugged. He waited until she was safely inside the building. He drove away.

24

He hadn't meant to kill her. Only rough her up—teach her a lesson. He stared down at the nude, lifeless girl sprawled at his feet. Betty Romirez. She was slender—almost frail—except for her tits. She really had a pair of jugs. Must have been a chore just to hold her head up. Too bad. Too bad she got greedy. Jacking prices on her johns. Skimming. She wanted an early retirement? She got it.

Her body, her arms and legs were covered with welts. Her face was pulp. He should have stuck to the coat hanger; he shouldn't have used his fists. The coat hanger, wrapped in tape, had only broken her skin in a couple of places. But the two big gold rings on his right hand, the silver on his left had really done a job on her profile. While he was sitting on her hammering away, she'd gone into convulsions.

James Larsen tucked in his custom-made monogrammed Zavarelli shirt and lit a cigarette. He walked over to the small lavatory adjoining his office and washed up. He dabbed at a nick he'd given himself shaving earlier, then walked back into his office.

He paused at his desk, dug his fingers into the seat of his trousers, thought for a moment. He picked up the phone, made a call and hung up. A few minutes later he got a call back. It was from his boss, Angelo Rusosco. Larsen explained about the girl. Rusosco was not happy. You had to come down hard on skimming, but murder was excessive. Besides, it was bad business. There was no money in dead gash. Larsen agreed, repeated it was an accident. Rusosco jumped on him for being clumsy. "Jimmy, you're an old dog better learn new tricks," he grunted ominously. Larsen redug his fingers into the seat of his trousers, swore it wouldn't happen again. Rusosco told him that he'd make a phone call and get back to him. In the meantime, he'd better clean up.

Larsen hung up, buzzed the bar on his intercom. He asked for Danny. A few minutes later Danny, one of the casino pimps, was knocking at the door. Larsen unlocked it, let him in. Together they rolled up the body in a rug, sat in silence waiting for Rusosco's call. The phone rang an hour later.

"Had to wake the chef. Barbeque's on. Make it snappy. You know, Jimmy, this is gonna cost you a couple of big ones," Rusosco added testily, hung up without waiting for a reply.

They carried the rug and its contents down the back stairway of the Pussy Cat Casino, loaded it into the tirewell of a casino ranch wagon and headed across town. Late-night traffic still jammed the main thoroughfares. They avoided Las Vegas Boulevard and Bonanza Road, kept to the side streets and quiet residential areas. In a small outlying community on the northwest side, they pulled into a private drive and circled to the rear of a large, red-brick colonial building. A somber blue neon sign in the middle of a spacious, well-manicured lawn read: Bay's Desert Chapel and Cinerarium.

A short time later they were driving back across town. Larsen held a shoe box in his lap. On the Strip, between the Dunes and Caesar's Palace, he rolled down his window. He lifted the shoe box, removed the lid and dumped out a pile of ashes as they sped along.

"Rest in peace," said Danny, who was driving.

"Some jugs," reminisced Larsen.

"What's your name?"

"Sandra Kane."

"Where you from?"

"Chicago."

James Larsen shifted in his chair, carefully scrutinized the girl standing in front of his desk. A real knockout. Body and face to match. She'd answered one of the modeling ads. No experience necessary. Just ambition, a little basic talent and a willingness to work. What a laugh. They all had the ambition—longed their little scuzzy hearts out for the bright lights and the big time. They had the talent, too—at least for the kind of modeling they were going to be doing: flat-backing and spreading for a bunch of tired slobs with limp dicks and fat wallets. As for a willingness to work —no worry there. If they didn't have it when they got here, they'd learn it soon enough; he'd see to that. This broad was something else, though. Clearly a cut above the rest. Strictly centerfold material.

"Chicago . . ." Larsen pronounced the name slowly, almost wistfully. "That ain't exactly the sticks. Maybe you know a thing or two?"

The girl smiled.

"Like maybe you know we don't do much modeling around here?"

"A thing or two," the girl answered, still smiling.

Hell, no need breaking this bimbo in with a pimp. She was ready to pull right now. He wasn't sticking her out on the floor, either. She was big-cash gash if ever he saw it. As a matter of fact, Rusosco wanted a couple of class numbers tonight; he was entertaining some big wheels in from the Coast. He'd send him this Sandra dish, her and one of the lead strippers, Margo or Yvette. A very tasty package. Maybe help jack him back in Rusosco's good graces.

He buzzed the old woman, Mrs. Shultz, upstairs and told her of his intentions regarding Rusosco, instructing her to give the new girl a thorough briefing on the "house rules" before sending her out. He didn't want another Betty Romirez screwing things up.

The girl thanked him when he told her she could begin work that night. She picked up her small suitcase and started to walk out of the office.

"Say, sweet meat," he called after her. "One other thing: Trash the wig. That's for street trade."

"It's not a wig, Mr. Larsen," she replied. She lowered her head, shook her hair, ran a hand through it—a luxuriant cascade of long, golden tresses.

He gloated over his good fortune as he watched her leave the room. Definitely a blue-chipper. He wondered if she was poking holes. Good idea to follow up fast. No doubt she could do a lot better than the Pussy Cat. The needle sure beat hell out of an employment contract. Unilateral, airtight and very long-term.

Shortly after midnight he got a phone call. He was downstairs at the time, amusing himself at the tables. He took the call on an extension in the cashier's office. It was Rusosco. As Larsen listened to his boss, his teeth clenched. He tightened his grip on a roll of chips he held in his left hand until his knuckles turned white. "Oshitogod!" he finally muttered under his breath.

Sandra Kane, the new girl he'd sent out tonight, had just rolled her john and taken a powder. She'd undressed him and skipped out of the hotel with his trousers, wallet and roughly fourteen hundred dollars. The aggrieved party was a business associate and personal friend of Rusosco's. A big *capo* from San Francisco. Rusosco was outraged.

Larsen knew where the blame would fall. "Oshitogod!" he muttered again.

"You hearing me, Larsen?" the voice roared over the phone.

"I'm hearing you."

"You goddamn well better be! You hired her ass in the first place—now you goddamn well better find her. I want that cunt's head on a platter!

431

You're so good at wasting hookers. Right up your alley. Only I'm telling you this: You don't bring me that cunt's head on a platter, I'm sending somebody for yours. *Capish?*"

"I *capish.*"

The line went dead.

Larsen slowly hung up.

That no-good fucking whore! She'd really put his tit in the wringer. Hers too. What a crazy-ass stunt to pull! She had to be whacko. He stood there for a few moments contemplating Rusosco's threat and coolly dismissed it. He was too valuable to be bumped off over an incident like this. The organization had too much time and money invested in him. He'd delivered for them, too. No, Rusosco was just blowing off steam—not that he blamed him any. That no-good fucking whore! He'd turn this fucking burg inside out to find her. And when he did—oshitogod!—when he did . . .

He strode quickly back to his office. The first thing to do was stake out the airport, the bus and train stations; seal the town asshole tight. She still could get out by car—nothing he could do about that. She didn't have wheels, though, not according to her interview, just got into town by bus today, didn't know a soul. Maybe a line, maybe not. Good chance she'd opt to lay low for a while, let things cool off. If she did, he'd find her. This was a small town.

It was after 4:00 A.M. by the time Larsen finally left the casino. He'd deployed all the pimps and hookers he could scrounge up for the stake-outs. Rusosco had loaned him additional manpower to comb the Strip. He had people monitoring calls at two of the major cab companies, even had the cops looking. Nothing to do now but sit tight and wait.

His rhoids were really killing him. Before he climbed into his silver Mark III, he unbuckled his belt, glanced around the lot, then plunged a hand down inside his pants, seeking a little relief with his manicured fingernails. When he withdrew his hand, rebuckled his belt, his eyes were watering.

As he drove along Charleston Boulevard on his way home to his suburban apartment, he mulled over the phenomena of his new life. The mob owned him. Not that he was complaining. They'd really bailed him out of a tight spot back there in Chi-town (thanks to past favors he'd done while he still was on the Force). They'd given him a new identity. A plastic surgeon had altered the angle of his nose, the shape of his eyes. He'd become James Larsen and had all the papers and credit cards to prove it. They'd also given him his present job managing the action at the Pussy Cat.

In exchange, the organization asked him to moonlight occasionally: to kill for them, swiftly, discreetly and with no questions asked. He was happy to oblige. He'd already made four hits. Two independent pushers in San Diego and Bakersfield, a newspaper reporter in Phoenix and a high-ranking union official in L.A. His background in criminology served him well. So did his temperament, now that he was off the sauce. He enjoyed his work, the personal sense of status that came from being an upper-echelon mechanic.

The matter concerning the hooker tonight really frosted his balls, though. It didn't relate directly to his work, but it did reflect on his judgment, and he knew the organization wouldn't forget. She'd made him look careless and stupid. Nobody could do that to him and get away with it.

He mused for a moment, remembered the old Jew and smiled. Nobody.

"What the fuck!" He did a double take, jammed on his brakes as he sped through the intersection of Charleston and Rancho Road, squealed to a halt. A broad standing on the corner thumbing a ride. Long blond hair.

He flipped the Continental into reverse, peeled back to the corner. It couldn't be her . . . couldn't be . . . But it was! No fucking mistaking a dish like that. What blind-ass luck! Hell—he was only a couple of blocks from his house! The stupid cunt was probably hitching to L.A. She didn't even have the smarts to crawl under a rock for a few days.

He switched off the dash lights so she couldn't see his face, waved, stretched across the seat and cracked the door open for her. When she opened it the rest of the way and leaned inside, he grinned and stuck the big barrel of his .45 in her face.

"Small world ain't it, sweet meat? Get in!"

She did as she was told.

He debated where to take her. No sense going back to the club—not with what he had in mind—the walls were too thin! Not his house either. Maybe a nice little joyride in the desert . . .

He swung off the main highway, followed a series of remote back roads for nearly half an hour.

"You had me fooled, sweet meat; I sure never figured you for a scumbag. You know that?"

He looked over at her as he casually wielded the big two-door around a stretch of gravel washboard and chuckholes. She sat motionless, staring straight ahead.

"You know that?"

She turned her head and looked at him.

"Yes, sir, a real scumbag, that's for sure. . . . Too bad."

Not in the eyes. She wasn't looking at him in the eyes. Her gaze was focused lower. . . .

"A nice-lookin' cunt like yourself . . . A real shame, cuz now you got to pay the price."

She was staring at his mouth—as if she were in some weird sort of trance. It made him feel creepy. He regripped the handle of his pistol. This chick was spaced. He didn't talk anymore, just concentrated on driving and keeping her covered.

On the other side of a dry wash he turned down a narrow lane and followed it for less than a quarter of a mile until it dead-ended by a small dump at the base of a ridge. He eased to a slow stop. The ground in front of the headlights lay strewn with refuse: bags of garbage, old mattresses and refrigerators, a junked pickup rusting on its side.

He killed the motor and shut off the lights. He motioned for her to get out, keeping the gun trained on her while she did, then climbed quickly out himself.

The air was cool, dry. A light breeze from the Spring Mountains swept across the mesa. A three-quarter moon, bright as any full he could remember, bathed the landscape in silver light. She walked in front of him for several paces, then halted on her own and swung around.

He could see her face clearly. He lifted the .45, took aim. Right between those beautiful eyes.

She was a cool one. No tears. No whining or whimpering. No nothing. Just stood there staring at him like she could care less. Totally whacko! He lowered the gun. Shooting her now was too quick. Too easy. She owed some big dues in the suffering department. Besides, he was starting to get turned on. He had to admit it. The way she was looking at him . . .

Joseph Blear switched the gun to his left hand, spread the fingers of his right, positioning his two big rings and made a fist. He'd have some fun first. Then he'd blow her away.

As he stepped forward, he noticed how the wind was really starting to kick up—how it had caught her hair, whipped it about her face, swirled it high over her head.

He drew back his fist.

She looked tense, frightened now.

He smiled. That was more like it.